Critical acclaim for STEPHEN LAWS

'One of the most inventive young writers on the British horror scene'

The Times

'It's nice to find a fresh, chilling voice among the multitudes of authors feverishly clawing to be the best imitation of Stephen King or Peter Straub. Stephen Laws is no imitator'

Knoxville News Sentinel

'Laws' work typifies a new generation of horror writing: [it] inhabits the world as we know it, and is all the scarier for it'

Maxim

'Great contemporary British horror writers are few and far between ... Stephen Laws is in the first division of doom merchants'

Alex Gordon in the *Peterborough Evening Telegraph*

'A new heir to the horror throne'

Starburst

Also by the same author
and available from New English Library

Spectre
The Wyrm
Ghost Train
The Frighteners
Darkfall
Gideon
Macabre
Daemonic

Stephen Laws lives in his birthplace, Newcastle upon Tyne, where he works as a full-time writer. The success of his early novels established him as a leading horror writer. He has now written nine highly-acclaimed novels.

Somewhere South
of Midnight

Stephen Laws

Kelmar
29a Victoria Street
Newton Stewart

£ 2·10

If you wish to return this
book in good condition - one
third of the above amount will
be refunded .

NEW ENGLISH LIBRARY
Hodder and Stoughton

First published in Great Britain in 1996
by Hodder and Stoughton
First published in paperback in 1997 by Hodder & Stoughton
A division of Hodder Headline PLC
A New English Library paperback

The right of Stephen Laws to be identified as the Author of
the work has been asserted by him in accordance with the
Copyright, Designs and Patents Act 1988.

10 9 8 7 6 5 4 3 2 1

All rights reserved. No part of this publication may be
reproduced, stored in a retrieval system, or transmitted,
in any form or by any means, without the prior written
permission of the publisher, nor be otherwise circulated
in any form of binding or cover other than that in which
it is published and without a similar condition being
imposed on the subsequent purchaser.

All characters in this publication are fictitious
and any resemblance to real persons, living or dead,
is purely coincidental.

British Library Cataloguing in Publication Data

Laws, Stephen, 1952–
Somewhere south of midnight
1. English fiction – 20th century
I. Title
823.9'14 [F]

ISBN 0 340 66610 2

Typeset by Palimpsest Book Production Limited,
Polmont, Stirlingshire
Printed and bound in Great Britain by
Caledonian International Book Manufacturing Ltd,
Glasgow

Hodder and Stoughton
A division of Hodder Headline PLC
338 Euston Road
London NW1 3BH

For Eve

May all your Midnights be Happy Places

Acknowledgements

I'd like to thank the following people for their assistance:

Dr M. J. Carter, Physics Department, University of Northumbria.

Neil McDonald, Meteorological Office, Weather Centre, Newcastle upon Tyne.

ADO Mike Reid, MIFireE, Emergency Planning/Hazardous Materials Officer, Tyne and Wear Metropolitan Fire Brigade.

Greg Holmes, Regional Health Emergency Planning Officer, Northumbria Ambulance Service (NHS Trust).

**Suicide note. Written by Harry James Stark.
Aged 47. Sales representative. Wife, Jean
Marjorie (41). Two daughters, twins: Hilary and
Diane (12 years of age).**

The wrong place, at the wrong time.

Someone told me that, shortly after it happened. As if it was supposed to be some kind of comfort. It wasn't. But then, how could it be? What makes people say things like that when they know you're dying inside? It's so complicated. Do they say it because they care, and they're trying to ease the pain? Or is it more to do with the fact that they're horrified by what happened to you, and they need to distance themselves from it by making a simple statement about fate? Perhaps they hope it will suddenly do the healing, stop you from looking like a walking dead person, and make them more comfortable when you lighten up?

I've wondered whether horror like that could be so random, so apparently without cause. But I've realised that it's not like that at all. There are reasons why the innocent suffer, I'm sure. It's to remind us about the Big Joke that God is always playing. Think about it. How many times have the innocent ones suffered? It's always the innocent, in wars, in famine, in ethnic cleansing. And how often do those who've perpetuated the vilest of crimes get away with it all? Oh no, there's a reason. There's a purpose in the suffering. It's to make those who ask the questions about the meaning of life think even harder, search their souls even deeper. All part of the Big Joke, you see. Because there is no meaning.

I've read all the reports, listened to all the debate about what happened. The longest recorded heat-wave that the country's ever experienced. Maybe the asphalt on the highway was softened by the unrelenting heat of the sun and the constant flow of traffic on that stretch of the A1 through Northumberland. And then perhaps the cool of the night cracked the asphalt after all that baking heat. Someone on the radio said that it was probably people driving too damned fast, and too damned close. A textbook case. Maybe someone's patience was frayed by the heat and the heavy traffic, and they'd taken a stupid chance when overtaking. Maybe it was what the television documentary people call 'road rage'. There've been instances in the past, widely publicised. Perhaps someone cut in front of someone else, that person gave chase and . . . well, perhaps one thing led to another, someone got bumped and the whole thing dominoed from there. Some people turn into bloody maniacs when they get behind a wheel. Others feel challenged when a more expensive car overtakes on the inside, and need to catch them and cut them up. Hell, I've felt that way myself. But I've also heard others pointing out that as the whole thing had happened at night, there was less chance of people wanting to take risks, more chance that people would be more careful and not prone to road rage.

All bullshit, of course.

It was between twelve and twelve thirty at night, and there wasn't much traffic.

I was there, you see.

The weather forecast was good. Temperatures that day had been in the seventies, and inland they were expecting it to reach the eighties by noon of the following day. Further south, the weather was beginning to break and showers were expected by evening. I remember hearing that on the car radio. But that was three hundred miles away from where it happened, and as much as some want the whole thing to be associated with a freak of the weather, they're all just plain wrong. Driving conditions were good that night, the weather clear.

I know what I heard, and what I saw.

And now I know what I've got to do.

Quite why I'm writing this is anyone's guess.

I'm not giving any excuses, and even though I know what I had in mind when I started writing, I realise I'm not giving any answers either. So I suppose that's the end of my note.

All I know is that there're no reasons, no point in living, and too much horror in my mind and in my memory to bear.

And yes, I killed our dog. You'll find it in the living room. No point in telling you about it, because you'll only think I'm mad.

I've got to go now.

They're waiting for me.

Goodbye.

PART ONE

DEAD AHEAD

Harry continued with the joke despite the protestations of his wife and daughters. The car headlights seemed somehow unreal on the road ahead, illuminating the cat's eyes and the white line but nothing on either side of the motorway, as if they were driving into a void, or as if the car wasn't moving, and the road itself was bearing down upon them.

'We're tired,' protested Jean with good humour. She checked the clock on the dashboard. It was eleven forty-five. Still another hour and a half before they reached the port and the ferry that was waiting there. 'The girls need some sleep . . .'

'So the farmer opened the cottage door . . .' continued Harry. His daughters – Hilary and Diane – threw themselves back in their seats, arms raised in mock desperation and groaning aloud '. . . and the travelling salesman said . . .'

'Dad!' Hilary leaned forward again, as if to swat his head. 'We've heard them all *before!*'

'He said: "There's a terrible storm. Can I stay the night?"'

'Just because you *are* a travelling salesman . . .' continued Hilary.

'Sales representative,' corrected Diane.

'. . . sales representative, doesn't mean you have to tell bloody travelling salesman – I mean representative – jokes all the time.'

'Language,' said Jean.

'What language?' asked Hilary. 'Bloody? You mean "bloody" is bad language?'

'You know what I mean.'

'So the farmer says: "All right, but we've only got the two beds. I've got one. So you'll have to sleep between my two sons in the other one".'

'What about "The Bloody Tower", then? That's not swearing, is it?'

'Or Baron Von Richtofen,' rejoined Diane. 'The World War One flying ace. They called him "The Bloody Red Baron". That's not swearing, either.'

'Someone's nose will be bloodied in a minute,' laughed Jean.

'See!' said Hilary. 'You're swearing now.'

'And the travelling salesman replied: "Christ, I'm in the wrong joke!"' Harry burst out laughing then, shaking his head, keeping his eyes on the motorway. 'That kills me every time I hear it.'

'We feel like killing *you* every time we hear it,' said Diane.

The car juddered. Harry gripped the steering wheel tight, straightening the car.

'Harry, be *careful*!' Jean rubbed at her elbow which had bumped against the door handle.

'Sorry. Bump in the road.'

'Shouldn't be bumps in the motorway, for goodness' sake. We should report it. Travelling at speed. Anything could happen.'

'Maybe it's the heat-wave. Warping the asphalt or something.'

'Only one thing warped around here,' said Diane. 'And that's Dad's sense of humour.'

'And then there was this time when a travelling salesman . . .'

'Oh *no*!'

Martin Russell shifted down a gear and brought his tanker-truck carefully down the slip-road towards the main highway at Junction 24. He always took this stretch carefully, after a nasty moment three years ago. He had travelled this road two dozen times since then, driving by the manual, as if making up for that mistake back then.

He had been careless. Nothing more, nothing less. And it was no use fooling himself and making up excuses when he had been in the wrong. He had been on the road from Scotland for two and a half hours solid after a bad night's sleep, had come on to the slip-road fast with a truckload of toilet paper and hadn't checked the main flow of the traffic properly, even though it was two in the afternoon and visibility was perfect. With the slip-road running out fast he was still travelling at sixty-five – and was about to pull out into the main flow of traffic when he saw that there was no gap. He had slammed on the brakes and left a 150-foot skidmark of fused rubber on the tarmac, with his front bumper a mere two feet from a hedge, and a herd of (until then) lazy cows galloping away across the field before him. Sweating and cursing, he had managed to reverse (there was no traffic coming down the slip-road behind him, thank Christ) and wait for a gap in the motorway traffic. His hands had still been shaking on the wheel fifty miles later. A bad mistake, potentially fatal. He should have known better; had always prided himself on his professionalism.

Tonight, the same slip-road. The same motorway beyond. Late, pitch black – and with very little glitter of passing traffic below and before him. But he was never going to take chances or let his attention slip again.

He was still braking when the face suddenly turned in the middle of the road, a hundred feet ahead. White and spectral, throwing up a hand in the glare as the headlights caught it.

'Bloody *hell*!'

Suddenly, time had snapped back again. It was still three years ago, and this time he was going to be made to pay for his mistake. Martin jammed his foot down hard on the brakes, the pressure valves hissing as the tyres shrieked on the tarmac again. The white face in the road remained in exactly the same position, body turned away, face looking back in the direction of the lorry. The truck screeched to a halt, shaking on its suspension. Martin's knuckles were white on the steering wheel, his eyes fixed on the white mask, caught in the headlights' glare. The mask seemed strangely blank, strangely calm with its big translucent eyes. No panic registering there, no alarm that in three more seconds its owner would have been pulverised and squashed beneath the heavy-duty tyres.

The figure dropped its hand. Calmly, it turned completely around now to face the truck. Apparently it had been heading down the ramp of the slip-road towards the motorway, seemingly unconcerned about anything that might come up behind. Now Martin could see that it was a young woman, with some kind of holdall over one shoulder. Her hair gleamed dark and long in the lights, the wind whipping it around her shoulders. Martin wound down his window angrily and leaned out.

'What the bloody *hell* are you playing at? Standing in the . . .'

Middle of the road, he meant to finish. But the girl was suddenly gone from the glare of the headlights. Beyond, only the remaining three hundred feet of the slip-road and the occasional glittering lights of a vehicle passing by on the motorway. Martin twisted in his seat. There *had* been a face there. He had seen the figure of a woman. Hadn't he? But surely she couldn't have vanished as quickly as that?

'I don't believe in ghosts . . .' he began.

'Neither do I,' said the figure, which suddenly clambered up on the passenger side of his lorry and pulled open the door.

This time the blank face was smiling. A pale white face with dark red lipstick, in a style that Martin seemed to remember was all the rage in the movies he had seen as a kid and which some of the trendier kids were now copying from those new-wave violent videos. The young woman was wearing a black leather jacket and dark jeans, standing on the footplate and hanging on to the door handle with one hand, ready to throw the holdall in next to him with the other.

'You okay?' she asked.

'Yeah . . . yeah . . .' mumbled Martin.

'Is that what you thought you'd seen? A ghost?'

'For a moment, I really thought I had.' Martin was suddenly angry. He had a right to be. Walking in the middle of the road, totally unconcerned. If he'd mashed her into catmeat under his rig, what then? But before he could really focus his anger, something he always had difficulty handling, the woman asked:

'You're not a rapist, are you?'

Martin was now too shocked to be angry.

'Not a *what*? Look, what the hell . . . ?'

'You don't look like a rapist. You look kind. Like a family man.'

'Listen, don't you know how dangerous it is to . . .'

Behind them, a car horn blared. Someone coming down the slip-road.

The woman cocked her head, still examining him.

'But that could mean you really *are* a rapist, couldn't it? The fact that you look so unlike one.'

The car horn blared again.

'I need a lift.' She strained to look at the car behind, before darting a glance back at Martin, as if she were using the car's presence to get what she wanted. The ploy worked.

'Get inside before we cause a pile-up!' snapped Martin, ramming the truck into gear.

The woman threw her holdall across the seat, sliding quickly and nimbly into the passenger seat after it and slamming the door, all in one swift and fluid motion. The next moment, the car had blared past them. Martin was focusing his attention out of his side window and heading the lorry down to the motorway.

'I've been on the road for three hours,' said the woman, stretching her legs. 'Not one lift. You're the first.'

Martin did not answer. He was too busy concentrating on the road ahead.

'How far are you going?'

'Just a minute,' he replied. 'Wait until I . . .' At last, there was a gap in the traffic and he was hauling the rig from the slip-road on to the motorway. The hedge flashed ahead of him in the headlights as the roads merged, the hedge that he had almost demolished on his way to join the cows three years ago. Quickly shifting gears, he settled himself back in the seat, composure regained.

'Do you know how lucky you are?' he asked at last.

'Lucky? Yes, I do. More bad luck than my share, but I've never complained.'

'I mean, walking in the middle of the road,' he said with disgust.

'But it stopped you, didn't it?'

'Nearly stopped my heart.'

'So how far?'

'What?'

'How far are you going?'

'Hartley.'

The woman made a noise, as if weighing something up. 'Yeah, okay. That'll do.'

'It'll bloody have to do. I should just pull over and throw you out.'

'But you're not going to do that. 'Cause you're kind-hearted. Like I said, a family man.'

'No, I'm not. I'm a rapist. With an innocent face. Like you said.'

He leaned forward and switched on his cassette deck. Country and western music blasted from the dashboard speakers. That would faze her. Middle of the Road music from a Middle-Aged Man. My cab, my space. For what she'd done, and for his lack of hardness in throwing the little cow back out the way all the other drivers he knew might have done, she'd have to suffer. One of his favourites: 'Daytime Friends, Night Time Lovers'.

To his immense irritation, she started to sing the lyrics, word for word.

'You like that?' he asked in annoyance.

She pulled a string of chewing gum from her mouth, as if to nail it to the windscreen with her thumb. Inches short, she reeled it expertly back in again. Martin watched, mesmerised.

'Road,' she said. Calmly.

A car horn blared ahead as Martin looked up front again. He jiggled the steering wheel. The rig wobbled on the motorway. Unnecessarily. His steering was steady, and the way was clear. He shook his head.

'What's your name?' asked the woman.

'John Wayne.'

'Liar.'

'It's Martin.'

'My name's Mercy.'

'Naturally. The Liverpool accent.'

'Not, not Mersey. *Mercy*. And don't say it.'

'Don't say what?'

'"The quality of Mercy is not strained." Everyone says that. My name's not got anything to do with my accent or where I was born.'

'So why Mercy, then?'

'I like it.'

'Fair enough.' Martin checked the clock on the dash. It was eleven forty-five, and with any luck they'd be in Hartley in about forty minutes. Just one side of his country and western tape. He looked back at the strange young woman. She was pulling at her gum again, mumbling the words to the song. Martin shook his head and concentrated on the road ahead.

The long-distance coach was three years old but had been serviced the previous day. Maintenance checks were rigorous at each end of its cross-country trip from Glasgow to London and back, and in the twenty-three years that the coach company (FlyWay MyWay) had been in business, there had only been two accidents involving their vehicles. One had been shunted from behind; a postal van badly negotiating a traffic queue. The other had been a crumpled wing when an empty coach was coming out of the depot. No one had been hurt. The company prided itself on its record.

Tonight, at 11:45 everyone on board the London Express from Glasgow was asleep. It had been a clear road for most of the way, but by this time of night most passengers had already succumbed to sleep. A movie was playing to an unconscious audience from a video screen near the front of the coach. The driver, George MacGowan, was heartily sick of the film: a badly dubbed jungle adventure, set in Latin America. He had listened to the damn thing five times, had asked them to change it at the Glasgow depot, but his plea must have fallen on deaf ears. Now, as the coach sped on through the night, he began to recite the dialogue to himself.

'*The jungle is the only law.*' Now what the hell was that supposed to mean? '*And if you break that law, the only payment will be your life.*'

George began to whistle the theme music now as it began to play brassily from the screen. He had caught himself whistling it in the shower and at the breakfast table.

The road ahead still seemed clear. Not much traffic at this time of night. He checked the overhead mirror, quickly scanning to see if anyone was desperate enough to be awake and watching this junk. Maybe he could switch it off, put on some music and . . .

A car overtook him, blaring its horn.

'Shit!'

George looked down at the road again, gripping the wheel. Behind him, several passengers stirred in their seats and then returned to their sleep. He hadn't seen that car coming up on the outside lane, but he hadn't been driving wide, so why the hell had it given him the horn? Bastard. He flicked his lights angrily as the car sped on in the fast lane, ignoring him.

No wonder there were accidents . . .

In Seat 47, with her overnight bag on the double seat behind her, Jane Teal shifted, looking for a more comfortable position, whimpering like a small child and reaching for her bag as if it were some kind of reassuring cuddly toy. Her voice also sounded like that of a child: a ten-year-old's voice issuing from the mouth of a thirty-five-year-old woman. Perhaps it was this more than anything else which seemed to make everyone around her treat her like a child. Or had she cultivated the voice to foster protection from those she met? Her dreams were troubled, surreal contortions of everything that had happened to her in the last forty-eight hours.

'You're pathetic, Jane. Can't you keep anything in your head?'

Her husband, Tom, towering over her in this dream as she remembered her father towering over her when she was young.

'You didn't put the date down in the diary, did you?'

'I'm sorry, Tom. I thought I had. I must have . . .'

'It's a dinner for six,' said Tom in her dream. *'Get that? Six. Comes before seven and just after five. So that only gives you a day to prepare . . .'*

'*A day's all I need,*' said Jane, anxious to make up for yet another lapse.

'*What the hell would you do without me?*'

'*I don't know . . .*'

'*And it has to be something special this time. Not like last time – but we won't talk about that, will we – because Yearby and his wife will be coming.*'

'*The deputy managing director.*'

'*Good! So something sticks in your mind occasionally, after all.*'

And in her dream, Jane saw that the kitchen had suddenly become a vast and cavernous space, with the units stretching up for miles on all sides. She was only a little girl, perhaps two feet tall, and everything towered above her. She struggled to cope with the meal she was preparing, but everything was going wrong. She couldn't reach the benches, couldn't get her hands to work properly; her fingers were too fat and clumsy. Steam filled the kitchen; the Led lights on the cooker glowed hellishly through the shrouds of steam. She began to weep uncontrollably as pans bubbled and boiled over. She screamed then, and found that somehow they were all here, all seated at the dining-room table. Mr Yearby and his wife were grinning at her, the others around the table laughing like maniacs at some joke that he'd just made. Tom was laughing too, but his eyes were fixed on her as she brought the first course to the table. His eyes were hard and bright, waiting for her to make a mistake, waiting for her to make a social *faux pas*. She saw his eyes move meaningfully to the wine glasses of the other guests; some of them were only half full. She smiled weakly and nodded. More wine. There were several bottles cooling in the kitchen . . .

Again, that laughter.

But this time the dream was truly a nightmare. Because everyone at the table was laughing at her. Some of the soup had spilled from one of the dishes she was carrying. They were pointing at the puddle on the carpet, and laughing. But Tom wasn't laughing. His face was just a hard blank mask, an expression that filled her with terror. Then the laughter became screaming. They were screaming abuse at her for being so stupid, and her screams joined theirs . . .

But now she saw herself from above, as if she were floating in the air. The laughter and the screaming had vanished. Now there was only the soft hiss of rain, and she saw herself walking through the night towards the bus station, saw herself carrying the hastily packed suitcase. From above, she was quite aware – but knew that the figure below had a blank mind, had been burned out as she walked to the bus shelter with the ticket clutched in her free hand. If a bus were to hurtle around the corner of the corrugated shed, it would smash into her and finish her torment, and she would never see it coming. But no bus came, and Jane watched herself reach the bus stand. The forlorn figure looked at the ticket and climbed aboard one of the buses. She found a seat and sat heavily, the suitcase slumping to the ground between her legs.

She began to wake then, expecting herself to be at home in bed. Waiting for Tom to come home from one of his late business meetings. Dimly, she felt the vibration of the bus engine in the seat beneath her. She reached out and felt the suitcase, saw the black window, felt the rough material of the seat – and realised where she was and what she had done. It was too much. She must go back to the dream, see if she could influence it, make everything turn out differently. Perhaps she'd be able to wake at home, after all. Not in this place. With all her problems solved, and Tom lying next to her with that lovely smile that had so entranced her when they first met.

Jane whimpered in her little-girl voice again, and went back to sleep.

Four seats behind Jane Teal, Roger O'Dowd lay across a double seat, head cradled in his arms, his lanky legs sticking out into the aisle. His holdall was in the overhead rack, but his most precious possessions were in the hardboard folder standing on the floor and resting against the head-rest of the seat in front. A hardboard folder tied with bootlaces at the side, containing two dozen watercolours, black and white prints and various sketches for fictitious advertising campaigns – all representing three years of hard work, and not counting the dozens upon dozens of roughs he'd discarded before deciding on this trip. Unlike Jane, he had no trouble sleeping, had often prided himself that he could sleep anywhere, any time. His dreams were not troubled, but that did not mean that his waking hours were trouble-free. Just before he'd finally nodded off, the words of his friend, Adam, had replayed in his mind.

'*You're joking, of course.*'

'*Why should I joke?*' he'd asked.

'*You're packing in your job, and you're heading off to the Big City. Just like that?*'

'*That's about it.*'

'*You're going to take your paintings and your drawings, and you're going to walk the streets, knocking on the advertising agencies' doors and asking if they'll give you a job.*'

'*Right again.*'

'*Anyone ever tell you that the streets aren't paved with gold?*'

'*I'll get nowhere if I stay here. I've got to go where the jobs are.*'

'*You're giving up steady employment, the prospect of an assistant manager's job? You're made, Roger. You're throwing everything away.*'

'*Throwing what away, exactly? Throwing nothing away, Adam! A management job in a supermarket, for God's sake! One step up from stacking shelves and collecting trolleys from the car park. Listen, Adam – it took me three years to get that university degree, part time. It was a long, hard slog. And I didn't just do it for the fun of it. I want out.*'

'*Well, if you say so. I'd better just get another drink for the madman.*'

'*Make it a double.*'

But Roger wished that he was actually as confident as he was trying to appear. He could tell that Adam was sounding him out. They had worked together for four years, and maybe Adam was just a little jealous that he'd taken the initiative, decided to do something about changing his lifestyle. Maybe he realised that if Roger upped the stakes and headed for the

Big City to tout his wares, he *might* just get himself a job – in spite of the odds – and he'd effectively be saying goodbye to a good friend. For just one moment, while Adam was standing at the bar, ordering more drinks, Roger really did wonder whether his plan of action was all pie in the sky. He finished the drink in front of him with an angry flourish. The hell with it! He'd go down there with his paintings and his sketches, and his copy of the diploma – give it a month and then, if nothing came of it, he could always head home again. Back to his family, back to his friends – back to stacking those supermarket shelves.

He shuffled in his seat when the car horn blared and the bus driver cursed, but it was not enough to wake him. He carried on sleeping, untroubled.

It was five minutes to midnight.

Ellis Burwell's gloved hands gripped the steering wheel of his Lotus Elan until the leather creaked. He was late, he was angry, and he had been unaware of the bus ahead of him until he'd almost rammed its rear bumper. His inner thoughts and emotions were at boiling point, and the sight of that bus trundling along in the lane in front of him had made everything erupt. The bus had moved out to overtake something, was even now heading back to the left-hand lane. But the very fact that it was there, and he had not seen it, together with everything that had happened that evening, enraged him. Burwell jammed his foot down hard on the gas and punched the car horn. He had a satisfying glimpse of the bus driver reacting in alarm as he flashed past, and then the bus was behind him.

The bus was gone, but the anger remained.

There was a long drive ahead of him, and he had to get back to the office and put everything right before anyone discovered what had happened to the money. The sight of Klark's grinning face, on the other side of the table at the Motorside Motel, made him grip the wheel again as if his hands were around the bastard's throat. He remembered the telephone call:

'*It's time again, Burwell.*'
'*But it's only a week since the last . . .*'

'One of your big troubles is that you just ... don't ...
LISTEN! I said, it's time again. And I mean tomorrow.'

'All right, all right. Where?'

'The Motorside Motel.'

'I don't ... I mean, I'm not sure where it is.'

'On the A1, in Northumberland. Just before Blackwell. I've
got business up here. You've got eyes. Use a map, you cretin.'

'What time?'

'Some time between ten thirty and eleven thirty. At night.
Natch.'

'All right ... I'll be there.'

'Of course you will. And the payment's increased this time.'

'What?'

'In line with inflation, Burwell.'

'Jesus ... How much?'

'Two grand.'

'But I can't get that much in the time you're giving me. I've
still got to cover my tracks on the last payment.'

'That's your fucking problem. Good phrase, in the circumstances, isn't it? A fucking problem? Got to keep your sense of
humour, haven't you, Burwell?'

'But I can't ...'

'HAVEN'T you, Burwell?'

'Yes.'

'Between ten thirty and eleven thirty. Keep laughing, lover
boy.'

Burwell jammed his foot on the accelerator and hunched
forward over the wheel. He had the keys to the office, and
should be able to get in there that night without any problem.
The computer work would take him a while, but with any luck
he should have everything transferred and switched between
accounts before morning. Now, in the headlights ahead, he
could see Klark's face when he'd finally arrived late at the
motel restaurant. Burwell had been there since 10.15. The place
had been almost empty – just a few long-distance drivers eating
a late evening meal before travelling on. He recognised them
straight away, knew that expression. Hungry men. Hungry, it
seemed, for something more than the food that had been served

up for them at this all-night stop-over. For a moment, as he sat with his coffee, he felt some dim kinship with them; travellers on the road, travellers of the night. He shrugged it off, refused to associate with them. He was much, much more than that. A man with management potential. He turned to look out into the night, could see only his own reflection in the window. Looking at himself, he remembered that night the previous week in the office. Everyone had gone home, and he had done what he usually did when he knew that he was alone. He wandered the building, looking at the paperwork on other people's desks, checking through the drawers that had not been locked. It was his way of staying ahead, of keeping one step in front of the other fuckers in the organisation who would do him down and take his place. His position was already precarious. But then Klark had come into his life, and everything had gone from bad to worse.

And then, as if summoned by his thoughts, Klark had suddenly slid into the restaurant seat opposite him. Without any acknowledgment of Burwell's presence, he rapped his knuckles on the table-top, looking around to make sure that no one was watching. He rapped them again, angrily, when Burwell hadn't taken the hint. Reaching into the briefcase next to him, Burwell took out a brown paper envelope and pushed it across to him. Klark quickly slid it into his inside pocket.

'Is it all there?'

'Yes. But I can't keep this up, Klark.'

'There you go again, weighing me down with your problems. You've had your fun. Now you've got to pay the price.'

'Please, Klark . . .'

'Please? That's what she said, didn't she? I mean, just before you did it.'

'Oh, Christ.'

'That's a good boy. Keep praying. Because the day you don't come up with the green stuff is the day the police are going to come knocking on your door. Now, fuck off.'

Burwell raised his hands in a hopeless plea.

'I said . . . fuck off.'

And Burwell had risen from his seat and left the restaurant, aware of the fact that Klark was sitting back in his seat with a satisfied grin on his face. He could feel his eyes on his back, watching through the floor-to-ceiling glass walls of the restaurant, as he crossed the car park and climbed back into his car. At first, despair threatened to overwhelm him, but something seemed to happen to him when he switched on the car engine. The throaty roar appeared to generate anger inside him. Screeching from the motel car park and back on to the motorway, the anger had been all-consuming.

The look in her eyes when she realised that he wasn't joking.

'*. . . please . . .*'

The terror as he kept on lunging into her, his hands around her throat.

'*. . . please . . .*'

And the knowledge that Klark had been watching – and recording – everything that was happening.

Consumed with anger and utter hatred, Burwell jammed his hand down hard on the car horn. It blared ahead into an empty road.

'And then there was the one about . . .'

'Right! That's it!' said Hilary. 'Put the radio on, Mum!'

Laughing, Jean leaned over and switched the dial. Heavy-metal music filled the car. Harry was immediately outraged, fumbling at the dash.

'Who changed the station last time we were driving? That should be fifties rock and roll, not Mega-bloody-Death or whatever they're called.' The night air was full of strange new frequencies and foreign tongues as he tried to find his station again.

'See!' cried Diane. 'He used the "bloody" word, Mum. Go on, tell him off.'

'Naughty boy,' said Jean.

'Nothing more obscene than a middle-aged rocker,' commented Hilary.

'Never too old to rock and roll,' smiled Harry, finding a Chuck Berry number and sitting back in contentment.

Hilary made a noise as if she might vomit. Jean groaned in parental disapproval of the sound.

'That is so *bad*,' said Diane.

'If it wasn't for Chuck and people like him,' said Harry, 'you wouldn't have heavy metal. It's a natural progression from rock. All the variants, all the permutations come from rock and roll.'

'Obscene,' said Hilary definitively.

'So what should I do? Take up knitting? Get myself a bath chair?'

Everyone except Harry was laughing now. He glanced around as they sped through the night. Now he could see that they were laughing at more than his last statement.

'So, what?' he asked, the humour infectious, a smile on his lips. 'What is it? *What?*'

'Stopped you telling corny jokes, though, didn't it?' laughed Jean.

And this time Harry was laughing with them.

Chuck Berry advised them that they were 'Riding along in my automobile'.

And Harry had never felt happier in his life than at this moment.

'So you're one of life's drifters?' asked Martin at last.

Mercy had been singing along with most of the country and western songs on his tape, and the sound of it was both restful and pleasurable to him. For the past ten minutes she had been staring out of the truck's side window into the night.

'Drifter,' she said dreamily, as if weighing up the word. 'Hmmm . . . No, that's not the right word. I move around, but it's not the same as drifting.'

'Of course it's drifting.'

'Look, you only drift if you don't have a purpose.'

'So what's your purpose?'

'To be happy.' Mercy looked back at him. There was a strange expression on her face, almost challenging.

Martin just nodded, not wanting to intrude further on her space. He faced front again, concentrating on the beam from the headlights in the road. 'Don't we all,' he said after a pause. 'But you've got to plan your life. Got to have a direction.'

'Why?'

'You've *got* to. If you just drift around, then you're just gambling that things will work out. Got to have an idea.'

'You mean a husband working nine to five. Three kids and a mortgage.'

'Nothing wrong with that, if it's what you want.'

'You got kids?'

'No. We can't have them.' He shuffled in his seat, feeling that he'd gone a step too far. It had been a source of great sadness in their lives. He looked back at Mercy, but she had returned to gazing out of the side window. No, it was all right. She was a stranger, after all. After this lift, they would never see each other again.

'I had a miscarriage once,' said Mercy, without turning from the window. Her voice was flat and unemotional.

Martin shuffled in his seat again and concentrated on the road. Maybe the conversation had taken a wrong turn. He wouldn't be surprised if the rest of the journey was made in silence. But then Mercy spoke again.

'So, are you a happy man?'

'Hadn't thought it through. Yes. Yes, I am, now I come to think of it.'

'Why?'

'What?' The question seemed almost childlike in its naïveté. Like a child asking a father how high the sky could be. For a moment, it threw Martin.

'Why are you happy?'

He looked at her, wanting to see the expression on her face. Was she mocking him? But he could see only the blurred reflection of the face in the window. It seemed blank.

'All right,' he said, after a while. 'I'll tell you why. Because I don't complicate things. That's why people are so unhappy all the time. They *think* too much. They want too bloody much out of life. So busy yearning and striving for a better house, for a better car. Always wanting things someone else has got, always wanting to climb the ladder. They're so busy scrambling for it that they just make themselves unhappy in the process.'

'But that's just ambition. You told me I was a drifter. If you don't go in for what you've just said – the house, the kids, the car, and all that other stuff – then you're just drifting.'

'No! Look, what I mean is – you've got to value the simple things, never take them for granted.'

'Like what?' Again that childlike simplicity in her questioning. *Daddy, why is water wet?*

'Like food. People forget it's a pleasure. They just grab a bite and hurry on. Give themselves ulcers in the process. Like sleep. Think about it. That's a pleasure.'

'Love?'

Martin paused, waiting for her to say more. When she remained silent, he said: 'Depends what you mean by love'.

Mercy looked back at him. There was a glint in her eye that he couldn't fathom.

'Trick question,' said Martin. 'You're talking about sex.'

'Might be.'

'Yeah, that too. Sex and love, together.'

'But sex is a pleasure on its own.'

'But not the same as when you're doing it with someone you love.' Once again, Martin felt uncomfortable; talking about such things so openly with a complete stranger, and a girl to boot.

'You're old-fashioned,' said Mercy. It was neither an accusation nor a statement, more an invitation for him to continue.

'So what if I am?' he replied defiantly. 'I'm happy.' And now he came to think about it, he *was* happy. This strange conversation had brought it home to him with a profound clarity. 'I'm really happy.'

'What do you want most in the world?'

Martin looked at her. Another strange question.

'Most?'

'Mm-hmmm.'

'That my wife should get well. She's got a . . . well, it's a degenerative muscular problem. I'd want her better again.' He cleared his throat. 'How about you?'

Mercy had turned to look out of the passenger window into the night.

'To find somebody.'

The statement seemed to go against everything she'd said before. But then Martin saw her expression, reflected in the window, and realised he'd misunderstood her words.

'Who?'

'Somebody I've been looking for. For a long time.' There was something hard-edged in her voice, something that spoke of a debt to be paid, an emotional debt perhaps. When she turned from the window to look at him again, her expression had softened. 'I envy you,' she said. 'I wish I could be like you.'

'What? You mean fifty years old, with a hernia?'

She laughed, and for the first time Martin saw just how beautiful this strange young girl could be. She leaned across to nudge his arm, a childlike gesture that matched the childlike quality of her questions. It made him feel good.

'So what are you carrying?' she asked. 'Back there in the lorry, I mean.'

'It's not a lorry, it's a truck.'

'So what's in it?'

'Amyl nitrate.'

'Sounds dangerous. Poisonous. The firm you work for isn't one of those that's been screwing up the rivers, is it?'

'You choosy about the kind of trucks you get lifts in?'

'You didn't answer my question.'

'They use amyl nitrate as an additive to diesel fuels. An oxidising agent.'

'Sounds flammable. Not sure I'm too keen about riding in a mobile bomb.'

'I've been driving stuff like this for twenty years and never had an accident with it. And, for your information, that tank back there is super-safe. Amyl nitrate is only a moderate fire risk and there's no real protective measures needed for its transport. That good enough for you?'

'Cross your heart.'

'*What?*'

'Cross your heart and hope to die. That it's safe.'

Suddenly, someone on the cassette tape began to sing: 'Come on baby, light my fire'.

Mercy began to laugh. The laughter was infectious. Soon Martin was laughing again. It had been a good idea picking this girl up, after all. Despite his initial irritation, he had suddenly found himself opening up to her. It felt good, being honest with a complete stranger. But despite his own understanding, the facts that he'd imparted to Mercy about his haul had been far from the truth. Martin had accepted the load in good faith, but was unaware that for the seventh time in his life he was transporting materials very different from those the foreman and general manager had advised him about. There had been scheduling problems back at the depot. There hadn't been time to clean out the tanker completely ready for its new load, and no other truck to take it to its destination. No other pressurised container would be available for at least twenty-four hours, by which time the firm might have lost its contract on this job. On the 'Hazchem' sheet and the official Trem card which all truck drivers were obliged to carry in the cab, it stated that Martin's load was amyl nitrate.

But he was carrying Acrylonitrile; highly toxic, alcohol-based and extremely flammable in contact with air.

It was almost midnight.

On the coach to London, Roger O'Dowd was having another flashback dream. This time, he was arguing with his ex-girlfriend, Paula. He'd believed that his decision about changing direction would please her. But he had been completely wrong on that score. She'd been pleased enough that he'd managed to achieve his degree, studying part time. But it seemed that she hadn't taken him seriously when he'd told her that he was going to pursue a career in graphic design, and intended to hawk his wares around the Big City.

'But you can't be serious, Roger. I mean, the drawing and the painting and the design – I thought it was like . . . well, like . . .'

'Like what?'

'Well, like a hobby.'

'A hobby? For God's sake, Paula. How many times have I told

you what I want to do with my life. I'd expect that kind of thing from Adam, but not from you. I'm not just doing this like it was . . . was . . . flower-arranging or something. I'm serious about this. I thought you understood that.'

'But you said yourself, there were no jobs up here.'

'That's why I'm going down to London.'

'What about what Adam was saying? These days they're looking for people who are . . . what did he call it? . . . computer literate. Not just the stuff you've been doing . . .'

'You mean "finished art".'

'Yeah, that. And what if you do find somewhere? What if you do manage to find yourself a job? What about us?'

'That won't affect us.'

'And that's where you haven't been listening to ME, Roger. You've been so busy with your bloody plans that you never stopped to ask yourself what I might want out of life.'

'How does my changing jobs like this affect US, for God's sake?'

'Because if you get a job in London, and you want us to stay together, then it means that I've got to go to London as well. Doesn't it?'

'Well . . . yeah . . .'

'Yeah. And that's where you haven't been reading between the lines, Roger. Because I'm not going to London. Do you hear me? If you manage to find somewhere to work down there, I won't be coming. My family's here, my friends are here. And I'm not uprooting and moving south, just because you want to spend your life drawing cartoons . . .'

'Christ!'

'Not a lot else to say, is there, Roger?'

'Not a lot, Paula. Not a lot . . .'

Jane Teal moaned in her sleep again, trying to get comfortable on her coach seat as she dreamed of what must be happening at home. She could see the front door opening, could hear Tom angrily calling her name. Even more angrily now when she didn't materialise to take his coat and his briefcase. She didn't want to be dreaming this dream, but was forced to watch as

Tom strode down the hallway. She watched him flinging open the door into the lounge, shouting for her. And maybe, oh God, maybe, she could will herself back home before he discovered what had happened. Jane struggled, trying to find a way by which she could return. She called his name, but now Tom was storming through the kitchen, grabbing a plate as he moved and smashing it on the floor. She winced at the sound, saw the fragments of bone china whirling like snow. Now he was striding up the stairs, and Jane prayed to God that he could transport her into one of those bedrooms. Perhaps she could pretend that she had fallen asleep, and hadn't heard him come in. He would still be angry, but at least she would be able to take her punishment and everything would be all right again afterwards.

But Tom was flinging the bedroom door wide, and she wasn't there.

His face was turning that unhealthy grey colour again, the colour she feared so much. Some people flushed red when they were angry, but with Tom it seemed that the colour drained away from his face. And the paler he became, the angrier she knew he would be. Again, she tried to call out to him, tried to reach for him, but Tom was suddenly gone from the doorway and had thrown open the spare bedroom door.

'*Jane!*'

I'm here, Tom. I'm sorry. I'm here. Why can't you hear me or see me? I'm here!

'*JANE!*'

Everything in the dream was whirling. Why couldn't she escape from it? Why couldn't everything be the way it was before?

Ellis Burwell's rage had become something else as he drove.

Overtaking the coach back there had been good for him. Sounding his horn into the darkness ahead had also helped. Now that the road was clear and there was nothing in front of him but his headlights skimming the surface of the road, his anger had simmered down to something that felt cold and controllable inside. Now he could concentrate on his predicament at work, putting his latest meeting with Klark to one side in his mind. Already he was working on a strategy.

And then the car radio crackled into life.

Puzzled, he glanced down at the Led lights on the dash. He remembered he had been listening to Classic FM when he switched the radio off. By rights, with the radio on again, there should be more classical music. Not this fierce and crackling static, not this sound like frying eggs and bacon. But also by rights, Burwell knew he shouldn't be hearing anything at all. He had not switched on the radio, and his dial was still in the 'off' position.

Burwell groaned, gripping the steering wheel tight and feeling the cold, controllable sensation beginning to slip away, feeling the heat beginning to bubble and build again as his temper flared. Three weeks ago, the car had been serviced and there had been two faults since that time which had needed repair. A passenger window that kept slipping from its frame by an inch, and an irritating rattle under the hood. Now the radio was buggered.

'Damn it. *Damn it!*'

He slammed his hand on the top of the driving wheel.

'Off means *off!*' he yelled at the hissing static on the radio. 'Did I switch you on? Did I? Did I switch you *on!*' Angrily, he stabbed at the 'off' switch. It had no effect. Angrier still, he jabbed at the tuning button. The Led light skipped from channel to channel. There was no difference, no variation in static tone. Just the same hissing, crackling sound on each and every frequency.

'What?' yelled Burwell, as if the sound were sentient. As if it were a whingeing child, demanding his attention, demanding that he do something before it stopped. '*What?*'

And then the car engine died.

There was no warning that there might be a problem, no rattling under the hood, no straining of the engine before it coughed and died. One moment, he was cruising at seventy, the next the engine was dead. He fumbled for the ignition and twisted the key. Nothing. He tried again, and again. Nothing.

'You *cunts!*' If the undiluted hate that radiated from him at this moment could be channelled and directed through the ether to the source of his anger, then surely two garage mechanics fifty miles away must even now be writhing in agony on the garage floor. 'I don't believe it! I just don't BELIEVE IT!'

He watched as the speedometer needle swung quickly from right to left. *Fifty . . . forty . . . thirty . . .* If he didn't act soon, he'd simply coast to a halt right in the middle of the fast lane. Yanking at the wheel, he steered across the lanes, praying that he could get to the hard shoulder without someone suddenly roaring out of the night behind him and slamming into his rear. He gritted his teeth, but the car was moving slowly towards the hard shoulder now.

. . . twenty . . .

It was going to be okay. He was centred in this stop-over lane now. The car would glide to a smooth halt . . .

. . . fifteen . . .

All the other electrics in the car seemed okay. Lights still glowed from the dash. But the fierce static still filled the interior as it finally rolled to a halt. There were emergency lights in the boot. First, he would get them out, plant them behind the car to show that he was here. Then he was going to march along the hard shoulder until he'd found an emergency telephone and blast the eardrums of the first person he spoke to. And then a certain garage was going to feel the full force of his anger.

And then the radio switched itself off again. The deafening static was gone.

Burwell sat there, looking at the dash. Waiting for something to happen. When the radio remained off, just as it should, he reached down and switched on the ignition.

This time, the engine turned over.

Quickly revving, in case it decided to die on him again, Burwell slipped the car into gear, then brought the clutch up to the biting point. Now it seemed there was nothing wrong with his car at all. Good sense and logic battled with his burgeoning rage. If his car had died once, and he had managed to get safely on to the hard shoulder, surely it might die again if he was to continue on his way. If it happened again, he might not be so lucky. Better by far to leave the car here as he'd

planned, make that walk to the emergency telephone and have
it towed away.

But then the FlyWay MyWay coach zoomed past again. The
coach he had overtaken in anger. Now it had overtaken him,
and anger overwhelmed good sense.

'You *shit!*'

Ellis roared from the hard shoulder, hardly bothering to
check if any other vehicle was emerging from behind in
the night.

'You *SHIT!*'

The next moment, he was gaining fast on the coach.

George MacGowan took only a brief interest in the car parked
on the hard shoulder. The coach flashed past, and he had
a quick glimpse of the man sitting behind the wheel, head
forward. Just some other poor bastard who had broken down.
There was never a good time to break down at all, of course,
but he didn't relish the idea of breaking down in the middle of
nowhere, in the middle of the night. He had no idea it was the
car which had so recently overtaken him with its horn blaring,
had no idea as he passed the car (reciting more dialogue from
the jungle movie) that, even now, it was slewing away from the
hard shoulder after him, approaching fast from behind.

'"That's why they hired a guy like me,"' murmured George,
lip-synching with the actor on screen. '"They know I got nothin'
to lose . . ."'

The video-screen image wobbled, and in the next instant the
picture was gone. Instead there was a hissing snowstorm and
an electronic crackling of static. George checked the rear-view
mirror. Everyone was asleep. Just as he'd thought, he was the
only one paying any attention to the damned thing. Leaning
forward, he flipped the video switch.

The screen still hissed and buzzed.

He tried again. This master switch should turn off the video
cassette and the television itself. But the television was still
on. He tried several more times and then finally gave up. If
someone complained, he'd have to pull into a lay-by and switch
it off manually, at the screen controls. Only a couple of extra

minutes added to the schedule, and they were right on time in any event.

Up ahead, well past his headlight beams, and on the other side of the carriageway, he could see someone else's headlights heading towards them. They seemed dazzling, much brighter than any of the other headlights he'd occasionally passed.

George checked the video screen again. Still flashing and buzzing.

And then the engine died.

No sputtering out, no sudden warning.

There was power, then suddenly there was none.

In panic, George stamped on the accelerator, trying to get more juice. Nothing. He twisted the ignition key. Nothing.

The car travelling towards them was approaching at top speed. Somehow, its headlights were even brighter than before, dazzling him and adding to his confusion. He felt suddenly sick with horror as the glaring headlights filled his line of vision. In that one instant, in a moment of stark fear, he knew that the lights could not be filling his windscreen like that if the vehicle was on the other side of the road. The lights could only be flaring and blinding for one reason.

The oncoming vehicle was not on the other side of the motorway.

It was on his side of the road.

Heading *his* way.

Somehow, some stupid idiot had taken a wrong turning from a slip-road – and his or her vehicle was heading the wrong way down the motorway, directly towards them.

The bus was losing speed. George frantically gripped the wheel, twisting to look at the rear-view mirror. But he could see nothing. The flaring headlights were impossibly bright, obscuring the mirror, and the only thing he could do was to swerve from his lane, and – just as Ellis Burwell had done – get the coach on to the hard shoulder and out of the way.

And then everything happened at once.

George MacGowan pulled the steering wheel hard over to the left, heart hammering, eyes dazzled by the headlights as . . .

*   *   *

. . . Ellis Burwell, filled with anger, floored his accelerator and began to overtake the coach on the inside lane. His car had just begun to pass the rear of the coach when the entire vehicle swung at him, vast and powerful and shuddering. He jammed his hand down on the horn.

And then the screaming began.

The screaming seemed to be coming out of the light that filled the windscreen, from somewhere beyond the coach, which should already have swung out of the path of the oncoming vehicle. But somehow the glare still filled the windscreen, and as the light grew to an unbearable intensity, it was as if the voices were somehow reaching a new pitch of fear. The sense of imminent impact was horrifying and inevitable. Squinting into the brilliance, fear threatening to rob him of all his strength, George tried to see in the rear-view mirror if it was the passengers behind him who were giving vent to the desperate shrieking. But his brief, terrified glance could see nothing in the mirror, only more of the dazzling brilliance as . . .

. . . Ellis Burwell's foot came off the accelerator as the screaming filled the interior of his own car. It was exactly the same sound as George could hear: desperate, shrieking voices. A multitude of screaming people, the pitches varying, rising and falling, all in terror. The sound of it numbed and terrified Ellis. He stamped on the brake, intent on letting the coach carry on, one hand flying from the steering wheel to his ear, trying to blot out the terrifying sounds before his eardrums burst . . .

George MacGowan frantically shook his head, clinging to the steering wheel, as the screaming went on and on and on . . . and he knew now, just *knew*, that those bizarre voices (could they possibly be *human* voices?) were coming from the source of intense light beyond his screen. And they knew – as did he – that nothing could stop the collision as . . .

George dragged the wheel hard over.

The coach swerved to the left again, towards Burwell's car.

One second later, and Burwell would have made it as his speed dropped.

But the rear end of the coach clipped his right wing.

Burwell's other hand flew to his face as his car was slammed from the motorway, spinning end to end. The side windows imploded, showering him with glass. Somehow, the screaming was going on and on – and now Burwell's own screams were joining the terrifying throng as the car slammed into the hard shoulder, mounted the grassed embankment and came to a shuddering halt. Burwell was screaming in fear and hate. It was as if the terrible screaming voices inside his car belonged to everyone in the world who had ever wanted to put him down or place an obstacle in his path. They belonged to the people who hated him, those who wanted him out of the way. To his mother and father, long dead. To Klark, the blackmailing bastard. He wanted them dead and gone, dead and gone as . . .

The coach's windscreen blew apart from an invisible impact. Somehow, the glittering fragments did not explode *into* the coach, nor out and away into the night. The glass shattered with an almighty, cascading roar and then, suddenly, was gone. As if the impact and the light had shattered and then instantly dissolved it all. The light and the voices filled the cab, and George's hands flew from the driving wheel towards his face as the light erupted all around him. It was as if some lead sheath had been removed from a nuclear reactor. He tried to scream, but his voice was drowned by the screaming multitude that had now somehow invaded the coach. The shock of the screaming voices and the brilliantly blinding light had brought the coach passengers instantly out of their sleep. Some added their own cries of distress to the maelstrom of noise as they struggled to rise; others clawed at their seats, too shocked to react further. Others froze, too terrified by the insane shrieking noise to say or do anything as . . .

Jane Teal awoke with her husband's name clenched in her teeth. In her dream, he had begun to destroy the furniture in the living room when he couldn't find her. She had been pleading with him to stop, until now merely whimpering in her little-girl's voice. But now the whimpering became a strangled scream as she clawed her way to consciousness, the reflection of her own face in the window next to her somehow adding an extra edge to her fear, making her recoil across the seat. She wanted the terror to end, wanted Tom to be taken out of her nightmares for ever as . . .

Roger O'Dowd was unaware that he was scrabbling above him, searching for the overhead rack. Still asleep, he was instinctively reacting to the horrifying voices and the terrible light by seeking to protect the thing that was most important to him: the folder in the overhead rack containing his portfolio of sketches and watercolours. Only when he was on his feet and his fingers were hooked in the rack did he finally erupt from sleep – just as the blinding light became like that from an open furnace door, making him cover his face with one hand as he hung swaying from the rack with the other. But there was no direct heat in the invading light. Far from it. The light emitted a bone-chilling and fierce *cold*, freezing everyone in the coach, but even though there was no heat . . .

George MacGowan screamed and clawed at his face as his eyes boiled in their sockets. And when he took his hands away again, his eyes finally exploded, smearing the dash-board in front of him. His hands spasmed and groped before him now, as if some hopelessly instinctive part of him was probing for the liquid remnants of his eyes, as if his twitching fingers could collect it all up and ram it back into the bloody sockets and make everything all right again. The light flooded into the ragged and empty sockets. Blood streamed from both ears as his body sagged back in the seat, then jerked forward again over the spinning wheel, like a puppet. The weight of his body dragged the wheel even harder to the left.

The angle of turn was too severe.

The coach swung low on its suspension, until the upper wheel rims gouged into the asphalt of the motorway and . . .

*   *   *

Jane Teal fell headlong into the aisle. Without her being aware of it, the Lord's Prayer had come to her, just as it had when she was a child, afraid of the dark. As her head connected with the stained carpet on the floor, 'thy Kingdom come . . .' was as far as she got. She flopped and rolled, catapulting back into the dream of verbal punishment from her husband. It was as if she had never woken. Her conscious mind, appalled and dismayed, gratefully grabbed its chance to return to oblivion as . . .

Roger O'Dowd's feet left the floor, making him swing out like some gymnast on the parallel bars, hanging on by one hand. His feet connected with an elderly man's head as he clambered to look back over the head-rest. His hair, carefully parted over a bald pate, flew up like a jack-in-the box lid; his spectacles smashed, and he flew backwards. Suddenly, Roger knew that he was going to die. And in that instant, his only ambition seemed to flare and then wither inside. He had wanted to break out of the mould that life had shaped for him, had wanted to create the kind of art that would change people's lives for ever, blow their minds. Now he knew with utter conviction that it was never going to happen. Somewhere, someone was shouting: 'My baby, oh good Christ, my BABY!' Roger clawed with his free hand to find some kind of grip; he failed, and his other hand was torn loose. He fell between seats, backwards and head down. The impact dazed him, but now he was bent double, feet in the air, and suffocating in the fetid darkness of the coach floor as . . .

A spray of sparks erupted from the coach's wheel rims as it slewed to the left. The next moment, the coach turned over, slamming down hard on its side. The interior became a catapulting, rolling nightmare as glass imploded from the windows on all sides. Hand luggage and bodies fell and twisted and rolled, as if in a gigantic, surreal spin drier. The coach flipped over on to its roof, then crashed onto its other side, turning side-on to the motorway as it slithered onwards in a shower of sparks. The shrieking of the voices would not cease. It joined the exploding of glass, the devastating roar, the shriek of buckling metal and ripping bodywork. George MacGowan was caught between the jagged window frame and the ground as the coach rolled, severing his body at the waist. Both halves of the torso whirled away through the broken side window, away from the coach and into the night, his arms signalling a wild semaphore as his upper half smacked on to the tarmac and slid to a halt like wet sacking. His lower torso vanished over an embankment and into a gully. The coach was still flooded with the impossible, blinding light; the inhuman screaming went on and on and . . .

'Oh my God,' said Harry, weakly, as the road ahead was suddenly bathed in incredible, enveloping, luminous light. His first reaction was the same as the ill-fated coach-driver's; the lights were the headlights of a car, travelling at speed towards them, on the wrong side of the road. And in the moment the thought registered, the light suddenly flooded out on all sides to engulf the motorway. And then, with the coming of the light, came the sounds that had engulfed the coach: the tortured screaming of voices and the cacophony of noise that followed the light, filling the Starks' family car with heart-chilling intensity. Jean clutched for her husband as he twisted the wheel, trying to get out of the way of whatever lay ahead, knowing instinctively that the danger was not *ahead* any more. It was here with them, now. The danger was *in* the car. In the rear seats, Harry's daughters grabbed for each other, crying aloud in distress at the *other* terrifying sounds of distress which had exploded into the car.

'Daddeeeeee . . .'

'Harry, oh God, Harry!'

'Hold on, hold on, girls!'

Harry twisted the wheel harder, trying to get out of the light and out of the screaming as . . .

Ellis Burwell scrabbled at the lock on the car door. His fingers clawed and wrenched, trying to pop the button up, but in his terror his hands would not do what he wanted. The car was still filled with light, even though it was stationary on the embankment. He could see nothing, could hear only the endless screaming of these voices in agony – still impossibly in the car with him. He had to get out and away from the car, because now he knew in his terror what the light must be. The car had caught fire, its interior was a blazing inferno, and that was why he could see nothing but brilliant light. And he was trapped in the car, burning alive. He was in shock, and although he could feel no pain, could indeed feel no *heat*, he knew that he was burning and that his flesh was shrivelling and peeling from him. The agonised screaming he could hear was the sound of his own voice as he burned. Burwell flailed at the driver's door, finally lunging away from it across the front passenger seat towards the other door, forgetting that he was still wearing his seat belt. The restriction around his waist and chest terrified him even further. He was trapped.

And then his car, nose pointing up the grassed embankment where it had been shunted by the coach, began rolling back down the slope.

It hit the hard shoulder, rocking on its suspension. Inside the car, Burwell began to sob, realising that he could still hear the shrieking voices, and that they couldn't possibly be coming from him. He scrabbled at the door again, suddenly realised that the seat belt was still fastened and hastily unfastened it – as the impetus of the car rolling from the embankment carried it straight back out across the motorway and . . .

Harry, still swerving to avoid the light inside his car, drove straight into the side of Burwell's vehicle. The impact smashed the Lotus Elan back in the direction from which it had come, spinning on its axis. Inside, Burwell bounced and jerked like a crash-test dummy as the car hit the embankment once more. Harry's car was smashed over on to its right side, tyres and bodywork screeching along with the shrieking of the invisible voices. The car rolled on to its roof in a spray of broken glass. Still sliding, it smashed into the underbelly of the coach, now lying horizontally across the motorway, straddling the lanes as . . .

*   *   *

The country and western song on Martin's truck radio suddenly broke up into a hiss of crackling static. Mercy was singing along again and reached for the dial, pausing when she saw the look on Martin's face.

'What is it . . . ?' she began to ask.

Martin's face was rigid, his eyes fixed. Obviously something was wrong up ahead. Mercy looked up.

'Something,' said Martin, applying the brakes. 'Something coming . . .'

And then the blinding light exploded into the cab. Martin threw a hand up to shade his eyes, steadying the wheel. Mercy cried out aloud in alarm, throwing herself back in her seat – and then the screaming horde erupted into the cab an instant after the light. Even above the tormented torrent of sound, Mercy heard Martin yell:

'*Oh my good Christ!*'

And even though Martin was braking, he had no way of seeing what lay in the road ahead of him. The luminous, all-enveloping light hid everything from sight. Instinctively, he knew that something was out there in the night, felt that it was heading straight for him at tremendous speed; but even though he braked, and braked hard, he still ploughed into the Starks' family car at fifty miles an hour, crushing it into the underbelly of the coach. The impact of the truck smashed the coach and the remains of the Starks' car aside. They slithered screeching up against the hard shoulder, demolishing the barrier.

Mercy dived for her door, blundering in the light, now pressing both hands to her ears and trying to keep the sounds of the hellish screaming outside her head. The impact slammed her forward and down. The breath was knocked from Martin's lungs as the steering wheel jammed under his ribs.

Then the tanker jack-knifed.

Groaning and juddering like some giant beast with a broken neck, the cabin slewed to one side as the connecting section between cab and tanker screeched under the strain. As the full weight of the load behind the cabin came to bear, the connecting rig was torn apart and exploded into fragments. The cab spun away, severed from its load, but did not turn over as the tanker slewed screeching across the motorway. With a great groaning and rending, the severed tanker-load carved a gigantic furrow out of the asphalt as it finally rolled on to its side, sliding to join the shattered coach on the motorway. The pressurised tanker was fractured, its load spilling out like the life blood of a belly-gashed dinosaur. Slowly, it began to flood the motorway.

For Martin, everything was happening in slow motion. And although he knew that he should be frozen in horror, some little part of him deep inside was amazed at how detached and distant he had become as the cab whirled around and around, spinning across the motorway, threatening to crash over on to its side at any moment. But the calm and quiet centre that had suddenly become his very being remembered something from years ago. He was seven years old, at the fairground. And he was on the waltzer with his sister and father. He hadn't thought about that fairground visit since then, but now it was crystal clear; indeed, he was reliving it. The cab was spinning around just like that waltzer; he could smell the ozone and the machine oil. And somehow the terrible screaming of voices was the screaming of the other people on the fairground rides, no longer truly terrified, now more a *controlled* terror. Martin tried to reach for Mercy, tried to tell her that everything was all right. But somehow his arm was leaden. Here inside the cab, everything was heavy and slow, even though the night was whirling and black and flaring beyond the cab windows. The overwhelming light had dimmed as they spun, enough for Martin to make out the interior of the cab. But Mercy was nowhere to be seen. Had she gone? Had she been flung out into the night? He saw the hand then, white and ghostly and crooked. Down by the passenger seat. She had been thrown down there, was struggling to clamber back, but the centrifugal force of the crazily spinning cab had pinned her down there, despite her slow-motion attempts to rise. Martin tried to say: It's okay, everything's okay . . . but then . . .

The Vauxhall Viva screamed out of the night, horn blaring.
    It collided head on with the spinning cab.

And Martin was back in real time now as the cab slammed over on to its roof. The windscreen and windows exploded. His head whiplashed back against the seat, the breath knocked from his body as the seat belt constricted him. Mercy's clutching hand was gone from sight.

The light and the voices were gone.

In a roaring tangle of disintegrating metal and flying glass, the Vauxhall and the truck cab ploughed off the motorway, destroyed an emergency telephone post and then, still locked in their embrace of destruction, rolled into a gully at the side of the motorway.

Cold night air was blowing on Roger's face as he struggled to be free of the weight that pinned him down. Had he passed out? For a moment, it seemed that he had been taken away from the terror that had so suddenly descended on him. There were no more screaming voices, no more of the hideously bright light. But the constriction on his chest brought claustrophobia and new terror. Where was he? He scrabbled at the weight, then realised that it was a seat rest. He shoved hard, and slid out from underneath. Somewhere, people were groaning. The voices that had invaded the coach? Broken glass lay everywhere; he felt a shard stab into his palm. Apart from the groaning, the silence seemed unnatural and ominous. Had the light affected his eyes? He could make no sense of the angular shapes and shadows. And then, as he crawled out from the fractured seat, he realised what had happened. The coach had turned over and was lying on its roof; the irregular shapes above him were the rows of seats. The jumble of shapes lying all around, glittering with broken glass, was suitcases and holdalls and coats and . . . human bodies?

He had to get out of here.

His leg hurt. Was it badly damaged? He had read somewhere once that people with really bad injuries didn't feel the pain at first because of the adrenalin that pumped through their bodies in shock. He groped at the leg, but could feel no warm, damp patch of blood or protruding bone. And as he did so, he saw a familiar shape in the darkness, a hardboard rectangle

that meant more to him than anything else – his portfolio
of artwork. Roger clawed at it, grabbed the edge. It was
jammed. Furiously now, he dragged it free, hugging it to
his chest as he crawled on elbows and knees towards the
shattered window. There was a smell of petrol, bringing an
added raw edge of terror as he scrambled. The window had
completely shattered, the frame bent and angular but big
enough to crawl through. Were they straddling the motorway?
Would he climb straight out into the path of an oncoming
car? How long before something smashed into them? And
now, somehow, he was outside in the night. Glass covered
the tarmac, glistening like snow and crunching underfoot as
he pulled himself to his feet. His leg did not give out beneath
him. Now he could see that his jeans were not torn, there
was no blood. Miraculously, he had come out of this alive.
At last, he could see where the coach had ended up, lying
across the hard shoulder with the motorway barrier buckled
and trapped beneath the shattered bodywork. Lying almost
parallel to it was another vehicle, a long-distance tanker. He
could not see the cab, but even in the darkness he could see the
skidmarks and carved furrow where the tanker had ploughed
into the coach and jammed them both off the motorway. A
great enervation overcame him then when he saw the extent
of the carnage. Suddenly, he was kneeling on the tarmac.
When he retched, it was as if the horror inside was trying to
get out.

When he looked up again, he saw a shape moving in the
broken window of the coach, the window through which he had
climbed. The shape raised a hand in his direction, imploring
help. For an instant, he saw a streaked face, a woman's face.
Then her head was lowered again, and in that moment Roger
saw her features reflected in the multi-coloured pool that was
spreading around the coach.

Petrol.

His first instinct was to get away from the coach as fast as
possible. But as quickly as it had registered, he was shamed
by his cowardice. He had to help the others, if he could. He
staggered back towards the coach, expecting the petrol to

ignite at any moment, expecting to be swallowed alive in a great roaring blast of liquid flame.

'Here,' he said when he reached the crumpled bodywork. He knelt quickly, glass crunching underfoot, and the woman struggled to take his hand. Roger heaved, and was surprised when she slid out through the gap easily. Her clothes were torn and there was blood on her forehead when he finally hauled her to her feet. In the darkness, and with the blood smearing her face, it was impossible to tell her age. She seemed groggy and concussed. 'Quick . . . come on . . .' Roger tried to squint through the darkness into the coach, tried to see if there was any other movement from within. But he could see and hear nothing as he began to half walk, half carry the woman away from the shattered vehicle.

'The screaming . . .' mumbled the woman. 'It was the screaming.'

'You're all right. Lean on me. You're going to be all right. We've got to find a telephone and . . .'

And then something ignited around the base of the coach with an oily whump. Roger flinched, looking back to see a lake of orange-blue fire surge around the coach. It flared and seemed to come alive. In seconds it had engulfed the twisted bodywork, orange clouds sucking hungrily into the shattered window through which they had made their escape, now greedily spreading to the other shattered windows and surging within. A horrifying image came instantly to mind. The flames were alive, they were predators. They had suddenly descended on the coach and were roaring through the windows to find survivors whom they could devour.

'Oh God . . .'

Roger braced himself as he carried the woman away. In a moment, he was sure, he would hear the screaming again as the flames reached the people who were still trapped in the coach. He shook his head, as if he could somehow block his ears and prevent the sound from coming. And perhaps it worked, because there was no frantic screaming and pleading for help as they moved away. Something seemed to split or crack inside the coach, a muffled retort like a gunshot. And then a great billowing of orange flame completely engulfed the vehicle, flames roaring from the shattered windows. Backlit by the flames, the shadows of Roger and the woman were gigantic on the tarmac as . . .

Harry Stark stared up at the stars.

They had never looked more beautiful. The sky was a rich, dark velvet; and those pinpoints were glinting and glistening with a lustre than was truly fascinating. Not since childhood had he been so entranced. For the moment, he could not recall what he was doing here. He could feel the ground beneath his back. It was soft. Perhaps he was lying on grass. Yes, he could see a stalk of grass on his right. It was caressing his face as if alive, now stroking his forehead. Harry tried to move, but the effort required seemed enormous, as if he were pinned to the ground by a great invisible weight. Suddenly, it became important that he find out where he was, and what he was doing there. A faint anxiety gnawed at his stomach. Something to do with other people, people who were important to him. Was he married? He could not recall. Groaning then, he tried to rise. There was a pain in his left arm. It would not take his weight as he tried to roll over. Instead, he rolled to his right. The sky swung in his line of vision. Looking around, he could see nothing but darkness. Had he died? Was this what it was like on the other side? Only perpetual night?

And then light flared fifty feet from where he lay, instantly silhouetting his surroundings. And in the one moment of surging, roaring flame, Harry remembered everything that had happened.

A sea of petrol flame was licking around the base of a coach. Harry could see the upside-down logo: FlyWay MyWay. The petrol was spreading from the overturned lorry which lay by the coach's side. Soon the fire would engulf the coach and the lorry . . . and the horribly mangled remains of the car that had been rammed between the two.

The car.

Harry's car.

At first, Harry thought that the screaming voices had

returned. The voices that had invaded his car, along with
the blinding light. But this time there was only one voice. The
sound of it terrified him. When he recognised the grief-stricken,
terror-ridden sound as his *own* voice, it terrified him even more.
Ignoring the pain in his left arm and the multiple pains in his
legs and the small of his back, Harry staggered to his feet. His
jacket and shirt were ripped and bloodied. His spectacles had
been smashed, the wire rim hanging from one ear. Warm blood
trickled from a gash on the back of his head, pooling around
his shirt collar and flowing down his back. He looked like
a scarecrow that had uprooted itself as he staggered across
the motorway, now gaining speed as great tongues of orange
flame began to rise from the lake of fire, clawing greedily at the
bodywork of the coach.

'No . . .'

The flames reached the shattered wreck of his car.

'*No . . .*'

The flames began hungrily to devour the ruptured engine
and the shattered hood, as if eager to gain entrance. Now, as
he half staggered, half ran across the littered motorway lane
towards the wrecks, he could see the windscreen. Crazed and
obscured, but with one ragged hole in the passenger side. As
if someone's head had jerked forward and punched a hole in the
screen there. The ragged edge of the fracture was stained red.

'NO!'

Flames were leaping up over the hood as Harry reached the
crumpled passenger door. The roof had been almost flattened,
the door frame compressed. When he yanked at the door
handle, it would not budge. He tried to look through the
crazed window but could see nothing inside. A hot blast
of air hit him squarely in the face, singeing his eyebrows,
blackening his skin. Yelling aloud, he lunged back and put
his elbow through the glass. Still yanking at the door, he
looked inside.

And what he saw in there almost turned his mind.

Still screaming, Harry yanked and tugged desperately at
the door handle. Flames roared and gusted at his feet. His
shoes and trouser legs were burning. Flames devoured the

crumpled hood, eager to reach the windscreen. Harry screamed and screamed as . . .

'Martin,' moaned Mercy. 'For Christ's sake . . . where *are* you?'

Her ears were still ringing with the sounds of the damnable screaming. Something very, very *bad* had happened somewhere – and it seemed as if they had driven straight into it. Being flung down below her seat had probably saved her life. There had been another impact, just as the light and the voices had fizzled to nothingness, and Mercy – still struggling to regain her feet – was glad that she had stayed where she was when something erupted through the passenger window next to where she had been sitting. Something that looked like a steel pole. The pole drove into the cab wall where her head would have been, puncturing a ragged hole. Instinctively, her hand had flown to her face as broken windscreen glass showered her. Then everything had tilted again, jamming her further down. Then blackness, and further disorientation.

Now it had all stopped.

Mercy waited in the darkness and the silence. Waited for the voices and the light to return. Waited for something else to smash into them. She struggled to control her breathing, poised ready to react if something else should happen. But there was only the ringing in her ears – no, not a ringing; more like a soft hissing sound. It sounded as if a pressure canister somewhere had split. Then she remembered the load that Martin was carrying.

Amyl nitrate, he had said.

Christ! I'll burn alive . . .

Unaware that the cab had been severed from the rest of the tanker and that the load itself was lying on the other side of the motorway, Mercy struggled to pull herself upright, finding immediately that something seemed to be wrong with her sense of balance. Had she been concussed? She pulled herself up to the seat and now could see what was wrong. The cab was lying at an angle, the driver's seat at the bottom of a forty-five-degree slope. Her own seat was at the top of the slope, and when she looked she could see that the passenger door had been torn off.

She clambered up over the seat, slipped and almost fell down on to the driving seat. Bracing her feet on the passenger seat and with one hand on the rim of the door frame, she looked back down for Martin. She could see grass pressed up close to the driving-seat window, which was still intact. But there was no sign of him.

'Martin! Where are you? Come on, we've got to get out.'

There was no movement. Only faint hissing sound. Mercy pulled herself up to the missing door frame and looked out into the night. What she saw there filled her with awe.

They had been smashed from the motorway and into a gully at the roadside. The remains of the car that had collided with them were fused into the rear of the cab, a hideous, compacted mass of crushed metal bodywork, shattered engine parts and wiring. Its windscreen had been punched out entirely from the frame and lay on the grass below her, miraculously undamaged. But of the place where the windscreen had been, there was no sign. Only a hood ornament and the remains of a grille gave a suggestion that the hideous mess of destruction that she looked on had once been a car.

Someone's inside that. The thought came to her, and immediately she felt as if she might throw up or faint or worse. With a sound of disgust that was also a sound of despair, Mercy looked across the motorway to the overturned truck, lying with its belly facing them. She was amazed that they had been flung so far and she'd barely suffered a scratch. There was something else on the other side of the lorry, something that had been rammed up hard over the hard shoulder. A coach?

Oh God, those people.

There was another car lying on its roof back there, perhaps fifty yards away.

And now as she came to look more closely, were those the remains of a further car, jammed between the lorry and the coach?

Oh God . . .

Looking quickly away, Mercy saw a reflective glint down below her. Beneath the mangled remains of the car, somehow in the grass of the gully. A sparkling; a blue-black and white rippling. At last, she realised where the soft hissing sound was coming from. There was a small stream at the bottom of the gully in which the mangled wreck of the car had rammed the cab, the surface of the water reflecting the soft blue of a neon sign further down the motorway. She leaned back into the cab, still balancing precariously on the seat and looking down into the darkness.

'Martin . . .'

The soft hissing seemed louder inside the cab now. That same rippling blue-black was blurring the window beside the driver's seat. Slowly, but surely, the cab was filling with water from the stream.

'*Martin!* Where the hell *are* you?'

This time, at the sound of her voice, there was movement in the darkness. A figure suddenly took shape as it leaned away from the bent steering wheel. Now, at last, she could see Martin, but could not work out why she hadn't been able to see his body crouched over the wheel. He groaned, passing a hand over his face, and the movement seemed to tilt him downwards. Like herself, he had been jammed into an awkward position on impact. Now he was fumbling and groping as his body twisted and dropped down against the side window. Water splashed over his arms. Mercy saw it flowing fast behind his head. If she didn't get him out of here quickly, he was going to drown. Cursing, she looked back out into the night for any sign of movement, any sign that other vehicles were stopping to help. But apart from the shattered wrecks on the motorway there was no other traffic. Surely someone *must* come along. But right now there was nothing. Mercy lowered herself back into the cab, still keeping a tight grip on the door frame. 'Martin, for Christ's sake. Are you hurt, is that it? Can't you move?'

Martin groaned again, and Mercy cursed once more. She would have to let go of the door frame, brace her foot on the steering wheel and lean right down. One slip, and she'd end up face down on top of Martin, trapped in the cab while the water rose to drown them both. Gingerly, she got down on one knee on the shattered dashboard, resting one arm across the steering wheel. The windscreen was spiderwebbed with cracks. Leaning down, she reached for Martin's arm. It was soaked with dirty water.

'You've got to help me a little bit. Or we're both going to die in here.'

Martin groaned again, but seemed to be nodding. He tried to sit up. Mercy leaned further down, dragged at his sleeve.

And then lost her balance completely.

The next moment, she was lying face to face with Martin in the water that now seemed to be gushing into the cab, her legs up in the air. The impact had cracked the passenger window around their heads, and the trickle had become a flood. Mercy panicked, twisted and tried to get a better grip. Water flowed into her mouth and she choked. Martin groped at her feebly, trying to help. But Mercy knew that if she didn't bite down on her panic, didn't do *something*, they were both going to drown in each other's arms in the bottom of this gully.

'Fucking *lorry*,' she spat, trying to rechannel her anger into energy. 'Had to get picked up by a lorry. Couldn't wait for a fucking *Mercedes*, with a *bar*, and a randy *millionaire*. No, had to get stuck down here in a hole, didn't I? *Didn't I?*' There was no way up; she could not twist around and regain her feet. There was only one way out.

The windscreen, cobwebbed with cracks.

Mercy shunted herself around, braced one leg – and then kicked hard. It was a stamp rather than a kick. But the first blow had the desired effect. It punched a hole clean through into the night. She dragged her foot back and kicked again, and again, uttering a sharp cry of effort with each blow. Glass sparkled and pattered down on top of them, splashing into the rapidly rising water. Martin made a glugging sound and Mercy realised that water had begun to flow over his head.

'No!'

Kick.

'*No!*'

Kick.

'NO!'

And this time, the entire windscreen crazed and fell apart,

showering them like broken ice. Mercy wriggled around, her legs thrashing in the night. She shoved with both hands, felt something slice across her forearm. She swore at it, kept shimmying backwards and felt her knees connect with the hood. Still crying out with the effort, she wriggled clear of the aperture she had created, but kept both hands fastened on Martin's sleeve. He seemed to be resisting her, fumbling at the shattered dash.

'Martin, for Christ's sake, *help* me!'

'Got to get the Trem Card and the Hazchem sheet.'

'*What?*'

'Got it . . . got it . . .' Martin had found what he needed, was cramming it into his soaked shirt-front.

Mercy yanked hard, cursing.

Slowly, ever so slowly, she began to drag him over the steering wheel and on to the hood.

If something snagged him now, or if his legs became trapped out of sight, she knew that she would never have the strength to pull him free. Martin seemed to be coming around at last. He groped out through the windscreen aperture, water streaming from his face, his hair soaked. Mercy slid from the hood on to the embankment, gravity pulling them apart. Quickly then, she jumped back up and grabbed him under the armpits with both hands. For a moment, it seemed that he would be stuck after all. But then he seemed to get a knee up on the windscreen rim. He shoved hard, and they both toppled from the hood on to the grass, their legs trailing in the softly trickling stream at the bottom of the gully. The soft hissing sound, just a moment ago so threatening and deadly, was now curiously comforting.

They lay there on their backs, gasping for air.

From somewhere over the embankment, from the direction of the pile-up on the motorway, Mercy heard a soft whump.

'You . . .' Martin had recovered now, was able to speak at last. 'You . . . got me out of there . . .'

Mercy laughed, the laughter turning into a coughing fit. Martin tried weakly to pat her back. When she had recovered, she said: 'That's the quality of Mercy.'

'Still a bad joke,' grinned Martin, and began to get up. 'Christ . . .'

Mercy looked up at him, saw that his attention was focused on the water that flowed in the bottom of the gully and swirled over their legs. No longer blue-black and white, the water seemed to be an oily orange-blue. Just another trick of the light. Martin leaned down and grabbed her arm. His grip seemed immensely powerful, totally at odds with the weak and groggy man that she had just dragged to safety across the hood of the lorry. He was looking back up the gully, trying to see past the wrecked cab at its crazy angle and the mangled wreck of the car that had rammed them there. He began to haul her up.

'Climb!' he yelled suddenly. 'Let's get out of here, *now!*'

Mercy hung on to him, struggling to clamber up the embankment, and was just about to ask Martin what was wrong when she saw what he had seen.

Roaring orange flame was rushing towards them down the gully.

In that instant, she knew that the orange-blue reflection in the water was petrol. It had spread across the motorway from the wrecked vehicles, and had somehow trickled over and around the edge of the embankment, into the stream at the bottom of the gully. Clawing at the grass, she recalled the soft whump, knew that something had ignited the petrol on the other side of the motorway. The fire had swept across to them, following its trail down the embankment and into the slowly flowing stream. In a matter of seconds the wrecked car, the cab . . . and they themselves . . . would be engulfed in the liquid fire. They thrashed to climb the embankment as . . .

Ellis Burwell staggered down the centre of the motorway, away from his shattered car. Dazed, shocked and confused, his hands were constantly exploring his body as he walked towards the coach and the lorry. He could not believe that he had not burned, could not believe that his clothes were still *there*. The car was on fire, he knew that it had caught fire, knew that the clothes had peeled and shrivelled away, knew that he had cooked and burned. The tie around his neck seemed fascinating. He played with it as he staggered on, fumbled at the lapels of his frayed jacket, explored the fabric of his ripped shirt. He patted his hips constantly, like someone trying to find loose change. Turning to look at his wrecked car, he expected to see flames leaping from its windows, expected to see a trail of footsteps from the car, a track of soot and ash from his disintegrating, still smouldering body. Then he heard the whump and staggered around again to see orange-blue flames leap up from around the overturned lorry. The sight of the fire froze him in his tracks. He watched in terror as it swept around the lorry to the coach. He recoiled when the coach suddenly exploded in flame. He had cheated the fire once. Would it find him now? Would it suddenly come sweeping across the asphalt? Burwell wanted to run, wanted to stagger off the motorway and climb the embankment, get away from this place as quickly as possible. But he could not will his body to move. He could only stand, hugging himself and watching the flames as . . .

Mercy's foot skidded on the slope. She pinwheeled to regain balance, knew that she'd fall backwards into the gully and be engulfed – but Martin had her arm again and held tight until she had regained her balance. At last, they reached the top of the embankment, their figures starkly illuminated from below as the lake of fire surged over the cab, exploded through the windscreen aperture and hungrily devoured its interior. They looked back to see the liquid following the course of the stream, onwards and beyond into the night. Thick black smoke gushed over them from the gully below.

'Jesus *Christ*!' exclaimed Mercy, waving the smoke from her face. Then Martin had her hand again and they were staggering down the embankment towards the motorway. Now they could see the course that the fire had taken. Spilling from the ruptured tanks in the lorry, it had engulfed both that vehicle and the coach next to it. Off to their right, following the slight cant in the motorway, the petrol had streamed across the road and into the gully from which they had emerged.

'Look!' said Martin.

Mercy followed his gaze, to see the lone man standing in the motorway, watching the flames and hugging himself.

The man seemed to see them.

For a moment, they just stood and looked. And then . . .

Roger and Jane staggered away from the burning coach, moving around to see the lorry which was spilling its lake of burning fire across the motorway, trying to keep as much distance between themselves and the pile-up as possible. Now, as they moved, they could see what had been crushed between the tanker and the coach. It was another car, horribly mangled. Somehow, the stream of burning petrol had not totally engulfed the vehicle; rivulets of fire had streamed around it, and they could see that flames were leaping over the buckled hood and in through the shattered windscreen. Smoke billowed and curled from the hood, and at first Roger thought that the frenzied movement at the passenger door of the crushed car was merely the flame and the smoke.

Then he saw that it was a man.

He was tugging frantically at the door handle, trying to wrench it open.

Jane saw him now, and moaned in horror.

The man was on fire.

His trouser legs and shoes were burning. Flame licked from the shattered car window, and she saw his hair frazzle and shrivel. Not heeding the pain, he continued his assault on the door. Even from this distance, they could see his smoke-blackened face. His mouth was wide open, and Jane realised that he was screaming like an animal, but they could hear nothing over the roaring of the petrol flame. In a moment, the flame would totally engulf the lorry, the coach – and the car between them.

'Get away!' yelled Roger, staggering forward and waving one arm, the portfolio still protectively clenched under the other arm. 'Get out of there!'

The man seemed to hear. He staggered in a half-turn towards them.

His face was a mask of horror and desperation.

He beckoned to Roger desperately.

And Roger saw, to his horror, that the man's hands were burning. He didn't seem to care, only wanted him to hurry over and help. But Roger's last vestiges of strength had been used up in his escape from the coach and his rescue of the woman. The man seemed to notice his hands then, looking at them stupidly. Then, in an utterly ordinary manner – so ordinary that it was utterly horrifying – he brought his hands together in a washing motion. As if he was at the kitchen sink, cleaning grime from his hands, twisting them together. The flames were snuffed out. He held his hands up to his face and looked at the smoke rising from them. Roger remained frozen in horror at the sight. And then the man turned back to the car again, the look of stupidity vanishing, the terror returning to his smoke-blackened mask of a face. He lunged awkwardly back towards the car.

And then it exploded.

The blast threw the man backwards across the motor-way as the vehicle was consumed in an orange-black fire-ball. A huge cloud of liquid sparks sprayed high like a fire-work display, pattering on the tarmac all around the blazing wrecks. A cloud of black smoke gushed skywards. Roger staggered, shielding his face, now ready to dodge aside as the burning rain fell from the sky. The three vehicles were almost entirely obliterated by the inferno. Roger began to move back, the heat fierce on his face. And then he saw the movement, only fifty feet away. A bundle of rags, rolling over and over on the tarmac, arms flapping before it came to rest.

It was the man with the burning hands.

The blast had flung him at least forty feet from the car wreck. Somehow, he had not been engulfed in the petrol spray. And when Roger looked again, he could see that the man was alive, struggling to rise to his hands and knees. Roger looked back at the woman, now on her knees with her hands over her head to protect herself from the falling rain of fire. Roger staggered back to her.

'Here!' he shouted. She looked up, her face as dumbfounded

as that of the man with the burning hands. Roger thrust the portfolio at her. 'Here, take it!'

'What . . . ?' Jane stared blankly at the folder.

'It's all right. You're safe now. But here, take this!' He took one of her arms and rammed his portfolio into her armpit. She looked at it, uncomprehending. 'Don't you lose it! Do you hear me? Don't you bloody *lose it!*' He looked up to see two figures on the embankment on the other side of the motorway. A man and a woman, staggering down the grass slope, clouds of black smoke gushing up from behind them. 'Help!' yelled Roger, turning back towards the man lying prone on the tarmac. 'Over here, for Christ's sake!' He began to stagger towards the man, seeing out of the corner of his eye that there was another figure standing in the middle of the motorway, watching him. It seemed to be hugging itself, as if seeking comfort from the horror all around. 'You too!' yelled Roger. 'Over here!' The figure didn't move.

And then he was almost on top of the burned man. For a moment, Roger just stood, looking down. He didn't know what to do, had no knowledge of first aid, was afraid to touch the man in case he hurt him. Instead, he stooped down just as the man raised his head.

'My wife . . .' said the man, trying to look back and holding out a hand.

Roger struggled to keep control at the sight of the charred hand. It was utterly black, still smoking.

'My daughters . . .'

'There's nothing you can do,' said Roger. 'It's all over. Look, just lie still and . . .'

'Got to get them out. Please help me to get them out.'

Roger remained kneeling in front of the man, unable to say anything as he turned on one elbow and looked back at the blazing carnage on the motorway.

'Can't . . . I can't . . .' Roger struggled to say something that might help, gestured weakly at the burning wrecks as the man turned back to him, the desperate plea still in his eyes. Angry then at his inability to be of any use, Roger looked furiously back at the man standing in the middle of the road watching them. 'Get to a *telephone*, then! At least, do *something!*'

Ellis Burwell fumbled weakly at his inside pocket, a hopeless gesture, for the mobile phone was still in the wreck of his car, smashed to pieces.

There was movement behind Roger now. He turned around to see that the two people from the embankment had reached him, were standing right behind him, apparently mesmerised by the sight of the burning wrecks and the great raging sea of fire. The woman Roger had helped from the wreck was still kneeling, holding his portfolio tight across her chest as if it were some protective charm.

'No cars,' said Mercy, and her voice sounded desperately tired. 'All this has happened, and there's not one car come by.'

Roger and Martin looked at her stupidly.

'I mean, no one's seen what's happened,' continued Mercy. 'It's like there's no other traffic on this fucking motorway tonight. No one to stop and help, or telephone.'

'Telephone,' said Martin, rubbing his face and now looking hard at Roger. 'You're right . . .' He paused, clearly inviting the stranger to give his name.

'Roger O'Dowd.'

'Roger. Right. Yeah, you're absolutely right. We've got to get to a telephone. Are you okay? I mean, you're not injured or anything?'

'Not me. But this guy's in a hell of a state. He needs an ambulance . . .'

'Jean,' said Harry weakly, pointing back with one of his terrible smouldering hands. 'Hilary and Diane . . .'

'Right,' said Martin uncomfortably, still addressing Roger. 'My name's Martin. This is Mercy. Look, Roger, why don't you head on up the motorway, see if you can find an emergency phone. I'll head on back in the other direction. There *was* a phone over there, but I think we smashed into it.'

'You'll never get back that way, Martin,' said Mercy. 'How are you going to get past the fire? Christ, why isn't there someone here to stop and help? Where's everyone gone?'

'I'll find a way. But if we both head in a different direction one of us is bound to find an emergency phone.'

'Okay.' Roger staggered to his feet.

'No,' said Mercy. 'You're still groggy, Martin. You'll fall face down in a burning petrol pool or something. I'll go. You stay and . . . and look after him.'

Martin almost protested, but then saw the sense of what she was saying. He was still dizzy. Looking into her eyes, he had no doubt that she would do what she said she would. Hadn't she already pulled him out of that cab wreck and saved his life?

'Okay . . . okay. But *hurry!*'

Roger and Mercy headed off in opposite directions. Martin watched them go, watched Mercy run past the man who was standing in the middle of the motorway, looking at them. Just past him, she paused, figuring out a route that would skirt around the burning lake of fire across the road. She hesitated, then chose, heading for the hard shoulder. Soon she had vanished into the darkness. When he looked back, Roger had vanished. His sweeping gaze brought the woman with the folder into focus, still on her knees. Was she praying?

'Are you all right?' he asked.

She did not answer. Her eyes were screwed shut, and now she was rocking backwards and forwards, clutching the piece of cardboard, or whatever in hell it was, her lips trembling and working.

'You're all right.' He answered his own question, but didn't sound confident about it.

When the man on the ground before him began to weep, he moved to touch him, the way a parent will move to comfort a weeping child. But the instinctive act was aborted when he remembered that they were both supposed to be grown men, and grown men did not comfort each other that way, no matter what the pain, or the loss. But the sound of the man's grief was somehow the worst thing he had ever heard in his life. And as he stared into the flames, and looked down on that bowed and flame-scorched head, something of it stripped away the hard edge that he'd tried to maintain for most of his adult life. It took away the manly shell that he'd felt was so necessary to protect himself – but more importantly those he loved – from the savage, cruel and mindless furies of the real world, furies that killed all goodness and love and innocence. The burned man's grief sliced away the protective shell that kept him from reacting to all the things that would otherwise have filled him with hopelessness. Suddenly, Martin was swamped in despair. The only realities seemed to be the cruel and unfair things. Cancer, famine, cot death. Innocent civilians being in the wrong place at the wrong time, and his father: dead at thirty-seven of a lung-devouring disease contracted in the coal mine where he worked. And Sheila, his wife, crippled by her progressively debilitating disease. All cruel and meaningless and unnecessary, like this damned motorway, where some stupid bastard had simply been driving too carelessly and too fast and on the wrong side of the bloody road.

There was no one to see. Not the man beneath him, shuddering and trembling in his terrible grief. Not the woman behind, who was praying to be out of here as soon as possible. So he gave in and began to weep too, at the utter futility of what had happened. He sank to his knees.

God knew how long it had taken, but when he heard the sound of the police sirens he was able to snap himself out of his utter desperation. He wiped his tears away, was able to touch the man's shrivelled hair beneath him, and say: 'They're coming . . .' As if this was somehow going to make everything right. But no one had seen him give in. Now he could put up his defences again.

He rose to his feet, none too steady, as the first police car and ambulance hurtled down towards him from the direction Roger had taken. And as he made that one gesture of pulling himself together, a thought seemed to leap unbidden into his mind. Something that he hadn't been able to think about since the crash, but which now seemed the most important question about everything that happened.

He remembered the impossible light that had flooded the cab.

But he remembered something else.

Who had been screaming?

PART TWO

SURVIVORS

Harry dreamed of gates.

Great ancient steel gates, which clashed and echoed. Dimly, he was aware that there were people on the other sides of the gates, clamouring to get through to him. People who had been separated from their loved ones. Even now, they were pushing up hard against the medieval barriers, thrusting their arms through the bars, groping and imploring. Begging someone to come and raise the portcullis. The sound of their voices was desperate, urgent. The clashing sounds and the voices seemed to be getting louder and nearer, louder and nearer . . .

And then he awoke.

There were lights above him; long strip-lights in a ceiling. And he was moving beneath them, lying on something that was being pushed and jostled. The voices were still urgent, but not the hundreds and thousands he had heard in his dream. He tried to turn and look, but he seemed to have no energy for that one simple incline of the head. Something rattled and clattered beneath him again as he turned a corner. At last, he knew where he was. The pale blue pastel walls, the smell of antiseptic and bleach. Now a figure passed close by. Unmistakably a nurse, her face tight and strained as she passed, but she managed a careworn, fragile smile when she saw that he was looking at her. And then she was gone, leaving behind a familiar trace of perfume.

At that moment, Harry wanted the truth to be that he had suffered a heart attack. Yes, that must be it. Jean had been telling him for ages to take it easier, that he should be thinking about winding down a little, travelling less, and not taking the money situation so seriously. She could work full time instead of part time. Nothing was worse than the kind of hassle he had been going through recently. He tried to hang on to those thoughts, but a formless anxiety began to erode them. There was something important to remember . . . Something about the car, and the motorway and . . . No! Something *had* happened to his heart. He had been at the office, and perhaps had felt the crippling pain in his . . .

. . . hands . . .

No! His arm, just like he'd read in that medical journal. First there would be a pain in the arm, then a tightness in the chest, difficulty breathing and . . .

. . . the light flooding the car, and Jean screaming his name and . . .

He must have lost consciousness in the office then. Keeled over at his desk. Now he was in hospital, had come round again. The ambulance had arrived in time to save him. They would wheel him down this hospital corridor to the intensive care unit and . . .

. . . the screaming of inhuman voices, the screeching of tyres and the roaring orange blossoms of flame . . .

. . . and Jean and the girls would be in the waiting room, anxiously wringing their hands as they waited for the doctor. Even now, the doctor was pushing through the waiting-room door with a smile of relief on his face, telling them as they rose to meet him that . . .

Staggering to the car wreck, wrenching at the door. Fire crackling over the hood of the car and through the shattered windscreen. The windscreen with the red stains around that ragged hole in the passenger side.

The doctor was telling them that everything was going to be all right. There was no need to worry. It had been a mild heart attack. Just a warning that he should take things a lot easier from now on, just as Jean had said. He was well on the way to recovery. He saw Jean sit down, hands moving to her face to hide tears of relief as the girls put their arms around her shoulders. He could see the tears streaming down their own faces, could see that they were both trying to be brave to make it better for Mum. In that moment, he was fiercely proud of Hilary and Diane.

'It's all right, Mr Stark.' The woman's voice was calm and gentle, but still a shock to his system. It cut through the images he was trying to overlay in his mind. He tried to turn again, and this time felt pain in his neck and shoulder. 'Just relax,' the calm but penetrating voice went on. 'Everything's going to be all right.'

'All right?' His own voice seemed alien to him. As if someone else were trying to use it. 'My wife, Jean. And my daughters. You mean they're okay? Oh *God*, I can't tell you what a relief that is . . .'

'Don't talk,' said the unseen nurse's voice again, but this time it seemed that some of the assurance had left it.

'I need to see them,' continued Harry. 'Please.'

This time there was no answer; just the strip-lights above and the clatter of the trolley on which he was being transported. He struggled to rise and felt a gentle arm on his shoulder trying to push him back down. This time, anger overwhelmed him and he resisted, feeling agonising pain in the hand that was trying to shove away the restraint. This time, he saw his hand – saw the plastic bag wound tight around it. He fell back, now raising both hands in front of his face, seeing that they were bandaged in the see-through plastic. The hands were hideously pitted and blackened.

And then reality flooded him.

The pain and the terror of remembrance were too much to bear. A stomach-clutching realisation of utter hopelessness and desperation racked him. He began to moan, incapable of speech, incapable of rational thought. And when he remembered what he had seen through the shattered side window, just before the flames engulfed his car and he had been blown across the motorway, he began to convulse.

'Dr *Fredericks*!' The unseen nurse's voice had lost its calm completely now as Harry's bandaged hands fell limply to the trolley and his body began to spasm.

'Patient in *shock* . . .'

Roger O'Dowd slept.

There had been no conscious decision on his part to rest, no desire to sleep. One moment he was awake, sitting up on the casualty ward bed where he had been taken by the ambulance staff; the next, he had fallen asleep with his head resting back against the cool wall tiles.

A fleet of ambulances had screeched up the motorway as he made his way back to the place where the collision had occurred. He had found an emergency telephone a quarter of a mile up the road, had telephoned in, but it seemed that the young woman who had gone in the opposite direction must have found a phone before him as the emergency services were apparently expecting his call. Now that the call had been made, he felt somehow different. As if all the energy was draining out of him. He had struggled back along the motorway, watching the great orange clouds of flame and the belching black smoke pluming into the night sky. Real time had somehow ceased during the collision and its aftermath, the world beyond that two-hundred-yard stretch of motorway seemingly frozen. Just like those science fiction movies he had seen as a kid, where visitors from space had made all the machines and the engines grind to a halt, as some kind of warning. Just ahead, he saw that the police had formed an emergency cordon across the motorway. At first, he thought he would have trouble getting through. A blank-faced constable had told him to turn back, then had seen him up close – the lacerated face, the bloodstains and the oil. Roger had begun to explain, but the constable had grabbed him by the sleeve, pulled him through the barrier and told one of the other men to drive him to where the ambulances waited. Roger allowed himself to be bundled into the back of a police car and slumped back across the seat. Someone was talking to him – perhaps the driver – but he seemed unable to focus on the words. There had been some kind of 'blank' period then. Without being aware that he had been transferred, he was now somehow lying on a stretcher in an ambulance, listening to the siren.

He seemed to remember one of the ambulance men shoving a newspaper reporter and his flash camera out of the way as they carried him from the ambulance to a wheelchair in the forecourt of the local hospital's casualty department. Roger had protested, telling the ambulance crew that he wasn't hurt – but they had insisted, wheeling him at breakneck speed through the corridors and into one of the wards. On the way, he had passed a clock on the wall.

It was 1.30 in the morning.

Once he was in the cubicle, screened off by grey plastic sheets, someone had told him that a nurse or doctor would attend to him soon. Roger could tell by the grim look on the ambulance man's face that the accident had been a very, very bad incident. He wondered how many had got out of there alive.

His head had slumped back against the tiled wall.

And in the next instant, he was asleep.

Someone was shaking him awake now.

'Please. Wake up. Please.'

Roger groaned. Consciousness seemed also to awake aches and pains in his arms, legs and back.

'All right, nurse . . .'

But it wasn't a nurse or a doctor.

For a moment, Roger just looked at the woman standing next to his bed. Her face was also streaked in engine oil, her hair awry. There was a bandage dressing on her forehead. Her blouse had been torn at the shoulder, and he could see a bloodstain in the fabric. Somehow, the oil on her face seemed to accentuate the beautiful blue of her eyes. At first, he just looked blankly at her. And then he saw what she was holding in her other hand.

It was his hardboard portfolio.

'See?' she said. Her voice seemed to be somehow much too young. A child's voice, trapped in an adult body. 'I didn't lose it.'

Roger struggled to rise.

'No, it's all right. You just stay still.'

'Thank Christ,' said Roger, smiling. 'Five years' worth of work in there.'

'I'll put it here?' The woman motioned to the near wall, and Roger nodded.

'Are you . . . ?' Roger groaned again, finally getting himself to a relatively comfortable position. Beyond the curtains, he could hear the sounds of controlled panic. Voices barking urgent orders, but trying not to sound alarmed and imply a loss of control. 'Are you all right?'

'Cuts, bruises. Banged my head a bit. But I wouldn't be here at all, if it wasn't for you. You pulled me out of that coach. Saved my life.'

'You were on your way out of there, on your own. Through the same window as me. You would have made it without my help.'

'I don't think so. How are you?'

'Not sure.' Roger felt his ribs, poked with grim humour at his limbs. 'I think I'm okay.' He waggled his fingers like a corny magician about to perform a trick. 'The tools of my intended trade are okay. And that's the important thing.'

'My name's Jane Teal. I just wanted you to know how grateful I am.'

'Roger O'Dowd. Like I said . . .'

'No one . . .' Jane seemed to be struggling with emotion now. She stroked a renegade strand of hair away from her eyes, using the motion to retain some control.

'No one else got out of that coach alive. I heard one of the doctors talking. We're the only two.'

'Jesus Christ . . .' The enormity of what had happened finally began to dawn on him. He wondered what would have happened if he had been sitting one seat in front or one seat behind. Would he be here now?

The curtain swished open.

Two nurses entered, with fragile smiles.

'Mrs Teal,' admonished the older woman. 'I wondered where you'd gone to. You shouldn't be up and about yet. Come on back with me.' The other nurse moved to Roger, gently pushing him back. An Asian doctor was coming forward now, moving quickly to him for an examination.

'My husband . . . ?' began Jane.

'I've telephoned him and told him that you're fine,' said the younger nurse, leading her away by the elbow. 'But even though you *think* you're all right, we have to wait for the X-rays.'

Just before she vanished behind the curtain, Jane looked back at Roger.

'I can't tell you how much . . .'

Roger smiled and waved a bloodied hand.

'Next time we'll *fly*,' he grinned.

Jane returned a nervous smile, and then was gone.

'Now then,' said the doctor. 'Let's see what damage has been done . . .'

Roger looked down at the portfolio.

Not a dent.

He tried not to think of the people who had been on the coach.

The crew of Ambulance Delta Five were trained to deal with difficult situations, not only from the practical and medical point of view, but also from a psychological perspective. In extreme circumstances, the injured could behave in a variety of ways, from the ennui of extreme shock to outright aggression. The crew had seen it all, from horrific conflagrations such as the sight that met them on this lonely stretch of the A1 in Northumberland to domestic disturbance to kids with their heads stuck in baking tins. And a tenet of the profession was to get on with the job and never take any aggression personally.

However, Ellis Burwell had proved to be far from Delta crew's favourite customer.

The first fire crew to arrive at the scene had yet to discover that the contents of Martin Russell's tanker were not what the ChemData fax from the company made them out to be, and would not succumb to their first fire-fighting strategy. Delta Five had been the first ambulance to arrive at the scene of the accident, and the first thing they had seen, apart from the great gouts of flame erupting from the shattered vehicles by the central reservation, had been the scarecrow figure of Ellis Burwell, still standing in the middle of the road and staring ahead. His shadow leapt out behind him when the ambulance screeched to a halt.

He seemed hypnotised by the flames.

Shock, obviously.

A gentle hand had been placed on his shoulder in an attempt to guide him to the ambulance. But the touch seemed to transform his trance instantly into a wild reaction. Burwell whirled, screaming aloud – and had punched the ambulance man. The other crew member had pounced on him then, forcing him to the ground. Kicking, thrashing and cursing, Burwell had been carried into the ambulance and restrained. As soon as he was lying on the trolley, he had returned to his spellbound state, staring up at the roof, while the other ambulances and fire appliances swarmed to the rescue.

Now, four cubicles away from Roger O'Dowd, Burwell finally seemed to break out of his torpor as a nurse cleaned his wounds. He had been lucky, like the others. A possible fractured rib, but nothing serious. Cuts and grazes mostly. The nurse who was attending to him was black, possibly Jamaican. In normal circumstances, he would have told her to piss off and send in someone who hadn't just got off the banana boat. But he allowed her to finish the task. She tried to make small-talk, but Burwell wasn't having any of it. Then, from somewhere beyond the screen, someone snapped: 'Who let the newspaper people in here?'

'What?' snapped Burwell, grabbing the nurse's wrist. She flinched, then expertly wrenched her hand away.

'It's all right, Mr Burwell. Just let me finish.'

'No it's not fucking all right. Ever since I came here, everyone keeps telling me it's all right. Dozens of people fried on a motorway – *I* nearly fried on the motorway – and everyone keeps saying it's all right. Now what the hell is this about newspaper reporters?'

The nurse tried to maintain a professional calm, sensing his innate hostility, an attitude with which she'd had to deal all her life. Carefully, she moved back to the curtain and looked beyond. Burwell strained to hear what she was hissing to someone else out there. There seemed to be some sort of commotion. Now someone was saying: 'Look, just a couple of interviews. He's okay in there, isn't he? I mean, only six people got out of there alive and . . .'

'Will you get *out*?' hissed that same invisible voice, just as the nurse pulled the curtain back again.

'It's . . .' and she stopped herself saying "all right". 'It's *sorted*, Mr Burwell.' She returned to her task.

'You're sure?'

The nurse nodded again, just wanting to get the job done as quickly as possible so that she could get out of there into the company of fellow human beings.

'I've got to get out of here. Things I have to do. I don't want anyone to know I'm here. For, you know, personal reasons.'

The nurse nodded and smiled unconvincingly.

Burwell listened to someone beyond the curtain being bundled unceremoniously out of the ward. At last, he relaxed.

'Is that true?' he asked.

'Is what true?'

'Only six people got out of there alive?'

The nurse nodded. 'So they say. You were very lucky.'

Burwell laughed. An ironic sound. It sounded like an invitation for her to follow it up. The nurse declined to respond. It had been her one chance to endear herself to him, and she had blown it. 'Hurry up,' said Burwell blankly. 'I want to get out of here.'

'With pleasure,' said the nurse.

Martin and Mercy met again in the X-ray department of the receiving hospital. They had travelled there together, in the same ambulance, after Mercy had returned to the scene of the collision, and Martin had passed on the Trem card and other details of his load to the crew of the first arriving fire appliance. He had struggled to find something to say as they'd travelled, but it seemed that neither of them had the energy to think of anything. Every emotion seemed to have been drained out of them. One of the ambulance crew had told them that they were being taken to Eastleigh Hospital, and Martin had been startled out of his blank mood when Mercy suddenly put a hand on his knee; another childlike gesture that was at odds with the worldly-wise young woman who had hitched a lift from him. He had put his own hand over it. It seemed massive by comparison, scarred and calloused by thirty years of hard labour. At the hospital, they had both been transferred to wheelchairs and hurried into Casualty, both absorbed in their own thoughts as they had been led in different directions.

But now, as Mercy came out of the X-ray department, still in her wheelchair, she found herself facing Martin, also still in his wheelchair, on the way in. The confrontation seemed to snap them both back into real time again. Martin's head had been bandaged, as had one of his hands. Mercy had a plaster bandage over a gash on her chin.

'Not after another lift are you?' asked Martin, giving a ragged smile. 'Only room for one in this wheelchair.'

The male nurse pushing Martin moved the wheelchair to one side as the other nurse pushing Mercy tried to get past. But Martin put a hand on Mercy's arm and brought them to a halt. Her face was so white that it seemed carved out of marble. He tried to give her a reassuring smile.

'Oh God,' she said. 'The car that hit us. The car that rammed us off the road . . .'

'What about it?' Martin tried to keep a note of reassurance in his voice.

'We never thought to look. Never thought to check . . .'

The nurse leaned down, trying to calm her.

'Just a moment,' said Martin to the nurse. Then turning to Mercy again, he asked: 'What's wrong?'

'The driver of the car was still alive. He was still in the wreckage. We never got him out. And when that petrol caught fire, he was still in there. I heard one of the doctors talking. He was *burned*. The ambulance people pulled him out. We should have looked, should have checked that . . .'

'Now listen!' snapped Martin. 'You could have got out of there, got away from the lorry and left me. But you didn't. You came back, and you pulled me out. We didn't have time to check out the car, remember? The petrol was flowing down the gully, and we only just got out in the nick of time. Do you hear what I'm saying . . . ?'

'God, Martin. He was *in* there, and he was burning . . .'

'Do you *hear* me!' Martin grabbed her arm and shook her. 'I wouldn't be here if not for you, and there was nothing . . . do you hear me? . . . *nothing* else we could have done.'

Mercy's face crumpled then. She bowed her head.

'Are you okay?'

She nodded.

'No broken bones?'

'Not as far as I know.'

'Bet you wish you hadn't hitched a lift.'

She tried to smile again.

'I'm glad you did.'

And then they passed each other, Mercy heading back to the ward, Martin into X-ray. Just before the orderly pushed him through the double doors, Martin leaned back and called, 'See you shortly for a coffee?'

'Three gallons,' replied Mercy, twisting in her chair. 'The first one's on me.'

Newsflash: 'And reports have just been received about a major incident on the A1 in Northumberland. Stuart Costigan is on the scene at this moment.'

'Yes, Peter. I'm here on a remote stretch of the A1, not far from the Alnwick by-pass, and it's the scene of one of the worst accidents in this area in living memory. A multiple collision occurred here just after midnight, and whereas it's not possible at present for the emergency services to determine just how the accident happened, it seems that eighty-seven people are feared dead. A long-distance overnight coach travelling from Glasgow to London was in collision with a tanker-lorry carrying flammable material, Several other vehicles were also involved. As you can see behind me, the fire services are struggling to control the blaze, which is still raging out of control. It would appear that the material in the overturned lorry ignited, and there now seems little chance of anyone surviving the inferno.'

'We understand that there were only six survivors, Stuart. Is that right?'

'*Early reports indicate that six people were taken to Eastleigh Hospital, none in a critical condition as far as we're aware. But that's still subject to confirmation.*'

'*And no explanations for the pile-up?*'

'*No. As I said, the emergency services are still struggling to contain the blaze and it will be some time before investigators are able to interview the survivors and examine the scene. The road conditions here are clear. The weather is temperate. No apparent reason for this terrible scene of carnage.*'

'*Driver error?*'

'*It can't be ruled out, although as I've said the investigation will have to take its course. What is certain, however, is that there will be renewed calls to have this single stretch of motorway dualled. The accident record here has been subject to much debate, and this latest terrible tragedy will only serve to fuel greater anger at the government's road budget cuts, which have shunted a dualling scheme north of Morpeth about fifteen years into the future. I'm sure that the A1 Safelink Group will have something to say about this terrible, terrible tragedy . . .*'

'*Thank you, Stuart.*'

Kenny couldn't work out whether working three shifts in a row had tired him so much that he was incapable of reacting to what was going on upstairs in the hospital, or whether working as an orderly for three years had simply desensitised him to the horrors of life. He remembered his sense of discomfort during that first year, particularly when kids were involved. Not that he had any family, or kids of his own. But he had always been sensitive about kids suffering. In recent years, that seemed to have worn off.

At first, when the Medical Incident Officer – in this case, the Senior Registrar – had been rushed out by ambulance on receipt of the Major Incident Standby alert to assess the extent of the damage, there had been an initial report back to expect multiple injuries. With ninety-eight per cent of their beds occupied, an emergency call had gone out from Eastleigh Hospital to other hospitals in the surrounding area for assistance, and off-duty staff had been alerted to attend immediately. But then

another call had come in from the Ambulance Incident Officer
to say that only six people had been recovered, and further
survivors seemed unlikely, even though standby arrangements should be maintained. A temporary 'body-handling'
area would be established on-site, guarded and supervised
by the police and the Coroner. Emergency Plan proceedings
demanded that the hospital would concentrate on survivors,
since carting casualties in various states of damage from an
incident like this into the hospital's morgue would be likely to
interfere with the physical (not to mention psychological) care
of those survivors requiring treatment, and tie up the staff.

But someone, somewhere, had cocked up. The remains
of the first body to be recovered from the scene of the
collision had been brought to the hospital, rather than left
at the accident site. An angry telephone call had been made,
but in the meantime Kenny had been instructed to get the
body of George MacGowan (identified by the wallet in his
jacket pocket), deceased coach-driver, downstairs and on ice
as quickly as possible. Poor bastard. He was in a hell of a
mess. Cut in half, by the looks of things, and in the absence of
anyone telling him otherwise, Kenny supposed that the bottom
half of George MacGowan was not lying on a trolley upstairs
somewhere, also requiring attention. The bloody thing hadn't
even been put in a body-bag, although someone seemed to
have tidied up the mess at the bottom end.

Yawning, Kenny pushed the trolley to one side and moved
to the double doors leading into the mortuary. The mortuary
attendant was on his way, but had yet to arrive. Who the hell
had designed these damned doors, anyway? No doubt someone
who assumed that there would always be two members of
staff on hand, one for the trolley and another for the doors.
The practical consequences of cuts in staffing and sudden
emergencies apparently hadn't come into the architects' or
health authority's equation. Bracing one foot against one of
the opened doors, Kenny manoeuvred the trolley through the
gap. The awkwardness of his situation made him bend, and
he realised that his face had come very close to what was
hidden under the not-so-white sheet that draped the body. It

seemed that he had been wrong about becoming desensitised. He wasn't sure whether his sense of discomfort was a good thing or a bad thing, after all. He straightened, shoving the trolley ahead of him and keeping the door ajar.

He knew that the body he was pushing had also been badly burned, and although he hadn't seen it for himself, he had heard one of the doctors talking *sotto voce* about the extent of injury.

Poor bastard. It just doesn't have *a face any more*.

The trolley jammed on the edge of the door. Kenny tried to shove it past.

And then a hand flopped out from under the sheet.

'Oh *shit!*'

Kenny felt his gorge rise. The hand was blackened and charred, fingers clutching. He shoved again, and this time the trolley slid into the mortuary. He pushed it on in, letting the door slap shut behind him. Now, he was angry. Angry at his lack of professionalism. Even if he had been working three shifts, he was needed upstairs after he'd parked this poor sod. And reacting like this wasn't going to help matters.

'Tired,' he said aloud, moving around the trolley. 'I'm just too bloody tired, that's all.'

Carefully taking the hand, he lifted the sheet and put it back underneath.

He found himself staring down at the spot where the face was hidden. Some part of him was suggesting that he should lift it and look. The small angry part inside which was accusing him of unprofessionalism. All right, it wasn't going to be pretty. But at least if he lifted it and made himself *see*, then he could remind himself why he was doing this job in the first place. He was doing it because he wanted to help people, for Christ's sake.

'Idiot,' he told himself, and walked back to the double doors.

Just before he reached it, he heard the hand fall out from under the sheet again. Sighing, he stood facing the door for a moment. Then he rubbed his face and turned. No, it must be his tiredness. Because the hand was still under the sheet where he had put it. But for a moment, he could have sworn he heard that same slithering, rustling sound as it fell out.

He was about to turn back again, when he saw the movement under the sheet.

He stood gawping, not really understanding what he was seeing for a moment, waiting for an explanation to present itself. But as he looked, it seemed as if the hand that he had just replaced was moving under the sheet; fumbling and sliding up from the corpse's side, now creeping over the chest area and moving slowly up towards the face . . .

Doesn't have *a face* . . .

. . . and the first thing that logically presented itself to Kenny was that the movement was not being caused by the hand. He had just felt that horribly charred appendage, and it was most certainly the hand of a dead man. No, this was something else. A cat, maybe? Yeah, a cat that had crept under the sheet and was crawling around under there. As the thought registered, he admonished himself for a fool. There were *no* cats in hospitals, and it was unlikely one would stray in here off the street without being seen. A rat maybe?

'Oh Christ!'

The thought was deeply horrifying. Rats down here? Creeping through the sewers? Maybe sniffing out where they kept the stiffs? Waiting for a new one, ready for a meal. But no, this was just as stupid. Corny horror-movie stuff, all engendered by too much work and too little sleep.

The creeping movement continued up to the no-face and paused there. Kenny watched when it began to explore. Tentatively, gently. As if surveying the extent of the injuries.

And then Kenny had it.

This poor bastard was *still alive*.

Things like this had happened before. He'd read about it in *Reader's Digest*. The vital signs were low, the heartbeat practically non-existent because of the incredible shock to the system. But sometimes people did come around again when everyone had assumed they'd given up the ghost. And here this man was now, horribly injured, still in shock. And when that charred hand finally fumbled across the ruins of his face and found that everything had been obliterated, he would throw the sheet back shrieking. He would thrash and scream, still mentally at the road accident. Traumatised and in agony, he would have a fucking heart attack or something. And everyone would say that it was Kenny's fault because he hadn't acted in time.

'You idiot,' said Kenny through gritted teeth. 'You bloody idiot. He's been chopped in *half*. No one survives something like that . . .'

But the fumbling movement was undeniably still there, and Kenny moved quickly forward to the trolley, not sure what he was going to do.

My God, he IS alive! Kenny cleared his throat. 'It's okay,' he said, in as professional a voice as he could muster. 'Don't worry. Everything's under control and you're safe now.'

The figure seemed to moan under the sheet. A muffled, *liquid* noise.

'Just . . . *relax* . . .'

Kenny pulled the sheet back from the face.

The hand that he had replaced under the sheet shot out from under the covering and fastened on his forearm. There might have been time to react, but Kenny could only stare at the horrifying visage, every last vestige of professionalism draining away, the terror of what was taking place before his eyes robbing him of his strength. And then the other charred arm snaked over as the horribly disfigured half-corpse heaved itself over to one side; in that same movement, the free hand clamped itself on the back of Kenny's neck, dragging his own face down to the bubbling riot of movement that had once been the corpse's face.

Kenny opened his mouth to scream.

But the scream never came, as his own face was engulfed.

At that moment, the strip-lights in the mortuary ceiling exploded simultaneously. A rain of yellow-orange sparks flurried in the darkness, drifting down over the nightmare scene that was taking place on the hospital trolley. Then there was only darkness and the final sounds of a life renewed and a life extinguished. Kenny's body was still held over the trolley, but his legs juddered and scuffed on the tiled hospital floor as the darkness suddenly became illumined. The light did not come from a single source; not from the horror that was taking place on the trolley, nor from the shattered strip-lights in the ceiling. The glow, faint at first, but now growing in intensity, seemed *luminous*. Coming from everywhere and nowhere, like the invisible lights that slowly bring out the details of a theatre for before the audience. Outlines at first of the other mortuary trolleys, of the stainless-steel benches with their indentations for siphoning bodily fluids. Now the benches were catching this luminous light, sparking and reflecting as it flared and expanded to engulf the mortuary entirely. There was no heat in the light as it swarmed and spread to the closed mortuary doors, expanding at the double windows.

It was the same light that had engulfed the motorway.

The glass in the windows cracked and shattered, finally exploding outwards into the corridor as the light flooded over the ceiling like a living thing with the sound of a great wind. The all-enveloping light swelled to fill the entire corridor. Pulsing there as it gathered strength, it suddenly exploded beyond the next set of double doors and into the space beyond. There were three flights of stairs there and an escalator. As the sound and the light erupted, the strip-lights blew apart just as they had done in the mortuary. The light filled the space instantly as sparks gushed and flared, seeping through the minuscule gap between the elevator doors, now surging to fill the entire elevator shaft, hungry to find more space. The light engulfed the three stairways, soaring, swelling and growing as it spread and surged and blinded and . . .

'No,' said Mercy quietly.

The radiographer, a woman in her late fifties with steel-grey hair tied uncomfortably in a bun at the back of her head, turned to look at her. Her face was expressionless. There was too much going on tonight without having to deal with temperamental patients. There was likely to be a flood of others in here soon.

'There's nothing to it. Really. You won't see or feel a thing.'

'No,' continued Mercy in a small voice. 'Something's coming.'

Delayed shock, thought the radiographer, moving forward as Mercy began to rise from the wheelchair, attempting to reassure her and guide her back to her seat. But Mercy's eyes flared with fear as she began casting wild looks around the X-ray room, at the ceiling and walls.

'It's all right, honey. You'll soon be . . .'

'No!' Mercy slapped the radiographer's hand away and leapt from the wheelchair, hugging herself tight and looking fearfully around. 'Something's coming *again!*'

Then she fled from the room, hitting the double doors with both hands and hurtling into the corridor beyond.

'Excuse me,' said a man's voice.

Burwell was buttoning his shirt, standing by the cubicle bed, ready to get the hell out of this hospital as fast as he could. He looked up, expecting to see a doctor or an orderly and making ready to tell him to piss off.

But the man who slipped almost surreptitiously around the plastic curtain, pulling it tightly closed behind him, was neither. His fashion sense seemed strange, to say the least: a pristine white shirt and collar, a funeral-dark tie and an anorak. The beard had been neatly groomed but because there were areas of cheek and chin where whiskers had refused to take root, it looked unkempt. The cheeks were florid, the smile too eager to please.

'Who the hell are you?' flared Burwell.

'Curtis. Don't laugh, but my first name's Tony. You know, like the film star.'

'So who the hell's laughing? Who are you? What do you want?'

'I'm with the *Independent Daily* . . .'

'Oh *fuck!*' Burwell began furiously fastening his buttons again, turning from Curtis as the newspaperman cast a furtive look over his shoulder at the plastic curtain. He moved forward, inviting Burwell to participate in a conversation.

'One hell of a smash back there. How are you feeling?'

'NURSE!' yelled Burwell, and Curtis hurried forward, both hands out as if to quieten an angry child.

'This is a big, *big* story. Could be some money in it for you if you . . .'

Burwell lashed out as the newspaperman tried to touch him, slamming an outstretched palm against his chest. Curtis was overweight and out of condition. The blow whumped the air from his lungs and he staggered back into the curtain, just as a nurse dragged it aside.

'I *told* you!' she snapped. 'We've got enough on our hands without your interference. Out!'

'Interference? For God's sake, woman, this is *news*.'

'How's this for a headline?' continued the nurse. 'Newspaperman admitted to hospital for involuntary enema.'

Curtis held up his hands in mock surrender. 'I *knew* I was going to like you.'

'Out!' repeated the nurse.

Curtis did as he was told but, as he turned back, the nurse saw the expression on his face change. Expecting it to be another fake ruse, she looked quickly back to see that Burwell was leaning forward over the cubicle bed, breathing heavily. His head was lowered to his chest.

'Mr Burwell . . . ?' She moved quickly forward, even as Curtis made an instant professional note of the name. But before she could reach him, Burwell suddenly lunged back from the bed. His eyes were wild and staring, and before he blundered into her and the plastic curtain, it seemed somehow that he could no longer *see*. She struggled to hold his arms, but his panic and his strength were too great. Shoving her hard to one side, he blundered out of the cubicle. The nurse remained tangled in the curtain, almost losing her balance as she clutched at the flapping folds.

'The light!' cried Burwell in despair. 'Oh Christ, that *light*!'

Curtis stared in alarm, unable to move as Burwell blundered straight into him. This time, his arms wrapped around Curtis, a drowning man clutching at anything to stay above the surface, or a man about to fall, clinging to anything he could get his hands on. Curtis cried out, arms trapped at his sides as they staggered into the waiting area. Other out-patients in the seating area stared in alarm; two orderlies began to run their way as the nurse extricated herself from the curtain.

'Get *away!*' yelled Burwell.

'*You* fucking get away!' yelled Curtis as they struggled in their mad dance. And then the weight of Burwell was too much for him, and he fell over backwards. His head smacked on the cold floor, his teeth clacking together. Burwell was on top of him, and the breath was knocked from Curtis's body so that he was unable to protest. Suddenly the nurse was there again, dragging Burwell away from him, now assisted by the two orderlies. Curtis lay where he was, looking up, as they dragged Burwell to his feet. He thrashed and kicked, and Curtis's breath came in great whooping, wheezing coughs. For a moment, he saw double; then he turned awkwardly on his side, raising himself up on one elbow to look as . . .

Jane knew that her husband had arrived.

She could feel that horrible *sick* feeling deep inside. She remembered the same feeling – or something like it – from when she was a little girl. That feeling of butterflies when she had done something wrong and was bound to be found out. The same feeling that had stayed with her, had grown and become frighteningly intense with the progress of years. She felt that way just before he was due home from work, as she frantically worked to prepare his meal, just the way he liked it. Or when she ran around the house, making sure that the bathroom was clean and that there were no tell tale threads or crumbs or marks on the carpet. It always grew worse just before he walked through the door.

Just as it had grown now.

Jane clutched at her stomach as she sat on the chair in her cubicle. The doctor had asked her to lie on the bed, but she feared what her husband might think or say or do if he caught her lying down like that. He didn't like to see signs of weakness. She wanted to show him when he arrived that despite everything that had happened in the terrible crash she hadn't complained and wasn't going to make a fuss. She looked up at the plastic curtain, certain that it would be pulled aside and he would be standing there. She prayed that he would be glad to see her.

But the curtain was not pulled back. Instead, she heard the sounds of commotion; of someone yelling something about a light. And it seemed that the sounds, and that one shouted word, were more connected to the way she was feeling inside than the imment arrival of her husband. Suddenly, the sickening butterflies seemed to wrench at her insides.

'Oh dear . . .'

Jane bent double in her seat, still clutching at her stomach. Was she going to faint? The prospect of Tom arriving, to find her collapsed on the casualty department floor, was enough to make her stagger from the seat, one hand out and clutching for the curtain.

'No, I can't . . .'

Something's on its way.

'. . . can't faint. I *won't* faint!'

Something terrible.

Jane had to get away from this place. If she stayed, that terrible inner fear would consume her.

Staggering to the cubicle curtain, she pulled it aside as . . .

Harry suddenly jerked awake in one of the screened cubicles, scaring the nurse who was attending to him.

'All right, Mr Stark. Just relax. We're going to admit you . . .'

'It can't happen again,' said Harry, the fear building inside. 'Please God, don't let it all happen *again*.' He struggled to rise.

'Mr Stark, *please*,' implored the nurse, trying to restrain him as . . .

'What the hell's going on out there?'

Roger winced as the doctor half turned from his job of stitching the gash above his eyebrow.

'Oh, sorry.'

The yelling came again. Something about a light, and this time the unmistakable sounds of a struggle. The doctor tried to concentrate, but the sounds seemed very close to the cubicle, making him uneasy. He managed to tweak the stitch he was working on once more and this time Roger grunted in pain. The doctor quickly finished as someone out there shouted: 'It's *coming!*'

And as the doctor moved quickly away from the cubicle bed, shoving the curtain to one side so that he could see what was going on and at the same time trying to keep it screened from his patient, Roger felt that same feeling again. It was just the way he had felt before the coach had skidded and turned over, the feeling of utter terror just before the light flooded the windscreen and then exploded into the coach. The feeling that something was headed his way at an impossible, life-threatening speed. He sat up, clutching at the sides of the bed, looking around for the source of his fear. Something was hurtling down upon him but he did not know from which direction. He felt trapped in the cubicle, trapped and vulnerable. Swinging his legs over the side of the bed, heart hammering, he tried to get control of himself. The doctor's attention was riveted on the fracas taking place not fifteen feet from them, clearly deliberating whether or not he should hurry over and become involved. A man was struggling with two orderlies and a nurse. Another man was lying on the floor.

And then Roger saw Jane suddenly stagger out from her own cubicle, clutching at the curtain, almost doubled over.

Her eyes met Roger's. And although there was no reason for it, no way he could possibly make the assumption, he *knew* that Jane was somehow experiencing the same terror of imminent impact with the same invisible, oncoming force. The doctor tried to restrain him as he pushed past, towards her. Jane's eyes remained locked on his own. She reached out for him and Roger lunged forward as . . .

Martin cradled the telephone close to his ear, not wanting anyone to listen in, afraid of how vulnerable he might seem if someone were to overhear.

'Yes, Sheila. I'm fine. Really.'

He looked back across the casualty department, into the waiting area, and the dozen or so other patients still waiting for treatment, apparently unconnected with tonight's Big Event. A teenager with a gashed hand. A drunk with a limp who had fallen asleep across two of the seats. A young couple cradling a weeping child.

'Oh my God, Martin,' continued his wife. 'I heard the news. I mean I *saw* the news on late-night television. But I never thought, never *thought* . . .'

'Look, I'm all right. Just a few scratches. And as soon as I make my calls to the firm, I'll be straight home.'

'I mean, I *did* think that something bad might have happened. I always do when there's been a smash-up or something and you've been in that area working and . . .'

'You're going to work yourself up and make yourself ill, if you're not careful.'

'But I put it out of my mind like I always do. It was on the telly. I mean I saw that lorry lying on the road. But you couldn't see what kind of lorry it was. Couldn't see any markings on it. It was just *covered* in flames. And it was *your* lorry all the time and I was watching and I never knew . . .' And she began to weep again.

Martin cursed himself. He had miscalculated. Assuming that she might find out about the crash, or be told by someone that he had been involved in it, Martin had telephoned home just as soon as he could. He had anxious thoughts as he dialled the number. Would the police have been there already, knocking on the door, getting her out of bed? Would she have seen something on the news and assumed that he was dead? In the event, she *had* seen the news but had not assumed that he'd been involved. Instead, he should have just gone home without telephoning her beforehand – that would have avoided all the upset.

'I'll be home straight away. Don't worry. Now come on. Cheer up. Just think, all that life insurance money and you won't be able to collect any of it . . .' His attempt at a light-hearted joke only served to make things worse. Sheila erupted into renewed tears on the other end of the line. 'Sheila, come on! They've got no ambulances to take me home, 'cause they're all tied up down on the motorway. So I've rung for a taxi. It'll be here in five minutes and I'll be home in twenty. You go and put the kettle on.'

When Martin replaced the receiver, he felt a tight constriction in his gut.

He paused. Had he been wrong about his injuries? Had he torn something inside after all? Something they hadn't seen on the X-ray? They had seemed satisfied that he was okay, but wanted him to stay for observation. Taking the conversations he'd listened in to as his cue, he had persuaded them that they'd have their hands full tonight and he'd be best out of the way. But had they been right? Was there something to worry about after all?

He hung up, then gingerly placed a hand on his stomach. No, this wasn't really pain, didn't feel like an injury at all. This was something else. Something he couldn't work out. Something that felt like . . .

Something like the feeling he'd had on the motorway. When he saw that light heading for them, just before the crash.

Martin shrugged it off. He needed coffee. Still rubbing at the site of the pain that was not somehow a pain, he walked past the waiting area, heading for the coffee machine. He needed something hot inside, something to kill the chill. As he moved, he concentrated on the faces of the nurses and doctors and orderlies, still waiting for an influx of seriously hurt survivors from the motorway pile-up. So far, only six people had been pulled from the wreckage, including himself. And the fact that none of those six had been seriously hurt – getting out with only cuts, bruises and scratches – seemed in some indefinable way to make their tension worse. Martin shoved loose change into the machine and watched as the paper cup dropped into its tray and began to fill.

As he bent to take the cup, he felt the cramp in his stomach again. It made him feel dizzy, made something seem to swell in his chest. He steadied himself against the machine and shook his head. Impatient with himself, he lifted the cup and took a sip, hoping that the caffeine would clear his head. But when he turned back to look out over the waiting area, it seemed worse than ever.

I'm going to crash again. The thought seemed to spring independently in his mind, as if something were using his mind-voice to warn him. *Something's coming at me, head-on.* He tried to lift the cup to his mouth again, and then everything happened at once.

A man, suddenly fighting with some of the nurses and yelling his head off.

Another man on the floor beneath them, looking as if he'd been knocked there.

A woman staggering from one of the cubicles, a young man lunging towards her as if she might fall at any moment.

Somewhere beyond, in the screened cubicles, more sounds of alarm as another survivor of the crash began to yell.

And then the double doors leading into a corridor burst open and Martin saw Mercy burst through them. She staggered to a halt, eyes wild, as the doors flapped shut behind her. She scanned the waiting area and the curtained cubicles, saw the people sitting there in astonishment, transfixed by the sudden violent activity. She was searching for something that terrified her. And then her eyes found Martin. Even from that distance, he could see the expression of vast relief, saw her take a deep, regenerating breath and start towards him. He made to move towards her, then was overwhelmed by a great wave of the sickening feeling – the sickening stab of unreasoning, outright *fear*, making him stagger back against the coffee machine. Mercy seemed to call to him, her own fear returning, and then . . .

Something exploded into the casualty department with the shocking violence of a bomb blast. Something that slammed through the double doors from 'B' ward, on the other side of the waiting area, shattering the strengthened glass in the windows. Out-patients sitting on the chairs nearest to the doors were flung to the floor by the shock of the eruption.

A hurricane blasted into Casualty.

Papers, pamphlets and medical brochures took instant flight from the tables and desks like a multitude of frightened birds, filling the air. A wind shrieked and gusted, snatching at the clothes of everyone in the department.

Curtis twisted on the floor in shock, looking back at where the double doors flapped and banged. His hair writhed and whipped like a nest of snakes as he squinted into the force of the storm, watched as people began to stagger and clamber away from the fury of the impossible wind. He tried to rise, but could not.

And then he saw it coming down the corridor from 'B' ward, straight towards Casualty. First a flare of light from around a corner, about fifty feet away. Then something that seemed to gush from around the corner, rippling and spreading in a kaleidoscopic flood on the ceiling. Something that looked like luminous smoke, or water, as it spread like an impossible upside-down tidal wave on the ceiling, surging towards the wildly flapping doors that gave admittance to Casualty. And as it came, an all-enveloping light seemed to fill the space behind it. Curtis could only watch in shocked awe as the details of the corridor behind the rapidly advancing wave vanished in the light-flare. He tried to raise himself, but the breath would not return. He lay there, propped on one elbow against the window.

Backdraft!

He had heard about the phenomenon before, had seen film footage during the course of his varied investigations over the years. A slow build-up of fire in a confined space, maybe a cleaning cupboard, with cleaning fluid and inflammable chemicals, greedily devouring the oxygen. Then some poor unsuspecting bastard opened a door, admitting a fresh draft of air – and a fireball would erupt from the confined space. A great wave of fire roaring and surging outwards to engulf everything in one great, gobbling roar. That kind of fire travelled high, on the ceiling. Just as it was doing now. In seconds, the hospital would be an inferno . . .

With an effort that he thought might burst his heart, Curtis rolled on to his hands and knees, the cries of everyone else drowned by the howling wind. He prepared himself for a headlong lunge towards the side exit. Already, he could see people blundering through the exit into the night, and then knew that the rolling fireball would explode in here and head for that greater source of oxygen. The exit would be engulfed, and him with it if he headed that way. Groaning, Curtis dropped flat to the floor again, covering his head.

And then the roaring wave of fire burst through the flapping doors, and everything dissolved from sight in a sodium flash of all-enveloping light. Somewhere overhead, a skylight shattered and glass began to fall in a splintered rain. Then the strip-lights began to explode one by one, and Curtis waited for the agonising pain, hands over his head. He waited for the searing blast that would engulf him and tensed, ready to roll and flap at the flames.

But somehow, there was no heat.

Only blinding light, and great dancing, flickering shadows.

And the sound of the hell-wind, now somehow slightly muted from its thunderous rage to a reverberating, grumbling roar, like the sound of an avalanche. Curtis could feel the floor shaking beneath him, as if he were experiencing some kind of earthquake. There was another sound now, a fierce crackling. He dared to look up from under his hands, and could hardly believe what he saw.

The doors were no longer flapping open and shut. They remained hard up against the walls, surrounded by broken glass. The entire floor of Casualty seemed to be covered in the shattered glass from the overhead skylight and the strip-lighting, each shard reflecting like a diamond. Despite the ominous thundering grumble of wind, the hurricane seemed to have passed, leaving only traces of itself behind as pages from magazines fluttered and unfurled in the air. Someone, somewhere, was weeping, and Curtis could see that there were still some people here, lying on the floor and sheltering each other from the impossible thing that was happening on the ceiling.

Could light be *alive*? Because that is what he could see there. Something that was not fire at all. Something that was not a backdraft surge, that gave off no heat. At first, it seemed to Curtis that he'd seen something like it before. Time-lapse photography of clouds moving super-fast through the sky. That was what it was like now, roiling and undulating and shifting; a mass of blue-white, luminous fog that also looked like fire. He saw a flickering within the glowing mass, a thin, jagged streak that looked like lightning; at the same time, the crackling sound emanated from the mass. The undulating light from above was casting huge, moving shadows, and Curtis turned to see that the man who had been fighting with the three nurses was standing in the same position and staring upwards. Even now, the people who had been restraining him were scrambling towards the waiting area and the people who crouched there, intent on getting them out.

The light-cloud on the ceiling seemed to billow, static filled the air – and the nightmare began again.

Curtis saw a spear of ragged lighting, thinner than a rapier, erupt from the cloud and streak like a living thing towards the curtained cubicles. It tore instantly through the plastic of one curtain, hitting something beyond. Sparks flew from a trolley as it made contact. A nurse screamed, and as a doctor fell through the torn curtain, someone on the trolley suddenly sat up as if electrified. The sparks showered and settled, and Curtis could see that the patient in the hospital smock was slowly climbing down from the trolley as the nurse staggered out to join the doctor, now falling senseless to the floor. Dazed, the patient staggered out of the cubicle and Curtis saw that both his hands were bandaged. Apparently unaware of what was happening over his head, or of the impossible lightning strike, the man staggered to a halt. Slowly, he raised his hands to his face.

'Bloody *hell* . . .'

Curtis could not believe his eyes.

The patient's hands had begun to glow.

The same colour as the luminous cloud mass on the ceiling.

And as Curtis watched, mouth open, he saw the luminosity begin to creep down the man's hands to swathe his forearms.

The crackling sound from overhead began to build again.

'Look out,' Curtis called. 'Get down before it . . .'

And then a nightmare tracing of lightning exploded from the ceiling in all directions. The nurses who had staggered to help the other patients dragged them to the floor as the air was filled with a chaos of electricity. Broken glass glittered wildly.

Curtis saw Ellis Burwell hit by one of the ragged lightning bursts. He saw him stagger away, hugging himself, head bowed. Smoke seemed to rise from his shoulders as he staggered to a halt, standing directly above where Curtis lay, now apparently immobile with pain and shock.

Roger O'Dowd had frozen in the act of reaching for Jane Teal. It was as if time had suddenly stopped. Jane's hand was outstretched to protect herself from the fall that she had not taken. She turned to look at him, and as if that movement had unlocked time once more, a craze of fractured light cut through the air – fast, but somehow *slower* than a real lightning strike, as if hunting for its target. It struck Jane in the chest, snapping back her head, but it did not knock her down. Instantly, the same strike seemed to leap from Jane to Roger. He spun away under the impact, reeling for a cubicle, falling to his knees.

Another spider's-web strand of fractured light zig-zagged across to the other side of the room, hissing with power. It struck Martin, lifting him from his feet and slamming him back against the coffee machine. Somehow, it seemed that the strike had also transferred to the machine itself. The glass frontage exploded in a shower of sparks as Martin fell to the floor. Paper cups began to cough out of the slot.

Mercy turned and ran.

But another crackling, luminous fracture found her as surely as a heat-seeking missile. It slammed into her back, lifting her from her feet and pitching her, face first, against the double doors through which she was trying to escape. She tumbled to the ground.

Curtis waited for the next random lightning bolt to strike him, watched as the living stormcloud on the ceiling undulated and writhed. It seemed to him that, whatever in hell it was, the churning mass was somehow pausing to *consider* its next target.

Not me, please God, not me.

His eyes were drawn to the first person who had been struck by the crazy indoor lightning. The man with the bandaged hands. The luminous light that had engulfed his hands now engulfed his entire body. But impossibly, he seemed unharmed as he stood there, still looking at his hands in awe. Curtis remembered a feature he'd written on spontaneous combustion years ago. Was this what was going to happen now? Was this poor sod suddenly going to erupt in flame and collapse in a burning bundle to the floor? Curtis began to crawl away, at the same time looking up at the man who stood above him. What he saw there made him freeze. Because this man too, also struck by the roiling cloud above their heads, had begun to glow with the same incredible luminous light. Crazily, Curtis remembered his younger days, when he'd been a night-clubber. Some of the lights in the clubs back then had been ultra-violet, making everything white shine in the darkness. It was like that now, only much more powerful. The man's white collar and frayed cuffs gleamed. And as Curtis watched, he slowly turned to look at the man with the bandaged hands.

Curtis watched as their eyes met.

On the other side of the casualty department, someone was rising from the floor.

It was the man who had been struck beside the coffee machine. Sparks were still spitting out of the serving hatch of the machine as he stood. He too was emitting the glowing light, and he was staring in his direction. Curtis squirmed to look around, looked at his hands to see if he was undergoing the same startling change. Was there somehow a reflection from overhead that was making this strange light-show? But Curtis seemed unaffected, as did those others still crouching on the floor beneath the living stormcloud.

The girl who had been flung against the double doors was slowly rising. She too was enveloped in the strange light. Now two others from the curtained cubicles, a young man and a woman, rising slowly and steadily, also surrounded by that bizarre glowing.

And Curtis watched as the six figures stood silently beneath the crackling, hissing indoor storm – and studied each other. He remained crouched, unsure just what the hell was going on, but convinced that something else was going to happen. Would all six of these people suddenly explode in flame? Would the ceiling suddenly cave in? Would the lightning strike again?

There was an expression on each of the faces.

Curtis looked anxiously from one to the other, still waiting for something to happen. What the *hell* was going on here? As he watched, the young girl was nodding. So was the guy from the coffee machine. Now the others. And even from this distance, Curtis could see the *calm* expression on each face. No fear, no pain, no terror at what was happening to them, and at what might happen next. Far from it – each of these shining faces seemed to bear the same expression.

Recognition and understanding.

And something else, as they stood there, faces calm and serious, nodding their heads almost imperceptibly.

Were they somehow silently *communicating* with each other?

Even as the thought registered with Curtis, the light seemed to drain away from each of the figures. There was no sense of the light dimming in a conventional manner. It was as if the light surrounding each began to *leach* away, evaporating and dissolving into the air. Suddenly, the crackling static sound was no longer there. And when Curtis twisted again to look, whatever had been roiling and undulating and rippling on the casualty department ceiling was gone. There had been no gradual dissipation, in the way that the remaining luminosity was dissipating from the standing figures. One moment, the impossible storm cloud was there – the next it was gone. Curtis could see the details of the ceiling – the shattered strip-lights and the skylight. Had the cloud escaped through the skylight like a living thing, while his attention had been riveted on the others?

And now the light surrounding the figures was gone,

plunging the casualty department into darkness and silence. Somewhere, a child was crying. Someone else called out a muffled name. Curtis squinted to see what would happen next, and could hear sounds of movement as the doctors and nurses began to pick their way across the new carpet of broken glass.

'All right, everyone,' said an authoritative voice. 'Just stay calm. Everything's all right . . .'

'Oh God,' said a voice above Curtis. 'I think I'm going to . . .'

Curtis looked up to see that the man above him was beginning to bend double.

'Don't you bloody *dare!*' he yelled.

Too late. Ellis Burwell emptied the contents of his stomach over the newspaperman, then slumped to his knees, retching. Curtis cursed and scurried out of the way, brushing at his anorak and climbing awkwardly to his feet. Now that his eyes were accustomed to the darkness, he could see the other people in the department. He could see doctors and nurses hurrying to help the injured, could hear someone at a reception desk telephoning for assistance.

'What about the emergency lights?' he heard someone ask.

'They've all blown,' came the answer from an invisible source. 'Every last bloody one of them.'

And Curtis stood, now uncaring of the mess on his hands and anorak, watching in the darkness as each of the six people who had been struck by something that only looked like lightning and which had emitted that eerie light seemed to come to their senses again. The man by the coffee machine groaned, holding his head like someone with a hangover. Curtis saw the silhouette of a nurse hurry forward to take his arm, guiding him to a seat. The girl, suddenly bending double like the man who had vomited on him, bracing her hands on her thighs, now standing up straight again and throwing back her head so that her hair danced around her shoulders. The man with the bandaged hands, standing still and straight, still looking at his hands with surprise as if they didn't belong to him. And the man and the woman by the cubicles, now being helped to the seating area by a doctor and a nurse.

A thought came to Curtis then. Something that didn't really make sense. But it seemed important. So much so that he said it out aloud, as if hearing the thought might suddenly *make* sense of it.

'Lightning never strikes twice in the same place.'

'Are you all right?' asked a nurse in the darkness to his left.

'All right? I'm not sure . . .'

And then Curtis pretended to stagger, just enough to make the nurse feel that he needed treatment. They'd tried to throw him out before all this happened. Far better to play hurt now and watch for a while. He allowed himself to be led through the double doors that had burst open to admit the storm. Glass crunched underfoot. The nurse who escorted him seemed nervous that the storm might still be there, perhaps hiding around the corner. But when Curtis looked up at the corridor ceiling, he could see that it was – with the exception of the burst strip-lights – completely unmarked. And yet he had seen that rolling backdraft gushing down the corridor. But on the bare white ceiling there was not a single scorch mark.

'What happened?' he asked the nurse, trying to maintain an edge of distress in his voice, already mentally writing up his feature for the early morning edition.

The silhouette of the nurse guiding him tried to say something, but seemed unable to speak. He felt something then in the guiding hand. Despite her instinctive professionalism, despite the fact that she was struggling to calm his own feigned distress, the nurse was clearly shocked. Her hand was trembling.

Curtis had come to create a story out of what had happened on the motorway. Now that first incident had yielded a bizarre second. But despite the excitement that was building inside, there was still one overriding question.

Just what the hell had *happened* back there?

Curtis intended to stay around for as long as he could, and find out.

*   *   *

'Kenny?'

Dennis Turner ran down the corridor towards the mortuary,
fully expecting that he would find Kenny in there, even though
he should have been upstairs helping out ages ago. How long
did it take to park a stiff down here, for God's sake? Maybe
the lazy sod had taken advantage of the situation to catch up
on some sleep and knew nothing about the panic upstairs.
The prospect angered Dennis. They had both been working
double shifts and it wouldn't have been the first time he'd
tried something like that. If he could stay on his feet all that
time, then Kenny should be able to manage it too. After all
hell had been let loose upstairs when the power had blown,
Dennis didn't feel inclined to be charitable. Some of the out-
patients up there had been hysterical and in need of calming
down, a task that was made doubly difficult when the other
bastard who was supposed to be on duty was nowhere to
be found.

His irritation with Kenny was fuelled by something else.
He hadn't been in the casualty department when the lights
suddenly blew, but he had heard what some of the other
nurses and orderlies had been saying after they'd managed
to get everything back to normal again. Wild stories about a
cloud of fire, and several patients having been electrocuted –
even though subsequent examination had revealed that not one
of them had been so much as scorched. The people he'd heard
talking were clearly disquieted by what they had seen, and
several witnesses to whatever in hell had happened seemed
to be in shock. And the edge of fear in staff whom he knew
to be utterly professional, and who had seen and coped with
hundreds of intense situations, had also served to set his own
nerves on edge.

The emergency lights had come on in the corridor leading
down to the morgue, but now Dennis could see that there were
no lights shining through the windows of the double doors.
Not only that, but there was no *glass* in the doors. He could
see it now, sparkling on the floor. Clearly, Kenny wouldn't be
in there, unless . . .

Unless he had been in there when the lights had blown, and

he had also somehow been affected – in the same way that the people upstairs in Casualty apparently had. He began to run then.

'Kenny! You in there?'

Dennis dragged the doors open. The glass screeched and cracked beneath the rims as he did so.

'Kenny?'

Dennis saw his own gigantic shadow leap across the room, backlit from the corridor lights. At once, there was a sparkling reflection from the floor, and he could see that the strip-lights in here had also exploded, showering the room with a glittering debris. But there was no sign of anyone. Only a trolley, about a dozen feet away and parked at an odd angle. On the trolley was a body covered in a sheet. A hand had fallen out from underneath.

There was something wrong here.

Dennis moved into the mortuary, towards the trolley. But the door began to swing shut on its spring-loaded hinge, plunging the mortuary into darkness. Dennis shoved the door back against the wall and looked for something to wedge it. Why the hell had Kenny left the trolley like this? He could get the bloody sack. Dennis had a cold feeling just then. Perhaps Kenny *had* been electrocuted, and was lying somewhere out of sight on the floor, behind one of the benches? Cursing his own flaring of inner fear, he fumbled in his pocket until he'd found a fountain pen. Stooping, he jammed it under the door so that there was a wedge of light shining into the mortuary and over the trolley.

He moved quickly to the trolley, pulling it around and shoving it to one side. The hand wobbled and seemed to beckon as the trolley moved. Dennis had undergone the training, but had never felt comfortable about the mortuary. The prospect that Kenny might be lying around here somewhere as a prospective customer did not serve to make him feel any easier.

'Jesus Christ, Kenny. Are you in here?'

The crooked index finger of the dangling hand seemed to be beckoning again.

Dennis did not want to touch the hand. But it was unprofessional to leave it just hanging there.

Why did Kenny just leave it hanging out like that?

Grimly, Dennis reached for the hand.

Plucking up the sheet, he grabbed it and threw it underneath.

But even as he began to walk away from the trolley and into the mortuary, peering into the darkness for any sign of his colleague, he knew that something was wrong.

Something was wrong with the hand.

Even though he had only touched it for a brief moment, he knew that it shouldn't feel like that. He knew that Kenny had been sent down here to put this half-body away over an hour ago. The guy on the trolley had been dead for at least two hours.

So there was no way the hand should still be warm.

He turned back to the trolley.

The light was shining from the corridor beyond, directly on to the sheet, like a spotlight. And now that he *really* looked, he could see that there was a stain where the head of the corpse would be. A stain where the sheet clung to the body's face. God knows what state that face would be in.

So the hand felt warm. So what?

'Kenny?' He began to check behind the benches, now acutely aware of the fact that there were other bodies in here, all filed away in their cabinets. Feet crunching on glass, he continued his search of the mortuary floor.

But the body under the sheet was always there. He could feel its presence. As if it were alive and somehow watching him. Dennis continued to ignore it as he searched. But now it was clear that Kenny was not in the mortuary. Cursing, Dennis moved back to the double doors and stooped to retrieve his fountain pen. He couldn't help looking back at the body under the sheet . . . and what he saw there made him stand up straight and fast, as if someone had commanded that he stand to attention.

The bloodstain on the sheet had spread.

And as he watched, it was still spreading. As the blood

flowed, it was making the sheet cling to the contours of the face. In the light from the corridor, he could see that it was seeping through the fabric, glinting like a patch of oil.

The hand had been warm, and now the body was bleeding. Someone, somewhere, had made a very bad mistake. This guy was still *alive*.

Dennis moved quickly to the trolley, pulling aside the sheet.

Instantly, he could see that he had been wrong in one respect. Whoever it was on this trolley, he was most certainly dead. No one could have suffered that kind of damage to the face and head and come through it alive. The face was gone, apparently torn from the frontal skull, leaving a chaotic and dark-glistening mass of bloody tissue. Only one eye remained in the horrifying ruin. Dennis flinched, dropping the bloody sheet on to the corpse's chest. Blood was still pooling in the empty eye socket. But how could that be? This body had been brought down here two hours ago. How could it still be warm, still be bleeding? Unless . . .

And then Dennis saw that the corpse was wearing hospital uniform, and realised that he could see the shape of a lower torso, and legs, beneath the covering sheet.

He saw the familiar dress-ring on the hand he had just touched.

When he saw the bloodied handprints on the uniform, prints that had been made by the thing that had ravaged and torn and finally ripped Kenny's face from his skull, Dennis blundered backwards to the doors. Then, when his mind finally accepted what his eyes were seeing, he turned and fled back down the corridor.

'Ambulance Delta Seven?'

The driver of the ambulance that had just pulled into the hospital grounds was on his way out of the cab when his radio crackled into life. Quickly, he responded; his crewmate was already on his way towards the rear entrance and paused to look back while the driver took the message.

'Delta Seven receiving.'

'*They want you out at the motorway, Gill.*'

'What? They've got five parked out there already, waiting for them to put the bloody fire out.'

'*Tell me about it. But they need you out there, Gill. Delta Three's at the scene, and has unspecified engine trouble. We're under instruction to have cover ready for the time our people can go in. So with Delta Three out of action, I'm afraid you've drawn the short straw.*'

'On our way, Control. Delta Seven out.'

'Motorway smash?' asked Gill's crewmate, heading back towards the ambulance.

'Got it in one.'

'Shit.'

'Right again.'

And as the ambulance performed a screeching U-turn out of the hospital grounds, neither of the men inside was aware of that which had dragged itself from the mortuary and was clinging to the undercarriage of the vehicle, wedging itself up tight, desperate to return to the scene of the crash.

'So, how are you feeling?'

Roger looked up from the bed as the man in the anorak pushed past the curtain and made his way to the beside chair. The man was holding an official clipboard, and he placed it on the small cupboard next to the chair. When he sat down, he sounded weary. Roger tried to push himself up on his elbows. He wasn't sure whether he had been sleeping or just day-dreaming. There seemed to have been a dream. Something about lightning and fire and people shouting. Perhaps he had nodded off after the woman called Jane had spoken to him?

'No, just stay as you are,' enjoined the man, holding out a hand.

Roger's eyes focused at last. The man was in his late forties, with a salt-and-pepper beard. A collar and tie, but no hospital uniform.

'How are you feeling?'

'Okay, I suppose. A little groggy.'

'Aren't we all. After what happened. So, no bad after-effects, then?'

Roger paused. There was something about this man that didn't really seem to scan. He was friendly, perhaps too friendly. There was something almost conspiratorial in his manner, and he just didn't seem to have the air of a medical man.

'Who are you?'

'Anderson. Joey Anderson. I'm a hospital visitor. Just doing the rounds.'

'Oh. Right.'

'So, you're okay, then?'

'Lucky. To be alive.'

'You were on the coach, weren't you?'

'Yeah. What about the others? I know about Jane Teal. I was talking to her earlier.'

'Jane Teal. Right. She was one of the survivors.'

Something definitely not right. Not right at all. Roger pushed himself up this time, despite the man's protestations.

'Only two of you came out alive, I'm afraid. You and Jane. A lorry collided with the coach.'

'Yeah . . . I know. I was there, remember?'

'The ones who didn't die in the smash must have died in the fire. So tell me about it. Tell me what you saw.'

'You're no hospital visitor.'

The man looked as if he might protest. But then he sighed, and sat back in the chair. He picked up the clipboard, something he'd taken from the reception desk when no one was looking, and began to toy with it in his lap.

'You're right.'

'Then who the hell are you?'

'Name's Curtis. I'm a reporter from the *Independent Daily*.'

'Then why the hell didn't you say so in the first place?'

'Because the last one I talked to wanted to do a runner when he found out. Then one of the nurses tried to throw me out.'

Roger began to reach for the call-switch.

'No! Look . . . All I want to do is find out what happened back there on the motorway. And then just what the hell happened here in Casualty. It's a story, for Chrissake. No harm in me finding out, is there? I mean, no one has anything to hide, do they?'

Roger paused.

'A major pile-up like that. The weather was clear, and there's no reason why it should have happened. There are eighty-seven people dead. And only six people got out of it alive. You're one of them. Now with a story like that you could be a celebrity . . .'

Roger grimaced and reached for the bell again.

'Okay, so you don't want to be a celebrity! That's fair enough. But all I want to know is what happened to you. Just your side of things, then I'll go.'

'What's to tell? I was on the coach, half asleep. On my way to London. Next thing I know, there's a light.'

'Light?'

'Shining full in the windscreen. Like headlights, only much brighter. Just as if someone was coming down the motorway towards us. On the wrong side.'

Curtis seemed a great deal more animated now. He fumbled in his pocket for a notepad and pen. 'You mean there was a car heading for you? You think that caused the crash?'

'I'm not telling you anything of the sort. I'm just telling you what it looked like.'

'Then what happened?'

'Then the driver started hauling on the wheel, like he was trying to avoid something. That was about it. Next thing, people were falling all over the place. I was catapulted out of my seat. The coach must have turned over then and everything was . . . was . . .'

'Yeah, go on.' Curtis leaned forward, noting the strange expression that had suddenly registered on Roger's face. A look of bewilderment, as if he had just remembered something very important, and puzzling.

'Like I said,' continued Roger, his attention now seeming to be fixed on some inner point. 'The coach turned over . . . everything was black . . . then I came around in the darkness and started to . . . started to . . .'

'There's something else, isn't there? Something you've just remembered.'

'What? . . .'

'Something you hadn't thought about until now.'

Roger swallowed hard, and tried to reach for the water jug on the cupboard. Quickly, Curtis moved to it, pouring a glassful. Roger took it, drinking greedily. Sighing, he sank back until his head rested against the bed frame.

'Screaming,' said Roger at last.

Still waiting to be told, and trying his best to be patient, Curtis said: 'Yeah, it must have been bad afterwards. All those people.'

'That's not what I mean.'

He paused again, looking at the ceiling. Puzzlement was still etched on his face, and Curtis was finding the suspense almost unbearable. Anxiously, he cast a glance at the curtains, willing that no one should interrupt them now.

'There was screaming *before* the crash. And it wasn't the people in the coach.'

'You mean one of the other vehicles? Maybe you heard someone in the . . .'

'No, I don't mean that! I mean, something was heading towards us. A light . . . *and* a sound. I can't explain it properly. But that screaming didn't seem . . . well, it didn't seem human. It came right at us, right at the coach. Real and solid. And then, just before the coach turned over, it was like that . . . bloody light, or whatever in hell it was . . . just exploded right through the windscreen. And the screaming was right behind it. Filling the coach. Then the coach flipped, and the screaming was gone.'

'Screaming,' said Curtis, and it was difficult to mask the disappointment in his voice. 'Yeah, right. Well, understandable. Thing like that. Big smash-up. Must have been very traumatic . . .'

'You don't get it, do you?' Roger's face was tight and drawn now as his memory came flooding back.

'What about the light? You say it looked like headlights. If someone did take a wrong turning and ended up travelling the wrong way down the motorway, it would account for what happened, wouldn't it?'

'That screaming wasn't normal. It was like it *hit* us!'

Curtis was absorbed in the theory now. He had enough to work on for the moment, certainly enough for the first edition if he moved fast. This other business didn't really scan, and was obviously a symptom of shock.

'What about what happened in Casualty?'

Roger looked at him blankly. Curtis was surprised by the blankness.

'Tricky things, burns,' he continued. 'But you look as if you came out of it okay.'

'What the hell are you talking about? I'm not burned.'

'But back there in Casualty. When the lights blew and the thundercloud came in . . .'

'You've got me mixed up with someone else.'

'But I saw you. You and the girl, the one that was in the coach with you. Look, I know it was a hell of a shock for everyone, particularly the people who got struck. But you must remember what happened in that reception area . . .'

'Like I say, you're thinking of someone else.' Anger was rising in Roger's voice.

'You were standing there,' Curtis went on. 'Right in the middle of it all. I got knocked to the bloody floor. And then I saw you get hit by something that looked like a thunderbolt. You were on fire.'

'Do you see any bandages for burns?' asked Roger, holding up his bare arms. 'Like I say, you've got the wrong man. And I think it's time you were going.'

'Are you trying to tell me that you can't remember anything about what happened back there in Casualty? And that you don't remember being slammed to the floor by a lightning strike?'

'I'm trying to tell you that it's time you buggered off, Mr Curtis, or whatever your name is.'

'Roger, isn't it?' asked Curtis, rising from his seat at last and looking at the graph at the bottom of the bed. 'Roger . . . O'Dowd. Right. Can I quote you on . . . ?'

'No, you bloody well can't!' snapped Roger. 'Quote me and I'll sue you.'

'No hassle,' said Curtis, smiling and backing away. 'No hassle at all. Thanks for the chat.'

Someone had come through the plastic curtain. Curtis bumped into him as he backed off. It was a uniformed police constable. Six foot four inches of 'don't get in my way'. Sheepishly, Curtis apologised and eased around him, out of sight.

The police constable watched him go. Then he turned to the bed.

'Mr O'Dowd?'

Roger nodded wearily.

'Do you feel up to talking? I know it's late and you'll need your rest after everything you've been through. But we really need to know what happened. Your view of it, I mean.'

Wearily, Roger exhaled, put his hands over his face and groaned when the constable's colleagues pushed through the plastic curtain.

A quarter-mile stretch of the A1 through Northumberland had become the Highway into Hell.

Joe Riggart had been a fire-fighter for ten years, and the one thing he'd learned from his time in the service was that each fire was always different, and always unpredictable. There were always textbook ways and means of approaching each incident, provided they could get the correct advance detail or the right reaction on the first visual contact. But sometimes the textbook approach just would not work, and tonight was one of those nights.

The substance being carried by the ruptured lorry-tanker was supposed to be amyl nitrate. By law, the tanker was supposed to bear a Hazchem code denoting the contents of its container. The driver had also managed to retrieve his Transport Emergency Card, Code 30G36. Both confirmed that amyl nitrate was the material that had leaked from the tanker and engulfed the motorway in flames, despite the low fire risk. As such, ordinary breathing apparatus and protective gloves were necessary, and there was no need in the circumstances for specialised protective gear. But the first attempts to smother the hellish scene with normal fire-fighting foam had been unsuccessful, turning the inferno into a nightmare Christmas scene of gigantic off-white snowdrifts and sheets of drifting, flecked-foam snow. Something was very, very wrong. Clearly, the petrol mixture from the other car wrecks was mixing in a volatile cocktail with what the lorry had spewed out over the motorway, and when three fire-fighters had suddenly keeled over for no apparent reason, they'd withdrawn from that blazing quarter-mile of motorway to reconsider their strategy. Their lack of success must mean that the company owning the tanker was not being entirely truthful about its contents. An urgent ChemData fax from a suddenly sweating executive had revealed its true contents: Code 61/30G45 – Inhibited Acrylonitrile, grossly in breach of the safety codes. Highly flammable, toxic, reacting with oxidising agents and completely untouched by the foam they were using. Gas-tight chemical protection suits were required, including breathing apparatus, and only alcohol-resistant foam from the pumps would put out the blaze. If anything happened to the three fire-fighters who had breathed in some of the stuff, there would be hell to pay.

Riggart and Tony Planer, now clad in orange, gas-tight splash suits with double-glazed visors, were handling the hose that was trained on the coach. The rest of their crew were concentrating on the shattered tanker beyond. But even using the alcohol-resistant foam, every time the damned truck flared up, everything around it was catching fire again. Each man from the five appliances called out to the scene were now wearing the same chemical protection suits and breathing apparatus. There was no telling what poison-acid cocktail might be emanating from these fires now.

As they worked, something was happening inside the coach again, beneath the enshrouding foam. When Riggart looked back quickly away from the wreck and over his shoulder, he could see through the visor on Planer's headgear that the expression on his face matched what he was thinking.

Because, given the new procedure, what was happening out here to the crashed vehicles on this motorway shouldn't be happening at all. The fire was still flaring through the foam. Riggart faced front again as the foam continued to cascade and smother the coach, only to see that the impossible thing was continuing to happen. The foam they were using couldn't – just *couldn't* – catch fire. But there it was again: a sudden flaring deep within the clouds of suds, like a thin tracing of blue-white electricity, sparking and igniting. Now the foam around the area, somewhere near where the driver's cab had been, was flaring and melting – and burning. Riggart shook his head in disbelief, and they pressed on. With the tons of foam they were spraying, the place was going to look like a winter wonderland, not like a godforsaken stretch of motorway miles from anywhere, with its tarmac bubbling under the onslaught of a heat-wave.

Riggart couldn't believe that they were going to find anything recognisable in the coach or the surrounding vehicles when they finally dampened everything down. Another ambulance had arrived recently to replace the one with engine trouble, but since the discovery of Acrylonitrile, they had all been pulled back to a safer distance. They were wasting their time here, anyway. No one was going to come out of the inferno alive. The flames that enveloped each vehicle were utterly consuming. Nothing could survive them; no teeth for dental experts, not a shred of clothing. He had seen fires like this before. At the end of them, only ash; and a lot of people worried about those they knew had set off on their journeys but hadn't yet arrived.

There hadn't been another of those bloody peculiar blue flares for ten minutes now, and it seemed as if the boys on the other side had finally managed to get the burning tanker under control. Clouds of black smoke had suddenly appeared over there. The sea of fire had been replaced by a sea of foam. Someone slapped Riggart on the shoulder. He turned to see the senior divisional commander, giving a cut-throat sign. Time to ease up on the hose. The SDC turned and began to run back towards the pump, and Riggart saw that the other crew was emerging from the black smoke sweeping over the motorway from where the tanker lay. He gave thought to the poor bastards who had been incinerated in the coach, felt the pressure vanish in the hose as the men at the pump switched off the foam-flow, and then . . .

Something erupted from the foam enshrouding the coach.

Something that howled and roared and hissed like a living thing before exploding with the impact of a bomb. Riggart only had time for a half-turn before the detonation slammed Planer and himself hard to the foam-shrouded tarmac. But in that instant, before the breath was knocked from his lungs and the visor of his breathing mask was cracked and fogged by the blast to the extent that he couldn't see a thing, Riggart had seen the impossible force that had so suddenly erupted to engulf the coach and the foam. He'd seen what was known as a 'Bleve' – a 'Boiling, liquid, evaporating, vapour explosion' – before. But this was something else; something much worse and in some way connected with the bizarre, blue-white electrical energy which had been flaring from within the impossibly burning foam. This was a concentrated eruption of that energy: a blue-white fireball that was unlike anything he had ever seen in his fire-fighting career. It was like a living cloud of energy. But despite the fact that it had thrown everyone standing to the ground and had pitched the SDC head first into the side of the appliance, where he now lay unconscious and unmoving, it was blossoming and flaring in an impossibly *slow* way. It was like seeing one of those time-lapse films of clouds speeding across the sky; fast, but too slow to be an erupting fire-cloud. There was something utterly, completely *wrong* about it. Riggart shook his head, tried to wipe his face-mask clear. The rational part of his mind was telling him that he was concussed, that he had only seen the fire-cloud for an instant and couldn't possibly trust his eyes. But some inner part of him, some instinctive sense, was reacting in fear. Riggart dragged his mask clear. No use staggering around blind even if there was a danger of poison in the air.

The cloud was still there. An eerie, boiling cloud of crawling blue fire. It was roaring with the sounds of an avalanche.

Riggart stood, utterly mesmerised, unable to comprehend the primitive way in which he was reacting to the sight of it. Almost at his feet, Planer was trying to clamber to his knees, still dazed by the blast. Across the way, he could see the other fire crew, some on their knees, others staggering and dazed just like himself. Astonished, Riggart looked back at the boiling cloud of living blue fire to see that it had enshrouded the entire coach and the foam that smothered it. The cloud hovered there, like a living thing, and through its roiling, chaotic mass he could also see the vague, skeletal outline of the burned-out coach as if he were looking at it through some bizarre form of X-ray machine. The cloud undulated, shivered, and then seemed somehow to turn in on itself in a way that defied human logic. The next moment, it was gone, leaving behind only crackling traces of blue lightning, flashing deep within the foam along the charred frame of the coach and tanker.

Riggart looked over to his own tender and saw that the SDC was still lying on the tarmac, face down. Two crew members from over the way were running towards him. Riggart reached down for Planer, shaking his head.

'I don't know what the $f \ldots$!'

He was unable to finish the sentence. The next detonation spun him away from Planer. The two running men were plucked in mid-stride as if they had been seized by invisible hands, and were flung back the way they had come. The blue-white cloud was alive and roaring again, bursting from the tanker and the coach. Now similar clouds of crackling, roaring energy were erupting from each of the burned-out vehicles surrounding the lorry and coach, each one detonating like a bomb and emitting that impossible, crawling blue fire. From Harry Stark's mangled car, from Ellis Burwell's Lotus Elan, from the other cars that had ploughed into the devastating scene of carnage. Seventeen separate detonations, each living cloud roaring into the sky, greedily amalgamating above the wrecks into one huge blue fireball, creating a wind that swept across the ground like a hurricane, plucking at the fire tenders and rocking them on their suspension, rolling fire crew over the tarmac and whipping the tons of foam into a massive blizzard of snow, engulfing everything in sight.

Seconds later, the fireball mass and the roaring wind were gone, dissolving into the night sky and leaving the foam to fall in a silent deluge.

Planer dragged his mask away from his face, just as Riggart had done. Just like Riggart's, the Plexiglas was cracked and fogged, something that Planer had never known happen in any blast he'd been in. Quickly, he checked to see if he was all in one piece and that nothing had been blown away by the detonations. He had still been lying prone when the last explosions had blasted across the motorway, had felt Riggart's hand on his shoulder helping him to rise. But then the hand had been snatched away and he had stayed where he was, slapping his hands over his head and feeling the impact of the explosions in the wet tarmac beneath him. When he looked anxiously back at the mound of foam that had been the coach and the lorry beyond, he could see no sign of fire. Had the bloody thing blown itself out? He wiped the suds away from his line of vision, unable to make out the men on the other side of the motorway, then remembered that Riggart had been standing right beside him when that last series of explosions had come, and clambered quickly to his feet, looking for him.

'Joe! Where are you?'

He pressed the mask close to his face again and sucked in oxygen. There didn't seem to be anything in the air, but there was no point in being unprofessional and stupid.

'Joe!'

And then he saw Riggart's headgear lying in the foam. It had been somehow ripped from him. He stooped and grabbed it, whirling around to look for him in the snowstorm. It was impossible to tell whether Joe had torn the gear loose, or whether it had been blown from his face by the blast.

'Joe. For God's sake! Where are you?'

Planer saw a figure then, about fifty feet away, by the edge of the motorway embankment. He couldn't be sure in the blizzard whether it was Joe or not, but whoever it was, he was in a bad way, staggering to the embankment with both hands to his head and face as if he were in agony.

'Joe!'

Clutching the headgear, Planer plunged ahead through the foam towards him, slipped and fell headlong on to the tarmac.

Joe Riggart had no idea who he was or where he was. He only knew that something bad had happened. Something had exploded and he'd been catapulted through the air, landing badly on something hard. His shoulder was dislocated, and the agony was excruciating. Vaguely, he remembered that this had happened to him some time ago; instinctively, he knew how to deal with it in a ruthlessly professional manner. As he dragged himself to his feet again, the pain made him ignore what had happened behind him and brought an intense focus to the road sign on the other side of the motorway. He loped, bent over and staggering, directly towards the sign, eyes fixed on the pole. Only feet away from it, he ducked even lower, swung his shoulder round and threw himself at it in a perfect rugby challenge. The pole slammed between his neck and his shoulder, jamming the joint back into place. Screaming, Riggart spun and collapsed against the embankment. Somewhere back on the motorway, he heard a great roaring, like bombs dropping. And as the agony of dislocation muted to a sick, horrendous gnawing of pain where the signpost had slammed into him, the sounds of the detonations seemed to cut through his temporary amnesia. He dragged himself to his feet again, and looked back across the motorway, memory flooding back. But there was nothing to see other than what he might have expected as a professional. No undulating, impossible stormclouds of flickering blue lightning. Just the smoke and guys on the ground and a snowstorm of foam. He straightened, and then the real pain exploded in his head.

If this was concussion, then he wished he were dead.

The pain was crippling. He doubled up and vomited, spinning away again and staggering as he blundered up the embankment. He clutched at his head, crying out at the stabbing agony as . . .

*   *   *

Planer got up out of the foam on his hands and knees and saw the figure claw at the embankment, grabbing handfuls of grass now and scrambling away. He swiped the falling foam away, sucked at the mask again, and saw that it was Joe Riggart, without a doubt. Looking back over his shoulder, he yelled for the others, unsure whether anyone had had a chance to recover or whether they'd heard him at all. Now, like a sprinter from the blocks, he lunged to his feet and charged through the foam, scattering suds. Riggart had pulled him away from a falling warehouse wall about a year and a half ago; he had never forgotten it.

'Joe!' he yelled again, but he inhaled foam as he ran, and his cry spluttered into a choking cough. As he watched, Riggart reached the top of the embankment, still grabbing handfuls of grass to steady himself. He stumbled then, falling forward. Planer saw one of his legs go up high, and knew that there was a gully or ditch on the other side. Riggart had blundered straight over the top of the embankment and fallen down the other side. He ran on, scattering foam as . . .

Riggart clutched helplessly at the grass as he fell heavily into the ditch, consumed by the pain that had exploded in his head and robbed his damaged arm and shoulder of any strength. He lay, gasping for air, looking up at the snowfall of foam. Weakly, he tried to rise.

And then he saw something else moving in the ditch.

At first, through his blurred vision and the pain that possessed him, he thought it was another fire-fighter or support services crewman, blasted across the motorway, over the top of the embankment and into the ditch, just like him. But there seemed to be something wrong with the shape that thrashed and kicked at the grass, not twenty feet from where he lay. Riggart pulled himself around to a sitting position; the effort made him gag, and he struggled to control his nausea.

'Are you . . . are you . . . ?'

He couldn't finish what he'd begun to say, but quite clearly this other poor bastard was far from all right. He could see a pair of legs, flailing, the boots kicking and scuffing at the foam-smeared grass. Not uniformed trousers by the look of it; so this was somehow a civilian who had strayed into the danger area. Or perhaps someone thrown clear of the crash. Riggart tried to drag himself forward towards the shape.

'Stay calm . . . you're going to be okay . . .'

And as if in answer to his strangled voice, another figure appeared out of the darkness from the unkempt shrubs and bushes down in the ditch. The figure lurched through the undergrowth, smashing it aside. At that moment, Riggart remembered that he had been with Planer only moments ago; no doubt he had followed him over the embankment. He raised his head to call out to his partner, and this time when his voice froze in his throat it wasn't with pain or exertion. It was with outright fear.

As the newcomer continued to lurch through the foam-flecked bushes towards the figure that kicked and thrashed in the ditch, Riggart was unable to make sense of the grotesque nature of the thing he was looking at. The symmetry was all wrong. It was human, yet not human. He looked, but could make no sense of it; it defied logic. A man without arms? There was a torso, and stumpy legs that seemed to struggle with the weight it was carrying. The figure seemed to roll awkwardly from side to side as it came, each step a massive effort, fighting gravity all the way. Riggart stared, trying to see where the arms might be, but there were none. But it was the man's face which caused the greatest spasm of unreasoning fear. It was much too white; a horrifying moon-mask, with dark craters where the eyes might be hidden. There was blood on the mouth, as if the figure had been eating messily. And as it took another lurching step, its head turned so that he could see a ragged tracing of blood all around the thing's face. It reminded him of something he had hated and feared as a child.

It was somehow the face of a clown.

A face that was much too white, with hideously extravagant make-up. Something like that face had sent him screaming from a circus tent when he was seven years old, leaving his father to make embarrassed excuses and run out into the surrounding fields after his son.

Its head swivelled again, and Riggart believed for one utterly horrifying moment that it had fixed its attention on him. But the figure seemed only interested in the thrashing form between them. Something like a smile creased the moon-white and hideously ragged face, and with a fixed expression that was somehow a hideous amalgam of delight, greed and bestial savagery, the figure threw itself forward on top of the spasming, kicking legs. Riggart cried out in fear and disgust, working himself back against the embankment. The figure was attacking the agonised bastard whom Riggart had been trying to save.

But attacking him *without arms* . . . ?

Riggart struggled to his feet, still stooped and holding on to tufts of grass to keep himself from keeling over again. And this time, what he saw transcended that first instinctive fear. What was happening not ten feet away from him was impossible to make sense of; it offended all sense of logic, to the extent that Joe Riggart could only stand there, swaying, and look and question whether the concussion he had suffered from the motorway blast had made him hallucinate. Was he really in the ditch, or in a hospital bed somewhere, dreaming this nightmare? Had any of this really happened, the motorway crash and all these hideous deaths? Would the alarm clock soon wake him and send him out on his first shift?

Only in a dream could he be looking at a lower torso and legs, kicking and jerking in the ditch; a lower torso without an upper body. Something that had been severed at the waist could not keep on moving all that time. And if anyone had been able to tell Joe Riggart in this dream that the self-same lower torso had been kicking and thrashing out of sight for the past two hours, then – as he was still dreaming – he would have accepted that logic and said: Sure, why not? And if he accepted that he was truly dreaming, then it must also be easy to accept that the figure that had blundered through the bushes *did* have arms after all. It too was a human figure, severed at the waist. Only this figure had no legs, and was only able to move around because it was walking on its *downstretched arms*, the knuckles raw and bleeding where the knotted fists served as stunted feet on the ground. And Riggart had been wrong about the first figure attacking the second. The first figure was merely trying to put things right, seizing the lower half as it rolled and spasmed and kicked in the ditch, jamming the apparently reluctant bottom half up hard against itself, so that the severed torso was made whole once more. Riggart nodded, a child in a nightmare dream. Of course it made sense. It had been cut in two, now it would be whole again. There was a sound of suction, like someone pulling his or her boot out of the mud in this filthy ditch, and Riggart could see that the thing was hanging on tight to its hips. As he looked on in fear and bewilderment, he could see the same blue-white crackling energy that he had seen in the fire-cloud, fizzling and crackling and crawling around the thing's waist, *soldering* the two halves together again. The legs were not kicking so wildly any more, as if the act of fusion were working at last. The legs slowed, and now it looked like some bizarre and mud-encrusted figure pulling on a pair of tight jeans.

'Right,' said Riggart. 'Get it together. Right. Now it's time to wake up, Joe.'

Everything was okay now. The dream was over. The figure in the ditch was struggling to rise, fighting to regain balance on its legs, arms pinwheeling. Now it was clutching at the embankment grass, just like him. Discarding everything he had seen, in order to restore normality and keep himself sane, Riggart held out a hand.

'Here, I'll help you.'

The figure staggered towards him, head down. At the last moment, it took his hand and looked up at him, full in the face.

The grip was like iron and ice.

The face was still the ragged moon-face travesty of a clown.

And as Joe looked, part of the ragged face was slipping. It was puckering and sliding from one of the ears and across a cheek, revealing a blood-raw mass of gelatinous muscle, cartilage and ruptured blood vessels. The face of Kenny, the hospital orderly, was sliding away.

'Just like me,' said Riggart. 'I lost my mask, too . . .'

'*Are you me?*' asked the hideous false-face. '*I'm looking for me.*'

'Jesus Christ,' said Riggart. 'Leave me alone.'

'*You look like me,*' said the thing.

It fell on him.

Planer felt like a fucking idiot, sliding and scurrying through the foam as he headed for the embankment. Somehow, he could feel the scorn and sarcastic comments from the other fire crew behind him. One of the disciplines they shared with the police was the ability – the outright need – to find humour in the most hideous and extreme situations. It was the only way to keep going and not get emotionally involved with the job. It was bad enough dragging your first baby out of a burning apartment, knowing that one hundred per cent of its skin was cooked and that although its mouth was working it could never scream because it had inhaled fire that had burned out its lungs. In your arms, you could feel its agony, know you'd gone in there against all the odds because you believed in this hellish job with all your heart and wanted to save people; but you knew that the kid was in the worst kind of torment, and the best that you could wish it was a quick death. But after the second and the third and the fourth, and worse cases beyond number, developing a ghoulish sense of humour was the *only* way to stay sane.

So Planer knew that the others were laughing and pointing as he struggled and skidded towards the embankment, even though in reality most of them had not even been able to rise from the tarmac and pull themselves together. Shouting for those others to follow and then cursing that they, unlike him, hadn't seen what had happened to Riggart, Planer finally skidded free of the foam and reached the embankment. Hand over hand, he clawed at the straggling grass until he'd reached the top. He turned back only once, yelling at the others: 'Come *on!*'

The snowstorm of foam hid everything from sight. Assuming that they must be running after him, Planer lunged down the embankment into the ditch. The other side was steeper than he'd anticipated. Sliding, he braced himself for impact; but the breath was still knocked out of his lungs when he finally hit the bottom. Thank God, he'd found Riggart straight away. Only feet away. He was okay. And he had found someone down here, someone to whom he was giving first aid.

Not Riggart.

Not giving first aid.

The thing pulled away from Riggart, still holding him by the shoulders. Something long and white and wet flapped from its mouth. Planer saw its face and recoiled in terror. There was no flesh on the face. It was a bloody mass of raw meat. And as Planer watched, he saw the thing let Riggart go; saw his partner sag back against the embankment, mouth working in terror and hideous agony. Planer was close enough to see that somehow Riggart now had the same hideous visage as the thing that had attacked him. Only his uniform and his shape and size told Planer that this was the man with whom he had shared so many dangerous times. He scrabbled away from them both, unable to utter a sound. Even though the thing had no face, Planer could swear that there was an expression of emotion there. No malice, no ferocious desire to do to him what it had done to Riggart.

Only fear.

Fear that Planer had suddenly interrupted whatever was happening, that he might take away from the thing what twitched and dangled from its gelatinous mouth. It fumbled at the white mass, grabbed it now with both hands, swung its head away from Planer and seemed to cram the indistinguishable mess over the ruin of its own face. Planer watched the elbows piston, up and down like someone taking a wash.

Quickly, and still in fear, the thing looked back at him, anxious that he might be creeping up behind it and trying to steal away that which it had itself stolen.

And Planer could only moan and shake his head and

throw a hand across his mouth when he saw that somehow – impossibly – the thing was wearing Joe Riggart's face. Even now, that flesh mask of a face was flapping away from where it had been crammed around the ears, chin and forehead. The thing hurriedly smoothed the mask back into place.

'*I'm me now!*' it hissed.

And then it vanished into the night.

Planer stayed there for a long, long time, watching the faceless thing that had once been his friend Joe Riggart die.

It was morning. Mercy moved quickly and silently.

There was no way she was going to allow them to admit her for observation. They had already dressed her cuts and bruises, seemed happy that she hadn't suffered any internal injuries, and there was no way she was going to sit in a hospital bed for weeks while doctors poked and prodded at her. There were things she had to do; places she had to be. And she would have been out of that hellhole a lot earlier if she hadn't been feeling so groggy towards the end. They seemed worried about that. But what the hell else did they expect? She had almost been totalled in that pile-up, and there was no way she was going to wait to be made 'heroine of the week' when the newspapers finally came sniffing around. She could barely recall what had happened in the casualty department afterwards, but clearly the nurses and other medical staff there had been freaked out. She vaguely remembered being in X-ray, and then not feeling very well. As if there was something she had to do, somewhere she had to be. And then there was a feeling of dizziness. Nothing else. The next thing she remembered was being led away from the darkened casualty department in a wheelchair at top speed. There were raised voices all around her, sounds of panic. Broken glass crunching under the wheels. Somewhere, someone had shouted that she'd been electrocuted. Electrocuted? What the hell had all that been about? She had been in a crash on the motorway. Then she seemed to have faded out again, coming around in the light once more. This time, she seemed to be in one of the main wards, and a nurse with a fragile smile was trying to take her clothes off and put her into a nightdress. For a moment, Mercy thought she was back in the children's home, and that the nightmare of those days was happening again. She had fought back, until the nurse backed off. Then everything had come into focus properly again, and a doctor had told her that something had happened to her back in Casualty. Someone had seen her being electrocuted or something. But she seemed to be fine. There must have been a misunderstanding, because there were no burn marks. She had been knocked down . . . by something (and Mercy had noticed the look of genuine unease on the young doctor's face) . . . but she seemed to be all right. They wanted her to stay in for a couple of days, just to keep her under observation and to make sure. Mercy had made all the right noises, and then as soon as their backs were turned, she was out of there. She had overheard someone talking about a power surge that blew out all the lights, but didn't know how that related to her.

Mercy remembered a time when she had been ten years old, playing with her friends on top of the concrete bunker that housed the rubbish bins for the block of flats where she lived. She had taken a step back to avoid another kid cartwheeling on the bunker, had fallen eight feet to a grassed embankment, and had landed flat on her back. The breath had been knocked out of her, but the strangest thing was the way she saw double for a few seconds, then couldn't remember anything for the next twenty minutes. According to her friends, she had simply climbed to her feet again and told everyone that she thought she'd better go home. They hadn't taken much notice when it was clear that she hadn't been badly hurt. Apparently, she had climbed the eighteen flights of stairs to home, had let herself in, had a conversation with her mother and brother about a television programme they'd watched the previous evening, and had then gone for a lie-down. None of that registered in her memory. She remembered the fall and the double vision, then waking in bed and feeling sick. The intervening time had been stolen from her memory.

It was like that now when she tried to remember what had happened in Casualty. She had a vague memory of flashing light and of a noise like rushing wind. Nothing else. She had asked the doctors what they were looking for as they examined her body, but none of them was letting on. And she had noticed the looks of incredulity on their faces when it was clear that her skin wasn't marked in any way.

Well, enough was enough. She had a life to lead, and it was time to be getting on with it.

She quickly slipped into the toilets just by the waiting area for Physiotherapy, was relieved to find that there was no one else in there, and then moved to one of the cubicles. Moments later, she was sitting on the lavatory seat, going through the handbag that she had stolen from one of the waiting rooms.

It seemed that the few personal belongings she'd had were burned up with everything else at the bottom of the motorway ditch. In the circumstances, there was nothing else for her to do. The handbag was there, and she needed the cash to get on her way.

But she wasn't a cow. There was personal stuff in the bag, and she wasn't about to tamper with it. She took the cash – about twenty pounds – and left the handbag carefully by the side of the toilet seat. Someone would find it and return it.

Flushing the toilet, she opened the door casually and saw that she was still alone. In two minutes, she was outside the entrance of the hospital, heading for the main road. The wad of five-pound notes in her back pocket felt solid and reassuring.

The Lord will provide, her shell-shocked mother had told her, just before she'd been taken away to the children's home.

Yeah? she thought. *Well, he must have forgotten my address somewhere along the way, Mam. So I just have to provide for myself, don't I?*

There was a bus-stop across the way. A shuttle-service coach was parked there, 'Town Centre' emblazoned on its side. That would do for now. Just get away from the place, find somewhere for a drink. And then plan her route. Some more hitch-hiking, but tankers carrying flammable liquid would not be high on her list.

Just as the thought registered, she looked back at the entrance and saw a familiar figure.

It was Martin, standing against one of the walls, trying with difficulty to light a cigarette. She felt something inside, something that was almost warm. She watched as he cupped the match in his hands and finally managed to get a drag out of the cigarette. Suddenly, she wanted a cigarette more than anything else. She took a step forward, then hesitated when she remembered the handbag she'd left back in the toilets. What the hell. No one had seen her with it, so even if someone did come screaming out of the main doors, there was no way she could be implicated. Smiling, she began to stride back towards the entrance.

A taxi pulled up. At first, Mercy took no notice. But then a woman climbed out of the back seat with some difficulty, and Mercy saw Martin stoop down to get a better look, then noted the look of recognition on his face. That expression turned into the gentle-giant smile she remembered from their first meeting. It somehow seemed a million years ago, almost in a different life. And then he threw the cigarette away as the woman almost staggered into his arms. Martin swept her up and swung her around. He seemed to dwarf her.

Mercy stopped, watching them embrace.

The sudden wave of warmth had gone. She felt like crying now, felt like a little kid who had just been spurned by an adult she cared for. And that other feeling suddenly made her angry. She spun on her heels, and headed back towards the bus-stop.

'Mercy!'

A doctor perhaps? They'd discovered that she'd discharged herself. Even now, two guys in white coats and several nurses might be running across the car park towards her. She looked down, increased her pace.

'Mercy. Wait!'

Someone had seen her stealing the handbag. The owner was pointing her out and a policeman was charging after her. She began to run.

'For God's sake!'

A hand clamped on her shoulder. She cried out, clawing at it and refusing to turn around. But the strength in the grip was enormous. It tightened, and suddenly she was swung around. She prepared to gouge out an eye, and deliver a kick to the balls.

'It's me! Take it easy. It's only me.'

Martin towered over her. Still trying to catch his breath, he kept his hands on her shoulders. Now those hands felt gentle.

'Sorry, I thought . . .'

'Where the hell are you going?'

Mercy looked back towards the entrance. The woman he had embraced was walking awkwardly towards them as if in pain. Brown, permed hair. A powder-blue coat that somehow reminded Mercy of her mother, despite the fact that her mother had never owned a coat like that. She was carrying a handbag close to her chest as if it were a protective charm.

'I . . .' Mercy struggled to balance out her conflicting emotions. 'I discharged myself.'

'Good for you. So did I.'

'You did?'

'Yeah. All that poking and prodding, when there's bugger-all wrong with me. I've got to get back to the depot, get the insurance worked out, make sure the bastards aren't blaming me for what happened. The police want to talk to me, but that can wait until I'm home and had a cup of tea. Have the police talked to you yet?'

'No . . . I mean, yeah. The police. Yeah.'

The woman reached them at last.

'You're the girl who pulled Martin out of the lorry.' It was a statement rather than a question. Mercy shuffled uncomfortably, not knowing how to respond. Now she could see what had made her initially uncomfortable, what had reminded her of home. This woman was in her fifties, but was dressed in a style that might have been fashionable thirty years ago. The clothes, the perm, even the make-up. She would be about Mercy's mother's age, and looking just how Mercy remembered her mother from those days. Mercy waited, hoping that someone would fill the gap in the conversation. Martin was smiling expectantly, also waiting. And then, unable to express herself, Martin's wife gave in to her overwhelming emotions. Mercy saw her face crumple, and almost recoiled when she suddenly stepped forward and seized her in an embrace, crushing her close. The smell of perfume was overwhelming. Mercy stood with her arms tightly at her sides. Martin was still smiling. When his wife pulled back again, she fumbled at her handbag, trembling fingers finding a crumpled tissue paper.

'I don't know what to . . . I mean . . . I should be able to . . . but I . . .'

'This is Sheila,' said Martin. 'I think she's trying to thank you.'

The sluices were opened then, and Sheila began to bawl into her tissue paper.

Mercy shuffled again, looking around the car park.

'Why don't you come back with us?' asked Martin.

'Well . . . I've got to get on . . . I mean, I was travelling to . . .' She was moving into automatic retreat. But even as she spoke, she began to feel something else. Something that was making her *want* to go back. Then Sheila seemed to come around a little, emerging from the tissue paper with sudden resolve.

'Yes, *yes*! You must come back.'

And there was something about her response, something that generated a host of conflicting emotions inside Mercy. This woman so reminded her of being young again. Part of her wanted – really *wanted* – to go back with these strangers, as if she could somehow recapture something of what had been lost in the past, as if what had happened on the motorway might somehow atone for the lost years, give her a chance of a new start. A crazy feeling, an irrational feeling, but it was a powerfully charged emotion nevertheless. But there was something else, too; something about the look of *need* in this woman's face. Perhaps it was only a need to say thank you, a need to show her how grateful she was. But Mercy remembered the same look on her mother's face. That need could be overwhelming, could be swamping. It reminded her of how her mother had controlled her, had used that need to order every aspect of her life. Mercy could never allow herself to get close enough to be controlled again. Ever.

And, of course, there was the person she was hunting. So much rage inside her; so much need to find him and make him pay for what he had done.

'No. Thanks, but no. I've got people waiting for me. Yeah, that's right. People who might be worried about me. So . . . gotta go, you know?'

Again, that look of need on the woman's face. Wanting to express herself properly, but unable to and distressed by the fact that she could not do it adequately.

Martin was nodding.

'Are you sure?' continued Sheila. 'Just for a little while. Just until you . . .' *Until you what?* The words dried.

'Here.' Martin reached into his pocket, found his cigarette packet. Tearing off a strip, he asked Sheila for a pen while Mercy looked around the car park, as if looking for a way to escape. Martin scribbled something on the scrap of paper he had torn from the packet. 'Here's our address. If you ever need anything. . . . anything . . . then let us know.'

Mercy shuffled uncomfortably again, took the proffered scrap and shoved it into her back pocket. As she did so, she felt the wad of notes. It made her feel uncomfortable again. This time, she was able to break away.

'The bus. Got to go before the bus leaves.'

As if in response to her words, the bus driver began to rev the engine. It was a good excuse to hurry. She waved as she hurried off. For a moment, it looked as if Sheila was going to call her back, try to express herself again. Martin did not move. He just stood and looked, but this time he wasn't smiling.

Mercy waved the bus to a halt just as it began to pull away from the stop.

Martin watched as she jumped aboard. She waved once, an embarrassed gesture, and then slung herself into a seat, facing away, not wanting them to see her inner thoughts reflected on her face.

Martin put an arm around Sheila as she began to snuf-fle again.

And then the bus was gone.

The doctors had given her something (she hadn't liked to ask what), and it was making Jane feel woozy. Good and comfortable and helping her to think that everything was going to be all right, after all. The bedclothes had been tucked in tight, just the way Mother used to do it when Jane was a little girl. One of the nurses had combed her hair, and that made her feel good too.

At first, the fear had been making her feel sick. Just after she'd spoken to Roger and had returned to her own cubicle and the nurse had told her that her husband was on his way. She had, in fact, been sick, when that fear had been too much to contain. But the nurses had only assumed it had to do with the shock of the accident – and with something else that didn't make any sense to her. Something about another accident in the casualty department when the electrical system in the hospital had failed. But they must have made a mistake there. She hadn't been involved in a second accident in the hospital itself. She remembered talking to Roger and going back to her cubicle. And then she supposed that one of the nurses must have given her something to calm her down. Because she had slept then, and hadn't woken until much later. She remembered dreams about thunderclouds and being very frightened in the dreams of something that didn't make much sense. Waking at last, she felt rested and comfortable and hazy.

Maybe everything would turn out all right. Perhaps the crash, terrible though it had been (and Jane marvelled at the way she had come to terms with it all as she lay there), might mean a completely new start. Maybe there were such things as fairy godmothers and wishes coming true. After all, there had been more than one bus in the depot. She could have chosen any one of them. But no, she had chosen *that* coach. The one that crashed. And Tom was on his way now, rushing to be at her side. He would see her in the hospital bed, would see the cut on her forehead, would realise just how much she had been suffering. The fear of his outraged reaction – that she could have just upped and *left* him – had dissipated. He would see and he would think about how he had been treating her. He would understand, and he would change; so very, *very* grateful that she was still alive.

It could only have been twelve or thirteen hours since she had boarded the coach, but as she lay there it could have been years ago. Then, her fear had driven her into retreat within her own mind. On automatic pilot, she had packed her bag and walked away from their house into the night. Too terrified even to think of the consequences of her actions, of where she was going or what she was going to do. Now it seemed that she was thinking about another woman who lived inside her skin. Even the fear that had so consumed her before she slept seemed to belong to a different woman.

I was nearly killed. By rights, I shouldn't be here. I was meant to board that coach. I was meant to survive the crash, so that Tom could realise what he was doing. So that he could see what he nearly lost. So that he could change.

The nice nurse who had combed her hair looked around the door and smiled. Jane returned the smile, interlocking her fingers on the neatly turned-down, snugly tucked-in bedcover.

'Mrs Teal. Your husband is here.'

And there was Tom in the doorway, smiling at the nurse.

A new beginning. Just like the way it was before Tom asked me to marry him.

'We're keeping your wife in purely for observation.' The nurse was whispering now, as if she didn't want Jane to hear. Which was silly, really, since they had already asked her nicely, even though she felt fine and the doctors had said there was no sign of internal injury or anything nasty like that. But Jane was pleased that the nurse was whispering, because it all added to the effect. 'Just a day or so, to make sure.'

'But she's all right, isn't she?' asked Tom. There was concern on his face, and it filled Jane with something like bliss to see it. The warm glow had spread to encompass her whole body. She felt like crying out loud with happiness, but mustn't do that in case Tom thought what had happened hadn't been serious, after all.

'Yes, she's fine. But shock can affect people in different ways. Sometimes it's delayed. And we want to be certain.'

Yes, yes. Good!

The nurse smiled again, turning to look at Jane.

'I'll be just around the corner here, if you want anything.' She smiled once more and was gone. Tom watched her go. Just like him, even now. Looking at the nurse's legs.

Boys will be boys.

He turned to look at her as he closed the door.

And Jane felt everything fall apart.

All her hopes for a new start. All her stupid dreams that what she had been through would mean something to them both. The new beginning. The smile had vanished from Tom's face. Now there was only that cold and expressionless mask which she had learned to fear so much. The face was blank, but the eyes told a different story, something she had learned only too well. With his eyes, he could control her in a crowded room. That look of barely contained fury, the sparking blue of the eyes that had regarded her so tenderly in the early days. She was a little girl again, clutching at the bedpane and shrinking back as Tom strode across the room, eyes blazing. He pulled a chair up roughly and sat close to her.

Jane struggled to contain the tears, could feel one leaking from the corner of her eye even now. Desperately, she swept it away with one hand, knowing just how furious he could become if he saw her crying.

'Sit up straight,' he demanded.

At once, Jane did as she was told. Bolt upright in bed, eyes wide in fear, hypnotised by the blue fire in those eyes. She wanted to say something, wanted to make it better. But nothing she could do or say would help. Now it seemed that she'd boarded the bus only minutes ago after all. How could she have fooled herself so badly? She had done a bad thing.

'So?' asked Tom, face still unchanged.

Jane tried to say something, but her voice was choked and dry.

'*So?*'

This time she jumped a little, and the shock of his raised voice made the words pour out.

'I nearly died, Tom. It was terrible. A terrible crash. There were lots of people. Dead, I mean. Killed. And I nearly died. Died.'

'Why didn't you die, you stupid fucking bitch?'

'You don't mean that, Tom.'

'Don't I? I come home, and you're not there. The next thing, I get a telephone call from the hospital.'

'It was awful, Tom. The coach caught fire and there were people screaming . . .'

'Why were you on that coach, Jane?'

'I nearly *died*, Tom.'

'*Why were you on that coach, Jane?*'

Jane couldn't control herself now. She began to sob, at the same time trying to control the noise. Her fingers moved to her mouth, trembling violently, as if she could cram the sounds back inside.

'Know what I think?' This time, his voice was calm and measured. 'I think you decided to leave. Decided to run away. Is that what happened?'

Jane began to shake her head furiously, fingers still crammed in her mouth.

'No? Well, I think we should have a proper talk about this. At home. Get to the bottom of it all. Find out what's going on.'

'I'm . . . not well, Tom. The doctors said . . . said they wanted me to stay . . .'

'There's nothing wrong with you, you whining little whore. So you're going to stop making that fucking noise, right *now!* And you're going to tell the nurse and the doctors that you want to go home with your husband. Where he can look after you. And no matter what they say, no matter how much they try to convince you to stay, you're going to insist. What are you going to do?'

'Insist, Tom. I'm going to insist.'

'Too fucking right you are.'

He stood up and headed for the door. When he had his hand on the handle, he turned back and gave her one of his meaningful looks. Jane knew what she must do, had learned what to do from past experience. It was time for everything to look normal again in front of other people. Hastily, she dried her eyes on the bedspread, straightened her hair and looked back. Tom smiled. There was no humour there. His eyes remained as cold and frightening as ever. He was showing her what she had to do. Clearing her throat, Jane smiled. A big, beaming smile, as if she were pleased with everything in the whole wide world.

'Good,' said Tom. This time he looked as if he really was pleased with her efforts. '*Good.*' She watched him open the door and call for the nurse.

Inside, she could feel something small and terrified, kicking and leaping like an animal caught in a snare.

Ellis Burwell logged out of his personal computer and sat back with a sigh of relief. The shirt beneath his jacket was soaked with sweat and was clinging to his flesh. His fingernails were hurting again, as if something had become jammed under the quick of each one. Tapping furiously at the keyboards had seemed to make them worse. And why the hell did his hands feel so cold all the time? Sweating profusely, and yet so cold. It was the shock of the accident, surely. What else could it be?

He had made it back to the office in time, before anyone else had come in. With only three weeks to go before the audit was due to take place, he couldn't afford to take any chances, and the window that he had left open in the computer programme dealing with one of his three 'slush fund' accounts had now been safely closed. Two of his personal stock market transfers would go a substantial way towards covering his tracks. He rubbed his hands over his face. They felt like the cold hands of a dead man.

Safe again. Nothing to worry about . . .

Until the next time, came that other little voice. *Until the next time that bastard puts the screws on to me for more cash.*

The intercom on his desk buzzed. Angrily, he snatched it up.

'I said I wasn't to be disturbed, Glynis . . .'

'I'm sorry, Mr Burwell. But Mr Purcell wants to see you in his office right away.'

The mention of the managing director's name made him sit up straight in the chair. 'Oh, right . . . right . . .' His mind began to race. 'Did he . . . did he say why?'

'No, just that you were to come straight up.'

Christ, he knows. Someone's accessed the files while I was away.

Burwell felt weak. A sudden, raging thirst had overcome him. More than anything else, he wanted a pint of something sweet. He reached for his cup, remembered that he had drained it – and then rose none too steadily to head for the door.

But surely no one can know. I've covered my tracks. I'm okay until the audit . . . and by then, I'll have everything back in place.

His secretary's face was blank when he passed her in the ante-office, preoccupied with the letter she was typing. He surreptitiously searched her face as he passed, looking for any kind of sign that she knew something but was deliberately keeping it from him. On the stairs outside, heading up to the seventh floor, he paused to lean against one of the blue pastel walls. The thirst was overwhelming and he considered making a detour to the men's room. But his stomach was cramped with fear now, and he wanted to get what was coming over with as fast as possible. He pushed himself away from the wall and headed for the next flight of stairs. But this time, it seemed as if his sense of balance had deserted him. His legs would not carry his weight, and in the next instant he had fallen to his knees at the foot of the stairs.

'Burwell? You all right?'

The voice from behind was instantly recognisable. Number twelve on Ellis Burwell's top-twenty hate-list at Purcell Advertising: James Tovey. Twenty-three years old and already scrambling up the ladder in his bid for the top. Smart suit and dyed blond hair, always looking for an opportunity to get one over on his colleagues. Without turning, Burwell desperately tried to regain his feet. Already, he had a mental image of what Tovey would be saying in his coffee break later that morning:

Just on my way up to see Paul about these roughs, and you'll never guess what I came across. Poor old Ellis Burwell, on his hands and knees on the staircase. Just about ready to keel over. White-faced, wobbly as hell. Got to be the booze, hasn't it?

There was a hand on his arm now, and Burwell wanted more than anything to shrug that grip away and stand up. But he was unable to do anything about it as Tovey suddenly came into view, leaning down and putting a hand under his other arm as he tried to lift him.

'Take it easy, Burwell. You're okay, I've got you.'

'Leave . . . leave . . .' Burwell could hardly speak now. Sweat was streaming down his face and his hands were still icy cold. Some distant part of him, something deep inside, seemed to be screaming. Was he having a heart attack?

The crash. On the motorway. Something happened to me, after all. They said I was lucky to get away with bruises and scratches. But something more serious must have happened. Something bad, and the doctors – those bastard doctors – missed it.

'Come on, Burwell. I've got you.' Tovey lifted him to his feet again and tried to turn him.

And for the first time since the accident, Burwell remembered something about the collision that had somehow completely escaped his mind. He remembered the sounds of screaming, the sounds that had exploded into his car, just before the light enveloped him. He could somehow hear the echoes of that screaming, from somewhere deep inside himself. But this time, there was no multitude of voices. There was only one small voice. A forlorn and distant echo.

'It's in me,' said Burwell, in a hollow voice. 'That voice is inside me.'

He could see Tovey's face now, turned to look full at him. He had expected to see a smirking grin, a look of glee that he'd been able to find him in this state. But Tovey's face bore an expression of what seemed to be real concern.

'Take it easy.' More than concern now; he was genuinely worried. Burwell's face had a complexion like melted candle wax. There were dark hollows under his eyes and something of real terror in them.

'But it's *in* me. For Christ's sake, it's *in* me!'

Burwell staggered and Tovey clutched him tight. But this time, Burwell pulled himself away hard. Tovey followed, thinking that he was about to fall; but Burwell seized the handrail and remained erect, swaying there like a drunk. His eyes were wild and staring, and he was immobilised by the sudden and instinctive awareness of something that was happening inside him. Tovey hovered, unsure of what he should do.

'Sit down, Ellis. On the stairs. I'll go and get someone.'

'They couldn't get away. They're still here.'

'That's right, they're still here. Now, just sit down slowly and . . .'

Burwell staggered again, and Tovey lunged forward. This time, Burwell grabbed at the air and seized Tovey's hand.

Tovey cried out aloud when he felt that ice-cold grip. This time, it was his turn to gasp. His eyes were now suddenly wide and alarmed. Because something was happening to his hand. Something that at first felt like an electric shock being transmitted from Burwell's hand to his own, but now not like electricity at all; now more like the very cold itself shooting into his fingers and down his forearm. Tovey tried to shake him loose, but Burwell clung fast as he righted himself, still staring deep into his eyes as if he wanted him to understand something very important. Now Tovey could not speak, could not resist or pull away, because that ice-cold shock had swept down his arm to his chest. In moments, it seemed to have engulfed his entire body. His chest had tightened as if his lungs had frozen. He had difficulty breathing, began to gasp in pain as Burwell clung to the handrail. The ice was in Tovey's legs now. Now it was his turn to collapse slowly. With Burwell still clinging to his hand, Tovey sat heavily on the stairs, breathing asthmatically, eyes imploring.

'You see?' said Burwell. 'You see, it's deep *inside*.'

And then Burwell dragged his hand away, clutching at the handrail. Pulling himself around, he began to climb the stairs again, like a drunken man, with his mind still fixed on that bizarre inner point.

On the bottom step, Tovey began to claw at his throat. His eyes bulged; his face was beginning to turn purple.

On the sixth floor, Burwell stopped and shook his head. He remembered covering the open window in his programme; remembered getting the call to go and see Purcell (and that memory brought with it a gnawing knot of anxiety deep in his stomach); but he could not remember leaving the office. Now he was on his way to see the managing director, but he had no memory of leaving his office. He felt strange. Thirsty as hell, still sweating like a pig – and with his hands feeling like blocks of ice – but somehow very strange. That accident had shaken him up worse than he had imagined. First meeting up with Klark again (enough to stress out anyone), then Armageddon on the motorway. But he wondered whether he was suffering from an undiagnosed concussion, enough to make him forget what he'd done in the last few minutes. Somewhere beneath him on the staircase, he could hear a sibilant hissing sound, but paid it no heed as he continued on.

Purcell's secretary told him to go straight through, and the knot of anxiety had become a crippling jag of fear as he pushed open the door and tried to muster as much of a show of confidence as possible. Suddenly, he no longer seemed to be in his body. In a curious way, he could see himself entering the office, pausing just beyond the threshold and looking over to the ridiculously old-fashioned desk that Purcell had bought from a previous company. He had been a messenger boy then, for another advertising agency; had brought tea and cigars from the corner shop to the boss, who had sat behind this self-same desk. When he had finally made it big, he had bought the company – and this ridiculous desk to remind himself, and anyone else in earshot, how he had persevered and got to the top. Purcell was sitting there now, doing boss impersonations, pretending to look at the artwork roughs that were spread over that desk, puffing on his cigar; in reality, waiting for Burwell.

Floating somewhere near the ceiling, Burwell watched the

figure that looked like him nervously clear its throat. Would those legs carry his weight as he crossed the carpet?

Purcell looked up. 'Ah, Ellis.' As if he hadn't been expecting him. 'Please, come in. Now what was it I wanted?'

He knows . . . oh my God, he's found out . . .

'Have a seat.'

Burwell watched himself walk across the deep pile of the carpet. Miraculously, the figure was walking straight and not falling to its knees. As it made it to the chair, he watched Purcell put the roughs aside and sit back.

'A little bird has told me . . .'

. . . oh God . . .

'That you've been up to no good.'

. . . oh Good Christ, no *. . .*

'You're a strange character, Ellis. Never really been able to work you out. But you're good at your job, no doubt about that. When it comes to finances, you're my man.'

'I can explain . . .'

Purcell waved a hand to silence him. Which was just as well, because Burwell had no idea what he was about to say.

'But what you've done today has made me see you in a different light.'

How long was the bastard going to draw it out? Was he going to give him a lecture before he reached for the telephone and asked his secretary to ring for the police? Burwell could feel something building inside the shell that was himself; some kind of pressure that was going to burst him apart at any moment. Something deep down inside, something that was screaming, just as someone or something had screamed on the motorway before the crash.

'You hadn't planned to tell anyone about what happened to you on the A1, had you? A multiple car crash, and you were right in the middle of it. Barely got out of there alive, and here you are – first thing in the morning, back at work, sitting at your desk.'

'How . . . ?'

Purcell smiled indulgently. He pulled out a newspaper,

which had been under the artists' roughs on his desk. Burwell could see the headline: Horror on the A1.'

'Did you know that only six people got out of there alive? Your name's in here.'

That bloody reporter ...

'I wonder how many of them are at work this morning. No, I'm seeing you in a different light, Ellis. Things like loyalty to the firm are old-fashioned, I know. But I was brought up to believe in those kind of principles, and I'm impressed. However, I have to tell you. You look like hell. And you might be underestimating the effects of shock. I want you to take the rest of the day off. Hell, take the *week* off ...'

The intercom on the desk buzzed. Purcell reached over and flicked a switch.

Burwell heard his secretary's tinny voice say: 'Sorry to disturb you, Mr Purcell. But there's been an incident on the staircase ...'

'Incident? What kind of incident?'

'It's Mr Tovey. He's been found on the stairs. By Mr Turner. He thinks he's dead.'

'Good Christ ... all right ... get an ambulance ... I'll be down in a second ... Ellis?'

'Something inside ...'

'What? Yes, well, never mind. I think you should get yourself home. Get someone to drive you. I've got to go ...'

When Purcell hurried from the office, Burwell remained in his seat, staring ahead. Still floating on the ceiling, he watched himself and wondered what was going to happen next. After a while, the figure stood up from the chair, turned and left the office.

Burwell wondered where it was going.

'Seen yesterday's newspaper?' asked Roger.

His brother emptied the last of the whisky bottle into his glass, jokingly wrung the bottle's neck as if he could squeeze some more out of it, and then dropped it into the waste bin. Roger had lost count of the times that Chris had performed that little trick over the years.

'You've travelled two hundred and fifty miles, drank a half-bottle of Scotch and three cans of ultra-strength lager, and now you want to read old newspapers rather than go out clubbing with me?'

'Seriously. Have you seen it?'

Chris slumped back in his chair, running a hand through his prematurely grey hair. He was four years older than Roger, but at twenty-eight years of age, his formerly black and wavy hair had given up the ghost. His girlfriend, Phyllida, said it made him look 'distinguished' or 'fucking old' – she couldn't make up her mind.

'Who needs newspapers? They're always full of bad news.'

'How about the news headlines on the television? Have you seen them recently?'

Chris took another gulp of whisky. This time, he gave a measured stare. 'You've got that sneaky look on your face, just like when we were kids. Yep, there it is. Something important that you've been wanting to tell me ever since you arrived. But you've been keeping it up your sleeve, just like the old days.'

Roger smiled and lifted his glass again.

'You don't change, Roger. Always gave you a buzz, didn't it? Having a secret, intending to tell everyone about it. But always in your own time. If you won ten million quid on the lottery, you'd still spend an hour and a half talking to me about the weather and the state of the government and the canvas you're working on, before you casually dropped it in to the conversation.'

'Makes me feel secure,' smiled Roger. 'Having an older brother who knows me inside out.'

'Bloody typical . . . here, you *haven't* won ten million on the lottery, have you?'

'Fat chance, but there's an element of luck in what happened.'

'If you want me to crack open another bottle of Scotch, you're going to have to get to the point, Bruv.'

'Not hear anything about that big smash-up on the A1?'

Chris sipped his drink again, thinking. 'Yeah, up north. Nasty.'

'Anything else?'

'Let's see ... it's a single stretch of motorway between Newcastle and Edinburgh, I think. Been subject to a lot of complaints about road smashes. They want it turned into a dual carriageway to make it safer, but the government have put it all back for fifteen years. There. How's that for attention to detail?'

'Commendable. But haven't you missed something else?'

'Nope. Nasty smash-up, though. Lots of people killed.'

'Ever occur to you that I might have been travelling on that stretch of motorway on my way here?'

'Well, yeah. You mean you saw some of it? No, that's not right. It happened three days ago and you just got here. Reckon the motorway must have been chewed up pretty badly. Oh, hell, for God's sake, Roger, enough is enough.'

Smiling his infuriating smile, Roger reached over the side of his armchair and hoisted up his artwork portfolio. Laying it across his knees, he began to untie it.

'On some details you're very good, but you wouldn't put Sherlock Holmes out of a job. You haven't asked where my travelling bag is, with all my gear.'

'Roger, I'm starting to get annoyed.'

'I lost the bag *en route*. And the reason I lost my bag was because of this ...' Roger opened the portfolio and pulled out a newspaper. Rolling it, he threw it across to Chris, who almost spilled his whisky as he caught it. 'Front page. Have a look.'

Christ unfolded the newspaper. '"Horror on the A1." So what ...?'

'Read it.'

'Roger!'

'About four paragraphs down.'

Exasperated, Chris read out aloud: '"It is feared that eighty-seven people have lost their lives in the worst incident on this stretch of motorway in the last twenty-five years. It is understood that only six persons managed to survive the initial impact, among them Jane Teal of Fulwell, Martin Russell, whose transport lorry is reported to have jack-knifed and spilled its load of flammable material, resulting in the conflagration, and Roger . . .'

Chris froze, and Roger got ready to laugh at his expense, just like the old days when they were kids. But his humour evaporated when he saw the change on Chris's face. His expression remained frozen as he stared at the report, and an unhealthy pallor suddenly crept over him. His skin seemed to be changing to the same colour as his hair.

'Chris, are you all right?'

'Jesus Christ, Roger. Jesus Christ. You were *in* that crash?'

'Yeah, but I got out of it okay. I was in the coach . . .'

'The coach?' Chris's mouth was a tight, hard line. 'Jesus Christ, the *coach*? It says here that almost everyone on that coach was burned alive. On the *coach?*'

Roger suddenly realised that he had made a major error of judgment with his older brother. Clearly, this was something they were going to be unable to laugh about.

'Take it easy, Chris. I'm safe. I got out of it okay . . .'

'You stupid bastard!' Chris threw the newspaper down and jumped to his feet. Moving from the armchair, he began to walk in a circle in the middle of the living-room floor, waving his arms, running a hand through his thatch of white hair. 'You stupid, stupid bastard! Why didn't you tell me straight away? You think it's funny? You think it's bloody *funny*? That you were nearly killed?'

Roger began to rise. 'I'm sorry, Chris. Really. But look, I'm okay. Everything's fine and I've got a . . .'

And then Chris did something that his brother had never seen him do, even when they were children together. He suddenly stopped, both hands braced on his thighs, bent double – and began to weep. Roger stood watching, hands wide apart, but unable to react. As if he had created something dangerous that he must put right, if only he knew how. Now they were not two grown men any more; they were children. Chris also seemed to sense that something had gone badly wrong. He pushed himself up straight again as they stood facing each other and wiped his face quickly, ashamed of the tears.

'Chris, I'm sorry. I should have told you ... I never thought ...'

'Crazy, isn't it? Ever since Ma and Pa were killed in that car crash ...'

'Oh *Christ.*' Roger hung his head, horrified now at his lack of sensitivity, and realising that he had inadvertently broken a dam of emotion that had been inside his brother these past five years. 'I'm so sorry.'

'... I haven't been able to let anything out.'

Roger remembered how he'd been back then when they got the news. Their parents had been travelling with friends to visit other friends. A ten-minute trip in the car. But a motorcyclist had jumped the lights and sent the car careening into another car travelling in the opposite direction. None of the passengers in the car, or the motorcyclist, had survived. Back then, Chris had been the strong one, organising the funeral, keeping Roger straight when he wanted to fall apart. This sudden show of emotion was somehow deeply disturbing to Roger, and he realised that unconsciously he had been depending on Chris's solidity through the years. Chris looked up to see his distress, then quickly crossed the room and took him in a bear hug, whumping the breath out of his body.

'Okay, you arsehole,' he said at last. 'Tell me all about it.'

Together, they killed another half-bottle of Scotch. And the more Roger told the story, the more he realised how he had underestimated his brother, the more shamed he felt about the jocular way he'd revealed what had happened. Since the death of their parents, their bond had deepened, something of which he had been aware only subconsciously. They lived two hundred and fifty miles apart, rarely saw each other, but the very fact that the other existed provided a solid stanchion of support. Chris saw that in his brother's eyes, realised that he felt the same way. He was a deputy manager in a technical components factory, based on an industrial estate five miles to the east, and had been living here for three years, ever since he had landed the job. Phyllida, his lover and partner for the last eighteen months, was an air hostess, currently somewhere between New York and

London, then away on a ten-day conference and training programme.

'So next time,' concluded Roger, remembering his conversation with Jane Teal, 'I think I'll fly.'

'Maybe you have won a kind of lottery after all,' said Chris. The alcohol might well have softened and smoothed the shock, but Roger knew that they would never regard each other as casually as they had in the past. 'All you have to do is write up the story and *Reader's Digest*, or one of the newspapers, are going to pay you a fortune for it.'

'Not on your life. Had a guy called Curtis from one of the rags, came snooping around in the hospital. Started asking me all these questions and . . .'

The screaming. The sounds of someone or something screaming, just before the light hit the coach . . .

'What's the matter? You all right?'

'What? Yeah . . . yeah . . . I was just thinking about something that happened . . . something . . . Anyway, I'm not going to be anyone's Survivor of The Week. There were other people who made it. Jane, maybe. The woman I pulled out.'

'Once they get hold of that part of the story, they'll turn you into a hero whether you like it or not.'

Roger made a dismissive sound and grimaced when he sipped his whisky again.

'Got anything . . . sweeter? Don't know what the hell's wrong with me since the crash, but I can't get enough sugary stuff. Had about fifteen cans of coke on the way down.'

'Good idea,' beamed Chris. 'Bacardi and coke. Got some duty-free from Phyllida.'

'Don't know about the Bacardi, but I'll go for the Coke.'

Chris got up and made his way on none-too-steady legs into the kitchen. While he rummaged in the fridge, Roger thought back to his conversation with Curtis. About the screaming that couldn't possibly have come from the passengers, the impossible light that had exploded into the coach. He hadn't mentioned anything to Chris about the sounds and the light, hadn't even mentioned it when he was being interviewed by the police, because he hadn't yet worked out in his mind what it all meant or whether the shock and the terror of the accident had done something momentarily to his mind. Maybe Curtis was right; perhaps he had misinterpreted what was happening in the terror of the moment. He needed more time to think about it. And he needed more time to think about something else that Curtis had spoken about back at the hospital: wild talk about an indoor storm, and the fact that Roger and others had also been impossibly struck by lightning. Now why the hell would Curtis say something as ridiculous as that when the doctors and nurses hadn't said a damned thing to him before he'd been interviewed by the police and discharged.

'Won't be a minute,' called Chris from the kitchen.

On a small table next to the kitchen door were two cups, a bottle of milk and a bowl of sugar. More than anything else in the world now, Roger wanted to clamber to his feet and head for that table, wanted to take a handful of sugar and cram it into his mouth, wanted to keep doing it until the bowl was empty and his craving had been satisfied. He was sweating now as he stared at the bowl. He drank more whisky, and found it bitter. From the kitchen, Chris cursed as he rummaged in the refrigerator.

'Hurry up, for God's sake,' called Roger, eyes still on the bowl. 'What's a man got to do for a *soft* drink in this place?'

Something was happening to his eyes. He could see swirling patterns of light, like the onset of a migraine, something from which he hadn't suffered in years. There was a kaleidoscope of colour in these fractured lights, swirling to a whirlpool centre. He rubbed a hand over his face, and the craving for sweetness was now almost unbearable. Something cracked in front of him and he almost leapt from the chair. It was Chris, pulling the tab on a can and now handing him the drink. Roger took it gratefully.

Chris watched in bemusement as he downed the entire contents in one long draft.

'Any chance of another?'

'Hope this isn't an indicator of how much you'll be eating and drinking while you're staying here, looking for a job.' Chris headed back to the kitchen, and continued their conversation. But Roger didn't hear a word of it.

His attention was riveted on the sugar bowl beside the kitchen door.

Jane knelt in the middle of the kitchen floor, her hands bunched into fists and thrust down between her legs. Mascara had streaked down over both cheeks, meeting at her chin. Her eyes remained focused on the door leading into the living room. The only light in there was coming from the television, but Tom had turned down the volume to a bare murmur.

She had been kneeling there for an hour and a half.

Tom was in the living room somewhere, perhaps sitting in the armchair that faced the television screen, but he had not moved in all that time, and apart from the instruction that she should remain kneeling where she was had said nothing further.

'Can . . . ?' Fear choked Jane's voice. He hadn't told her that she could speak. Biting her lip, she closed her eyes and tried again. 'Can I stand up yet, Tom?'

'No.'

His voice sounded dull and flat, but it seemed shockingly close and made her wince. She could feel tears coming, and knew that this would be the worst possible thing to do.

'Do you know why you're kneeling there?' asked Tom.

'No . . .' The word was a barely controlled sob.

'No?'

'I mean yes!'

'Then why?'

Jane struggled to find an answer, knowing that a wrong reply would incur further wrath.

'Why can't you answer a simple question?'

'I'm . . . I'm frightened.'

'Frightened of me, Jane? Why should you be frightened of me? Have I ever laid a finger on you?'

'No, you've never touched me.'

It was true. In their four years of marriage, Tom had never struck her. His violence was more skilful, more terrifying.

'Then answer my question.'

'I don't know, Tom. I swear to God and the Blessed Virgin that I don't know.'

'It's because of what you did. And I'm still waiting for an explanation.'

'I couldn't help it.'

'Couldn't help it? That's what little girls say when they've been naughty. But you're a twenty-five-year-old woman, Jane. You're supposed to be a fucking *grown-up*.'

'I'm not well. You know that. Sometimes I can't help myself.'

There was silence from the living room and Janet felt the terror rise in overwhelming waves. Had she said the right thing or the wrong thing? Her hands began to tremble violently in her lap. She screwed them up tight, just the way she did when the period pains became too much. The suspense was unbearable. When she spoke again, the words came tumbling out, tripping over her tongue.

'It's like you've always said. I need you to tell me what to do. Need you to show me the best way. Everything becomes too much for me . . .'

Tom laughed. A low, sarcastic sound that silenced her.

'Life's too much for you . . .'

'I know, I know. And it just seemed that I couldn't manage any more, when you were at work, I mean. And I didn't want to telephone you there, like you've told me. I didn't know what I was doing. I went for a walk and I don't know how I got on the bus and then there was that terrible crash. I was nearly killed, Tom. Nearly killed. And I banged my head. That's why I can't think straight, can't remember . . .'

'You'd packed your bags, Jane. You were leaving.'

'I don't remember it, Tom. I really don't remember. My head, I hurt my head . . .' Tears were not far away, and now she knew that he could hear it in her voice.

'Always the last resort, Jane. Cry-baby tears.'

She hung her head and sobbed. And the more she tried to control it, the worse it seemed to become. Suddenly there was movement in the doorway, and she looked up quickly, wiping her face and smudging the mascara even further.

Tom was standing there. He was naked.

'All right . . . all right . . .' His eyes had that glazed look that so frightened her, but there was something like a smile on his face. 'I'm prepared to believe you. Prepared to be kind. But you're going to have to be punished first. You know that has to happen first, don't you?'

'Yes . . .'

'You *want* to be punished, don't you?'

Jane began to nod then. Eagerly and gratefully, like a small child desperate to please.

Tom beckoned to her, and she scrambled forward over the kitchen floor on hands and knees.

Suddenly, she was seized by a terrible thirst – and the need for something sweet.

'Anthony!' exclaimed the editor-in-chief of the *Independent Daily* as Curtis stepped into his office. He held both arms wide, as if Curtis were his best friend, unseen for a dozen years. There was a big smile on his face.

Right away, Curtis knew that Roland was furious and that he was in deep shit.

Roland never, *ever* smiled like that unless something had gone very seriously wrong.

Groaning inwardly, Curtis closed the glass door, not wanting his colleagues to overhear any of the details that might follow. Roland was gesturing to the seat in front of the desk and then, as Curtis headed for it, he suddenly sprang to his feet with an agility that belied the fact that he was at least three stones overweight. The bottom three buttons on his shirt popped open to reveal a white and hairy belly.

'No, Anthony,' he continued in the same jovial tone. 'Why not sit here? Right here in the boss's seat. Big man like you. Front-page headliner. Seems more appropriate.'

'Cut the sarcasm, Roland. Just tell me what I've done wrong.' Curtis sat wearily in front of his desk.

'What you've done wrong?' asked Roland, the essence of

gentility. He too sat, hands on the blotter in front of him. The fingers seemed to need a pencil to crush. 'What makes you think that, I wonder?'

'Roland. Please?'

'Well, you've just done your job, surely? Big front-page story in that first edition. Major pile-up on the motorway. Dramatic photos. Large-scale tragedy. Nothing wrong there. So far. And you managed to get into the hospital and talk to some of the survivors. Capital. On the strength of that alone, I reckon you should be up for a major regional award. Big ticket in the band of your hat, just like the reporters on those old Hollywood movies . . .'

'*Roland!*'

'But then we get this other stuff. About what happened in the hospital. The fireball exploding into the casualty department. The ceiling on fire and people running around screaming. Very dramatic. *Then* we get the business about something that looked like a stormcloud indoors, and people being struck by lightning. Bodies flying all over the place in a shower of sparks. *Very* dramatic, on-the-spot reportage . . .'

'It happened, Roland.'

'No it bloody *didn't*, Tony!' And now the act was over as Roland punched the desk-top and jumped to his feet again. The colour was rising in his face, and he jerked his tie loose as if it would prevent the top of his skull blowing off. 'We've got a writ from the hospital trust, telling us that what you wrote was . . . effectively . . . a load of bollocks. There was no fire, and no one was struck by your bloody lightning bolts!'

'What the hell are you talking about? I was there, for Chrissakes. I saw it!'

'Not according to this!' snapped Roland, snatching a legal document from the desk and waving it at him. 'A fireball or an explosion or even indoor fucking lightning would cause serious damage. But the only thing that happened there was a few broken strip-lights.'

'They're the ones talking bollocks. I saw six people knocked over by some kind of . . . electrical discharge, or something.'

'No one was hurt the way you describe. There was a short in

the electricity supply, according to this. Nothing more. And the trust take a dim view of your beefing up the story that way.'

'They're clamping down in case there's any civil action from anyone who was hurt. And even if I *was* over-dramatising – which I wasn't – why the hell are you chewing me up like this? A writ, for God's sake? So what? Wouldn't be the first time. Anyway, I was a witness, Roland. I was *there!*'

'Really? You were there? I mean, you were actually in the same fucking *building*? I mean, that's what you're trying to tell me, if I'm not mistaken?'

'Of course I was there. What the hell's the matter with you?'

'I mean, you were *there*? Not on some other planet, perhaps?'

'Will you get to the point and tell me what's *really* bugging you?'

'What's bugging me is *this*, Anthony. You see, while you were creeping around like an ace reporter, making up stories about fireballs and lightning, something else was going on in the very same building. Something that the other majors have managed to discover for themselves. Namely, Anthony, that someone was murdered in the hospital – had his face torn off, no less – and a body was stolen from the morgue. All while you were prancing about, jiving up stories about fuses blowing and electricity failures.'

'What?'

'Now you can see why I'm pissed off. I mean you *can* see that, can't you, Anthony?'

'There were other people there . . . in Casualty . . .' Curtis's mind was racing as the words stumbled out of his mouth. 'They saw it . . . but someone else was . . .'

'Murdered, Anthony. Yes. And our man on the job didn't know anything about it. Or about Boris Karloff, the Body-snatcher. Here . . .' Roland picked up a copy of their rival newspaper from the desk and threw it at him. Curtis caught it clumsily, and began straightening the crumpled pages.

'I'll get on it.'

'Exquisite,' hissed Roland, and now it seemed that the

outburst of anger had drained him of his last vestige of energy. He sat down wearily, tugging at his collar again. 'Just what I want to hear. A news hound on the trail of a story.'

Curtis didn't hear him.

There were too many conflicting thoughts and images in his head.

Images of a fire that didn't burn, of people who should be dead but had somehow survived.

And of one survivor, who had spoken of the sounds of screaming.

Selina had been having a bad time this morning with the kids. The girl who had promised to babysit for her had been overdue for an hour and a half now. Paulie had the gripes and couldn't be consoled and Yolande had smashed one of the kitchen windows when she had thrown the coffee mug at her for being scolded. Selina had to admit – it had been a hell of a shot. But it had been the only moment of light relief this morning. The bastard who did landlord impressions had told her that if he didn't see any cash in hand by Tuesday then she – and her multi-coloured kids – would be out on the pavement. So she had to get to work soon. Paulie decided to turn up the volume and began to howl at her from the mat in front of the television; and from the kitchen came the sound of something else smashing on the linoleum and a giggle from Yolande.

'For Christ's *sake!*' snapped Selina, lunging back to the television and turning it up louder to drown the noise.

And then someone hammered on the door.

For Selina, it was the proverbial straw not so much breaking the camel's back as squashing it flat. Whoever was on the other side of the door was going to really get it, a real full-frontal. Stiff-legged, stamping on the floor as she walked, Selina marched to the battered door, threw back the bolt and yanked it wide open.

'Where is he?' asked Mercy, from the other side.

The imminent explosion of rage suddenly imploded and vanished with a gasp of astonishment. Eyes wide, Selina seemed unable to register who she was looking at for a moment. Mercy remained standing in the doorway, one hand on the frame. Her face seemed blank and unemotional, her skin somehow too white. But the eyes were the same: the coal-black, intimidating eyes that Selina remembered from their days together in the children's home. From behind, Paulie began to squawl again. Selina blinked, as if finally registering who she was looking at.

'Selina, I asked where he is.'

'Christ, yes . . . yes . . .'

Paulie decided that enough was enough. This time, he began to yell his lungs out.

'Come in, Mercy,' said Selina, turning impatiently back to the rug and sweeping her son up with a practised swoop. 'And for God's sake close the door. Any more complaints from the neighbours and we'll be out on the bloody street again.'

Mercy did as she was told, but remained with her back to the door, as if she would block Selina forcibly if she tried to get out.

'Who is it?' came Yolande's voice from the kitchen. When there was no answer, she ran out into the living room and saw who was at the door.

'*Mercy!*'

And as Yolande ran across the room, it seemed that the appearance of this four-year-old child had somehow instantly melted something cold and very dangerous inside Mercy. She stooped and held her arms wide as Yolande ran into her embrace. The dark eyes were softer, and for a moment Selina felt something inside that tasted of jealousy. Yolande bombarded her with questions about where she'd been and what she was doing here, but Mercy managed to field them all with practised ease. As she answered, she looked at Selina, still waiting for the answer to her question.

'I wasn't expecting you so soon,' said Selina at last, dropping Paulie into a battered high-chair. She set about preparing something for him to eat, taking out a small can of baby food from the cupboard. 'How did you get here? Car?'

'Like the old song, "Planes and Boats and Trains". Nearly didn't get here at all.'

'What do you mean?'

'It's a long story.'

Selina grimaced, as if she'd heard too many long stories in her life already. 'Fair enough. So you're here.'

'And you know where he is?'

'That's why I wrote to you. I didn't forget.'

'And you're sure it's him?'

Selina paused in the act of emptying the tinned food into a saucepan on the hob of the battered cooker. For a moment, it was as if she were struggling with some inner fury, as if unbelieving that Mercy could be so stupid as to think she'd be unable to recognise him, even after all this time.

'It's hardly likely I'd be wrong now, is it?'

'It's been ten years.'

'And he's still the lanky, weedy fucker that he was back then. He hasn't changed. Same bad skin, same hair parted all the way from ear to ear over the top of his bald fucking head. Couldn't believe it when I saw him. Kerb-crawling. Must have moved down here in the last few months. Just like him. Get to find out where the fanny is.'

'You're still . . .'

Selina looked up when she'd lit the gas flame. Mercy watched the flame at the end of the match, waited for it to burn her fingers and distract her from her stare. She must be feeling the pain, but she simply let it burn and then crushed the match between finger and thumb as if she were squashing an ugly insect.

'On the game? Yes, I am. You going to give me grief about that again?'

'No.'

'Good, 'cause the last time we had that argument was the last time we spoke to each other. Six months ago.'

'Six months too long. I'm surprised Yolande remembers me.'

Yolande had retrieved three battered dolls and was telling Mercy their names as they talked.

'No one's taking my kids, Mercy. And as long as I can pay my way, that's all that matters. Income support payments and money from the sad old fuckers who like to have me toss them off. It pays the bills and keeps the social workers away from the door.'

'I didn't come down to have a go at you, and you still haven't told me what I need to know.'

'He brings his car down to the Strip. That's what the working girls call the main road in this town where the business is done. Maybe once or twice a week. First time I saw him he was talking to Iris. Couldn't believe it, thought I was having a bad turn. But then later that week I saw him kerb-crawling again. Tried to flag me down, but I just kept on walking. But it was him. Must have done his time and then resettled.'

'He'll never do enough time.'

Again, Selina saw the look in those coal-black eyes. They had frightened her when she was a child; they were frightening her now.

'If I show you where he is . . . I mean, if I take you down there and we hang around waiting for him to show. What are you going to do?'

Mercy didn't answer. She was smiling as she helped Yolande play with her dolls.

'Got any sugar?' she asked at last.

Puzzled, Selina said: 'Sugar? Yeah. I mean, what . . . ?'

'A bag of sugar. I need a bag of sugar.'

Selina paused to stir the food in the pan. Paulie began making noises again when he smelled the food. Opening the cupboard before her, Selina found a two-pound bag, unopened.

'You want tea or coffee, or something?'

'No. Just the sugar. Throw me the bag.'

Still puzzled, Selina hefted the two-pound bag across the room. Mercy caught it with both hands, and Selina could only watch in amazement as she tore open the top of the bag, sat cross-legged on the floor with her back to the door as Yolande played with her dolls – and then began to take handfuls of the sugar, cramming it into her mouth.

'Fucking hell, Mercy,' said Selina. 'You diabetic or something?'

Mercy smiled when she spoke, and Selina could not help shivering at the sight of her chalk-white face, the black eyes and the greed with which she devoured handful after handful of sugar.

'Or something,' said Mercy.

Harry stood at the garden gate, looking at the house.

The grass hadn't been cut for a long while. He remembered that Jean had harangued him about it before they'd started out on their holiday. The heat-wave was burning brown patches in the tangle. The flowers hadn't been watered; rose petals littered the path, reminding him of . . .

. . . broken glass on the casualty department floor . . .

. . . something. He examined the windows, wondering if one of the net curtains might be pulled back and someone would rush out to meet him with open arms. There was a patch of guttering up there that needed repair. He pushed the garden gate, watched it swing up against the stopper and then come juddering back.

The black suit was making him sweat. Not good clothing for this kind of weather. He wondered how those Greek widows could possibly put up with it day after day in their kind of weather. A bead of sweat ran from his brow to the corner of his mouth. It tasted like . . .

. . . blood . . .

. . . salt. To wipe its trace from his face was simply too much effort. Instead, he remained where he was, looking at the detached five-bedroomed house that had wiped out their savings when they'd bought it. He remembered the long discussions before they'd gone for it. Jean had called it a haven. She had been the one who had convinced him, despite his protestations about the erratic nature of his sales job. There had been only three years left on the mortgage. Now the insurance policy had paid it off after the accident.

Somewhere, a girl laughed.

Harry looked up anxiously, scanning the garden, expecting to see Hilary or Diane running across the grass. The sound came again, from behind him. He turned to see a young man and woman, hand in hand on the other side of the street. They turned a corner, out of sight, unware of his presence.

He turned back to the house, placing his bandaged hands on the rim of the gate. He looked at his hands for a long time, thinking back to what he'd recently been through.

He had just come from his wife and daughters' funeral. But it was as if someone else had been occupying his body through the entire service. Or perhaps he too was dead. Yes, that was it. He had also been killed in the motorway collision. He was a ghost. And that was why everything in the church had seemed so distant. Jean's sister, Iris, had organised the wake at her own home; in the circumstances, having it at the family home seemed too potentially traumatic. Everyone had been understanding. Iris had even suggested that perhaps he should come and live with them for a while, give him a chance to recover. Her husband, Bryan, was only too happy about the proposed arrangement – perhaps *too* happy. There was a sort of desperate glint in the eyes of his permanently smiling face which made Harry decline the offer with thanks. Not that he could possibly consider it, anyway. Sooner or later, he would have to go back to the house. Better sooner than later.

He remembered catching sight of himself in the mirror of his sister-in-law's living room. People were milling around, friends and family, drinks in hand, pecking at the small buffet that Iris had laid out on her dining table. Harry didn't blame them for feeling uncomfortable in his presence. What was there to say? As best he could, he tried to put them at their ease, tried to say the right things when someone offered a condolence. Even as he did so, he felt like an actor, felt as if he was outside himself. And the person he saw in the mirror didn't look like him at all. It looked like someone impersonating him. The black, curled hair. Perhaps too long for a man his age, but his daughters had insisted that he wear it that way because it suited him (he had drawn the line at their suggestion of a pierced earring). The white face. Recent pictures in the family photograph album showed a man with a healthy complexion. This face looked as if it was someone related to the man in the album. A brother, perhaps. Someone who had been shut away in darkness for years, and who had only been let out today for a special occasion. There was a glass of sherry in one of the awkwardly bandaged hands. It looked clumsy and ridiculous.

Somehow, the person acting his part had been able to see him through the rest of the proceedings. Tearfully, Iris had tried to make him stay longer after everyone had gone. But Harry had been insistent. Back home, now. Sooner or later. Iris had called him a good man, a good husband and father, had crushed herself tearfully to him. The desperate look in Bryan's eye seemed to have softened now that he was heading for the door.

Harry couldn't remember the journey from their house to his own. It was four miles, but he couldn't be sure whether he'd taken a cab or a bus, or whether he had walked. Perhaps he had driven the car . . .

. . . the screeching of tyres, the screaming, a smashing of glass and the ugly squealing of metal and asphalt. Flames billowing over the hood of the car and roaring through the shattered windscreen . . .

No! That was a stupid thought. He didn't have a car any more, hadn't bothered to see about a replacement since . . . since it had all happened. He looked at his bandaged hands again. This time, he shoved the gate open and walked purposefully up the garden path towards the house, hearing the gate bang shut behind him. Still with that out of body feeling, he was experiencing almost second-hand the confusing riot of emotions as the man who looked like him approached the front door. Did he feel as if he were being watched? Were they in there now – the three of them – waiting for him to come in so that they could upbraid him for being late and making them worry? Had there been some sort of terrible mistake? Perhaps they weren't dead after all, and everything could go back to the way it was before. Or was it the terror of *not* being watched? The empty and horrifying prospect of there being nothing at all in this house, ever. Perhaps the house itself was somehow alive and watching him. Was that it? Had this house, so loved and cherished as their haven, somehow absorbed their personalities? Would he find comfort there, after all?

He struggled with his key-ring, the bandaged hands clumsy and shaking.

No matter how he tried, he could not fit the key into the lock.

The man who looked like him was making a noise now. Harry was standing right next to him, watching. It was the noise that a small and deeply frustrated child might make. A desperate whining and whimpering. Harry watched the efforts to open the door become frenzied and manic. The whimper began to rise in pitch and volume.

And then Harry drew himself back and flung the keys at the door.

Screaming, he shoulder-charged it. The door thundered and shook in its frame under his onslaught. There was pain as he threw himself at the panelling, time and time again. But pain meant nothing to him now. On the fifth attempt, the door flew open and he staggered inside.

'Hilary!'

Harry staggered into the living room, spinning around and then rushing to the french windows to look into the garden. She wasn't there.

'Diane!'

He blundered into the kitchen. Empty. Throwing open the kitchen door so that it smacked hard against the wall, he ran down the hall, turned past the forced door and thundered up the staircase.

'Hilary!'

The bedrooms were empty.

'Jean!'

There was no one in his study.

He thundered down the stairs again, breath catching. His shoulder was agony, his hands on fire again.

'Jean! For Christ's sake, where ARE you . . . ?'

When the police came fifteen minutes later, alerted by concerned neighbours, they found him kneeling on the living-room floor. His head was bowed forward, his forehead touching the carpet, the bandaged hands over his head like those of a child fending off blows.

Harry watched his sister-in-law in the kitchen, trying to find things to do. She kept glancing at the kettle, and he thought: *A watched kettle never boils*. The voice in his head didn't sound like his own; it sounded like someone he had known a long time ago, someone very young.

His brother-in-law, Bryan, was standing by the front window, looking out forlornly as if hoping for rescue. He turned to see that Harry was looking at him and said, sheepishly: 'Doctor should be here soon. Not long now.'

'I told you,' said Harry quietly. 'I don't need a doctor.'

In the kitchen, Iris started opening and closing cupboard doors, as if she were trying to block out other sounds.

Bryan shrugged and tried to smile. 'Best take the police's advice, eh?'

'It was my fucking front door, Bryan. I can break it down if I feel like it.' Even as he spoke, Harry began to feel a strange new sensation. As if he were suddenly looking down the wrong end of a telescope. Bryan seemed to be miles away, by the window; Iris even further away in the kitchen. And when he looked at his hands on the armrests of the chair, they somehow seemed enormous. It was a good feeling. It kept the utter, abject and terrible desolation at bay. If he stayed here, in this place at the other end of the tunnel, he would never again have to become that mad, screaming animal that had kicked down the door.

Bryan held out his hands, as if he somehow expected Harry to leap from the chair and knock him to the floor with flailing fists.

'Okay, Harry. Okay. But we only want what's best for you. I know how you must be feeling . . .'

'Strange how many people have said that to me. Even stranger coming from you, Bryan. No offence. I mean, we've never seen eye to eye. Always stayed friendly, for the sake of our families.'

Bryan tried to find something to do with his hands, but could not.

'And no one knows. *No one.* Tell you what it's like. It's not a state of mind, not even an emotional state of mind. It's just like someone poured petrol all over me and set it alight. Now if that was to happen to you, I mean literally being set alight with petrol . . . how would you react if someone said to you: "Pull yourself together. Snap out of it. It's just a state of mind."'

'Now come on, I'm not saying anything like that at all.'

'No, you're missing the point, Bryan. Like always. You see, the point is that when you're burning alive like that, you don't look at things the same way that everyone else does. Your flesh is peeling off as it burns, you're in utter, *utter* fucking agony. And you can't hear anyone saying anything to you, you can't hear the best-intended advice, and the solace, and the good wishes, and the helpful hints. Because you're too busy screaming inside. And when it's like that . . .'

'Harry, for God's sake. Keep calm.'

' . . . when it's like that, you only want to do one thing. You want the pain to end. You just want it to stop, because you literally can't stand it any more. You just want to throw yourself off a bridge, because when you hit that cold water all the way down there, it's going to snuff out the flames and the agony. For ever. See?'

'They shouldn't have let you out of hospital. You're not ready yet.'

'Try to see, Bryan. Try for once in your life to see things the way that someone else sees them, and not through your own cosy, ordered little . . .'

'For *Christ's sake!*' Something shattered in the kitchen, and Harry turned slowly to look down the long, long tunnel to see that Iris was bent almost double in the middle of the kitchen, hands clutched to her face as the grief finally poured out of her. To him, it looked as if she were trying to hold her face together. Harry could see her mouth opened wide, the fingers interlaced across it. She had thrown a plate to the floor. Its fragments gleamed bone white on the linoleum. Harry remembered how Jean had washed the floor with the mop before they set off on their holiday.

Bryan rushed into focus and took her by the arms. He tried

to pull her close, but Iris would not straighten up. Harry remembered when the girls were young, very young, and one of them had perhaps banged her head or jammed a finger. He remembered rushing to one or the other, to comfort them. Iris was like that now, her breath held, a lcng, long pause before the crying came. Jean had always been anxious that the crying would never come, and as if in answer to his memory Harry seemed to hear his late wife yell: 'Breathe! Breathe!'

Just the way she'd done the time that Hilary had jammed her finger.

And then Iris let out a long howl of anguish. With its release, she was able to straighten at last, and Bryan took her in his arms, hugging her like a bear, her own arms crushed against his chest. Now it reminded Harry of the time that Jean and he had danced a slow dance together on New Year's Eve when the kids had gone to bed. They had moved slowly into the living room and towards the rug in front of the fireplace for a slow burn of beautiful passion and . . .

And the tunnel seemed to quiver then, as the memories threatened to haul him back to the place where the mad beast ravened. For the first time, Harry felt that he was on some kind of elastic band. One wrong move, and he could be catapulted back to a place where he didn't want to be.

'Twang,' he said without emotion.

Iris turned from Bryan to look at him, and the howling began again. Harry wondered whether he should feel bad about her grief. This distancing factor allowed him to think callously, as if it was not him thinking at all.

Bryan moved Iris carefully back into the living room, and this time he could not prevent one of his cold glances finding its way to Harry. Good old familiar Bryan. This was the face Harry was used to. This was the Bryan who had once told him that he didn't think they were bringing the girls up the right way. It had been at a party, with too much to drink all round. And Harry had taken Bryan confidentially into the garden, very politely, as if to ask for further advice on the point he had made. Then he had told Bryan that if he ever said anything like that to him again, he would take one of the barbecue skewers from the ever-so-neatly-bricked barbecue and stick it up his arse.

Somehow, Harry could not take his gaze from the kitchen. Bryan and Iris were somewhere behind him, perhaps on the sofa, and Iris's sobbing had fractured and broken down into a series of moaning gasps. There was something there, something about the kitchen that was making other things happen inside Harry. Something deep down. He frowned, trying to make sense of it. Was he going to be ill? No, he didn't think he would vomit, but the feeling was very much like it. There was a tingling in his arms and legs now.

Yes, a heart attack. Good. Hit me hard, and I won't come around again. I don't have to go back to the way I was; to the pain and the anguish. I can stay in this out-of-body state until the pains cramp my chest, then I can keel over and and join Jean and Hilary and Diane.

But no, it wasn't his heart. He could feel that it was beating faster, but he somehow knew instinctively that he wasn't going to have a heart attack.

The kitchen. Something in the kitchen that he needed.

He stood up slowly. The feeling was a *craving*. He needed something very badly. Behind him, he seemed to hear Bryan saying something, his voice cracking as he spoke. But Harry couldn't hear him as he staggered to the door frame. He felt weak, and prayed to God that he was dying. But the inner need had taken over.

'What?' he asked aloud, as if the compulsion were somehow an exterior, sentient thing. He scanned the kitchen. 'What do you need?'

Bryan seemed to have lost his temper completely now. He was shouting, but Harry still couldn't make out the words. He looked at the benches. Like the floor, spotlessly clean and wiped down in preparation for the holiday, since Jean always liked to come back to a nice clean house. It made her feel good and took the sting out of the fact that the holiday was over. Without being aware that he had made the decision, Harry staggered into the kitchen, his foot catching the shards of plate, sending them spinning and clattering over the floor.

'. . . you're forgetting, you bastard . . .'

Now he could vaguely make out what Bryan was trying to tell him.

'. . . Iris has lost a sister, too. And her nieces and . . .'

The kettle began to boil.

Was that what he needed?

Harry moved to it, but the inner craving was not satisfied. It wanted . . . wanted . . .

And then Harry knew what he had to have. He blundered to a cupboard over the kettle. His hands looked alien as they moved through the steam, dragging the door open. What he wanted was right there. He had to have it straight away, before something awful happened.

Iris had managed to surface from the worst depths of her grief, drawn back by Bryan's rage. She knew that he was protecting her, was angered by what seemed to be a lack of concern for Iris's own space in this terrible, terrible time. But he had got it wrong again, was saying the wrong things *again*. She grabbed his arms as they sat on the sofa, shaking her head. And when Bryan saw the warning glint in her red-rimmed eyes, he realised what she was thinking. Angry again, misunderstood again, Bryan stood up quickly, an awkward, hurried movement. He did not know where to put his hands as he turned in the middle of the room. Everything he did seemed to turn out wrong. Hand to his forehead now – a place for one of them, at least – as if he had a bad headache, he moved to the kitchen door, seeing Harry grabbing something from the cupboard.

It was a bag of sugar.

And as Bryan watched in astonishment, Harry tore the bag open with both clumsy, bandaged hands. A spray of sparkling white dust enveloped his face as he crammed the ruptured bag to his mouth. Whirling from the kitchen bench and the wreath of steam from the kettle, he nuzzled and crammed the sugar into his mouth like a mad dope addict with handfuls of cocaine.

The doorbell rang and Bryan turned, his expression still dumbstruck. He could see across the living room, and through into the hall. A blurred figure was standing on the other side of the fluted-glass front door. He seemed to be holding a bag. The doctor, no doubt. And none too soon. Bryan turned back to look into the kitchen.

Harry was still standing with his back to the bench. Sugar lay around his feet like a snowfall. It was on his shoulders like dandruff. And his face was still buried in the shreds of the packet as he crammed the white powder into his mouth like a wild animal. The doorbell rang again, and this time Bryan pushed himself away from the door jamb, aware that Iris was weeping once more. This time, it seemed controlled; bitter, but controlled. When Bryan opened the door, the doctor saw his white face and automatically assumed that he had been summoned to take care of *him*.

Bryan gestured with a weak wave of the hand that he should enter.

A woman was weeping on the sofa.

And in the kitchen, the doctor could hear an animal feeding.

'Bottoms up!' exclaimed Sheila's cousin, Ron, encouraging Martin to lift his own glass. Martin smiled and complied, but didn't feel like drinking tonight. There seemed to be something wrong with his taste buds since the accident. The alcohol tasted too bitter, and he'd switched from beer to whisky, and finally to Sheila's favourite – rum snatch. He normally found it sickeningly sweet, but now it seemed to suit him.

He looked up over the top of his glass as Ron slapped him heartily on the shoulder again and turned to say something to his wife, which made her screech with laughter. They called her 'The Banshee' in the family. Martin's eyes connected with Sheila, watching him as she spoke to the neighbours on the other side of the table. He smiled and drank again, turning away now lest she see what he was really thinking. Immediately, he was engaged by one of her other cousins, Sylvia. A widow with three wayward sons, one of whom had died when the car he'd stolen had wrapped itself around a lamppost three years ago. Clearly, she felt bonded with Martin since the motorway pile-up, and proceeded once again to tell him so. He didn't hear a word she was saying, but nodded and mm-hmmed at the right moments, too preoccupied with his own thoughts.

Martin didn't like parties, and this was the second one he'd decided to endure, without causing a fuss. The first had been their wedding reception, for obvious reasons. When Sheila had first mentioned how much everyone wanted to have the party, just to show him how they felt about his near-miss on the motorway, he had turned the proposal down flat. The newspapers had made a big enough fuss, those bloody reporters trying to make out that everyone who had survived was some kind of hero, or something. Eighty-seven people dead, some of them horribly burned alive. And all they could rabbit on about was the 'bravery' of the survivors. With Mercy, it was different. She really had saved his life, and his only regret after the event was not being able to get the address or telephone number of the place she was headed. More than anything else, he just wanted everything to settle down and get back to normal again. But Sheila had insisted, and when he'd stood firm he had watched her crumple up. In that moment, he knew that this party was about something else, something altogether more important insofar as Sheila was concerned.

Sheila was frail; her strength and vitality sapped by the rheumatoid arthritis that had blighted her body from the age of thirty. Until then, she had been so beautifully vital, carefree to the point of foolhardiness. Her tendency to do the unexpected thing at the unexpected moment had been what so attracted Martin in the early days. He considered himself too stolid, too ordinary in his endeavours. She was a magical person in his life, his true other-half. But since the illness, that hunger for life, that joyful risk-taking, had ceased as Sheila had become gradually possessed by the pain. As time went by, she had become dependent on the very stolidity than Martin had considered such a burden, and from which he thought he had been freed. The motorway accident had done something to Sheila. It had somehow focused and intensified

her fears and reliance. Martin had come close to death, and
the prospect of his loss had been shattering for her. He had
seen all of this when he had refused her the party. The fear of
losing him, the realisation that she had become so reliant on
him, the knowledge of having lost the person she used to be
and – despite his protestations to the contrary – therefore his
love. This party was more than just friends and neighbours
celebrating the fact that he hadn't become a road accident
statistic. It had become, for reasons both basic and complex,
her way of showing him how much she loved him. Martin
couldn't spend time arguing that it was unnecessary to have
a party to show him that, didn't have an understanding of the
complexities of Sheila's feelings. But instinctively he knew that
he must agree; he must allow her to show him.

And so the party had taken place, and Martin was aware
that no matter who she was talking to her eyes were on him,
making sure that he was enjoying himself.

There were perhaps twenty people here, in their two-up,
two-down terraced council house. No complaints from the
neighbours tonight about party noise, he had been told. For
one thing, everyone knew that he was a hero and heroes were
allowed a knees-up; for another, all the neighbours were *here*
at the party. Martin wondered what they would think – what
Sheila would think – if he told them that the haulage company
that employed him was facing an aggressive official inquiry
about the cause of the accident. Now he knew that he had
been transporting something much more dangerous than amyl
nitrate, and the knowledge that he had been used that way
made him feel like going to the company office and shoving
someone through a plate-glass window. His lorry hadn't been
the cause of the accident, but his spilled load had caused the
fire that had killed most of the people involved. And in the
absence of a satisfactory answer to what had happened on the
A1 that night, Martin was aware of the fact that he was the
easy target. Now the bastards who didn't know just what the
hell had happened out there were trying to find a reason, trying
to find someone to blame. And perhaps he was the obvious
choice. Maybe, just maybe, he could have done something to

avoid the skid and the jack-knife? He hadn't the heart, once Sheila had put the party idea to him, to tell her that he had been banned from driving pending the findings of the inquiry. He would be paid for the duration, an average for the hauls he had undertaken in the last year, but he was beginning to feel like the proverbial soft thing between a rock and a hard place. Telling Sheila now would surely devastate her. Far better to let the party happen, and try not to think about the possible consequences for the moment.

'Don't you think so?' asked the woman who was talking to him, quite drunk now. For the life of him, he couldn't remember her name. Three kids, one dead in a car smash. He raised his glass to his lips, buying himself a few seconds to think.

'Oh yeah,' he said at last.

It was the wrong thing to say. Her eyes glazed in horror, her glass froze on its way back to her mouth.

'You can't *mean* that?'

'Well, no. I mean . . . No, of course not.'

'Are you sure? I mean, you're *sure*? People did think that when Gene died, you know? All right, I know he had that wild streak of his dad's. I *know* he stole that car. But he didn't deserve to die, did he? Not that way. No one could say he deserved it, just 'cause he took someone else's car.'

Martin suddenly pieced together what the question had been. 'No . . . I mean, yes . . . when I said yes, I meant that's what some people, you know, *unthinking* people, would say. Typical, isn't it? But you're right. What you've said there is absolutely right.'

'Sorry, I'm – you know – still a bit touchy about it all. You were being ironic.'

Martin nodded. He hadn't a clue what ironic meant, but he nodded anyway.

'Christ, Martin. Sheila's so lucky. That horrible crash, and all those people dead. Only half a dozen got out of there, you know? You never can tell. It's like a lottery. Like that night when Gene . . .' She stuttered over her grief then, still undimmed after three years. Another sip of what she had in her glass prevented her from dissolving into tears. Fortified,

she continued: 'Why Gene? I keep asking myself that. Some
people have these terrible accidents and they live through it,
but Gene didn't. Why *is* that? The roads were clear that night,
just like for you on the motorway, but he didn't and you . . .'

I did, thought Martin. *And Gene didn't.*

At once, his sympathy for this sad woman dissipated.
Despite his protestations about the party, it was supposed
to be, after all, a celebration of the fact that he hadn't been
killed. But this stupid woman hadn't considered the logic of
her argument. Martin wasn't clever, often prided himself on
the fact, but he could see that there was only one question in
her mind, even if she had managed to mask its implications.
Why did you live and my Gene die? If she got within three
feet of Sheila he'd remind her that she had two sons left who
had spent the last three years trying to love her, but couldn't
because all she had time for was the memory of Gene, the
car thief.

'Excuse me,' said Martin. The politeness of his departure
was lost on her. She nodded, sipped again, and began to look
for someone else who might remember what a good boy Gene
had been, despite the rape accusation. (Apparently, the victim
had asked for it.)

Pete McFarland and his son were nearest to him, and he
realised that he hadn't been able to speak to either of them
properly since the do had begun. Pete was a shy man, a
background figure until his wife had died. She had been the
driving force in the family when their thirteen-year-old son,
Ben, had contracted motor neurone disease. She had been the
one who had held them all together and Pete had taken the
back seat, partly out of a refusal to come to terms with what
was happening, hiding behind the old working-class ethic that
the man was supposed to bring in the money and the woman
was meant to look after the family. In reality, he was terrified
by his own emotions, and knew that he couldn't cope if he had
to do the day-to-day caring. Then, in a cruel double twist of
fate, Katie had fallen prey to a rapacious cancer. The woman
who hated smoking, who had never smoked in her life, and
who had insisted that he have his five-a-day drag outside in

the back yard, had been savaged by lung cancer. Dead within five weeks. Everything had come into savage focus for Pete. He had been flung into coping with Ben's situation. Enough insurance money to cover his giving up work. Done. His wife buried. Done. The immediacies of his son's need and care as he lapsed progressively into total paralysis. No choice but to do it. And his newfound commitment, late in coming and borne from grief and the need to make up for his weakness in the past, was one of the bravest things Martin had ever seen. Grief had united Pete with his son, had bonded them in a way that would never, perhaps, have happened if Katie – the lost and uniting love of their lives – had lived.

Pete was standing there now, pretending to enjoy himself with a glass of sherry in his hand, smiling at half-heard conversations across the room which did not involve him. Ben, whose condition had now deteriorated to the point where he could no longer control his continual neck spasms, struggled to focus his attention on any one given point. Soon, his losing battle and his frustration would lead them both to leave.

'What's the matter, then, Ben?' asked Martin as he bent down, glass in hand, and fixed Ben in the eye. 'You getting bloody legless again?'

Ben convulsed with laughter, smacking his hands on the wheelchair arms. Pete looked vaguely uneasy at the remark, and it was this that so amused his son. It was a joke they had shared many times.

'You've been at Sheila's punch when no one's been looking,' continued Martin.

'Regular piss-head,' said Ben, and laughed again when the language drew a disapproving stare from his father. When Martin laughed, the awkwardness in Pete seemed to melt. He raised his glass, now with only a smear of sherry in the bottom.

'Come on, Pete. Let your hair down. Have another.'

'What hair?' laughed Ben.

'Used to have hair, you little bugger,' laughed his father. 'You've seen the photographs. Right down my back.'

'None on your head,' said Martin, taking his glass. 'Just growing down your back.'

With Ben's laughter ringing in his ears, Martin headed for the table in the middle of the room on which Sheila had laid out bottles, cans and hors d'oeuvres or horses-dooves, as Martin liked to call them. 'Try something different,' he called back. 'Sheila's punch is like rocket fuel. I'll join you.' In a trice, he had filled two glasses with the ladle in Sheila's cut-glass punch-bowl (a wedding present from a long-dead aunt, never used until tonight), and brought a Coke for Ben. Pete looked uncomfortable when he returned with the drinks, as if punch were much too exotic for him. Martin had warmed him up, didn't want him to become self-conscious again. 'Come on, Ben. Make your dad drink it. Tell you what. Both together, Pete.' Pete managed a lopsided grin, and when Ben grabbed his sleeve with a gnarled hand and began tugging hard, he knocked it back in one. Martin did the same.

Pete feigned the effect of liquid fire going down his gullet. Two seconds later, he wasn't faking at all. Martin laughed hard when he saw his expression change.

'Don't tell Sheila.' He wafted a hand in front of his face, as if his mouth might catch fire. On the turntable someone had put 'Light My Fire', an apt choice. 'I put a bottle of brandy and a bottle of vodka in there after she'd mixed it.'

'Real firewater,' said Pete. And for some reason, the innocent remark had a profound effect on Martin.

Completely out of the blue, it brought the horror of what had happened on the motorway back to him. In that moment, he could see the lake of devouring flame greedily consuming the motorway and the vehicles – and the coach, with its trapped passengers. His lorry had been the reason for the horrifying conflagration; what he had been carrying, the chemical that had spilled from the ruptured tank, had hideously burned those poor people to death. He couldn't bear the memory. For the first time, he became aware that he had been keeping all his emotions firmly locked away in a room in the back of his mind. Something else was happening now. Something that didn't make any sense at all. Was it something to do with the rum snatch, or the punch? He had to have something sweet. It was more than a craving. If he didn't get something really sweet in the very next moment, then something important within him would surely die. His mouth was bone dry, and so was his glass. The punch-bowl on the centre table was suddenly the most important thing in his life. Crazy, but it seemed as if the sweetness could resolve all his problems. There were bottles of lime cordial all around it, and lemonade, and ginger beer, and Coca-Cola. Perhaps the bottles of vodka and brandy he'd sneaked into the punch were the reason for his thirst? Suddenly, he experienced a rerun of his previous conversation with the woman whose name he couldn't remember. Pete had been talking to him and Martin hadn't registered any of it. It made him feel bad because he'd been trying to make him feel at ease, to open him up.

'. . . and he said he would never do it again.'

Was this a punchline for a joke, or something deeply serious about Ben that he mustn't misunderstand? He wouldn't make the same mistake again. Ben was clearly waiting for a response, eyes shining in anticipation. And that almighty thirst possessed Martin.

'I know . . . I know . . .' said Martin quickly. 'Watch this. This'll get the party going.'

And while Pete and Ben watched in astonishment, Martin strode quickly to the punch-bowl, twisted the tops off two bottles of soft drinks, seized one in each hand and then upended them into the punch-bowl. His actions were drawing attention now. Out of the corner of his eye, he could see that Sheila was looking over as the person she was talking to suddenly caught sight of what was going on.

Christ almighty, what am I doing? What the hell is WRONG with me?

'Tonight's party piece . . .'

Martin braced himself like a weightlifter about to attempt a new world record. He smacked his hands together, bent at the knees, then gripped the sides of the punch-bowl as if it weighed half a ton. With a mock cry of effort, which was less an act than anyone else in the room could know,

he lifted the punch-bowl from the table, bringing it to his
mouth.

He drank.

The punch slopped and gushed around the sides of his
mouth, splashing down his shirt-front, soaking him. There was
no sound in the living room as he gulped great mouthfuls of
the sugary-red liquid, and the tidal wave around his face began
to splatter down over his shoulders and on to the carpet that
Sheila had so meticulously cleaned before the party started,
despite the pain it caused her. Pete looked horrified, and the
silence seemed to go on and on as Martin continued to drink,
not pausing for breath.

And then Ben started to laugh. An explosion of sound as he
rocked backwards and forwards in his wheelchair. Pete looked
down at him aghast. Someone else had started to laugh at the
back of the room. Then another guest, and another. And suddenly, the room erupted in loud, appreciative laughter. Sheila's
look of astonishment melted, became something else. She was
looking at Martin as she hadn't looked at him in a long time.
Her husband, the man who didn't like parties and who had so
often been taken aback by her tendency to do unexpected and
silly things before the pain had changed everything, was doing
something utterly, ridiculously silly. She began to laugh too,
even though the carpet was being ruined. Despite the pain, and
the grief that had threatened to overwhelm her when she had
so nearly lost him, Sheila laughed long and loud. The laughter
was augmented by a loud round of applause and cheering, as
Martin finally dropped the punch-bowl back on the table. He
wiped both hands across his face and staggered back as if he
had just dropped a hundredweight barbell. Behind him, Ben
was shrieking with laughter and Pete was chortling at his
son's reaction. Soaked, and with the applause still ringing in
his ears, Martin turned to where Ben sat in his wheelchair.

'Three cheers for Martin Russell,' said someone from the
back of the room.

Martin turned to look down at Ben.

Pete looked at Martin, smiling.

And something about the expression on Martin's face wiped

the newly found smile completely from Pete's face. Martin wasn't laughing. His face was almost grim, as if looking at Ben were causing him great consternation. Ben seemed too convulsed with the great joke to notice it.

'Hip, hip, hooray!'

Martin dropped down on to his haunches, directly in front of Ben, his shirt and trousers soaked. His eyes were glittering as if he had suddenly gone mad. He reached out slowly, and touched the side of Ben's face. Pete moved forward, unsure now of just what the hell was going on.

'Hip, hip, hooray!'

Martin kept his hand on Ben's face, cupping one cheek in his great scarred, calloused hand.

Suddenly, Ben's eyes shot up into his head. This time, he was spasming not with laughter but as if he had just received an electric shock. His arms and legs began to jerk and thrash, his head whipping from side to side. Pete lunged down and smacked Martin's hand away from him.

'Hip, hip, *hooray!*'

Martin staggered back and away, as the people nearest to him began to clap him on the back and shoulders. No one but Pete had seen what had happened. Everyone was still in the thrall of the extravagant party trick.

'Please!' Pete yelled, trying to be heard over the sounds of the partygoers. 'Someone, please! For God's sake, phone for an ambulance! My boy's having a *stroke!*'

And this time, Pete's pleas were heard, the laughter and banter dissolving again as he tried to pin his son's flailing arms. One of Martin's neighbours, a young man trained in first aid, hurried through the crowd, pushing Martin and the others to one side. Pete was trying to jam something into Ben's mouth as foam bubbled from his champing jaws.

But Martin heard nothing of the commotion as he walked through the horrified crowd. He had quenched the terrible thirst for the moment, and he could feel something happening inside him. His arms and hands were trembling in the aftermath of the bizarre surge of power that he had felt transmitting itself from somewhere deep inside him, out through his fingers and into Ben. He had been drawn to Ben, knew that he had to give him something, and the after-effects of whatever he had done had made him dizzy and nauseous. He put his hands to his face, hearing someone on the telephone next door, frantically phoning for an ambulance. His fingers trembled against his cheeks. The face felt like it belonged to someone else; the fingers also belonged to the hands of a stranger.

Should he vomit into the sink, get rid of whatever was inside him?

No!

The voice that shouted inside his head was not his voice.

Was he losing his mind? Was this how it all began? Martin braced both hands on the kitchen bench and lowered his head. Something was happening to him. Something bad. But he had no idea what, and for the second time since he'd been a child, he felt like weeping.

'But you're all right?' asked Jane's neighbour. It was a statement rather than a genuine enquiry, a trademark of Maureen Golightly from number forty-seven.

Jane sat in the middle of the sofa, knees together, fingers closed tightly around the cup and saucer as if they might fly from her lap at any moment. She had been doing the washing up when Maureen had marched across the street towards her. Plainly visible through the front window, she had been unable to shrink from sight and pretend that she wasn't in. Now, she sat as if she were a nervous guest in someone else's living room. She cocked her head when she smiled, as if she were straining to listen to a complimentary comment coming from the next room.

'Oh, yes. All right. Yes, I'm all right.'

'Good,' continued Maureen. 'I mean, when we read about it in the papers, none of us *dreamed* that someone we knew might have been in that terrible crash.'

Oh God, please. Why don't you go away? I've told you that I'm all right, so please just leave. Just LEAVE!

'Honestly, Jane. You know what it's like in The Mews. So quiet, and nothing ever happens; apart from the public footpath at the rear of the Lewis's property where – you know – that poor girl was attacked, and no one, and I mean *no one* in their right mind is going to walk up that way again – so when something as terrible as *that* happens you just thank God that it wasn't you driving on that road, and then you find out that someone you *do* know was there! I mean, right there! And in that coach too. Oh, my poor dear, what must it have been like for you? I can't begin to imagine. Did you get to know any of the other passengers? All of the others died, you know. Eighty-seven of them. And what a terrible, *terrible* way to die . . .'

Tom doesn't want me to socialise with you, or any of the other neighbours while he's out at work. And if he knew you were here I don't know what might happen. Please, please, why don't you go away? I know what you want. You're empty on the inside, just like me. And you want what happened to me to be a part of you, too. You want to share in it all, without having any of the fear or the hurt. And oh God, please, please just finish your cup of coffee and go home again . . .

'. . . an accident waiting to happen. That's what Ron's always said to me. That stretch of road should have been dualled a long time ago. Did you read the accident statistics in the newspaper? It's a disgrace, an utter disgrace. Why anyone should choose to travel on a coach on that route, I don't know. I wouldn't. I mean, I wouldn't drive on that stretch *at all*. I'd take the by-pass. I know it's a fifteen-minute detour, but far better fifteen minutes out of your life than not having a life at all . . .'

You want to know why I was on that bus. And if it wasn't for that newspaper and that Curtis reporter, you wouldn't have known that I was on the bus at all. And oh sweet Jesus, what is Tom going to do when he finds out that everyone knows?

Jane glanced at the wall-clock. Four thirty. Another hour and a half to go. Surely Maureen wouldn't stay that long? The little girl who lived inside her spent a great deal of time looking at the clock during the day, dreading the time when the big hand came around to six. Because six o'clock was when Daddy came home. All day and every day she watched the clock in the kitchen. The hours crawled slowly by, and each time the little hand moved around the face one whole time to reach another number, it made the knot in her stomach screw tighter. Sometimes she struggled to the bathroom and vomited out the little food she'd been able to eat during the day . . .

'. . . you look much too thin. I think they should have kept you under observation. You know, just for a few days. To make sure that you're all right . . .'

Jane knew that she'd looked that way ever since they moved into The Mews; knew that Maureen had been gossiping about the state of her health endlessly, but hadn't been able to find out just what had been happening. The motorway accident had been a perfect opportunity to invite herself over, offer false sympathy and obtain all the information she craved, so that she could turn Jane's life from a living hell into something ten times worse.

Maureen shuffled forward until she was sitting on the edge of the sofa, confident that Jane would be opening her heart. Jane found that movement deeply intimidating, and thought she was about to burst into tears. Maureen saw her eyes filling, and for a moment her fake expression of concern almost melted into outright pleasure.

'More coffee . . . ?'

Jane had to get away, had to do something.

'No more for me. I'll never sleep tonight. You can tell me, you know. All about it.'

The sugar bowl on the tray before them was empty. For the first time, it seemed, Jane remembered that there was no sugar anywhere in the house; had faint memories of creeping down from her little-girl's room in the night and eating handfuls of it from the packet. Surely that was a dream?

'Let it all out, Jane.' Maureen reached out to take her hand. 'That's the only way, darling. Don't keep it all bottled up inside.'

All Jane could see was that hand reaching out for her. She shrank back, as if contact with it might be poisonous. But Maureen had now homed in on those tears, wanting to see them flow, wanting to hear Jane pouring out her heart. Jane shrank back further. But the hand was still moving towards her. Maureen had ceased to exist. There was only the hand, disembodied and greedily hunting for her own hand.

'You want to feel the way I'm feeling?'

The fear and the grief and the knowledge that her one brief act of bravery in finally walking out on Tom had been snuffed out by the horror on the motorway suddenly inverted all the emotion inside Janet to a point of white-hot, burning intensity.

'You want to know what it *feels* like?'

Some small part inside her was appalled at the ferocity of her anger. She had never felt like this before, as if something had taken possession of her soul. And the white heat of emotion was suddenly in her hands now as she lunged forward and seized Maureen's hand in both of her own. Maureen's eyes widened in surprise at the sudden movement.

'Can you feel it, then? Can you *feel it?*'

Maureen opened her mouth to respond, but seemed awed by the anger that had so suddenly consumed Jane. Suddenly, it seemed that Jane was the third person in the room, somehow outside her body and observing the two figures who sat face to face, one clutching the other's hand. Maureen tried to pull away now, but Jane held fast.

In that moment, something *jumped* between them.

Something that felt like an electric shock, transferring itself from Jane's hand into Maureen's own hand. The shock of it catapulted Jane back into her body again. She recoiled in her seat, the grip broken. Maureen thrashed back across the sofa, clutching her hand as if it had been burned. The look of shock on her face had become an expression of outright terror. Her mouth was working, but she was unable to speak.

'I'm sorry . . .' began Jane, but then realised that she didn't know what she was sorry for. The fear was still palpable, now somehow externalised, not festering and eating at her alone, but somehow in the air all around them. She reached for Maureen again, this time in real need of support and terrified at the strangeness she was feeling. But the situation had been utterly reversed. Now Maureen was shrinking back

in fear from Jane's hand. At last, she was able to find
her voice.

'Stay away from me! Don't you *touch* me!'

Maureen staggered to her feet, knocking her coffee cup and
saucer to the carpet, clawing at the back of the hand that Jane
had touched as if it had been smeared with something that was
corroding the skin.

Impossibly, the sofa cushions on which she had been sitting
had begun to smoke. Grey wisps of it were curling from the
fabric, as if a cigarette had been dropped between them and
was smouldering there. Maureen lurched away from the sofa,
upsetting the small coffee table. She saw the smoke curling
there and began to smack at her own posterior, half turning
to look, still wide-eyed in fear and now convinced that her
skirt was on fire. But there were no flames. Only the same
faint wisps of smoke from the hem of her dress, and now
from the sleeves of her blouse.

'What did you do to me? What did you *do* to me?'

'Nothing ... something ... something burning ...' Jane at
last found the strength to do something, struggling to her
feet and grabbing at the sofa cushions. Pulling both of them
on to the floor, she began swatting at them to put out the
non-existent flames. But just as the smoke from the cushions
was diminishing, it seemed to be increasing around the sleeves
of Maureen's blouse and from the hem of her dress.

'Oh God ... oh God ... I'm on fire. For Christ's sake, I'm
on fire.'

'Where? *Where?* I can't see anything!'

Maureen began to perform a whirling dance in the middle
of the living room. It suddenly occurred to her to unbutton the
blouse. She clawed at the buttons, and several popped, flying
over the carpet. Jane ran into the kitchen, turned on the taps
and began to fill the bowl in the sink. Through the doorway,
she could see Maureen tearing off her blouse and throwing
it to the floor. Now she was struggling with her skirt. The
smoke was rising thick and fast around her body and she
was giving small whoops of distress when, seconds later,
Jane half lunged, half staggered through the doorway into the

living room. Maureen's skirt dropped around her ankles at the same moment that Jane threw the contents of the washing-up bowl over her. The mini-tidal wave completely soaked and obliterated an expensive perm. The shock of the cold water left Maureen gasping, hands held rigidly down by her sides. The water soaked her bra and knickers, splashing down over the smouldering skirt.

'Are you hurt?' Jane quickly studied her body, looking for any signs of burning. There were none. Now the smoke was gone. And the shock of the dowsing seemed to have killed Maureen's fear. Instead, there was only rage and humiliation.

'Here . . . here . . .' Jane ran from the room. Seconds later, she had brought her muslin dressing gown from the upstairs bedroom. Maureen took it, face set and furious.

'Are you hurt? I don't know how . . . are you burned?'

Maureen said nothing. Instead, she swept her sodden skirt and blouse from the floor and stamped out of the living room. Jane stood at the window and watched her crossing the street to her own house, anxiously looking from left to right in case any of the neighbours should be watching. Her own front windows shivered when Maureen slammed the front door.

Dumbfounded, Jane turned to look back into the room. Hurrying across to the sofa, she checked again that there was nothing burning there. But there was nothing to be seen. Even the smouldering cushions that she had thrown to the floor appeared to have no scorch marks or burn holes. After a while, she looked at the water stain in the middle of the carpet – and then at the clock on the wall.

Five o'clock.

Daddy would be home at six.

Only one hour to clean up the mess and have the place looking the way he wanted it to look. The gnawing fear was back in her stomach. Frantically, she hunted for towels to soak up the water. There was a portable fan heater under the sink. She could plug that in and aim it at the stain. Everything would be all right again by the time he came home. Everything would *have* to be all right by then.

And as the heater hummed and blew hot draughts in her

face, Jane knelt on the floor, soaking up the water with the towels and praying to God that Tom wouldn't find out that Maureen had been here today.

Sweet.

She had to have something sweet.

Moaning, Jane continued to mop.

The second hand moved inexorably around the face of the hated clock.

When the front door opened and Curtis saw the white-faced man who stood there, blinking in the sunlight, he asked: 'Is Mr Stark at home?'

And then he realised his mistake. The face was white and drawn, there were dark hollows under the eyes and the hair was dishevelled, but this was still the man whom he had seen and then later surreptitiously photographed at the hospital after the motorway disaster. He had looked pretty rough then, but seemed to have really deteriorated since that time. Still, what should he expect of a man who had lost his wife and two kids in such a dreadful manner? However, that fact shouldn't stop him from pressing on with what he had to do.

'Who are you?' Stark shaded his eyes against the dim sunshine. He looked like some pathetic vampire disturbed in its sleep during the day, and wary of the sunlight.

'My name's Curtis, from the *Independent Daily*.'

'Curtis, yeah. The reporter. Goodbye.'

Stark began to close the door and Curtis stepped forward, as if to put his foot in the way. Stark's rheumy eyes sparked with anger. Now unheeding of the daylight, he lunged through the half-opened door and seized Curtis by the lapel of his anorak. His hands were still heavily bandaged, but he nevertheless managed to get a good grip. The lapel ripped and the impetus of the sudden lunge made Curtis stagger back until they were both standing on the garden path.

'No trouble, Mr Stark! No trouble . . .'

Curtis fumbled at the hand that held him. Beneath the bandages, Stark's hands seemed to be made of stone or steel.

'I should just break your *bloody* . . .'

'No trouble!'

Stark stared at him, as if debating just how he could inflict the worst kind of damage. At last, the dangerous glint in his eyes faded. Giving a hiss of disgust, he turned back to the door.

'Don't you want to know what happened?' asked Curtis.

Stark whirled round as if any sound from this unwelcome visitor, any sound at all, would give him the excuse he needed to hurl himself back and tear him limb from limb. Curtis backed off, holding out both hands in defence. But he was adamant that he would speak to him.

'Don't you want to know what happened on that motorway? Don't you want to know what caused the crash?'

Stark paused, deliberating.

'Don't you want to know who was responsible for the death of your family?'

'You're telling me they've found out what happened?'

'Can't we talk inside?'

Stark looked at him again, long and hard.

'If this is some kind of trick, just to get another interview, then you know what I'll do to you. Don't you?'

Curtis looked uncomfortable, but nodded.

'And if you ask me how I *feel*, I won't tell you. I'll show you. You understand that too, don't you?'

'Fair enough.'

Stark turned and re-entered the house. Adjusting a tie that had suddenly become too tight around his neck, Curtis followed.

There was a smell inside. Not completely unpleasant, and at first Curtis couldn't identify it. As they walked into the living room, a dog looked up from a basket beside the television set. It hadn't reacted to the fracas outside, so he guessed that it was one of the more placid mongrel varieties. Was it simply dog musk? No, Curtis had had pets before the divorce, and the smell wasn't like that at all. It wasn't human, either. Not like the smells he'd endured interviewing some of the unfortunates whose stories he'd covered in the past, those who had given up hope and, as a by-product, had stopped attending to their own hygiene. The television set wasn't tuned into a receiving channel. Static flashed and hissed angrily from the screen. Stark walked straight over to it and switched it off. The dog whined and lowered its head.

Curtis looked at the plates and cups on the table in the middle of the room. He remembered how he'd been when his wife left him. Eating and drinking until there wasn't a clean dish or cup left, and then having to wash everything up at once. Stark moved to an armchair, absently waving a hand behind him at one of the others. Curtis took the hint, and sat gingerly, hoping that Stark hadn't allowed the dog to pee on the cushions.

'So who was it?' asked Stark, gripping the arms of the chair. 'What's the name of the bastard who was driving the wrong way up the motorway?'

'No one knows who he or she was – or just *what* the hell it was.'

Stark lowered his head, and stared at his lap. Slowly, he began to shake his head, and Curtis could see the bandaged hands gripping the arm rests. He was preparing to pull himself upright again as the great rage began to consume him once more.

'Look!' Curtis shifted uneasily, ready to make a dash for it. He had bluffed his way inside with the suggestion that he had some answers. Now he knew that he'd better think fast. 'I'm not here to interview you. Well, not really. Not yet. But I do know something about what happened that night. Something that doesn't make sense. I saw things myself, later at the hospital, saw things happening to the people who survived that smash – including *you* – things that I bet you can't remember. And before you decide to beat me up and throw me out of here, why don't you just listen to what I have to say? It won't take but a few minutes. After that, you can throw me out.'

Stark looked up. His flashing eyes were moist, sparkling in the dim light.

'You do want to know what happened,' continued Curtis. 'Don't you?'

'I want to know.'

Curtis tried to relax.

'Good. Then why don't we just . . .'

'You've got five minutes, Curtis. That's all. And don't push your luck.'

'Five minutes. Right. What about a drink?'

'*Five minutes!*'

'I'm not here to probe into your misery, Stark. That's been covered, and the public have a short memory. No, I'm more interested in just how that crash happened. And I'll tell you something for nothing. When that inquiry reaches its conclusions, they won't have found the real reason either. There was such a mess of vehicles all piled up on each other and the fire was so intense . . .' Curtis paused, waiting for some kind of reaction from his listener. There was none. He continued. '. . . was so intense that most of the physical evidence has been destroyed. Points of impact, skidmarks. All wiped out by the burning fuel that spilled out of that tanker. Even when you and the others get to give your testimony, there won't be much to add. They're still trying to check out the registrations on those burned-out shells, but when it comes to which of those drivers was driving down the wrong side of the road, it could be one of several. They *think* the coach was the first to be hit, but like I say they can't be sure. And since it was heading from Glasgow to London, at least they know it was heading in the *right* direction.'

'Your time's nearly up, Curtis. And you haven't told me a bloody thing.'

'Something bizarre happened on that stretch of road. Whatever it was, it's still happening.'

'One minute left.'

'All right, I wanted a big scoop out of that crash. I'm sorry, but that's my job. I got into the hospital, and saw something in there. Something that happened to each of the six people – the *only* six people – who survived the crash. At least one of them swears blind that he doesn't know what I'm talking about. But I was there, in that casualty department, and I saw it – whatever it was. I saw what it did to them all, and to you.'

'What the hell are you talking about?'

'Something that looked like a storm. Something that looked like thunder and lightning *inside* the hospital. Something that smashed through doors and ripped across ceilings without leaving a trace. I was there, Stark. In Casualty when it happened. You were on a stretcher in one of the cubicles, ranting and raving. In shock, probably. Then that thing that looked like a stormcloud exploded into the room. You, and the five others, were all struck by something that looked like lightning. It blew the truck-driver guy clean across the room. Except that he, and the artist fella, just don't remember a thing about it.'

'This is some kind of trick, Curtis. Some kind of bullshit so that you can screw some more juice out of the story.'

'No, I swear to God! I was there, Stark. I was there, and I *saw* what I *saw*. All right, I'll come clean. There's a story there, and I want to know what the hell is going on. But what happened was so incredible, I've just got to find out what it was. Not just for the story, but for *me*. So please, tell me, can you remember anything about it?'

'It never happened, Curtis. Not what you said. I would have remembered.'

Curtis sighed and slumped back in his chair like a deflating balloon.

'And you still haven't got to any point,' continued Stark.

'Okay, you don't remember. By the time I catch up with the others, they won't remember anything either. At the moment, I've got a bunch of strange stuff that doesn't add up to anything. A mystery that just grows and grows. But it doesn't have an explanation or a reason. I just know that something's going on and that it's building up to something big.'

Perhaps it was something in Curtis's voice which prevented Harry from rising, crossing the room and dragging him out by the frayed lapel. Perhaps for the first time, there was something genuine there. When the reporter paused to collect his thoughts, Harry just sat and watched and listened.

With weary resignation, Curtis said: 'Ask the hospital and they'll say just what you've said. That nothing happened. They'll accept that there was a power short; some burned fuses and a little damage. But they won't tell you what I've told you. Because they don't understand what the hell happened, and none of the people who were "hit" were hurt. Don't have so much as a scorch mark. And they don't remember any of it – which is pretty handy. So if no one can remember, there's little prospect of law suits. Which suits the hospital just fine. Seems like most of the staff there were hugging the floor and holding their hands over their heads when that thundercloud appeared. I'm the only one who saw it. Okay – forget that stuff for the moment. Let's look at the other bloody peculiar things that have happened since that smash.'

'Like for instance?'

'Like for instance, a hospital mortuary attendant was attacked and killed in the morgue just minutes before that indoor storm appeared. And not just killed. Whoever did the killing ripped the poor bastard's face off. And then stole one of the bodies that had been retrieved from the crash. The coach-driver. An hour later, a fire-fighter was killed back there on the motorway. Can't get the full details, because it seems the fire crews are just as badly shaken up as the hospital staff. You see, that fire-fighter *also* had his face torn off. So, I ask myself: Did the same person who killed the mortuary attendant kill the fireman? And why? And what the hell would he want to steal that body for?'

'You said you were here to tell me something. So far, all I've heard are ramblings and hangover hallucinations.'

'Something's happened to the fields on either side of that motorway. I've been out there to have a look. And the people who live nearby are just as scared as everyone else. They don't really want to talk about it. But seeing's believing. You see, there's not much around the place where the crash happened. Two farms three miles to the east, another two miles west. That motorway just cuts through scrubland, pasture and next to bloody nothing. But the grass all around that collision point has died. I don't mean it's been burned by the spilled fuel. You can see where that's happened on the embankment. No, I'm talking about beyond the embankment. For maybe three hundred yards on all sides. Everything's withered and died.

Some of the farmers had sheep and cattle in those fields. Half of the sheep stock have died overnight. No reason. Vets can't give an answer. They just wandered back, lay down in their byres and died. Some of the horses were in foal, and they've all lost their colts. Stillborn. The farmers are not happy men. They'd like to sue someone over the crash, but it's hardly likely that forty-nine sheep are just going to drop dead of fright from a crash that's happened a mile and a half away.'

'Time's up,' said Harry.

'One of the survivors, Roger O'Dowd. A graduate. He told me about something that happened just before the coach he was in turned over.' Curtis paused, waiting for Stark to say something. Harry looked at him blankly. 'Something bloody strange. First there was that blinding light in the windscreen. But then something else hit the coach. His words, not mine. *Hit* the coach.'

'So? What?'

'Screaming. People screaming. Not anyone in the coach. He said it was as if the screaming sounds exploded into the coach from outside. Shook him up when he remembered . . .' Curtis paused as Stark slowly raised a hand to his brow, as if he had suddenly developed a bad headache. 'You see, up until that moment, he'd forgotten all about those sounds.'

'That's enough, Curtis. I want you to leave now. There's nothing more to talk about.'

'You mean you didn't hear it? Didn't hear the screaming?'

'Look, that's it. Just leave me alone . . . leave me . . .' Harry hunched forward in his seat, both hands to his head now. Something about his manner reminded Curtis strongly of Roger O'Dowd's reaction. What had he expected? That Stark would refuse to listen to him, or at best that he would hear what he had to say and then throw him out? Certainly not what he'd wished in his heart; that Stark should be reacting this way, just as O'Dowd had.

'You remember now, don't you? You'd forgotten all about that noise, just like O'Dowd. Just as if you didn't want to remember, or something inside was *stopping* you from remembering . . .'

Something inside.

Harry felt a wave of nausea then. His mind was whirling with confused images. He had spent so much time trying to block from his head what had happened that day. Now it seemed that Curtis had opened something in his mind, some kind of floodgate, and the terrible memories were flooding through. And yes, he remembered the horrifying screaming sounds as they exploded into the car. He jammed his hands against his ears when he heard Hilary and Diane screaming again.

Daddeeeeeee!

Curtis recoiled back into his seat as Harry suddenly lunged out of the chair. The dog leapt out of the basket and stood, cringeing and whimpering as Harry blundered across the room. The kitchen door slapped open and the dog began to slink around in fearful circles as Harry staggered into the kitchen and fell against the sink. Curtis recovered and followed him, to find him gagging and convulsing as whatever was inside him tried to come out. But nothing would come. Unsure, Curtis moved to try and help, then hung back and looked at the dog as if it could somehow tell him what to do.

'Look ... look, Stark. I'm sorry. I didn't mean to bring it all back ... to make you feel bad ...'

And Curtis recoiled again, the dog yipping with fright and scurrying from the kitchen back into the living room where it vanished behind the sofa, as Stark lunged back from the sink. Staggering as if drunk, he pulled the cabinet door beneath the sink open and dropped to his knees. With frenzied, clawing hands, he began to pull cleaning-fluid bottles and cartons from the shelves. They clattered on the kitchen linoleum around him. Curtis watched, hypnotised, as a can of spray-polish rolled lazily towards him. Stark seemed to be sobbing now, and suddenly it was as if he were reacting like a drug addict, deprived of a fix. There was something in the cupboard he needed desperately. A carton of fabric conditioner burst open on the floor, spreading a pink pool of liquid around his knees. Curtis stepped forward. He would have to do something. And then Stark found what he was looking for. With a strangled gasp of joy, he stood again, trouser knees soaked in the pink liquid, clutching a bottle of pine-scented disinfectant.

'Come on back into the living room.' Curtis carefully edged towards him as he fumbled at the screw-top of the bottle with his heavily bandaged hands. Wrenching the top off the bottle at last, he let it drop to the floor. 'Sit down and let's have another talk about it. I'll telephone for someone, a doctor maybe . . .'

And then Curtis cried out aloud, lunging to grab his arm as Harry lifted the bottle of disinfectant to his lips and began to drink greedily from it. His head was flung back; Curtis saw bubbles erupting in the neck of the bottle as he poured it down his throat.

'Jesus, Stark! *Stop it!*'

Stark was a lot stronger than Curtis could have imagined. As he grabbed his left forearm, the crazy man jerked his head away from him and continued to drink, bearing all of Curtis's weight on the arm. Curtis cried out again, yanked hard, and this time managed to pull him away from the sink.

'You bloody fool! You'll kill yourself!'

Suddenly aware that this was just what Stark intended, Curtis dragged him again. But this time his foot skidded in the fabric conditioner and he fell heavily to the lino. Stark turned to look down at him and drank again as he struggled to rise.

'Some chance!' snapped Harry, wiping an arm across his mouth and then flinging the half-empty bottle into the sink. His eyes were wide and wild. And at that moment, Curtis believed that he had done the stupidest thing in his journalistic career. He had voluntarily walked into the home of an absolute and utter maniac without taking any precautions at all. Crazed by the death of his family, Stark was about to commit suicide – prompted by himself – but maybe not before taking one of the kitchen knives from the sink's draining board and ramming it into him.

'You don't have to do this, Stark! There are people who can help you.'

'Really? *Really?* So what the hell do you know about any-thing, Curtis? Want something to write about? Want to add some more fucking spice to your lunatic stories? Well, how about this? For the past three weeks I've been addicted to the stuff in that cupboard. First it was sugar. Bags of the stuff. Then flour. Get that? Flour. Sometimes I looked like a white-faced clown when I looked in the mirror. Then cleaning fluids, now disinfectant! So what do you make of that? I'm a cleaning-fluid junkie. Not the heavy stuff yet. Not the heavy drugs, like Domestos or Sterno. But I'll get there eventually. Soft drugs first, then hard drugs. See? I can't stop myself. I'm hooked. And you want to know something else? It doesn't affect me. Doesn't hurt me. Stuff that should burn the lining out of my throat and my guts just slides down as easily as whisky or vodka. The worst thing it does is give me the shits. Now what do you make of *that*, Mr Reporter? Know the funny thing about it? I *want* it to kill me, I *want* it to finish what I'm going through. But it's like some great big funny fucking joke is being played on me.'

Stark staggered back against the sink then, both hands braced behind him on the rim. Now it seemed that the burst of ferocious anger was taking its toll. Or perhaps the stuff he'd just guzzled was going to have the obvious effect. Curtis scrabbled back and managed to rise, all the time expecting the man in front of him to slump to the floor again, hugging his stomach and screaming for help. There was a long, long silence. From somewhere in the living room, the dog was still whimpering.

'Stark . . .'

'Get out,' said Stark in a voice that was now so quiet it was barely audible.

'You've got to get help.'

Harry looked up. The glint of rage in his eyes had gone. Now he just looked ill, old and tired. But there was control in his expression.

'I don't need anybody's help. Least of all yours. Get out.'

'But for God's sake, that stuff you were drinking . . .'

'Won't hurt me. For a newspaper reporter you don't listen very well, do you? What are you expecting? You want to see me throw up, cough blood and start screaming for a doctor? Well, you won't see it, 'cause it isn't going to happen. There's nothing more for you here, Curtis. So get the hell out of my house.'

Curtis shook his head, tried to think of another way of rationalising everything and getting this utterly crazy situation back on an even keel.

'Don't,' said Stark, quietly again. 'Just go. If you don't go *now*, I swear to Christ that I'll kill you.' The words were quiet and calm, with none of the ferocious anger behind them. But Curtis knew that Stark meant it. Holding out both hands to placate him, he backed out of the kitchen and into the living room. Harry followed him slowly, watching all the way as Curtis tried to wipe the pink liquid from his anorak and trousers as he moved, watching him warily in case he should suddenly turn wild again and lunge after him.

'Let me make a call,' began Curtis. 'See if I can't get someone to . . .'

Harry shook his head, sadly and wearily, but still with a promise there that he would do what he said he'd do. Curtis stumbled in the hallway. From behind the sofa, the dog yipped again. Safely beyond the front door and standing on the garden path, Curtis looked back at Stark standing in the hall.

'I've got to send someone, Stark. Don't you see that? Christ, man, you've swallowed poison. No matter what you think, it'll do you harm. You're just . . . just not thinking straight.'

Stark sighed again. 'If you send anyone here, I'll kill them. Then I'll kill you.'

Frustrated, confused and afraid, Curtis backed away down the garden path to the gate. Fumbling with the latch, he saw Stark slowly close the front door on him.

'Shit, shit, *shit!*' Curtis hissed at the sky.

Impotently, he turned and strode away without looking back.

'It's okay,' said Harry, returning to his chair. 'It's all right, Felix. You can come out now. Everything's okay, baby.'

The dog whimpered from behind the sofa, but would not come out.

Diane christened him that. Always liked to give the wrong

*kind of name to a pet. No 'Fido' or 'Rover' for her. Had to give
the dog a cat's name.*

'Come on, boy. Come on out.'

This time the dog pushed itself halfway out from behind the
sofa. Its head was still hanging low, looking up at him from
under ragged eyebrows. Its tail wagged furiously, wanting
everything to be all right. It had been put into kennels for
the duration of their holiday, but even when Harry had finally
arranged for it to be brought home again after the funerals,
it seemed that the animal could sense what had happened. It
slunk around the house, head held low, and would not eat.

'Come on over. Come to Daddy.'

Felix pushed himself out and darted across the room,
jumping up to land on Harry's lap. He cradled it as it strained
its head up to meet him, now furiously licking his face. It was
the first real show of affection from the animal since he'd
come home.

Daddy.

It was the one word that cracked Harry apart inside. A
word that no one would ever apply to him again. He turned
from Felix to look at the photograph on the bureau beside
him. Jean, Hilary and Diane. All standing with their heads
close together, all with their forefingers placed in a shushing
gesture on the little indent between nose and upper lip. It
had been a family joke. Once, a long time ago when they
were very small, Harry had told them that before anyone was
born, every person knew the secrets of the universe. But then,
just before that moment of birth, an angel was made to place
its forefinger over their lips, making that little dent, so that
the newborn baby would forget everything. That story had
become a good-hearted family joke, used every time a family
discussion about the meaning of life became too heavy. But
the sight of the beautiful smiling faces in the photograph had
a profound effect on Harry as he sat there.

In a sudden burst of clarity, he saw himself for what he had
become, knew for a fact that he must be losing his mind. He
had become, literally, mad with grief. Tears flooded his face
and the dog furiously licked the moisture from his skin. He

hugged him tight, began to stroke his head again, and then realised that he could not feel him for the bandages on his hand. Felix was the one living thing that still bound him to his family: the family pet on whom they had all lavished affection. There were other photographs in the family album, of Hilary and Diane and Jean cradling Felix when he was a puppy. Photographs of family holidays with the dog prancing and jumping around them in a summer-filled garden. And in that one moment when he needed to touch Felix, he couldn't feel a thing. Weeping, he began to claw the bandages from his hands. Still nervous at his outbursts, Felix jumped down again from his lap.

'No, please . . . no, Felix . . . it's all right, boy. Come on back. Come back to me . . .'

The bandages came loose more easily than he expected. Streamers of cotton began to coil and gather around him as he tore at them. He had been told that he'd need treatment twice a week for several weeks, perhaps ultimately skin-graft treatment because of the extent of the burned tissue. Someone had suggested that he was lucky to still have the use of his hands. Harry's cold expression had ended that attempt to comfort him. But no matter what the state of his hands, he had to feel something living. He waited for the pain to begin as the bandages unwound, but there was none.

'Come on, Felix. Jump up, boy . . .'

The last bandages fell away from both hands, almost simultaneously.

And Harry could only sit and look at them in astonishment.

For a brief moment, the grief and the loneliness were banished as he held both hands up slowly in front of his face. He turned them, looking at the palms, then the backs, then the palms again, over and over, unbelieving. He had been expecting raw and bloodied meat, or hideous grey scar tissue.

But his hands were unblemished.

There were no marks on them; no burns, no shrivelled, puckered skin. No raw and festering wounds. They were covered in new skin. They looked as if they'd been scrubbed clean, and his nails given a manicure.

This was too much to take in. Nothing made sense any more. Was it all a dream? Something like hope flared inside him. Yes, it was another impossible thing. First he had been thrown clear from the car after the immense impact, almost without a scratch. That couldn't happen in real life. Then he had been eating and drinking impossible things, chemicals that should have killed him. But there was no effect. And now these clean and newborn hands when he had seen them burning and withering as he clawed at the burning car door. Harry's face crumpled; tears began to stream down his face again.

'It's a dream, Felix. Oh, thank Christ, I'm only dreaming.'

The dog barked, as if to confirm it.

'Oh, thank God, thank God! Felix, come here. Come here, darling.'

The dog swivelled its backside, wagging its tail furiously in sheer pleasure. Gathering itself, it leapt into Harry's lap. With joy, Harry grabbed it by the ruff of the neck and pulled it to him in an embrace.

Something exploded in the room with frightening force.

Something that flared a brilliant white and filled the air with a flat and shocking retort.

Harry recoiled in his seat from a blow that stunned him. In the same instant, as he was blinded by the brilliance of the detonation, someone or something dragged Felix out of his hands with a savage yank. The dog made a high-pitched squeal of pain and was gone. Harry's new hands flew to his head. There was pain, but now he was confused. Before he could locate where the pain came from, it was gone. At first he thought that he had been hit across the head, then the small of the back, now over the forearms. But the pain was gone before he could localise it. In the next instant, eyes still blurred, Harry leapt from the seat, flailing at whomever his attacker might be. As he flailed, his eyes focused again. There was no one behind the seat, no one around it. He spun on his heels, flailing again. But now he could see that there was no one in the room.

'Light-bulb . . .'

Harry staggered and looked at the ceiling. But the bulb hadn't exploded and showered him with sparks; there was no dangling electrified wire. Leaning against the chair now, he shook his head and recovered his senses. He remembered months ago trying to change a damaged light fixture in the living-room ceiling. Foolishly and despite Jean's protestations, he hadn't switched off the mains first. The shock he'd received from the bare wire, that buzzing, *dragging* feeling at the nerve ends, was the way he had felt just now, albeit much worse. There was no doubt about it, he'd received an electric shock. He looked around at the foot of the chair for a loose wire. There was no sign of anything.

'Felix, it's okay, boy. Everything's all right . . .'

He smelled burning as he turned to look across the living room. The first thing he saw was the smoke curling from the floor, confirming what he'd thought about a shock and a bare wire. In the next instant, he saw what the smoke was emanating from.

It was coming from Felix, lying on the carpet.

His hind legs were twitching, and now Harry could hear his strangled whimpering.

'Oh, *God!*'

Harry scrambled across to the dog, falling on his knees beside him. Felix's eyes had rolled back up into their sockets; his tongue was thrust out between his teeth as saliva pooled around his head. The smoke was rising from around his throat, and Harry could see that he had been burned badly there; a great patch of fur was gone, the raw grey-pink skin beneath puckered and shrivelled.

'Oh, Felix. What's *happened?* . . .'

He stroked the dog's head.

Something cracked beneath his fingertips. He jerked his hand back as the dog spasmed and kicked. He heard a long, low exhalation and watched as his dog died at his knees.

Harry looked at his hand in blank horror. Then he looked down again at the smouldering patch around Felix's neck. Slowly, he lowered his hand over the patch and flexed his fingers. There was no doubt about it. The burned patch was the same shape and size as his hand. Harry could see the five indentations where his fingers had held the dog to him.

Impossibly, he had killed his own dog – just by touching it with his new, clean hands.

'A dream.' Harry nodded emphatically. 'Just another part of the dream. None of this is happening.'

He stood up again, holding his hands away from him as if they didn't belong on the ends of his arms. He backed off, still nodding. Suddenly, everything made sense as it never had before. He was more than asleep. He had somehow fallen into another nightmare world where there was only death and agony and torment. Everything had been taken away from him, even his own sanity. He looked at his hands again. Was this the way? Holding his breath, he raised his hands to his face.

'All right. All right. I'm coming, Jean.'

As if his hands were filled with invisible, healing water, Harry cupped them and raised them to his face. Taking a deep breath, he covered his face with his fingers, and waited for the shocking blow that would send him back to where everything was all right again.

But there was no shock. No sudden blinding light and smell of burning.

Only the smell of his own new, clean skin.

Harry moaned, rubbing furiously at his face.

'Do it to me! *Do it!*'

But there was to be no release.

And then everything became clear. Things that should have killed him were unable to do the job, and now he knew that the only way to get out of this sleep-world was to take something that would, through sleep, carry him right back into his own world. That was the answer, that was the key.

Nodding, Harry stepped over the smouldering body of the family pet and headed for the hall.

As he climbed the stairs, he felt something gnawing inside him. Something deep, deep down was trying to fight against this new resolve. Shaking his head now, denying the inner impulse to turn from his newfound purpose, he blundered

up the stairs, still holding his hands out in front of him. He
had to get back to where he was before the crash happened;
maybe the evening before they set off. The means of getting
there was upstairs in the bedroom. As he reached the landing,
the inner impulse was thrashing and fighting. It was strong,
but not strong enough. Was it screaming? Yes, in a blur Harry
sensed that it was screaming – and the sound of it was familiar.
Then, it had been one of many voices, voices that screamed
with shock and pain as the light flooded the car and they
were catapulted into the nightmare. Now it was screaming in
rage and frustration, knowing that it could not prevent him
doing what he was about to do. As the bedroom door swung
open and Harry staggered into the room, he could see things
inside himself that he had been unable to see before. Through
a dark, internal prism, he could see that one of these voices had
somehow collided *into* him on the motorway. It was still there,
hiding deep inside. It was that one voice which had compelled
him to cram all that bloody stuff into his mouth; the sugar,
the flour, the household detergents and God knew what else.
All to serve its purposes, whatever those might be. He could
sense that it was struggling inside, to prevent him doing what
must be done.

'No,' said Harry calmly, as he sat on the edge of the bed,
next to Jean's bedside cabinet. He opened the top drawer and
felt the thing that was inside him struggle and fight and try
to get him to stop. 'There's no stopping me now. This is the
only way. I don't want this to be happening any more.'

Again, he felt something inside. This time there seemed to
be a threat. Was it trying to let him know that it could hurt
him if he didn't stop?

Harry laughed. 'So hurt me. You think I can be hurt any
worse than I'm hurting now?' He unscrewed the stopper from
Jean's bottle of sleeping tablets with his new and nimble
fingers. The bottle-top didn't smoke or flare. All part of
the dream. Obviously, as in all nightmares, Harry was only
allowed to kill the last thing in the world that meant anything to him.

Now he could feel a different emotion deep down. As if the

voice inside, the voice that couldn't speak, had realised that
its empty threat had not worked. Now it was desperate.

'I'm going back to sleep,' Harry explained calmly. 'So
that I can wake up properly and everything will be real
again.'

The voice inside spasmed. It cramped Harry's stomach. He
recognised the feeling. It was pure terror.

'Hush,' said Harry, and crammed a handful of tablets into
his mouth. He didn't need water to swallow. 'Why should you
be afraid of a few pills, after all the stuff you've made me
swallow?'

There was paper and a notepad on the bedside cabinet. He
hadn't noticed it before. When he turned it around to look
at the writing, he could see that it was a shopping list that
Jean had started. He popped more pills into his mouth and
swallowed. Inside, the voice was squirming and thrashing.
But at the centre of Harry's soul was a calm and pure resolve.
He knew what had to be done. Turning the paper around to
face him, he picked up the pen.

A suicide note?

No, just an explanation.

He carefully folded the paper below Jean's list, turning it
back. Then he began to write.

*'The wrong place, at the wrong time. Someone told me that,
shortly after it happened. As if it was supposed to be some kind
of comfort . . .'*

With each word, the thing inside fought.

With each word, Harry marvelled at the calm voice that
came from his pen. He recognised the words as the true
voice of Harry Stark, husband and father of two. But he had
become something else now as he swallowed the pills. He was
no longer a person. The real Harry Stark was asleep. And
this walking-dead Harry Stark was going to put everything
right again, by changing places with him and bringing his
family back.

'Goodnight,' said Harry at last, when he had finished the
note and swallowed the last of the pills. Calmly, he folded the
note and left it on the bedside cabinet, placing the empty pill

bottle on top. Then he lay back on the bed and folded his arms across his chest.

The voice inside that could not speak thrashed and spasmed and fought.

'Everything will be all right in the morning,' said Harry.

And as the voice continued its fight, Harry drifted away into a deep, safe place.

PART THREE

TRAVELLERS

Mercy and Selina stood in the shop doorway, sipping coffee out of paper cups and watching the rainwater reflecting the blue, red and white neon signs from the gutters and the cracked pavements.

They had been there for an hour, the rain beginning on cue as soon as they arrived. Selina had changed into her 'working uniform' – a short leather skirt and sheer tights, and a bra halter that barely covered her nipples. But what she referred to sarcastically as 'the goodies' were hidden beneath a heavy fur coat, only to be revealed on offer when a punter passed by, or kerb-crawled past in his car.

'How much time did he do, in the end?' asked Mercy.

'Seven years,' replied Selina. 'Some kind-hearted psychiatrist managed to sweet-talk an appeal board into letting him off with the other three. Willie told me.'

'Willie?'

'Look, Mercy. It's best you don't ask too many questions. It's the old cliché, isn't it? The less you know the better.'

'I've come halfway across the bloody country for this, Selina.'

Selina hugged the fur coat tight to herself with one hand and sipped angrily at the paper cup. Her first sight of the bastard had fired her with rage, enough rage to get in touch with Mercy, even after all this time. Now she was beginning to regret that she'd ever done it.

'Willie's my pimp, and I asked him to find out . . .'

'Your *pimp?*'

'Yes, Mercy, my pimp! You know, P.I.M.P.'

'But you never used to do that, always used to work on your own if you had to. At the pubs and the clubs . . .'

'Get real. That's not the way it works down here. We're not in that smoke-stacked, cobbled-lane nowhere town that we grew up in. The business is organised on the streets. Don't have a pimp and you don't work. Try to work without one, and you'll get your face slashed. It's as simple as that.'

'I never thought you'd . . .'

'I *don't* want to talk about it, right? That's enough, that's it.'

They were silent then, drinking their coffee and waiting.

And while they waited, Mercy thought back. Another replay in her mind. Back to when she was eight years old again, in the holiday camp in hell they'd called a children's home.

Did you tell anyone you were coming up to my office? Mr Deinbeck had asked.

Mercy remembered shaking her head, unable to speak. Deinbeck was the boss, the man in charge of the children's home to which she had been sent, and she knew that she had to do everything she was told. So when, after the first six weeks, he had singled her out for special praise that day, she had felt good about herself in a way that she had never experienced before. When he had whispered to her, asked her if she believed in 'secrets', she had nodded again. Not because she understood what he meant, but because she had been told to be polite. Then, making her feel special again, he had told her that if she came up to his office at half past nine when all the other girls were asleep – and told no one that she was coming – he would have a special surprise for her. Again, she had done as she was told, not even confiding in her one and only, new and special friend: Selina.

No one saw you come?

Mercy had nodded.

You're sure?

Mercy nodded again.

Good, said Deinbeck, as he moved behind her and opened the door again. He looked out into the hall, checking to see that no one was around. Then he closed the door again and locked it, smiling his sickening smile and smoothing the strands of hair over his head as he moved towards her.

Hadn't she known, even then, at eight years old? Hadn't she been told how to react, what to do if someone older wanted to take you somewhere alone? Even her mother had told her about that, and God knew motherly advice was never something she had been strong on. Hadn't she been afraid when she'd climbed out of bed and tiptoed up those stairs? Yes, she remembered all of that. But somehow, she had forgotten it all. After she had been taken away from home and put in this place, all she wanted – all she had ever wanted – was for someone to care about her. And here it was, the most important man in the building, the man who looked after *all* the children, and he thought that she was special and he wanted to look after her. Everything else had been crowded out of her young mind in the desire to be wanted and cared for.

Mercy bit into the paper cup, the steam from the coffee wreathing her face, when she remembered the smell of him as he had lifted her. Two meaty hands pinning her arms to her sides as he carried her to the couch by the window. The smell of aftershave. So strong and pungent, as if he were trying to cover up some other stink on him. The moaning in his throat as he had pinned her down.

Then the horror.

The hands, tearing at her. The suffocating weight and the gibbering demands that she be good. The hand over her mouth when she began to cry. The stabbing, tearing pain of him doing it. And even though it was finished quickly, it seemed that it had gone on for ever. Trembling, he had kept his hand over her mouth as she wept, shuddering, beneath his sweating palm. With his other hand, he had crammed the money into one of her hands. Ten pounds. His face was like stone now. He was going to take away his hand. If she cried out or wept or made a sound, he would have to send for someone. Someone important, who would listen to what he had to say, about how bad she had been. And then she would be taken away and locked in a room by herself with only bread and water. Then her mother would be told that she had died and that she would have to stay in that room for ever. She would never see another soul so long as she lived. But if she was a good girl, and kept quiet, and was nice to him again when he wanted; why, then he would treat her as the most special girl in the home. Money, much more money. And lots of other nice things that she had only ever dreamed about. But it was none of these promises which made her keep this hideous abuse secret. It was outright fear, and the belief that he could do the horrible things he said he could do.

She had endured it for six months.

And then, one day, the police had come to interview her best friend, Selina. Deinbeck, it seemed, had more than one special little friend in the home. Selina had told them everything. Suddenly, Mr Deinbeck was gone; and the police were interviewing all the children. Mercy remembered those interviews well. Right up until the end, Deinbeck's fearful hold over her had prevailed. Terrified, she had denied that anything had happened, even when an internal examination verified that she was not a 'little girl' any more. But the testimony of the other six children, including Selina, and of two previously suspicious and now guilt-ridden social workers, had been more than enough to put Deinbeck behind bars.

Selina and Mercy had become close friends after that. Perhaps the presence of the monstrous Deinbeck in their lives had served to bind them. They had run away from the home together, twice, once spending a month on the streets of London before being retrieved. Then, when they had been able to after all those years, they had gone their separate ways.

Now Deinbeck was out on the streets again.

Mercy looked at Selina hugging the fur coat tight to herself and wondered why they had drifted apart. There had been arguments about what Selina did with her body, but it was more profound than that. She had never been able to understand the feeling she'd experienced then. Was it simply that they both needed to forget what had happened to them, including their fairy-tale journey to the big lights to start a new life?

'We never did . . .' began Mercy.

'Who the fuck is *this*, then?' The voice startled Mercy. Coffee spilled from her cup as she turned to look at the woman who had suddenly emerged from the rain beside Selina. She was a good ten years older than them both, and therefore still young. But her face was etched in sharp lines. Heavy make-up and lipstick couldn't disguise the fact that she was old beyond her years. She wore a red leather jacket and skirt, beaded by the rain, and long black, straight hair that was supposed to convince punters that she was Cher. She sounded as if she had gravel in her voice-box.

'Friend,' said Selina, trying not to look nervous.

'Willie's not said anything to me about new meat, darling. And if he hasn't said it, then that means she's not working our patch. It's as simple as that.'

'I told you, Michele. She's just a friend. She's not working.'

The woman turned her gaze on Mercy. A bead of rain had smudged her mascara.

'Good girls should be at home with Mummy and Daddy.'

'So what's keeping you?' asked Mercy, unblinking.

Michele's eyes glittered coldly; she made a move towards her handbag.

'She's not on the game!' Selina knew what was in the handbag, had seen Michele use it once when a punter got difficult. 'Honest, Michele. She's just here . . . to keep me company.'

Michele snorted in disdain, but her hand relaxed. 'You think I'm stupid. Well, I'll tell you what, darling. I see her going anywhere near a punter, and she won't want to look at her face in the mirror again.'

A car cruised to a standstill in the rain beside them. Inside, the driver had a scarf across his mouth in a weak attempt at disguise. He looked across hopefully and Michele stood for a moment, as if daring Selina or Mercy to do anything about it. Then, slowly, she turned to him, her blank face suddenly friendly.

'Lost?' she asked, moving to the car, bracing a hand on the roof and leaning down to look inside.

Selina turned away, breathing out in relief. 'I knew this was a bad idea. What the hell is she going to say to Willie?'

'Fuck Willie,' said Mercy.

Selina turned to her angrily. 'Don't you screw anything up for me, Mercy. Whether you disapprove or not, I'm doing what I *have* to do. And I didn't bring you down here to get me cut up.'

Michele climbed into the car. It slid off into the rain.

'You're sure he'll come?' asked Mercy at last.

'No, of course I'm not *sure*.'

Mercy finished her coffee, dropping the cup at her feet. Her face was expressionless.

'What are you going to do?' continued Selina. 'I mean, if he does turn up?'

'I just want him to know. That's all.'

'I don't understand. Bloody hell, Mercy, I've *never* been able to understand you.'

'I want him to know what it's been like for me. I want him to know how he made me feel. I want him to feel the same pain.'

'Now wait a minute! I didn't bring you down here to do something stupid.'

'Then why did you telephone me in the first place?'

'Not to *do* anything! You weren't the only one, you know. It happened to me, too.'

There was an uneasy silence then. Selina began to hop from foot to foot.

'What are you going to do?' She demanded at last.

'Nothing. Don't worry, I'm not going to kill him if that's what you think. I just want to see him, face to face. That's all.'

'You're sure? That's all?'

'Sure.'

'I don't believe you. And I'm not staying here, helping you to do it. I made a mistake, Mercy. Maybe it wasn't him after all.' She stepped out into the rain and began to walk away. She stopped and looked back, hoping that Mercy would follow. But Mercy remained in the shop doorway, smiling at her now in a way that Selina did not like one little bit. She remembered that dangerous smile of old.

'I thought you needed the money tonight, Selina. Thought you needed the punters.'

'You're cramping my style. Come on, let's go home. It was a long time ago. Time we put it behind us.'

'Now I know you're not being honest with yourself. Don't you remember the way you felt when you rang me up? I've been feeling like that deep inside ever since I was eight, ever since the bastard took me. That kind of feeling is never going to go away until I look at him face to face, and tell him what he's done.'

Selina shook her head. 'I know what you're like. That's not enough for you.' She turned and began to walk away again. She had made a bad mistake getting in touch with Mercy. Head down, she looked at her shadow moving over the wet roadway, watched it drifting through the blurred neon, praying that she'd hear Mercy's footsteps behind, hurrying to catch her up. Tears were coming now, against her will. She was confused. Maybe some part of her, deep down, really did hope that Mercy would come and do what she herself hadn't the guts to do. Hadn't she felt that familiar, bitter hatred swelling inside when she'd seen Deinbeck cruising past in his car? Hadn't she wished him dead? And wasn't that the reason she had telephoned Mercy? Moaning, she wiped the tears from her face. As she did so she saw Michele climbing out of the car at the end of the street. Surely the quickest blow-job in the history of the profession. Michele slammed the door, her face like a mask, and began walking towards her. Selina slowed. Sorting through a riot of confusion in her mind, she knew that she couldn't leave Mercy in the shop doorway, literally at the mercy of Michele's razor. Thinking quickly, she increased her stride.

'Michele.'

'Wonder what Willie's going to think?'

'Look, you're right. She shouldn't be out here tonight. I'm going to take her back home. Really. She's just a friend with . . . with a few hang-ups. But she's not on the game. Doesn't even like me being on the game. (*That's it, Selina! Play it up!*) She followed me out tonight, been trying to talk me out of it. You know, real do-gooder. Wants me to get a job, and blah-blah. Real fucking airhead she is. We had a fight about it back there. But I'll take her back now, okay?'

'So she's not a working girl?'

'That's right. I mean, no she's not.'

'Not on the game?'

'Definitely not.'

'So what the fuck is she doing right this minute, Selina?'

Selina looked back.

Mercy was leaning down to the window of a car that had stopped beside the shop doorway. As Selina watched, she reached for the door handle.

Selina could not see the driver. But she recognised the make of car. But no, it couldn't be. This surely couldn't be Deinbeck's car. Was God playing a bad joke on her? Having a good laugh at the fact that the moment she had walked away from Mercy, Deinbeck should be cruising past, looking for trade?

'Oh, Jesus Christ, *no!*'

'Oh, Jesus Christ, yes,' said Michele with a voice like grinding stone.

Mercy opened the door and began to climb into the car.

And then Selina broke into a run, back down the street.

'Mercy!'

The car pulled away from the kerb, slewing through the neon and turning in the street.

'Mercy, come back!'

Selina staggered out into the street, one of her stiletto heels broken. She stooped awkwardly to yank it from her foot. Then the other. But it was pointless running any further.

The car had disappeared into the night.

She turned to look back, hopelessly.

Michele was walking slowly towards her, her hand already inside her bag.

'Martin?'

The sound of his wife's voice stabbed a needle of guilt through Martin's heart. The half-empty flour bag dropped from his trembling fingers into the wash-basin, and a cloud of white dust puffed around him, fogging the mirror. He fumbled and pulled the bag out from under the running tap.

'Yes?'

'How much longer are you going to be in there, love?'

'Not much longer.'

'I need to go.'

'Just two minutes.'

He strained to listen, then heard her unsteady footsteps descending the staircase. When the door to the living room closed with a soft bump, he exhaled.

What the hell is happening to me?

He looked in the dusted mirror. There was flour caked around his lips and down over his chin. His fingers were thick with the grey-white mixture, where he'd been holding his hands cupped beneath the running tap and letting the water flow over the flour until it was wet enough to cram the resultant paste into his mouth.

Why am I doing this?

He crumpled the half-empty bag shut and carefully shoved it back into his pocket. Grabbing a facecloth, he wiped the mirror and cursed when it left streaks. Repeatedly wetting and wringing out the cloth, he was finally able to wipe it clean. Quickly then, he cleaned out the wash-basin with his hands, making sure that there were no telltale signs of the flour mixture caked in the plug-hole. Finally, he washed his hands and face. On his way back to the door, he spotted speckles on the carpet around the wash-basin pedestal. Using toilet tissue, he brushed them up and flushed the tissue away down the toilet bowl. Physically, he felt a great deal better. When these mad cravings came over him, he could not ignore them. But he was distressed and confused in a way that he had never previously been in his life. There was no sense to any of this. No matter how hard he tried to ignore the cravings, they would not go away. A practical man, with a practical view of life, he was unable to explain what was happening. And worst of all, he felt guilty. Unable to tell Sheila what was happening, he had resorted to locking himself away like an addict getting his fix. The sense of guilt was crucifying. He had tried to tell her, but was too ashamed.

He paused at the top of the stairs, looking back into the bathroom to make sure that all traces of his secret activity had been covered up. Maybe these cravings would go away eventually? It wasn't as if he was taking anything that could really harm him, was it? Not like drugs or booze. He ran a hand over his face and shuddered. The skin felt cold to the touch again, like a stranger's face. He started down the stairs. Before he reached the bottom, the telephone in the living room rang. He heard Sheila answer it, then saw the look of amazement on her face as he entered.

'No, I don't believe it. After all this time? So the doctors . . . ? No! Pete must be . . . I can't believe it, it's just *wonderful*! I mean, after what happened at the party everyone thought that . . .'

Intrigued, Martin sprawled on the sofa, watching and listening. Sheila's eyes were filling with tears now. She was dabbing at one eye as she spoke. He leaned forward, anxious to find out what was going on.

'That's just the best news I've heard in a long, *long* time.'

'What?' hissed Martin. Something that might have been a fleck of flour flew from between his teeth. Guiltily, he quickly wiped a hand across his mouth. 'What is it?'

'Ben McFarland,' said Sheila, putting her hand over the mouthpiece. 'Pete must be overjoyed. This really is the *best* . . .'

'*What?*'

'Just a minute, Betty. I've got to tell Martin.' When she looked back at him again, a tear brimmed and spilled down her cheek. 'Ben McFarland, Martin. He can walk. Happened last night. Pete had put him to bed, heard him calling, and when he went into his room, there he was. *Standing*. This morning, he's been walking. Doctors just can't believe the illness is in remission.' She turned back to the telephone.

Martin sat back on the sofa, Sheila's conversation now fading. He felt strange, somehow only able to think back to the party. Something had happened back then. He remembered Ben's eyes rolling up into his head, remembered how his arms had flailed, the panic when everyone thought the boy was having a stroke. Even the ambulance crew had looked grim when they finally arrived to take Ben and his father away. Within a couple of days, after tests, Ben had been allowed home again, apparently none the worse for what had happened, and their understanding from Pete had been that the doctors could find no sign that he'd had a seizure of any kind. Could the fit have been a prelude to him suddenly improving? Maybe some kind of chemical change, some kind of . . .

'No,' he said aloud, but Sheila was too preoccupied with her telephone call to hear him. 'Ben's going to get better. It'll be like he was never ill.'

He knew it with a certainty that made his head swim. He sat forward again, crushing his palms against his forehead. His hands were trembling, and he remembered how they had trembled when that *something* had transferred itself from him into Ben. He remembered the feeling deep down inside. The feeling that he *had* to touch Ben, *had* to transmit whatever was inside him, directly into the boy, to make him . . . make him . . .

'I made him better.'

Martin crushed his hands together, wringing them before his face to control the trembling.

'Something came out of me. Came out of my hands. And made him better.'

When Sheila tearfully and joyfully hung up the telephone, she turned back to give him more details of the miracle.

'Martin?'

He was no longer sitting on the sofa.

'Martin, where are you?'

Martin was long gone, out on to the street and away.

He needed time to think.

There were too many complicated images flashing around inside his head. Every time he tried to think sensibly about what was happening, things would blur and fly away. Nothing that had happened to him since the motorway smash made any kind of sense. There were times when he sincerely believed that he had dreamed everything that had happened. Even the girl, Mercy. He had once questioned Sheila about that day in the hospital, wanting to be sure that she had also seen the girl, could confirm that Mercy was real. The way Sheila had looked at him then had been the reason that he was keeping everything else to himself. That look of doubt was too much for him to handle. She was relying on him to be strong, relying on him to look after her. What would she think if she knew that he was losing his mind, was cramming sugar and flour and God knew what else into himself every time her back was turned?

The heat-wave showed no sign of abating, and when Martin turned on to the main street from their own road there was almost a carnival atmosphere. Women in short, light dresses; kids on roller-skates; men in short-sleeve shirts as they went about their business. Normally the sight of people feeling good just because the weather was fine would have made him feel even better. But today it made him feel worse. He felt apart from everyone he passed on the street, as if they all belonged to some other world. The crash had changed everything, had made him different in ways he could barely understand.

Maybe it's gone now, he thought at last, as he moved on with his head down. *Yeah. Maybe it's burned itself out or something. It was in me. And then when I touched Ben, it came out through my fingers and went into him. That's it. I've passed it on . . .*

He thought the words, but remained unconvinced. There was something there, deep inside. So deep that he could barely sense it. But it was there all right. Hidden and waiting. Sometimes, in his sleep, he felt sure that he had almost touched that inner place and found out just what it was, and what it really wanted. He felt sure that he had been having *conversations* with it while he slept, even though he could remember nothing about what had been said the following morning.

Schizo. That's what it is. I've read about it. Ordinary people one minute. Then a bang on the head or something and WHAM! That's it. Next thing you know, you've got two people trying to live inside your head. Well, listen to me, whoever or whatever you are. There's only room for me in my head. So get used to the bloody idea, 'cause you're moving OUT!

This was something he knew. Something he had tried before when things became tough. You just got tougher, right back at whatever it was that was standing in your way. He nodded as he walked on through the crowds. His assurance lasted for fifty yards before he realised the hopelessness of what he was doing. He was getting angry with *himself*, getting angry with imaginary things. You couldn't fight unreal things that way. He looked up. Just ahead was a butcher's shop, the place where Sheila bought most of their meat, since the man there gave a square deal. But Martin's attention was focused on the girl who had been left outside the door while her mother went inside to make her purchases. The sight of her made Martin stop in his tracks. For a moment, he considered crossing the road to avoid her.

The girl was in a wheelchair.

She was younger than Ben, but obviously disabled to a much greater degree. Her head was thrown back, her eyes unfocused.

I will NOT cross the road!

He marched on ahead, refusing to look down when he passed the wheelchair.

Coincidence. That business at the party. All right, I know strange things are happening to me. But that doesn't mean to say that any of it has anything to do with Ben getting better. That's just me putting everything together wrong. Things like this don't happen. Not to someone like me. So, let's just stop thinking about it and . . .

He paused then, suddenly overwhelmed by a memory that had emerged from nowhere. With the memory came a sudden stabbing cramp of pain in his stomach. He saw himself standing in the waiting area in Casualty. He had just been on the telephone to Sheila, telling her that everything was okay. He was buying himself a coffee from the machine, but now that same cramp of pain in his gut was making him dizzy, reminding him of the way he had felt just before that light . . .

Why do I keep forgetting about that light?

. . . had exploded into the cabin and sent them spinning, as the screaming . . .

And why, oh God, why, do I keep forgetting about that terrible, terrible screaming? It's as if everything that happened to me keeps drifting in and out of my mind. Sometimes I remember, then I forget. But how could I forget that screaming . . .

. . . filled the cab. Martin was feeling dizzy again, just as he had in the hospital. He moved to a nearby wall, turned and braced his back against it. It felt warm. But it couldn't melt the cold knot that had suddenly developed inside him. The knot of pain was something like fear, but as it hardened and tightened, he realised that it felt just the way it'd felt in the hospital waiting area.

'Something coming . . .'

Again, something was hurtling out of the darkness, from God knew which direction, straight for him. Something that had to do with what had caused the motorway crash. And then Martin's fragmented memory began to come together, his amnesia beginning to clear. He saw . . .

A man, yelling and fighting with nurses.

Another man, lying on the floor beneath them, struggling to rise.

A woman staggering from a curtained cubicle; a young man following her, grabbing for her. More yelling from another cubicle.

And then Mercy, suddenly bursting through those double doors in panic. She looks around wildly, in terror. She sees Martin and, even from this distance, he can see how relieved she is to have found him. She starts forward.

And then something explodes into the waiting area. Something that feels and sounds like a hurricane, as it blasts papers and pamphlets into the air in a great stormcloud of torn paper.

And then something else . . . something else is coming . . . something . . .

'Excuse me, are you all right?'

Martin shuddered back into consciousness again. He was still standing with his back to the wall. An elderly lady with a shopping trolley was standing beside him, head craned up to look at him in concern.

'Yes . . . yes . . . I'm fine. Thanks.'

'Are you sure?'

'It's . . . it's the heat, I think. I just needed a rest.'

'I've got a fizzy drink in my trolley if you need one.'

Martin forced a smile. 'No thanks, darling. You're very kind. But I'm all right.'

'As long as you're sure,' smiled the woman, and she moved off.

Martin fumbled for the handkerchief in his pocket, found it and wiped his face. His shirt was soaked with sweat; he could feel the outlines of the bricks on his back. Breathing out heavily, he pushed himself away from the wall and began to walk back the way he had come.

Something had happened in the hospital. Something that no one had told him about. And he knew that he only had part of his memory back. Mercy had been there. Had it involved her, too? Maybe she could tell him what happened next? But why the hell hadn't she said anything when they met in the hospital car park for the last time?

Perhaps because nothing DID happen? Maybe it's all in my crazy mixed-up mind.

Martin dismissed the thought. It wouldn't do any good to wonder about what Mercy might or might not have seen. He had given her their address in case she ever needed anything, but she hadn't told them where she was headed. So there was no way he could get in touch with her to discuss it all.

The girl in the wheelchair was still parked outside the butcher's shop.

Again, that spasm inside Martin. Angrily, he tried to beat it down as he walked towards her. There were people coming the other way, blocking the pavement. Martin was forced to stand just behind the chair while a family of four passed by. Patiently, he waited but did not look down.

And then the girl made a noise.

It was only a small sound; an exhalation of air, perhaps.

But it was enough to make Martin look down into the girl's upturned face. The child's hair was blonde, the eyes a beautiful blue. The kind of blue that Sheila had once described as periwinkle blue, although he wasn't sure whether a periwinkle was a flower or a jewel. Whatever, the word seemed to suit the kid's eyes. They were beautiful, but not focused on him. Rather, they were focused on the sky, as if waiting for someone or something to catapult her out of the chair and into a place where she could fly as free as a bird. The way was clear now. Martin could pass.

Except that he could not pass.

That *feeling* was in him now. The tightness in his stomach that was close to fear, but was not fear. Just the certain knowledge that something was hurtling towards him, just as it had on the motorway, just as it had in the hospital waiting room – just as it was hurtling down on him now. Something about the girl's eyes was crystallising and focusing that feeling, and the more he stared down into her eyes, the clearer everything was becoming. Yes, something had come into him on the motorway, and again in the hospital. But he had been wrong to think that it was bearing down on him again from some outside direction. It was firmly rooted, deep inside him; whatever it was. And he was bringing it *out* from inside. Whatever this thing might be, it was no longer controlling him. He could control *it*. And as he stood and stared down at the girl, he was summoning it, making it swell and build inside his fingertips until they seemed to fizz with power. The girl made a noise again. Could she see him? Was she trying to communicate?

'I have to know,' Martin said quietly.

Slowly, he moved around until he was facing the wheelchair. The girl's head was still turned to the sky. He looked back into the butcher's shop. The girl's mother was being served, and could not see him from where she stood. Martin knelt down, just as he had knelt in front of Ben.

The feeling inside him wanted to come out. But Martin knew that he could control it. It would come when he wanted it to come. Leaning forward, still on his haunches, he stroked the girls's cheek. There was a sharp snap where his fingertips connected, just like a static electricity shock from walking on a brand-new carpet. The girl juddered once, and for a moment it seemed that nothing was going to happen. Martin stood back, still feeling the tingling in his fingertips. Quickly, he looked

around. No one had seen him touch the girl. He looked back
to see that she seemed not to be moving at all.

Oh my God . . .

He couldn't see her breathing.

He clasped his hands together. In that moment, he felt the
power dissipating, fading back *into* him. It seemed to have
emanated, he realised, from just beneath his breastbone; and
the power was fading and retreating to that same inner point.
Sweat suddenly broke out on his brow. Wiping his face, he
backed off until he reached the kerb. A horn blared as a
passing driver thought that he was going to step backwards
into the road. Startled, Martin whirled, and then looked back
at the girl again. She was completely still.

Oh, sweet Jesus, what have I done?

And then the glass door of the shop juddered open, and the
girl's mother emerged with a bag of shopping.

Filled with horror, Martin watched the woman hang the
plastic carrier bags over the handles of the wheelchair and
then look down to kick off the brake so that they could
continue on their way. Should he say something? Should
he step forward? He tried, but could not move. What the
hell could he say? Excuse me, I think I've just killed your
daughter? His heart was hammering, his throat dry.

The woman looked down at her daughter.

Fear stabbed like ice in the secret place beneath Martin's
breastbone.

The woman looked troubled, not understanding what she
was seeing. Eyes wide in alarm, she moved quickly around
to the front of the wheelchair, her back to Martin.

'Bronya! Bronya, love, are you all right? Oh Christ, are you
all right . . .'

*Oh dear God in heaven, what have I done? WHAT HAVE
I DONE?*

And then the girl looked down from the sky with a slow and
gracious movement. Her muscle co-ordination was smooth and
controlled. Looking directly at her mother with eyes that were
completely focused for the first time in eight years, she said:
'Hello, Mum.'

And smiled, as if she had just returned from a long journey. The smile transferred to her hands, as she brought them up before her face. She laughed when she saw them, as if having these things on the ends of her arms was somehow the most marvellous thing in the world.

Martin heard the mother gasp. A sobbing intake of disbelief. For a moment, it looked as if she might fall backwards, and the prospect broke Martin out of his immobility. Quickly, he moved forward and took her arm. The woman seemed not to notice, her attention still riveted on her daughter's smiling face.

'Can you see?' the woman asked him, without turning to acknowledge his presence. 'Can you see what I can see? Please God, tell me that I'm not dreaming. Not after all we've been through. God wouldn't play a trick like that, would he, mister? He wouldn't be so unkind.'

'No,' said Martin, and his voice was choked with emotion, tears suddenly streaming down his cheeks. 'I don't think he would play a trick like that.'

A crowd was beginning to gather, wondering just what was going on. Martin became aware of people around him. Gently letting the woman's arm go, he slowly moved backwards, watching as the mother sobbed again and threw herself into the girl's lap. He saw the girl stroking her mother's hair, just before the surrounding crowd blotted them from sight. Quickly now, he turned.

Elation flooded him like a drug.

Like a joyous child, he began to run back home down the crowded street.

Ellis Burwell's car slid into the Civic Hall car park.

It was fifteen minutes after eleven at night, and his head-lights revealed that there were only three other vehicles in the space for 150. During the day, only council officials were allowed the use of it, but at night the spaces were available to the general public. However, the general public had finally grown weary of having their cars stolen or broken into, and so the place was little used in the evening. The setting seemed to appeal to Klark; he had used it for meetings with Ellis three times in as many months. Burwell wondered whether he had chosen the last meeting at the motorway motel to cause maximum inconvenience.

Ellis did as he had been instructed. He drove over to the far side of the parking area, to where shrubs and trees hid him on two sides. Behind him, the Civic Hall itself; in front, a railway embankment. No one to see their secret meeting. He parked the car and switched off the engine. His window was down. Even at night, it was unbearably hot. He sat in the darkness for a long while, the only faint spot of light coming from the cigarette between his lips.

And he remembered.

She'd said that her name was Dawn, but he guessed that it was one of many professional names. What the hell did a name matter, anyway? She was just what he was looking for this time. In the past, it had been like a lottery for him. First of all, drawing his ticket from a shop window, or the inside of a telephone box. Then making the call, and wondering whether the disguised description might, after all, live up to his expectations. More often than not, he was disappointed. But it was needs must in his case, and the spilling of his seed was the most important thing. His winning ticket had come from another whore. After their business had been transacted, he'd asked if she knew any black girls on the game. He'd never had a black woman before. The girl, who had stoically put up with his verbal and physical abuse, had looked at him for a long time as she put her skirt back on again. And then she'd nodded, watching while he counted out the notes on the bedside table. At the time, her expression had seemed curious to him. Now he realised what had been going on in her mind. Yes, she knew of someone. Her name was Dawn, and she worked out of a flat on Etal Street. He'd asked if she had a card, and the bitch had laughed in his face, asking him if he thought this was a tax-deductible business.

On the following day, his birthday, Burwell had found the flat. A ground-floor apartment that looked on first approach as

if it might be derelict. But despite the mounds of garbage and
street detritus lying around the entrance, this was the place.
Sometimes the tattiest of wrappers contained the best birthday
presents. Sure enough, she was waiting for him, gift-wrapped.
Her colleague must have told her to expect him.

She was black, and very beautiful. And her sliding scale of
charges was very reasonable.

Burwell drew on his cigarette. He had begun to tremble.
He still couldn't understand what had happened to him, what
kind of impulse had overcome him. Even now, he could
remember only brief snatches of what had happened next.
In his mind, he could see what looked like photographic stills
of it all, but couldn't remember the living, breathing, moving
actuality of it.

They were doing it. Straight. Missionary-style. Nothing
exotic.

And then he had told her that he wanted to sodomise her.
He remembered using the word, because it had a good sound.
But she'd refused. It wasn't on the list of goodies for sale.

Somehow, his hands were around her throat. His excitement
and his passion suddenly focusing into blazing anger. But the
anger was somehow controlled and burning with a ferocity
that made what he was doing feel even better. No matter how
much she squirmed and thrashed beneath him, he tightened
his grip. His climax was coming, and if he didn't hang on to
her he would lose the greatest experience of his life. Tighter
and harder. Now the pleasure surging and swelling, like a
crimson tide.

And when he'd finished, and had rolled away from her, she
was lying still and staring at the ceiling.

That's when Klark had walked into the room, and Burwell
thought he must be having a dream. The girl couldn't possibly
be dead, because then this stranger wouldn't just be walking
into the room as he was doing, waggling a finger and smiling
as if he were mildly chastising a naughty boy. He had walked
over to the girl, leaned over to look into her eyes, and then
had tut-tutted. When he told Burwell that he should put his
trousers back on again, he had done exactly as he was told.

And that's when the nightmare had begun.

Klark had been on the other side of the apartment wall, with his video camera rigged up so that the lens was pointing through a hole in the ragged wallpaper. The entire thing had been recorded. Clearly, this had been a regular operation, a nice little sideline in blackmailing to supplement the other activity. Ever one for an eye for a killing, Klark had allowed everything to proceed.

And Burwell had been paying Klark for it ever since.

He shuddered. Despite the warmth of the night, a deep chill had settled on him. He leaned forward and stubbed out his cigarette.

'You're always on time,' said a voice from the darkness.

The sound was supposed to startle him. Klark loved dramatic entrances. As Burwell stared ahead, a figure emerged from the shrubs directly ahead. It moved to the front of the car, hitched up a leg and sat on the hood. Burwell could see no details, only the silhouette; but he knew from the voice and posture that it could only be Klark.

'Did you bring it?' Klark asked, just like an actor playing a blackmailer in a movie.

'Some of it.'

'What the fuck do you mean, *some* of it?'

'I mean I couldn't get all the money you wanted.'

The silhouette stood up angrily, and slammed the flat of its hand on the hood.

'I told you I wanted five hundred tonight! Not tomorrow, or the next day! *Tonight!*'

'The auditor's coming in next week. I've only just managed to cover my tracks. If I start to access the system again, they're bound to find out about me and . . .'

'Just how you get the money doesn't matter to me, Burwell. You're misunderstanding our relationship again.'

God, oh God, how easy it would be to just switch on, rev the engine and drive straight into him. Ram him back through those trees and keep on going. Hear him fall beneath the wheels, listen to him being chewed up underneath me while I drive back and forth all over the bastard.

'When I need the money,' continued Klark, 'I ring you on the telephone and you just *bring* it to me. Understand?'

'I just couldn't get it. It was too short notice. I need some more time.'

'How much have you got, you arsehole?'

'Two hundred.'

'*Two* hundred! You shit. What *are* you, Burwell?'

'I'm a shit.'

'Let me see it. Get out of the fucking car and put it on the fucking hood.'

Burwell picked up the carrier bag from the passenger seat next to him and slowly climbed out of the car. Leaning on the open door, he swung the carrier over and dumped it on the hood.

'Plastic carrier bag from the supermarket? Not only a shit, Burwell, but a cheap shit. What about the fancy briefcases you brought all the other money in?'

'You kept them all, wouldn't give me them back. Now I can't afford any more.'

Klark laughed as he grabbed the carrier bag. 'Cheap shit. What are you, Burwell?'

'A cheap shit.'

Klark rummaged in the bag. 'Two hundred, you say?'

Burwell nodded, the movement unseen in the darkness.

'Well, I'll take you on your word. Feels like two hundred, and smells like two hundred. But if I get where I'm going tonight and find that it's just one little itty-bitty penny short, you're going to suffer for it, my friend.'

'It's got to stop. I can't get any more . . .'

The silhouette froze. This time there was no cruel humour in Klark's voice, just a cold and deadly menace.

'You'll get the money when I need it, Burwell. Our *arrangement* will continue the way it's always been since that night you enjoyed yourself so much with poor little Dawn. So far, you've done as you're told. And since this is the first time that you've let me down, I'm going to be kind-hearted and give you another chance. A *last* chance, Burwell. I want the other three hundred in two days.'

'But I *can't* . . .'

'Two *days*, Ellis! Same time, same place, right here. And I don't care if it's in a briefcase or a plastic carrier bag or wrapped up in last night's newspapers – you'll get it and you'll bring it to me. Otherwise, the video goes to the police. Do you understand, Ellis?'

'I . . .'

'Do you *understand*, Ellis?'

'I understand.'

'Good. Now fuck off. And mind what I've said.'

Ellis stood by his open door for a long time after the silhouette had vanished into the darkness. Finally, he climbed back into his car.

Then he began to punch the steering wheel until his knuckles were raw and bloodied, and tears of frustration flowed down his face.

Chris O'Dowd was worried about his brother.

It was true that before now he hadn't seen Roger for over four years, and then it had been on a couple of family occasions following the death of their mother in the car smash. There had been a lot of water under the bridge since that time, and people could change a lot in the interim. They had spoken on the telephone, of course, and it had seemed to Chris that Roger was just the same younger brother he had always known. The sudden decision to return to college and take his arts degree after packing shelves in a supermarket for all that time could have seemed, in retrospect, an unusually out-of-character thing for him to have done. But at the time, Chris had applauded his courage, and had been doubly delighted when Roger had passed his degree course. But was that sudden and ultimately successful change of career direction an indicator of something altogether more serious? A sign, perhaps, that there were other, hidden problems?

Roger's behaviour was not only strange, it was downright bloody bizarre.

For three weeks now, he had been taking the train into the city and trudging the streets, calling in on the advertising

agencies who had deigned to give him an interview. Chris
had to admit he had done his homework on which agencies
to approach and which individuals would be the best to target,
given his skills in finished artwork. Right from the start, he had
acknowledged Chris's brotherly advice that it wasn't going to
be easy, and that he might get nothing out of his initiative.
He had clearly thought through all the potential difficulties.
And as the days passed, and he returned to the apartment
with nothing to show for his travails but worn shoe leather,
he had grown quieter, more withdrawn. At first Chris thought
that it was the obvious reason: his enthusiasm and optimism
were waning with each rejection. But there seemed to be more
to it than that. He was sitting in front of the television,
turning down his offers to go out. Chris had even found
himself over-compensating for Roger's withdrawal. He had
told Phyllida all about him, of course. About the zest, the
practical jokes when they were younger, all the details of their
boyhood spent together. But none of it seemed to apply to the
young man who had turned up on his doorstep.

There was the accident, of course. Chris had made allow-
ances for this; had even tried to engage Roger in conversation
about it. There was nothing like a sudden brush with death
to make someone aware of their own mortality, and perhaps
it was this that had made him suddenly so withdrawn. But
Roger could not, or would not, open up. Even so, Chris could
give him the benefit of the doubt and assume that the crash
was the cause of his strange behaviour – if it were not for
the other things that Roger was up to when there was no one
around.

First, it had been the sugar bags.

Fair enough, his brother had a sweet tooth. But he seemed to
be going through a bag of the bloody stuff in a day. And Chris
was sure that he was buying more packets, and not telling him
about it. He had found several empty bags in the garbage. He
must be eating it by the handful. Then, other things had started
to go missing from the kitchen cupboards – fruit conserves,
spices, paprika. Now the same thing was beginning to happen
with bags of flour.

But the most worrying thing of all was what had happened the day before yesterday.

Chris had walked into the kitchen, engrossed in a paperback book and wanting to make himself a coffee. He was wearing a ridiculous pair of dinosaur slippers which Phyllida had brought him back from one of her flights abroad, so perhaps that's why Roger hadn't heard him come in. And Chris had supposed that Roger was in his room, so both of them got a shock. But Chris still couldn't believe that Roger was doing what he thought he was doing.

He was standing at the kitchen window. There was a unit there, just beneath the window ledge, containing all the household cleaning materials. And Roger was looking out of that window, with his back to Chris. His head was back as he held something up to his mouth. He was drinking, and just as Chris had suddenly been startled by the unexpected sight of someone else in the kitchen, so Roger had also been startled. Choking and gagging, he had whirled round, keeping the bottle of whatever it was firmly hidden behind his back.

Roger, a secret boozer? Well, that didn't disturb Chris too much. They had put away quite a bit between them since his arrival, and if he needed topping up occasionally, who was he to say no? Chris had mumbled his apologies and left. And in the moment of turning away, he thought he had seen a flash of the label on the bottle which Roger was trying to hide, reflected in the window behind him.

But it surely *couldn't* be a bottle of household disinfectant? It *must* be a vodka label, or another liquor bottle label that he hadn't seen before.

Later that day, when Roger had left to do an afternoon session of trudging the streets of the big city, Chris had first examined all the bottles on the drinks tray. None of them bore a label similar to the label he thought he'd seen. For a long while, he refused to look in the cupboard beneath the window. Finally, exasperated and worried, he had given in. And as soon as he opened the door, he saw the label.

And, just as he had suspected – even though he had been consciously trying to tell himself that he must be wrong – it was from a bottle of disinfectant that he used to clean the bath. For a moment, he remained there on his haunches, looking at the bottle and trying to make sense of what was happening. Why should Roger go to all the trouble of emptying out a disinfectant bottle, and then filling it with booze so that he could have a sly slurp when no one was looking? There were bottles of the stuff on the tray in here; he could have a drink any time he felt like it, morning, noon or night. Chris had shaken his head. What if the bottle wasn't washed out properly? What if there were traces of the cleaning fluid in there? Roger could burn his guts out. And what if Chris should suddenly decide to clean the bath before Roger had a chance to replace it? Chris knew nothing about out-and-out alcoholism, other than what he had gleaned from the occasional newspaper report or television programme; but was the secrecy part of the compulsion, part of the buzz? He took the bottle out and jiggled it. There was still liquid in there. Screwing off the top, he sniffed.

And recoiled.

No, that couldn't be right.

He sniffed again. Then he stood, made for the sink and poured some of the fluid out. He must be right. Christ, Roger *hadn't* cleaned out the bottle properly. He dipped one finger into the sink and brought it to his tongue. Gagging, he spat out, quickly turning on the tap and splashing a handful of water into his mouth. Fumbling for a glass tumbler on the draining board, he filled it and then rinsed, hawking and spitting until he had got rid of the taste.

There was no alcohol in that bottle at all. It was pure disinfectant.

But that made no sense whatever.

Chris had tried to put it out of his mind. He must have been wrong. He hadn't seen the label properly after all. People just didn't drink neat disinfectant. It would kill them. No, it had been something else; perhaps Roger had taken the bottle out with him that afternoon, and Chris had only assumed that he'd heard the cupboard door close when he'd left Roger in the kitchen.

He struggled with his inner conflict. Something was wrong with Roger, but he could not understand it; could not get close enough to find out. His indirect approaches weren't working and he felt uncomfortable about a direct interrogation. In a way, he knew that moving away from home after their mother's death had been an attempt to overcome his grief, to get on with his life and make his way in the world, which he had successfully accomplished. But he also felt a sense of guilt about having walked away from his brother. They were both grown men, and not joined at the hip. It was up to both of them to make their way. And he was not his brother's keeper. But Roger's arrival had somehow focused his memory of those times. His grief had been made even more palpable, not dimmed by the years, when it seemed that history might have been repeating itself in a cruel way. Not only had he lost his mother to a car smash, but the baby brother he had left behind had also almost lost his life in the same way. The prospect had shorn away the years and shaken him badly. Confused, Chris was unsure how to handle his brother now.

Maybe there was a way ... maybe ...

When the front door banged against the wall, Sheila almost dropped the plate she was drying.

'Martin? Is that you?'

'Yes. Where are you?'

'In the kitchen. What's wrong?' Sheila turned to look for him, not liking the sound of his voice. He sounded distressed, the words coming out with great effort.

When Martin blundered into the kitchen, she did drop the plate. He looked terrible. He was gasping for breath as he leaned in the doorway. His face was flushed, his hair awry. And any thought she'd had about asking where the heck he had suddenly disappeared to after the telephone call was gone. The shattering of the plate seemed to break Martin out of something too. Suddenly he realised how he must look to her.

'No, Sheila. Don't worry. Everything's all right. Everything's *better* than all right.' He was trying to smile, but his eyes still seemed wild.

'You're frightening me, Martin. For God's sake, what's *happened?*'

'Sit down . . . here, sit down.'

Martin stumbled across the kitchen and gently took her arm. He could feel that she was trembling; she could feel how hot he was. Guiding her to a chair by the kitchen table, he hurriedly dragged another over and sat so that they were face to face. Sheila groaned. She had sat down too heavily, the pain grinding in her spine. Her look of agony spurred Martin on.

'If you've ever trusted me before, love, trust me now. Take my hands . . .'

'Martin, you *have* to tell me . . .'

'Take my hands, Sheila.'

She took them, firmly convinced that he was about to confess something to her. Something terrible. The prospect made her trembling worse. Even now, she could see that he was preparing himself to tell her the painful truth. He had closed his eyes, and was concentrating hard, as if looking for the right words. His jawline was taut; she saw a muscle twitch in his cheek. And God, his hands were *so* warm. They seemed to be getting warmer as he sat there. Other wild fancies were flying through her mind as she looked at his face. He was sweating; she could see beads of it on his forehead and running down his neck. Had he been running from someone? Had he done something bad? Was he in trouble? She opened her mouth to speak again, and it seemed that Martin had sensed it. He jerked her hands, a gesture that meant she was to remain silent. She closed her mouth again, feeling tears beginning to well. And there was pain in her hands now, where he was holding her. No . . . not pain, exactly. It had begun like the old pains; pins and needles at first, which then became intense and focused, like a bad toothache in the bones. But this sensation was different. Now it seemed that her hands were tingling. Now they felt too hot . . . or was it too cold?

'I'm going to make you better,' said Martin, eyes still closed in concentration. 'I know I can focus what I've got. I *know* I can. And I'm going to take away what's in you, Sheila. I'm going to make you well.'

She had heard him speak like this before, when the pain became too much to bear. But even the experts had told them there was nothing to be done. She swallowed her emotion and began to tell him that just having his love would be enough to help her through . . .

And then something happened in her hands.

Something *snapped!* and Sheila felt herself pushed back hard in the kitchen chair. So hard that it rocked on two legs and almost went over backwards. Martin quickly lunged forward and grabbed her again to prevent her from falling. Sheila was dazed. She looked quickly at Martin and found that she couldn't focus properly. What had happened? Had he *hit* her? No, he had been holding on to her hands with both of his when she had been slammed back like that.

'What . . . ?' Then her vision cleared, and she saw Martin leaning forward, his face only inches from her own. He was staring at her hard, as if waiting for her to say or do something. His hands were sweating, and it seemed that the tingling sensation in her own hands had disappeared. 'I don't understand, Martin. What did you do? What happened . . . ?'

And then his face crumpled as the well of emotion inside suddenly burst through. He dropped his head into her lap, still holding her hands. He was sobbing now, and she pulled her hands free to stroke his head. She was still stunned, still anxious about what was going on. She had never known Martin weep like this before. Surely, something must be terribly, *terribly* wrong.

She pulled his head up again to look into his eyes.

And saw that Martin was weeping tears of joy.

'Martin, please . . .'

'You're well, Sheila. I've made you well again.'

She was holding his face with both hands. And something felt different about the way she was holding him. There was no feeling of cramp in her fingers. And no sickening ache in the base of her spine. No, that couldn't be right. She *always* had that pain. She shifted in her seat, knowing that it would send a spear of pain like broken glass up her left side. But there was no pain, not even any hint of discomfort.

She twisted her neck.

No spasms. No broken glass under the skin.

Martin saw her eyes widen, and then clasped her hands tight to the sides of his face.

'It's true, Sheila. It's not a dream. It's *true* . . .'

It sat in the darkness, hunched beneath the sagging branches of a willow tree.

A restless wind kept the branches in a constant, sweeping motion, the tips so low that they almost touched the ground. Through the wavering, ragged screen, it could sometimes see the cemetery beyond. The clouds were moving fast through the night sky; moonlight came and went swiftly, illuminating the gravestones.

It had been drawn to this place somehow. Its first sight of the church steeple and then the gravestones on the other side of the rough stone wall had seemed to ease its suffering. Something about this place, whatever it might be, seemed to offer comfort. It offered a promise.

A promise of coming home.

The thing had clambered over the stone wall, dislodging part of it as it tumbled over. It had rolled into the gully on the other side, clambering hand over hand until it found itself underneath the branches of this tree. And it had remained there for hours, looking through the branches and not understanding what it was, or why it was here.

Its hands were clamped to its face. Its efforts had dislodged the mask, and the skin kept sliding away from beneath the ears. Keeping its hands there, it had begun to croon: 'I am me . . . and no one else . . . I am ME . . . and NO ONE ELSE . . .'

There were fragments of memory: a jigsaw that it struggled to put together in what was left of its mind.

Travelling through the night. Somewhere important that it had to go, had to be. Lights in the road. Comfortable lights . . . '. . . this is the jungle, and the only law is the law of the jungle . . .'

And then, other lights.

Dead ahead.

And then screaming; a terrible, terrible screaming — as something smashed into it. Something smashed right into it.

The thing began to scream then, clutching its head and trying to wrench away the agonising memories. And as its hands left its face, the mask of skin slid from the shattered visage beneath. The thing groped for it, moaning and sobbing. But it had fallen somewhere in the darkness. Like an animal, it began to claw at the grass and the dirt beneath it.

'I am me, me, ME!'

Its claw-hands found the clammy mass. Moaning, it crammed it back into place, trying to smooth the gory, mud-splattered mess back into place. But now it was disintegrating beneath its claw-fingers. And the more frenzied its attempts, the more torn and ragged the mask was becoming.

'Oh no, no, no, no . . .'

It would no longer stick. The mask of flesh came apart in its claws, sliding and tearing and falling apart to the grass beneath it. Moaning, the thing put its claws to the ruins of its own face and began to weep.

'Another me,' it said at last. 'I have to find another me.'

Still weeping, it staggered off through the gravestones and into the night.

'That's forty-three seventy-one,' said the blank-faced girl at the check-out counter.

Jane took out her purse, aware of the fact that there were four more people in the supermarket queue behind her, all impatient to be getting on. Casting anxious looks back at the woman directly behind her, she began to take the notes out of her purse. Tom hadn't allowed her a credit card. She wasn't capable, so he gave her money when and if it was needed. Afterwards, she had to present him with a list, accounting for every penny, and another list, showing the alternate brands on sale and their comparative price. Just to make sure that she wasn't wasting their money. Jane began to count the notes out on to the plastic shelf while the girl on the other side chewed gum and looked out into space.

'Thirty-nine . . .'

She began to count out the loose change. There should be enough.

'Forty . . .'

And now she realised that there was only small change left. She didn't have enough.

'Oh . . . oh dear . . . I don't think . . .'

The girl turned her blank stare on Jane.

Jane began to fumble in her coat pocket, even though she knew there was no money in there. Her colour had begun to rise.

'I don't think I've got . . .'

The woman next to her turned away impatiently and tutted, bringing her wristwatch up to her face in an extravagant gesture of annoyance.

'. . . got enough.'

'Haven't you,' said the girl. It was a statement rather than a question. 'Then some of it'll have to be put back, won't it?'

'Yes . . .' stammered Jane. 'I'm sorry. Yes, I'll put some of it back.'

'Just tell me what you don't want, and leave it here.'

'No, I'll take it back where it came from. It's only right . . .'

'So what don't you want?'

Jane pulled out a tin of peeled tomatoes, a bag of brown granary mini-loaves, two bags of flour (which she then put back; she *had* to have those), another bag of dried pasta.

'How much is that?' She could not control the waver in her voice.

'Let's see . . . you need to get rid of another one-fifty's worth.'

The woman behind Jane said: 'Oh, for *God's* sake!' and Jane flushed dark red. The others in the queue were grumbling now; a woman with two kids and a trolley full of shopping angrily jerked the trolley away and headed for another queue.

With trembling fingers, Jane took out two cartons of yoghurt and a packet of rubber washing-up gloves.

'Right,' said the girl, taking the cash from the counter and shoving some loose change back at Jane. 'That's it.'

Jane began to pick up the groceries she had set aside.

'What you doing?' asked the blank-faced girl.

'I'm going to put them back.'

'Just leave'em. Someone else'll take care of it.'

'No, I did wrong. I'll put them back.'

'Do you *mind*?' asked the stern-faced woman. 'We're all in a hurry. She said someone will take care of it. Why don't you just put all that stuff in the carrier bags, make room for someone else?'

Anger began to rise beneath the shame. Head down, Jane pushed past the woman and down the queue, her eyes averted from the gaze of the others and with her arms full of groceries.

'You're holding everyone *up*!' snapped the woman.

'Oh, for Christ's sake,' said the girl, turning her blank gaze on the others and holding up her hands in a 'What can I do?' gesture. 'I've keyed in the entry wrong. I'll have to get the supervisor to sort it out.'

'Look, can't you do me next?' asked the stern woman.

'I told you. What with all the fuss and that silly bitch, I've keyed in the register wrong. You'll have to wait.' The check-out girl pressed the 'assistance' switch and a light began to flash on and off above her head.

'Oh, *really!*'

Jane hurried down the supermarket aisle. First the granary loaves, back on the shelf they'd come from. At the end of the aisle, she turned and headed for Dairy Products. Two yoghurts down; only the pasta, the tomatoes and the rubber gloves to go. On her way to the pasta shelf, she slipped and almost fell. Head down, not wanting anyone else to see the colour of her face, she felt the two conflicting emotions fighting inside. Shame and anger; anger and shame. She headed down the next aisle, found the pasta and slapped her packet down hard. She doubled back, crossed another aisle and found the tinned products, where she deposited the peeled tomatoes. But she remembered that the Household Cleaners and Hygiene section was on the other side of the store. Quickly, she turned at the bottom of the aisle and headed back towards the queue she had come from. She did not raise her head, but could sense the irritation of the customers there. At least she was coming back now and they could get on with it and . . .

. . . and Jane walked straight past them, heading for the other side of the store.

'Look,' the stern woman asked the girl behind the counter. 'I'm in a hurry. I can't stay here all day.'

'Gotta wait for the supervisor, madam.'

'Oh, *really!*'

Jane found the basket with the rubber gloves and dropped the packet inside. Turning then, she began to run back. This time, her feet skidded and she *did* fall to her knees. The pain was sharp and brought tears to her eyes, tears that were almost ready to fall due to her humiliation in any event. A young man and his wife stopped and helped her to stand again. She politely shook off their gestures of concern and hurried on, tights laddered. Reaching the queue again, she kept her head down and hurried past. The customers gave her plenty of room, as if her stupidity might be contagious. Jane began to push her remaining groceries into the plastic carrier bags at the end of the check-out conveyor belt, aware of the hostile stares on her back. The supervisor arrived, no older than the girl behind the counter. Judging by the attitude of both, there was no love lost between them. Leaning over, she began to stab her fingers at the register board.

'Just my luck to get stuck behind a *brain-dead*,' said the stern woman, as the register cleared and the girl began to push her own groceries off the conveyor belt and down into the tray where Jane was putting the last of her purchases into the bags. Jane swung the trolley away and headed for the exit, face still down.

When she reached the exit doors, the tears were flowing down her face and she was sobbing.

At the check-out, the stern woman was paying for her groceries by cheque; another delay further irritating those behind her. She couldn't have cared less.

And then something happened in one of the aisles.

There was a scream, and in the next instant a woman came skidding around the corner with her trolley. Several other shoppers followed, and when the supervisor pushed her way past the queue, she could see the looks of surprise and outright fear on their faces. They remained clustered at the end of the aisle, looking back at something that was clearly alarming them.

'Something caught fire on the shelf,' gasped the young woman with the trolley, pointing behind her. 'Back there . . .'

And even before the supervisor had turned the corner to look down the aisle, she could see the flames and smoke rising from the bread shelves beyond. Flaring, crackling gouts of flame from over the top of the shelving units. Sparks and soot began to float in the air. In the next instant, there were further screams and a flash of light from the Dairy Produce section as something suddenly burst into flames amidst the yoghurt. Flames crackled and spread, even in the refrigerated section. Then the smoke alarms in the supermarket were activated; klaxons began to sound, and an unemotional voice overhead told everyone to leave by the nearest exits as quietly and as quickly as possible.

Something flared on the shelves containing the dried pasta. A packet seemed to explode into flames, the fire spreading hungrily and quickly as if a petrol trail had been poured along the shelves, or as if it were hunting for something. There was more screaming as people began to run for the check-out counters.

A tin of peeled tomatoes exploded, its contents now somehow containing liquid fire. They cascaded high in the air, spreading fire to the shelves on the other side of the aisle and landing on the shoulders of an elderly lady, setting her hat and coat alight. Moaning, flapping her arms, she sank to her knees as assistants ran to help. Other tins on the same shelf began to explode like hand grenades as the fire spread and grew. A fractured tin smacked hard against a teenaged assistant's head, cartwheeling him into a pyramid of cornflakes packets.

And a plastic bucket containing rubber washing-up gloves suddenly erupted in a gout of blossoming orange flame. A fireball coughed into the air, hungrily spitting sparks into the overhead rafters. Somewhere, a baby began to wail.

Customers stampeded, crying aloud in fear as assistants tried to shepherd them out safely and the flames behind them spread.

Two hundred yards from the supermarket, Jane made her weary way home with two heavy bags of shopping. She did not hear the shouting, or the commotion, or the klaxons from the supermarket as people spilled out into the street. She could still feel the shame and the misery, but somehow they had been swamped by the rising anger. The anger was like a fire within. And with the fire came a great hunger. She needed to eat . . . something . . .

Her thoughts were on the kitchen, and what she might find in the cupboards there as she continued homeward.

'Hello, Eastleigh Casualty Department?'

'Yes, who's speaking?'

'This is Anthony Curtis from the Independent Daily . . .'

'I'm sorry, Mr Curtis. We've been given instructions to give no further comment to you on the motorway incident pending the official inquiry. So I'd be grateful if you would . . .'

'I'm not asking for any further comment! This is a bona fide medical matter. Someone's in trouble, and I think he needs your help.'

A pause. Was this another attempt to create more trouble for the hospital?

'Who needs help, exactly?'

'Harry Stark. One of the survivors.'

'I'm sorry, Mr Curtis. I'm going to ring off now. Any further enquiries you may have on ex-patients relating to that incident should be directed to the trust's solicitors or to legal advisers representing the patients concerned . . .'

'I was at Mr Stark's home not too long ago. I don't think that he's in his right mind. He might do something to himself. He's clearly suicidal.'

'I'm sorry, Mr Curtis . . .'

'Well, fuck you, then. I've done my bit. Ring off if you like, but it'll be on your head. I'm telling you, Harry Stark is a sick, sad man. And unless you get someone round to see him *straight away, I don't think you'll have to worry about any other after-care arrangements you might have made for him. Right? Goodbye.'*

'Mr Stark . . . you say he's . . .'

'56 Parade Street.'

'Mr Curtis, if this is an attempt to . . .'

'Goodbye.'

And then Curtis denies the administrator the pleasure of ringing off when he slams the receiver down.

Mercy watched him as he drove.

Could this really be the same man? When he had pulled up beside the shop doorway and leaned over to wind down the window, the sight of him had cramped her stomach with fear. For an instant, she thought she might actually just throw up then and there in the street. The spasm of fear did something else to her. Suddenly, she was an eight-year-old girl again. Because the face looking at her through the car window did not seem to have aged at all. In her mind's eye, she had already assumed that he would have lost more hair, would look more worn. Maybe the time he'd spent in prison had aged him even further. But no, he was just as she remembered him from those hellish days. The weasel-like eyes, the angular nose and the hair still parted across his bald pate. Even the voice was the same when he said: 'Looking for a friend?'

That same nasal sound.

Mercy had swallowed her fear and walked over to the car, looking back along the street to see that Selina was still heading home, head down and not looking back.

'For a price,' said Mercy, trying to control any waver in her voice.

'Tenner for basic? And twenty-up for anything special?' Clearly the going rate on this street.

Mercy nodded. 'Sounds good.'

Deinbeck leaned across and opened the passenger door. Mercy looked at Selina once more, saw that she wasn't coming back, and then climbed in beside him. Quickly, he pulled away from the kerb and turned the car, back the way he had come.

There was something going on in the street back there now, but Mercy paid no heed. Her attention was riveted on the man in the driving seat. The voice was the same, the face was the same. But could this *really* be Deinbeck? He seemed too damned small. The Deinbeck she remembered had towered over her. But that had been when she was a child, of course. And now that she had grown up, her perspective had changed dramatically.

But it was him all right. No doubt. This was the man who had abused her so hideously.

Suddenly, she was aware that she had no plan.

I don't trust you, Mercy, Selina had said. *You'll take it too far.*

Just what was she going to do? Ask if he remembered her, wait for a moment's doubt, then see a growing recognition? Then what? Grab the steering wheel, drag it over so that the car swerved from the road and smashed into a brick wall, killing them both?

'Hand-job should be the same as oral,' said Deinbeck, eyes still on the road. 'That's what I think.'

'You know the rates,' Mercy heard herself say, and inwardly marvelled that she could sound so calm. 'If you don't like it, stop the car.'

Deinbeck laughed. And Mercy remembered that laugh so clearly. A sniggering, clever-clever laugh.

'Can't blame a man for trying.'

'Where, then? The car, or your place?'

'And I can't blame *you* for trying, either,' sniggered Deinbeck. 'Can't fool me, sweetie. I know it's going to cost me more if I take you home. So the car can be our love-nest, eh?'

'Whatever you say. Where?'

'Here's as good as any place.'

He pulled the car from the main road into a badly lit side street. He seemed familiar with the place as they bumped over the rough ground. No doubt he had spent money here before.

So what else are you going to do, Mercy? Lead him on, then tell him? Then yell and scream and swear at him and rake your nails over his face, hoping that you might take an eye out?

Most of the houses down here seemed to be boarded up. They passed a car that had been propped up on four piles of house bricks, its wheels removed.

Or maybe I'll just be civilised? Wait until he stops the car and then talk to him. Tell him what he's done, the scars he's left. Tell him that the time he's spent in prison can never make up for what he did to me and all the others. Then he'll crumple up and start weeping pathetically. He'll beg forgiveness, but I'll just climb out of the car, slam the door and walk away. Will I do that?

The car slid to a stop in darkness. The nearest street lamp was a good fifty feet away. Plenty of shadow in the car. Deinbeck killed the engine, pulled on the handbrake and then turned to smile at her in the darkness. She could smell his stale breath, see his weasel eyes glittering with the same kind of anticipation she remembered as a little girl.

Will I fuck!

'Okay, then.' He wiped one hand across a dry mouth. His fingers were trembling. 'Oral. For twenty notes.'

So what are you going to do, Mercy? What happens next?

She felt the anger building inside her as she watched him begin to fumble with his belt. The anger was coming from deep down inside. It was coming from more than her memory of that time, and of the hideous abuses that he had inflicted on her. It seemed as if the child Mercy had been was somehow different from the adult Mercy in a much more profound way. They were two different entities. The child she'd been and the adult she had become. The older Mercy now fiercely protective of that child, and now . . . vengeful. But she still did not know what she was going to do.

Deinbeck unzipped his flies and looked at her. She could hear the breath catching in his throat. He licked lips that were dry with anticipation.

'Money first,' she heard herself say. 'Isn't that the way it's done?' Her voice seemed to be coming from a long way away, from down a distant tunnel.

Deinbeck gave a nervous laugh, fumbling now in his rain-coat pocket.

*A country and western song on Martin's truck radio, sud-
denly breaking up into hissing static. Martin's rigid face, eyes
fixed. Something wrong up ahead in the road.*

Deinbeck found the crumpled notes and proffered them to
her. Mercy saw herself take the notes and shove them into her
jeans pocket.

'Come on, then,' said Deinbeck. 'Do me.'

'Something,' Martin had said. 'Something coming . . .'

Mercy was outside her body somehow. It seemed as if the
anger had boiled over and in the process her soul had been
pushed out of the body it inhabited. She could see herself in
the passenger seat, could still feel the rage as she watched and
knew that something was about to happen. She was about to do
something, born from that rage. But she still had no idea . . .

And then was filled with horror when she felt and saw
herself leaning across towards Deinbeck in the darkness.

No . . . no . . . for God's sake, NO!

She tried to prevent her *doppelganger* from moving, but
the rage was still there, still consuming them both. She saw
Deinbeck lick his lips again as he yanked his erect penis from
his trousers.

She saw herself reaching for him – and the Mercy that
floated outside her body began to scream at what she was
doing. But her screams were unheard and the anger and the
intent of the girl she was watching were unstoppable. She saw
the blank expression on her face. And in the next moment, was
catapulted back into her body once more. But in that instant,
the two Mercies were united; the rage and the power were all
that she could feel. She would do what had to be done, and
that was all there was to it.

Her hands had begun to tingle.

Something inside was coming out through her fingertips.

She took Deinbeck in her right hand.

*The blinding light exploding into the cab. Martin struggling
to control the spinning wheel. Mercy crying out in alarm and
throwing herself back into the seat.*

'Come up to my room, Mercy. And don't tell anyone.'

Some inner part of her was still screaming. Some part

that was deep, deep down and could do nothing to stop her.

She took Deinbeck in her mouth.

He began to moan as she worked, lifting his buttocks from the seat, moving his hand to the back of her head.

A screaming horde erupts into the cab an instant after the light. Martin yells as he stamps on the brakes and the luminous, all-enveloping light burns out their vision. Something intangible but real smashes into them at an impossible speed. Now Mercy has a revelation in the depth of her anger and her horror. Something crashed into HER then. Not just into the cab. Whatever it was, it smashed into her psyche and her soul in ways that she cannot understand, but knows instinctively. And it's been there ever since. She remembers what she was thinking before the crash; what she wanted most in the world. Remembers how much she hated Deinbeck.

And that hate was channelled and focused in Mercy's hands as she held him and as her mouth worked. The hate was transferring to his very essence, into the very part of him that he was a slave to, the very part of him that had been the instrument of so much abuse. The tingling in her hands had become fire.

Deinbeck screamed.

But Mercy did not stop, the anger keeping her at the task. The hateful memories flooding back into her mind.

'You're my special one, Mercy. You'll always be my special one.'

Mercy diving for the cab door, blundering in the light, squashing both hands to her ears and trying to keep the sounds of the hellish screaming outside her head. The impact slamming her forward. The centrifugal force of the crazily spinning cab pinning her down there, despite her slow-motion attempts to rise.

Deinbeck was beating at her head, clawing at her hair in agony. She held him tight with one hand, clawed his hands away with the other. He spasmed, bucking and writhing in the driving seat. Her hands were still on fire, and she knew that the fire was coming out of her and into him. Her head was jerked away from him. In anger and hatred, she darted back to take him in her mouth again . . .

But Deinbeck had somehow pulled up a leg. His knee caught her under the chin and Mercy's jaws snapped shut as she was smashed back against the passenger door. In agony, still thrashing in terror, Deinbeck lashed out with his foot. Mercy fell against the handle and the door juddered open. She fell outside on to wet and cracked tarmac.

The anger was still consuming her. Face contorted, she clambered to her feet, dragging herself up the side of the car screaming obscenities at Deinbeck inside. Part of her felt that she had been cheated, prevented from finishing whatever it was she had started. But when she looked inside the car, she could see that whatever she had done to Deinbeck was still happening.

He thrashed and struggled in his seat as if he were having a fit. His head was jerking wildly from side to side. Spittle flew from between his clenched teeth. His face was a rigid mask, eyes bulging and wild; the lid of hair over his bald pate flapping up and down. His feet were drumming on the floor of the car, his arms convulsing and clawing like those of a mad puppet.

Mercy staggered away from the car, still looking.

The anger inside her seemed to be waning. Her hands were no longer burning; now they were merely tingling, as they had been at the beginning. Suddenly, she felt sick. She began to spit, clearing the foul taste of him out of her mouth. She gagged then, bending double. And when she looked back, she could not believe what she was seeing.

Something was happening to Deinbeck.

He was *shrivelling*.

The wild thrashing had begun to subside. Now his limbs were twitching erratically and his head had ceased to jerk from side to side. There was a sound like a sigh, and it looked as though something was happening beneath Deinbeck's raincoat. There was movement there . . . no, not movement. He was exhaling, and as he did so his chest was receding. And receding . . . and receding. More than that, his chest was crumbling and caving in before her eyes. His fingers were bunching in towards the palms; she could hear a crackling sound and watched as the fingers began to disintegrate like charcoal. Black, carbonised ash pattered on his lap and on the passenger seat. His lips were drawn back in a silent, frozen scream of pain and terror. And now Mercy could see that the same thing was happening to his face. The skin was blackening and stretching tight, as if he had suddenly aged fifty years in seconds. Now his face was the face of a corpse, decomposing before her eyes. His eyes disappeared into the shrivelled sockets, turned to black powder and spilled out into his collapsing lap. The hair over his pate had come loose. It slithered in one large hank to the floor like something alive that needed to escape.

Deinbeck, the love-doll.

And now Mercy had punctured him to let all the air out.

But she had done much, much more than that. And her mind could barely take it in as she continued to stagger away. There was moaning now. And she could not be sure whether it was coming from her or from the thing in the car.

Deinbeck's head fell forward, something cracked with a sound like a log on a fire – and then it fell away from the disintegrating stump of his neck, tumbling between his knees. Everything within the raincoat above his waist crumbled into an indeterminate mass on the driver's seat. There was still movement in the horrifying mass, but Mercy could take no more.

She turned away in horror, filled now with the certainty that there was something *alive* inside her. Something that had come into her on the motorway. Something that had collided with her – and had stayed inside her. She hugged herself tight, willing whatever was buried deep inside to leave.

'Oh, God . . .'

She took a final look at the car, still trying to convince herself that she had done what she'd done, seen what she'd seen.

Was she going mad?

Turning, she fled into the night.

* * *

The Reverend Jameson turned from the altar and faced the
congregation.

'Draw near with faith. Take, eat, this is my body . . .'

And the first of the communicants stood up from where
they kneeled in the front pews and began to file out into the
central aisle.

He had prepared the wafers for the first sitting and now
walked to the steps leading up to the altar just as these first
communicants came to the front of the church and began to
kneel at the rails. He knew that he should be maintaining his
concentration on the service, and the blessed importance of
what he was doing. But he still found himself wondering,
even as he moved forward to give the first kneeling person
the sacrament, what Martin Russell was doing in the third row
from the front.

He was sitting there, with his wife. And throughout the
service he had sat with his head down. It was difficult to tell
whether he was singing the hymns or not. But quite clearly,
he was obediently following what his wife was doing at each
stage of the communion service. He was such a big man, it
was impossible to tell whether he was kneeling, as his wife
was at the appropriate moments, or whether he was sitting.
Jameson knew Sheila Russell quite well. She was a regular
churchgoer, had been so ever since childhood. So it had not
been the crippling pain of her illness which had turned her
to religion. When they had talked about it, at one of the
church social events, she had obviously been genuine in her
declarations that she should count her blessings. She wasn't
in a wheelchair, was still able to get around under her own
steam; and had a husband who loved her deeply.

But in the twelve years that Sheila had been attending
the church, the Reverend Jameson had never seen Martin
at a service. He knew him by sight, of course. But today
was a first.

'The body of Christ.' He moved down the line as the second
row of communicants began to file out into the central aisle,
waiting for the first to receive the wine and then move away.

Maybe Sheila had been working on Martin over the years?

He had never shown, as far as Jameson was aware, the slightest inkling of an interest in the religious side of life. He seemed to be a good man, but always made excuses to leave the room if Jameson was visiting Sheila on his rounds. Could it be that now, after all these years, he had seen the light? Or perhaps he was attending as an act of love for his wife? Jameson realised that the speculation was making his attention wander, offered a quick mental prayer for forgiveness, and then moved back to to the altar to collect the goblet of wine.

'The blood of Christ . . .'

Sheila was kneeling . . .

I've told her that she mustn't do that. It's much too painful, and the Lord doesn't need her to suffer that way if there's no need for it.

. . . but her face seemed calm and devoid of pain today.

You're a brave, brave woman.

Martin looked up then, directly at him. Their eyes caught and held. Quickly looking away again, the Reverend Jameson moved down the line. The second row began to take their place on the altar steps vacated by the first row.

Has Martin been confirmed? I don't know. Can he take communion? The subject's never come up before.

The second row received the body and the blood of Christ. The third row began to file out. Jameson could not stop himself. He had to see. He looked up and observed something so unusual that it made him pause in the act of proffering the goblet to one of the communicants.

Sheila was standing up from the prayer mat and moving down the row to the centre aisle.

But there was no struggle to rise. No strained look of pain on her face, the expression that had so worried Jameson in the past. No stiff and painful gait as she clutched at the row in front to support her as she moved. If anything, her face seemed almost . . . well, *radiant*.

Jameson became aware that the elderly lady kneeling before him was looking up in concern, her mouth open and ready to take a sip from the goblet.

'The blood of Christ.'

'Amen.'

And when he moved to the next person, he looked up again to see that Martin was following his wife, moving to the centre aisle behind her. Why was he so fascinated with all of this? There was something going on here which was intriguing, but Jameson could not understand it. Martin followed his wife with an almost embarrassed air, looking around him all the time as if expecting criticism. They joined the line of people waiting to take their place at the altar steps.

'The blood of Christ.'

'Amen.'

Angry with himself, Jameson struggled to keep his mind on the job. He refused to look, knowing that they would be drawing near soon.

And sure enough, there they were. Sheila, kneeling on the steps, looking ten or fifteen years younger. More than that, it seemed that she was concentrating her smile on him, as if keen that he should notice . . . what?

That something has happened, the smile said. *Something that I need you to know, something that I . . . no, we . . . must share with you.*

Martin was kneeling next to her; even on his knees he was towering over everyone else. Anxiously looking at Sheila, he seemed like a child completely out of his depth, focusing all his trust and his attention on the person he loved most. There was something more about his expression. Jameson realised that his first assumption was wrong. Martin wasn't here against his will at all. He could tell just by looking at his craggy face; Martin *wanted* to be here in the church. But he didn't understand everything that was happening in the service. The Reverend Jameson reached the end of the line and moved back to the beginning again.

'The body of Christ.'

Would Martin cup his hands to receive the wafer? Would he merely copy his wife's actions, not understanding the need to be confirmed before he could take the sacrament? Surely Sheila would have told him.

Even now, Sheila was cupping her hands as Jameson moved down the line. And Martin was bowing his head, his hands held down by his sides.

'The body of Christ,' said Jameson when he came to Sheila, placing the wafer into her cupped hands. Her eyes were closed. He placed his hand on Martin's head, the traditional blessing for those who were not confirmed.

'The blessing of the Lord Jesus Christ.'

Did he feel something then when he touched his head? Martin remained unmoved, head still bowed. Perhaps it had been some kind of static shock from the altar carpet. Jameson moved on down the line.

When he had shaken the last hand and patted the last child's head in the vestibule, it did not surprise him to find that Sheila and Martin were still inside the church, standing by the noticeboard. Martin continued to look out of place, pretending to take an interest in the parish notices. Sheila was sitting on one of the plastic chairs next to him, hands folded in her lap, patiently waiting. She smiled when he walked towards them, and then stood quickly. Again, it was a fluid, almost spry movement, without pain.

Drugs, thought Jameson. *It's got so bad for her that her doctor has prescribed some kind of pain killing drug. Perhaps it's given her a lift . . .*

'Reverend . . .' Sheila's voice seemed breathless with excitement. Behind her, Martin shuffled uncomfortably, then held his head up and moved to stand beside her as Jameson drew close.

'Sheila. Nice to see you again. And I see you've managed to kidnap Martin this morning for the . . .'

'Reverend, something wonderful has happened.'

Sheila seemed almost *too* happy. So much so that Jameson began to worry. Was she pumped so full of drugs that they were inducing some kind of euphoria?

'And you've come to tell me all about it.'

'That's right,' said Martin. There was a sense of strength and purpose in his voice, clearly overriding his discomfort.

'Well, why don't we sit down first. Take the weight off . . .'

'I don't need to sit,' said Sheila. 'Don't need to use a stick. Don't need to suffer any more. Look at me.' She turned, arms held apart, as if showing off some new dress.

Jameson looked at Martin, trying to glean some kind of hint from his face that his own diagnosis of Sheila's situation was correct. Martin's face remained resolute.

'Well, I hope you don't mind if *I* sit. I've been on my feet all morning.'

He moved to the plastic chairs by the noticeboard. Sheila followed eagerly, pulling her chair up close when he sat. Martin remained standing, clearly waiting for Sheila to speak.

'Something wonderful,' said Jameson. 'So, tell me, Sheila. Tell me all about it.'

'Look at me,' she said, holding out her hands. She turned them, palms up, palms down, over and over again. As if she were about to practise some kind of conjuring trick. She cocked her head from side to side. 'Do you see? No pain, Reverend. No pain at all. Now watch . . .'

'Sheila, do you really think you should be doing this?'

'Now *watch*!'

She stood up quickly and tried to touch her toes. She was bending at the waist, but her fingertips were still a good distance from her feet.

'Never could do it when I was fit and healthy,' she continued, sitting again. 'But I *can* bend at the waist. And, Reverend, there's absolutely *no* pain. None at all. It's all gone away. I've been made better.'

Jameson looked up at Martin, cricking his neck in the process.

'You mean that the doctor has found something to . . .'

'No, not the doctor! They couldn't do anything for me. You know that. They told me that it would be a progressive illness. The best I could expect was for it to get worse in gradual stages, and to keep taking the painkillers. But . . . well . . . it's *gone*! I've been completely cured. I haven't taken so much as an aspirin since it happened.'

'The doctors have confirmed that?'

'Oh, no, I haven't been near a doctor yet. Who needs them? I had to come and tell you first about the wonderful thing that's happened.'

'I don't understand, Sheila. You say you're cured, and . . . you look wonderful. But how . . . ?'

'Martin did it,' said Sheila proudly, looking up at him. 'My Martin did it. He cured me, Reverend. Him.'

Now Jameson knew. Something had happened all right. But not something wonderful after all. And perhaps that was why Martin was here. Perhaps Sheila had been prescribed a new drug to ease her suffering, something that was clearly giving her great relief and enhanced mobility. But quite obviously it was also affecting her state of mind. It all seemed perfectly clear now, deeply sad, but clear. Jameson said nothing, waiting for Martin to give him confirmation of what was happening.

Martin coughed and shuffled his feet.

'Well, go on,' said Sheila, smiling up at him. 'Tell him.'

'It's true. I don't know how or why. But I've got . . . something.'

'The laying-on of hands,' completed Sheila, smiling. 'He's been given the gift of healing.'

'Perhaps we need to have another chat with your doctor, Sheila. I mean, you look marvellous. But perhaps whatever's . . . happened . . . is making you over-stretch yourself if you can't feel the pain. You might damage yourself if you don't take care.'

'You don't believe us,' said Martin, and now he was angry. 'We've come to tell you, and you don't believe a word of it.'

Jameson started to rise. 'Now let's be calm about this. Come on over to the vicarage. Have a cup of tea.'

Martin strode forward until he was looming over Jameson. His face was furious. Jameson slowly sat back, feeling a gnawing of anxiety now, unsure of which way this bizarre conversation was going to go. He knew that Martin was not a violent man, was in fact a gentle man by all accounts. But he clearly believed the fantasy too.

'I'm not sure what it is,' said Martin, and his voice was trembling with controlled emotion. 'Sheila says it comes from God. Says that she's heard about this sort of thing before. The power to heal. The laying-on of hands. Me, I just don't know. I've never been one for religion and all the holier than thou stuff I've seen and heard ever since I was a kid. All I know is that something has come into me. And now, I can heal people. I mean, *really* heal them. Maybe I'm wrong, and Sheila is right. About this God thing, I mean. That's why I'm here. To find out.'

'Martin . . .' Jameson spoke as calmly as he could, 'there's no need for anyone to get upset. Like I say, let's find somewhere nice and quiet to talk this through.'

'You don't believe me.'

'I didn't say that.'

'Do you still have that stomach trouble, Reverend?' asked Sheila. 'The pain and the acid with your hiatus hernia?'

Jameson turned to look at her, to see that although she was talking to him she was looking at Martin.

'Seriously,' said Jameson, now very concerned at the disturbing course the conversation was taking. 'We need to talk . . .' He turned back to Martin.

Just as Martin placed a hand on his head in a gesture that was identical to the blessing Jameson had given him on the altar steps.

Something snapped inside his head.

And he was gone from that place into a darkness without dreams.

Klark was in very bad trouble.

He had paid out a deposit on the Ecstasy tabs using Ellis Burwell's cash and had borrowed the remainder from Tonsa, a black bastard who specialised in short-term loans at spectacular interest rates. Two nights ago, at a rave, Klark and the two associates he'd entrusted to mingle in the crowd to sell the drugs had been targeted by undercover cops. Both of them had been collared after a fight, and Klark had escaped by punching a hole in a back-room window and climbing down the drainpipe. All the tabs, except the three in his overcoat pocket, were gone. He had seven bloody quid to show for it, with the remaining cash to be paid to his drug contact (not an understanding man), and the loan to pay back to Tonsa (whose known reaction to late payment in the past had involved taking a blowtorch to someone's balls).

Klark needed the rest of Burwell's money *now*, and cursed himself for being such a kind and considerate man in letting him off full payment last time they had met. To cap it all, he'd cut his hand on the back-room window and it hurt like hell. Each aching throb in his palm served to fuel his anger as he turned into the Civic Hall car park.

There had been something wrong about the last telephone call to Burwell.

When he had demanded the money, knowing that Burwell had previously told him he couldn't get his hands on it for a further two weeks, he had expected the same whingeing pleas. But Burwell had seemed calm, somehow much more in control than he had ever sounded before. As if he knew something that Klark didn't, and it was just pleasing him no end.

'*I need the rest of the money now, Burwell.*'

'*Ah yes, the money.*'

'*You've got it, then.*'

'*Got so much money I just don't know what to do with it. Can't think of anything I'd like better than giving it all to you.*'

'*You been drinking?*'

'*No, I've been thinking. About things that have happened recently. Things I'm able to do. Worried me at first. Hell, no – it scared the living shit out of me. But even though I don't understand it, I know that if I concentrate hard enough – think back to the motorway – I can use it to my advantage. It's all happened so suddenly. My understanding of it all, I mean.*'

'*What the fuck are you talking about?*'

'*I can't expect you to understand. But I can show you, Klark. I can show you just what I mean. You miserable little cocksucking, shit-eating, low-life bastard.*'

Silence then, as Klark was too strangled with rage to speak. When he did, it was a torrent of obscenity and threat. Burwell remained silent throughout.

'*You want the rest of your money?*' asked Burwell at last,

when Klark had run out of breath. '*Then be at the usual place tonight. Ten o'clock. I'll be there. And I want the original video, any copies, and the negatives of any photographs you might have taken as well. Do you hear me? I want everything. Bring it all along and I'll give you two thousand. A once-and-for-all final payment. And that'll be the last cash you'll get out of me, you fucker. Oh, and Klark? Something else. I'm going to wipe my arse on that money before I give it to you. Shit for a shit. Know what I mean?*'

Before Klark could launch into another furious tirade, Burwell had hung up.

And now Klark had some very special plans for Burwell. He didn't understand how or why the bastard had suddenly found the courage to say what he'd said. But he was going to be very, very sorry.

As usual, Klark had arrived a half-hour early for the meeting. He always liked to have the edge; liked to have time to think and plan what he was going to say. He enjoyed seeing Burwell grovel. Tonight, he would be grovelling like he never had before. Klark looked around before he entered the car park. No one about. Good. Quickly, he turned into the entrance and kept close to the darkness of the bushes at the side of the road. A train clattered past on the embankment, casting its flickering light over the empty car park. At the far end, he looked back once more to make sure that he wasn't being observed and then flitted across to the bushes by the embankment. That would give him a clear view of the entrance and Burwell's car. Pulling his coat collar tight around his neck, he stood there waiting and began to savour his plan.

'Boo,' said a voice from the darkness.

Klark cried out in alarm. Staggering out of the bushes and on to the tarmac, he threw his hands up over his face, expecting an attack.

A silhouette stepped calmly out of the bushes after him, carrying a briefcase in one hand.

'You're early, Klark,' said Burwell.

Furious, Klark straightened and took a threatening step forward.

Burwell raised his other hand. Was that a *gun*?

'Yes it is,' said Burwell, levelling it at him. 'And if you take another step forward, first I'll shoot you in the balls and then I'll shoot you in the head. First shot will be in your brains, won't it? 'Cause there're no fucking brains in your head, are there, Klark?'

Klark gritted his teeth.

'You haven't got the guts for that kind of thing. I know you, Burwell.'

'Not any more you don't. I've changed.'

Burwell sounded the same as he had on the telephone. Unconcerned and totally in control. For the first time, Klark began to feel unnerved.

'Have you got everything I asked for?'

'Do you think I'm stupid?' Klark jammed his hands into his pockets. 'Give me the fucking money, Burwell. Give it to me *now*!'

'Yes, you *are* stupid!' snapped Burwell. 'Because I mean what I say. Give me the video and everything else and you can have the cash in this case. A once-and-for-all payment, like I said.'

'I'll take what you've got. But you won't get the video, because I haven't brought it with me. You think you'll buy me off with two thousand? You're a nice little earner, Burwell. I've got no intention of letting you buy me off. Our arrangement is going to last for a long, *long* time. And if you shoot me, what then? The police find the body. Go around to my place, look for clues. And find all the tasty little video cassettes and the photographs I've got hidden away there. Including you. So give me the case – and then fuck off.'

Even in the darkness, Klark could see that Burwell was trembling with rage.

'The money,' said Klark, maintaining his nerve. There was still a chance, if it *really* was a gun, that Burwell's trembling finger might squeeze the trigger by mistake. Klark smiled then, as Burwell's hand lowered. The smile broadened when his head was also lowered in defeat.

He stepped forward.

Burwell held out the briefcase.

Klark tightened his grip on the switchblade in his overcoat pocket. He would teach the pathetic cunt a lesson tonight; would cut him up a little. Not too badly, just enough to act as a reminder and to keep him in line.

'Naughty boy,' said Klark. 'Naughty, *naughty* boy . . .'

Before he could take the case, Burwell suddenly let go of the handle, letting it fall to the ground.

The knife in Klark's pocket clicked.

And Burwell seized his outstretched hand, his head suddenly snapping up with an exultant look on his face, eyes blazing.

The effect was instantaneous. Klark yelled in surprise and pain as something seemed to slam into his chest. The next moment he was rolling on the ground, hugging his hand to his chest. Something seemed to have wrenched out his innards. His hand was burning as if it were on fire. His eyes were misted when he struggled to look back at Burwell. He was still standing there, looking down at him, the case at his feet.

Something in that case. Something . . . electric shock.

Klark twisted on the ground and tried to reach into his pocket for the switchblade, unaware that in his fall it had pierced his thigh. Blood was already beginning to soak his trousers. But the effort seemed to have another effect, something altogether worse. Not only did it make the pain in his guts bad, but it seemed that the fire in his hand was spreading along his arm to his chest. He slumped back, now feeling the fire in his lungs. He couldn't breathe.

'The video cassette!' snapped Burwell, suddenly striding forward until he was standing over him. From here, it would have been such an easy thing to take the knife out of his pocket and jam it up between Burwell's legs. But Klark was unable to move. The pain was worsening; he was fighting for breath. And now he was consumed by terror. 'The video!' Burwell leaned down and took him by the collar, dragging him up from the ground until they were face to face. Klark's eyes were bulging in pain and fear. Spitting into his face, Burwell slammed him to the ground and began to rummage through his pockets.

When he came to the knife in his overcoat pocket he dragged it out. It carved a furrow in Klark's flesh as it came free; a pool of blood spread around his crotch, thick as dark soup. But the pain was as nothing to what he was already experiencing. Burwell saw the dark glinting of blood on his hand in the darkness and threw the knife aside.

'Where is it, Klark?' he yelled. 'Where *is it*?'

'What . . . what . . . have you *done*?'

Burwell was about to fly into an uncontrollable rage. Steeling himself, he looked apprehensively around to make sure that there was no one out there who might have heard his voice. Turning back to Klark, he began again, controlling his voice so that each word was tight and stabbing.

'You're dying, Klark. Hear me? Dying. And there's only one way – *one* way – you can save yourself. Are you listening? Tell me where you've got the video. Tell me that, and I'll save you. If you don't, I'll let you die. Do you hear me? You'll *die!*'

'God . . . Burwell . . . God, what have you . . . ?'

'*Tell me or you'll die!*'

'My apart . . .'

'*Where?*'

'My apartment . . .'

'Where do you live, you bastard! *Where!*'

'Ouseburn. Wharf Seven.'

'I know it. Which number?'

Klark moaned, fumbling feebly at his throat. His eyes were beginning to roll up into his head. Burwell seized him by the collar, lifting him until they were face to face again.

'Which *number*?'

'Sixty . . . seven . . .'

'Sixty-seven? Are you saying sixty-seven?'

Klark tried to nod his head. And then Burwell flung him back down again, this time going through his jeans pockets. He discarded the three tabs of Ecstasy and the small amount of cash, letting the notes drift away across the car park in the wind. Finally, he found a key.

'Is this the key?'

Klark was beginning to spasm, his legs twitching, his eyes showing white.

'It had better be, Klark!' There was fear in Burwell's voice now. Had he over-played his hand? Why had he thought that Klark would be goaded into bringing the evidence? How could he have been so bloody naive as to think that his ploy would work the way he wanted it to. 'It had *better* be!' Gripping the key tight, he shook his fist at Klark.

Klark made a sound then. A choking, gargling sound in the back of his throat.

'Then *die*, you fucking parasite! Go on . . . *DIE!*'

Something roared over to Burwell's left, making him flinch. A train hurtled past on the embankment, illuminating the car park in a thunder of black and white. He looked down at Klark, saw the spreading pool of blood and remembered the flick-knife.

Fingerprints!

Staggering, he stooped to grab it from where he had thrown it and jammed it into his pocket, next to the toy pistol – and began to run.

He prayed that his torture would soon be over.

Roger staggered back from where he had been kneeling over the toilet bowl and slumped on the bathroom floor.

On both elbows, he backed off until he had reached a wall and lay there, regaining his breath. His skin felt clammy when he wiped his hair away from one eye; his lips were dry and cracked. Not for the first time since his arrival in the big city, he wondered just what in hell was happening to him. He had tried to vomit, tried to jettison whatever it was that was inside him, making him do these bizarre things. But nothing would come.

Even though he had consumed a pint of pine-scented fabric conditioner in the last hour, and should therefore be barfing his brains out.

The crash. It has to be something to do with the crash. Some kind of trauma, maybe. Perhaps I've inhaled something. Something from the burning lorry.

He sat up straight, bending forward at the waist to lower his head.

Take deep breaths. It'll soon be out of your system. There's too much at stake to see a doctor. Anyway, you're not registered for a practice down here . . . and you don't really want to know if there's anything wrong. Do you?

He knew that he was making excuses for himself. He hated doctors. If he ever picked up a virus, or was feeling the worse for wear, the last thing he'd do would be to seek medical advice. He knew that it was an unreasoning attitude, but ever since the death of his parents he seemed to have developed an aversion to them.

Anyway, if it had been something serious they would have found it in the hospital after the crash. They gave me tests then. Surely they would have picked it up if there'd been something?

No, it was psychological. He was sure of it. Maybe the stress of slogging around the streets with his portfolio, rarely getting past the receptionists even when he'd been given half a promise of an interview. Of the seven possible contacts he'd established before setting off from home, he had only been able to get in to see someone at two agencies. At one, the guy had been interrupted by the telephone five times while Roger was trying to talk him through the artwork he'd brought. At the end of the interview, he'd promised to think about it, see if there were any openings . . . and let him know. Roger had left the building with no high hopes. At the second agency, the woman he'd talked to had made it plain from the beginning that she was uninterested in finished artwork. There might be openings for computer-literate artists, but not for people wearing berets with paint-smeared smocks. And so on and so forth . . .

It had to be the strain, so soon after what he'd been through on that hellish stretch of the A1.

He staggered to his feet, wondering whether he should try again. Uttering a groan of self-disgust, he blundered out of the bathroom, letting the door slap back against the wall. Chris's two-bedroomed attic flat was perfect for a struggling artist.

Is that what I am? he asked himself. *A struggling artist?*
He braced both hands on the banister rail before him. *Good
Christ, I don't know just what the hell I AM any more . . .*

The stairway below him led down to the main door. At the
top of the stairs, where he now stood, was an open-plan living
room. Leading off from that, a bathroom, a kitchen and two
bedrooms. And in the far corner of the living area, a slanting
skylight from knee height to ceiling. A perfect working-place
for an artist, taking advantage of the natural light. Chris had
even brought in an easel one day and set it up there in the
recess. A second-hand item he'd spotted on his way home
from work one day and a goodwill gesture that seemed to
have been under-appreciated. Roger was aware that he hadn't
reacted properly to the gift, but he had been too preoccupied
with what was happening inside him. Guilty afterwards, he
had set up the limited amount of materials he'd brought with
him around the easel. There was even a stretch of canvas
pinned up there. *Just in case the muse should strike*, he had
smiled thinly at a pensive Chris one evening.

He shook his head, then ran both hands through his hair.
Clearing his throat of the sour taste, he moved across to the
easel and looked out through the skylight, down to the street
below. The attic flat was on the sixth floor. Down below, old-
fashioned wrought-iron railings fronted the Victorian building.
Beyond, a grassed area that was jokingly referred to by the
locals as the common, where owners walked their dogs and
for the most part left the results lying around for everyone else
to stand in. Consequently, no one laid down picnic blankets on
the grass, even when the weather was as hot as it continued
to be today.

Heat . . . and light . . .

A blinding light, hurtling down the motorway towards them.

*People screaming . . . screaming and rushing down on
him . . .*

There were echoes in his head, echoes that somehow hurt
him. Roger staggered back from the skylight, clutching both
hands over his eyes. The feeling was coming again, this time
much faster. Only minutes before, it had sent him reeling into

the bathroom, and now it was coming again, even stronger than before.

'No . . . it's too early . . .'

He should be feeling like this again only after three or four hours.

'Christ, not *yet!*'

Instinctively aware that the process within him was somehow accelerating now, Roger reeled again and fell against the easel. Somehow, he did not knock it over. Instead, he clutched it to himself as if it could save his life. The burning feeling was swelling in his chest, beneath his breast bone. Now he could feel the familiar tingling in his hands.

He remembered what he had been dreaming about just before the crash. In his half-slumber, he had been looking forward to his arrival in London. With supreme confidence, he knew that he had a talent in his hands; a talent to create, a talent to *connect*, to draw people into what he'd rendered. Confidence and ambition were a burning passion.

Burning.

Now, in his hands.

Dimly, Roger saw himself set the easel back into position again. His vision was blurred, too slow it seemed to keep up with his motion as he stooped to his materials on the floor and began to prepare his brushes. They needed cleaning . . . needed to be prepared . . . needed to be . . .

And then he was at the canvas, his materials mixed, a sable brush ready. Surely it would take him some time to prepare before he was ready to start? Had he done all that and been unaware? Dimly again, he realised that he had lost some time. Was he dreaming? He had tuned out, whirling within the burning sensation that possessed him.

His hands were no longer tingling.

They were on fire.

Clawing above his head for the overhead rack on the bus; instinctively reacting to the horrifying voices and the terrible light by grabbing to protect the thing that was most important to him: the folder containing his portfolio of sketches and watercolours.

The white of the canvas was the same as the blinding light on the motorway.

He had to make sense of it; make sense of what was inside him.

Anguish and passion; focused to an inner point of white heat. Furiously, he began to work.

The light that was like an opened furnace door, making him cover his face with one hand as he hung swaying from the rack with the other. But there was no heat in the invading light, and Roger suddenly realised that the feeling inside him wasn't burning after all. He remembered now as he worked. It was a bone-chilling, fierce cold, freezing everyone in the coach.

Roger's hands were burning . . . were freezing . . . but they were independent of him now. With a frenzied life of their own, they were creating a swirl of colour that made his senses swim. Was he controlling them, or were they controlling him?

Roger's feet leave the floor, making him swing out like a gymnast on the parallel bars, hanging by one hand. His foot connects with a man, smashing his spectacles, sending the man catapulting backwards. Someone, somewhere, is shouting: 'My baby, oh good Christ, my BABY!' Roger claws with his free hand to find some kind of grip; fails, and his other hand is torn loose. He falls between seats, backwards and head down. The impact dazes him, but now he's bent double, feet in the air, suffocating in the fetid darkness of the coach floor.

And with that intense memory, Roger was propelled deep into a dark place behind his eyes. Even as the swirling colour faded, he knew that his hands would continue to work, to create something . . . something . . .

'*To blow people's minds,*' he had told Adam in the pub, before he had set off on his quest. '*To make them see something they've never seen before. To draw them right in, make them feel it – really FEEL it – and blow them away . . .*'

The last thing Roger saw was his hands.

Twin white spiders, working together and fuelled by the passion that had been so much in his mind when he had impacted with the light on the motorway.

*   *   *

'. . . Roger . . . All right? . . . Roger . . .'

He emerged from the place behind his eyes to realise that he was desperately thirsty. His body was aching and his hands felt strangely cramped. The light was blinding, and he shielded his face as the voice became louder in his consciousness.

'Roger, are you all right?'

Chris's voice, sounding very concerned.

Where the hell am I?

Suddenly aware that he was standing, not lying down, Roger reached out and touched wet paint. He rubbed his eyes, and colours began to swirl before him. He tried to see what they were and then something seemed to scream a warning at him. He turned quickly away, heart hammering, unable to understand why he was so frightened. There was something there. Something that he shouldn't see because it would open things inside him that he preferred not to know about.

Where the hell AM I?

Chris's flat. Not daytime any more. The skylight was behind him, but night had fallen.

'You been working in the *dark*?' Chris's voice again, coming from the other side of the room.

Struggling to orientate himself, and still uncomfortably aware of the painting on the canvas, Roger quickly stooped and picked up the length of old blanket that Chris had provided for cleaning his brushes. Unheeding of whether the blanket still had wet paint on it or not, he scooped it from the floor and draped it quickly over the easel, completely covering what he had been working on. Feeling guilty, and not sure why he should, he rubbed his eyes and stepped around the easel to look for his brother.

'The dark?'

'Roger, what the hell is the matter with you? I come in from work, switch on the light, and you're standing behind that easel in the pitch black. What were you doing? I mean, you couldn't have been *painting*. Not in the darkness, surely?'

'Oh, yeah.' Roger tried to smile, but his mouth seemed unwilling to accommodate the expression. 'In the dark. That's

right . . . I'm . . . you know . . . experimenting with something.'
Now he could see that Chris was standing at the top of the
stairs, still with his coat draped over one arm and his briefcase
in the other.

'But you're all right?' Chris's tone seemed to suggest that no
matter what Roger's answer might be, he was still unprepared
to accept that everything was all right.

'Never better. How about a drink? You want one?'

Chris watched his brother walk across the room to the
drinks tray, keeping his head down and his face averted.

'Scotch,' said Chris, throwing his coat and briefcase on to
the nearby sofa. He remained standing there as he watched
Roger pour his drink. 'You having something?'

'Maybe a beer or something first. Got a hell of a thirst.'

'Try carrot juice. Might help you see in the dark.'

'Fun-*nee*! Don't you know that artists are supposed to be
eccentric?'

'Eccentric, yeah.' Chris joined his coat and briefcase on
the sofa. He stretched, groaning when his joints popped and
cracked.

'Hard day at the office, dear?' asked Roger. He was trying
too hard, and Chris knew it.

'This is working out okay, isn't it? I mean . . . you being
here.'

''Course it's working.' Roger brought his drink over and then
headed for the kitchen. Chris sipped the Scotch and listened as
his brother vanished from sight, filling a glass with water.

'Beer's in the usual place.'

'I know. I need water first.'

Chris listened to him filling and drinking from his glass
three times before he spoke again.

'I think you should give this job-hunting a rest. Just for
a while.'

'What makes you say that?'

'Just . . . you know, after the accident and all. Maybe you're
a little stressed out. Need to have some time to yourself before
you start hawking your wares all over the city.'

'My cash is limited, Chris. I don't have a lot of time.'

'I can give you cash . . .'

'No, I don't need it. Thanks. I want to pay my way.'

'Well, look, let's just forget about the money you're giving me by way of rent. You know I didn't want to take it off you in the first place.'

'It's important to me that I pay my way, Chris.'

'Yeah, but if we just forget about that part of it. Then you can use that money more usefully. And maybe you need to be getting out and about a little more. I've got a few friends at the local boozer. Some more at the squash club. Maybe I could take you down there to meet a few people . . . ?'

'No, thanks.'

'But you can't just carry on the way you are. It's not good for you. You need to . . .'

'I *know* what I *NEED*!' Roger was suddenly standing in the kitchen doorway, eyes glaring. There was something about his eyes, something about the way they caught the light, which disturbed Chris. That gleam didn't look healthy, as if reflecting some kind of inner fever.

'I'm trying to help you, Roger.'

'You're trying to tell me what to do, Chris. Just like when we were younger.'

'For fuck's sake! Look at you. You're running on empty and you're heading for a . . . for a . . .'

'For a what? Go on, say it!'

'I don't want us to fight.'

'SAY IT!'

Chris finished his drink in one swallow, banged down the glass and stood up to face him.

'All right, I think you're headed for some kind of breakdown. You need help, Roger. I don't know what's happening to you, but . . .'

'Thanks for the moral support, brother.'

'*Roger!* Do you think I'm blind or something? Don't you think I know what you've been doing since you got here?'

'Oh, yeah? Maybe you'd like to tell me?'

'The stuff you're eating and drinking, for Chrissakes! Sugar, flour, all kinds of crazy stuff. And now kitchen disinfectant and fucking toilet cleaner!'

Trembling with rage, Roger stormed across the room.

Christ! thought Chris. *He's going to hit me!* He braced himself, ready for Roger to throw himself at him.

But Roger grabbed the banister railing at the top of the stairs and glared at Chris as he swung around, thundering down the stairs away from him.

'Where are you going?'

'*Out!*'

'Roger, for God's sake, don't run out like this. We need to talk . . .'

'I'll make other arrangements. Find somewhere else. I'm sure you don't want to share your place with a lunatic.'

'Roger! Come back . . .'

The door slammed, and Roger was gone.

In misery and pain, it slept during the daytime.

The darkness somehow served to ease its terrible suffering. It felt more at one with the night, seeming to remember that it had been travelling in darkness between two places where the light at either end was joyous and welcoming. But not here, not in this place that was no-place; this in-between place where everything was agony and suffering. The light of the day stripped it raw, exposed its shredded nerves to unspeakable torment.

When the first rays of a new dawn had begun to creep through the tree branches in which it hid, the thing had once again become aware of its vulnerability. It had been hunting in the night. Hunting for itself and for the place where it was supposed to be. Its search had been unfulfilled, and the burning light of the day meant that it would have to find a place in darkness, a place where it could hide until the hideous light went away again.

It had found shelter in a concrete culvert.

The culvert had been built into the side of a hill, connecting with a series of storm drain pipes that took a stream from the highlands directly beneath the nearby villages and out into the woods that bordered the A1 motorway. There was a grating across the upper half of the culvert entrance, and the thing thrashed through the shallow water towards it. Crackling traces of blue-white energy sparked in the water around its legs as it moved; fierce spider's web discharges snapped and crawled in and around its shredded, bloodied clothes, like miniature lightning strikes, as the energy within it reacted to the conductive properties of the water through which it ploughed. With one wrench, the thing tore the grating loose and discarded it. There was darkness within. A place where it could rest.

And as it lay there, deep within the darkness, listening to the stream trickling past its legs, those thin spears of blue-white energy would occasionally leap between the thing and the water, lighting the interior of the storm drain like a photographer's bulb. This was a light of which the thing was not afraid. Just like the light ... the light ...

The light on the motorway.

The thing struggled in its half-dream to remember the light. But once again, the chaotic ruin that had been its brain could not focus long enough to make any sense.

Once, something snuffled at the entrance to the culvert.

The thing had turned its head to look. And the animal – whatever it had been – fled in terror.

The long day had passed.

And the thing became aware that the hateful light had gone. It could come out again into the no-place darkness. Free to continue its search.

It clawed through spider's leg branches, paused to listen and knew that it was close to the place where it had first been lost. There was a sound in the night air, a rushing of wind where there was no wind. It followed the stream, thin vein-like traces of energy crackling in its legs, raising steam from the trickling water. Clawing uphill through bushes that ripped its skin and its clothes, it sensed that the place was not far away. The rushing sound was closer. Falling to its knees, it crawled the rest of the way to the top of the rise, and looked down.

There were faint glittering lights down there, travelling fast. Those lights were making the sound it had heard before: the sound of rushing air. Somewhere down there on that long and winding stretch was the place where it had become lost. If it could find its way back to that same place, would the door still be open? And would it find itself down there, waiting, arms held wide? The remaining musculature of the shredded and raw mass that was once its face tried to form a smile, but only managed to show the bloodied teeth in a death's-head grin. It clambered over the rim and began to descend, slipping and sliding and grabbing at hanks of grass to slow its progress. It had to reach those moving lights, whatever they were.

It was sliding too fast, the grass slipping through its claws. The thing scrabbled to halt its progress, barely aware that something was looming out of the night below. A fence, bordering an allotment site.

The thing smashed through the fence, its legs tangling in broken boards, jerking it up and forward so that it continued the rest of its slide face first. Wire and splintered wood snared one of its legs, bringing it to a halt just as it slammed into the side of a roughly built henhouse. Inside, the hens began to screech and bicker. The rest of the allotment was on even ground, the slope continuing beyond the boundary fence thirty feet away. The thing thrashed at the wire that held its leg. In the darkness, something snarled.

The thing finally clawed its way free. Thrusting the shattered wood and chicken wire to one side, it rose on unsteady legs, its sights still fixed ahead. It could no longer see the glittering lights, but knew that they were still there. Just below. It staggered towards the boundary fence.

And from the darkness, something snarled again.

The thing stopped and cocked its head.

'Are you me?' it asked.

There was only another answering snarl.

'Come here. If you're me, come here.'

It searched the darkness for the source of the sound, but could see nothing. Only the dim shapes of cabbages and potato plants, all laid out in neat lines up to the boundary fence by an amateur gardener. It stepped forward, still looking. The thing no longer had eyes. They had boiled and burst in the motorway crash. But the power that had enabled it to become whole again, the power that propelled it through the night, had also given it the power to 'see'.

'I need me. Come here.'

And something hurtled out of the darkness around the side of the henhouse. Something that hit the thing square across the shoulders and slammed it back down to the ground. The Doberman's jaws fastened around the back of the thing's neck and it remained there, its legs planted firmly on the thing's back, pinning it down, tearing and worrying. The dog was on a chain, fastened to the henhouse itself, but long enough to allow it to cover the allotment site. After several break-ins during the night, the owner was taking no chances. The thing braced one hand and began to rise, the dog's legs slipping from its back. But its jaws remained fastened as it slid.

'Are you me?' asked the thing again, above the ferocious snarling and growling of the Doberman.

Then one of the thing's claws fastened on the dog's collar, dragging it around to the side. Part of the thing's torn flesh came flapping away in the dog's jaws. The dog shook it away, lunged to take the thing's restraining arm – and then the thing twisted to fasten both claws around its neck. The Doberman thrashed and howled as the thing rolled on top of it, in turn pinning the animal to the ground with its body weight.

Sparks flashed from the dog's skin where the thing gripped it.

The dog screamed in pain, thrashing to be free.

Grunting, the thing lowered the remains of its face to the dog's head.

The dog snapped its jaws viciously, stripping away the remaining flesh from the thing's bottom lip to its chin.

But in the next instant, the thing had fastened its own bloodied teeth on the dog's throat.

The shrieking Doberman took a long time to die. But there was no one around in this out-of-the way allotment to hear its diminishing screams of pain and terror.

And when, at last, the Doberman had ceased to kick and spasm, the thing sat back briefly to take a rest. It listened.

The sounds of rushing wind were still there, just over the rise.

'You're me.'

The thing stooped to the Doberman's corpse and began to work around its snout and nuzzle. Then behind its head and around behind the ears.

The sounds of wet, ripping cloth.

And the thing stood, smoothing the mask into place.

Except that this mask would not stay in place. The size and the shape were all wrong. No matter how much the thing used its claws to keep the mask in place, it kept sliding away from behind the ears. There was not enough to cover the bottom half of the face. The eye-slits would not fit. And the more the thing scrabbled to keep it smeared to its face, the more shredded the material became. It began to sob.

'You're me. You MUST be me.'

The mask disintegrated.

In fury, the thing crumpled it in its claws, shredding and tearing at it in anger before throwing it down on to the dog's corpse.

'You lied! YOU LIED!'

Weeping, the thing staggered across the allotment to the boundary fence. The wood split beneath its claws in a spray of angry blue sparks. It tottered on the rim of the next slope, looking down on the motorway.

The lights were still there.

There was still hope.

Moaning, the thing began its descent once more.

'Jane, who have you been talking to on the telephone?'

'No one, Tom! No one's telephoned all day! I promise.'

'I tried to ring you five minutes ago, and the fucking phone was engaged, Jane. So you must have been talking to someone.'

'I swear to God, Tom. No one's telephoned. And even if the phone rings, I never answer it, just like you've told me. When it rings three times in quick succession, then I know it's you and that's the only time I answer the telephone. I swear.'

'You wouldn't lie to me, Jane?'

'I swear!'

'Good. That's very, very good. Because I was only testing you there. I didn't ring five minutes ago. You know why I do this, don't you?'

'Because you love me, Tom.'

'And why else?'

'Because you want to protect me.'

'From whom?'

'From other people, from myself. You're all I've got, Tom. And if I didn't have you, I don't know what I'd do.'

'Look what happened when you tried to run away. Do you know why that coach crashed and all those people were killed?'

'I was ill, Tom. I wasn't in my right mind . . .'

'Answer me, you bitch! Do you know WHY all those people died?'

'No, Tom.'

'They died because you ran away. You were selfish. Only thinking of yourself, as usual. So you got on that bus. And someone was watching you all the time. Can you guess who was watching you?'

'God was watching me, Tom.'

'That's right. God was watching you. And then, when you wouldn't see sense, wouldn't listen to what I've always told you, he made that coach crash. He made that bus turn over and he made that lorry smash into it. He made them – all those people – burn. He punished every single one of them. And all because of what you did. Do you understand that, Jane? If you hadn't run away like you did, God wouldn't have punished all those innocent people. It's your fault, Jane. You know that, don't you?'

'It's all my fault, Tom. I'm bad. And I need to be looked after. I need you to . . .'

And then, a sudden change in her husband's voice when the door of his office opens and someone comes in. 'That's right, darling. I know it's inconvenient, but I knew you could pull the stops out. Dinner for five of us from the office. Tell you what, I'll take them all for a snifter at the pub round the corner, give

*you a chance to get organised. How about that? Then I'll bring
them around at . . . what time do you think?'*

'You want me to prepare a dinner for five people tonight?'

*'And you and me, of course.' And then Tom laughs heartily
as if Jane has made a wonderful joke. 'So, seven in all. And the
time, darling?'*

'Tom . . . I don't know if I can . . . I'm not sure . . .'

*'Eight o'clock? That would be marvellous. I'll try to keep them
sober . . . excuse me, love. Just one moment.' And Jane hears
good-natured mumbling as Tom talks to whoever is there, now
on his or her way out of the office. She hears a door close. 'Are
you still there, bitch?'*

'Yes, Tom.'

*'Do I have to repeat myself again, spell it all out for you?
Or are you capable of remembering that one small message?'*

'Dinner for seven. At eight o'clock. Yes, Tom.'

'Then get a move on.'

'Yes, Tom.'

*'And Jane. You had better make a good job of it. I'm
warning you.'*

'Yes, Tom.'

'God is watching.'

'Yes, Tom.'

And the line goes dead.

And as soon as Jane put the telephone down, she stood back
away from it as if it might somehow be alive and sentient,
still somehow connected mentally with Tom. The line might
be dead, but was Tom still there even with the receiver back
in place? Was he listening to what she might say? Could he
somehow see her standing there, both hands to her face in
shock, waiting for the wrong kind of reaction?

She sat down heavily on the sofa, hands still clasped to her
white face.

Dinner for five. Seven, counting us.

It was like the dream she'd had on the coach. Or was it
a dream? Had there already been a dinner party like the
nightmare party she recalled from the coach ride? She didn't

know what was real and what was imagined any more. She looked around the living room, as if expecting that there might be someone there to whom she could turn for help. Finally, with trembling fingers, she reached for the bottle on the coffee table. Screwing off the top, she drank deeply, then lowered the bottle to look at the label.

'Dewson's Fabric Conditioner. Keeps your woollens as good as new.'

She stared at the label. The words there made no sense to her at all.

She drank again. But this time, as the liquid burned her oesophagus, she choked. When the coughing had subsided, there were tears. She began to weep as she hadn't wept since childhood. Racking, mournful pleas for help that was never going to come. She was alone. And in a living nightmare. Things were happening to her that she could not understand. Things that she was unsure were real at all. Perhaps everything, including the bottle she was holding in her hand, was just what Tom had always told her. Things were only happening in her mind and nowhere else, and there was only her husband to direct and protect her.

Dinner . . .

'Oh, sweet Mary, Mother of God.'

Wiping the tears from her face, Jane staggered to her feet again and headed for the kitchen. There was hardly any time, and if everything wasn't just right, wasn't just the way Tom liked things to be . . . She shook her head, not wanting to give head-room to such thoughts. The possibility was too awful.

Drinking from the bottle again, she lurched into the kitchen.

For a moment, she staggered on the threshold. Everything seemed to zoom in and out of focus for a moment.

Oh God, don't let me faint. Don't let me faint . . .

She lurched towards the freezer and prayed that there was a joint of meat in there.

There had been no answer to the bell, so the burly paramedic pounded on the front door. Both he and his partner had tried

looking through the front window, but couldn't see anyone
inside. Clearly, there was someone at home. The television
was playing to itself (a football game that they were both
pissed off they had to miss because of their shift work, but it
was being videoed at home) and the volume was turned down
low, so there was no way that anyone at home wouldn't hear
the front doorbell ringing.

'Mr Stark!'

The paramedic stood back again and looked up at one of
the bedroom windows. No twitching of curtains. No signs
from inside.

'Mr Stark, are you there?'

The hospital administrator had tried telephoning Stark after
the warning from Curtis, the reporter. After all, wouldn't
everyone look a bloody fool if some twitching newspaperman
was overreacting and an ambulance came screaming up to the
front door while the poor sod inside was just settling down in
front of the match with a couple of cans of lager? But there
had been no answer to four calls, and that's when the alert
had gone out.

'He's in there,' said the second man. 'He must be.'

'So either he's ignoring us or . . . ?'

'Or he's overdosed like we were told. Your shoulder on the
door or mine?'

'It was my turn on Wednesday.'

'Yeah, but that door was just on a latch. No problem
breaking that down. This one's got studs in it or something.
What if he's got a double Yale lock?'

'I'm a paramedic. I'll see to any of your injuries. Trust
me.'

Grimacing, the first paramedic stepped forward, deciding
on one last thump on the door before the heavy treatment.

But before his fist could connect with the door, it opened.

The paramedic recoiled, realising that he had almost knocked
on someone's face.

'Yes?' asked the white-faced man on the other side of the
door. His black hair was dishevelled, as if he had just got
out of bed.

'Mr Stark?'

'Who are you?'

'Mr, er, Harry Stark?'

'Last time I looked at my birth certificate I was. What can I do for you?'

'Well . . . it's not what you can do for us. It's more like . . .'

'What we thought we'd have to be doing for you, sir,' said the second paramedic.

'Look,' said Harry, 'I'm in the middle of the match. Must have dozed off and missed some of the game. So the last thing I need is puzzles on the doorstep. What are you after?'

Nonplussed, still looking over Harry's shoulder into the hall and through the front windows into the living room as if he expected to see someone lying there in distress, the first paramedic said: 'We got a call. Someone told us that you weren't . . . that you . . . well, you know. That you were unwell, and that maybe you needed an ambulance.'

'All I need is a little peace and quiet to watch the football.'

'Have you . . . ?' The second paramedic shuffled uneasily. 'I mean, you haven't . . . taken anything, have you?'

'I've taken more than enough crap from you two, for a start.'

'Okay, Mr Stark,' said the first man, backing off. 'Someone somewhere has either made a stupid mistake or else is playing a joke in very bad taste. We're sorry to have bothered you.'

Without another word, the white-faced man closed the door.

Returning to the ambulance, the second man said to the first: 'Maybe we should have asked to come in. Had a look around or something.'

'Why? That bastard Curtis is just trying to stir up another story. Let the management sort him out.'

'I mean maybe we shouldn't just walk away.'

'What the hell are you on about?'

'Didn't you see his face? Christ, he looked terrible.'

'After six cans of lager and falling asleep in front of the television, *everybody* looks terrible. Even me.'

'Still, maybe we should . . .'

'Look! We got an emergency call. If that guy had OD'd, he'd be on the bloody floor.'

'But it took him a long time to answer the door . . .'

'After six cans, I'm surprised he got to the door *at all*.'

The second man laughed at last.

The mobile radio crackled into life as they made their way down the garden path, giving details of a severe asthma attack not one mile away. In seconds, the ambulance was on its way, and the false alarm about Harry Stark was all but forgotten.

And standing with his back to the front door, sweat streaming down his face, Harry clenched his fists tight and gritted his teeth.

Had they really gone? Or had they just moved the ambulance around the corner? Had they parked it there out of sight, and were they even now leaning out of the windows and looking back at the house, waiting for some sign that there was something wrong, that he hadn't played the part convincingly? He remained there, pressed hard against the door; waiting for the hammering to begin again.

Each waiting moment was agony.

'No,' he said, through gritted teeth. 'No, you bastard. I won't.'

The pain gripped him again. At the base of the neck and right down his spine to his hips. He jerked away from the door, bending at the waist and gagging. Spittle drifted from his mouth to the carpet like a single strand of gossamer.

'*No!*'

He flung himself upright, slamming back against the door. This time, unheeding of the paramedic who might be waiting outside, he hammered his balled fists against the panelling in a torrent of anguish and rage. Let them come.

His breath came in sobs. And God, how he wished he could vomit. He was alive, and that was bad enough; but surely he could be allowed the dubious relief that hanging over a toilet bowl or a sink might provide? He knew how many sleeping tablets he had consumed, knew that it was impossible for him to be standing here like this; yet he was standing, and sobbing, and praying and . . .

It came again. The same compulsion.

'*No!*' cried Harry again. He would not give in. By rights, he should be dead. And now that he was aware of what was within him, he had even more cause – if that was possible – to be dead.

The overdose should have killed him. But instead, it had done something else. Now he knew that the chemical shit and the ridiculous household oddments that he had been force-feeding himself had been for a purpose. Something that he could never understand. He had been made to eat and drink all that crap to feed and nurture and protect the thing that had ... that had ... *imploded* into him on the motorway. Without all that stuff, it would have died.

It was in there now. Deep inside him. Not in his guts, not in his brain. But somewhere; deep, *deep* down. If Harry believed that he had a soul, then he imagined that this thing was somehow wrapped around it, clinging there and feeding from it. Growing stronger. Until it could ... could ... what? That much he could not guess. But the drugs he had taken to kill himself, to ease his pain, had also done something else.

They had taken the thing that was within him to the point of extinction. Having come so far, it had fought back with all the strength it possessed.

It had brought Harry back from the brink of death. Had fought and absorbed and somehow *assimilated* the overdose; had come out of hiding within him to fight, and eradicated the effects of the drug from his system, just as it had fought to survive in the last few moments before the motorway collision, when it had taken its last desperate chance. Like the others with which it was travelling, it had done the only thing possible at the moment of impact.

It had survived.

Just as it had fought to survive when its host had decided to kill itself.

It had saved the host, and saved itself.

But not without a price. Because, in that struggle, the mental and psychological barrier that it had used to block its presence from its host had been severed. Now Harry knew that it was inside him. Now he knew that he was not going mad. It could not work on him secretly any more, pretending that it didn't exist and that the extravagances of Harry's behaviour were mental aberrations.

It was *there*.

Again, the impulse.

'I won't,' said Harry, beads of sweat running down his face. 'I won't do what you want. I *won't!*'

He shoved himself away from the door again. There was a scream inside him, but he would not allow it out. It was somehow a further defiance of the thing inside that sought to control him. He staggered into the living room. Like a drunk, he lunged at the curtains, dragging them across the windows. Sobbing for breath, he sank to his knees. Looking up, he saw the television. The screen was green, or almost green. Things were running there, chasing something.

One of those running things was running harder than all the others behind.

As it ran, there was a sound from the screen. The sound of a great crowd. As the figure ran, the sound of the crowd was growing, louder and louder, urging it on. The running figure twitched, and something flew into a net.

And the sound of the crowd became a roar.

The motorway. The light. The screaming.

The sound of the roaring crowd from the television was a sound of jubilation. The sound that Harry had heard on the motorway was a sound of terror and utter desperation. But the intent of that roaring, screaming sound did not matter. The sound made Harry remember again.

'Daddeeeeeee!'

He crushed his hands over his ears, stumbling on his knees and bumping against the bureau. Something fell to the floor with a clatter beside him.

It was the photograph of Jean, Hilary and Diane. All with their heads together and with their index fingers on the indent between nose and top lip. The family joke. And as he looked at it, it seemed that Harry could hear them all saying the phrase that had brought so much jocularity to the family.

'*Only The Angels Know.*'

He cried out in anguish.

As the sound of the crowd on the television set went on and on, Harry utterly hated the thing that was inside him. He knew with unworldly conviction that it was there and could hear him. It had been recovering somehow inside him, being fed and growing strong. It had survived – whatever in hell it was – but his wife and children had not. Harry did not want to live. He wanted to be dead; with his family. But the thing inside him wanted him to live. It was dependent on him, and could not survive if he died. And it had made him live. Had saved him from the overdose, and had therefore saved itself.

And Christ, how he *hated* it for that.

It had not caused the accident. But he was alive, because *it* did not want to die.

They had collided with these things on the motorway. And whatever in hell they were, they had *jumped* at the point of impact. Harry knew now that each one of the human survivors of that crash had *another* survivor inside themselves. Each had one of these *things*, hiding deep down inside.

Again, the impulse.

Harry fought to resist. But it was doing it to him even now. Somehow, it could apply a pressure to the base of his skull, just where his neck met his shoulders. It could stab him there, with a pain that seemed to flow like an electric current right down his spine. Harry hugged himself tight, moaning in pain.

'You won't kill me ... you can't kill me ... *oh God!* ... because if you do, you'll kill yourself ...'

Suddenly, he was on his feet again, lunging back across to the bureau. The pain eased as he tore open the drawers and began pulling out the contents. A telephone book, old Christmas cards, electricity and gas bills. Harry paused, breathing heavily. The pain began again.

'Bastard!'

He began clawing through the drawer once more until he found what the thing inside required.

A sheet of paper and a stub of pencil.

He felt nausea rising in his gorge. But it seemed that the

thing inside even had control of that. The feeling passed.
Wiping the sweat from his face, he blundered to the living-
room table and sat heavily.

He fought again, trying to reassert his will.

The pain stabbed in his spine.

Harry gave in . . . and let the thing control his hand.

He began to scrawl on the paper.

And when he had finished, Harry sat back. The thing had
taken away the pain completely now. With his head thrown
back, he gulped in air and waited until his breathing had
calmed. It seemed that the thing was allowing him that
breathing space. Finally, wiping the sweat from his face, he
looked down at what he had scrawled on the paper.

Find the Others

The last time Curtis had been in church, he was drunk.

And if the truth were known, he could do with a drink now.
He wondered whether the communion wine up there on the
altar table was the real stuff, or some watered-down variety. He
seemed to remember taking communion on that last occasion,
even though he had never been confirmed. Something in his
mind about doing it to be sociable. His memory of the event
was blurred. It had been a christening. The baby daughter of
his ex-wife's friend. Whatever he had done, his wife's friends
had never spoken to him again, and it had been one further
nail in the coffin of his marriage, now long since over.

Curtis looked around. Was this a typical congregation?
Maybe everything he'd heard and read about the church
being a dying institution had been misinformed. Or perhaps
the recent events on which one of his colleagues had reported
were the reason for the very real sense of expectation on the
faces that he was looking at this morning. The place was

packed with people of all ages. He'd had difficulty in squeezing into one of the rows. But now that he was here, three from the back, he could study the faces carefully. Everyone's attention was focused up front. Even the children seemed affected by the air of expectation. There was no crying or snuffling, or running around in the aisles, the way he remembered from his youth: tight-lipped Sunday-outfit Christians gritting their teeth in the name of loving patience while the kids played frisbee with the offertory bowl.

So far there had been nothing out of the ordinary. Curtis recognised the Reverend Jameson from the photograph his newspaper had printed with the initial story. The photograph must have been a few years old, but the guy standing up there by the altar was still clearly recognisable. Perhaps there was a shade more grey in the hair. Curtis listened as the service proceeded, looking from the vicar to the faces around him as they followed what he assumed was the communion service. He remained unmoved by what he perceived to be the hollow phoniness of it all. How could some people be so gullible?

The newspaper report had meant nothing to him. There had been some kind of falling-out between the Reverend Jameson and the bishop about the changes that had taken place in some of the services. There had been complaints that a revivalist aspect had suddenly crept into what should be traditional Church of England worship. To Curtis's mind, it was all a big 'So what?'

And then another colleague had drawn his attention to a follow-up article. The specific problem with the bishop had been the introduction of a laying-on-of-hands ceremony, a form of spiritual healing. But this was not being carried out by the resident vicar.

It was being done by a certain Martin Russell.

There was no photograph to accompany this second article, and surely there must be several dozen Martin Russells in the telephone book. But something continued to nag at Curtis. Could this be the same lorry driver he had seen catapulted across the casualty department by lightning-that-wasn't-lightning? The same man who had refused to speak to him when he'd gone to his home to interview him. Curtis had pushed the article to one side. But the thoughts had continued to worry him. Finally, driven by the memory of the dressing-down by his editor for missing out on the stolen-body story (which seemed to have dried up altogether, with no new developments), he had sought out the church in question after checking with his colleague who had covered the first story to make sure that he wasn't professionally treading on his toes. At least he could check it out, establish that the reborn Martin Russell wasn't the same as the lorry driver, and then let it go.

'Please stand,' said the Reverend Jameson, and Curtis suddenly found that he was the only one still sitting. Quickly, he joined the rest of the congregation, peering over the shoulder of the man in front to get a view of what was going on. 'Blessing and power and glory and honour be Yours for ever and ever. Amen.' The congregation also gave an amen. Was someone coming into the church from one of the side doors behind the altar? Curtis struggled to see, but the man in front shifted position and blocked his view. Then, at an unheard, unseen signal, everyone sat down. Curtis was left standing alone. But now he could see that he must have been mistaken. There was no one up there except the vicar, still in the same position in front of the altar. For a moment, their eyes met. Curtis sat quickly. Could it be that the reverend had sensed that he was a newspaperman? Had that been a sudden and frosty appraisal?

'I'm glad to see so many familiar faces,' continued the Reverend Jameson. 'And new faces, too. They say that all publicity, even bad publicity, is good publicity. That's certainly been the case recently, and no doubt many of you will have seen the recent newspaper reports about the ... difference of opinion between the bishop and myself. I don't want to elaborate any further for the benefit of the tabloids ...'

Was he suddenly looking at Curtis again?

'... but the problem is still outstanding, and it would seem that the Church authorities are unwilling to even listen to what I have to say about the wonderful thing that has happened here. What I can say to you today is what I've said already to the diocese administration and the Church Commissioners. A marvellous thing has happened. A wonderful blessing has been bestowed on us. In an age of cynicism and pessimism, it seems that there is no place any more for miracles. But a miracle *has* happened. God's hand has reached out and touched a very special someone. And that someone has come here, to this church, to pass on that blessing. Now, it may be that the Church authorities will continue in their efforts to try to stop what is taking place here. That they will try to tell you that this is not a gift from God. But I believe with all my heart that they are wrong. I have seen with my own eyes . . . indeed, many of you have seen for yourselves . . . the healing miracle which has come among us. And so long as I live and breathe and believe, I will do everything in my power to ensure that it is not taken away.'

Jameson was looking at someone in the front row now, and smiling. Someone who had not been there a moment before.

Curtis recognised the back of the head, and something seemed to lurch inside him. Had he been writing an article, he might have been tempted to describe it as his 'heart missing a beat', but then would have discarded the cliché. Cliché or not, he had felt something jump up and down inside him at that moment.

No, surely not . . .

But the curly red hair looked just like the hair he remembered. The shape of the head looked the same. A big man. Curtis strained forward, willing the figure to give a half-turn and confirm that he was wrong. There was a woman sitting next to the figure, now turning to look up at her companion with adoring eyes. She looked the same type as Russell's wife, but was it her?

Come on . . . turn around . . .

No. Why should this person be the lorry driver? It made no sense.

Neither does what you saw in that hospital, Curtis. Or what you've heard about. Screaming voices on the motorway. Thunder and lightning like nothing on earth. Dead sheep and

horses for miles around the crash. Mutilated and stolen bodies.
Why shouldn't this be Martin Russell? Of course none of it
makes the remotest sense. But doesn't the fact that it's too
crazy to be true, too crazy to fit into any kind of pattern, make
it eminently possible that this Martin Russell is the same man?
Why the hell else are you sitting here? You gave in to that crazy
logic, didn't you . . . ?

It *was* the same Martin Russell.

He had shifted slightly in his seat as Curtis strained forward.
And there could be no mistaking it. The same uncomfortable
expression on his face. As if things were going on which
were way above his head, but he was going to see it through
anyway.

Curtis sat back, mind whirling.

Martin stood and moved towards the altar rail, and Curtis
examined the expressions of naked joy on the faces all around
him. They seemed convinced that *something* was going on.
And for those faces to look so ecstatic, then surely they
must have seen or experienced the magic of this so-called
laying-on of hands. Martin kept looking back at his wife in
the front row, drawing his strength from her presence. And
when Curtis looked back at him again, he noticed that there
was a difference in the big man's face. There was no doubt
that this was the lorry driver, but there had been a change.
Curtis strained to examine the face while the crowd continued
to applaud and Martin shuffled uncomfortably.

Skin colour, concluded Curtis at last. *He doesn't look as . . .*
robust as the last time I saw him. He had an outdoor type of
tan that last time. A man used to spending a lot of time in the
open air. Sort of quality leather. Now he looks sallow, as if he's
been ill. There are dark circles under his eyes which weren't
there before.

Martin held up his hands and the applause died away.

'I was never a religious man,' he said. 'Anyone can tell you
that. And I'm not a religious man now . . .'

Curtis noticed his wife shuffle uncomfortably; saw the vicar
look down at his shoes.

'No,' continued Martin, with a brief glance in both their

directions. 'It's true. And I'm not here to lie to anyone. I haven't been to church since I was a boy. Never looked at a Bible. I've always tried to do the right thing, and my wife has always insisted that I'm a Christian by proxy. Someone else once told me something about ... humanism, I think it was. And what they had to say seems to be more like what's been going on in my head over the years. But that doesn't mean to say that I *disbelieve*. I love my wife, and I respect what she believes. I respect what the Reverend Jameson stands for. But it's no use me standing here now and telling you all something that's not quite true.'

It seemed to Curtis that Martin's eyes had begun to sparkle as he talked. The embarrassment was gone from his expression and his posture.

'But I do know something that's true.'

Martin coughed then, a racking cough that made his wife wince.

'And it's this: I nearly died ... by rights I *should* have died. But I didn't, and when I came through it all, I was changed. Something had happened to me. I had been given a power. A power to heal. Now ... my wife firmly believes that the power comes from God. She says she *knows* it. Because I was able to heal her. I was able to take away her pain, and the doctors still can't tell us how it was done. One of them even used the word miracle. The Reverend Jameson feels the same way. He's felt that power, and he's been healed. And he tells me that he also believes this power comes from God, because it's a power that does *good*. My wife is the most important person in the world to me. She has the faith that I've never been able to find. So when she tells me the power comes from God, I'll take her word for it. She trusts the reverend here. And he also says it's a power for good. So I'll take his word for it, too. All I know is that I can heal ...'

'Draw near with faith,' said the Reverend Jameson, making the sign of the cross. The congregation began to sing a hymn.

The people in the front row were filing out into the aisle. As they moved forward to the altar rail where Martin stood, the second row were also beginning to file out, just as they would if receiving holy communion.

And Curtis watched as Jameson stood next to Martin. Two young men had moved from the front row and taken up position behind the people who were moving to the altar. Once the altar step was filled with kneeling people, Jameson began to move, making the sign of the cross and moving to the next person. Martin put his hand on the communicant and Curtis watched as he closed his hollowed eyes and concentrated hard. The two young men stood facing Martin and Jameson, also moving along so that they were always directly behind the person being touched.

Nothing seemed to be happening.

The first three people Martin touched remained kneeling in an attitude of prayer, standing after he had passed and moving back to the aisle as their place was taken by someone waiting behind.

But the fourth person – a woman about seventy years old – suddenly seemed to convulse as Martin touched her. She moaned and swayed backwards as both young men swooped forward and took her arms, carefully moving her away from the rail and carrying her back down the aisle to a seat. Someone in the congregation cried:

'*Hallelujah!*'

The singing, at first hesitant and expectant, suddenly swelled into loud exuberance.

Curtis looked at Martin. His eyes were closed and he had taken a step backwards. Was that partly outstretched hand trembling? His wife was still in the front row, had not joined the others. Curtis could see the look of joy on her face and could not somehow match it to the look on Martin's. Surely this guy was in *pain*? The young men hurried back down the aisle to the altar rail, took up their positions once more, and now the vicar and Martin were moving down the line again.

Suddenly, Curtis saw another face near the front of the church, intent on what was happening. This figure seemed disinclined to join in with the service, and Curtis found himself examining the figure, trying to work out where he had seen him before. The man was perhaps in his late fifties, with iron-grey hair that curled around the collar of his expensive three-piece suit. There were two other men sitting on either side of him, looking more like debt-collectors than churchgoers. The man with the iron-grey hair occasionally smiled as he watched. Curtis *knew* that face. He was sure of it. But no matter how he tried, he could not place it. His attention drifted back to what was happening by the altar rail.

He stayed for the whole service.

And in that time, twelve people reacted in the same manner as the elderly lady. A convulsion, a spasm, and the young men hurried forward to make sure that the communicant didn't do a back-flip from the altar steps to the cold marble floor. When it was all over, and everyone had returned to their seats, Martin moved back to his wife and sat silently as she continued to sing her heart out. His head was lowered so that Curtis could not see his face. He seemed to be exhausted.

The communion wafer and wine were taken after the laying-on of hands. As far as Curtis could tell, it seemed that the service itself was unchanged. There had merely been a gap in the proceedings before communion was taken so that Martin could do his stuff. At the end of the service, the congregation rose for the final hymn. The vicar came down the centre aisle, giving a blessing as he moved.

'Go in peace to serve the Lord.'

'In the name of Christ,' said the ensemble. 'Amen.'

They kneeled for a final prayer before dispersing.

But Martin and his wife were already gone from the front row.

And the man with the iron-grey hair and his two escorts had vanished.

Curtis hung around in the aisle until the last person had shaken the vicar's hand and left the church. Jameson seemed not to notice him as he turned and headed for the vestry.

'Reverend!' called Curtis, following him and putting on his most affable smile. His voice seemed inordinately loud now in the empty church. For reasons he could not understand, it made him uncomfortable. The vicar did not look round, but continued on his way to the vestry doors at the side of the church. 'I wonder if I could have a word . . .'

'What word would that be?' asked Jameson in a mild voice. He still did not turn.

'About . . . you know, what's happening here. You see, I've got a friend . . . someone close . . . who's very ill. And it would mean the world to me if your friend might be able to . . .'

'The world,' said Jameson. He had reached the vestry door and paused with his hand on the handle. This time he looked back, but there was no reproach in his expression. 'That's what you write about, isn't it? The world and its sorrows.'

'No, you don't understand. I've got this friend . . .'

'Why don't you try and do some good in your job? Give something back to the world. The way Martin has been given the ability to give something good back to it. You saw what's happening here. Why do you want to debunk it?'

'All right, I wasn't being truthful just now. But believe me, I *don't* want to debunk it. I just want to find out exactly what's . . .'

'Goodbye,' said Jameson.

He vanished into the vestry, closing the door firmly behind him.

Curtis looked at the panelling for a long time.

Finally, he turned and looked back at the silent altar.

Burwell had been standing opposite Wharf Seven of the Ouseburn development for only ten minutes, but it felt like hours and his agitation was getting worse by the moment. The luxury apartment block stood on the quayside, overlooking the River Tyne where the Ouseburn tributary met its big sister. Burwell had found a stand of designer shrubs and trees directly across the road which hid him from sight.

How long could it be before someone stumbled over Klark's body? If he was lucky, the bastard might lie there undetected until the next morning. But what if someone taking a short-cut should see him? (*They might think he's just drunk, and leave him alone. Some chance.*) Or what if someone should drive into the car park and run over the body? Burwell cursed under his breath, trembling with anxiety. Now he wished that he'd dragged the body into the bushes. (*A train went past. Travelling fast, but someone might have seen me if I hadn't got away when I did.*)

He couldn't take the chance of waiting any longer. With Klark's criminal record, he felt sure that it wouldn't take the police long to discover his identity. So if his body was found that evening, the panda cars would be screeching up to Wharf Seven in short order.

Heart hammering, mouth dry, Burwell stepped smartly out of the bushes and marched across the street. Briefly fumbling at his fly to suggest to anyone watching that he had skipped into the bushes to relieve his bladder, he kept his head down as he pushed through the revolving glass door. There was no one in the reception area. Two choices now: the elevator or the stairs. If the elevator was already there, he'd risk taking it. But when he stabbed the button, he could see that it was on the tenth floor. It started down, but his anxiety would not allow him to stay and wait. He pushed through the door to the stairwell and started to climb. There was a strong smell of disinfectant here.

To kill the smell of the shit who lives here. Well, they won't have to bother about that any more . . .

He gripped Klark's key tight in his fist as he climbed, as if it might suddenly acquire a life of its own and fly from his pocket. With each step, he expected to hear a door bang open and the sound of people ascending or descending to meet him. But his luck held all the way to the sixth floor.

He paused on the landing, one hand on the door that led to the apartments on this level. His fingertips had begun to tingle, in the familiar manner of the new power that he had somehow miraculously been granted. The tingling seemed to be affecting his gloves, as if the leather were somehow shrinking around his hand and fingers. He closed his eyes and willed the feeling to go away. He had quickly learned to master it.

Control your breathing. Come on. Everything's working out fine. Klark's out of your life for ever. Just find the videotape, and get out of there. After that you can start a new life.

He pushed the door open.

Klark's apartment was the very next door on the landing.

What if there's someone else in there? Oh Christ, why didn't I think of that? What if he's living with someone, or he's got one of his working girls in there?

He stood before the door with sweat pouring down his back. He yearned for some of the crazy stuff he'd been forcing into his mouth these past few weeks.

Then I'll have to do what I did to Klark. It's as simple as that.

He knocked.

In his mind's eye, Burwell saw the door judder open on a chain. There would be a face there. A woman's, perhaps. Or maybe even a child. And then he would tell them that something bad had happened to Klark, that he'd been sent by him. That the police would be here soon and there were things to do, things to get rid of before they showed up. He would show that face the key and the wallet that Klark had given him as evidence that they should believe what he was saying. Then the face might say, *Maybe you mugged him and stole the wallet and the key. Maybe you're going to come in and rape me or something* . . . Then Burwell would say: *For God's sake, there's no time! Klark'll fucking kill you if you don't let me in. You know what he's like.* The door would close then. He would hear the chain rattle as it was unlocked. It would begin to edge open . . . and then Burwell would thrust his arm through the gap, clamping his hand on the face as . . .

He knocked again.

He needed to piss.

There was no one inside.

Fingers trembling, Burwell took out the key.

'Hello . . .' His voice refused to work properly as he edged the door open.

Thank you thank you thank you thank you . . .

There was a table light on by the window, but there was no one in the apartment. Quickly, Burwell shut the door and looked around. The place was several shades gaudier than he would ever have imagined. The sofa and chairs had leopard-skin coverings. Everything seemed to be coloured gold or black. A full-length airbrushed portrait of a naked woman in stilettos, squatting. A copy of *Playboy* strategically placed on the gold and black coffee table to disguise Klark's real activities with a fake glamour.

Burwell started with the nearest cupboard, pulling open the drawers.

And as he hunted, his mind began to race.

Filled with anger, flooring the accelerator as he overtook that bloody coach on the inside lane. And right now, right at this moment, more than anything else in the world, he hates more than he has ever hated in his life. He hates that bastard Klark. His foot on the accelerator is like having his foot on Klark's neck, squeezing the life out of him. His hands gripping the steering wheel are also somehow around Klark's neck. More than anything else, he wants to KILL . . .

He began to throw underclothes on to the floor behind him.

His car passes the rear of the coach and then the entire vehicle swings out towards him, vast and powerful and shuddering. The car horn screams, and then that scream is joined by a screaming that comes out of the terrible, terrible light. The light that engulfs the car and the coach. And the screaming is like a multitude of voices, all in terror of an imminent, horrifying impact.

There was nothing in the cupboard and there was a ringing in Burwell's ears as he lunged across to Klark's wardrobe. He began to tear his clothes from the hangers, ripping the fabric of shirts as he fumbled in pockets, throwing everything over his shoulder. He rummaged through the drawers, checked for secret compartments, rapped on the back of the wardrobe to see if it was hollow, checked on top, and then dragged it away from the wall to look behind. Nothing. He continued to ransack the apartment.

He stamps on the brakes, a hand flying to one ear to try to block out the sounds of the screaming, which have somehow burst into the car. The coach looms gigantically at his side, clips the car's wing and everything whirls and twists as his car is slammed from the motorway, spinning end to end in a welter of imploding windscreen and side windows. Burwell is screaming with the invisible horde; screaming and screaming and . . .

'Where is it? *Where is IT?*'

Burwell saw the kitchen and staggered towards it over the mess he had made on the floor.

Keep calm, for fuck's sake keep calm. If anyone downstairs hears you . . .

He began to search the cabinets.

The car has slewed on to the motorway embankment. He scrabbles at the door lock, trying to get out. The light and the screaming are still in the car with him. He must surely go mad, and hears himself screaming with them. Now he knows that the light must be fire. The car is burning . . . and he is burning . . .

Burwell was on the verge of panic and knew it. In a moment, he would be unable to help himself. He would start throwing the tinned food around, smashing the place up.

The car rolls back down the embankment, back across the motorway and into the oncoming traffic as Burwell scrabbles at the door lock and his seat belt . . .

Sobbing, he collapsed to his knees on the kitchen floor.

He would never find it. Perhaps – and the possibility filled him with despair and horror – perhaps it just wasn't here. Perhaps he had another place where he kept his important stuff.

No, I won't believe that. I saw his eyes when he was dying. He said it was here and he meant it. He really thought that I could stop what was happening to him.

Burwell tried to draw strength from the memory of the dying bastard's eyes.

And then a great craving filled him. The craving that he had been unable to understand since the road accident. He looked up at the opened cupboard doors. Was there a bag of flour in there? Was that it?

No, something else.

What, then? Spices? Cayenne pepper?

There was a sink unit with a double-doored compartment beneath it.

Yes . . .

On all fours, Burwell scrambled to the unit and dragged the doors open. In a cardboard box, he found what he was looking for. Mirage Window Cleaner. 'Grip and Spray for a See-Through Day. Warning: Keep Out of Reach of Small Children. Do Not Take Internally.' Gripping the trigger attachment on the plastic bottle, Burwell jammed the nozzle into his mouth and squeezed, using it like an over-sized fresh-breath spray. Instinctively, he knew that what he was doing was all part of the Big Change that had happened to him. Somehow, it was feeding his newfound ability. And he knew that if he started to ask himself questions about it all, started to doubt his sanity, then he was risking everything. He didn't know how or why he was able to do what he'd done. But if he started to look too closely, then maybe it would all go away. Had he died in that burning car? Had he somehow been reborn? He refused to give the thoughts any head-room. All he knew was that the power was in him, and that rather than cringe in terror from it, he had learned quickly how to use it to his advantage. Klark was dead. And once he was out of this place with what he wanted, he could continue to use the power to get him everything he'd wanted in life.

Just so long as he kept cool, and didn't ask himself too many questions about how and why this power had been given to him.

He finished sucking on the window-cleaning spray, and saw something else in the cardboard box under the sink unit. B-B Barbecue Fuel. He paused, wondering whether his strange cravings now extended to something that might not only poison him but cause spontaneous combustion. Barbecue fuel, here in a sixth-floor apartment block. How the hell could the bastard have barbecue parties up here?

But then he knew what he must do.

He had turned the apartment upside down and there was still no sign of the evidence. There was only one way to make sure that it was destroyed.

Destroy the apartment.

Discarding the window cleaner, Burwell grabbed the red and yellow bottle and pulled himself up again. Wrenching off the stopper, he could see that the bottle was almost full. With a grinning rictus on his face, he made his way out of the kitchen. Pausing only to look with satisfaction at the torn clothes strewn over the floor, he began to splash the fuel around him. At any moment, he expected to hear police sirens down below on the quayside. His face a leering mask, Burwell continued with his task. There were two pints of fuel in this bottle. More than enough. Returning to the kitchen, he found a box of household matches, upended the cardboard box and emptied anything remotely flammable on to the floor. Starting back for the lounge area, he turned and saw the cooker. Eyes glittering, he hurried back and turned on all the gas rings.

Back in the lounge, the smell of the fuel was having a strange effect on him. It was filling him with a craving once more. Burwell laughed aloud and hurried to the main door. Opening it a crack, he could see that his luck was holding. Didn't anyone else live in this place? He closed the door again, leaned back heavily against the wood and slid down on to his haunches. The video and the negatives were in here somewhere.

He scratched a match on the box. It flared into life. And in that curling orange flame he saw . . .

. . . *himself, staggering down the centre of the motorway, away from his shattered car. Dazed, his hands constantly explore his body as he walks towards the overturned coach and the lorry. The car he was in must have been burning, but he has survived it untouched and cannot understand how his clothes have not peeled and shrivelled away, cannot understand why his flesh hasn't cooked and charred. Turning to look at his wrecked car, he expects to see flames leaping from its windows, expects to see a trail of footsteps from the car, a track of soot and ash from his disintegrating, still smouldering body. Then he hears the whump of igniting fuel and staggers around again to see orange-blue flames leap up from around the overturned lorry. The sight of the fire freezes him and he watches in terror as it sweeps around the lorry to the coach.*

Suddenly and with shocking force, the coach explodes in flame and . . .

Burwell cried out in pain as the match burned his finger. It dropped to the carpet.

Instantly, bunsen blue flame began to pool at his feet.

Shocked into reality again, Burwell dragged the door open behind him. The sudden draught of air sent a wave of engulfing blue flame surging over the torn clothes and debris in the centre of the room. He skipped around the door. Just before he pulled it shut, he saw the curtains at the picture windows flare and flap into exploding orange blossoms.

The stairs. Use the stairs again.

Head down, Burwell descended the way he'd come, expecting to hear the sounds of the inferno in Klark's apartment. But everything was uncannily still.

Somewhere above on the stairwell a door banged.

He froze, waiting for the sounds of footsteps. There were none.

Two minutes later, he was outside on the street outside Wharf Seven. Without looking back he walked on into the night, head down.

Forty minutes later, somewhere in the night and on his way home, he heard the first fire engine klaxon.

His hands were tightly balled into fists in his pocket.

Grinning again, he began to formulate his plans for career advancement at Purcell Advertising.

Vinny watched the bastard artist come out through the front door of the terraced block, slamming it behind him before marching off down the street.

He had been sitting on the park bench on the Common which fronted the building for over an hour, partly because there was nothing else to do and partly because he was still deeply pissed off after an argument with his girlfriend. The stupid bitch had taken out a loan with a local moneylender at two hundred per cent interest, and when he'd confronted her about it, she'd pointed out that she wouldn't have had to take out a loan *at all*, if he was able to bring some money in to pay the bills once in a while. Not for the first time, he'd thought about walking out on her; and he still didn't believe that the kid was his either.

So for the time being, he'd decided to sit here and smoke a little something to make him feel good again. There were bushes to right and left and he knew that the local coppers didn't bother patrolling round here, so maybe he'd just sit and wait and see if he could get any answers.

Hidden in the darkness, he'd seen the artist bastard suddenly move into view in the attic flat window. Because it was the only movement, Vinny watched him for a long while. No way of seeing what it was the guy was working on, but it was a painting. He was using brushes and there was an easel there, or something. And as Vinny sat there watching, with the shadows creeping across the Common, he found that he hated the man up there, hated everything he stood for. There he was, poncing about in front of a canvas, waving his brushes like he really thought he was someone. And when he'd finished painting the vase of flowers, or the kids playing in the haystack, or the fucking cows chewing grass and staring up at the fluffy white clouds, he'd take his painting to one of those fucking galleries. And they'd give him . . . what? Two, three, four thousand? Probably more. And there was Vinny. No chance of a job just because of his so-called criminal record, no chance because he was neither white nor black thanks to his long-gone and unmissed parents. Living off income support and having to keep the bitch and his so-called son happy all the time. Why the hell should it be like that? Why the hell should that bastard up there be earning thousands while someone who was willing to graft hard like him had to be grovelling around for every penny? Vinny knew someone who lived just below the attic flat. Not a friend, exactly. Just someone who had a contact for Love Dove and other stuff, and who sometimes let him and a few others hang out there. Dropping out and tuning in, he liked to call it, like he was some sixties freak. And the last time he'd been there to score he'd heard all about the guy upstairs. What he did for a living and how his artist brother had come to stay a while.

Night had fallen, and Vinny had continued to watch the bastard working. How the hell could he work up there now, without a light on? All part of the fucking 'artistic process', no doubt. He was still there. Vinny could see him moving around.

He smoked some more, and lost all sense of time. He watched as some guy let himself in through the main door and then shortly afterwards the attic light had come on. Vinny saw the bastard artist recoil, suddenly framed in the attic window. Then he'd moved out of sight. Was the guy who'd come in through the front door the guy who rented the place, coming home and finding his fruitcake brother working in the dark? This was like being at the movies, or something, watching a story taking place.

And then, moments later, the front door had banged open and the artist had come storming out like he'd had a fight or something. There was no doubt that it was the artist. Vinny hadn't been able to see the guy's face, but he recognised the red shirt and the blue jeans. And now, just like a movie unreeling before him, the story continued. Because now the door was opening again and the guy he assumed was the brother came out on to the pavement. Vinny watched him look one way and then the other. He shifted in his seat, grinning. He'd almost jumped up and shouted, 'He went *thataway!*' Giggling, he put a hand over his mouth and watched as the second guy started off down the street in the opposite direction. 'Wrong move,' laughed Vinny. 'You ain't going to find him that way.'

The attic light was still on up there.

There'd been some kind of fight, and the two brothers had gone off into the night.

Something was whispering in Vinny's ear.

'What?' he asked aloud.

Now's your chance. See, there was a reason why you came and sat here. You'd been anywhere else, you wouldn't have seen all this happening. But the fact is, you are HERE. And it's all been laid on a plate for you.

'What?'

Don't you see, you prick! They've both gone out. There's

*nobody else up there. And if you're, like, super-quick, you can
at least get in there, find something, and get that fucking loan
paid off before the interest gets so high someone comes around
to cut your balls off.*

'Right!' Vinny slapped his thighs, rose unsteadily and took
in a deep breath of the night air. The next moment, he was
loping across the Common to the terraced houses. He paused
while a car passed and two couples strolled in front of the
house. He used the time to check out the window below the
attic flat where his contact lived. There was no light on up
there, so with luck there'd be no one home, or if there was
they'd be spaced out lying on the floor. The last thing he
wanted was for anyone to recognise him once he got inside.
Maybe if someone came in or out while he was on his way up
he could pretend he had just come along to score? That would
be a good cover.

When the street was clear, Vinny jogged the rest of the
way to the main door. Its so-called 'visitor monitor' lock
was no problem for him. In seconds, it was open. Head
down, still jogging, he made his way quickly up the stairs,
checking each door as he moved, looking all around for any
sign of movement. The overhead wall-lights cast his shadow
gigantically down across the stairwell as he climbed.

On the fifth floor, where his contact lived, he was faced with
a dilemma. He felt good in his head, but he'd lost his sense of
direction. There were three doors here on the fifth landing, so
it didn't take a genius to guess that there might be three doors
up above on the sixth. Which of those doors would be the one
he wanted? What was he going to do – make a guess and then
just knock on one? Then, when it was answered, say, 'Excuse
me, wrong door?' Then maybe the second door would be the
wrong guess, too. Great. Two witnesses to give the police a
perfect description, right down to the scar across the bridge
of his nose, the legacy of a broken beer glass in a pub fight.

'No. Wait,' Vinny whispered to himself, spinning in a little
dance. Both hands to his head, he tried to orientate himself.
'You're not thinking straight.' It was easy. His contact's
window was facing out across the Common, so that would

mean the attic window with the light on was directly *above* that. Facing the same way. So that meant . . . the door on the sixth landing would be in the same position as the door on the fifth. Grinning in the darkness, Vinny loped up the last two flights of stairs.

'Shit!' He didn't know whether to be angry or satisfied.

There was only one door on the sixth floor. The one he wanted. All that hard thinking when there had been no need for it.

Looking down the stairwell, he waited and listened.

No sounds.

He moved to the door and jemmied it open. He'd learned his trade well, using the iron in his inside pocket and snapping the lock, making hardly any noise at all.

Quickly, he slipped inside and closed the door behind him. The first thing he could see was the easel in the attic window.

He reached for the light-switch and then paused. What if one or other of those guys was coming back down the street right now? Wouldn't they see the light go on and think something was wrong?

They can't see the light from either side, you stupid bastard. They'd have to be out front there on the Common, like I was.

No, leave it on. Best be safe. Get in here, then get out. Quick as fuck.

He checked all the usual places for cash or credit cards. Drawers, cabinets, gewgaws (it was a phrase his grandmother liked to use a lot) with lids on, standing on the mantelpiece of a hearth that had not seen a fire since Victorian times. Clothes hanging in the wardrobes. He couldn't spend much more time here, and he didn't really want to take a video or a cassette recorder. Too bulky, and no transport tonight. His nerves were fraying; he had to shit. And then, in a leather jacket hanging behind the very door he'd forced, he found a wallet with twenty quid in notes and several credit cards.

'Bingo!'

He stuffed the wallet into his pocket and reached for the

door. Then he remembered the easel standing by the attic window.

How much is that artist bastard getting for each one of those?

Hundreds, maybe thousands, came the other voice in Vinny's two-way mental conversation.

Then I'll take it, flog it.

And what the hell do you know about the art business?

Shut up. I'll find someone . . .

He loped across the attic room towards the easel.

Like who? Leave it. You take that with you and you're marked. You'll never be able to shift it. You don't know any art dealers who'll take a stolen painting, man!

Vinny crept around the easel and sneaked a look around the curtain, out over the street below, aware of the fact that he would be framed up here for all to see if he wasn't careful.

Leave it, Vinny. A moment ago you decided that a video recorder or a cassette player would be too conspicuous, would slow you down. How you going to look with a three-by-four painting in a plastic bin-bag under your arm?

'Suspicious,' whispered Vinny, looking down at the Victorian railings that fronted the building and then along the street on both sides, half expecting to see the two brothers walking back home, arms over each other's shoulders and differences resolved. He squatted down then, below the level of the windowsill, and looked back up at the painting. It was backlit from behind, and he could make nothing of it.

So he'll get hundreds, maybe thousands for this thing? And I'll get my Monday morning cheque from social security and it'll go straight to the bitch and her crying-mouth brat.

Vinny reached into his pocket and took out the iron, moving around to the side on his haunches until he was out of the window's sight-line. Glancing back down again, he took the easel by its frame and pulled it towards him gradually, edging it away from the window.

He hefted the iron.

Well, you'll not get much for this thing, you bastard. 'Cause

*when I'm finished with it, there'll be nothing left to wipe your
arse on.*

He pulled the easel around so that he could get a full view
of what had been painted. He raised the iron.

Were they clouds he'd painted? Swirling, multi-coloured
clouds? Or was it blood running out of a wound, sort of
gushing and spiralling down into a ragged hole? Or was
it something swirling *up* into a ragged hole? Vinny's arm
remained aloft as he stared at what Roger had made with
his burning hands.

The more he looked, the less he could make sense of what
he was seeing. And something, somewhere (maybe the second
voice in his head that always argued with him) was telling him
to look away. Something vague and deep down was telling him
not to look any more at what was there. But the more he looked,
the more he could feel himself being drawn into the painting,
wanting . . . no, not wanting, now *needing* to make sense of
the way the abstract planes and colours swirled and merged
and moved on, pulling him into the vortex of movement. There
was something at the centre of the hypnotic, sucking whirlpool
of shapes and angles. Something that was taking substance
as he looked and was drawn deeper and deeper into what
was there.

'. . . something . . .'

Vinny couldn't look away.

The shapes were coming out to meet him as his eyes drew
him ever deeper towards them.

The iron fell from nerveless fingers. Its ragged end bit into
the unprotected part of his foot, between the hem of his jeans
and the laces of his trainers, before falling to the floor. Blood
oozed from a three-inch gash, but Vinny felt no pain.

The real pain was in his mind.

Because, at last, he knew that having looked on what had
been painted, he could never look away again. His eyes had
been seduced by a juxtaposition of colour and angles and
shapes that could not be looked upon without something
happening to the mind of the onlooker.

Vinny was looking at Madness.

And having looked, he knew in that last pure spark of utterly horrifying knowledge that he must go and dwell in that canvas for ever.

The screams were heard two blocks away.

The lights were very near.

As the thing staggered through the bushes, frightening sleeping birds from their resting places and scattering them into ragged flight through the night sky, it kept its vision on the place where the lights rushed and swept through the darkness.

There was a word in its head as it thrashed through brambles and encountered the splintered remains of a long-abandoned cattle byre. But the word seemed to make no sense to the scrambled mess that had once been its mind.

'Road,' it said aloud. 'This is the Road.'

Angry that it could not fully grasp the word and what it meant, the thing trudged through the byre, snapping rotted wood in its claw-hands, stamping down hard on whatever impeded its progress. Splintered fractures of blue energy crackled and dissipated into the ground with each step.

It knew that it was close to the place where it might find itself again.

It called to the lights that travelled on that . . . road . . . and waited for a response. There was no answer. Just a rushing of wind as each light suddenly appeared out of darkness, passed by and was lost in the darkness once more.

Moaning, the thing climbed an embankment. For a moment, the lights were lost to view and the thing felt an even greater desolation settle about it. Clawing at the grass, the thing hauled itself to the top of the embankment.

Standing there in the night like a scarecrow that had uprooted itself from the nearby fields, and swaying in the wind that ruffled and fumbled at its clothes, the thing looked at the lights that were approaching from its left. There was another word in its mind, just as confusing as the road word.

'Motorway . . .'

The light grew larger and brighter as it neared.

Slowly, the thing raised its arms, as if to embrace it.

The light filled its vision, and the thing cried out aloud its need to be saved, its need to return to the way it was before.

A lorry horn blared. Harsh and loud, like some gigantic beast as the vehicle roared past the thing, spraying it with grit and dust. The scarecrow tottered by the roadside, almost flung to the ground in the vehicle's passage. Whirling, the thing turned to see the light fade into the distance as the lorry continued on its way.

'Don't leave me!' yelled the thing, staggering after it. 'I don't belong here. I have to . . .'

To what?

Holding its ravaged head, the grief-stricken thing tried to think.

'To . . . to get where I'm going.'

The thing shook its head again, claws still fastened there as if it might finally tear the ghastly visage free and throw it aside.

'No . . . I mean, get back to where I was . . .'

It staggered out across the motorway, still yearning for the light that had passed it by.

'DON'T LEAVE ME!'

Another horn blared, this time right behind the thing. It whirled and was blinded by the headlights. Tyres screeched as the car swerved to avoid it. The thing held its arms wide to be taken. But the screeching careered around it and the lights vanished past it into the darkness. The horn blared again as the car continued on its way, the driver furious at the behaviour of the stupid drunk who had wandered out into the road.

More light, and again a horn blared.

The thing staggered backwards and forwards across the road as each new light blinded it as it bore down. Now, it was weeping. None of these lights wanted it. They were all avoiding it.

Darkness again.

The thing stumbled on the shale on the other side of the motorway. Falling to its ragged knees, it clutched at the barrier rail and howled its anguish. Other lights were rushing past, but none of them stopped.

'I'm not at the right place yet . . .'

That must be the answer. It could sense that the place where it had emerged into this hideous torment was further down the . . . road? . . . motorway? . . .

It had to keep moving until it found that place.

It stood again, swaying.

And began walking down the hard shoulder of the motorway.

Heading South.

Jane was in a state of abject panic.

She still had three hours left to prepare the meal, probably longer if Tom was able to keep his colleagues at the pub as he'd said he would. And, thank God, there had been a leg of lamb in the freezer, which was now defrosting, but before even thinking about the food, she knew that she'd have to clean the house thoroughly. She had cleaned all the rooms, including the bathroom, first thing in the morning; just as she did every morning. She had cleaned the windows, polished everything, vacuumed, just the way Tom liked it. If he had time when he came home, and wasn't feeling really tired, he'd inspect the house to make sure that she hadn't missed anything. If he felt that she was slipping, then corrective measures would have to be taken. Sometimes she prayed that he would come home tired, and sometimes her prayers were answered. But she knew that she must never allow herself to become sloppy. Although the house had already been cleaned from top to bottom, she would start again, just to be sure. Clean everything that had been cleaned. Then the lamb could go in the oven. Baked with butter and herbs; redcurrant, orange and mint sauce. Two hours at gas mark five in tin foil, then opened out and cooked for another thirty minutes. Get the vegetables prepared. Everything should be okay. There would be time.

She took the plastic bucket out of the utility room, filled it with water and then splashed in disinfectant. She dipped the mop into the bucket and swirled it around. The smell of disinfectant seemed to fill the room. It made her head swim. Dizzy, she leaned against the draining board and waited for her head to clear. She knew that there were chemicals in the mixture to make the finished result smell like a Chinese rose garden, but it seemed to her that the fake floral scent was a poor substitute for the wonderful cleansing smell beneath. She shook her head and tried to continue with her task of washing what was already a spotless linoleum floor. Lifting the mop out of the bucket, she swirled it on the floor and was overcome again by the powerful smell of the cleansing agent.

Almost against her will, she stooped to look at the suds.

The mop clattered to the floor.

Jane dipped her fingers into the soapy mixture. The smell on her fingers was wonderful.

She tasted it.

Wonderful.

And then, kneeling on the lino, she pulled the bucket towards her and began dipping her fingers into the mixture, hungrily bringing her fingers to her mouth as she set about satisfying the craving within.

Was she dreaming? It seemed that time was somehow inverting, turning in on itself. She was back on the coach, in Seat 47, with her overnight bag on the double seat beside her. Outside, neon motorway lights flashed past as she drifted in and out of a half-sleep and remembered what had happened to her.

Tom, towering over her and telling her that she was pathetic, couldn't follow simple instructions or keep a damned thing in her head. Why hadn't she put the dinner date in her diary? He'd given her ample time to prepare a dinner for six. And she had better make damned sure that it was something special this time, because the deputy managing director, Yearby, and his wife would be coming along. Not some cheap burger-bar rubbish like the last time.

And in her troubled dream, as the coach sped on towards its final destination, Jane saw that her kitchen had suddenly become a vast and cavernous space, with the units stretching up for miles on all sides, way beyond her little-girl reach.

She struggled to cope with the meal she was preparing, but everything was going wrong. She couldn't reach the benches, couldn't get her hands to work properly; the fingers were too fat and clumsy. Steam filled the kitchen; the LED lights on the cooker glowed hellishly through the shrouds of steam. She began to weep uncontrollably as pans bubbled and boiled over. She screamed then . . .

And suddenly she was awake again.

She was still sitting on the kitchen floor, but the bucket had been tipped over on to its side. The kitchen floor was soaked, and she was sitting in the middle of a soapy pool. The detergent had saturated her dress and legs. Her fingers felt strange, and when she looked at them, she could see that the fingertips were prune-like as if she had had them in water for too long. Her throat felt sore. There was a ringing in her ears.

And the kitchen clock showed that she had lost an hour and a half.

She had sat down beside the plastic bucket, and ninety minutes had disappeared from her life.

'Oh God, NO!'

She struggled to rise. Her legs slid beneath her on the slippery floor and she fell flat on her face, the blow knocking the breath from her body and soaking her blouse. She began to weep in fear.

All this work to do, and all that time wasted.

What would Tom say?

Oh my God, what will Tom DO?

Sobbing, Jane clambered to her feet.

And now she was unsure whether she was dreaming or whether she was still in the real world. She couldn't remember cleaning up the house again; couldn't remember preparing the food. She remembered the panic, remembered the terror that had descended on her, but now she was sitting at the table. Candles were lit, the dining room seemed to be as tidy as Tom liked it to be. And when she looked around, she could see familiar faces. Mr Yearby and his wife. Laughing and talking to the people on either side of them. Jim Kelly and his girlfriend.

Still in a detached blur, Jane tried to remember her name, but couldn't come up with it. She wore a lot of gold; bracelets and chains. Her hair was cut close around the ears and over the eyes in the way Jane remembered that French singer, Mireille Mathieu, had worn hers.

She realised that a spoon was lifted to her lips. She looked at it, wondering. Then she put the sweet into her mouth. It tasted wonderful. Could she dream a taste? Had she really cooked the food, received their visitors, and been unaware of all of it until now? There were empty spirit glasses on the table. The bottles of red and white wine were half empty. No one seemed interested in Jane at all. She looked down at herself. She had changed into an evening dress, had even managed to paint her fingernails, but couldn't remember any of it. She looked around the table again, and this time saw Tom. Lovely, affable Tom. All smiles and eyes glittering with amusement as he listened intently to what Yearby's secretary had to say. Sue Clayton had vivid red hair, ringlets beautifully curled around her ears and falling down over her shoulders. She seemed uninterested in her sweet, idly pushing her spoon around the plate as all her concentration was focused on Tom. Jane had seen that look between them before, but was terrified to think about it. She looked at the others, all of them now laughing at some joke.

This must be a dream. No one can see me. I'm not here.

Something made her look across at Tom again. Even in her dream-state, she felt a stab of anxiety when she saw that despite the fact that Sue was still telling him her secret story, eyes concentrated on her plate, Tom was staring across at his wife. His face was smiling, but his eyes were hard, cruel and bright, waiting for her to make a mistake, waiting for her to make a social faux pas. She watched his eyes move meaningfully to the wine glasses of the other guests; some of them were empty. Jane smiled weakly and nodded. This was, after all, only a dream. So he couldn't really hurt her. But if she did as she was told, the dream surely wouldn't turn into a nightmare. More wine. Jane drifted to her feet and moved around the table, taking first the bottle of red and then the bottle of white to top everyone up. She couldn't feel her feet, she might as well be floating inches above the carpet. Holding both empties, she headed for the kitchen. There were several bottles cooling in there.

Again, that laughter.

But this time the dream was truly a nightmare. Because everyone at the table was laughing at her. Some of the wine had somehow spilled from a bottle down the front of her dress. Everyone began pointing at the puddle on the carpet around her feet, and laughing. It looked as if she'd peed herself. But Tom wasn't laughing. His face was just a hard blank mask, an expression that filled her with terror. The laughter became a screaming then. They were screaming abuse at her for being so stupid, and her screams joined theirs . . .

No, this can't be right. This has happened before. And last time, it was soup that I spilled, not wine.

And Jane sees herself walking through the rain towards the bus station, carrying a hastily packed suitcase. There is a bus ticket clenched in her hand.

She shook her head, desperate to escape from the spiralling dreams. If she didn't escape, then in a moment she would find herself on the bus. Then there would be the terrible burning light and the screaming. The horror of the bus crash. The fire and the death. Then Tom coming to her again, knowing that she'd tried to run away . . . and something like lightning in the hospital which leapt across the ceiling and stabbed into her chest . . . and then the knowledge, the knowledge forgotten until now that . . . that . . .

'There's something inside me. Oh God, there's something hiding inside me. It talked to the others then. The others who survived . . .'

And suddenly, Jane is back in the dining room.

There is no laughter now, and from the looks on their faces it seems that they were never laughing at all. They've all become quiet as if in response to her words. There's an embarrassed cough from someone when it becomes clear that she isn't going to qualify the strange things she's just said, or make a joke. The dinner party conversation resumes as if she doesn't exist.

She sees Tom's eyes again.

This time, he is furious.

In panic, Jane leaves the room. This time, she feels the carpet beneath her feet as she enters the kitchen. Staggering to the bench, she tries to remember what she came in here for.

'Wine . . . more wine . . .'

She feels the chill of the bottles as she takes them from the refrigerator, and realises at last that . . .

This was not a dream. She could feel herself breathing. Could feel the sweat in the small of her back, struggled to contain the nausea. Did that mean that none of the other things had happened? Was this the first nightmare dinner party? Had that first dinner party *ever* taken place, or had she imagined it? Jane screwed her eyes shut and tried to make sense of the fragmented and frightening images that flashed through her mind. Perhaps . . . perhaps this was some kind of second chance. Something had happened to her. She had been given some kind of foresight into what might happen. If she didn't walk away from tonight, didn't buy that bus ticket, didn't get on that bus – then there would be no motorway crash. And none of the nightmare things that had come afterwards.

Jane steadied herself, nodding her head. That must be the answer.

She pushed through the kitchen door into the dining area again.

Everyone had gone.

'No . . .' Jane closed her eyes. They were there. She knew they had been there. She opened her eyes again and saw the soup tureen and the plates and the glasses. Then she heard the hubbub of conversation from the living room and thanked God that she wasn't losing her mind, after all. She walked through, and there they all were, sitting on the sofa and in the easy chairs. The smiles seemed forced when she moved around the room, filling their glasses.

She could hardly bring herself to look Tom in the eye when she refilled his glass. But she could sense his expression, and was forced to raise her bowed head to look directly into his eyes.

'Coffee now, dear. I think everyone's ready. *Don't you?*'

Eyes like marbles. Cold and piercing. Frightening.

And now she was back in the kitchen. Again, there was no memory of leaving the room. It was as if by the simple command of his eyes, Tom had transported her from one place to the other in a cold and glittering *twinkle*. The coffee machine was already bubbling but she couldn't remember putting in the coffee or switching it on. Drawing deep breaths, she caught sight of her reflection in a window pane. Tears weren't far away, and her mascara had streaked on one eyelid. Moaning, she tore off a strip of paper towel and dabbed at it. No use. She would have to go upstairs.

Checking the coffee machine and looking back at the door as if Tom might suddenly explode through it with that terrifying expression on his face, she hurried into the hall and crept up the stairs. The heavy pile of the carpet hid the sound of her footsteps as she anxiously glanced back down through the banisters. The bathroom was at the top of the stairs and she prayed that no one was in there. Breathing a sigh of relief, she saw that the door was ajar.

Jane hurried across the landing towards the door.

And heard the moaning.

At first, she thought it was coming from her, and hurried through into the bathroom, afraid lest anyone downstairs heard her. But she was just about to close the door when she realised that the sound was coming from the spare bedroom. It was a man's voice. Moaning low. And now there was a woman's voice, too. That man's voice . . . it sounded like Tom . . .

. . . and the woman's voice sounded like Sue Clayton.

And back in the dream, Jane shakes her head, already knowing what that moaning must mean but refusing to accept what she has suspected for so long. She looks at her hand, still in the act of closing the door. The hand freezes.

'You don't have to know. Jane, you don't have to *know* . . .'

Jane has no control over her actions. Suddenly, she is floating through that doorway and up the stairs to the second landing. The moaning is still audible, reaching a crescendo, as if both voices don't want to make a noise at all, but are unable to help themselves as they rise to a peak of ecstasy. Like a ghost, Jane drifts past the master bedroom. There are horrible memories for her in there, but the ghost that she has become is detached and unmoved as she reaches the second bedroom door.

She sees her hand reach out.

Sees the door swing inward.

From inside, there is a sharp intake of breath. The woman's voice. The man is still moaning, unheeding of anything except his need.

And Jane sees them in the full-length mirror, without having to enter the room. Sue is standing against the bedroom wall, arms around Tom's shoulders. His head is bent into her neck as he heaves between her legs. His trousers are still on, fly unzipped. Her dress has been bunched up to her waist. Sue's eyes lock with Jane's own. They are filled with horror. She slaps Tom on the shoulders, wanting him to stop. And now it seems that Tom has at last sensed that there is something wrong. Jane sees him begin to turn his head to look back.

But Jane the ghost drifts backwards, away from the door until she can no longer see their reflection. The next moment, she is drifting down the stairs. Somehow, there is no emotion. Jane knows what should be happening. There should be screaming, or weeping. But there is nothing inside because this is, after all, only a dream.

She drifts into the kitchen.

The coffee is bubbling. The ghost sets about pouring it out. She prepares a tray with the requisite number of cups. And then she drifts into the living room. The others are still here, barely acknowledging her entry, continuing with their laughter and conversation as she puts the tray on the coffee table. Out of the corner of her eye, she sees the door into the hall open. Sue swirls in, moves quickly back to her wine glass and starts a conversation with Mrs Yearby. Jane looks up. Sue is stroking her throat with her forefinger and does not look at her. She laughs too readily at a semi-humorous remark from Mrs Yearby. Janet moves to the others, handing out cups.

Two minutes later, Tom enters the room.

Without looking at her, or speaking, he takes two cups from

*the tray. One for himself, and another for Sue. She might as
well not be there as he joins Sue and Mrs Yearby in their
conversation.*

Jane stands and looks around.

*Jim Kelly and Mireille are both standing and sipping their
coffee, looking down on Mr Yearby as he lights his cigar
and continues their conversation. Jane can't hear the words.
She sees their mouths moving, but the sounds are muffled,
seeming to come from a long, long way away. Mrs Yearby
and Sue and Tom are all sitting together now. Sue and Mrs
Yearby on the sofa, Tom on the easy chair. No one is looking
her way. Perhaps, in this dream, she didn't really see anything
happening upstairs after all . . .*

Jane lifts the coffee cup to her lips.

Except that it isn't a coffee cup any more.

It's a bottle of domestic cleaning fluid.

She pauses for a moment. Does this count as a social faux
pas*? Smiling then, she takes a deep swallow.*

'Oh my *God!*' said Mrs Yearby, suddenly looking Jane's
way. Her face betrayed a confusing mix of emotions. Was
Jane really doing what she thought she was doing, or was this
some strange kind of joke that would make sense in a moment?
Would the reasons for her strange behaviour throughout the
evening suddenly become apparent? Would everyone suddenly
get the joke? Jim and Mireille turned to look, their mouths
opening in astonishment. Jane smiled, lowering the bottle and
wiping her lips. Now everyone in the room was looking at her.

'The coffee tastes bitter,' she explained. 'This is much more
to my taste these days.'

'*Jane!*' Tom put his coffee cup down, trying to decide
whether to rise or not.

'I heard a joke once, when I was a little girl,' replied Jane.
Her eyes seemed far away. 'A long time ago. What happens
to you if you drink bleach and Fairy Liquid and toilet cleaner?
Do you know?'

'*Jane!*'

'It makes you go clean round the bend.' Jane giggled. 'Do
you get it? *Clean round the bend.*'

And now Tom was on his feet, striding across the room as she lifted the bottle to her lips again. He seized it from her, a gout of the liquid spilling down her dress. Still smiling vacantly, she looked at the stain and then back at Tom. This time, he was trembling with suppressed anger, aware that the guests were shuffling uneasily behind him. Jane looked back at him, the fragile smile still there. No terror in her eyes. And the fact that she was no longer frightened of him sent a spasm through Tom, something that he could not understand.

'Am I in a dream, Tom? Or is this a dream within a dream within a dream? No matter, really.'

'Jane ... dear ... come into the kitchen. I don't think you're well.'

'Not well? No ... I don't think I've ever been well. Not since I met you.'

'Perhaps ...' Mrs Yearby gave a nervous cough and began to rise. 'Perhaps it's time that we all went home. After all, it's getting late and ...'

'Yes,' said Jim, looking at his watch. 'Lots to do tomorrow.'

'No, please,' said Tom, turning his smile on them. 'Everything's fine. I just think that Jane needs a little rest ...'

Jane suddenly became aware that Tom was gripping her arm.

And in the dream within a dream within a dream, Jane sees Tom standing by her hospital bed; hears him saying: 'There's nothing wrong with you, you whining little whore. So you're going to stop making that fucking whining noise, right now! And you're going to tell the nurse and the doctors that you're going home with your husband.' And now, she's kneeling naked on the living-room floor – on this very carpet – as Tom towers over her, and he says: 'You want to be punished, don't you?'

And suddenly, she is seizing her neighbour's hand and screaming: 'You want to feel the way I'm feeling?' as the power inside streams out of her hands and into Maureen. Now Maureen is staggering away in terror as the sofa cushions against which she has been sitting suddenly begin to smoulder. Her blouse and skirt suddenly billow with flame ...

'Do you mind!' snaps the woman in the supermarket queue.

'You're holding everyone up, and you must be punished! Do you understand that, you bitch! You must be made to SUFFER!'

The terrible light on the motorway.

The screaming.

The coach, suddenly erupting into flame.

Tom felt something cold on the hand that was holding Jane. He looked back at his wife, the fixed smile still on his face. Jane's face was blank, and she was gripping his hand. That hand was somehow terribly, terribly cold, as if transmitting ice into his veins. He yanked his hand away.

'I don't have to touch any more, Tom. I did before. But now I don't. So you see? I don't *quite* understand it, but as long as *I've* touched something *you've* touched . . .'

'Jane, pull yourself together!'

'Yes, I do believe it's time to go,' said Mr Yearby, rising from his chair. 'Thank you for a lovely evening, Mrs Teal.'

'Too late now,' said Jane. 'You really shouldn't have eaten the food I prepared for you, Tom. You see, I touched it. And now . . . well now, it's *in* you! Isn't it?'

Unable to control himself any longer, trembling with rage, Tom slapped Jane hard across the face. Behind him, everyone moved quickly in an embarrassed rush for the door. Mr Yearby seemed crimson with anger and embarrassment as he held out an arm for his wife to follow.

'I'll get the coats,' said Jim, opening the door into the hall. 'I think I know where they are . . .'

And suddenly, Mireille bent double. Clutching at her stomach, she reeled against Jim. In alarm, he caught one arm, but was unable to prevent her from sinking to her knees. She moaned, a deep and distressed sound, the sound of a woman in labour perhaps.

'*Jim!*'

She began to retch as the others milled in the doorway, unsure of what to do.

Tom was still holding his own hand where Jane had touched him. Somehow, it was tingling. Anger dissipating, he moved to the others.

Just as Mrs Yearby gave vent to a shriek . . .

... and in her spiral of dreams, Jane watches calmly as Mireille, or whatever her name is, begins to vomit blood on to the carpet. That will make a terrible mess, and she feels sure that Tom won't like it. And now she comes to think of it, she isn't sure whether there is anything left in the cupboard to clean it up with; she's drunk everything in the house. Jim seems to be yelling for an ambulance, but Mr Yearby – like a good husband – is only concerned about his wife as she staggers back into the room, her hands held up in front of her face. Smoke is beginning to curl from her waist and her arms and her hands as she totters back like some peculiar mannekin, mouth open, making goldfish motions.

'Jesus Christ, Tom!' screams Sue, running to him. 'What's happening . . . ?' He hugs her close, the way that he has never hugged Jane. And the sight of that embrace seems somehow to focus something inside her. Lowering her head, she stares hatefully at them. On the easy chair where Mrs Yearby has collapsed there is a sudden single flapping sound, dull and muted, as if all the seat springs have suddenly broken. Out of the corner of her eye, Jane sees the easy chair erupt into a blazing fireball, making light and shadow leap all over the room. Flames and flecks of soot writhe across the ceiling. Something is hopping and dancing around the sofa, now screaming and flapping its arms as it collapses to its knees beside the chair in its own shroud of flame. Jim screams, leaping back from the suddenly burning shape on the carpet and reeling in the doorway. He clutches his own stomach, his face a grimace of agony, like some kind of hideous mask now, lit from below.. The sounds bubble and die in his throat as he clutches at the lintel, falling out of sight into the hall beyond. There is more flickering, dancing light in the hall as Jane watches Tom and Sue back away from her towards the kitchen door, afraid to pass the atrocity that lies burning in the doorway and the hall.

'Oh Jesus God, Jane . . . please,' sobs Sue. 'I don't understand . . . please . . .'

'Ask Tom to tell you about punishment, Sue. Have you told her all about it, Tom? Have you laughed together about MY punishment?'

Tom cannot speak in this dream. His eyes are wide, reflecting the burning light.

'Don't say you don't understand, Tom. You're in charge. You know everything. So go on . . . tell her.'

Sue clutches at her midriff.

'Indigestion, Sue?'

Now Sue is yanking herself out of the embrace, clutching at her stomach with both hands as she staggers away from Tom. Her eyes remain fixed on him, a look of mind-numbing agony and a desperate plea. A plea to make it stop, make it stop, make it . . .

Jane screams.

Even in this deep, deep dreaming place her true feelings are suddenly able to erupt. In the space of a single second, the years of humiliation and pain and sorrow and anguish focus deep within her; deep where the light has given her its power, gouting forth in a blaze of hate and revenge.

Sue explodes in a sheet of flame and with a roaring of sound. Her burning body catapults away from them, smashing against the far wall and falling in a flapping blur of disintegration and voracious flame to the floor beside the kitchen door.

Tom is backing away from Jane, hands held out imploringly.

The room is filled with flame. The doorway to the hall is engulfed. The curtains have ignited, the wallpaper is peeling and burning. A firestorm erupts from the place where Sue's body has been flung, making escape into the kitchen impossible.

'Feel it, Tom,' *says Jane. But her voice is too quiet to be heard over the roaring of the flames.* 'Feel the way I feel . . .'

Tom reaches the far wall, claws at his hand again when the icy tingling begins to feel like fire. He calls to her across the room, his shape obscured by flying ash and soot and fire. Now he clutches at his stomach, hugs himself and tries to stagger back across the room to her. His mouth is working. Is he begging her for help, the way she begged him not to hurt her any more? The carpet between them is burning fiercely. He cannot get back across the room to her.

Jane turns and walks to the doorway leading into the hall.
Behind her, she hears Tom screaming her name.
She steps through the flames.
The fire shrivels her tights, melting the fabric around her calves and knees. Her skin blisters and burns, but as she is still in the multiple dream she feels no pain. As she steps over what remains of Mireille and Jim, the flames from the blazing corpses ignite her dress. Orange blossoms envelop her left side as she walks down the hall. Casually, she swats at the flame. Her dress has almost disintegrated, but the flame is snuffed out as she heads for the front door. She looks at her hands and sees the red-white blisters there. She can feel her hair burning and puts her blistered hands to her head as casually as if she were combing it. She can feel bare patches, and raw skin beneath her burned fingers. Behind her, the sounds of Tom's screams have been drowned out by the roaring flames. There is an explosive crash of glass, the drinks cabinet suddenly cracking and splintering apart.
Such a mess, and nothing in the kitchen cupboards to clean it all up with.
Jane opens the front door and the clean air outside seems to rush past her, eager to get inside and fuel the flames.
She walks into the night, unaware of the people who are emerging from the surrounding homes to look on in shock and horror.
Finally, she turns and looks back at her home – at Tom's home.
She is unable to recognise the blazing mass as the place where she once lived.
Fire coughs from the front door like a living thing. Suddenly, the windows on either side burst across the lawn as the fire greedily licks over the upper window frames towards the roof. Deep inside, something explodes, and Jane sees the roof begin to cave in.
She sits awkwardly, pulling her burned limbs into a cross-legged position, the way she used to do at school when she was a little girl.
She watches the fire.

No one comes to her.
Soon, she hears the sound of fire engines.
And as if on cue, she finally falls asleep into a safe place.

Curtis had just met his deadline on the story to which he had been allocated.

In the middle of the heat-wave, it had been discovered that the regional water authority had somehow turned a wrong tap, and at a time when some local areas had been forced to resort to stand-pipes, the equivalent to an entire reservoir had emptied straight out into the sea. Curtis's attendance at the church service where Martin Russell had performed his conjuring act had severely cut into his time, and he knew that if his editor found out that he'd been moonlighting on *that* out-of-bounds story again, there would be hell to pay.

Printing out his final copy, he swivelled in his chair to look at the pile of papers on his desk. The mess was inches deep, like some kind of forest mulch, with the lower layers beginning to decay. He slapped his hand randomly on the pile and came up with a scrawled message that was the last thing he wanted to see.

'Shit!'

There had been another telephone call from Eastleigh Hospital's legal advisers while he had been out. Now they were threatening further legal action for his persistent time-wasting. The note had been signed by his colleague, Brenda. She was hurrying across the office away from him when he called out.

'What the hell's the . . . ?' Curtis checked to see that the editor's door was shut and that he couldn't overhear their conversation. Brenda turned. 'Brenda, love. What's up with the hospital people?'

She looked over her spectacles at him. 'I've told you before, Tony. Call me "love", and I'll not only take offence, I'll break your arm.'

'Please?'

'Did you get them to make an emergency call on someone?'

'Yeah . . .' Curtis anxiously looked back at the editor's office.

Roland was on the telephone. No chance of him hearing or seeing anything.

'Well, you've pissed them off. There wasn't any need for it.'

'What do you mean? The guy was about to kill himself.'

'I don't know anything about that. All they said, when the ambulance got where you sent 'em, was that the guy was fine and dandy. And also pissed off because they'd disturbed him watching the football match.'

'*What?*'

'For the record, Tony, I didn't take that message, or leave you a note. If Roland finds out you're still sniffing around the motorway crash story, he'll not only cut your balls off but he might start looking for accomplices.' She turned and left.

Curtis stared hard at the note again.

'Maybe it's me. Maybe I'm the one who's going mad.'

He crumpled the note up and threw it in the basket. It missed, joining the pile of scrunched-up paper which lay strewn around the empty basket like origami snowballs. He swivelled again, one complete turn bringing him back to face his desk. He grabbed the copy of the newspaper he'd had on his side desk since the crash, the motorway smash-up special, containing all the fantastic detail that no one but himself seemed to have seen. He flapped the paper open, skimming his own copy and looking at the pictures of blazing vehicles and the rescue services struggling on the embankment as flames roaring behind them silhouetted the figures of humans and vehicles. It looked like something out of Dante's inferno.

Six people who should be dead, but aren't.

One of them suddenly has the power to heal the sick. Another drinks stuff that should kill him and he's still standing on two legs.

A body torn in half in the crash, stolen from the mortuary.

A mortuary attendant with his face torn off. Same thing to a fireman on the motorway a couple of hours later.

Indoor thunder and lightning that no one saw. The storm-that-wasn't.

Dead cattle and sheep all around the area of the motor-way smash.

He flicked through the newspaper, baffled and angry. It was like having a dozen pieces of a jigsaw. They all belonged to a pattern. But each piece belonged to a *different* bloody jigsaw. Nevertheless, he knew that something out of the ordinary had happened out there on the motorway that night. More than out of the ordinary. Something truly bizarre had happened.

'It's *still* happening,' he mumbled to himself.

His eyes rested on the daily horoscope column. He hunted for his own star-sign.

'Aquarius: Today is a time to rest your batteries. In a work environment, it seems that nothing out of the usual is likely to take place. Far better to take life and work at a steady pace, and hold yourself in reserve.'

He laughed at the irony.

Beneath the horoscope was another regular item: 'On This Day: In 1889, The *Betsy Kane* runs ashore at the mouth of the River Tyne, its cargo of sugar almost entirely dissolving. Local wit Newby Carter is inspired to pen the novelty poem "Sweet River". In 1945, multi-millionaire Jack Draegerman is born in humble lodgings in Walker Road, Newcastle. In 1987, fifty-three people are killed in still unknown circumstances in a local cinema, "The Imperial".'

Curtis wondered what the column would have to say about the motorway crash in due course. And then his eye caught the last item.

'The Aquanids return. A shower of meteors on this day, 4 May, every year. From the Eta Constellation of Aquarius. Not as active or as strong as the Perseides shower, which comes on 11 or 12 August every year. In fact, the Aquanids are one-tenth as strong.'

Curtis sat looking at the final entry for a long time.

'I will not believe this. I will not believe that the motorway was hit by a fucking meteorite.'

He read it again.

And remained silent and still for an even longer time.

Then he groaned, and threw the newspaper across his desk.

'No, no, no.'

Stretching back in his seat, he pulled on his neck joint until it cracked.

'And I will definitely not . . . I mean absolutely *not* . . . even countenance that . . . that . . .'

That what?

'All right, so what am I saying? It wasn't a meteorite. I'm saying it was . . . what? . . . something else?'

Yes. What?

'No, no, no . . . I mean, come *on*!'

What?

'So it's always been in the back of my mind. Too stupid to give it any head-room.'

What?

'I'm trying to tell myself that they collided with a UFO or something.'

What do you mean? A flying saucer? With little green men?

'I know it, I know it. But think about it, Curtis. The glowing light. And the screaming from nowhere. And the strange things that have happened since.'

Wouldn't there be UFO wreckage after the smash? Surely someone would have found something?

He looked up from his desk. His editor was still in his office, still on the telephone. He tried to think what his reaction might be to the headline that Curtis had in mind right now.

'No, I won't . . . I mean, I can't . . .'

The telephone on his desk rang.

He had to dig through the papers on his desk until he found it.

'Curtis, *Independent Daily*.'

'*This is Harry Stark.*'

He rubbed his face to make sure that his latest idiotic premise hadn't catapulted him into some kind of dreamland.

'Stark. Yeah, right.'

'*I need to talk to you . . .*'

'So you're still alive. Can't say I've become bored since I met you.'

'*I need to talk to you! Stop fucking me around. You've got something I want. And I've got something you're after.*'

'And what might you have that would interest me?'

'*The truth . . . or part of it . . . about what happened on that motorway.*'

'Don't tell me. It was little green men in their flying saucer.' Curtis's mouth had suddenly become dry. The last remark was more than a piss-take or a wry aside. His heart began to beat faster as he waited for Stark's reaction.

'*Don't talk bloody stupid, Curtis. Meet me in an hour. There's not much time before . . .*'

'Before what?'

'*Just meet me on the swing bridge. One hour.*'

Stark hung up. Curtis listened to the disconnected line buzzing in his ears. After a while, he replaced the receiver.

'On this day,' he said, 'Everything turned upside down and now I don't know what the hell is going on, or what I'm doing chasing this bloody senseless, ridiculous story.' He checked that his editor was still on the phone and then reached for his anorak.

'*—Martin . . . Martin, love . . . wake up . . .*'

Martin had been at the bottom of a deep, dark sea. There were thoughts down here that didn't belong to him; thoughts like a school of fishes, drifting and turning suddenly in the current when they thought there might be a predator heading their way. He couldn't tune in to these thoughts, couldn't hear what they had to say. But he could feel them, and could see the occasionally glimmering shoal as it turned in the darkness. Then he heard a voice that he recognised, somewhere up above on the surface. More than anything else, he wanted to stay down here where he could hide and rest. But the voice belonged to the woman he loved most in the world. And once called, he could only obey. He swam upwards to the sound of her voice.

'*—Martin . . . come on, love. Wake up . . . Martin . . . Martin . . .*'

The room was too bright. Why did she have all the lights

on in here in the middle of the day? Martin struggled to sit upright on the sofa. He hadn't meant to sleep, but he had felt so tired on his return from church that it was making him feel ill. It seemed that he'd crashed out as soon as he'd sat down. He looked at his watch, but his vision was too blurred to make any sense of what he saw. When he looked over at the doorway, Sheila was leaning around the frame, looking in on him.

'Yeah? S'marra . . .' he mumbled.

'You've got a visitor. Make yourself presentable.'

'Sheila, for God's sake, I'm *dog* tired . . .'

'It's the Reverend Jameson.'

Martin buried his face in his hands and groaned. 'Tell him I already gave at the office . . . I mean, the church.'

Jameson was already coming into the room. He'd changed into his civilian gear after the service. Black shirt, white collar and tweed jacket. He tried to smile, but it didn't work. When Sheila saw his expression, her own smile fractured and began to fade.

'I'm sorry, Martin. I know you must be exhausted after . . . everything you did this morning.'

'Don't tell me. You've had some dissatisfied customers. My healing didn't take and they want the money that they put on the collection plate back.'

'Martin!' hissed Sheila, in shocked admonition. Even though she had persuaded him to go to the church to pass on his blessings, she could not stop him from coming out with these irreverent comments.

'It's all right, Sheila.' With a look of world-weariness, Jameson moved to the chair opposite Martin, looking to him for permission to sit.

'I'll go and make some tea,' said Sheila, and headed back to the door.

'No, please,' continued Jameson. 'I've something very important to tell you both.'

Sheila looked frightened, quickly moving to Martin and sitting on the arm-rest of the sofa. Jameson sat with a deep sigh. His hands moved to his face in imitation of Martin's waking-up gestures, and for a moment he looked like the one who needed two weeks' bed rest.

'This is very difficult . . .'

'Then best just say what you have to say,' said Martin. 'And say it straight.'

'Right . . . right. You know that I've been encountering a lot of opposition from the church authorities and the General Synod about what we're doing at St Cuthbert's.'

'They're blind,' said Sheila. 'All the good that's being done, and they just want it stopped.'

'Well, it looks like they might get their way.'

'No,' breathed Sheila. 'They can't.'

'Oh yes they can. I've always known that to a great extent we were fighting a losing battle. They're about to make their big move. The archbishop.'

'But surely he can see that it's not wrong?'

'The Church has no place for miracles any more, Sheila. In a historical context, telling stories about past miracles is one thing. Having them happen under their noses in this day and age is quite another. They can do any number of things. Defrock me, for instance. And desanctify the church.'

Sheila's hand moved to her mouth. Her eyes had suddenly become wet.

'You mean Martin has to stop? That he can't use the blessing any more?'

'There's a way,' continued Jameson. 'A way to beat them. But it's not easy. And the greatest burden, I'm afraid, will be on you both. And on your marriage.'

Martin saw that Sheila was on the verge of tears. He leaned across and took her fragile hand in his own calloused one.

'Like I said, Reverend. Tell us straight.'

'You have a great power, Martin. Your wife and I have our views on where that power comes from. I know that you're not convinced, but that you're . . .'

'Open to persuasion. Go on.'

'In my view, it would be . . . would be a *sin* if we allowed you to be prevented from using it. There are others in the Church, others like myself, who have the same view. Despite the fact that the weight of Church authority is against us. And you must never underestimate what kind of power we're up against. There is a place, where some of my other colleagues carry out their work. They minister to the poor, to the suffering. It's not exactly a hospice or a refuge, but the work that takes place there is vitally important . . .'

'Let's get this right. You want to send me to a bloody *monastery!*'

Sheila stifled a sob. This time she did not complain about the profanity.

'No, it's not a monastery. It's a holy order. But the work that's done there is very much tied in with real life and its problems. It's not divorced from the real world in the way you might think. I know the people who work there, and I've discussed it with them. If you were to go there, then people who are sick and dying could be *brought* to you. As far as the Church authorities are concerned, you've ceased to carry out your . . . practice. But, in secret, you'll be there. Your powers will be protected and you can continue to carry out your work.'

'So Sheila and I just pack up lock, stock and barrel. Put on our habits or whatever, and just move in there?'

'And that's where the problem lies. I told you that there would be heartache involved. Like I've said, the Holy Order isn't a monastery and the workers there aren't monks in the conventional sense of the term. But it is a men-only order. No women are allowed within its precinct.'

'You're barking mad,' said Martin firmly. 'You want me to walk out on my wife and go and be a bloody monk in some godforsaken place. Well, that's *it*! As far as I'm concerned, the Church authorities or whoever the hell they are *have* won, after all. As of now, it all stops. You almost had me convinced with this religious business. But that's the end of it.' He squeezed Sheila's hand harder. Her fingers had begun to tremble.

'Don't get me wrong,' said Jameson hurriedly. 'It doesn't mean that you'll be separated. You'll still see each other regularly.'

'That's enough. Time for you to go now . . .'

'No,' said Sheila, her voice muffled by the handkerchief she was using to dab at her eyes and mouth. 'Let him finish.'

Jameson cleared his throat, obviously troubled. 'During the week, Martin would be at the Order. It's not too far away. Two or three hours by car perhaps. And then, at weekends, he would be brought home. Look on it like . . . a job of work. Working away from home, as it were.'

'Balls,' said Martin.

'And he'd be protected?' asked Sheila. 'I mean, nothing would happen to him?'

'Of course not.'

'Wait a moment, Sheila! You can't mean that you're listening to any of this?'

'Look at me. Go on, Martin. Take a look at me, and then look at that photograph over there on the mantelpiece. Remember what I was like before you healed me? Back then, it was misery. Plain and simple misery for me, and for you. Now there's no pain and I feel better than I can remember. You gave me my health back, Martin. You *cured* me. All because of the power you were given. And think of all the other families out there who are suffering. All the people with pain and the misery. Don't you see? You can change all that.'

'I'm not clever, Sheila. You know that. And you know how I feel about the religious stuff. We had a church wedding, the way you wanted. And the promises I made to God then about us didn't matter. It was the promise I made to *you*. I promised I'd never leave you. Till death do us part, remember?'

'But you're not leaving me. Like the Reverend Jameson says, you'll be away during the week. Home at the weekends.'

'I don't want us to be apart. I need you.'

'What about those long-distance lorry hauls? Have you forgotten what you used to do for a living? Sometimes you'd be away from me for a *fortnight!*'

Martin opened his mouth to speak, then realised that his wife had him over a barrel. He couldn't argue against the logic of what she was saying. There had been occasions over the years when he'd been away for three weeks at a time. He looked deep into her eyes, saw the tears, but saw also the joy that was there. He squeezed her hand and looked back at Jameson.

'There's still the official inquiry about the motorway crash coming up. I'll be needed for the court appearance.'

'Of course,' said Jameson. 'You'll have to be there.'

'And Sheila has to be looked after. What about money?'

'I promise you. You'll both be well looked after and Sheila will have no money problems. I guarantee it.'

Martin looked long and hard at the vicar.

'I won't have anything happen to Sheila while I'm away.'

'She'll be under our full protection.'

'And weekends at home are guaranteed.'

Jameson laughed, a ragged sound. 'You're not going to prison, Martin.'

Martin looked back at Sheila and smiled when she smiled. 'Best get me fitted for one of them monk's habits, then.'

'It's not like that.'

'When do I start packing?'

'Now,' said Jameson.

Sheila squeezed his hand, and smiled again.

The thing had arrived.

It had no perception of time as it staggered and trudged along the motorway's hard shoulder. It could sense that its place of arrival and departure was very close, and had continued on its ragged path, heading south. The lights continued to pass it as it moved, but now it did not mourn the fact that they seemed unaware and unheeding of its presence. It knew instinctively that it had a kinship with those rushing lights, but it no longer felt desolation about their refusal to acknowledge its presence. Those lights were 'travellers' too, all heading for their own destinations, just as it was heading for its own. Once, one of the lights seemed to slow, almost to draw alongside. There appeared to have been a voice then, expressing concern. It had half inclined its head so that the light shone on it. Then there had been an exclamation of horror and the light had continued on its way. The thing did not care any more. Its destination was close . . . so very close . . .

At last, it had found the place.

The road here was gouged. There were great furrows and mounds of excavated earth. Bright orange cones had been laid out in a double line ahead of the thing, and it watched the lights all slow down and converge into the narrow lane before roaring off into the night. But it could sense that this was the place, and a great feeling of joy overcame its ravaged frame.

'I'm here!' it called into the night. 'Take me with you! I'm here!'

It staggered out into the road again. More horns blaring and the screeching of tyres. The thing blundered back to the hard shoulder. Now that it was close, it must not put a foot wrong, and it felt sure that, far from being angry with it, those blaring sounds were meant to act as a warning to keep on its path until it had found its home. The hard shoulder had become an embankment. The metal barrier here had been smashed and removed so that the thing was able to wander up on to the rim of the motorway. Now it was moving along the grassed rim, looking down on the road and the single lane that had been demarcated by the cones. The remaining trees here were burned to black skeletal sculptures. The thing's feet were becoming clogged with black, wet ash. There was a memory here now, as it walked. It had been here before. Not once, but twice. Before it had wandered; before the realisation had come upon it that it must get back to its . . . what? . . . birthplace?

A light, burning bright in the windscreen.

Screaming. A hideous explosion of shattering glass and screeching of tyres as everything turned upside down. Whirling and flying. And then . . .

Crawling through a gully. Frantically thrashing in torment to find what was missing; clawing through the undergrowth and the bushes to find the rest of itself, to make itself whole. The agony of fusion. The crawling blue-white light. And then a man in a uniform. A man who was wearing his own terrified face.

Down there.

The thing tottered to a standstill, and knew that it had found the place.

Even in the darkness, it could see the gully in which it had crawled. It was directly beneath it. On the other side, at the rim of the embankment, forty feet from where it stood, was the single-lane motorway.

The impact point.

The place where it had arrived.

The place where it could continue its journey.

The thing half fell, half scrambled down into the gully. The grass here had been burned down to the bare clay. Scrambling up the other side, its claws dug into the furrowed earth. It pulled itself erect and stood swaying in the night wind. This was where the lights were coming.

Grinning its hideous, ragged grin, the thing flopped into a grotesque cross-legged position and waited to be taken away.

Curtis saw Stark while he was still a long way off, standing on the swing bridge, and wondered whether he'd chosen this meeting place for dramatic effect. Every time a film crew or a documentary team were filming something up here in the North, they'd have a shot of the protagonists hanging over the rail of the Tyne Bridge, or perhaps the high-level bridge, or the swing bridge. Curtis wondered whether Stark had been a film fan before the horrific crash.

The swing bridge was just downriver of the Tyne Bridge; a little sister of a bridge which had closed and opened regularly when the Tyne had boasted a shipbuilding industry. Regular maintenance had been required then because of frequency of use; regular maintenance was still required to stop its mechanism from rusting through lack of use.

Harry was standing at the mid-point, where steel ladders led to the bridge's control cabin above. He was looking down at the river, head over the rail. As Curtis walked over the bridge from the Newcastle side, he expected Stark to look up at any second. But he kept his gaze directed towards the dirty water below. Was he contemplating jumping in? And if he did, what would Curtis do? Ring for an ambulance again? He could imagine the response.

Do us a favour, Curtis. YOU go jump in the river and don't bother us again.

Fifteen feet away, Curtis saw Stark suddenly look up as if a voice over his shoulder had startled him from his reverie. He looked across at the Gateshead side of the river, seemed to mumble something, and then turned to look directly at Curtis. His face was still as spectral and white as Curtis had last seen it. His expression did not change as Curtis finally drew level and put a hand on the rail beside him.

'Surprised you're still here,' he said. 'After all that stuff I saw you swallowing.'

Stark seemed to be studying his face, but said nothing.

'Okay, I'm impressed,' continued Curtis. 'Good trick. I don't know how you did it, but you made me look a complete arsehole. And the hospital authorities are about to sue said arsehole for causing them so much trouble.'

Stark turned from him again, still without responding, and looked out across the river once more.

'Look, Stark. We're in the middle of a heat-wave. I'm hot and bothered, carrying more weight than is good for my health, and it's a long walk from the office to the river. Not only that, but if my boss finds out that I'm still chasing up this story, I'm likely to be out of a job for good. So a few words of encouragement wouldn't go amiss. You know – like, "The reason I asked to see you, Mr Curtis, is . . .", and then a whole lot of interesting stuff.'

'I remember . . .'

Stark's voice seemed to crack, as if he hadn't used it for a long time. He grimaced, hawked and spat over the side of the bridge into the river. Curtis winced. Was that *blood*?

'I remember more about what happened. Since you came. And then, afterwards . . . after you left and I did what I did . . . it's told me a lot more.'

'Come again?'

'Been thinking,' continued Harry, as if he hadn't heard him. 'Watching the stuff float by on this river. Bits of wood. Bottles. Stuff. Like life, really. Like that night on the motorway. River's like a road.'

Curtis moaned and stood with his back to the rail while Stark continued.

'You see, it could have been anyone that night. On the motorway, I mean. If we'd been five minutes later, we would have missed it. Even five minutes earlier. Could have been delayed setting out. Could have had a flat tyre. Or we might have stopped for Coke and chips, like the kids wanted when we passed that service station. Or we needn't have gone up to Scotland to see Jean's relations and then decided to drive straight back down for our holiday. I think about that a lot. We had plenty of time to get to the ferry. Or if I'd just stopped for a little while ... then none of this would ...' He cleared his throat. 'It could have happened to anyone. But it happened to us.'

'Look, I'm sorry. I really am. But you said you had something to tell me. About what happened.'

'There's something in me,' said Stark, turning to look him directly in the eye.

'You need help. I don't know why those paramedics couldn't see that there was something wrong with you, but you need specialist help. Christ, after something like that you should be getting counselling at the very least.'

'You're not *listening!*' Harry's eyes were wild, but Curtis could see a control there that hadn't been apparent until now. 'I said, there's something *inside* me. Look ...' He fumbled in his inside pocket and pulled out a piece of crumpled paper. It was A4 size, and when he straightened it out Curtis could see that both sides of the sheet were filled with cramped, crowded handwriting. 'See this? It's a suicide note. I wrote it just before I took an overdose. You were right. I did try to kill myself, but not in the way you think. All that stuff I told you I was drinking and eating, the stuff you saw me drink. None of that can harm me. The thing that's inside me *needs* that stuff. Needs it to help keep it safe inside, to help it to grow and recover ...'

'What the *hell* are you talking about?'

'Shut up and listen! After you left, I couldn't take any more. I wrote this suicide note and I went upstairs. Took an entire bottle of Jean's sleeping tablets. They should have killed me, *would* have killed me if not for the thing that's buried deep inside me. You see, if I die it dies, too. It's like a parasite. It knew that I was dying, so it fought . . . and *fought* to bring me back. There's all kinds of weird chemical shit going on inside me, I think. By rights, that bottle of pills should have finished me. But the thing counteracted the drugs, fought against them. I know it wasn't easy. And there are times . . . times when I think that I really *did* die. And the bastard brought me back to life, just to save itself. It's a survivor, you see. Just like me. The difference is . . . I want to die, and it wants to live. Now that I'm alive again, there's a sort of side effect. You see, it's been hiding deep down inside. It's not alive in the way we know. I mean, it's not like some kind of slug in my guts. It's more like a kind of energy. I reckon if I was X-rayed, you'd see nothing there. But it's deep down. Maybe hiding in the place where my soul is. It didn't want me to know that it was there. It's been hurt by the collision, and it's been hiding and growing strong, making itself better day by day as the chemicals I've been pouring into myself have been feeding it somehow. And I would never have known it was there if I hadn't tried to kill myself. 'Cause in the course of bringing me back to life, some kind of barrier between us has been dissolved. Now I know it's there, on the fringes of . . . this is hard to explain, like on the fringes of my conscious mind. And I can sense things about it. Not everything, but piece by piece, hour by hour, I'm finding out more.'

He paused, as if to give Curtis a chance to call him a lunatic, or a junkie, or a sad, sick man. Curtis leaned on the rail and said nothing, waiting for him to continue.

'It's a traveller,' continued Harry at last. 'One of seven. It – they – collided with the southbound traffic on that motorway. The sounds of screaming I heard. The sounds you say the others heard. That was the sound of the travellers. They were in just as much terror, just as much pain, as we were.'

'The light?'

'That was them. Heading straight for us. God knows how or why. But out of control, I think. Then they . . . collided. And they *jumped*.'

'Jumped?'

'At the moment of collision, they somehow jumped into

seven people. Like *that!*' Harry snapped his fingers. 'They didn't have a chance to choose who they were jumping into. They just did it. Seven surviving travellers jumped into seven human hosts. There were more than seven travellers. Not sure how many, but several dozen perhaps. Maybe the others jumped, too. I'm not sure about that part. But if they did, the humans they jumped into were killed in the smash – and that meant they perished, too. That word. *Perish.* I get that word a lot while I'm trying to tap into the thing. Doesn't use the word "die". Prefers "perish". Funny sort of fucker, isn't it?' Harry laughed, a cracked and brittle sound. 'So I'm one of the lucky seven.'

'There were only six survivors, Stark.'

Harry looked at him again. He hadn't expected the journalist to take what he had said so calmly; had partly expected that he would listen and then walk quickly back the way he'd come, dismissing him entirely.

'What do you mean?'

'I mean what I say. There were only six of you, not seven. And in the hospital, I saw the six of you being ... being *hit* by the lightning strikes from that bizarre stormcloud.'

'I don't know anything about that. Nothing about there only being six. The thing inside me says ... except *says* isn't the right word for it ... that there are seven. More than that, it says that the Seventh Survivor is somehow more important than any of the others. And God knows what that means. And the storm business? I believe you now, about what happened in the hospital, I mean. But I still don't remember it. Maybe if I keep trying, I'll find out more. It's like a two-way flow going on inside me. This thing wants things from me, wants me to do things, *forces* me to do things. But I can fight back, and sometimes I can get stuff out of it. It's bloody unwilling, but sometimes it can't hide things from me if I dig down deep enough into it.'

'When you were struck by that lightning ...' Curtis had a faraway expression on his face, he turned to look out across the river. 'I remember the expressions you all had on your faces then. Know what I reckon? I think that whatever is inside you all was . . . communicating. For a moment, the things inside were all somehow able to talk to each other.'

Harry took another piece of paper from his pocket. This one was even more crumpled than the other. He showed it to Curtis. Three scrawled words.

'"Find the others"' Curtis read aloud.

'It made me write that. I didn't want to do what it wanted. My body, my hand. But it made me write those words. That's why I'm here. Listen, Curtis. I don't want to be here. I only want to die. There's nothing for me now. But it *made* me come. Sometimes it can do that. It puts some kind of physical pressure on me inside when I resist it too much. It feels like it's wrapped around something inside me, in my rib-cage and at the back of my head. And when it squeezes, it's . . . agony. As far as I'm concerned it can go to hell with the others. But here I am. It needs to find the others . . . and I know you can help me.'

'Why? Why does it need to find them?'

'To save them. I get the feeling that it knows more about what's going on than any of the others. They're all in some kind of danger that I can't work out yet. I'm trying to find out, but it keeps that part hidden. I'll wear the bastard down eventually. But all I do know is that it needs to get all the survivors physically together again. I don't think any of the other human hosts know what's in them. Maybe, in time . . . wait a minute . . .'

Curtis watched as Stark gripped the bridge rail with both hands and squeezed tight. He leaned forward, as if he might suddenly vomit into the water below.

'Yeah, I know . . . come on, then . . . come on . . . No, I can't get much more out of it.' There was a sheen of sweat on his face. His breathing seemed heavier as he leaned away from the rail again. 'Just that something's gone wrong for them. More than the crash, I mean. Something to do with their survival after the crash. Survival in us, that is. But it's vitally important that it finds the others.'

'I know where three of them are. Four of the six, that is, counting yourself. I still don't know what you mean by a "Seventh Survivor", though.'

'There's a Seventh, believe me. Who are the others? Where are they?'

'Let's see . . . Jane Teal. Housewife. She lives locally. Roger O'Dowd, an artist. He's moved away from his flat, but I've got a forwarding address in London for him. One of the others was checked in as Elton Blackwell. Didn't think it sounded like a real name at the time. I sneaked a look at the credit cards in his wallet. Real name's Ellis Burwell. God knows why he gave a false name. There was a young woman, Mercy something-or-other. She checked herself out of hospital and just vanished. And then there's Martin Russell.'

Curtis stopped speaking. When Harry looked at him, he could see that the newspaperman was staring at where Harry was clutching the bridge rail.

'What?' asked Harry.

'Why are you wearing gloves? We're in the middle of a heat-wave, and you're wearing gloves.'

'You know,' said Harry, his voice low with astonishment. 'How the hell do you know about my hands?'

'Jesus Christ. Are you saying that you can do what Martin Russell can do? You can heal people just by touching them?'

'*Heal* people?' Harry burst out laughing, throwing back his head. It was a wild and desperate sound. 'Oh yeah, I suppose you could call it that. If you can call death the answer to everyone's problems.'

'No, no, no. Wait a moment. I'm talking about what I saw him do in a church. He's found God or something. I went down to watch him in an unofficial service that's causing a big stink with the Church authorities. I saw him touching people, and healing them.'

Harry's laughter died.

'If I take one of these gloves off, my friend, and if I so much as touch you with one finger . . . you're dead.'

They stood looking at each other for a long time. Traffic rushed past them on the bridge. Seagulls were picking at the detritus that floated down the river.

'It happened when I took the bandages off my hands. I was badly burned trying to, trying to . . . anyway, I was badly burned. I should be getting further treatment. Skin grafts. Except that I don't need them. My hands are healed. New skin. Like a miracle. But the first thing I touched – our dog – I killed. It was like an electric shock.' He held up his hands and looked at them. 'Want to know something funny? When the thing saved me from suicide, when I found out what I could do . . . I put my hands around my own neck. Thought it would do the trick. Big joke. It doesn't work on me.'

'You think the thing inside you has given you that power?'

'That part seems cloudy in my head. But what else could it be?'

'So the thing inside our lorry-driver friend is also giving him some kind of power. So why does yours kill, and his heal?'

'I don't know. Not yet, anyway.'

'And if you've both got this kind of . . . power, then what about the others? Christ, what will they be able to do?'

'You'll help me, then?'

'Why does one want to kill, and another want to heal? It doesn't make sense.'

'I don't know, Curtis. When I do, you'll be the first to find out. Believe me. But you'll help?'

'Yes, I'll help you. Won't be easy, though. I can't tell the people I work for what I'm doing. They'll send me off to the funny farm. No offence.'

'None taken.'

'Christ, aliens and flying saucers . . .'

'What?'

'Well, that's what we're talking about, aren't we? You know, I had a feeling about this from the very beginning. The storm in the hospital, the light on the motorway. I just kept shoving it all to the back of my mind. And then, today, just before you called – I came across that business with the meteorites.'

'What the hell are you talking about?'

'The Aquanids. It's a meteor shower. Pretty mild, but it takes place on or about the same day every year. There was a shower on the night of the crash.'

'Forget it, Curtis.'

'What do you mean, forget it? It all adds up.'

'Get real. This isn't about flying saucers, meteorites or men from Mars.'

Curtis was suddenly exasperated. 'Get real? You're the one who's telling me that you've got an alien survivor hiding inside yourself. You're the one who says he can kill at a touch.'

'We didn't collide with a UFO or a meteorite. And the thing inside me isn't an alien.'

'Then what the hell *are* we talking about?'

'I don't know yet. But whatever we collided with – and whatever these things are – it's not the way you think it is. So forget about all that crap.'

'So you don't know what it *is*, but you know what it *isn't?*'

'Exactly.'

'That doesn't make sense.'

'You don't say.'

Curtis needed a drink now more than he'd ever done in his life. He looked down at the dirty water and thought about what Stark had said. Yeah, he was right. He could see what he meant now, the river looking like a road. He slapped the rail and looked at him again.

'Come on. We've got some visiting to do.'

Mercy had no idea how long she had been walking.

For a long time, she had kept her head down, looking at her feet as she staggered through the night. She seemed to remember that someone had called out to her, asking if she was all right. But she hadn't looked up; had just kept on moving. There was too much going on inside her head, and moving like this through the darkness kept the nightmares at bay. It had always been like this for her. If there was a problem, then the way to solve it was to put as much physical distance between it and herself. Maybe that was why she spent so much time on the move.

With each step, she told herself that what had happened to Deinbeck hadn't happened at all. It was all inside her head. She had spent so much time wondering what she would do when she found him. There had been so much hate, so much rage. Everything inside her had become focused on the need to find her abuser. Finally, when she'd found him ... well, perhaps something had happened to her mind. Maybe she'd had some kind of breakdown and had only imagined what had taken place.

She looked at her hands as she walked.

And then saw Deinbeck in his car; saw his head thrashing from side to side as the skin darkened and spittle flew from his lips; saw his limbs jerking and twitching as if there were an electric current going through him. She remembered the strange sensation in her hands as the power had flowed from her ...

'No, it didn't happen!'

She screwed her hands into fists and beat them on the sides of her thighs with each step.

'It *couldn't* happen!'

What had happened to Deinbeck had been what Mercy wanted. She had wanted him to die the most hideous, agonising and tormented death imaginable. Wasn't that the reason behind her search? To pay him back for everything he had done to her, to Selina and to all of the other kids in his care? A deep, secret part of her was rejoicing at the spectacle of Deinbeck's spectacular disintegration. But the greater part of her felt cheated and afraid. Cheated because her mind had played such a grotesque trick on her and conjured up that wild hallucination; also cheated because no matter how hard she tried she could not dig into her mind and *really* remember what had happened to Deinbeck in his car. Had she walked away? Or – and this was what filled her with such a feeling of sickness and horror – had she somehow *allowed* him to take her? And if so, what in fucking hell was she doing or thinking about? Had she *wanted* to be abused again?

'No, no, no, NO!' she yelled at the night.

And she was afraid, too. Afraid that the confrontation with Deinbeck had done something irreversibly bad to her. It had turned her mind, and now she was wandering like a madwoman in the night.

Mad. Oh Christ, that's what's happened. I'm mad and I'm stuck in that place inside my head where I'll keep seeing those

*things that can't happen. Think about it. Think of all the mad
things that have happened, that you've been doing to yourself.
Think of all the crap you've been forcing into your face, like a
bloody madwoman. Only mad people do things like that. I'm
not in the darkness. I'm not walking anywhere. In a moment,
I'll be able to see what's really happened to me. I'll be in an
institution somewhere. I'll have been trussed up in a strait
jacket, and thrown into one of those padded cells. And I'll kick
and scream and start biting the walls. But I'll never stop seeing
those terrible things that can't happen.*

She stopped and held her hands to her face.

She dug her fingers deep into the flesh, feeling the pain,
trying to convince herself that she was real, that she wasn't
where she feared she might be. She took her hands away and
opened her eyes again.

It was night.

There was a warm breeze blowing.

And she was standing on a motorway embankment, looking down.

Fear stabbed at her heart again. It was a very real pain,
like a fragment of glass. Her hands flew back to her face and
she moaned. She really was trapped in the nightmare after all.
Somehow, she was back where she had started. In a moment,
Martin's lorry would come down the slip-road she'd glimpsed
just before she'd blocked her vision. She would walk out in
front of it, and he would have to slam on the brakes. Then
she'd walk around and climb up to the cabin again. Moments
later, they'd be *en route*, having that same conversation about
music and nine-to-five jobs.

Then there would be the light.

And the screaming. (*Why did I forget about that? Why
have I just remembered after all this time? Because you're
mad, Mercy. And you're living in your own nightmare. That's
why.*)

And then Martin would say: *Something's coming* . . . And
they would be catapulted right into the shrieking, exploding
nightmare again. She was on some hideous kind of merry-go-
round, forced to relive the same nightmare, over and over

again. She'd find Deinbeck, do the impossible thing to him again. And then she'd be walking through the night, right back to the motorway, where Martin's lorry would come roaring down the slip-road and . . .

The headlights picked her out clearly, standing on the other side of the motorway barrier, and at first Munby thought she was waiting for them to pass so that she could run across to the other side. But then Asa said: 'Hitch-hiker!'

And Don laughed from the back seat. 'Put your foot down and flatten him!' The laughter turned to choking when a mouthful of beer from his can went down the wrong way. Munby glanced back, angrily complaining about stains on the seat of his father's car. Then Asa's hand was on the wheel.

'Come on, Munby. Stop the car.'

'Get your fucking hands off. What do we want to stop for?'

'The hitcher!'

'Some fucking hippie kid smelling of joss-sticks and with fucking lice in his hair. I'm not having him in the car.'

'It's not a fella. It's a girl. You're not looking.'

'And I don't want a girl in the car either. Fuck it, Asa! I don't want to pick up any hitchers. We're only going as far as the next turn-off.'

'Come on!' Asa dragged at the wheel. Munby swore again and slammed on the brakes. The car swerved into the hard shoulder and screeched to a halt a hundred yards past the figure. Don strained to look back through the rear window.

'What's she like? Nice tits?'

Asa wound down the passenger window and looked back out along the hard shoulder to where she stood.

'Not bad. Stuck-up bitch, though.' He leaned back in and banged on the car horn.

'Shit, Asa! Whose fucking car is it, anyway?'

'Your dad's,' laughed Don, drinking again. 'Remember? And he told me that Asa could do what he liked with it.'

Asa laughed when he looked out again. He had expected the hitcher to come running along the hard shoulder towards them when it became obvious they'd stopped to give her a lift. But she really *was* a stuck-up bitch. Because now she was just sitting down on the motorway barrier, as if she expected them to come to *her*.

'Reverse up,' said Asa. 'Come on. Let's go and collect her.'

'Fuck off!' Munby braced his hands on the steering wheel.

'What's the matter with you? Poor girl stuck out here in the middle of nowhere. Needs to get home.'

'You stupid twat. You forgetting what happened to Kelly that time?'

'What's Kelly got to do with anything?' asked Don impatiently. 'Wanker.'

'He picked up that tart from Whitley Bay. Said she was hitching. Then she started crying rape. Got himself in to big trouble. Should have just kept on going. Saved himself all that hassle.'

Asa laughed again. 'But he *did* try to give her one. You forgot that part.'

'That's not the point. Picking up some bint in the middle of the night in the middle of nowhere. It's asking for trouble.' Munby made to drive off again.

Asa grabbed the wheel once more.

'Reverse up. Come on. Who the hell's going to touch her?'

'If I thought you were putting me in the same boat as Kelly,' muttered Don darkly, sipping from his can again, 'I'd kick your fucking teeth down your throat, Munby.'

'Come on, Munby. Have a heart.'

Mumby looked at Asa again and knew he had lost the argument.

'No fucking funny business, Asa.'

'No fucking,' said Asa. 'And no funny business.'

Don laughed like he'd heard the greatest joke in the world.

Muttering under his breath, Munby reversed up the hard shoulder.

'How far you going?' asked Asa when the car finally drew level. The girl was still sitting on the barrier, staring out across the motorway, and had not registered their presence.

Don wound down his window and leaned out.

'It's a trick, isn't it? We stop to give you a lift, 'cause we think it's only you. And then ten other people jump out of the bushes and try to get into the car. Saw that done once.'

The girl said nothing, still looking out across the motorway. A car zoomed past in the night, horn blaring.

'Fuck *you*!' shouted Don, craning his neck to watch it vanish in the darkness.

'She's spaced out,' said Munby tightly. 'Look at her. Come on, let's get out of here . . .'

Asa leaned out of his window and yanked open the rear passenger door. Don gave a whoop and almost fell out.

'Well? You want a lift or not?'

Still without looking at them, the girl stood up from the barrier and walked to the rear door. She seemed to be trying to solve some mysterious inner problem. Don scrambled back across to the other side of the seat. The girl climbed in and sat, looking ahead.

'Come on, then,' said Asa. 'Let's go.'

Munby gripped the wheel tight, face set and angry.

'What?' asked Asa angrily. 'Come on, let's get a move on.'

'The *door*,' said Munby, through gritted teeth. 'She hasn't shut the *door!*'

Grinning, Asa climbed out, gave a chauffeur's mock bow to where the girl was sitting, and then closed the door with due ceremony. Jumping back into the front passenger seat, he slammed his own door closed with such force that it rocked the car on its suspension. Munby opened his mouth to complain again.

'We know, we know,' said Don. 'Dad wouldn't like it. Now, come on. Drive.'

There was silence in the car then as Munby finally pulled off the hard shoulder and joined the motorway again.

'Where you going?' he asked the girl, when it became clear that no one was going to break the silence.

'Home,' said the girl, in a faraway voice.

Both Asa and Don began to laugh.

Munby gripped the steering wheel and moaned again.

*   *   *

On impulse, Chris finally made his way to the Irish Paddock, and there was Roger sitting at the bar in the same seat. It was the first place they'd come to for a beer after Roger's arrival. He paused at the doorway, looking in. The night was hot, and someone had propped the door open with a bar stool, trying to get a little air. Tonight it seemed that most of the patrons preferred to sit on the pavement outside. Only a dozen diehards remained inside, the jukebox playing its usual selection.

Instinctively, Chris knew what it meant, Roger's being here. They might have been apart for a long time, but they were still brothers; and now, despite everything that had happened, it seemed to Chris that neither had changed to the extent that they didn't understand each other any more. Roger was here, in the same seat, because he wanted to be found.

Pax.

Chris moved casually into the bar, stood next to him and caught the barman's attention. Roger's drink was almost finished.

'Two pints of Murphy's.'

'And two whisky chasers,' said Roger. Now it was as if there had never been an argument.

'Make it Bell's whisky,' said Chris, pulling up the stool beside Roger.

'Come here often?' asked Roger, finishing his beer.

'Just when I'm hunting for runaways.'

'You were right. Something's happening. To me, I mean.'

'I shouldn't have said what I said.'

'Why not? You were right, Chris. I think something is fucking around with my head, and it must be to do with the motorway smash. Some of it is . . . scary. Like the stuff I've been eating and drinking.'

'I was wrong trying to tell you what to do. Older-brother syndrome. Being a know-all pain-in-the-arse is part of the problem.'

'Maybe the job-hunting is just putting me under extra stress. Maybe if I give myself a rest from it.'

'Rest, hell. What you need is some serious partying.'

'Starting tonight?'

Chris paid for the newly arrived drinks, placing the whisky and the beer in front of Roger. 'Starting tonight. *These* are the kind of chemicals you need inside you.' When Roger drank, Chris studied his face and struggled to retain his light-heartedness. God knew what damage he'd done to his guts, and maybe getting stoned on booze was the worst thing he could do to his stomach in the circumstances. But right now, it was a question of literally going with the flow. Tomorrow, he could set about trying to fix Roger up with some professional help. He had some friends with contacts.

Two skinfuls later, they were headed home. They'd talked a lot about their youth, about their shared experiences, youthful ambitions and dreams. Retelling old stories that had perhaps been embellished in the telling over the years, but which reinforced their bond and made them feel comfortable.

And then Roger had talked about the motorway crash, and he'd spoken in more detail than he'd done before. Perhaps the alcohol was making it more vivid in the telling. The headlights directly ahead, evidence that some stupid bastard was driving on the wrong side of the road. The sounds of screaming. And then the nightmare of the coach turning over. The rescue. The burning fuel and the horror. No wonder his head had been screwed up.

At the corner of the street, looking down to where Chris lived, they could see that there had been some sort of incident. There were three panda cars parked outside the Victorian terraced building. Blue lights flashed. There was a straggling ring of late-night revellers gathered on the pavement around the entrance to the place. Impatient police officers were trying to move them on. Police radios crackled. Some of the people living in the terraces were leaning out of their windows, looking down.

'Maybe someone heard us arguing,' joked Roger as they walked on down the street.

'Christ, I didn't realise we were making so much noise.'

'What do you fancy to drink when we get inside? Drain cleaner and Coke?'

'How about Domestos and ginger ale?'

'Fairy Liquid and lime.'

Now that they were closer, they could see that they might have difficulty getting through their own front door. The police had sealed off the entrance and the surrounding area with red tape streamers. Something seemed to be happening on the pavement beside the railings, but it was difficult to make anything out because of the milling crowd and the uniformed police who were trying to disperse it. As they walked, they first heard and then saw an ambulance screech around the far corner of the street and pull up. Paramedics emerged from the rear, carrying a stretcher.

'Got to be the guy living below me,' said Chris.

'Why's that?'

'Real low-life. Has all kinds of trash in there. Surprised there hasn't been any trouble with the police before now.'

They had reached the entrance. Two constables were standing at the top of the main stairs, with their backs to the door. As Chris pushed through the crowd and called one of them over, Roger moved further down to try to see what was happening on the pavement. The flashing blue lights from the panda cars, and now from the ambulance, made the scene seem surreal.

'Excuse me,' began Chris. 'We live here . . .'

And then Roger saw the paramedics lay the stretcher on the pavement. There was broken glass everywhere, crunching underfoot, and a dark pool, reflecting the blue light. And someone had thrown what looked like a tarpaulin sheet over the railings. As he pushed forward, Roger saw at last that there was something under the sheet, something that dripped and was making the pool on the pavement . . .

'*Jesus Christ!*' It was Chris's voice, registering real alarm.

Roger jerked around and saw that his brother was standing back from the policeman behind the tape, and was looking up now at the building.

'But that's *my* apartment!'

Roger followed Chris's line of sight, and saw what had so alarmed him.

The attic-room window was shattered. Another police constable was framed in the ragged aperture, looking down at the street below.

The tarpaulin had been thrown over the railings directly beneath the window.

Roger felt something inside then. Something that was drawing him forward, despite the irritated demands from the police behind the tape that people should move on. Over someone's shoulder, he looked again at the tarpaulin.

This time, he saw a hand.

It was hanging below the rim of the sheet. Blood dripped from its fingertips. In horrified fascination, Roger saw that the same blood was dripping on to something appallingly familiar, lying on the pavement beneath it.

It was his canvas. The painting he had been furiously working on before Chris had arrived home and they'd had their fight. The canvas had been torn and ripped; the blood from the dripping hand had soaked and obliterated the painting itself. And the impulse in Roger was an overwhelming desire now. He could not prevent himself lunging forward through the crowd, shoving the man in front of him to one side. The man cursed and one of the policemen saw what he was trying to do. But Roger was moving too fast and he ducked under the tape and eluded the constable's grasping hand. His heart was hammering, and all he could think about was the way he'd felt when he'd come out of his trance – or whatever in hell had been happening to him – and had seen the first whorling spiral of colour that he had created on the canvas. The way the pattern he'd painted drew in the eyes, seemed to suck at the soul, and the terrible fear that he mustn't look too closely or something *terrible* would happen.

Something terrible *had* happened.

And he had to see.

He ducked and twisted. Someone yelled, perhaps one of the paramedics. Blue flashing light blinded him for a moment. And then he reached the tarpaulin, grabbing for its edge. In one sweeping movement, he yanked it away from the spiked railings.

Behind the cordon, someone screamed.

Someone else seemed to have fainted. The crowd stirred and pulled back. Someone yelled: 'Give her *room*, for Christ's sake!' Two policemen seized Roger by both arms. Someone else yanked the tarpaulin from his hands and hurriedly began to throw it over the railings again.

'Get him out of here!' snapped another voice. 'Have the lab people taken their photos yet? No? Then how fucking long has he got to stay hanging there before we can take him down . . . ?'

Roger was bundled away to one of the panda cars. Dimly, he was aware of Chris's voice somewhere behind as he tried to push through the crowd towards him.

'Couldn't have picked a better spot to land if he wanted to do himself in,' mumbled one of the paramedics. 'Straight through the window and down on to the railings. Hell of a dive.'

As Roger was bundled into the back of the police car, he could see only the stranger's face. Someone had painted the face; painted it in savage streaks with his own blood. But the expression in the dead eyes was what hypnotised him. Because something in those insane, staring eyes of glass contained a trace of what the stranger had seen in Roger's painting before he had thrown himself through the attic-room window.

Roger remembered the old wives' tale of the retina of a dead person retaining the image of the last thing it saw.

Vinny had seen hell.

And Roger had created that hell with his own hands.

Ellis Burwell was having a good day at the office.

The heat-wave showed no signs of abating. The company took pride in its air-conditioned offices and therefore felt that there was no excuse for extended lunch breaks to escape the heat. Nevertheless, Burwell was striding through the municipal park at the rear of the premises. It was a half-term holiday for schools, so kids were running about, playing on the battered play equipment, climbing on the monkey bars. Mothers sat on benches, pushchairs carefully parked beside them as they chatted. Burwell walked with something like a

smile on his face. He seemed to be trying to find a way to make
it fit, as if this expression were so new and so alien to him that
he was having difficulty getting it to hang right. There was a
newspaper under his arm and a paper bag in one hand. His
shirt-sleeves were rolled up, for the first time in twenty years.
There was a lightness in his step today which had drawn
bemused attention from those with whom he'd worked over
the years.

*Maybe the sour bastard's in love for the first time? Yeah?
Well, Lord help the poor soul, whoever he or she is.*

*I reckon someone he hates has died and left him some
money.*

Has he been given a raise?

*Maybe . . . maybe he knows something we don't. That would
be more like him. Always sitting in front of that console, with
his spreadsheets and his facts and figures. I bet the whole
company's going to the dogs. We're all going to end up on
the dole and that sod will have made himself safe. I bet that's
it. We're all off to hell in a handcart and he knows it . . .*

Burwell found an unoccupied bench and sat down with
a sigh. Opening the crumpled paper bag, he took out a
sandwich. Despite the peculiar cravings, his appetite had
never been better these past few days, after the gnawing
anxiety had worn off. He bit into the sandwich and then
opened the newspaper to read the story he'd already read a
dozen times that morning.

Drug Link to Car Park Death and Arson.

Investigations are still proceeding following the
mysterious death of Henry 'Klark' Clarkson in
Newcastle's Civic Hall car park on Wednesday, although
police now believe that a drugs motive is likely.
Clarkson (33) was found dead in the early hours of the
morning, with a knife wound to the leg. The findings of
a post-mortem are still awaited, but it is understood that
the wound was not the reason for death. Although initial
speculation suggested that Clarkson himself may have

been responsible for setting fire to his luxury apartment
for reasons unknown . . .

Burwell chortled over his sandwich. He liked that bit. Something he'd never considered. Thank God for the ingenuity of
the tabloid press.

. . . for reasons unknown, it is now felt that the horrific
arson attack which completely gutted the sixth-storey flat
at Wharf Seven, Ouseburn, and which also resulted in
the deaths of Norman Holister (56), Myra Holister (61),
Terry Bland (32), Patricia Bland (21) and three-year-old
Teresa Bland might have been a revenge attack by rival
drugs gangs. Clarkson was convicted on three separate
occasions for possession of and dealing in controlled
substances. Police are investigating these links further and
expect that . . .

Burwell finished his sandwich, sucking the crumbs from his
fingers. When they were clean, he held them up before his face,
inspecting them as if they were the most wonderful things
on earth.
They are *wonderful* . . .
He touched his face with them.
Only other people. Not me.
He had never believed in miracles; never could have believed
that he might be given the power of life and death over others.
And although he still refused to think too deeply about what
had happened to him and how it had happened to him – in
case the magic should decide to go away again – he felt
sure that it had something to do with the motorway crash.
He remembered the way he'd felt back then, just before the
smash. He remembered that he'd been thinking about what
he'd wanted most in the world, with an intensity of passion
that he'd never felt before. The coach-driver had cut him up
on the road, and that had lit the fuse of his anger. Maybe he
should have died in the crash. But maybe the fates had been

listening in; maybe they agreed that he'd been given nothing but the shitty end of the stick from the beginning. So maybe they'd stepped in to save him from being smashed to a pulp, or burned to a crisp. And maybe they'd found in his heart and his head what he wanted most – and had decided to save him, and give him the ability to rebalance the scales of his life and put things right, by getting even with anyone who had ever crossed him or got in his way.

Burwell read the newspaper article again, sighed, and tucked the paper under his arm. Crumpling up the paper bag, he lobbed it into a nearby waste bin. It went straight in. A perfect shot.

See?

The fates were with him in everything he did.

So much to do at work. So many plans to set in motion for his climb to the top.

Beaming, he walked past two mothers sitting on another bench. Both had children in pushchairs, parked securely next to them; both kids were obligingly asleep. Burwell paused and looked down at the nearest child. The mother looked up at him and smiled.

'Sweet kid,' said Burwell.

He leaned down and patted the sleeping child on the head.

The mother smiled again and returned to her conversation.

Still beaming, Burwell walked on with a spring in his step.

So much to do.

Three minutes later, fingers tingling, he heard the woman's screams somewhere behind him as she tried without success to rouse her child.

It was a *good* day.

What was it about churches that made them seem so much emptier than other empty buildings?

Martin remembered when he was a kid and his old man had taken him to the cinema, one of those big ritzy places. All plush red stair carpets and marble columns, with gigantic curtains on either side of the huge screen, rippling waves of plasterwork and chrome on the walls and ceilings. Not like the cinemas these days at all. Most of all, he remembered what it was like when the movie was finished and everyone began to stream outside as the lights came up. Sometimes, he and his father had been at the back of the queue, and he had looked back into the massive auditorium. A vast, opulent, cavernous space. And although there were no longer any people there, there was no sense of *emptiness* about the place. It was as if the magic images he had seen up on the massive screen were all still somehow present; invisible, but tangible. Floating somewhere in the air; alive and waiting for the next time the place filled up with an audience, so that they could be replayed on the screen.

Churches weren't like that for Martin.

This church he was standing in now – the self-same church where he had administered the blessings – was emptier than empty. No feelings of a presence, no hint that the ever-present God whom Sheila loved and trusted so much was invisibly watching. With his suitcase in his hand, Martin felt small and hollow and empty despite his large, six-foot-four-inch frame; like a child about to be sent away at the behest of a so-called loving God who couldn't even put in a brief showing now to let him know that everything was all right.

It hadn't taken Sheila long to pack his only suitcase. After all, he was only going to be gone for a week. And then he'd be home on Friday evening again for a long weekend. It wasn't really like saying goodbye, at all. It was, as Sheila herself had volunteered, just as if he were going away to work – like one of his long hauls in the truck. But Martin couldn't forget the tearful farewell of only an hour ago, and a part of him knew that he would *never* forget it. After everything that had happened, everything they'd been through, the last thing he wanted was to be leaving her. This was Sheila's way of thanking God for giving Martin the gift, so that he could pass the blessing on to others. But, more than anything, he wanted to be staying home and holding her and knowing that she wouldn't be in agony from one simple touch. Jameson had arrived in his car, had quickly put the suitcase in the boot, and in moments they were gone. He hadn't looked back, but had seen Sheila standing in the darkened doorway, her slight reflection in the rear-view mirror. He'd told her not to wave, but she had anyway. And at the last, he knew that she had gone indoors to weep, as Jameson's car turned the corner, heading for the church.

It hadn't felt right, the way he had left home. Jameson had looked anxious, darting glances into every dark corner as if someone might be watching. It made Martin feel as if he were doing something shameful; made him feel as if he were sneaking away like a bloody thief.

The Brothers of the Holy Order would be making their way secretly to the church, and Jameson had convinced them both that it would be best if Martin were collected (how he hated that word, collected – it made him feel as if he were a thing rather than a person) from the church rather than their home. There was a walled courtyard at the rear of the church where the car could pull up. Far better than the street outside their house.

Martin walked down the centre aisle of the church. The echoes of his footsteps reinforced his sense of loneliness and emptiness.

'God?'

His voice seemed to be swallowed up in the vast space of the building. The sound intimidated and angered him. When he spoke again, it was almost a shout.

'Come *on*, then! I'm here. That's what you want, isn't it? They all tell me I've got this power because you gave it to me. And you want me to use it. So, come on. Show your face, and let's have a chat about it.'

He reached the altar steps, turned and looked back the way he had come. Jameson had vanished into the darkness on their arrival, calling back that he was going to check the back yard to see if the car had arrived. Martin hadn't watched him leave, did not know through which of the many oak doors he'd vanished.

'What's to stop me just walking out of here? Eh? Answer me that.'

He dropped his suitcase. The sound bounced amidst the pews.

'Know something? I think you got it wrong with me. You should have picked some churchgoing soul who believes in . . .' He held his hands wide. '. . . in all of *this*. It would have been far better if you'd given me some other kind of power. What about loaves and fishes? Wouldn't that have been better? Put my hands on one thick slice of Mother's Pride and some fillet of cod . . . Hey presto! Baskets full of the stuff. Then I could have opened a restaurant or something and everyone would be happy.'

He laughed. It was a hollow, echoing sound, and it seemed to mock him.

'So *tell me*, then! Why the hell shouldn't I just walk out of here?'

'Because,' said the Reverend Jameson from the darkness, 'whatever the reason for your having been blessed with this gift, you've been able to take away your own wife's terrible suffering. And she wants you to share that gift of healing with others.'

Martin started at the sound of Jameson's voice, watched him as he made his way down one of the pews.

'Are they here yet?' he asked.

'Yes. They're waiting in the yard.'

Martin stepped down from the altar steps and hefted his suitcase again.

'How do you know about the big man in the sky?' he asked. 'How do you know that there's anyone there?'

'Shall we go?' said Jameson, and he turned and headed for one of the side doors.

Martin looked around the church once more, swinging his suitcase.

'Thanks for the chat. We must do it more often. Let's not be strangers, eh?'

There was a small corridor beyond the oak door. It smelled of damp and disinfectant. Martin watched Jameson's silhouette up ahead. The sounds of their progress were close and muffled in here, a complete contrast with the great echoing reaches of the church behind them. For a moment, Martin wondered whether he should say something about his outburst back in the church. What was the point? Jameson knew the way he felt. A sudden flow of warm air seemed to sweep from ahead.

'Watch this last step,' said Jameson, and then they were both in the rear courtyard. In the past, this yard had been used to park hearses for funeral services, but there had been complaints from the congregation about the surreptitious way in which the dear departed had been removed from the church *en route* to the place of burial or cremation, so the facility was now little used.

There was a car parked there, waiting for them.

Martin was impressed. It was a silver Mercedes. Top of the range, with smoked-glass windows to ensure privacy. A chauffeur was standing at the passenger door, holding it open. He wore a traditional grey uniform and cap. Two other men were standing at the rear. Both looked like businessmen, not monks, in sober grey suits with carefully parted hair. One was smiling, the other looked deadly serious. They reminded Martin of the types who could be seen trying to look unnoticeable around prime ministers and presidents. Looking everywhere except where the cameras were pointing, and somehow making everyone *aware* of the protective hardware readily at hand beneath their coats. Was that what these two characters were? Professional security men?

'No expense spared,' said Martin. 'Are we going to a monastery or a film première?'

Jameson's attention was centred on the wooden double gates at the other side of the yard, as if there might be spies out there somewhere, watching for them.

'Mr Russell,' said the smiling man. 'Thanks for coming.' He gestured to the rear door. The chauffeur also smiled.

'Seems to me the Church can't be short of cash. Do people know where the money in the collection plate is going?'

'Did anyone see you arrive?' asked Jameson, and Martin turned to see that his remark was addressed to the man who wasn't smiling.

'What do you think?' asked the man, without looking at him.

There was something more to this remark, an edge of hostility that surprised Martin.

'Mr Russell?' said the smiling man. 'Please?'

Jameson was shrinking back into the doorway again. His head was down, and in the darkness Martin could not see his expression. But something seemed to be wrong.

'Where are the details?' he asked, looking from the vicar to the men by the car. 'You said I'd have the details of where I was going, who I'd be seeing, where I'd be staying. I haven't seen any of that yet.'

'It's all in the car,' said the smiling man. 'We can fill you in on the way.'

'I'm not talking to you,' said Martin. 'I'm talking to him there. The one with the face-ache.'

The man who wasn't smiling looked at Martin then.

Martin looked at Jameson, was able to see for the first time the look of fear on the vicar's face.

And he knew then that something was wrong.

'So tell me,' he said. 'Come on, Jameson. What the hell is going on?'

Jameson did not answer. He stepped back again, reaching for the door. 'For God's sake. Just *do it!*' In another moment, Jameson would be back in the church, the door firmly closed.

Martin lunged forward and seized the edge of the door, dragging it out of Jameson's grasp. With a startled cry, the vicar fell back into the shadows.

And then someone was on Martin's back. A pair of hands was braced on either shoulder, shoving down hard. It was a brutal, professional movement. Despite his burly frame, Martin's legs buckled under the expert pressure and he fell to his knees.

'Hold him!' hissed someone in the darkness. 'For Christ's sake, don't fuck up!'

Martin roared, grabbing at the hands and twisting, trying to rise.

'Shut him up! Someone *shut him up!*'

Something stung Martin in the back of the neck. Christ, had he been *stabbed?*

He tried to twist again, but it seemed as if all his energy had dissipated with that one sharp pain. The world was tilting, voices were still hissing urgently, but something had slowed the sound down. Like a tape or a record that was running down, the sounds slurred into a deep bass grumbling as if his head were under water. Something glinted on the periphery of his vision.

In the moment before consciousness left him altogether, Martin recognised the shape that had glinted in the dark.

It was a hypodermic needle.

PART FOUR

SOUTH OF MIDNIGHT

PART FOUR

SOUTH OF MIDNIGHT

'Something up ahead . . .'

Look out!

Mercy cried out as she clawed at the air, waiting for the light to explode through the windscreen and for her face to be cut to shreds by whirling glass. She knew that the cab of the lorry would now tilt, catapulting her to the floor. But there was no screeching of tyres, no explosion of glass. There was no light and no screaming. Warm night air caressed the bare forearms that she'd thrown up to protect her face. Suddenly, she was aware that she was standing. Carefully, gingerly, she lowered her arms and looked around.

She was standing at the side of a country road. The silhouettes of trees slowly waved their branches from either side in the warm breeze. The sky was a deep, dark blue, and when she looked up she could see stars studded like cats' eyes in the velvet expanse. A crescent moon looked more like a movie special effect than the real thing, as if all she had to do was find a ladder and she could climb up there and unhook it from the sky. As she watched, a shooting star scratched a path through the heavens. There was a rushing sound that wasn't the wind, and when she listened carefully, she realised that it was the sound of motorway traffic. She might be standing on a country road, but there was a main thoroughfare close by. There were no street lights on this stretch, and it was impossible to make out much detail, but she could see that there were grass verges on either side of the road.

Was this a dream?

She felt her face in the darkness, convinced herself that she wasn't imagining anything.

Something bad had happened.

Deinbeck, in his car.

'Oh *God* . . .' She tried to force the memory out of her mind, tried to convince herself that *that* had been a nightmare. Then she remembered standing on the motorway once more, convinced that the bad dreams and the motorway crash were about to begin all over again in a terrifying, recurring cycle. And then . . . and then there had been something else . . . something about a car that had pulled up in her dream. She seemed to remember voices. But she had been disconnected from it all then as she struggled to escape back to reality.

Don't say much, do you? one of the voices had said.

What's your name? asked another.

How can I drop her off if she won't say where she wants to go?

Know what I think? I think she wants to party . . .

Asa, you said you wouldn't! I'm in enough trouble as it is . . .

So who's making trouble? Tell you what. Let's have a question-and-answer session. First question. Do you mind if I touch you?

Asa!

She doesn't have to do anything she doesn't want to. So, come on. Do you mind? See? She doesn't mind.

Mercy crowded the fragmented voices out of her mind and walked ahead, down the grass verge. There was a dark shape further down the road. At first she thought it might be a gate, but as she drew nearer she could see that it seemed to be a car.

So if I undo these buttons, that'll be okay? I mean, just say stop if you want me to stop.

Laughter. *Asa, you dirty bastard.*

Stop him, Don.

Keep driving Munby, you prick.

It was a car. And as she approached she could see that there seemed to be something wrong with it. It wasn't parked properly. It looked as if someone had suddenly swerved off the road on to the grass verge, dragging the wheel. Mercy stumbled in a furrow that had been carved out of the grass by a sliding

tyre. Moving to the side, she could see that the driver's door
and one of the rear doors on the verge side were wide open, as
if the people inside had scrambled out and run away as soon
as the car had stopped.

More laughter. *Slide over, Don. Come on, you bastard, I can't
get her down.*

I'm going to stop the car, Asa! I'll stop . . .

*You stop and I'll kick your teeth out. Now . . . see this? You
want it, don't you? If you want it, just say nothing.*

She's not saying no, Asa.

There was something on the grass verge, about four feet
from the opened rear door. Something that looked like a deeper
shadow. Mercy stopped and stared at it. Was there someone
standing over there in the trees, casting that man-sized, man-
shaped shadow on to the grass. No. How could anything be
casting a shadow in this darkness? There was hardly any
illumination. She moved slowly towards the dark patch. Was
someone hurt? A passenger from the car maybe? No, that
couldn't be right. That wasn't a body. It had no substance.

*If you want me . . . to stop . . . you just . . . just have to . . .
say No!*

Just say no! Laughter that dies as the onlooker watches.
Hurry up, Asa. Me next. A fumbling of clothing.

And Mercy suddenly realised what she was looking at on the
grass verge. She stumbled back from it, bumping against the
opened car door. At first, she had thought that it was Deinbeck,
and that all of the dreams were somehow merging. But the
sight of the hideously disintegrated face was now focusing
everything inside her. She could not hide from the reality any
longer. It was as if something deep, deep down inside
her were taking charge, forcing her to see things as they really
were, for only in accepting those realities would she survive.
The face was not Deinbeck's, but the horrifying remains bore
testimony to the fact that someone else had suffered the same
fate as him. Mercy looked down at the crumpled blue jeans and
the denim jacket. Whatever had been inside that clothing had
crumpled and fallen apart, just as Deinbeck had disintegrated
in the front seat of his car. The trainers had fallen away from

the trouser legs as if there had never been feet in them. There was a tangled, powdered mass on the grass where hands had once been. But Mercy's attention was riveted on the blackened, skeletal mass that had once been a face. Somehow, it looked as if the head had *burned*. There was still the vestige of a scream on the terrible half-visage.

And then Mercy felt the discomfort between her legs.

And remembered what had happened in the car. Moaning, she slid down the side of the vehicle to her haunches, pressing her fists into the pit of her stomach. Now it was like a video replay in her mind, but she was watching from a distance. It wasn't happening to her, it was happening to someone that looked like her.

'No . . .'

She had tried shouting at them to stop. But she knew that it had already happened, and there was nothing she could do as the boy in the denim jacket and the jeans forced her across the back seat and heaved between her legs, squashing the other boy into a corner. He was laughing and drinking from the can, urging the other on. And as she watched it happening, she suddenly felt an echo of the rage and the power that had flowed out of her and into Deinbeck. It was there in the car now, flowing out of the girl that looked like her as she gripped her assailant's hair in both hands and yanked his face up. He was screaming now and the boy with the beer can was suddenly yelling in terror as he lashed at them both, trying to kick himself away in the close confines of the car's back seat. The boy on top of her was shrieking and trying to pull himself up and away, but Mercy could see her hands fastened in his black, curly hair. Smoke was beginning to wreathe her assailant's frantically thrashing head. His arms were flailing.

'No . . .'

And the boy in the front seat was yelling now as he twisted the steering wheel. Suddenly, the rear door flew open and the boy with the beer can was gone, tumbling into the night. Mercy had fallen down between the seats, but was still clinging to her attacker. Suddenly, she realised that he was no longer screaming. She recognised her own voice. The car was swerving, suddenly impacting.

Somehow outside the car now, Mercy watched as the second rear door flew open. Someone was climbing out of the back seat. A human figure that held its hands as if it were somehow suffering from the worst headache in the world; a figure that was *smoking* as it staggered three steps from the car and then pitched face forward on to the grass verge. The smoke was thickening around the figure as it spasmed and clutched in agony at the grass. It made no sound. There was movement in the back seat, and Mercy saw someone sit up and look out. Was it her?

And now, here she was, crouching by the side of that same car. In real time, and aware that there were no dreams, only a truly living nightmare, she looked at the charred remains of her attacker. For a moment, the boy had become Deinbeck – and he had suffered Deinbeck's fate as a result. She pulled herself upright again and remembered the driver. She looked back into the car and beyond the open door, but there was no sign of him. Then she became aware of the weeping.

She turned to face the bushes and the trees by the verge.

'Come out.' She was startled by the volume and clarity of her voice in the still night air.

The weeping turned to a low moaning.

'I said come out.'

'Please . . . *please* . . . don't hurt me.'

'Do it. Now.'

'I told them not to do it. I said, right from the beginning. I didn't even want to pick you up.'

'Come *out*!'

Mercy watched as a figure came out of the greater darkness towards her on its hands and knees.

'Don's dead. I think his head must have gone under . . . under the back wheel or something.'

'Where are we?'

'Please don't do what you did to Asa. *Please*.'

'You fucking bastard. Tell me where we are, or I *will* do it to you.'

She had meant to frighten him into submission, but his reaction made her recoil in shock.

Munby shrieked.

It was a sound that cut through the night air, pierced Mercy's ears with something like real physical pain. It was the sound of sanity finally crumbling and splitting and falling apart. The sound an animal might make when it is caught in a trap and knows that a horrifying, inevitable death is only moments away. Munby stumbled to his feet and staggered backwards, hands held out to ward her off.

'No. Wait. I just want to know . . .'

He turned and plunged into the surrounding bushes.

'Stop! Wait! I didn't mean it . . .'

But it was too late. Mercy listened to him plunge on into the darkness, laughing and crying and making crooning noises in the back of his throat.

She moved back to the car. Through the window, she could see that the keys were still in the ignition.

'Shit.'

She'd never passed her test, but she'd driven an old boyfriend's car before.

'Shit!'

One guy back there somewhere in the road with his head pulverised. Another looking as if he'd been dead for several years. Another one half (if not fully) insane, thrashing around in the undergrowth. How was it going to look for her if the police pulled her over?

'*Shit!*'

She ran around the car and climbed into the driving seat. The engine turned over straight away. Slamming the door, she braced both hands on the wheel and closed her eyes.

Something was happening to her.

It wasn't a dream.

She couldn't pretend that it hadn't happened, that it *wasn't* happening.

Somehow, three people were dead – and at least two of them had died because of what she'd done. For a moment, the memories and the implications threatened to overcome her.

Gritting her teeth, she fought off the phantasms and rammed the car into first gear.

She looked over at the bushes into which the driver had vanished, as if expecting to see him in there somewhere. There was no sound. Only the soughing of a warm wind and the rushing of motorway traffic nearby.

'*Shit!*'

She pulled away from the verge.

She refused to look in the rear-view mirror for the shadow-man on the grass in case he suddenly began to sit up. In her mind's eye, she could see him – could see *it* – staggering into the road after her.

She forced herself to look ahead.

She had to find a telephone box.

'Mrs Russell?'

Sheila looked at the two men standing outside her front door and felt a stab of fear. The bearded man in the anorak and tie was smiling, and there was something familiar about him. But even though she was unable to place the face, the sight of the man made her feel deeply uneasy. The colleague standing behind him had a curiously blank look on his face, as if he were thinking about other things. Neither of them looked as if they were selling door to door or collecting for charity. The car parked at the kerb was a battered Nissan saloon. There were no advertising logos on it.

'Yes?'

'Is your husband at home?'

'Why do you want to know?'

'We were wondering if we could speak to him for a moment.'

'Why?'

'Well . . . this gentleman behind me here is Harry Stark. He's one of the survivors of the crash.'

'If he needs to be healed, you'll have to speak to the Reverend Jameson.'

'No, he doesn't need to be healed. We just need to talk. About what happened.'

Sheila began to close the door.

'Please, Mrs Russell.' Curtis stepped forward. He could see the look of anxiety on her face. 'It really is very important that we talk to him.'

'Martin isn't here. And even if he was, he wouldn't talk to you.'

'We're not here to cause trouble. We're here because . . . well, because . . .'

'We know what's happened to him,' said Harry, suddenly tuning in. 'And he's in trouble, Mrs Russell. Something has happened to everyone who survived that motorway pile-up and we're all in trouble.'

'You're from the newspapers,' said Sheila tightly, suddenly remembering where she had seen the bearded man's face before. 'I remember now. You came and tried to interview Martin after the crash. And you've been making all that trouble in the papers about Martin's gift. Get away from our house. We won't speak to you.'

'All right, Mrs Russell. It's true, I'm a reporter for the *Independent Daily*. But I'm not responsible for the articles on your husband's church work. I only want to . . .' Sheila slammed the door. Curtis swore under his breath and looked back at Harry.

'I don't think he *is* at home,' said Harry, looking up at the bedroom windows.

Curtis rapped on the door. 'Mr Russell? It's vital we speak to you. Mr Stark has something very important to tell you. Very important. Can you hear me, Mr Russell? Please . . .'

'Go *away*!' Sheila's voice came to them from inside, muffled and anxious. 'I'll call the police.'

Curtis fumbled in his pocket, found a piece of paper and a pen. 'Mrs Russell, I promise you that we're not trying to make any trouble for you or your husband. Believe me.' Leaning on the door, he scribbled a note. 'I'm putting my name, address and telephone number on this piece of paper. Can you hear me, Mrs Russell?'

'Go away!'

'If Mr Russell doesn't want to see us face to face, perhaps he'll talk to us on the phone. Please, it's very important. I'm putting this note through the door now. Please.' He shoved the paper through the letter-box and stood back.

'Come on,' said Harry. 'We're wasting our time here ...' Curtis turned to look and saw Harry suddenly grimace. He clutched at his stomach as if experiencing a sudden bout of indigestion.

'Are you all right?'

Harry bowed his head in pain, but held up his other hand to Curtis to indicate that he was fine. He began to breathe deeply.

'Shit, you aren't having a heart attack or something, are you?'

'I'm ...'

'For Christ's sake, Stark. Don't die on me now.'

'I'm *fine!*' Harry's head snapped back in anger. Colour had risen in his face, but it seemed that his pain had passed. 'It's that bastard inside me. It doesn't want me to leave. It wants me to stay and talk to our lorry-driver friend. But I'm not about to smash a window, climb in there and drag him out by the throat – so *leave it!*'

Curtis knew that the last angry statement was aimed at the thing inside Stark.

'What now?' Harry asked in a calmer voice.

Curtis shook his head in mock disbelief. 'How the hell am I going to write this all up?' He looked back at the door in the vain hope that Mrs Russell had relented and was about to open it with a welcoming smile on her face. 'What now indeed. Well, if we can't get to Mr Russell yet, I think we should try someone else on the list.'

'Who?'

'We know the whereabouts of two others. Roger O'Dowd's two hundred miles away – so I reckon we pay a call on Jane Teal.'

'So let's go.' Harry was rubbing his hands, as if the skin were itching beneath the gloves. Curtis looked at him warily. Harry saw his look of concern and gave a dry, brittle laugh. 'Don't worry, I'm not going to take them off.'

'No pun intended, Stark.' Curtis moved to his car and opened the door. 'But please keep your hands to yourself.'

Harry said nothing, and climbed into the car.

'Reverend Jameson, it's Sheila Russell.'

'Yes, Sheila. What's wrong?'

'I'm sorry to telephone you – I know you said that people might be listening in – but something's happened here and I'm really worried. I would have come to the church to see you, but they might still be outside.'

'They, Sheila?' And Jameson cannot keep the fear out of his voice. 'Who are "they"?'

'Two men. I've seen one of them before. His name is Curtis, a newspaper reporter . . .'

And from the other end of the line comes something that could be a crackling of static interference or a sudden intake of anxious breath.

'He pushed a note through the letter-box with his address and telephone number on it. They wanted to speak to Martin. But I wouldn't let them in. I didn't know what to do.'

'Did you tell them anything, Sheila? Anything at all?'

'No, Reverend. Just like you told me. I only said he wasn't here. Do you think they might be wanting to cause more trouble in the papers?'

'They . . . they may have been. What did they say? Did they say they'd come back?'

'No. They want Martin to telephone them. What should I do?'

'Oh Christ . . .'

'Sorry? Reverend? Are you still there?'

'Yes, yes . . . you did the right thing, Sheila. If they come back or try to telephone you or contact you in any way, just say nothing. I'm afraid things aren't . . . I mean, I'm just so sorry that . . .'

'Reverend? Are you all right? You sound ill.'

'Ill, yes. I'm not . . . feeling too good. But listen to me. Do as I say. If they get in touch again, say nothing. Leave it to me.'

'Is Martin all right? Have you heard from him?'

'He's . . . in good hands. And he's fine. Now, leave everything

*to me, dear. Don't come to the church. I'll be in touch with you
again when I've . . . when I've . . .'*

    'Reverend?'

    'Say nothing, Sheila.'

    And the line goes dead.

Martin was suddenly awake.

    There was no gentle return to consciousness, no hazy aware-
ness that he was emerging from sleep into the real world once
more. One moment, he had been unconscious. The next he
was awake.

    He was lying in bed, looking up at the ceiling. But there was
something wrong. He'd spent enough time in his own bed to
know that this wasn't the same ceiling. Their own bedroom
ceiling was Artexed – it had taken him ages to get it just right
for Sheila – but this ceiling was off-white with a tracing of
cracks. There were old spider's webs up there, too. Martin
tried to sit up, but was overwhelmed by giddiness and nausea.
His head fell back to the pillow, a bad taste in his mouth. He
raised his hands to his face. The skin felt cold. There was a
strong memory now. A memory of standing in a church at
the altar steps and yelling angrily at an invisible God. Had
he been struck down for blasphemy? He tried to rise again,
taking it easier this time. With a groan, he swung his legs over
the side of the bed and sat still for a while until the dizziness had
abated. When he finally looked around he could see that he was
in a room about twenty feet square. There was linoleum on the
floor and the walls were bare plaster. There was one window,
with a closed Venetian blind. Daylight was shining through the
slats. But here in the room, the darkness was relieved only by
a single light-bulb hanging from the ceiling.

    'Hello? . . .'

    His voice was dry, and he needed water. He heard an
answering sound beyond the flimsy wooden door at the bottom
of his bed, like a chair scraping as someone rose. Then the door
opened slowly and a young man with curly blond hair and wide
eyes looked in on him.

    'You're awake?'

Martin tried to speak again, but this time his voice broke up in a coughing fit. The young man seemed nervous. Licking his lips, he held up a hand to placate Martin.

'Just a moment. I'll go . . . go and get somebody.'

'Never mind that. Just tell me where the hell I am.'

'Someone will be right back.'

And then Martin remembered what had happened in the rear yard of St Cuthbert's church. At first it seemed blurred. Had he really seen that expression on Jameson's face? Had someone really stuck a hypodermic syringe in the back of his neck? He felt his neck. There was a sore nodule there, making him wince when he touched it. He now knew that he had not dreamed it all.

'You *bastards!*' He pushed himself up from the bed. The nervous young man slammed the door and Martin heard a key turn in the lock. He took an angry step towards the door, and his legs gave way beneath him. He fell back over the counterpane, cursing.

'I'll get someone . . .' came the young man's voice from beyond the door. Then the sound of feet clattering on bare boards as he ran to get help.

'Jesus *Christ!*' He felt the sore spot gingerly once more. Rage flared again, but he was still unable to pull himself together. He sucked in air, and concentrated his attention on the door. Just a minute, that was all he needed. And then, when he'd got his strength back, he would go over there and tear it off its hinges. After that, he'd tear the head off the first person he came across. But first, he had to lay his head down, just for one more moment until his senses cleared . . . until he had his strength back . . . until . . .

Martin slept.

The same ceiling.

The same spider's web cracks in the plaster. Was this a dream inside a dream? His mouth still felt cracked and dry, his throat was sore. Groaning, he rose to one elbow. This time, someone said: 'He's awake again.'

There were three people in the room, and Martin recognised one of them.

It was the stony-faced individual from the rear yard of the church. He had the same expression on his face.

'You bastard . . .' Martin tried to rise. A gentle but firm arm guided him back.

'Take it easy, Mr Russell. There's nothing to worry about.'

Martin slapped out at the hand and pushed himself back until he was leaning against the headboard. The owner of the restraining hand stood back. He was big, perhaps six feet four, wearing a black polo-neck shirt. His face was tanned and heavily lined. There were scars on the nose and cheekbones. The eyes were small but steady. Martin's attention returned to the stony-faced man.

'You stuck a bloody needle in me.'

'Just something to calm you down.'

'I'll get off this bed and fucking calm *you* down in a minute.'

'Please,' said the third man. He was sitting in the chair next to the door. 'Give yourself a chance to recover. Then I'll explain.' The man looked to be in his late fifties with thick, iron-grey hair that was curled extravagantly. Martin couldn't believe it was like that naturally. It looked like a perm. The grey hadn't extended to the man's thick black eyebrows. He was wearing a smart three-piece suit, a trendy tie and had his fingers folded before him in a cat's-cradle of showy dress-rings.

'I'm really sorry for the way things turned out, Martin,' said the man, absently examining one of the dress-rings as he talked. 'Truly. This isn't what I'd had in mind at all.'

'Who are you?'

'Would you like to make money, Martin?'

'I asked who you are.'

'With a talent like that at your disposal you could make a fortune. At first, I couldn't be sure that what I was being told about your . . . abilities was true. One of the people who works for me was cured at your church, you see. He'd been diagnosed with multiple sclerosis. When he came to see me, after you'd touched him, he told me what had happened. He wasn't a religious man, you understand. But he'd heard about you in the newspaper. I undertook tests. Hired the best specialists. They confirmed it all. And I've watched you too, at the church.

Oh yes, I've been there. Watching. If there was ever a God-given gift, then it's yours.'

'There we go again. The God-given bit. Now who the hell *are* you?'

'But you haven't thought through the potential, Martin. Instead of wasting your time in an out-of-the way church in a rundown town, you should be aiming higher. There are people out there, people who are ill, who are prepared to pay for your kind of talent. All you need is someone with the business acumen, someone with the right contacts. You could be a very, *very* rich man.'

'And you can handle all of that for me. Is that right?'

The grey-haired man paused for a moment. For the first time, he looked up from his dress-rings – and began to chuckle. He looked at the other two men in the room to see if they were sharing his secret joke. The man in the black polo-neck smiled and nodded his head, but the blank-faced man remained impassive. And it seemed that the blankness was reinforcing the seated man's mirth. He guffawed with laughter, throwing his head back to look up at the ceiling.

'You see?' he said at last. The remark was addressed to the two men. 'You *see*? Everyone always thinks they know better than me. I come up with an idea, and there's always someone secretly thinking that they know better. But I'm right again, aren't I, boys? That's why I am what I am.'

'What's the joke?' asked Martin.

'The joke?' Suddenly there was no more mirth in the man's voice. His face looked set and threatening as he leaned forward in his chair. His eyes fixed on Martin. 'No joke. Just a matter of sound business sense. You see, there are those in my . . . organisation who would prefer me to handle the company's affairs in a more traditional manner. Like, for instance . . . here's someone who seems to have a very special ability to cure people of their illnesses. Let's go see him and make him a business offer. Maybe a fifty-fifty deal. We supply the paying customers, he does the business. Everyone's happy. But that's just . . . what would you call it? Limited perception? Yeah, that sounds like the right term.'

'You've brought me here to make me a business offer?'

'You're not listening, big man. Now don't fucking interrupt me again.'

The grey-haired man was silent then, trying to stare Martin out. Martin gritted his teeth and kept his gaze level. It was a difficult task. There was something about this well-dressed thug who liked to act the part of a businessman. There was something in his demeanour which seemed to suggest that he was more than capable of carrying out any kind of threat he wished. The man sat back again, and turned his attention once more to the rings on his fingers.

'I've seen you in action. I know what you can do. Lots of people might ask too many questions about the hows and the whys of what you do. While they're busy asking, the opportunity is stolen from under their noses. I like to act. So I have. I don't have time to fuck around. I like making money, Martin. But sometimes it's the *way* that I make money that gives me the buzz. Sometimes my associates find my methods a little difficult to understand, so I don't expect you to fully understand either. I don't do deals, Martin. I just get what I want. So first of all, you're going to work for me. That's what you're here for. That's what you're going to do. We're going to bring in the world's richest sick people. You're going to heal them, and we're going to make a lot of money.'

'No you're not.'

The man was suddenly silent, mouth set tight at the interruption. He cracked a knuckle. The sound was sickening.

'What?'

'I'm just not going to do it, that's all.'

'Like I said,' continued the man. 'We're going to make a lot of money. But it isn't going to stop there. Like I said, there's no room for limited perception. Now that you're here, now that you'll be working for us . . .'

'Dream on, you bastard.'

'. . . now that you'll be *working* for us, and we have this little place all to ourselves, I can afford to bring in some special medical people. After all, let's not just take your special talent for granted, Martin. What if we can find out how you do what you do . . . ?'

'Gerry and the Pacemakers,' said the blank-faced man.

The grey-haired man paused. When he spoke, he had great difficulty containing his irritation. 'What?'

'A song, by Gerry and the Pacemakers. "How do you do what you do to me?"'

'Shut the fuck up.'

'Sorry.'

'So . . . we find out how you do your conjuring tricks, Martin. Then we distil it. And find out if we can reproduce it. Now how's that for long-term vision?'

'How's this for a short-term answer? Go and screw yourself.'

The man bowed his head wearily. Sighing, he slowly stood up.

'You'll do it, Martin. Because if you don't, we'll kill your wife. It's as simple as that.'

'You *bastard*!' Martin flung himself from the bed. But the man standing at his side was fast. Seizing Martin by one arm, he twisted and flung him back across the counterpane. Instantly there was a knee on his chest and a forearm across his throat.

'I'm leaving now,' said the man nonchalantly. 'Our first customers will be here soon. They've travelled a long way. And you *will* heal them, Martin. You see, your first lesson starts now. My two colleagues here are going to hurt you. They're going to hurt you very badly. And then we're going to talk again.'

Martin tried to yell, but his voice was constricted by the forearm across his windpipe. He was afraid now. He was trying to use his rage to kill the fear. But the fear was real and sickening as the man nodded at his blank-faced colleague and walked calmly to the door.

'You'll do what I want, Martin,' he said, opening the door. 'Believe me. You will.'

Smiling for the first time, the formerly blank-faced man reached into his pocket for something and moved towards the bed.

The door clicked shut, and Martin thrashed to rise.

'You're a long way from home now,' said the scarred man, taking his arm away from Martin's windpipe. 'But make as much noise as you like. 'Cause there's no one within twenty miles of this place to hear you.'

'*You . . .*'

'Make it sound good, Martin,' said the smiling man. He took something out of his pocket which glinted. 'We want him to think we're earning our pay.'

'I don't believe it . . .'

Curtis climbed back into the car and stared ahead, out of the window.

Fumbling in the dash, he found a packet of cigarettes and lit one up. When he sucked in the smoke, he seemed to be wanting to achieve some kind of world record for keeping it in his lungs. He finally let it out with an explosive sigh. He gagged, cursed, and then wound down the side window.

'Here's me, wondering about all the chemical shit you've been eating and drinking. And here's me, sucking this shit in all day.' He took another deep drag and let out another smoke-wreathed sigh. 'But I still don't believe it.' He strained to look back the way he had come. 'See that house down there? The one that's completely burned out? Well that, believe it or not, is . . . or rather *was* . . . the home of Mr and Mrs Teal. Mr Teal and several party guests are dead, believed burned alive. And the sole survivor, Mrs Teal, is in Eastleigh General Hospital. According to the neighbours, she's in a coma. Staggered out of there with second-degree burns. Hasn't spoken a word to anyone about what happened. Eastleigh Hospital! Back to the place where they've got the indoor weather problem. And where they'll lock me in a padded cell if I ever darken their doors again. Anthony Curtis, trouble-maker for NHS Trusts, and *persona non grata*. This, Mr Stark, just gets weirder and *weirder*. I don't suppose you've got any ideas about why . . .'

He turned to look at Harry, and was silent.

Something was wrong.

Harry was staring ahead out of the window. His face was

white and there were beads of sweat on his forehead. As Curtis watched, a trickle of sweat ran down behind his ear and curled under his chin.

'What's wrong? Are you ill?'

Harry swallowed hard, eyes still staring ahead. 'Worse than ill.'

'What do you mean? What is it?'

'I'm dying. We're *all* dying.'

'Take it easy. It's the strain. It's time we got you to a doctor.'

'You're not listening. I said I'm dying, and it's true. So are the other survivors, but they won't know it yet. And it's pointless getting doctors involved. There isn't a doctor alive who could work out what's happening, and how to stop it. There's only one way. I was . . .' He managed a gasp of a laugh. '. . . was *digging* around inside to find out more information from the thing, and it just came right out and told me that I'm dying.'

He paused, as if gathering his strength.

'We're acting as a host for these fucking parasites,' he continued. 'Like I said, we're being made to eat and drink all that stuff to help them recover. But we're still dying. And when we die . . . when we perish . . . so will the parasites.' He laughed again, then winced in pain. 'It doesn't like being called a parasite.'

'Maybe painkillers . . .' said Curtis, desperate for something to say.

'Now I know why it wants me to find the others,' said Harry, eyes widening as it suddenly became clear. 'Bloody hell, now I know . . .'

'*What?*' demanded Curtis with agitated impatience.

Harry was nodding his head now at his new inner certainties.

'Stark! For God's *sake* . . .'

'We've all got to go back,' said Harry quietly. 'Back to the motorway. To the exact place where the collision occurred. There's a *gap* there, where the smash happened, but it will close soon. The things inside us are just about fully recovered. We've got to get them all together at the point of impact. If we do that, they'll be able to go back to where they come from. They'll be able to leave our bodies and return. But if we don't do that . . . we'll die. So . . . so . . . so *what?*'

Curtis recoiled in shock at Harry's sudden outburst.

'So *what?*'

Harry raged as if he had suddenly lost his mind.

'I wanted to die, remember? Wanted to be with Jean and the kids. So what if *you* die?'

Curtis realised that Harry was talking to the thing inside him, and continued to watch the outburst in astonishment.

'So why the hell should I care about you? You brought me back again. Just to do what you want. Well, listen to this, you fucking *parasite*. I don't care. I don't care whether I die, or you die, or whether any of the other survivors – human or otherwise – die. It might be important to you, but it means *shit* to me! You got that?'

'Take it easy,' said Curtis, leaning towards him. Stark's colour was changing as he raged. There were red blotches on his cheeks and forehead.

'You . . .' And then Harry doubled forward in his seat, clutching at his midriff, face screwed up in pain.

'Stark!'

'Come on then, you parasite. Do your worst! You just keep on hurting me that way, and maybe you'll kill me yourself, after all. That's fine by me. Come on . . . do it again, you bastard . . . do it!'

Helpless, Curtis's hands hovered over Harry's back. He recoiled again when Harry suddenly flung himself back in the seat. His face was raised to the car roof, his breathing erratic. But the expression of pain had gone.

'Christ, Stark. Look . . . I don't know what to do . . .'

'It's all right. It's okay. The pain's stopped . . . the bastard has stopped. Now, it's . . . it's . . . Jesus, I don't believe it.'

'What?'

'I wouldn't have believed it possible. I mean, it doesn't make any sense.'

'*What?*'

'I can feel it inside. Feel what it's doing now. I just . . . don't understand it.'

'Tell me what it's doing, Stark.'

'It's *weeping*. Jesus God, it's . . . weeping.'

'Maybe you hurt its feelings,' said Curtis sarcastically, becoming overwhelmed once more by the bizarre nature of the scenario he found himself in.

'No . . . no . . . look, I'm sorry. What? I didn't know . . . I . . . oh God, I don't want to feel like that. I'm sorry for you, but I don't want to feel that kind of pain. Don't you know that's why I tried to kill myself?'

Curtis waited, fighting down his impatience to know what was meant by this new exchange.

'Yes, I know what it's like. But why don't . . . why don't you give me more? Why do you have to hold so much back? I know there's something there I'm not *supposed* to know. But why is that? Why is it so important that I don't find out *what* you are? All right . . . all right . . . sweet Jesus . . . I see it. Oh God, I see.'

'*What?*'

'A moment. I just need some time. It's . . . gone to ground inside me again. It has to recover, and I know I'll not get much more from it now.'

Curtis waited impatiently.

'The thing,' said Harry after a while. 'It's in pain. But not physical pain. It let its guard slip just then, and I felt a little of what it's feeling.'

'And what's that?'

'It's grieving.'

'For what?'

'For the Seventh Survivor.'

'Six, Stark. There were only six . . .'

'The bus driver. Jesus, I got some kind of flash about it in my mind. The thing inside me is trying to locate it . . . I mean them . . . and whatever is going on in his mind is fucking hideous.'

'George MacGowan? The driver of the coach they reckon was the first to be hit? I mean, that *is* who you're talking about?'

'I don't know his name. I just know that, according to my little visitor, it's him.'

'All right, there *were* seven people pulled out of that hellish tangle. Six we know of. But Christ, Stark. George MacGowan was cut in half. Literally. They couldn't find his lower torso.'

'It's him. I'm telling you. Somehow, he's alive and out there.'

'Oh, shit . . .' Stark looked across to see an expression of dawning incredulity on the newspaperman's face.

'What?'

'No. I've just thought . . . I mean, I'm sorry, I don't believe . . . I've gone along with a lot, following up this story. And now it's just going from crazy to crazier.'

'You've just thought of something,' said Stark wearily. 'Something that makes sense of what I've said.'

'Makes sense?' Curtis laughed, and lit another cigarette. 'Makes *sense*? You tell me that George MacGowan is alive and out there somewhere with one of those things inside him, when I know for a fact that the poor sod was sliced in half and ended up on a mortuary slab. But I also know that a body was stolen from the mortuary. My boss carpeted me for missing that little detail while I was chasing my stormcloud. The hospital clamped down on everything and I wasn't able to follow up the story. But doesn't the crazy logic of whatever's happening suggest that the missing body should belong to our bus driver?' He blew out more smoke and felt a wave of enervation pass through him. All these bizarre fragments, and not much sense.

'The thing's grieving,' continued Harry. 'I recognised the same kind of pain. It's . . . it's what I've been feeling since the accident, for my own family. It feels the same way about the thing that's in the coach-driver. Jesus . . . I think . . .'

'Go on.'

'I think the thing in me, and the thing in him . . .'

Harry wiped a hand across his face, as if he too was now having problems with what he was saying.

'Come on, Stark. Extra suspense is something I can do without at the moment.'

Harry turned to look at him, his face deathly white.

'They're lovers. I think the thing in me and the thing in MacGowan are *lovers*. And the reason it's grieving is it knows that something bad has happened to MacGowan and the thing in him. The coach was the first to be hit. The thing that jumped into the coach-driver was the first to make that "leap". But something bad happened. The transition wasn't . . . I can't quite grasp this part . . . but the transition wasn't successful, in the way that the other six were. The minds of both survivors have been badly damaged.'

'Why is the Seventh Survivor so important? You said the thing thought it was more important than the others. What did that mean?'

'I don't know yet. But we have to find it – and the others.'

'I thought things were bad enough. Now we've got a mutilated corpse with mental hang-ups, wandering around out there somewhere.'

'And it's dangerous, Curtis. Very dangerous.'

'Oh, *thank you*. Things just get more interesting all the time.'

'Jane Teal,' said Harry. 'We have to find her.'

'What happens when we do?'

'Christ knows.'

'And it seems he isn't about to tell us,' replied Curtis.

The car pulled away from the kerb.

'I'm going to give up the lease on this place,' said Chris, for the seventh time since the accident had happened. He stood looking at the boarded-up attic window, then sipped from his coffee cup. 'Just the thought of it makes me . . .' He shuddered, and sipped again, looking over to where Roger lay on the sofa, and felt a familiar twinge of anxiety.

Roger looked terrible. Perhaps it was just the shock of seeing that poor sod impaled on the railings downstairs, or the problems that had come to haunt him since the crash. His face looked haggard, his complexion wan and unhealthy. Chris knew that Roger was still looking after himself, still washing and showering, but his hair looked matted and greasy. He'd assured him that he had stopped eating and drinking all that weird stuff, telling Chris that the compulsion seemed to have gone. But Chris wasn't sure. It really seemed that things had taken a turn for the better when he'd found him in the pub that night. But the hideous death of their burglar seemed to have set Roger right back at square one. Maybe the terrible nature of the death had sparked off something relating to the crash. After all, practically everyone on the coach had been burned to death. Maybe this recent event had brought Roger's near-escape back into focus, prompting the realisation that he was, like everyone else, mortal.

Chris had tried to tempt him with a breakfast drink, but Roger had waved the offer away.

'Look, this isn't big brother telling you what to do again. But maybe you need to get out of the house. Christ, I know *I* do. Just the thought of that bloke going through the window . . .'

'You've *got* to go out, Chris. You've got a job, remember?'

Chris paused. Was the headway they'd made after their argument about to be lost again? 'Get some fresh air. Have a walk down to the market. I'll meet you in the pub at lunchtime, if you like.'

'No . . . thanks, Chris. But no. I don't know why I've been kidding myself with that portfolio. The money's nearly run out, so's my time. Why the hell should I go trudging the streets again? There's always a job waiting for me in Newcastle, stacking supermarket shelves.'

Chris mentally debated whether he should take him to task, then decided against it. Finishing his coffee, he grabbed his jacket from the back of a chair and hoisted his briefcase from the floor.

'Okay. If you change your mind about the lunchtime drink, you know my number. I might call in here at lunchtime, anyway. See if you change your mind.'

'Okay.' Roger covered his face with both hands and didn't see his brother's expression of resignation as he swung around the banisters and headed down the stairs. He stayed where he was, listening for the sounds of the door. He tried to envisage the staircase leading down, counting out the steps in his head. Now across the lower landing to the main door. Now . . . the outside door. He seemed to sense a slight vibration, supposed that it was the door – and then swung from the sofa, groaning.

The crash seemed to have happened a lifetime ago. And in all that time, Roger had been in mental agony. Right up to the day of his fight with Chris, he had felt sure that he was losing his mind. Then, after their reconciliation at the pub, it seemed that he might be able to put the phantoms to rest. Just being able to speak to his brother about the night of the crash appeared to have released something pent-up inside. The booze had helped, allowing him to express himself in a cathartic and cleansing way. But the time of healing had been brief indeed. The nightmare was still back there at the apartment, more intense than ever.

He screwed his knuckles against his eye sockets as if he could rub out the memory. It was no use. He could still see the reflection in the burglar's eyes. And each time he had a flash of the dead, insane, blood-streaked face, it was like another glimpse of the painting he had executed in front of the attic window.

Executed.

A perfect word.

He had not been able to talk to Chris again about what was going on in his mind. Because the death and the look in the corpse's eyes were evidence of an even greater insanity. What was he going to tell his brother now? Was he going to tell him that he believed he'd somehow painted something that was a perfect essence of insanity? Just one glance and it was enough to send your mind reeling. Look any harder, and it would pull you right in as you tried to make sense of its crazy perspective and colour scheme. Moments later, and you'd never be able to look away again, never be able to free yourself from the madness. And perhaps, within minutes, you wouldn't be able to live with the mental agony of what you'd seen.

So you see, Chris, the poor bastard threw himself out of the window.

Now Roger knew that he was insane himself. Because he believed all of it. He had seen those mad eyes, understood what they held. And if he believed that, what hope could there be for him?

He pulled himself to his feet and walked across the attic room to the boarded-up window. The easel was still there. It had been thrown to one side. The police had spent time with both Roger and his brother and had more or less agreed a scenario while they were being interviewed. Vinny (or whatever his name was) had been through the apartment (they'd found other stolen possessions on him) and had come across the painting. He obviously thought he could fence it and had been in the process of taking it off the easel when he'd heard someone downstairs. Thinking the owners were returning, he attempted to escape through the attic window, slipped, and hey presto. Except that it didn't take a Sherlock Holmes to see that almost all the glass in the window had been shattered, and it would take a running leap at the window to have that kind of effect. The railings below were also a good fifteen feet from the wall, so the body must have been travelling at some speed to have landed squarely on the spikes.

Roger looked at his hands and remembered the way he had felt on the night of the crash. He had been half asleep before the nightmare. But he remembered that even in that drowsy state, he had felt a distillation of everything that had made him give up his day job and go chasing his dream. He'd wanted to create something with his hands. Something to . . .

'Blow people's minds,' he said aloud, remembering the phrase that had drifted through his mind.

He began to shiver. Was that what had happened? Had something out there in the night heard him? Had it granted his wish, in the most hideous way imaginable? He looked at his hands as if they were alien, as if they had been grafted *Hands of Orlac*-style on to his wrists.

'No, I won't believe it.' His words were choked with emotion. He refused to allow himself to believe that he was at the mercy of some cruel God or gods. Just because he felt these things with a deep-rooted and profound instinct didn't mean that they were true. He had to prove to himself that he was suffering from some post-crash trauma. There was only one way.

He set the easel up straight and anchored it. Stooping, he plucked a canvas from the roll on the floor and began to pin it up. There would be no natural light, but that hardly mattered. He would paint something else. He would defy the nightmare and convince himself that his mind really was playing tricks.

Perhaps he could kill this nightmare now, once and for ever.

It was the only way.

At first, Mercy thought the telephone box had been vandalised. One of the glass sides had been smashed and there was a glittering frost of shards on the floor. She thought about continuing on past but decided to risk it. There was a service station up ahead, but no sign of anyone around. Bringing her foot down unnecessarily hard on the brake, she gritted her teeth when the tyres screeched on the tarmac. She remained that way, gripping the steering wheel and expecting someone to come running out of the service station to see what the noise was all about. When there was no movement, she yanked on the handbrake and climbed out of the car. The motorway was nearby, but she had yet to join it. As she ran around the front of the car, she could see a roundabout further down the road past the service station. It was dimly lit on this stretch of road. She reckoned to have left the laughing, crying driver and the remains of his friends a mile and a half back.

She yanked open the door of the telephone booth and muttered a prayer of gratitude when she lifted the receiver and heard a dialling tone. Fingers trembling, she fumbled for the crumpled piece of paper in her jeans pocket, then force-fed coins into the slot. On the first attempt, she misdialled. Forcing herself to keep calm, she ejected the money and tried again.

'Hello?' said the voice on the other end of the line.

'Selina, thank God you're there . . .'

'Mercy? You BITCH!'

'I know you're angry. You've got every right. But listen to me, I need your help.'

'Do you know what you've done? Have you any idea?'

'I'm not sure, Selina. I only know I need somewhere to go.'

Selina laughed, a forced sound without humour. 'You have got to be joking. I knew it was a mistake telling you about Deinbeck. Now I wish to God I'd never set eyes on your face.'

'Selina, please . . .'

'Don't give me that, Mercy. You killed him, you bitch. I knew you wanted to get even. Christ knows, I wanted to get even too. But you KILLED him. It's all over the papers here. You killed him and then you poured petrol on him and burned him.'

'Is that what they're saying? I suppose they would. But Christ, Selina. It wasn't like that, and I have to have a place where I can . . .'

'And do you know what kind of trouble you've got me in on the streets? I can't work here any more. I've been told if I show my face again, they'll carve my initials on it so I won't pick up a punter ever again. Do you know what that's like, Mercy? I can't pay the fucking bills, and I've got two kids to feed. Did you ever think about any of that before you set out to get Deinbeck? No, you fucking didn't. Because that's you all over, Mercy. The thought never crossed your mind, you selfish cow.'

'Selina. Help me, please.'

'I don't want to see you around here, Mercy. Not ever. I'm not going to the police, but if they come snooping around here, I'll tell them.'

'Selina . . .'

'I mean it, Mercy. I'll tell them. Don't ever come round here again. Don't telephone. Don't write. Just stay away from me and my kids!'

The line went dead. Mercy stared at the receiver in her hand for a long time.

She had nowhere to go.

Except . . . ?

Fumbling in her back pocket, she found the other piece of paper that had been given to her a lifetime ago by a stranger. She looked at the address and telephone number. Suddenly there was a glimmer of hope. A forlorn chance perhaps. Martin Russell had been with her in the crash, when the nightmare had begun. She had no one else and nowhere else to turn to. Maybe, just maybe . . . he could make sense of what was happening to her. She reached for the dial, then decided against it. What was she going to say? How could she make any sense of what was happening? Even as she thought about it, the hopelessness of making contact with him threatened to plunge her into despair. No . . . she had to go to him. Speak to him face to face. It was the only way. She looked at the address, then shoved the note back into her pocket. She glanced at the car and deliberated whether she should leave it there and hitch-hike again.

If she were to use the car, how long before someone reported it missing? Had the guy she'd left weeping and laughing back there stumbled across someone yet? Had he told them everything that had happened? And what would happen if she was picked up by the police? She might have got away with Deinbeck's death (if Selina kept quiet), but how would she explain the death of the two kids who had picked her up?

She had to get back to Martin. Something inside her, deep down, seemed to know that this was the best thing – the only thing – to do. She'd have to risk using the car. Hitch-hiking would take too long.

She looked down to the roundabout, and thought about the long drive north on the motorway. It brought fractured images of the crash back to her. Shuddering, still unsure of whether she could handle the vehicle on a stretch of road like that, she hurried back to the car.

As she started the engine, she realised that the bizarre cravings had left her. Did that mean she was getting better, or getting worse?

Gritting her teeth, she headed the car down towards the roundabout, and the motorway beyond.

Quinn O'Farrell left the secure block where Martin was being entertained by his employees and walked across the open grassed area towards the main compound.

Halfway across, he stopped to take a deep breath of fresh air, then reached into his jacket pocket for a cigar. He really should spend more time in the country, taking advantage of the good clean air. He worked out often in his private gymnasium, but nothing could beat the country life. He should get out of the city more often. He patted a firm waist beneath his waistcoat. Not bad for fifty-three. One of his underlings had dropped dead on the squash court last week at the age of thirty-nine. Never touched the booze or the cigarettes. Stupid faggot. Too late now.

He stood with his hands on his hips, blue smoke wreathing his head as he looked around the compound. He'd done a good job here. One square mile of land on the fringes of Kielder forest. All owned by him, signed, sealed and delivered these past four years, even though the signatures on the deeds were those of legal advisers to the Brothers of the Holy Order. He still managed to raise a laugh thinking of the time when the conservationists had tried to challenge ownership of the land, wanting it returned to woodland. His organisation had invoked the wrath of the European Court of Human Rights when it had been pointed out that the Brothers of the Holy Order were a devoutly religious group, devoted to exploration of the inner spiritual self, their retreat a haven of peace and meditation away from the travails of the so-called civilised, urban world. O'Farrell still remembered the horrified reaction of the others in his organisation when he'd lodged his complaint. What if investigations revealed the true nature of the retreat? Wasn't he just calling attention to their activities? But it was a gamble that had paid off. The conversationists had beaten a hasty retreat when the ownership of the land had been validated beyond any doubt. And no one was any the wiser to the fact that the fenced-off, barbed-wired, square mile that had been cleared in the forest with its purpose-built log cabins and plain, white-walled church served a completely different purpose; nor that the forty-five people dressed in monks' robes who lived here were engaged in activities most decidedly non-spiritual. This was the way O'Farrell liked to live; it was the way he had created, and kept, his empire. None of the stupid bastards he employed seemed to appreciate his one simple strategy: *Take it, shag it and throw it away*.

O'Farrell had his own name for this tract of land, which both described the facility and its real purpose: 'The Wholly Smoke Joint'. For the past four years, it had been operating as the most successful illegal drugs facility in the United Kingdom. *Not so much 'roll your own'*, he had once said to one of their foreign backers. *More a case of 'grow your own'*. Only two of the log cabins were used as lodging facilities for those who worked there. Protected by virtue of its religious-community status, so recently endorsed by European bureaucracy, O'Farrell's brainchild had become one of the most successful ventures of his business empire, thirty per cent of which was legitimate, the other seventy per cent deriving its substantial earnings from extortion, corruption, prostitution and drugs.

O'Farrell looked across at the helicopter on the landing pad, the same helicopter that had brought him here for a break four days ago. It was this helicopter which transported the stuff out of the compound to the various undercover distribution points, and which had brought a famous rock star for a week's spiritual rest recently. This same star, noted for his love of all things green, had been very vocal against the conservationists' attempts to reclaim the retreat, prompted, of course, by O'Farrell, who owned eighty per cent of said rock star and who had provided the retreat so that he could get smashed out of his head for a week.

As O'Farrell watched, three figures emerged from one of the low log cabins and headed for the church. All were dressed in the same brown habits and cowls.

'Hey!' he called, blowing out blue smoke. The three turned to look at him. 'Piss be with you, brothers!' One of the three made the sign of the cross, and O'Farrell burst out laughing as they turned and pushed their way through the main doors. He liked to laugh. He'd find out who the comedian was later and give him a raise.

O'Farrell felt good.

No matter what the other advisers in his organisation had counselled about Martin Russell, he knew that his tried and tested strategy was the only way. They were menials, and were always going to have blinkered vision. Not one of them could take a risk; and for O'Farrell, risk was always the name of the game. None of them could see the potential in the story of the man who could heal with his hands; none of them *believed* it. But O'Farrell had a nose for these things. And when he'd sat that day in the Reverend Jameson's church, unbeknownst to most of his menials, he had seen the truth with his own eyes and had instantly weighed up all the angles.

One: it was true, this big man had some kind of power.

Two: the established Church didn't like what was being done here. And of all the establishments he'd had to deal with over the years, the Church was always one he'd kept at arm's length, because it was potentially the most powerful. Sooner or later, they'd find a way to put a stop to these activities.

Three: that meant that O'Farrell would have to act before (1) someone else, not least the big man himself, realised that there was a potential gold-mine here and moved the operation away from this backwater church to a more organised environment; or (2) the Church, or someone else in authority, metaphorically cut the poor fucker's hands off and locked him away somewhere where his power could never be exercised again.

That left only one course of action.

First of all, an approach to the man who seemed to have more control over Martin Russell than anyone else, the parish priest: the Reverend Jameson. The method of approach had been something entirely appropriate to the circumstances. They had put the fear of God into him. That part had been very entertaining. Then, to sweeten the pill, O'Farrell had brought out the cheque book. The combination had been as successful as he'd known it would be. He laughed aloud when he remembered the looks on the faces of those who had advised him to make a civilised approach to Russell with a bona fide business deal. The wide eyes and open mouths as he'd torn up the written scenario and told them all what he had already done. His way guaranteed something else that was essential to the operation of his plan. With Jameson's now-willing assistance, he could retain a strong edge of respectability in terms of Russell's whereabouts. First of all, the Church was pleased because he'd vanished from the scene to some weirdo religious order that no one seemed to know, or care about. Secondly, Jameson himself – that symbol of respectability – was always there to substantiate Russell's situation and keep his wife happy. That last element seemed to make everyone in the upper management of O'Farrell's organisation very twitchy indeed. But they were wrong again. The fear of God and twenty thousand pounds in his bank account had apparently made the Reverend Jameson very convincing indeed.

Martin Russell was here in the compound.

And now that he *was* here, O'Farrell's plan was simple. It was a time-honoured, successful strategy.

First of all, destroy Russell's self-respect by using pain, fear and degradation. The added threat to his wife was a bonus, of course. But the first part of the strategy was the most important. It had always worked well in the past, no matter who the subject was. Then, the drugs. O'Farrell had experts. They could make Russell compliant, obedient and eager to serve in a matter of weeks. Then they could start flying in the poor dying sods from Saudi and Europe and America, and Martin would be only too pleased to assist.

He knew that they all thought it was overkill; knew that in their opinion he had just made it hard for himself and the organisation. Who was to say that the big, dumb, lorry-driving bastard wouldn't just have clapped his hands at the prospect of a cheque for ten million and said: 'Right! Who's first?' They didn't understand. It was a question of *control*.

Striding across the compound towards the gleaming white walls of the church, O'Farrell finally gave in to the temptation to unbutton his waistcoat. This heat-wave showed no signs of abating, but his business suit was like a symbol of authority. After clawing his way up to respectability, he would remain a three-piece-suit-and-tie man whatever the fucking weather. Throwing the cigar butt into the dry dust, he pushed through the church doors after the three monks.

As the doors banged closed behind him, O'Farrell stood and watched the three men up ahead, weaving their way forward past the glass frames housing the fruits of his business. He had passed through the front doors of a church into an indoor gardening centre. Instead of pews and an aisle to the altar, there were rows of hi-tech glass frames housing the precious plants that were being fed by special nutrients and cosseted in constantly maintained atmospheres. Each species received specific treatment. The monks here were gardeners of a very specialised sort. Overhead, ultra-violet lights had been rigged to encourage maximum growth. Even the walls of the church had been soundproofed to hide the constant thrum of the underground generators that kept this lush and exotic series of contained gardens in bloom. For a moment, O'Farrell wondered whether he shouldn't construct an altar of sorts in here. After all, the fucking idiots who took this stuff were worshipping it, weren't they? There was nothing judgmental in his attitude; after all, the same fucking idiots were for the most part paying his bills. Maybe there should be pictures of him up there, on the walls, like Christ. Just to remind everyone here that *he* was God. Was Christ God, or what? What the hell . . . Anyway, it would be evidence, wouldn't it? Pictures of him? Best not take any chances.

He walked on ahead, looking from side to side with approval at the misted glass of the greenhouses on either side. At the end of the church was a purpose-built office facility, screened off from the rest of the place, an extension beyond with various living quarters for O'Farrell and his guests. It was cool and air-conditioned in there, and he could make the telephone calls he needed to make in comfort.

When the door set into the white wall directly ahead banged open, and Molineux came hurrying towards him, he saw an expression of anxiety and confusion on his face.

'So what,' said O'Farrell, raising his voice unnecessarily to obtain just the effect he was after, 'is so fucking vitally important?'

Molineux straightened, stopping in his tracks, eyes wide behind his spectacles. He cleared his throat and tried to look confident.

'It's a telephone call. For you.'

'What the fuck are you talking about, Molineux? *No one* rings me here at the compound.'

'The call's been rerouted four times and scrambled to make sure there's no trace. It's not good.'

O'Farrell pushed past him, swinging the inner door wide

open. The blast of cool air felt good, but did nothing to cool his temper. As he stormed inside, he heard an 'Oof' as the door slapped back against Molineux. The two monks who were checking the thermostats straightened and looked alert when they saw who had entered.

'So tell me. Who is it?'

'Cullen. From Central.'

'And what the hell does he want?'

Molineux feigned a coughing fit to avoid answering the question. A moment later, O'Farrell had reached the top of the metal stairs and was on the platform containing the office equipment for the complex. A monk was holding out a telephone receiver for him. O'Farrell seized it, then gestured impatiently to the out-of-place, extravagant drinks cabinet nearby. The monk hurried to pour out a whisky the size of which could have anaesthetised O'Farrell's entire board of (non-executive) directors.

'So *what*, Cullen?'

'It's Jameson. Something's happened since we picked Russell up.'

There was a pause then, as if Cullen was scared to continue. Suddenly aware that his hesitation was being matched by O'Farrell's own dangerous silence, he blurted out the rest.

'He telephoned our screened number. Said he had to talk to you. Someone got in touch with Russell's wife asking to see him. She panicked and rang Jameson. He rang us.'

There was more silence at O'Farrell's end of the line.

'It was a newspaperman.'

'Yeah?' said O'Farrell at last. 'So what? Jameson's had newspapers breathing down his neck since the Russell business first began.'

'He . . . he didn't sound in control.'

'What the fuck am I paying you for, Cullen? Handle it.'

'He didn't sound right in the head, Mr O'Farrell. If it's not played right, I think he might tell the newspaperman everything. He kept talking about a "crisis of conscience".'

'The bastard is trying to screw more money out of us. Seems we didn't put enough "fear of God" into him. Put him on.'

O'Farrell twisted the telephone wire around his fist as he waited. A great coldness had descended on him. Rage always manifested itself that way with him. There was no boiling over, never any heat generated by his anger. It was always ice cold. Those who feared him knew from his face when the line had been overstepped. It seemed to drain of colour.

White-faced, O'Farrell waited for his connection to the priest.

'It's no use,' said Harry weakly, and Curtis looked over from the driving seat to see that Stark was having trouble breathing. 'I can't go on at the moment. I need . . . need to lie down, or sleep, or something . . .'

'Look, we're not far from the hospital. Take deep breaths. You'll be okay.'

'I'm not okay. Turn the car around and take me home.'

'That thing wants you to find the others, doesn't it? I'm hardly going to be able to bring her to you. So you've got to go to her.'

'She's in a coma. What good will it do? I won't be able to speak to her, won't be able to . . . oh *Christ*! I'm not ready, you bastard. Not strong enough. I need some more time.'

Curtis looked over again, hastily correcting his steering when a car horn blared ahead. At first, he thought that the last remarks had been addressed to him, but now he could see that Stark was talking to the thing inside. Stark caught his eye and nodded.

'Something will happen when I come into contact with another Survivor. I don't know what, because the bloody thing won't tell me. But *something*. And whatever it is, I just don't have the strength at the moment. I've got to rest . . . *Christ*, you shit! I've got to rest and get some strength. Then we can try again.'

Curtis could see by the look on his face that it was pointless carrying on to the hospital. In truth, he had no strategy worked out anyway. There hadn't been time since the visit to Martin Russell's home. He had been hoping that getting Stark and Russell together would have borne some kind of fruit in an investigation which, instead of resolving itself piece by piece,

was getting progressively more bizarre as time went by. But
since that dead end, and the discovery that Jane Teal's home
was burned out, he hadn't conceived any kind of plan to get
to her in hospital. Quite clearly, Anthony Curtis, ace reporter,
wasn't going to get through the front door. So that meant that
Stark would have to try to see her on his own. But first, she
might still be comatose, in which case, the whole thing was
a waste of time. Second, there might be a no visitors rule if
she was still critical. Third, if Stark *did* get to see her, then
the ace-reporter wanted to be there to record what happened.
That latter part was even more important after what Stark had
just said.

Something will happen.

'Okay, I'll take you home. Hang on.' He took a turning that
would head them back to Stark's place.

'No, not my home. I can't face the emptiness of the place.'

'My place, then. You'll have to put up with the mess, though.
I wasn't prepared for visitors.'

Stark muttered assent, his head dropping until his chin was
on his chest.

'You're not going to die on me, are you?' asked Curtis.

Harry made a noise that was almost a laugh.

'Chance would be a fine thing,' he said.

The next moment, he was asleep.

Curtis circled the roundabout and took the exit that would
lead to his own home.

He wondered what his editor would say about his absence
from the office.

Ellis Burwell took another mouthful of Scotch and looked out
into the night from his living-room window. He rolled the
empty glass in his hands, and then moved back to the bottle
for a refill. Was it the whisky which had killed the bizarre
cravings? What the hell. He poured another and looked out
again across the city that he'd come to believe at one stage
would be his for the taking.

He hadn't asked any questions about how he'd acquired his
power. It was simply *there*, and he had been able to use it to get

rid of Klark. For that alone, he should be grateful. That day in the park, he'd seen a new future stretching ahead of him. But then, back at the office, it seemed as if God had been playing a great big joke on him. Drinking again, he thought back to that afternoon.

It hadn't been easy getting an appointment with Purcell. Most of his time had been taken up with the auditors. Thank God, he had managed to cover his tracks as regards the funds that he'd appropriated and then returned. And thank God he wouldn't need to be stealing any more cash for the blackmailing bastard. But no thanks were due to God for what had happened when he'd finally managed to get a ten-minute appointment with the boss.

'*Yes, Burwell. Make it quick. I've a meeting at three, and I haven't looked at my briefing papers yet.*'

'*It's about my job.*'

'*Yes?*'

'*I'm not being paid enough. I want my salary doubled.*'

'*Have you been drinking?*'

'*No, not drinking. Just thinking. And you will increase my salary. Come to think of it, I want it trebled. And there are lots of changes I'd like to see.*'

'*Are you out of your mind?*'

'*Come to think of it again, I believe I'm being a little unambitious. I think you should appoint me as your deputy. Forthwith. Get rid of that prick Bailey. I'll move into his office. That should give you a chance to train me. Once I've got the hang of it all, we can think about your retirement.*'

'*Miss Grieves, could you telephone Dr Fairley, please . . . ?*'

'*Leave that intercom alone, Purcell. You're not listening.*'

'*You're not well, Burwell. I should have seen it from the beginning. These mood swings since the motorway crash. Miserable as sin beforehand. Then happy as a lark afterwards . . .*'

'*Are you forgetting what happened to Tovey? James bloody Tovey. Dead as a doornail. And do you know how? With these hands, Purcell. I touched him, and he died. See? That's what I can do. I can do it to you now. One touch, and you're dead.*'

'*Tell Dr Fairley that I want him up here as soon as possible. Mr Burwell isn't well.*'

'*Not well? Not WELL? You fucking idiot, don't you understand? I can kill you. I can kill ANYONE, just by putting a hand on them. I can kill you. NOW!*'

'*And why would you want to do that, Burwell? You should have done as I said and taken some time off. Now I want you to sit here quietly while I go off to my meeting. Dr Fairley will give you something. Then I want you to take a long rest. As much as you need, until you're feeling well enough to work again.*'

And suddenly, the reality of his situation hit Burwell. What was he going to do? Kill Purcell? Then what? Threaten someone else who wouldn't believe in his new power? Or maybe get two people together, kill one and terrorise the other? How was that going to work? How was that going to set him on the path to fame and fortune? Crushed, he had been forced to go along with Purcell's assumption. Slumping into a seat, he had feigned the weariness of illness; had allowed himself to be treated by the doctor when Purcell had gone off to his meeting, and was now at home on enforced sick leave.

He drank again and continued to look out into the darkness.

He had been given the power.

But he did not know how to use it.

Angrily, he slammed the glass down, grabbed his coat from the back of a chair, and let himself out into the night.

Maybe there were answers out there somewhere.

'*Now then, Reverend Jameson. Confess all, my son. It's good for the soul.*'

'*They said . . . you said . . . there'd be no violence. But that man who came in the car. My God, he used a hypodermic needle. It all went so . . . so very badly wrong.*'

'*The way I hear it, Reverend, you lost your bottle. Russell saw it in your face and changed his mind about coming. Now that wasn't part of the plan at all, was it? And who do we have to blame for that? Why, no one but yourself.*'

'*But his wife. She telephoned me. Said that a newspaperman*' *and one of the other motorway crash survivors had come to see her. They'll be asking questions, Mr O'Farrell.'*

'First of all, I told you not to use my name on the phone, even if we are screened, you hypocritical shit. Secondly, we had a nice long talk about how you were going to handle any more press enquiries. Don't you remember our cosy little tête-à-tête? Don't you also remember that nice little cheque for twenty grand?'

'I don't know any more. I didn't think that it was going to be like this. I can't manage . . .'

'Now listen to me, you whining fucker. You deal with all the enquiries in the way we agreed. Russell is staying with the Brothers of the Holy Order, on a spiritual sabbatical, at a secret address. That's all. And if I get wind of the fact that Mrs Russell is getting twitchy because of you, then you know what I'll do to you. Don't you?'

'She relies on me. She trusts me. But I don't know if I can . . .'

'DON'T YOU?'

'Yes, oh yes, sweet Jesus, I'm sorry, I'm sorry . . .'

'Now wipe your sweet little eyes, Reverend. And if I hear once more that there's a crisis of conscience, you are a fucking dead man. Better than that, you'll pray to the Big Man in The Sky for death. Because there are things we can do to you that are worse than you could possibly imagine. Worse than being in Hell. Believe me.'

Roger suddenly became aware of voices, juke-box music and the clinking of glasses. There was a beer glass in front of him, half full. His hand was reaching out, in the act of lifting it.

Suddenly also, he was terrified.

He lowered his hand to grip the brass-and-chrome rail that ran around the bar at which he was seated, afraid that he might suddenly fall backwards from the seat. He seemed to recognise the bar, and when he looked around fearfully, he could see that he was somehow back in the Irish Paddock pub. For a moment, he wondered whether this was a fantasy or a dream. He closed his eyes. But when he opened them again, it was not to find himself in bed, or sprawled on the sofa in Chris's apartment. He gripped the rail tight until his hand hurt. The pain confirmed the reality of his situation. Anxiously, Roger checked his watch. It was twelve fifteen, and daylight was shining through the pub windows.

What the hell was he doing here? And what was the last thing he could remember?

Jesus, I can't remember a bloody thing.

There was a band of pain from temple to temple. He remembered that he often suffered that kind of pain when he had been working too hard on a painting.

Painting . . .

There was a glimmer of memory now. He tried to bring it into focus. Had he been working on something? He reached for the pint glass, and finished the beer in one great swallow. The barman saw him and came over.

'Same again?'

'What? Oh, yeah. Please . . . Listen, do you have any idea what time I came in here?'

'Couldn't say, pal. Place is full to the rafters, what with the heat-wave and all.'

Roger nodded and tried to remember. There were fragments of a conversation with Chris there. Something about him wanting to give up the lease, after what had happened . . .

'Roger?'

Chris called up the stairs as he let himself in. There was no answer as he made his way up.

'Roger, you still here?'

Apprehensively, he reached the top of the stairs. There was no one in the living room and he could see through Roger's open bedroom door that he wasn't in there. Sighing, he dropped his briefcase on to the sofa. He felt awkward about what he had done that morning, after leaving Roger, and wasn't sure how his brother would react when he found out that he'd been in touch with his squash partner, a psychiatrist. Sean Spence was a fit bastard, winning two games out of three every time they played. And Chris had worked on that angle to make him feel guilty and give Roger a free 'assessment'. He had managed to fix a ten o'clock appointment for the following morning, but didn't know how he was going to broach it with his brother. Assuming that Roger was still going to be here after their conversation that morning, he'd decided to come home at lunchtime to try to sort things out. The prospect of a discussion after work had been nagging him, and he knew he wouldn't be able to work that afternoon with it on his mind.

When he looked up, he saw that Roger had set the easel up in the attic window alcove again. It was facing away from him, but he could see that Roger had apparently pinned a canvas up there. The sight of it made him feel uneasy. If he had been Roger, able and eager to begin painting again, he certainly wouldn't want to work in the very spot where their unscheduled visitor had torn a previous painting from the board and then fallen out of the window to his death. Why not move it away, maybe set it up in his bedroom where he could get some natural light from the window? Was this just more bizarre evidence of Roger's unhealthy state of mind?

Chris walked over to the easel. Yes, Roger had obviously been working on something, because he could see his materials on the floor. He stopped halfway, suddenly remembering their youth together. Even then, Roger had been the artistic one. He remembered the fights they'd had if he tried to sneak a look at one of Roger's drawings or paintings before it was finished.

He looked back at the easel.

He shuddered, thinking of the new coat of paint their burglar had given the last canvas with his blood.

Chris turned away.

And then turned back to the easel, wondering . . .

'The painting,' Roger said aloud.

'Excuse me?' said the barman.

'Nothing. I was just thinking aloud.'

The barman turned away, wondering whether he should refuse to serve this guy after that last drink. His skin was the colour of candlewax, and even though the heat-wave showed no signs of relenting, it was fully air-conditioned in here so he shouldn't be sweating like that unless he was suffering from delirium tremens.

All the pieces had come together in Roger's head. The look in the dead burglar's eyes. The blood-soaked painting, all details of the nightmare he'd wrought with his own hands obliterated. His determination to start again, and kill the lie. He remembered beginning the painting. It had started as a landscape, nothing particularly extravagant, with blue skies and birds and a high feel-good factor.

And the skies were magenta; whirling crescents of clouds that drew the eye to the swollen yellow eye that was the sun. It was the eye of a Great Beast, the eye of the Gorgon. Once looked on, it was impossible to look away. It drew the eye in closer, to look deeper at the Mystery that dwelt at its centre . . .

Something had happened while he worked. Had he gone to sleep? No, it wasn't that; more as if he had drifted into some kind of coma. There were fragments in his mind, fragments of a terrifying struggle as he fought to paint what he'd set out to paint. Instead, there was only the . . .

The eye of the Gorgon swelled to fill those magenta skies as the eye of the beholder was drawn in. It was impossible to look away now. All that mattered was to find out what existed at the core of the painting. Deep, deep down was the Answer to Everything . . .

Roger knew now that his insane instinct had been proved true. He was able to paint something that would blow people's minds. The power came from what he had been wishing at the moment of the crash, a wish that had somehow been granted by the forces that had erupted that night. And even though he was creating the damned thing, his mind had found a way to screen itself from the act of creation. His conscious mind had taken one step back so that the creator would not also be driven mad.

He struggled with the other fragments in his mind.

He had finished the painting, remembered reeling away from the easel, dropping his brushes to the floor in a splatter of magenta and yellow. He had to get away, out of the apartment before the thing crawled off the easel and clawed its way back into his mind.

A rushing blur then, of hurtling downstairs, of the street outside swinging at him from crazy angles as he ran past startled passers-by.

He remembered something else, and stood up so quickly that he knocked his stool over. A wave of dizziness and nausea overcame him. He clutched at the bar rail.

'Right,' said the barman. 'That's enough, pal. I think you'd better be getting home.'

Okay. If you change your mind about the lunchtime drink, you know my number. I might call in here again at lunchtime, anyway. See if you change your mind.

Roger spun from the bar and ran for the door, scattering lunchtime drinkers in every direction . . .

Chris thought about the session he had fixed with his shrink friend. What was the technique that psychiatrists sometimes used to assess their patients' mental state? Great splodges of ink blots on paper. Then asking them what they thought they looked like. The Rorscach technique. Yes, that was it. He looked over at the easel, and saw now that Roger hadn't covered the work-in-progress before taking his stroll. What if the work he was now producing reflected his mental state, in some kind of Rorscach ink-blot way? Wouldn't Sean be able to tell something from one of his paintings? But how to persuade Roger not only to see him, but also to take a painting along? No, it was going to be hard enough to convince him in the first place, let alone go along with this most recent idea.

He paused again, looking at the back of the easel.

What if he just had a look himself? What if he took a really good look at what was there, memorised the details and the colour scheme? Maybe he could describe it all to Sean after they'd had their meeting (provided it ever took place, of course) and see what he made of it. Nodding, he strode over to the easel . . .

Roger ran across the main road away from the pub without checking the traffic. A taxi screeched to a halt only inches from him, close enough for Roger to slam an instinctive hand on to the bonnet as he catapulted over the traffic island in the middle of the road and caused another car heading in the opposite direction to hit its brakes. Two horns blared simultaneously. But the commotion was way behind Roger now as he grabbed the steel fence at the roadside and used it to swing down the side street that would lead to Chris's apartment.

His breath was harsh, his hair flying as he pumped his arms and legs.

Two women were directly ahead, carrying shopping, unsure of whether they should step to the right or the left as he came pounding down the pavement towards them.

'*Out of the way!*' he yelled at the top of his voice.

One woman jerked to the left, another shrank to the right, and Roger hurtled between them. A plastic carrier bag split under the impact, spilling vegetables on to the pavement. The sounds of outrage were quickly behind him as Roger grabbed a lamp-post and swung around the next corner, dashing across the road that brought him on to Chris's street. Now he was filled with terror. The exertion brought fragments of fear leaping back into his mind.

The news that their parents had died in the car smash.

An image of their bloodied faces through a shattered car window.

Dad saying: 'Why didn't you join us, Roger? You should have died on that motorway, just as we died on that road. We've waited for you so long, why didn't you come to us?'

'Oh, Jesus!'

Ahead, he could see the railings where Vinny the burglar had met his end. The tines had embedded so deeply that they couldn't simply pull the poor thieving bastard off; they'd had to use cutting tools. He remembered listening to the sounds of the cutters while he was upstairs in his bedroom, remembered clasping his hands over his ears, but he couldn't keep the sound out. Not wanting to leave the building because it would have taken him right past the operation at the front door, he'd got drunk instead.

He looked up as he ran, breath ragged. There was a raw pain in his lungs. From here, it was still not possible to

see the boarded-up window. The street curved as he ran
and . . .

Something up ahead in the road.

A brilliant white light, and screaming . . . and the explosive,
rending crash of the coach turning over. Glass flying. And the
smell of petrol and the eruption of devouring fire and . . .

. . . and there was Chris's car, parked in his reserved space
just a little way down the street.

'Oh, *Jesus!*'

Chris walked, head held down, into the kitchen. For a moment,
he stood with both hands on the kitchen bench. And then he
looked up.

At the knife-block on the bench.

There were four knives in there. Two broad-bladed for heavy
duty, two smaller, one with a long, slender and keenly sharp
blade, the other with serrated cutting edges.

Chris leaned over.

He took the knife with the long, slender blade out of the
block.

Roger's shoe clipped a crack in the pavement. Pain stabbed
through his foot and his arms pinwheeled as he fought to
control his headlong momentum. For an instant, it seemed that
he must fall to the ground, smashing his face on the pavement.
But he managed to stay on his feet, reached the steps to the
controlled-entry door, and fumbled in his pocket for the spare
keys. Gasping and wheezing for breath, he cursed desperately,
slamming the flat of his hand on the visitor monitor set into
the wall. Then he'd found the keys, jammed the appropriate
one into the lock and was through into the main hall. With
the echoing sound of the door slamming behind him, he took
the stairs three at a time. He would have yelled had he had the
breath and the energy, but stars were spangling in his eyes
now as he climbed and . . .

. . . *saw briefly the whirlpool of hideous colour that sucked the*
viewer in towards the Eye and . . .

. . . clutched at the banister on the first landing, shaking the hideous fragments from his mind. Even now, a small part of him was trying to convince his conscious mind that this couldn't possibly be happening; that he was in a nightmare and that all he had to do was draw breath and scream to wake from it and find that everything was in order, and he had a day of stacking supermarket shelves to look forward to. But he could not find the breath to scream, and the pain in his lungs told him that he wasn't dreaming, as he lunged from the banister and took the next flight of stairs.

Chris's apartment door swung at him like a portal into hell. Roger lunged at it, fumbling with the keys as he moved. But the door was unlocked; it swung wide with a clatter and Roger blundered up the inner stairs to the apartment above. He still could not find sufficient breath to call out Chris's name as he dragged himself around the top banister.

There was no one in the living room.

Everything was as he remembered it from that morning, before the blackout. Wheezing, he stumbled to the sofa. There was a ringing in his ears.

The easel stood in the boarded-up window bay, its back to him. Uncovered.

Giving a wide berth to what lay on the canvas, as if it could suddenly pull itself free and look around the edge of the easel with the nightmare stare of the Gorgon, Roger stumbled into the kitchen. Chris wasn't in there. Pausing, drawing breath to call his name, Roger decided to check the bedrooms. He swung back to the living room.

And Chris was standing in the doorway directly behind him, the knife in his hand.

'*Chris!*'

Chris reeled away from him, knife held high.

'*Jesus, Roger!*' His eyes were wild and staring.

Roger staggered back, grabbing at the kitchen bench for support, bracing himself.

Chris took a step forward.

And then, trembling with rage, he yelled: 'What the fucking *hell* are you playing at? Bursting in here like that! You scared the living shit out of me, Roger!'

'You're okay? I mean . . . you're *okay?*'

'Yes, I'm okay. Which makes only one of us! What in Christ's name are you doing?'

'What are *you* doing with that fucking knife?'

'I'm going to make a fucking sandwich. It's fucking lunchtime, remember?'

'But . . . I mean . . . but you weren't *here*. Why didn't you answer me when I called?'

'I did! You were making so much bloody noise, you didn't hear me!'

'Then where were you, for Christ's sake?'

'Roger, I was in the bloody toilet, taking a crap.'

'With a *knife?*'

'I got caught short. It was in my hand. I left it on the shelf in there. Next thing I hear is some idiot banging away at the visitor monitor, then the door crashes open and in you come.'

'You're sure you're all right? I mean . . . the painting?'

'What about it?'

'You didn't look at it?'

A shade of guilt seemed to pass over Chris's eyes then. Roger was suddenly aware that his hands were still raised in a defensive posture. Guilty too, he lowered them.

'I nearly did. Then I remembered what you were like when we were kids. You were a huffy little bastard, even then. Didn't speak to me for a week once when I sneaked a look at one of your masterpieces without permission. I guess old habits die hard.'

'Oh, God . . . oh, sweet Jesus . . .' Roger leaned against the door frame, sweat soaking his white face. His shirt was clinging to his back. Chris looked at the knife in his hand, then back at Roger with real concern.

'Look, Roger. Here. I'm putting the knife back in the block. There. See? Now, come on over here to the sofa.'

Roger allowed himself to be led into the apartment.

'I've got a friend. He's a professional . . . well, he's an expert. Helps people out with their problems. Post-traumatic stress.' He was struggling to avoid using the word psychiatrist. 'I think you should have a chat with him. Nothing intense. Just a talk to straighten things out. Like you said, that motorway crash was . . .'

Roger froze when they were level with the easel again. He turned to look at it.

'Come on, Roger. Sit down. Take it easy.'

'There's something I've got to do first.'

'Roger, please . . .'

'A moment. It won't take a moment.'

He pulled away from his brother and slowly approached the easel as if it might somehow be sentient and aware of what he was going to do. Chris held his hands wide in frustration and helplessness. He watched as Roger crept right up to the back of the easel, then stooped to grab the stained dustcloth that had been spread at its base to catch any falling drops of paint. He was lifting one leg of the easel as he began to slide the dustcloth towards him, carefully, inch by inch.

'What are you *doing*, Roger?'

Roger held up one hand for silence, as if this were the most delicate operation he'd ever performed.

'I don't want the painting to fall off the easel while I'm doing this.'

'Why?'

'It might fall facing us. And then we'll see it.'

From behind, Roger heard a long intake of breath. Lifting the other leg of the easel, he repeated the process until the dustcloth was completely free. Standing quickly, he stood back – and then threw the cloth over the easel, as if he were trapping an animal.

'Roger . . .'

'Not yet.'

Quickly, Roger moved around to the front of the easel. Chris watched in astonishment as he began to fumble under the covering sheet for the clips that kept the canvas on the frame.

'Roger, take the fucking cloth *off* and you'll be able to see what you're doing.'

'You don't understand.'

'You're right. Jesus, Roger. Look, you've got to see this guy. I've fixed an appointment for tomorrow.'

'You think I'm mad.'

'Me? Naaaa! Now, whatever might give you *that* idea? Let's face it, since you came down here life has been . . . well, frankly *boring*. Not much going on at all. What with you acting as quiet and refined as a choirboy.'

Roger had succeeded in freeing the canvas from its frame. In one quick motion, he tore it free and crumpled the whole thing within the enshrouding dustsheet. Stooping, he grabbed a can of cleaning agent, then strode past Chris back into the kitchen.

'*Now* what are you doing?'

'I'm making it safe.'

'You're *what?*'

Chris watched as Roger crammed the bundle of dustsheet and painting straight into the sink. Screwing the top off the can, he poured the cleaning agent over the entire jumble. Chris could find nothing to say as his brother began to knead the bundle as if he were washing some scruffy shirt in a sink. Magenta and yellow oozed between his fingers, quickly dissipating when Roger turned both taps on.

'Stop it.'

'I'm nearly finished. It won't take long.'

'I said stop it, Roger. You're not well. You need help.'

'We've been through all this before, remember?'

'It doesn't matter what's already been said. I just know that you need help. I want you to stop this now, and come with me.'

'To see your shrink? You think he can "cure" what's happening?'

'He can help.'

Roger was carefully slipping his fingers under the sodden sheet now, finding the soft canvas. He began to pull it apart. Clots of paper began to block the sink and the water was rising. He unhooked the detritus with his forefinger and kept working.

'My painting killed that burglar, Chris. He saw it, and it killed him. I know how that sounds. Know it just makes me out to be even crazier than you think. But I know it's true. And it's all to do with that motorway crash. Something came into me then. It's still there. I don't know what it wants, but it's given me a power . . .'

'Come away from that fucking sink!'

Chris grabbed Roger's shoulder and spun him away from the bench to face him.

Roger grabbed his brother with a magenta-coloured hand. Chris countered, trying to manoeuvre him away from the bench again. And this time, Roger punched him on the jaw. The impact sent Chris reeling back into the living room; his foot caught in a fold of the carpet and he fell heavily backwards. Roger stood in the doorway, breathing hard. There was a look of anguish in his eyes like nothing Chris had ever seen before. Behind him, the water began to overflow from the sink to the kitchen floor.

'You mustn't stop me,' said Roger in a ragged voice. 'I've got to destroy what I've created.' Turning, he moved back to the sink and began to clear the drain again.

Chris rubbed his chin. There was a tightness in his chest now. Something that felt like despair. It reminded him of the day when he'd heard that their parents had died and knew that it was up to him to break the news to his younger brother.

He began to rise.

And then the telephone rang.

Chris let it ring, still lying on the floor, watching and listening as Roger went about the business of destroying the canvas in the sink.

The telephone kept ringing.

Rising groggily, Chris staggered to the sofa, lifted the receiver and slumped down.

'Yeah, hello?' His voice was desperately weary.

'*Can I speak to Roger O'Dowd, please?*'

'He's . . . he's not available at the moment. Who's calling?'

'*My name's Anthony Curtis. I'm a reporter from the* Independent Daily. *It really is quite urgent.*'

'This isn't a good time. Maybe you could call back.'

'*If I said it was a matter of life and death, would that make a difference? I know it's a corny old line, but in this case it happens to be true.'*

'What do you want?'

'Who am I speaking to?'

'His brother, Chris O'Dowd. He's living with me.'

'Right. I got your number from his friend at the supermarket, Adam.'

'Believe me, it's not a good time. If it's about the motorway crash or something, ring later . . .'

'He's been acting strangely since then, hasn't he? Eating and drinking things from the kitchen and the bathroom? Cleansing lotions, sugar, flour, detergents.'

Chris had been in the act of hanging up. He froze.

'How the hell do you know about that?'

'He may also think he's going mad. And he may feel he has . . . something inside him. Something that gives him a power. Right again?'

'Do you know what's *happening*? Christ, can you help him?'

'He can help himself. If he does as I say. The first thing to know is this: your brother isn't mad. Something is happening to him. Something that's also happening to the five . . . sorry, six other Survivors. I'm with another of those Survivors now. Harry Stark. He's here in my apartment right at this moment, sleeping. Has your brother told you about Jane Teal? She's the woman he pulled out of the coach wreck. She's back in hospital, comatose. My guess is that she's fallen prey to the same syndrome.'

'So tell me, for God's sake. What's happening?'

'You have to persuade your brother to come back up North. I've . . . we've . . . got information, but nothing I can tell you over the phone. I will tell you this. Your brother – just like all the other Survivors – is dying. He doesn't know it yet, but he's dying. And unless all the Survivors get together again, there's nothing anyone can do to prevent it.'

Roger was standing in the doorway. Water dripped from his hands to the floor.

'It's done, Chris. I'm sorry. But it had to be done. It just wasn't safe.'

Chris held the receiver away from his ear.

'There's someone on the phone for you.' The voice crackled in his ear again. 'What?'

'Tell him it's the reporter – Curtis. We met after the accident.'

'It's a reporter. Anthony Curtis. Says you know him.'

'That shit. What the hell does he want?'

'Roger . . .' Chris's face was like a mask. The red mark on his chin would soon be a bruise, but he didn't feel the pain any more. 'I think you'd better talk to him.' And something about Chris's expression was enough to propel Roger to the phone.

'Curtis?' snapped Roger. 'What do you want?'

'I want what you want. Answers to what's been happening. And I think we can find them, Roger. Before you go mad.'

'Keep talking.'

Chris watched Roger as he stood in the middle of the room, listening.

For the first time, he wondered what really *was* inside his brother.

'We're in business,' said Curtis when Harry finally woke from his deep sleep.

The sleep had not refreshed him. The parasite exuded anxiety and urgency which even permeated his subconscious. He swung his legs from the bed-settee and tried to make sense of the reporter's words.

'What?'

'Third time lucky.'

'Speak English, Curtis.'

'I spoke to a Survivor. Roger O'Dowd.'

'The kid from the coach . . . ?'

'One and the same. And I've persuaded him to come back. He'll be here as quick as he can.'

'How long?'

'From London to here? A four-hour drive, maybe. Quicker if he gets the train.'

'How . . . how did he sound?'

'Do you mean has he been suffering the same symptoms as you? Well, he's been eating and drinking the same kind of weird stuff. And there's something else going on, but I couldn't get it out of him, or his brother, on the phone. Neither of them seemed to need much convincing about coming back up North. I know O'Dowd hasn't got the same ability as you, though. He can't kill by electric shock. Maybe each survivor is able to do something different. You and the electricity . . . even though I've yet to see evidence of your own gift . . .'

'What the hell do you want me to do, Curtis? Take off my gloves and show you how I can kill someone? Maybe somebody's pet, or a wino . . .'

'All right, all right. I'm taking your word for it. So, there's you – then there's Russell, able to heal with a touch. O'Dowd can do *something* that seems to be neither of those things. I reckon . . . I reckon you've all got a different ability. God knows why. I mean, it doesn't make sense that you should have these powers, unless there's a reason for it. Why does the thing inside *you* want to kill?'

Harry moaned, bowing his head.

'You want a basin or a bucket or something? You going to be sick?'

Harry shook his head.

'Get me . . . get me some paper. And a pen.'

'What?'

'It's what you've just said. The thing's reacting to it. It wants . . . wants me to write . . .'

Hastily, Curtis looked around the untidy room. Fumbling in his pocket, he found a ballpoint pen. Yanking open a cupboard drawer, he began to search for paper.

'Quick!'

'I can't find anything . . . Here!' Seizing an old envelope, Curtis hurried back to Harry, who grabbed the pen and paper from him feverishly. The reporter stood back. If anything, Stark's face looked even whiter than before, as if it had been carved from marble. Beads of sweat appeared on his brow as he screwed his eyes shut. Was he fighting the thing inside, or concentrating on making a contact with it to allow the message to be communicated? Curtis could feel his heart hammering, and realised for the first time why he had cut so many corners and taken so many risks in the pursuit of this bizarre story. He was excited. He hadn't felt this way for ages, believing that twenty years in the business had turned him into a complete cynic. Now he felt alive; could feel the exhilaration and . . . yes, the *fear* . . . inside him.

Harry began to straighten the envelope across one knee. Quickly, Curtis lunged to a nearby bookcase, found a hardback and shoved it between Stark's knee and the envelope. Tension mounting, he stood back to watch.

Harry began to write.

It was as if he were somehow disabled, his hand clutching the pen awkwardly. He moaned, and then gritted his teeth. Curtis watched his crabbed hand as it continued to scrawl. When the spasming hand dragged the pen from the paper and began to scrawl on the book, Harry seized the wrist as if it had an independent life. Curtis stooped and quickly turned the envelope over. Harry lifted his writing hand and slammed it back down on the envelope, continuing to write in his spidery scrawl.

Finally, with an explosive sigh of relief, he slumped. The pen fell to the carpet. Curtis winced when his other hand screwed the envelope up, as if to destroy the message it contained. Stark took several deep breaths and then wiped his face. Curtis could barely contain his impatience at this delay. Harry smoothed out the envelope and read what was there as Curtis anxiously peered over his shoulder, trying to see. Before the reporter could focus on what had been written on the first side of the envelope, Stark had flipped it over to read the other side.

'Come on, Stark! What the hell has it written?'

'Here . . .' Harry handed it to him, then leaned forward, holding his head in his hands.

Curtis looked at the large, scrawled handwriting.

Not me. Or the others
the Fire. The Storm
Between.
Bus man has it.
Find the Others.

Curtis looked back at Stark, who remained hunched forward, head in hands.

'What's all this supposed to mean?'

Harry did not answer.

'This is all jumbled nonsense, Stark. It doesn't mean a bloody thing. "The Fire. The Storm Between." What the hell is that all about?'

He waited for a response. There was none.

'Stark . . . ?'

'Will you just *shut up*! I'm trying to think. Trying to listen in.' Harry looked up, rage flaring in his eyes. Curtis knew that he was also trying to make sense of the message. He looked down once more, fingers massaging his temples. 'It's like I said before,' he continued quietly. 'When the message comes through, when the writing starts, there seems to be . . . a link, or a bridge between us. More meaning than is in the words. I just need time to get my head around it. The thing gives out . . . I don't know . . . emotions like colours. It's hard to explain.

Just leave me for a moment . . . here, give me back the note.'

Curtis handed it back, watching as Harry smoothed it out and stared at the creased brown paper.

'I need a drink,' said the newspaperman, leaving the bedroom to find a bottle. Returning with a large Scotch and soda, he stood in the doorway and saw that Harry had dropped the note on the floor between his feet. He remained seated on the edge of the bed, staring down at it.

'It's not the thing . . . or the things . . . that give the power.'

'What?' Curtis swallowed a large mouthful of Scotch.

'The first part of the note: "Not me. Or the Others". The parasite inside me . . .' Harry winced, then gave a low laugh. 'Oh, *how* it dislikes that term. Well, fucking tough. The *parasite* inside me isn't responsible for my power to kill with a touch. Neither is the thing inside Martin Russell. It didn't give him the power to heal. It has no control over it. Same with the others, whatever it is that they can or can't do. There's your answer, Curtis. The things have no hidden motives. They only want to survive.'

'Then where the hell *do* these powers come from?'

'From "The Fire". From "The Storm Between".'

Curtis opened his mouth to voice another confused objection. And then his voice died to a whisper. Eyes wide, he drank the remains of the tumbler of whisky straight down. Now he knew. 'The Storm . . . in the hospital. The thing I saw. That's what it's talking about, isn't it?'

'Yes. The Storm Between . . . and The Fire . . . the same thing.'

Curtis began to pace the room.

'The lightning strikes. The energy that zapped you all. That's where the power comes from. That's why you're . . .'

'You're rushing ahead too fast, Curtis. And you're not getting it completely right.'

'Right . . . right . . . now wait just a second. Just a second.' He dashed from the room, returning with the whisky bottle.

'No use getting pissed, Curtis. I need you sober for what's ahead.'

'I won't, I won't. Now come on . . .' The reporter grabbed a chair from the other side of the room, returned and slammed it down in front of Harry. Sitting so that he could lean forward over the back-rest, he poured himself another drink. 'So tell me.'

'What I'm getting from this note is . . . feelings. Emotional waves. I don't know the specifics, so it's no use asking me detailed questions. What I'm telling you is all there is.'

'Okay.'

'We know about the collision. We know about the things that jumped into us, even if we still don't know what they are.'

'No little green men and flying saucers. Right.'

'Wherever these things are from, they're not from our own here and now. They're from a completely different reality. Funny, but when I try to get more about that, the thing *really* clamps down. As if the most important thing, the most vital thing, is that I don't get to find that part out. Anyway . . . it, and they, are on a completely different plane to us. Normally, those two planes would never meet. But something happened that night on the motorway. The traffic . . . the human traffic, that is . . . was headed South in its own plane. The other traffic . . . the things . . . were headed North, or whatever the equivalent of North might be where they come from. You see . . . you see . . . Shit! I'm trying to make sense of it.'

'Take it easy, Stark. Take your time.'

'This business of planes . . . I suppose a better word is dimensions. I don't know. Maybe these things are from the fucking fourth dimension or something. But it's like . . . we're occupying the same space as they are. The same physical space. But we never come into contact, because we're occupying different dimensions in that same physical space. The thing screens off what it's like "over there". But it's utterly different. Nothing like here.'

'Alien?'

'There you go again with that word.'

'Sorry.'

'Normally, neither side is aware of the other. Both sides coming and going. I suppose we're travelling *through* each other all the time. Does any of this make sense?'

'It makes sense. Go on.'

'This part is confused. But I think . . . it thinks . . . that there was a *rift* between the two realities that night. Maybe a combination of factors on both sides. Over here, the heat-wave, the atmospherics – maybe even that meteorite shower you were talking about.'

'The Aquanids?'

'Yeah. And over there . . . well, I can't make sense of the feelings I get about that. But there was more of the same on that plane, or in that dimension. A combination of circumstances, maybe not so important in themselves. But together, fusing with the combination of circumstances over here . . . all those conditions coming together and causing a fracture between their reality and ours. Suddenly, those other Travellers . . . hah, now there's the word it prefers me to use . . . the *Travellers* were heading North in our dimension, in our physical space, on a direct collision course with us. That's when the crash happened. Somewhere South on the motorway, just after midnight.'

'The power, Stark. What about the *power*? The Fire, and the Storm.'

'The Storm Between. When that collision took place, there was an eruption of energy. I can't find the right way to describe the feeling I'm getting. But The Storm Between is the way the thing describes it. It's as if there's a huge flux of energy between the two realities, maybe keeping those realities apart. I don't know. When the fabric of those realities was ripped, when the collision occurred, there was a massive release of that energy.'

'The light that everyone saw?'

'Yes, that was the beginning. Christ, these parasites are clever bastards. In the split second of that impact, they were able to ride that energy, were able to use it to make the jump in to their human hosts. But there were side effects. The energy zapped through me and the others and . . . Christ . . . oh, Christ . . .'

Harry bent forward again. His words dissolved.

Curtis shuffled uneasily. He wanted to hear more, but Harry's sounds of anguish were almost too much to bear. He poured another drink, and looked out of the window. He tried to think of something else; of what kind of power had enabled Jane Teal to incinerate her husband and their guests.

'Burning,' said Harry, raising a tear-streaked face as if he had heard Curtis's thoughts. 'They were burning, Curtis. My wife, and my daughters. In the car.'

Curtis drank another tumblerful of whisky and looked at the floor.

'I tried to save them. Tore at the car door. Tried to get them out. I didn't care what happened to me. My hands were burning . . .'

'Maybe you need to rest for a little while,' said Curtis, without looking up. 'We can continue later . . .'

'No. You want the truth. Well, listen. Because now, for the first time, I know it.'

Curtis looked up, trying hard to hold Harry's anguished gaze.

'My hands were burning, but I didn't care. I wanted those hands to save them. Everything in me was concentrated on these hands.' Harry held them up. 'And what I wanted, more than life itself, was to get them out of there. *That's* why I have the power, Curtis. *That's* why my hands can do what they do.'

'I still don't understand.'

'That energy – the storm-fire, the cloud, whatever – was all around the crash site. In the air, in the vehicles, and in the survivors. Sometimes visible, sometimes not. But it's an energy force that doesn't belong to this plane, to this dimension. And it's also somehow a kind of *psychic* energy. It was in me. In my mind. And in that moment, when I needed my burning hands to have the power to save Jean and Hilary and Diane . . . somehow I was granted that power. In the event, way too late.'

'You talk about that energy as if it were alive.'

'It's not. It was the strength of my emotion. It connected with that power surging all around me and in me. Like I said, the ability I've acquired was merely . . .' He gave a weary ironic laugh. '. . . merely a side effect. It has nothing to do with the things that are surviving in us.'

'So you reckon that the powers the others have acquired all come from that energy, from the stormcloud?'

'My guess is that whatever the other survivors are capable of relates to whatever their deepest personal desires or ambitions or fears were just before impact.'

'Heavy stuff.'

'Two realities smashing together. Unreal becoming real.'

'What about the rest of that note? "Bus Man has it. Find the Others."'

'MacGowan. The coach-driver. He's the key to putting everything back together again.'

'Take this part slowly,' said Curtis, refilling his glass. 'You want some?'

Harry shook his head wearily and continued. 'You told me that MacGowan was . . . what? . . . cut in half?'

'They couldn't find the lower torso. At least, that's the last I heard before the hospital clamped down on everything.'

'The energy – the Storm Between – made him whole again.'

'That doesn't make sense.'

'The coach was the first to be hit. MacGowan took the full brunt of that pyschic collision. Even though he was physically mutilated, the power must have flooded his body. Normally, he wouldn't have survived. Hell, he *couldn't* have survived. But the forces somehow kept him alive between the two realities. The Storm was still *in* him, even when they took what they'd presumed to be a dead body to the hospital. At some stage, that power erupted from him like a huge discharge of electricity. It had something to do with MacGowan's agony. That agony allowed the energy inside him to explode out. Wait a moment . . .'

Curtis watched as Harry hung his head again. He seemed to be gathering energy, perhaps trying to commune with whatever was inside himself.

'The Travellers were still in a state of shock. Temporarily safe inside their human hosts, but still shocked and frightened and not knowing what to do. But they've got a . . . what the hell is the word I'm getting? . . . a *kinship* with that Storm Between energy. As it erupted from wherever MacGowan was, they sensed it and *reached* for it. It also sensed them, like electricity hunting for conduits. And it found the Survivors.'

'I saw you all, in that light. I saw you all *communicating*.'

'Not the humans. The Travellers inside us were communicating. Using the Storm Between, before it blew itself out. Maybe sharing their knowledge for survival. Afterwards, we knew nothing about it. And the bus driver was energised. Enough to get away from the hospital.'

'You mean MacGowan crawled out of the hospital and went looking for the *rest* of himself?'

'I don't know. I'm just telling you that the thing inside knows he's been physically repaired. Enough to be walking around, at least. But the other damage that's been done is the reason for the thing's despair.'

'What kind of damage?'

'Mental. Maybe spiritual. The first of the travellers jumped into MacGowan, the first of the human survivors. But because they were the first, in that millisecond, they were both mentally damaged in the transfer. Neither MacGowan, nor the Traveller that jumped into him exists as a separate entity any more. They've been *fused*. And both have lost their identities and their minds in the process. They're both in hideous mental agony. The thing just wants that pain to end for them both.'

'"Bus Man has it"?'

'The Storm Between energy dissipated in the hospital when it had found its conduits. It was still there in the fire consuming the motorway wrecks. I read after the crash that the fire service had a hell of a job putting out the fire. That's because I think they weren't dealing with an *earthly* fire. It had to burn itself out in its own time. Most of that energy dissipated as the fracture between the two realities healed over. But there was – and still is – a trace of that energy left. And it's the means by which my Traveller believes it can get its own kind back to where they came from.'

'It's in the bus driver. The energy.'

'We've got to get all the Survivors back to where the crash took place, including MacGowan; which isn't going to be easy. Something will happen then. Something to do with that energy. Maybe it will open up the gap again.'

'What's going to happen when the Survivors meet up? You said something would happen.'

'I don't know. Not yet.'

'O'Dowd's on his way. Jane Teal in hospital. Martin Russell not wanting to speak. MacGowan out there wandering somewhere. And God knows how we find the other two. There must be a way to . . .'

Harry looked up, waiting for Curtis to finish. He had frozen in the act of lifting the glass to his mouth once more. Now he was beginning to nod slowly.

'Well, well, well.' Curtis filled his glass again, eyes sparkling.

'What?'

'Something's just connected in my head. When I went to see Martin Russell performing his miracle healing in church I saw someone there. Someone I thought I recognised, but I couldn't put a name to the face. With everything that's been happening since then, I put it all to the back of my mind. Now it suddenly fits.'

'Who was it?'

'A really nasty piece of work called Quinn O'Farrell. Big businessman. Started off by organising street gangs, worked his way up. Now he's super-rich and has a huge business empire. All of it supposed to be legitimate, but everything he's involved with has a nasty smell. No one's been able to pin him down on anything, but he's an evil bastard. And suddenly, there he is, sitting in St Cuthbert's church and taking a big interest in Martin Russell. Now why should he be doing *that*? I think . . . I think . . . we need to be trying out something sneaky. How do you feel?'

'Tired.'

'Well enough to pay another house call?'

'What have you got in mind?'

'Well we can't get past Martin Russell's wife. But maybe we can try their vicar friend again.'

'I thought you said you got nowhere last time.'

'Last time I was being polite. Now I think it's time for some strong-arm tactics. And I think that the O'Farrell connection might be worth a little bluff.'

'You're having an easier time accepting all this than I thought you would.'

'Hell, just call me Mr Gullibility.'

'Maybe I've got some kind of communicable mental illness. Ever thought of that?'

'Believe me, Harry. You've got to have half a screw loose to work in my profession at all. Shall we go?'

Somewhere on the streets outside, they could hear an ambulance or a police siren. It seemed to be calling them out.

Harry nodded. Slowly and wearily, he rose from the bed.

The thing crouched in bushes at the side of the motorway.

Before the hated day had come, it had rummaged in the gully at the roadside, dimly aware that it had been here once before. The grass was charred and blackened as it hunted; the sounds of the lights passing up above ever present. It had felt sure that someone would come for it, or that a door would be opened, enabling it to return to where it came from. But it was still waiting for a sign. There were more images in its head, making no sense; some of them seeming to hold a promise of return, others filling it with fear.

Travelling in darkness.

A light up ahead.

'. . . drive carefully, George. It's a big responsibility, all those people in your coach. And it's a long drive . . .'

The utter terror. Knowing that a headlong crash was imminent. Sensing something directly ahead and not being able to avoid it.

'. . . kiss the kids for me, love. I'll be home after the return trip. Soon as I can . . .'

And then a succession of faces, screaming.

The agony and the fear.

Something about those faces. They were all different faces. But they were all its face, somehow. It had to get home.

. . . get home . . .

It knew that there was no shelter down here. When the daylight returned, it would have nowhere to hide. In the gully, it found a sheet of tarpaulin and a dozen tattered black bin-bags filled with rubbish. Tearing the bags open with its claws, it scattered the garbage and gathered the fluttering rags of plastic.

There were shrubs down here in the gully, not enough to provide cover in themselves. The thing tore them out by the roots, dragging them to the bushes at the top of the embankment and cramming them around the deepest thicket, creating a primitive hide. By the time a dull orange line had begun to spread along the horizon, the thing had covered its hide with a roof and walls made from the torn tarpaulin and the black plastic bags. It crawled inside, making sure that no light could enter. It left a small, ragged strip in front of its 'eyes', enough to be able to look out on the motorway.

As the dawn began to break, it shrank back into the safety of its nest.

Then became aware that someone or something was coming.

It was nothing to do with the lights that occasionally flashed by. This was something different. Something moving altogether more slowly, and headed its way. The thing shuffled impatiently in the hide. Was this what it had been waiting for? Was this the moment of release? Unable to contain itself any longer, it gingerly tore a small hole in the ragged black plastic on one side of the shelter, the side from which this promise of escape seemed to be emanating. Hissing in pain, it shrank back from the light that speared inside. But overwhelmed by this new instinct, it moved back to the small gap it had torn and peered painfully out. Through a barbed tangle of skeletal branches, it could see down the hard shoulder of the motorway.

Two silhouettes were making their way down the hard shoulder towards the place where the thing was hiding.

The thing watched them come.

Should it wait until both of the strange figures found it? Or should it burst out of its hiding place now?

The thing could see that the larger of the shapes had a small four-legged silhouette on a rope or a chain. Was something being brought to it? Unable to understand, the thing shrank back into the darkness and frantically deliberated what to do. What if this source of salvation should pass by without seeing where it was? It raised its claws to the raw meat of its face.

'Is one of you me? Is that what it is?'

It moved back to the ragged slit. The two figures were

less than fifty feet away and would be passing directly by at any moment. The thing raised itself to its haunches, peering eagerly out. The hated light still backlit both figures, so that it was impossible to see anything other than silhouettes.

The thing gathered itself to brave the light and emerge from the darkness.

'Bronson! Don't pull like that, or I won't take you walkies again!'

The thing paused at the sound of the taller silhouette's voice. Was it talking to it? Was there some meaning in those words which it was supposed to grasp? Confused, it stooped to look through the gap again.

The smaller silhouette was jumping and twisting its body, as if it could sense that there was something waiting up ahead.

'What is it, boy? What's wrong?'

The thing could see that the taller silhouette had stopped now, about twenty feet away, keeping a tight hold on the chain as the smaller silhouette jumped and snarled.

Unsure, the thing began to sob.

'Who's in there?'

Perhaps it had been provided with a choice of a new face? Was that what was going on? Maybe the large silhouette had its face, perhaps the smaller one? The thing looked from one to the other. But what if it made the wrong choice? If it took the wrong face, perhaps it would never get home again. The smaller shape began to make a loud, piercing noise which only served to confuse the thing further.

The bigger figure began to back away, pulling the struggling, barking shape with it.

The thing knew that it was about to lose its chance. It raised its claws to the black plastic wall.

The dog lunged, twisting its head. Its owner hung on tight, dragging the animal back fearfully.

Then the thing caught sight of the dog's head. The way it had twisted had shown the thing full details of its snout, its head and face, its eyes and its bared teeth, all highlighted by the rising sun. The sight of the animal made the thing pause. It remembered struggling with one such animal, believing that it had its face.

But of all the faces it had taken, that was the one that the thing knew without doubt was the wrong face. The shape, the size, everything. That face had been just like the snarling face he was looking on now. The thing was confused and afraid. Did that mean the bigger figure had its face? Why then was the smaller figure being brought to it?

It sank to its haunches once more, its claws covering its terrible head.

Confused, frightened and alone, it began to weep.

Soon, it became aware that both figures had gone away for ever.

It could not contain its anguish, and howled its pain to whoever or whatever might hear.

The Reverend Ben Jameson, a man who had spent years frowning on over-indulgence of all kinds, poured the last of the brandy into the glass and made his unsteady way back to his seat. It was the same upholstered seat in which he composed his sermons. On cold winter nights his housekeeper might have a roaring fire in the grate, and everything might seem to be reasonably well with the world. Those days seemed a long, long time ago. He sat wearily, and the empty fireplace before him somehow seemed to match his feelings. No need for roaring coal fires in this heat-wave. The ash stains on the hearth were somehow the loneliest things he'd ever seen.

He sipped the brandy, praying that it would quench the ghastly hollowness inside. But the liquid was like fire, and as it burned its way down his thoughts were filled with the Old Testament images of fire and brimstone which he'd spent a lifetime in the ministry trying to allay.

He had been weeping a lot, and tears were close to the surface again.

In the space of a few days, he had lost everything he'd held valuable.

He felt damned.

Sitting and staring at the ash streaks in the grate, and sipping the last of the brandy, he didn't hear the first knock at the door.

When it came a second time, loud and impatient, it roused him from his torpor. He turned to look back across the front room as the knocking came again. He'd made no appointments to see parishioners here at the vicarage, not since everything had gone so horribly wrong. He checked his watch. Three in the afternoon. Door-to-door salesman? Surely not at the vicarage? Someone in trouble, requiring spiritual assistance? He knew that he couldn't handle anything like that, and decided to ignore it, turning back to the empty fireplace.

And then the thought came to him that it might be someone from O'Farrell. The thought filled him with anguish and horror. He froze in his chair, the glass held tight in his fist. In panic, he looked across at the window. If someone decided to move away from the door and look through it, they'd be able to see where he was sitting. Jameson pulled himself out of the chair and shrank back into the far corner of the room, praying that whoever it was would go away.

'I know you're in there,' said a voice from behind the front door. 'We saw you come in.'

Oh, God . . .

The knocking came again. This time, it sounded like the flat of a hand.

'Come on, Jameson. We only want to talk to you . . .'

Did he recognise that voice? He was still trying to place it when he heard the sound of metal scraping on metal, a jangling noise like the sound of a keyring. He moved carefully to the edge of the living-room door and looked into the passage that led to the front door. There was a mumbled curse from the other side, then more of the metallic scraping.

In the moment that the door swung open, Jameson remembered the owner of the voice. It was the reporter called Curtis, the man who had tried to speak to him at the church, the man who had tried to speak to Sheila Russell.

The same man was now letting himself into Jameson's home.

Enraged, Jameson came around the door into the passage, letting the brandy inside him fuel the anger.

'How *dare* you!'

There was someone with Curtis, a man who looked as ill as Jameson felt. He saw a flash of a white face with dark, hollowed eyes as Curtis stepped into the passage and the other man closed the door.

'Get out of here at once, or I shall call the police!'

'So call them. Let's all have an open, frank discussion about Martin Russell.'

Jameson blundered back into the living room to the telephone table. Colour rising in what had been a pallid face, he yanked the receiver from its cradle, holding it like a weapon as Curtis and the man behind him slowly entered the room.

'I'm not joking!' Jameson waved the receiver at them, his other hand hovering over the numeral 9 on the set. 'You are intruders. You have no right . . .'

'Cut the crap, Reverend,' said Curtis, ignoring his threats and looking around the room as if expecting someone to be hiding here. The man behind him shuffled uneasily, looking at his feet. Jameson noticed his unease, and redirected his threat there. Harry pretended not to see.

Curtis moved to the centre of the room, ready to psych this so-called man of the cloth out. He had been around people long enough to sense when someone was running scared. He could almost smell the fear exuding from Jameson. There was no time for detailed mind-games. He decided to use his master card straight away and hope that it hit home. If it didn't, then that was the end of his gamble.

'I know what you've done.'

'You can't just let yourself in here. What are they? Skeleton keys or something? That's against the law. Now, for the last time . . .'

'Quinn O'Farrell.'

'Oh.' Before their eyes, it seemed that the suddenly rising colour in Jameson's face was beginning to fade. 'Oh.' He was unaware that he was lowering the receiver, seemed now to be interested only in a spot on the carpet in front of where Curtis was standing. 'Oh, God.' His face looked bleached now as he sat heavily in the chair next to the telephone table. He looked at the receiver as if he could not understand what it was for or how it had come to be in his hand. He tried to replace it, and missed. The sight of it dangling by the flex seemed to break something inside him. 'Oh, God, *forgive* me . . .' He bent forward then, holding his head in his hands and rocking back and forth like a keening child.

Curtis looked at Harry and gave him a thumbs-up. Harry could not share his enthusiasm.

'Feel like confessing, Reverend?' asked Curtis at last, playing his bluff card for all it was worth, and to Jameson it seemed that the newspaperman was only echoing O'Farrell's words. He looked up in despair.

'I know I've done wrong. I know I've failed.'

'Tell us all about it.'

'How much do you know?'

'Most of it,' lied Curtis. 'But we want to hear it from you.'

'The money wasn't the main thing. That's what O'Farrell would say. That I'd done it for the money. He's wrong. I did take the money, but only after he'd threatened to kill me. Do you know what it's like, to be threatened that way? He meant it. Would have done it. Look . . .' Jameson pulled up a sleeve and showed them his forearm. There were cigarette burns there. 'Do you know what it does to you inside? It's worse . . . *worse* than the pain. It kills everything that was good in you. Everything you believe in . . . Christ, I can barely bring myself to go into the church. Sweet Jesus, help me, I'm so ashamed . . .'

'So tell us.'

'Martin healed one of O'Farrell's employees. We didn't know it at the time. He came along and was healed like the others. Someone must have told O'Farrell about it. He came to see for himself . . .'

'I was there. I saw him in the congregation.'

Jameson looked across at the brandy bottle, as if hoping that it would magically refill itself. 'Afterwards, a few days afterwards, O'Farrell and some of his . . . people came to see me. I wouldn't let them in. I thought it was going to be more of the same fuss from the newspapers. Then they broke in, like you. And then they . . . then they . . .' He waved hopelessly at his scarred arm. 'They told me what I had to do. What I had to say to Martin and Sheila about getting away from the Church authorities and moving to a retreat. God help me, I helped to organise Martin's abduction. They said that he would never know. That they would maintain the sham, keep Martin convinced that he really was doing God's work based with the Brothers of the Holy Order. But then, when the time came to take him away, and he seemed reluctant . . . Oh my God, they just *took* him. I don't believe they ever intended to keep up a pretence with him. I think they were just going to take him whatever happened. Bring people to Martin, people who could pay their price to be healed. Perhaps I wanted to believe that everything would turn out all right.'

'The Brothers of the Holy Order?' asked Harry, moving forward and gripping his midriff as if suddenly suffering acute indigestion. 'Where are they?'

Jameson looked at him in puzzlement. 'I thought you knew everything . . . ?'

'But you took the money, didn't you?' said Curtis quickly, afraid that their bluff would be exposed by Stark's words. 'You hypocritical bastard.' Jameson looked back at him as the newspaperman continued his attack. 'You're supposed to be a man of the cloth.'

Jameson crumpled again, and Curtis breathed an inner sigh of relief. 'I'm so *sorry* . . . The money's still in my account. I haven't touched a penny of it yet. Can't even give it to charity. It's . . . tainted money.' He began to sob once more.

'I'll tell you what you're going to do, Jameson.'

The vicar continued to weep.

'Jameson!'

Startled, he looked up at him through red-rimmed eyes.

'This is what you're going to do. You're going to telephone O'Farrell . . .'

'Oh God, no! I can't do that! He'll kill me. You don't know what he's like.'

'You're going to *telephone* him and . . .'

'—Please . . . no . . . sweet Jesus . . . I can't . . .'

* * *

'*Mr O'Farrell. This is . . . is . . .*'

'*I know who you are, Reverend. And I can't believe that you've forgotten our last telephone conversation. I told you . . . TOLD YOU . . .*' A pause then, while control is regained. '*I told you not to try and get in touch again, Jameson. It seems to me that you need another visit, and one or two further reminders about how we're playing this business with Martin Russell.*'

'*You mean, like more cigarette burns on the arms?*' says Curtis. '*More death threats?*'

'*Who the FUCK is this?!*'

'*Anthony Curtis, from the* Independent Daily. *And don't hang up, Mr O'Farrell. Not if you know what's good for you. You're just going to have to take a chance that I'm not taping the conversation. As it happens, I'm not. But there you go, life is full of risks.*'

Silence.

'*We need to talk about Martin Russell. Because, I know . . . we know . . . that he's being held against his will. We also know where he's being held. You see, the Reverend Jameson's had a change of heart. I think he's found his faith again, know what I mean?*'

'*Who is this, please? We appear to have a crossed line.*'

'*Nice try, O'Farrell. But I'm pleased you haven't hung up. You just chew over what I've said. And it's no use sending strong-arm men around to the church. You won't find Jameson there. He's in a safe place now. Where you and yours won't find him. And there's no point in contacting Sheila Russell. She knows nothing about this.*'

Silence.

'*I'll be in touch again. To fix up a meeting place. We need to talk, O'Farrell.*'

And then the line goes dead.

'What did you mean?' asked Harry. 'About needing to talk?'

Curtis had a look on his face which Harry found difficult to understand. He seemed elated as he replaced the telephone receiver, clapping his hands now as if he'd pulled off some neat trick. He looked over his shoulder, towards the room where Jameson had retired to lie down.

'Got him. Got the shit.'

'What are you talking about, Curtis?'

'I should have known when I saw O'Farrell's face that there was something rotten going on. This has been big, so far. But it just gets *bigger* . . .'

The newspaperman turned to brace both hands on the sill, staring out of his apartment window. There was nothing to see but a bare stone wall opposite; clattering sounds drifted up from a loading bay somewhere below. Curtis had driven them back to his home after their confrontation with Jameson, guessing that O'Farrell might be wise enough to send some of his 'employees' round to the vicarage. Now the vicar was lying next door, in a state of semi-collapse. He had allowed himself to be led away, had complained that all he wanted to do was sleep. Curtis had found it difficult to keep the edge of contempt out of his voice as they bundled the vicar into his car and drove here. Since their arrival, Jameson seemed to have become more incoherent, as if the enormity of his betrayal had finally begun to damage his mind. Curtis had managed to bully O'Farrell's number out of him, had forced him to make the call.

But suddenly Harry didn't know where Curtis was coming from at all.

'What did you *mean*, Curtis? About needing to talk?'

Curtis remained at the window, buried in his thoughts.

Harry grabbed him by the shoulder and spun him around.

'What did you *mean?*'

Curtis seemed to snap back to reality. 'What? What the hell's wrong with you . . . ?'

'With *me*? Get real, Curtis. And talk to me. Just what the hell have you got planned?'

'I'm going to meet up with O'Farrell.'

'Why?'

'To talk to him, reason with him. Find out what's going on.'

'That doesn't make sense. We know from Jameson that Russell is being held against his will. You've told me that O'Farrell has a reputation for being dangerous to deal with.'

'So what do we do? Tell the police? What then? They move in, maybe even get Russell back. But then the authorities clamp down, just the way the hospital clamped down on me when all those impossible things began to happen. You could end up in a padded room, Stark. Ever think of that? And even if they *do* believe all the stuff you've been telling me, what then? You'd end up locked away for good. Sedated, strapped down, while the medical people examine you and test you and God knows what else.'

'You don't want to let go of the story, you bastard. You're stringing it out.'

'Think straight! No one's going to believe what happened to you.'

'You want to add to the fucking story as it goes along. This O'Farrell business is like another dream come true for the time when you write this all up. That's what this is about, isn't it? Anthony Curtis, ace reporter. Centre stage. "I was there when it happened". You fucking idiot. My life . . . our lives are at stake. There isn't much time.'

'I thought you said you didn't care whether you lived or died any more?'

'*You* . . .'

Harry seized Curtis by the lapels and swung him around. The newspaperman was overweight, but nonetheless his feet left the floor. Harry's face was a mask of fury as he flung him across the room. Curtis collided with a chair, knocked it over and fell awkwardly. When he looked up, Harry was bearing down on him.

'Wait!' He held up an arm to ward him off, realising that he'd gone too far.

'If you think this is a *game*, Curtis . . .'

'No, no, no. Look, I'm sorry. I shouldn't have said that. But think about it, Stark. Yes, you're right, of course I want this story. But I'm not stringing it out. Really. You said it yourself, there's not much time. One survivor in hospital, and no way to get her. Three others God knows where. But we know that Russell is being held by O'Farrell. You said yourself . . . *it* said . . . "Find the Others".'

'You're forgetting about O'Dowd. He's heading north to meet us. I say we stay put, wait and see what happens when he arrives.'

'And what happens if O'Farrell decides to do away with Russell? Where does that leave you and the other survivors? You said they *all* have to be together if they're ever going to get back.'

'You're saying that O'Farrell will *kill* Russell? You make him sound like Al Capone.'

'I've done features on him before. He's a ruthless bastard, hiding his shady activities behind a great screen of so-called respectable business enterprises. Everyone's amazed he's got this far without being arrested for something.'

'All the more reason to keep well away, then. He's hardly likely to do anything to Russell if he knows that Jameson's cracked and is spilling his guts. No, I say leave it for the police. Things will be clearer when O'Dowd gets here. Maybe we'll find out something more.'

'Maybe O'Dowd won't get here.'

'What?'

'I didn't tell you everything. Perhaps I was being over-optimistic about O'Dowd. Maybe he'll think twice about coming up here.'

'Curtis, what kind of games are you playing?'

'I'm just saying that we need to talk to O'Farrell. Tell him that we're on to him. Ask him to let Russell go.'

'You *are* stringing this story out, you sod!' Harry lunged again. Curtis grabbed the chair, shoving it between them. 'Taking that kind of risk just doesn't make sense,' Harry went on. 'He'll cut your stupid throat, if he's as bad as you're making him out to be.'

'He doesn't know who else is involved. Doesn't know about you. He won't be able to risk it.'

'So . . . what? You just arrange to meet him somewhere, ask him nicely to let Russell go? He says "Fine", and everything turns out okay?'

'Something like that. I've got all the cards.'

'Wrong. If Russell's being held against his will, O'Farrell

won't risk him telling all to the police. Far better to knock him off. Tell you to get lost. They know nothing. Or just knock you off, too. No, Curtis. Your plan is completely cock-eyed. You're going to wait here with me until O'Dowd . . .'

Harry bent at the waist, clutching his stomach. Curtis had grown accustomed to these spasms of pain. The thing inside Stark was making itself felt again. Groaning, Harry took a step back.

'You've . . .' Harry was talking to the thing inside. '. . . you've got to be . . . got to be . . . *joking!*'

He reached for a nearby bureau, gripping the edge and clinging on tight as if he might fall over at any second. Curtis hadn't seen him in so much pain from the parasite before.

'No . . . *No!*'

Shaking his head, his face twisted and grimacing in pain, Harry sank slowly to his knees, still hanging on to the ridge of the bureau with one hand and clutching his stomach with the other.

'*NO!*'

Curtis rose slowly, thought about going to help him, before a slow smile of understanding crept over his face.

'It agrees with me. Christ, I don't believe it. The thing inside you . . . it's disagreeing with you, and *agreeing* with me.'

Harry held out the hand from his stomach, as if he could reach over and grab Curtis, bringing him down. His face was spectral white, the hollows even darker than before. Curtis's smile began to fade when it seemed that the pain was not going to cease.

'All right,' he said, sternly. 'All right, whatever you are in there . . . that's enough.'

Harry gagged, still clinging to the bureau, head bowed in agony.

'All right, you fucker. That's enough. Leave him alone.'

'Christ . . . Curtis . . . help me . . .'

Curtis shoved the chair aside and moved quickly to Harry's side. Harry clutched his arm, making him wince as the fingers dug through his anorak sleeve and into his flesh.

'You've made your point,' hissed Curtis. 'Just let him be.'

'Curtis? . . .'

'I said *leave him ALONE!*'

Groaning, Harry sank forward to the carpet. Curtis took his weight and began to haul him to his feet. He was too heavy. Leaving him, he moved to the sofa, swept the newspapers and magazines strewn on it to the floor and then hurried back. Harry seemed on the verge of passing out altogether, trying ineffectually to assist as Curtis dragged him to the sofa. Finally, he managed to heave him on to it. Gasping for breath, he stood back and looked down.

Harry looked even worse than he had before.

'This isn't for you, Stark. This is for the thing inside you. Are you listening?'

Harry was showing the whites of his eyes as he drifted off into unconsciousness. His breathing was heavy and ragged.

'I don't know if you can hear me or not. But there's no point in hurting him that way. He may be right. And I may be wrong. But if he is dying, what's the use of hurting him like that? He dies, you die. Simple as that.'

He moved to the overturned chair, righted it and sat facing Harry.

Now he wasn't so sure that his way was the right way after all.

Stark had accused him of wanting to string the story out. And he knew that at least a part of that accusation was true. Suddenly needing another drink, he looked around for the whisky bottle. He returned to his seat and drank straight from the bottle, looking long and hard at Stark's prostrate form.

A disgraced priest, unconscious in one room.

A man with a demon, unconscious in the other.

'Christ,' said Curtis to himself, 'how do I headline this one?'

As night fell outside, and midnight neared, Curtis sat and drank and wondered which way was the best way.

'Street scum,' said Ellis Burwell. 'That's all you are.'

He snatched the bottle back when the vagrant reached for it, and drank deeply, letting the vodka burn his gut, and then moved around to the back of the park bench. He grinned. The vagrant, out of his mind, struggled to look back. He groped for the bottle again, mumbling. The prospect of the bottle was making him drool; gossamer threads filled his ragged beard.

'Gimme . . .'

Burwell leaned away from the back of the park bench as the vagrant groped. The man began to sing, as if entreating Burwell to join in, change his mind, and for God's sake give him a *drink*.

'King of the world,' said Burwell, standing straight with drunken dignity. 'That could be me.'

He drank again, looking around the park. It was two thirty in the morning, and there was only one street light fifty yards away. The vagrant began to sing 'King of the Road'

'Not king of the road, you stupid bastard. King of the world. Because . . . because I've got the *power*. In my hands.'

He held the bottle out to the vagrant.

'I could kill everyone in the fucking world if I wanted to. Did you know that?'

'Gimme . . .'

'Did you know THAT?'

He seized the tramp's outstretched hand and began to laugh.

Night had crept up on Curtis.

The whisky bottle was long finished, but it still dangled from one hand as he sat in the same seat watching Stark sleep. There had been no sound from Jameson in the next room since he'd been brought here. Curtis wondered how much of that brandy the less-than-Reverend Jameson had consumed before they'd arrived at the vicarage.

He had been thinking long and hard, about his real motives for wanting to meet up with O'Farrell, and not handing the matter straight over to the police. After all, it seemed that Jameson was compliant at last, crucified with guilt and more than willing to tell everything. As such, it ought to be a straightforward matter of handing everything over to the authorities. But then the whisky had taken his thoughts in other directions as the shadows had lengthened. He was still deep in those thoughts, had not moved to switch on a light.

If he accepted everything Stark told him, and he'd seen enough since the night of the motorway crash to convince him that this *wasn't* all just a fantasy, then what did that mean for the cynical way he looked at life? Did the existence of the 'Travellers', and what Stark called the Storm Between, with all its side effects of healing and destruction, confirm the complicated networks of human belief in an afterlife? Or did it mean that everything everyone thought about an afterlife – whether based on organised religion or personal belief – was utterly wrong? What did the Travellers believe, wherever they came from? Clearly, in saving themselves the way they had – by hiding in the bodies of their human hosts until they'd grown strong enough to 'escape' – they'd revealed what could only be described as supernormal powers. Did they have a god? Curtis remembered that day in church, and the sight of Russell healing. What did that imply about the possibility of there being a 'human' God? The whole bizarre series of events seemed to throw up more questions than answers.

Stark had said that the energy flux that was the Storm Between had interacted with the emotions of the survivors at the point of impact, resulting in some kind of astonishing wish-fulfilment. What did that say about the nature of human emotion? Curtis thought about the stories he'd written over the years, thought of the accidents and the murders and the tragedies. For the first time, it seemed that he was aware of the true nature of anguish and grief ... and maybe even love. Were those emotions real and tangible, did they have *solidity*? Had they been raging invisibly all around him at the scenes of his reports, an expended flux of energy, invisible yet somehow concrete? *Real* energy. Somehow, when expended by the people who had created those energies, could they become *independent* of the people who had created them? And, once expended, could those forces really shape the world? Unseen, and dismissed by the cynical and the weary and the hopeless? But somehow the greatest forces in the world?

There was a noise somewhere in the darkness. It brought Curtis out of his contemplation. But when he looked around, he wasn't sure what he'd heard or where it came from. Joints creaking, he rose from the chair, stood and listened. There was no repetition. But he'd heard something . . . and it had sounded *stealthy*. Rubbing a hand over his face, he moved to a standard lamp and switched it on. Harsh, angular light illumined the room like a roughly hewn jigsaw of orange and black.

He moved to the window and looked out. Had it been something below? No, it had sounded a lot closer than that. Maybe he was just spooking himself with these crazy thoughts. He looked at the empty whisky bottle, still clutched in one hand, and then headed across the room for another.

And then he saw the white envelope that had been pushed under his door.

For a moment, he stood watching it, as if it were alive.

When he opened the door and looked out into the communal corridor, there was no sign of anyone.

'Hello?'

No answer.

He closed the door and picked the envelope up. There was no inscription. quickly, he tore it open and read the closely typed message inside. Instantly, he broke out into a sweat.

> CLEVER BOY. WANT TO TALK?
> WHITLEY LEISURE COMPLEX, KING
> ROAD. TONIGHT. JUST AFTER TWELVE.
> NICE AND OPEN THERE.
> IF YOU'VE GOT COMPANY, FORGET IT.

He moved to the cabinet and took out another bottle of Scotch, pouring a large measure. The fact that O'Farrell had found out where he was so quickly after the telephone call was deeply unnerving. His number was unlisted, his address confidential. Had Sheila Russell passed it to Jameson? Had he then passed it on to O'Farrell? Or was O'Farrell simply much better organised than he'd ever imagined? He returned to his seat, looking at Stark sprawled on the sofa-bed. He looked at the note again. O'Farrell was a clever sod, all right. No return telephone call (*if* he'd somehow sussed Curtis's ex-directory number) just in case he had fixed up a recording device. And a terse note delivered by an unseen flunky.

Curtis drank.

He had cast the die. For good or bad.

He toasted the thing that hid in Stark's sleeping body.

'Well, at least *one* of us thinks I'm right.'

'Do you believe in miracles?' asked the nurse, as she checked Jane Teal's temperature readings and the intravenous drip in her arm.

'The human kind, or the religious kind?' asked her colleague, unnecessarily tucking the bed clothes in at one side.

'You mean there's a difference?'

'Yeah. The human kind we see every day. Like Dr Rafferty taking that tumour out of little Graham Dinaggio's skull. He's human – despite the way he treats his secretary – but it was amazing, what he did. Or down in Physio – Mr Fellowes. You know? The one they said would never walk again after his stroke. Now he's walking. That's a human miracle. That was all about people who've been trained well, trained to heal, and that's what they do. But more than that. Mr Fellowes *wanted* to walk again, more than anything in the world. His strength of will had a lot to do with it. So that's a human miracle, in my book. They said he wouldn't walk again. And he can.'

'And what about the religious kind?'

'Ah, well . . . Is this a trick question?'

'No, I'm serious.'

'Well . . . that's like visits to Lourdes, and stuff like that. Isn't it? People who can't be helped by human means, who are cured by . . . well, by religious faith, I suppose.'

'Religious faith?'

'This *is* a trick question, isn't it? You're taping everything for Sister, so it'll go on my next assessment.'

'Don't talk rubbish. I'm serious. I want to know what you think.'

'Ahem . . . testing, testing, one, two, three. Very well, for the record: faith. They tell me it can move mountains. And I'm sure that people, deeply religious people, have cured themselves of incurable diseases by a process we've yet to understand, i.e. a largely subconscious/unconscious cross-over from the mind to the physical immune system engendered by personal, religious *faith*, which harnesses the body's own complex power of recovery and destroys the physical ailment, in whatever form. How's that? Did I pass?'

'What if I told you that Jane Teal had second-degree burns when she was admitted to hospital?'

'I'd say that someone made a mistake. There are no burns to be treated. I would know. I've been looking after her this past week.'

'Well, I'm telling you. She was admitted urgently to the burns unit. They gave her emergency treatment. Checked her burns the following day. Healed.'

'This is another bloody assessment test. And it's getting near the end of my shift. So if you don't *mind* . . .'

'I'm telling you the truth. Here . . . look at her head. See there? *That* was burned raw. And I know, 'cause I saw it myself. Now she's grown new skin . . . *new* skin . . . and there's hair there, too. Know how long it takes hair to grow, once it's been burned off?'

'So what's the punchline to this joke?'

'There isn't one. I'm telling you the *truth*. No one knows just what's happened, or how it's happened. But it's true. So . . . that goes back to what I asked you in the beginning. Do you believe in miracles? And if you do, is this a human miracle or a religious miracle?'

'I wonder what happened to her?'

'She's the only one who knows. And it doesn't look like she's going to tell us.'

'It must have been terrible. I mean, all those people dead – and her the only one getting out of it alive. Doesn't seem possible that she could have walked out of it.'

'Maybe she left a chip pan on or something.'

'A chip pan for a posh dinner party? I don't think so.'

The first nurse gazed down at Jane Teal's pale face. She looked like a twelve-year-old girl.

'It looks like . . . I don't know . . . but it looks to me as if . . . well, as if she's *smiling*.'

'Don't think there'll be much of that if and when she wakes up. I don't fancy the job of telling her that her husband and best friends are . . .'

'Ssshh! She might be able to hear. Look at her. Hello? Jane, love? Can you hear me?'

'Know what I think?'

'What?'

'I don't think she *wants* to wake up. I think she's happier than she's ever been.'

At first, Harry thought he was in his own bed.

'Jean?'

As soon as he called for her, he knew that she was gone. Again, the unutterable grief descended on him. He would have crushed his face into the pillow, but this was not their bed and he could not release the intimacy of his grief into someone else's resting place.

'Let me die, you bastard. Let me go.'

But it would not let him die, would not let him go. He could feel it deep within, stirring and goading, anxious that he rise and continue with the task. He could feel its own grief at what was happening to the Traveller it loved, out there, alone and lost and in agony.

'Your grief *isn't* my grief!'

Angry now, Harry threw himself from the sofa-bed, clutching at the arm-rest in the darkness to prevent himself from falling. He would not allow the blurring to take place inside him. The parasite was using him, had no real regard for his pain, just its own.

At last, he realised where he was.

'Curtis?'

There was no reply.

He staggered to his feet. He needed water. In the stark orange-black, he saw the door to the bathroom and made his way there. After he had drunk two pints direct from the tap, he came back to the living room and remembered Jameson.

Pushing open the bedroom door, he saw the vicar still lying across the bed.

'You still alive?'

Jameson moaned and turned over.

Harry moved back to the living room.

'Curtis?'

When he checked his watch, he saw that it was 11.30. Pitch black, so it must be evening. How long had he slept? And where the hell had the ace reporter gone? At that moment he remembered their argument about meeting O'Farrell, the thing's agreement with such a ridiculous course of action, and then he saw the crumpled note next to the telephone. He stamped across the room and grabbed it angrily. It was the note that had been slipped under the door. Something else had been added.

> Stark: Maybe I'm wrong. But for better or worse, I think it's worth a try.

'You stupid, *stupid* idiot! What *good* is it going to do?'

Crumpling the note in his fist, he looked at his watch once more. Then he turned back to the bedroom.

'Jameson! Wake up! You're coming with me!'

Mercy was heading north.

For the first hour she'd been tearing hell out of the gears, bringing the clutch up heavily and stalling frequently. But now she was on the motorway, on the straight, and cruising in fifth. Soaked in sweat, she wiped the hair frequently from her eyes. Suddenly, she realised that her arms and shoulders were aching badly. She had been clutching the steering wheel as if it might suddenly come alive and fly out of her hands. She forced herself to relax and looked at the petrol gauge. It was half full, and she prayed that she wouldn't need any more before she got where she was heading.

Ever since setting off, she'd expected to hear the sounds of police sirens somewhere behind her. But so far, she had been lucky.

The headlights picked out the road ahead.

And even though she didn't want to think about it, they reminded her of that night.

Then, she had been headed south.

Now, north.

Maybe Martin had been right. She didn't know where the hell she was going in life at all.

But she had set out to do what she'd planned, hadn't she?

He's dead, Mercy. Deinbeck's dead, and he won't be raping any more kids.

She shook her head. Yes, the shit deserved to die. But she hadn't intended to kill him. Just to make him *know*. Just to make him really *feel* the horror of what he'd done. She shuddered then, remembering how she'd felt just before, and during, the crash.

Mesmerised by the headlights, she stayed in the left-hand lane. She realised that Martin had been half right. But it was the important half. Up until the time when Selina had telephoned, she had been drifting. It was her way of dealing with the hurt that had been done to her. Her way of being independent. Now she realised that independence was just a way of describing her reluctance ever to get into a relationship or a situation where someone or something might have power over her. She had always wanted to be part of *something*. Something good. But experience had taught her that most things turned to shit. Far better to move on, before things turned painful. A good strategy, if it brought happiness. But it had brought her nothing but a rootless misery. And then, when Selina had telephoned with the news of Deinbeck's whereabouts, everything in her life had suddenly become focused. Confronting him was a way of saying goodbye to everything that had happened to her, and a way of moving on. When Martin had suggested that she was unfocused, he had been wrong at *that* moment. As they'd talked in the cab, she had never been more focused in her life. She was heading south. She was going to find the bastard. And somehow, in a way that she had yet to determine, she was going to put right the wrongs that had been done to her in the past. At her very core, she had felt that a confrontation with the person who represented everything bad about her past was going to turn things around.

Now Deinbeck was dead.

And, by Christ, was she turned *around*.

But what now?

Something up ahead!

Mercy cried out, twisting the wheel.

Tyres screeched as the car swerved into the hard shoulder, churning up a spray of flying gravel. She stamped hard on the brake and the car slewed to a grinding halt, jerking her forward over the wheel. The engine stalled. Wide-eyed, she stared ahead. There was nothing in the road. The headlights picked out the hard shoulder and the empty motorway ahead.

'Shit, shit, *shit!*'

She hammered at the steering wheel with the flats of her hands.

And then the bad feeling came over her again. She felt sapped, nauseous, as if there were something alive deep inside her, eating away like a cancer. Kicking open the door, she leaned out and vomited. Through that purely physical, wretched, retching act, she suddenly *knew* that there was something deep inside. Something that was hiding inside. Was it . . . was it a cancer?

Was she dying?

When she had finished, she climbed back inside and slammed the door.

Just where the hell was she going, and what would she do when she got there?

'Just drive, Mercy. For Christ's sake, just *drive!*'

Starting the engine again, she rammed the gear lever into first and screeched from the hard shoulder back onto the motorway. If anything had been coming up behind her, then her journey would have ended. But there was nothing behind.

She wanted to feel as if she were heading home.

And for reasons both basic and complex, Martin Russell was home.

The car vanished into the night.

Heading north.

Curtis parked his car in the forecourt of the Whitley Hotel on King Road. When he climbed out he could hear the sea not far away. He remembered covering a joke story for the *Independent Daily* on a seafood restaurant not far from here. The brother of a famous rock star had opened the restaurant; its centrepiece had been a glass tank full of piranha fish. One night, the tank had been broken and customers had fled from their tables as a miniature tidal wave of flapping, squirming fish had snapped at their ankles.

The Whitley Leisure Complex was directly across the road from where he stood. A long, low building, its stucco white walls were covered in graffiti. It had been built on a site between two hotels, and in the late sixties and early seventies had been the 'in' place for holidaymakers looking for recreation in style. There had been a definite snob factor back then. It advertised its services for the young, upwardly mobile holidaying executives looking for a gymnasium/swimming pool/sauna of taste for tasteful people; it was most definitely not for the families of shipyard workers from the Clyde, who would have to make do with the three-mile stretch of beach beyond the promenade, not two hundred yards from where the complex had been built. But now the building was derelict. The windows and doors had been boarded up, the long, low walls left for the graffiti artists. Now that Curtis thought about it, hadn't the leisure organisation that had owned the place and gone bust been gobbled up by one of O'Farrell's subsidiary companies?

He scanned the street in front of the building. There were no parked cars. No suspicious figures waiting for him. He looked around to see if there was anyone standing in a hotel entrance, or on a street corner. There were late-night bars along this stretch, and night-clubs further along the promenade. So even at this time of night there was a regular stream of traffic on the main road a hundred yards from where Curtis stood. It helped to make him feel less vulnerable. He looked back at the Whitley Hotel. Perhaps O'Farrell was in there now, watching him from a window? Or perhaps he was occupying a room in one of the hotels on either side of the derelict building? He decided to hold his ground, and see if anything developed.

Twenty minutes later, he was still waiting for something to happen.

Nervously jangling the car keys in his anorak pocket, Curtis took heart from the drunken foursome who good-naturedly jostled past him on their way to a seafront night-club. There were people around. O'Farrell surely wouldn't try anything physical. He crossed the road as nonchalantly as he could and stood in the building's forecourt. Empty beer cans and fish-and-chip wrappers had swirled in here, driven by the wind from the promenade. What would he do if a limousine suddenly pulled up and a bunch of guys looking like extras from *The Godfather* told him to get in?

'I won't bloody get in,' Curtis mumbled to himself. 'I've seen the movies. I know what *not* to do.'

But he knew that the best response he could muster was also a cliché from the movies he'd seen as a kid. Tell them that he wasn't operating alone, that someone else had all the information on the case and would turn it straight over to the police if he didn't turn up by a particular time. Sitting there in the darkness and scanning the street, Curtis went over the options again in his mind.

A car rounded the bend, its headlights sweeping over him. He stood up and tried to look causal as he moved to the roadside. The car kept on going, zooming past him with its radio blasting through open windows like a mobile disco. Curtis turned back, leaning against the building's front wall.

Another twenty minutes. It was now after 12.30, well past the time dictated in the note. Why go to these lengths to get him down here? He lit another cigarette and turned to look back at the leisure centre. For the first time he became aware that the main front doors weren't boarded up at all. From across the road, it looked as if they had been blocked with the same steel shutters that covered the windows on either side. But now that he was up close, he could see that the doors were open. The deep shadow of the alcove leading to the doors had been misleading. Curtis paced slowly back and forth in front of the entrance, peering inside. He could see the same street detritus of newspapers and old cans just inside, but nothing beyond. Surely O'Farrell, or whoever might be representing him, wasn't actually *in* there? It was pitch-black and full of garbage, for God's sake.

'No . . .' he said aloud. He walked back to the road, looked up and down again – and then returned to the entrance. Venturing up the two steps, he craned his head to look into the darkness. It was possible to see the shapes and shadows of walls, and something that might have been an inner window aperture, but not much else.

He looked back into the street.

Nothing.

'Hello?'

His voice echoed back at him.

'Anyone in there?'

Nothing.

Cursing, and now irritated by his own anxiety, he quickly moved into the entrance lobby and, bracing one hand on an inner wall, called: 'O'Farrell?'

'Took your fucking *time* about it!' hissed a voice from the darkness.

Curtis barely had a chance to react as the fist took him behind the ear. His head rebounded from the inner wall and he pitched forward into the black, unconscious.

Rough hands dragged him inside.

Outside, two dozen party revellers came down the road, singing and carousing and dancing. A car passed by, horn blaring when one of the revellers danced a jig in front of it before diving back to the pavement. Finishing his beer, he ran across the street and lobbed the can into the entrance to the leisure centre. It rebounded from the inner wall in a jangle of clattering echoes, coming to rest against one of Curtis's shoes.

The partygoers passed on.

The street outside was empty.

The slithering, bumping sounds of Curtis being dragged

deep into the dank, foul-smelling depths of the building went unheard.

'Had a good night then, Reverend?' asked the taxi driver, as they turned into King Road.

In the back seat, Jameson just looked at him with a blank face.

'I'm not a religious man myself,' continued the driver. 'But I do like to see a man of the cloth enjoying a few bevvies.' Still receiving no response from the vicar, the driver turned his attention to the white-faced man sitting next to him. 'You staying at one of the hotels down here?'

'Why don't you just shut up and drive?' asked Harry.

'No need for that, mate! Just making conversation.'

'Fifty yards further down. Stop there.'

'I can take you into the hotel car park.'

'Just stop the car.'

Sullenly, the driver pulled up at the kerb and told them how much was on the clock. Harry crammed a crumpled note and a fistful of change into his hand. It was more than treble the charge, but Harry didn't care and the driver wasn't about to complain. Seconds later, they were standing on the pavement opposite the derelict leisure complex as the taxi sped away into the night. The driver never looked back.

'Why . . . ?'

Harry looked at Jameson. He had explained to the vicar what they were doing before they'd left Curtis's apartment, but this was the first time Jameson had spoken.

'Why don't we just tell the police?'

Jameson was right. That was exactly what they should do. But Harry couldn't get out of his mind what Curtis had been saying about how the authorities might react if they got wind of what had happened to the survivors of the motorway smash. Death was one thing, an escape from the torment. But being locked in a padded cell and wearing a strait jacket, or being treated like a human guinea-pig by scientists, was altogether something else. Maybe Curtis was wrong about that, but he could not shake the images from his mind.

'Come on,' he said, and began to cross the road.

Jameson remained standing at the kerb.

Harry stopped halfway across. 'Come on, Jameson.'

'I didn't want to do what I did. You know that, don't you?' The vicar seemed on the verge of shamed tears again. 'God help me. I was so frightened . . .'

'God help you if you don't get your arse in gear, Jameson. Because if I have to come over there and get you, I'll kick you to the other side of the street.'

Head bowed, Jameson crossed the street.

At the entrance, Harry looked down each side of the building for evidence of figures in the darkness. Curtis must surely have arrived by now. Like Curtis, Harry was familiar with the area and knew that the leisure centre was derelict.

'Stay here!' he hissed, and quickly hurried down one side of the building.

It was longer than he'd anticipated, perhaps five hundred feet. There was a series of concrete out-buildings at the rear. At one time they had housed generators and a chlorine filtration unit, now boarded up like the building itself. He moved around the back, calling Curtis's name, then quickly ran up the other side of the building to the entrance. Jameson was standing in the same position.

'Have you seen anyone?'

Jameson shook his head in resignation.

Muttering, Harry moved back to the entrance, then saw that the battered main doors were wide open.

'Not in there. Surely not in there.'

Jumping up the two steps, he strode in, trying to see into the darkness.

'Curtis? You in there?'

There was no sound, no movement from within. Harry turned to look at Jameson's silhouette. The man seemed to exude despair.

'This can't be right . . .' He started down the stairs again.

And from within the derelict building, he seemed to hear a whisper of movement. Perhaps a gust of air blowing a newspaper? Or a cat, scavenging somewhere inside for rats?

He paused, listening again. There was no further sound. He carried on away from the building ... and then paused. He couldn't walk away without checking. Turning back, he moved into what had once been the reception area and tried to make out the layout within.

'Curtis?'

There was a reception booth directly ahead, wooden boards nailed across its frontage. On either side, a tiled corridor. Once the tiled walls had been a pristine blue and white; now they were covered in graffiti, cracked, crazed and smeared with filth. Litter and garbage covered the floors. Someone had started a fire in the left-hand corridor at some time in the past. The floor was littered with soot, ash and the remnants of a mattress, rusted coils and springs protruding from the mess. Harry chose the right-hand corridor, moving carefully.

'Curtis?'

There was a faint light at the end of the corridor, and when he reached the corner he could see why. Part of the roof had caved in here and was open to the sky. A criss-cross of rusted girders, rotted plasterboard and crumbling masonry formed a frame for the stars that studded a dark blue velvet expanse above. Standing at the end of the corridor, Harry could see right into this section of the leisure centre. There was a swimming pool here, perhaps fifty feet square, with changing cubicles along the far wall. No doubt it had been drained when the company who owned the place had gone bust. But since the roof had collapsed, exposing the interior to the elements, the pool had almost filled with rainwater. The stagnant, stinking water gleamed in the darkness, rubble, girders and other detritus jutting from the surface. Harry could hear the dripping echo of water somewhere, as if he had somehow emerged into a cave, the twisted and jagged silhouettes of the wreckage in the pool looking like contorted, bizarre stalagmites.

'Curtis?'

There was no one here.

He turned to go.

And something snapped past his cheek like an angry bee. He felt its sting, and recoiled in alarm.

'What the *hell*!'

He put his hand to his face and felt an abrasion, a long scratch that was somehow burning. Had he walked into something in the dark?

The bee zinged again, and this time something exploded from the tiled wall beside his head with an ear-splitting crack. Tiny particles stung his face. Instinctively, he ducked to his haunches. Confused, he searched the murky interior – and saw something flash in the darkness. This time, something snatched at his jacket, and he felt the same burning pain stab in his side. He knew now that someone was shooting at him. There had been no roaring detonations, no ratcheting echoes. But some fucker was *shooting* at him. He tried to scramble back round the corner of the corridor, on all fours, but had travelled several feet before he realised that he had missed it in the darkness. He was now heading along the stagnant poolside, deeper into the building. Another shot snap-cracked into the tiled wall.

'Jesus!'

Leaping to his feet, he ran full tilt down the poolside. The sounds of his flight were amplified in the enclosed space, and the building seemed full of clattering, crashing echoes. He knew that the next shot would slam him back against the stained wall, and then it would all be over. Fear tight in his chest, hyperventilating as he ran, Harry saw murky light crawling up ahead. It was reflecting from the surface of the stagnant pool on to a wall directly in his path. There was no way to turn but left, and that would take him around the edge of the pool and down towards where his attacker was standing. Harry hit the wall with the flat of both hands, not knowing which way to turn.

There was a shadow on the other side of the pool, darker than its surroundings. He cried out and dropped to his knees as another flare of light sparked from his attacker's silencer. The shot impacted on the wall behind him, ricocheting into the darkness in a series of screaming echoes. Harry flung himself flat. There was a girder protruding from the pool, two feet from where he lay. It projected four feet into the air from the surface of the water, and he tried to squirm around so that his body would be shielded by it. Calmly, as if it had all the time in the world, the shadow began to walk around the pool in his direction. Harry squirmed again, trying to head back in the direction he'd come, still trying to use the girder and its surrounding debris in the water as a shield. It was useless, and he knew it.

'Stop it!' yelled a voice from the other end of the swimming pool. 'For God's sake, *stop it*!'

Harry's head jerked up to see that another man-shaped shadow had materialised from the surrounding darkness. He knew from its posture that it was Jameson. Perhaps he had heard the commotion, or perhaps he had suddenly found the courage to follow him into the darkness? Harry saw across the pool that his attacker had paused and was looking back to where the vicar stood. There was a fearful sense of calm and control about the figure.

The echoes from Jameson's voice faded to nothingness.

'Stop it . . .' he said again in a small voice that still seemed to carry to where Harry lay.

The attacker's shadow raised an arm.

'Run, Jameson!'

This time Harry heard the pneumatic cough of the silencer, like a panther's sneeze.

'No!'

Jameson was flung back from the poolside, his spreadeagled body smacking against the tiled wall. For a second he seemed to hang in that cruciform position. When he fell, there was a wet stain darker than the shadows on the wall.

In terror, Harry scrambled on all fours, shrinking down behind the detritus in the pool. If he could get sufficient impetus, he could rise to a crouch and make a lunging dash back towards the corridor along which he had entered the building. Unhurried, the shadow on the other side of the pool turned from where Jameson lay and approached.

There was another shadow on the far side of the pool. Not far from where Jameson had fallen. It loomed out of the darker shadows with such impetus that Harry flinched, his foot skidding on the poolside. There were *two* of them, and now he was trapped. As he fell heavily, the bulky shadow reared and ran towards the man with the gun. The new shadow was holding something in its hand, something that looked like a length of wood or a rusted pipe. Breath knocked from his lungs, pain burning in his side, Harry saw his attacker's shadow suddenly pause and look back towards the new shadow which pursued it.

'Bastard!' yelled Curtis, flinging the pipe or the wood as the man with the gun raised his arm and fired again. Curtis's shadow vanished in the jumbled darkness and the projectile whirled end over end in the shadows. Harry's attacker sidestepped, but was not quick enough. The projectile clipped his shoulder and he cursed in pain. But the movement had caused his foot to skid on the cracked tiles. Its footing momentarily lost, the shadow pinwheeled and stumbled. Clumsily, it stumbled awkwardly again, one foot going over the edge of the swimming pool. With another loud cry of surprise, it plunged sideways into the water.

Stagnant water flurried in the air as the figure struggled to rise.

Harry tried to get up, but was still winded. He managed to get to his knees and tried to brace himself for a run to safety. But luck still eluded him. This end of the pool had been the shallow end. Although filled with wreckage, the water here was no more than knee deep. And as Harry looked, he saw the shadow stand up, cursing and shaking water from itself.

It still had the gun in its hand.

Standing erect, the figure fixed on where Harry lay, not twenty feet away. There was no girder or wreckage to hide behind. It was a clear sight-line between Harry and his attacker.

Calmly, the figure trudged through the foaming, stagnant water towards him.

As it came, it raised its gun hand. It took care with each measured and deadly step, not wanting to stumble on anything under the water.

Harry could see only the hand, levelled at him, as his

attacker closed the gap between them. He moved with such grim determination that Harry froze where he lay.

The outstretched hand, with the gun – ready to spit fire.

Fire.

And Harry could see his own hands now, burning, as he clawed at the wreckage of their car, trying to free Jean and Hilary and Diane. And God, oh God, how he wanted those hands to save them. How he screamed and prayed as those hands burned. And he could see those same hands as they caressed Felix, the dog; saw the animal's smouldering body with the handprint and knew ... knew then ...

Squirming to one side, Harry yanked the glove from his right hand.

Somehow, even though he could not see it, he was sure that the figure was smiling.

Lunging over the poolside but keeping one arm and leg braced so that he did not fall over the edge, Harry plunged his uncovered right hand into the water with a fierce and feral cry.

Instantly, the derelict building was lit by a blinding blue-white flash.

Sparks leapt and exploded from the wreckage and girders and fallen masonry that jutted from the surface of the pool, bouncing and ricocheting from the walls and floor and the hissing surface of the water like an indoor firework display gone horribly wrong. Harry felt the power surging from his hand, the water forming a direct conductor to the body of his attacker.

In the middle of the pool, Harry's attacker jerked and spasmed maniacally. The gun flew from his wildly flailing body. Harry peered up through the pyrotechnics just as his attacker's hair erupted in flame, enshrouding his head and obliterating the features. The figure's jacket smouldered, great gouts of blue-black smoke erupting from the sleeves and the shoulders and around the figure's neck. The building was filled with the hissing crackle of a terrifying, expended energy, the blue-black and white flashes lighting the hellish scene as if from the windows of an express train thundering past.

Harry kept his hand in the water.

The figure twitched and flailed and jerked like a burning marionette, kept on its feet in the water by the power that surged through it.

At last, Harry pulled his hand out and rolled away from the edge.

The noise and the light were instantly gone. There was a soft splash as the smoking body fell lifelessly back into the water.

Harry rose to his knees and gagged at the hideous smell of burning and the waves of smoke and steam that drifted up through the ragged hole in the ceiling from the surface of the water below. Moving on his knees to the wall, he tried to rise, but had no strength. From the other side of the pool, he heard coughing, and looked back to see a familiar silhouette waving its arms through the smoke as it blundered around the edge of the pool in his direction. Curtis's attention remained fixed on the floating man-shaped mass in the water as he approached. When he reached Harry, he stood over him, one hand braced against the wall and looking back at the pool.

'I don't . . . I mean I can't . . . I mean, bloody *hell*, Stark.'

'Jameson . . . ?'

'Dead. Jesus, he's dead. And it's my fault. I should have listened to you.'

Harry looked up to see that the newspaperman had a bad gash in his head. The blood had seeped down through his hairline and soaked one side of his face. Harry gingerly felt his side again. Blood glinted dark on his fingers when he looked. But it seemed that, just as the first bullet had cut a burning groove in his cheek, this bullet hadn't penetrated his side. It had carved a bloody furrow.

'He must have brained me. When I woke up, I was staring into the barrel of a fucking gun. I swear . . . I *swear* he was just about to pull the trigger when he heard you. When he left me, I just played dead. Waited for a chance. Christ, Stark . . . what did you *do* to him?'

'What's the hit-man jargon?' said Harry in a flat voice. 'I burned him.'

'You can say *that* again.'

'Help me up . . .'
'On one condition.'
'And what's that?'
'You put your glove back on.'

Curtis slept like a dead man.

He could not believe, after what he'd been through, that sleep could have come so easily. O'Farrell's clear intent to do away with him was threat enough to have him watching every corner and every shadow of the room until morning came. But he slept anyway after he'd cleaned up the gash on his head, and when he finally came round he saw that it was well into the afternoon. Harry was lying on the sofa-bed again, and for one bizarre moment it was as if Curtis had never left the room, never gone to the leisure centre on that ill-fated mission. He could not fool himself, however, that it had all been a dream. Struggling to his feet, he grimaced at the sour taste of last night's whisky and headed for the bathroom.

Having cleaned his teeth, he moved into the kitchen with the idea of making something to eat. And then he remembered Jameson, and the ugly stain that had been left on the tiled wall. The memory cramped his stomach, an ugly knot of anxiety that killed any need for food. The vicar shouldn't have come. He hadn't asked him to come. The greedy shit had taken O'Farrell's money and assisted with a kidnap. The way he had started to crack apart at the seams, it was surely only a matter of time before O'Farrell made a move to have him eliminated. Why, then, did Curtis feel so sickeningly guilty about his death?

He moved back into the living room and glanced at Stark. He was looking worse all the time. The grey-white face was pinched and drawn. The hollows under the eyes were more pronounced. Could it be that using his power had sapped his vitality even further? Until last night, Curtis hadn't seen evidence of that power, but Stark's pyrotechnic display had been the final proof – if proof were needed – of the veracity of this whole crazy story. He stood looking at the unconscious figure, wondering whether he should leave him or let him sleep longer.

A winking light on the telephone answering machine drew his eye. Fear turned in his stomach. He had underestimated O'Farrell very badly. The ease with which he had been able to trace his address bore testimony to that. After the horror of last night, was this a further development? He moved to the machine and pressed 'play'.

'You are not Mr Popularity with the Boss, Anthony.' It was Brenda, from the office. 'Now YOU know what you're doing, and I know what you're doing. But if HE knows what you're doing . . . ? Need I say more? For the record, I told him you'd phoned in sick, so that gives you two or three days. After that, you're on your own. Needless to say, this will cost you a packet in the favours stakes . . .'

The message finished.

'Brenda, you're the best.'

What now? The police? Two dead men in a derelict building. How long would it be before someone found them? Or would O'Farrell organise a clean-up job? Things were out of control. Stark had been right from the beginning. It was time to hand everything over to the authorities, no matter what. Curtis wanted the story, but he had almost ended up dead. And no story was worth that risk.

There was a knock on the front door.

This time, the fear was so real that Curtis felt as if he might throw up. He turned to look at the door, wanting it to be some other sound: someone tripping in the corridor, or something being dropped, or a landing window banging shut. Anything but . . .

The knocking came again, sharp and urgent.

Curtis took a step forward, not certain what to do. Should he keep quiet and pretend there was no one at home? What if O'Farrell had found out about last night and sent someone around to finish the job? On the bed, Harry groaned and began to rise. Curtis held out his hands imploringly, but Harry's eyes were closed. He rubbed his eyes, this time hearing the insistent knocking.

'Mr Curtis?' It was a woman's voice.

'Who . . . ?' began Harry.

Curtis waved his hands in front of Harry's face to quieten him.

'Mr Curtis, it's Sheila Russell. Martin's wife. I need to talk to you.'

Curtis moved quickly to the door.

'Are you alone?'

'No.'

'Who's with you?'

'It's a complicated story. Please let us in.'

'Let them in,' said Harry.

'Oh yeah?' whispered Curtis, turning back to look at him. 'Have you forgotten what O'Farrell tried to do to us last night? What if someone's got a gun in her back?'

There was a peculiar intensity in Harry's eyes. He still looked like death, but it was as if he had suddenly found new reserves of energy. Curtis started to object again, but was halted by his expression. Did Harry somehow *know* who was on the other side of the door?

'Open it.'

Reluctantly, and with as nonchalant an effort as he could muster, Curtis threw the door open.

Sheila Russell was startled by the sudden opening. She was clutching the piece of paper that Curtis had shoved under her front door as if it were some kind of protective charm. She held it out to him as if it explained her presence. Curtis stood aside to let her enter, and then saw the young woman who was standing behind her. Something about her face startled him. There was no actual resemblance to Harry Stark, but this woman also had the same parchment-coloured skin, and the hollows under the eyes, as if she were suffering from the same malaise. Sheila turned to look back at the girl, urging her to follow.

'Jesus,' said Curtis, closing the door behind them and suddenly putting it all together. 'You're one of the motorway crash survivors.'

The girl didn't speak as she entered the room, did not even seem to register Curtis's presence. Her attention was centred on the man who had risen from the sofa-bed.

'Yes,' said Sheila. 'This is Mercy. She was the hitch-hiker who saved my husband.'

'What . . . ? I mean, how did you find her? I didn't think we were going to do it.'

'I didn't find her. She found us. Martin gave her our address before she left. Look, Mr Curtis . . . can I sit down? I'm not feeling too well, and I'm very, *very* worried about . . .'

'Yes, yes. Please.' Curtis pulled up two chairs. Sheila sat gratefully, but Mercy ignored his offer and remained standing, looking across the room at Harry. 'Tell me . . . us . . . all about it.'

'Mercy arrived last night. She's been driving for a long time. From down South, I mean. We had a long talk last night. And some of the things she's told me were . . . well, they didn't make a lot of sense. But she wanted to see Martin, and, well . . . her arrival has just focused something else. Something that's been worrying me dreadfully . . .'

'Your husband's gone away. To a religious order, where he can carry out his healing without interference.'

'How do you know that?' asked Sheila, alarmed.

'Because the Reverend Jameson confided in us, told us everything.'

At the mention of the vicar's name, it seemed that a floodgate had been opened up in Sheila. 'What's wrong with him? I telephoned him after you tried to see him. He didn't sound right. The things he said. As if something had gone terribly wrong, when he'd always been so much in control before. I was supposed to get a telephone call from Martin, to let me know that everything was all right. But I've heard *nothing*, Mr Curtis. And now I can't get in touch with the Reverend Jameson any more. He won't answer his telephone, but he told me that he would *definitely* . . .'

'He's dead, Mrs Russell.'

Sheila looked at him as if he'd gone mad.

'I'm sorry, but it's true. What he told you . . . about the religious order . . . wasn't true, I'm afraid. Your husband has been kidnapped. And the man responsible killed Reverend Jameson, and tried to kill Mr Stark and myself last night. We're going to have to let the police . . .'

'Midnight,' said Mercy.

'What?' Curtis looked up, to see that the young woman was still staring across the room at Stark. 'What did you say?'

Something was happening.

Mercy's eyes were glazed. Her hands were held at her side as if she had sleep-walked into his apartment. Sheila also saw that something was wrong, rose to her feet and took one of Mercy's arms.

'What is it, love? Come on, sit down. You must be exhausted after everything you've been through . . .'

'Just after midnight,' said Harry from the other side of the room. 'Just after midnight, tonight.'

Curtis looked at Harry to see that he had the same glazed expression on his face. Trance-like, his eyes were fixed on Mercy.

The same white faces, the same hollows under the eyes.

And Curtis suddenly became aware of the subtle change in the atmosphere of his room. He could feel something, barely tangible but real. As if there were a generator of some kind here, giving off a vibration that could not be heard, only sensed. But the energy was real, and it was here now, somehow in the air between Mercy and Harry. Sheila started to say something; Curtis saw the growing look of fear in her eyes, and carefully guided her away from Mercy to another chair in the corner of the room. At that moment, he remembered that night in the casualty department of Eastleigh Hospital, when the bizarre power had surged and the survivors of the crash had stood looking at each other while something inside each one of them communicated with the others.

It was happening again now, between Mercy and Harry. Their proximity had generated something.

'Mr Curtis?' Sheila Russell sounded on the verge of tears. 'What's *happening*?'

Curtis looked from Mercy to Harry, and back again. He sat next to Sheila, without taking his eyes off the two people in the middle of the room.

'There's a lot I have to tell you, Mrs Russell.'

'I don't understand . . .'

'There's a lot I don't understand either. But listen to me . . .'

Curtis shuddered. He could feel the fine hair on the nape of his neck prickling in the presence of this strange and unknown energy.

'. . . there's a *lot* I have to tell you.'

He spoke softly.

In the middle of the room, the things inside Mercy and Harry remained in silent communication.

'Midnight,' said Burwell, reeling through the park under-growth, the bottle of vodka halfway to his lips. He had been out all night, had bought himself another bottle at a supermarket, and supposed that it was mid-afternoon, although he had no idea. His wristwatch had been lost somewhere along the way, but he didn't give a damn. Puzzled, he lowered the bottle and wondered why that word had come into his mind. Shaking his head, he raised the bottle again and . . .

Chris looked up from the steering wheel to the rear-view mirror. Roger was slumped in the back seat. He had been feeling ill before they set off and Chris had insisted that he try and get some sleep. He looked terrible.

'What did you say?'

Roger grunted, rubbing a hand over his white face.

'What?'

'You said something about "just after midnight".'

'Did I?'

'Go back to sleep, Roger. We're nearly there.'

'Sleep . . . Right . . .'

Chris turned his attention back to the road, as . . .

Jane Teal's lips moved in her sleep, but not enough to register anything on the monitors beside her bed, or to alert the nurse on night duty as . . .

Martin Russell tried to rise from his bed. A hand slammed him back to the mattress as the injection was prepared.

'Just . . .' mumbled Martin.

'Just shut up,' said a harsh voice, holding his limp arm as

the other figure approached with the hypodermic. 'You've got a busy day tomorrow.'

'Busy day,' grinned Martin.

'That's right, you dopey fucker.'

'After midnight.'

'Never mind the time, Martin. You just be a good boy and do as you're told.'

Martin didn't feel the needle in his arm.

He returned to sleep as . . .

The thing felt something dragging it from the fearful torpor it experienced during the day. It was the sound of familiar voices, somehow near, but as soon as it awoke they receded into the darkness. Terrified, it struggled to rise inside its makeshift hide. Had it received the call? Was it time to go back?

'Wait . . . wait!'

It erupted from the hide, its ravaged head and shoulders thrusting out into the hated daylight. It raised claw-hands to its face and tried to see where the voices had come from. But even as it struggled to look, the voices faded away.

'Come back! Please, don't leave me!'

There was no answering cry. Only the rush of the vehicles that travelled along the road, but were not aware of the thing set back from the motorway. Had it missed its chance? How long would it have to wait before they came again?

'Please . . .'

Unable to bear the daylight any longer, it slumped back into the hide, covering its head with its skeletal claw-hands. Thin shafts of light speared through the darkness. Miserably, straining to listen, the thing grabbed handfuls of detritus and shrub and set about repairing the damage to the roof only inches above its head.

'. . . please . . .'

'Is this it?'

Chris looked back to where Roger was sprawled, folding up the street map at last. They'd had no trouble getting to Newcastle; it was a straight enough route, but they had got lost in the suburbs. There had been new development since the map had been published, adding to their difficulties, and Chris had been forced to stop several times to ask for directions. At last, they had found Curtis's apartment.

'This is it. But Roger, maybe we should find . . .'

'Please, don't say it again. I don't know what the hell's wrong, but I can just feel in my gut that a doctor isn't going to be able to help me.'

'You don't *know* that. This bloody story of Curtis's . . .'

'I need to know what's going on, before anything else. Come on, let's get on with it.' Roger fumbled at the door handle, but was so weak that he could barely turn it. Quickly, Chris climbed out and helped him from the car. Was it possible for him to have lost so much weight in two days? His arms felt thin. Keeping hold of one arm, he steered him to the main entrance of the apartment. There was no controlled-entry system here, and they pushed through into a communal stairwell.

'Third floor, I think,' said Chris, looking at Roger with concern. 'Can you make it?'

Roger just looked at him. They started up, the sounds of their progress echoing preternaturally loud from concrete stairs and iron balustrades. On the first landing, Roger had to pause for breath. Halfway up the third flight of stairs, he suddenly stopped. Chris hung on, waiting for him to recover before they continued. Then he saw the strange expression on his brother's face.

'What is it? What's wrong?'

'I . . . I don't know. I feel . . . peculiar.'

'You're overdoing it. Wait here. I'll go up and get someone to give me a hand. We'll carry you the rest of the way.'

'No, I don't mean that. I mean . . . something is happening, or going to happen, when we get to Curtis's place.'

'What do you mean?'

'I don't know, Chris. Just . . . something.'

Roger took several deep breaths and then started up once more. It took them almost ten minutes to reach the third landing. Curtis lived at 34(d). The first door along the corridor was number 30. No more than a few yards past the door, hunting for the right apartment, Roger stopped again.

When Chris looked at his face this time, he could see fear clearly etched on his brother's features. The sight of it filled him with an unreasoning apprehension about what they were going to find when they got there.

Roger drew a deep breath and allowed himself to be led on to 34(d).

Chris paused in the act of knocking. Were all the answers on the other side?

And suddenly the door was flung wide.

Chris recoiled in shock.

'Jesus,' said the bearded man who had suddenly appeared. Clearly astonished, he turned back to someone in the room. 'You were right. They *did* sense someone outside.'

Before Chris could react, Roger had suddenly pushed past him into the apartment. The bearded man let him in, then turned to Chris.

'You'd better come in.'

'Curtis?'

'That's me. But quick, before anyone sees you.'

Inside, Chris was instantly confused. A middle-aged man was sitting on what seemed to be a sofa-bed. There was a younger woman sitting next to him. In the far corner, a woman in her late fifties was sitting with her hands in her lap like a nervous patient in a dentist's surgery. Roger had moved to stand in front of the couple sitting on the sofa-bed. Chris remained at the door as the man called Curtis stood beside him, watching.

Chris waited for someone to say something.

Everyone in the room remained silent in a bizarre tableau.

'Would someone mind telling me what . . . ?'

'Quiet,' demanded Curtis, cutting Chris off. He was aware that the bearded man was waiting for something to happen. Angered, he looked over at Roger who was still standing, looking down at the couple on the edge of the bed. They stared up at him.

'Roger, what the hell is going on? Do you *know* these people?'

'Please,' said Curtis, putting a hand on his arm.

Chris angrily shook it off. 'This is fucking ridiculous! We've come a long way. The least we expect is some answers.'

'You'll get them. Believe me. But I just need to see if they'll . . .'

'It's happening,' said the woman from the corner. 'I can feel it again. They're starting to talk to each other.'

Curtis left Chris where he was standing and hurried to join the woman, so that he could get a better look at the three faces. Impatiently, Chris followed him.

'Yes,' said Curtis, again without taking his eyes off them. 'I can feel it. It's like . . . I don't know . . . static electricity or something. But it's stronger now that O'Dowd's here. It's as if their abilities to communicate with each other are enhanced now that there are three. I think . . . I think they're growing stronger. Building themselves up for the time when they'll need to escape, and go back.'

'Roger, would you tell me what in hell you're doing?'

Chris put a hand out to touch his brother. Curtis called out in alarm, but the next instant Chris pulled his hand away as if he'd received a mild electric shock. He moved around to get a better look at his brother. He seemed to be in a trance, staring down at the other two. Suddenly he could see a similarity in the expressions on all three faces which chilled him. No, not on the faces after all. It was the unhealthy pallor of the skin and the hollowed eyes. Were they all suffering from the same illness, whatever in hell it might be?

'They're survivors,' said Curtis, reading his mind. 'Your brother, and the two on the sofa-bed. Harry Stark and Mercy Something-or-other. They're communing with each other now. They won't be able to hear you.'

'Roger!'

'It's no use, believe me. These two have been like that for over an hour. Just a few minutes ago, they stopped staring at each other and began staring at the door. They knew that Roger was on his way up.'

'Someone has a lot of explaining to do.'

'Well, that seems to be my job,' said Curtis. 'But I've had a bad enough time with Sheila here already. I'm not sure you'll take it all in.'

'I believe you,' said the woman, looking at Curtis.

Chris looked at her.

'Oh, I'm sorry,' said Curtis. 'This is Sheila Russell, the wife of Martin Russell. Another survivor of the motorway crash. And therein lies one hell of a problem for us. Getting to Martin Russell, that is.'

'He has a power,' said Sheila in a small voice. 'In his hands.'

'His *hands*?'

'They all have a power,' continued Curtis. 'Just like your brother.'

'He said he'd killed someone. With one of his *paintings*, for God's sake.'

'Then he probably did.'

'Wait. Wait a moment. This is too much. Would someone like to start from the beginning and tell me what . . . ?'

Suddenly, Harry Stark turned to look at Curtis. The movement was as slow and deliberate as that of a marionette. Curtis froze, looking at Harry's glassy eyes. As he watched, the glaze seemed to dissipate, the eyes focusing on him for the first time in more than an hour.

'Harry?'

'Water,' said Harry weakly, licking his lips and rubbing a hand across his face.

'We'll . . . we'll all need water. Lots of it. We're not . . . not finished.'

'I'll get it,' said Sheila nervously, heading for the kitchen.

'Harry, what's happening? What are you all *talking* about?'

'I don't have . . . Christ, I'm dry . . . don't have a lot of time. They still have a lot to do, building each other up. Getting strong. But listen, Curtis. Listen *very* carefully! Tonight is the only time it can be done. Just after midnight. Round about the time the crash happened. It doesn't have to be the exact time, but *definitely* before twelve thirty . . .'

'You're not making sense.'

'Just *listen*, and don't ask any more questions! Tonight, between midnight and twelve thirty, is the one and only chance they've got to go back again. The weather conditions here, the conditions over there – whatever they might be – will be almost the same as on the night of the crash. All the survivors have to be at the point of impact, on that motorway. If any one of us *isn't* there for what they're calling the bonding, then it won't work. We'll all die. After twelve thirty, the rift that exists between the two realities will have closed. And there'll never be another chance. We have to get all the survivors there before then. But listen, Curtis. George MacGowan, the hybrid thing that he's become, is the most important one of all. The power of the Storm Between is still in him. They need that power to make the jump back.'

'How the hell am I going to find him? Or the other guy we know nothing about? Or Russell, come to that? All *that*, before half past twelve tonight. You're joking.'

'Shut up and listen. They're stronger now that there are three. But they need another survivor, a fourth, to make "the Call".'

'The what?'

'If we get four of the survivors together, they can make a call. I don't know what that means, exactly. But in my mind I'm getting an impression of something that's like a psychic distress signal. The others will hear it, wherever they are. And they'll know what it is and what they have to do. They'll come to where the "call" originates from, they'll be drawn to find the others. But the three of us here aren't strong enough. We need a fourth.'

'What do you want me to do?'

'You'll have to get Jane Teal, Curtis. Whether she's comatose or not. You'll have to get her and bring her here.'

'You mean *kidnap* her from the hospital?'

'I mean *get* her, Curtis. It's vital. Vital that . . . that . . .'

'Here's the water,' said Sheila, bringing a tray with a pitcher and glasses.

'Curtis?'

Harry's eyes had glazed over again, his words drifting away as he turned to look back at the other two. Sheila brought the tray to the sofa-bed, put it on the mattress and poured out three glasses.

Chris watched astonished as, without breaking their joint gaze, Roger and the two others took the glasses and drank greedily. When they were empty, Sheila looked at Curtis. He nodded, and she poured again.

Again, they drank.

'What the *hell* were you talking about?' asked Chris at last.

Curtis gave a weary sigh. 'Had any experience of kidnapping?'

'*What?*'

'Here we go again. Just listen. Once upon a time . . .'

What am I doing? thought Curtis as he continued on down the hospital corridor, head lowered but eyes fixed ahead for the 'Ward Seven' sign. *What in God's name am I doing here?*

Directly ahead, a nurse turned a corner and headed straight towards him. Lowering his eyes, Curtis began to work at the surgeon's cap as if he were having trouble with the fastening. His forearms masked his face as the nurse passed.

Last night someone tried to kill me. Today I'm about to kidnap someone. Is this really worth the story you think you're going to get, Curtis? What happens if you're stopped in the act? What happens if you're arrested? How's that going to look for you?

Hospital security had been stepped up in recent months. A spate of child-snatching incidents nationally and a stabbing in a London hospital had made hospitals more vigilant. And Curtis suspected that Eastleigh hospital was being much more vigilant than anyone else these days after what had happened there. There was a security guard at the main entrance and it seemed that visitors were being monitored at the main entrance.

But no one seemed to have given a thought to the loading depot at the rear of the hospital where hospital supplies were delivered. There were two lorries parked in there when Curtis slipped through the rear gates, and no sign of their drivers or any hospital workers supervising delivery. The lorries had provided a perfect 'cover' for Curtis as he'd slipped through the loading bay doors, thanking God that he wasn't going to have to shin up any drainpipes, after all. His car was parked several streets away, and he'd already taken off his trademark anorak then, throwing it in the boot as he'd taken out the holdall. Rolling up his shirt-sleeves had provided that casual touch which belied his nervousness. After all, everyone was sweating in this weather, weren't they? The difference for him was that he was sweating with fear. There was no one in the loading bay. Moving quickly, he unzipped the holdall and took out its contents: a standard hospital issue white coat and surgical mask. Back in his apartment, Curtis had managed to acquire a whole wardrobe of 'official' uniforms from gas inspectors to train guards, all of which had served him well over the years. Slipping on the white jacket, Curtis had shoved the disposable holdall into a corner of the loading bay and entered the hospital through the heavy duty rubber and Plexiglas doors. Once inside and unchallenged, it seemed that his presence there was unquestioned. Three doctors, two nurses and numerous visitors had passed him without acknowledgement or comment.

Still sweating, Curtis followed the signs for 'Intensive Care'.

You can't go through with your plan. It might affect other patients. What about that, you heartless bastard? And then, the other voice inside. The voice that had seen the world's pain and tried to make some kind of sense out of it all in his reports. *The doctors and nurses in here are well trained. They'll know how to react. Nobody will suffer. By the time they find out that there's nothing wrong, I'll be long gone.*

Curtis saw the sign up ahead. As he approached, the double doors opened and another nurse headed his way.

'Good morning,' he said, pushing through as she passed him. It was a dangerous chance to take, speaking to her, but Curtis needed it for the confidence that would follow. And he needed all the confidence he could muster to go through with the plan he had in mind.

''Morning,' replied the nurse absently, as she passed on.

Pausing on the other side of the double-doors, Curtis quickly looked around. A short corridor leading to the Nurses' Enquiry desk, where one nurse was currently talking to someone on the telephone, and therefore oblivious to him. Behind her, a large white noticeboard. Although he couldn't read what was on that board from here, he knew from previous experience that it would contain a list of patients on the ward and important 'care' notes for those nurses arriving to relieve their colleagues on duty. Head down, Curtis walked quickly down the corridor, praying that the nurse would stay on the telephone.

As he reached the end of the short corridor, Curtis saw what he wanted on the right hand wall. It was at shoulder-height, and perfectly placed for what he had in mind. Passing the nurse behind the desk, he glanced at the notice board. There were five patients in intensive care. One of them was Jane Teal – in Room Nine.

And what if one or all of the other four have a relapse because of what you're about to do? What then?

Room Five . . . and the nurse was still on the telephone . . . Room Seven, a nurse tending to someone in there . . . and there was a Day Room, its television playing to no one . . . Room Eight, its blinds drawn . . . and the nurse was still on the telephone . . . Room Nine.

The blinds were drawn.

Did that mean that someone was in there, treating her?

Curtis looked back. The nurse picked up some paperwork and moved out of sight.

Give it up, Curtis. Give it up before they lock you up and throw away the key. And then the other voice: *You've got a room full of Survivors back home. A room full of what Stark calls 'Travellers'. There's another one in here. And once you've got her out of this place, that'll be another part of the jigsaw in place, another step in the right direction. Another . . . another . . .* And then the first voice, intruding once more. *Another development in the story that you're helping to create. Anthony Curtis, Ace Reporter, on the trail of the Story of the Century.*

Gritting his teeth, Curtis knocked and pushed the door open.

Jane Teal was lying in bed, apparently asleep. There was an

intravenous drip in her arm. She looked calm and composed. But there was no one else in the room with her. Quickly closing the door again, Curtis headed back the way he had come.

Room eight . . . room seven . . . room six . . . room five . . .

And the nurse had gone from sight. He could hear her moving around in a kitchen not far from the desk.

Curtis moved to the left hand wall, his attention centred on what he had first seen on entering. Looking back in the direction of the kitchen, he paused.

Now, or never.

Drawing a deep breath, he raised one elbow – and jabbed it hard at the glass fire-alarm disc set into the wall. The glass *crumped!* and in the next instant, the fire klaxons were sounding shrill all over the complex. Instantly too, the nurse came out of the kitchen into the corridor, and the doctor and nurse in Room Seven appeared anxiously at the doorway.

Jerking forward as if he had suddenly burst through the main doors, Curtis found a sight-line where he could be seen by all three.

'Quick!' he hissed. 'There's a fire. We've got to get them all out of here!'

Afterwards, when Curtis had gone, Chris finally gave in and decided to have the drink that had been proffered. Curtis seemed to have taken his responsibilities as a hard-drinking newspaperman seriously. In deference to the cliché, he had the best-stocked drinks cabinet Chris had ever seen.

When he'd poured, he looked across at Sheila Russell, wondering whether he should offer. But her demeanour precluded it. Chris drank and looked at the silent three in the middle of the room. Harry Stark and Mercy sat on the bed, and Chris had eventually pushed a chair against the back of Roger's legs until he'd sat on it, facing them. The pattern of their silent conversation/observation seemed to recycle itself in regular phases. Harry looking at Mercy looking at Roger looking at Harry. After a quarter of an hour or so, at some kind of invisible agreement, they'd switch: Harry looking at Roger looking at Mercy looking at Harry. After another fifteen minutes, they'd switch back. Every time Sheila moved to fill their water glasses, they'd drink without taking their eyes off each other. Visits to the bathroom seemed to be unnecessary.

'Do you believe all this?' asked Chris at last, when the silence became unbearable.

Sheila looked up calmly. 'Some of it.'

'Which parts?'

'I believe that Martin's been taken against his will by the man called O'Farrell. That the Reverend Jameson had something to do with it, and now he's dead. I believe that Martin has a special power of healing, because I've seen it . . .'

Chris snorted in disdain, drinking again.

'You mean your husband's suddenly a miracle worker?'

'You asked me what I believe. I'm telling you. What *you* believe is up to you.'

'What else do you believe?'

'That these other people here have also somehow gained powers.'

'Yeah, yeah. Aliens from outer space have got into their heads!' Chris drank again. The whisky suddenly tasted bitter.

'I don't believe that. And neither does Curtis. You heard what he had to say, about Mr Stark's *feelings*. But you asked me what I believe. So I'll tell you that I don't believe that part of it. About what's in the survivors, and in my Martin.'

'So what *do* you believe?'

'That the power comes from God.'

Chris poured another drink and grimaced. 'Know what I think? That's even crazier than the bug-eyed aliens from space theory.'

'You asked my opinion. That's it. All I want is for Martin to be home and safe again. Whatever Mr Curtis believes, I think he can help.'

'How can the so-called power that's in Mercy be from God? If God's supposed to be all-loving and caring, how come he gave her the power to burn up those people the way she told you?'

'They were evil . . .'

'Oh, here we go. A "vengeance is mine, saith the Lord" speech.'

'You're angry because you're frightened.'

'Too true I'm frightened. I'm just supposed to swallow all this stuff. Roger! For God's sake, speak to me.' Chris moved to touch him, then remembered what had happened last time. 'For God's sake . . .'

'Yes,' said Sheila quietly.

Exasperated, Chris turned away angrily.

And then there was a quiet knock on the door.

'Not before time.' Chris strode to it. 'Let's have another party guest, even if we have to *kidnap* someone . . .'

He swung the door wide.

And then the rules of the party changed entirely.

Ellis Burwell knew that he was dying.

At first, the instinctive knowledge had filled him with a mean-spirited rage. He had fought it with the angry ambition that had fuelled him since the day Klark had died. Now even the hateful frustration that had consumed him at his not being able to wield his power in any effective way had dimmed. With a pint of vodka inside him, he had staggered to a park bench. Many hours ago, a park attendant had advised the police that he'd found a vagrant on another bench a half-mile away, dead of liver failure. The police who had carted the body away had not questioned his less-than-expert advice.

Ellis had slept, the alcohol taking him to a place inside that promised rest and restitution. When he awoke, the needs of his unknown inner traveller had taken from the vodka everything that it needed, to the extent that he had no hangover.

But he *knew* that he was dying.

The vodka bottle was still cradled in his lap. He had slept sitting upright, head bowed. The day had waned. Long, deep shadows were stretching across the green lawns before him from the trees at the western periphery of the public park. Kids were still playing football in the now-muted warmth of the heat-wave. Their shadows leaped and danced smoothly in pursuit of the ball. Their cries of effort and joy were utterly alien to Burwell. He lifted the bottle and held it up before him. The sinking sun made the remaining liquid spark. He

did not want what was in there. But something deep inside –
something that needed no false elation, only a chemical fixative
– demanded that he drink.

He finished the contents in one swallow, then threw the
bottle over his head.

He was free of Klark, the single greatest problem he'd ever
faced. That alone should please him. But he was not pleased.
He'd been given something special, and asked no questions in
case the magic went away. But what good was the power he
had been given if he couldn't use it? He pushed himself up from
the bench, cursed at the playing kids, and staggered off into the
lengthening shadows.

He needed more alcohol, but when he fumbled in his pocket
for moncy, he discovered that he only had loose change. It
seemed that the discovery was having an instant physical effect
on him. There was a cramp in his stomach which seemed to
flood his entire body. Burwell staggered, feeling nauseous but
unable to throw anything up.

*There's something inside me. Something to do with the
power*.

For the first time, he became aware of another presence,
hidden deep down inside. The revelation was terrifying. He
sank to his knees on the grass, screened from the playing kids
now by a border of bushes.

I'll die here. And no one will ever know . . .

A feeling of desolation overwhelmed him, bringing tears
of self-pity. But before he could embrace the emotion, the
thing inside *turned over* again. Burwell hugged his midriff,
moaning. With that last movement, he also became aware of
the thing's own pain. These physical symptoms were somehow
a side effect of whatever the thing inside was suffering. It was
trying to break loose, trying to be free of him. Aware now of
what kind of host it had chosen, dimly aware of how he had
used the power of the Storm Between to further his own ends,
and needing to be free of this hideous entrapment. But more
– the thing inside was reacting in desperation to something
else . . . to something that was happening, even now, to its
companions. It had been roused by the distant knowledge that

other travellers were attempting to unify, attempting to pool
their strength to allow them all to . . . to . . .

'Return . . .' moaned Burwell.

With that one utterance, he had an inner flash of realisation
and emotion. The *others* had somehow communicated a hideous sense of urgency. That had stirred the thing within into
its spasms, but worse . . . those others had somehow been
prevented from doing what they had to do, and that realisation
was causing the thing's pain.

The thing's pain muted, as if it were forcing itself to remain
calm. Breathing heavily, Burwell also felt his own physical
discomfort begin to ease.

Get up . . .

There were no words, but the intent of the thing inside was
clear. The trauma had brought it closer to the surface than
it had ever been before. Now it could exert the same kind of
influence that Harry Stark had endured.

'What . . . ?'

Get UP!

Pain stabbed again, this time directly from the thing, which
was using it like a goad.

'*Christ!*'

Burwell staggered to his feet again as the pain ebbed.

There's another nearby. In worse pain. Find it . . . him.

'I'm drunk, that's all. Delirium tremens. I'm not really hearing
voices. I'm just ill . . . that's all. Just ill . . .'

FIND HIM!

Moaning, Burwell staggered away through the park into the
creeping night as the thing inside struggled to find the scent of
the other survivor which . . .

*. . . thrashed and moaned in the makeshift hide beside the
motorway. Its ravaged hands covered its head, where the thin
needles of daylight had pierced the cage. These needles were not
as sharp or as painful as before. It was late afternoon, and the
thing knew that the darkness would come again eventually. But
it was still in mental agony. In its horribly mutated symbiosis,
it could not make sense of the new sense of urgency that had*

suddenly descended upon it. Its two identities fused, the thing was already in a torment of psychic agony. Beyond physical pain, it began to tear at its ravaged head when this new fear suddenly overwhelmed it.

'. . . coming . . .' it moaned through its hideously shredded mouth.

It took the claw-hands away from its head and fearfully looked up at the hole in the hide. The hateful light was still there, although it was dimming.

'Someone's coming . . .'

It wanted to burst out of the hide and rush towards whoever or whatever was now coming its way. It imprisonment in this terrible place was nearly over.

'Go away!' the thing hissed at the needles of light. And then, quickly and fearfully, it put a claw over its shredded mouth, hoping that its rescuer would not hear it and misunderstand.

Moaning, the thing put its claws over its head again.

The waiting was unbearable.

'. . . must get to the others,' mumbled Jane, and Curtis looked up in alarm from where he was manoeuvring the trolley.

The damn thing had jammed in the double doors and he looked anxiously back down the corridor to make sure that the two nurses who had quickly transferred her from her hospital bed could not see what he was trying to do. Using the anxiety that was being fuelled by the insistent ringing of the fire alarm, Curtis had managed to convince them that he was a male nurse, had almost panicked when he'd seen that the intravenous drip was going to have to be moved. But one of the nurses had seen to that, and when she'd snapped at him: 'Right, standard procedure! Exit B!' Curtis had snapped back 'Right!' and shoved Jane Teal and the drip-stand out of her room and through the double doors through which he'd originally entered. Similar procedures were being repeated with the other patients in intensive care, and even as two grim-faced doctors held the double doors open for him, Curtis was expecting a shout from behind him at any moment: 'Hey, YOU! What do you think you're DOING?'

But no one shouted as he rattled on down the corridor.

He knew just where he was going, but began to doubt now that he could ever get away with his ridiculous scheme. Fighting back the internal voice that was shrieking at him, he struggled again with the doors, hoping that he could get past and down to the elevator beyond. It led straight down to the loading bay through which he'd initially entered the hospital.

Do you really believe that you can bluff your way all the way down there?

SHUT UP!

Now, Jane Teal had decided that it was time to emerge from her coma. Perfect timing.

'It's all right . . . really, it's okay. Just relax.'

'But the others,' mumbled Jane. 'Something's happening. We have to be together and they're being taken away . . .'

Perhaps it had been the noise and the clattering of the trolley. She began to rise sleepily on one elbow.

'Shit!'

Curtis yanked hard and the trolley slid bumping through the doors. Jane lurched and almost fell out of it. Grabbing her arm, Curtis managed to pull her back, looking around at the same time to make sure that there were no hospital staff here to interfere. The next moment, the IV drip swung on its pedestal and shattered against the corridor wall.

'*Shit!*'

Curtis dragged the trolley after him, the wheels crunching on broken glass. Ducking low, he peered back through the double-door windows. But no one seemed to have heard or noticed and, thank God, there was no one in this stretch of corridor at all. They reached the elevator, and Curtis stabbed the 'down' button. What if there was someone in there? He looked back at the IV drip, its broken bottle hanging from the rack, liquid dribbling on to the floor. He reached for the tube into Jane's arm. There didn't seem to be any damage there, but he knew nothing about IV or what kind of fluid they had been putting into her. Would the breakage harm her? He couldn't just rip the tube out of her arm, but neither could he let it stay in there. Would she get an embolism or something? The elevator light pinged!

Quickly, Curtis disconnected the stand and shoved it aside. It clattered to the floor by the side of the elevator. Gritting his teeth for fear that someone had heard it, he shoved the loose wire under the cover. Jane was moaning, moving her head from side to side. There were beads of sweat on her marbled face. Then the elevator doors were open. Curtis hissed in relief. It was empty. Shoving the trolley inside, he looked back just as the double doors clattered open and three white-uniformed figures hurried through. Turning his back on them, Curtis jammed his hand on the '*down*' buttŏn.

The doors remained open.

The figures hurried on in his direction.

Come ON!

You're never going to make it.

Shut UP!

Gradually, the doors began to judder shut. They were moving too slowly. Curtis waited for the hand that would suddenly grab the edge, yanking the doors back. Then there'd be an exclamation as someone saw the shattered IV bottle and stand. Then the three figures would step into the elevator, one of them recognising the patient. Then someone would grab his shoulder and spin Curtis around. Then someone would say: 'Wait a moment. I know you. You're that bastard from the *Independent Daily*! Just what the hell do you think you're . . .'

The figures hurried past, unheeding of the elevator and its occupants. The doors closed and the cabin juddered as they started their descent. Curtis suddenly became aware that he too was soaked in sweat. He wiped a hand across his face.

And when his hand moved away from his face, he started back in shock.

Jane Teal was sitting bolt upright on the trolley. Her upturned face was like the face of a statue, and the eyes were fixed on him. But there was something about her face which held him spellbound as the elevator continued on its way down. No, not the face, he realised. It was the eyes.

Her eyes were like glass. They caught the light from the

strip above, and reflected the light back so that Curtis couldn't see the irises. In that one instant, he understood two things. First, that in an unfathomable way, these were not the eyes of Jane Teal. They were somehow reflecting whatever was inside her. He could feel it, just as he had felt the bizarre *current* passing between Harry Stark and the others when they were communicating. He could feel a vibration emanating from the figure that sat staring at him. Suddenly, it was as if he were lying on the floor of the casualty department again, watching them all communicate with each other. He could *feel* the presence of the Traveller inside Jane Teal. Secondly, he knew that while she might still be in a coma, the thing inside had somehow fought its way to the surface. Why? But before he could open his mouth and ask, Curtis *knew* why. The thing inside Jane Teal had reacted in fear. Trapped inside her comatose body, it had become aware of its entrapment, knew that somehow it was being taken away against it or Jane's will. In that sudden surge of fear, it had been able to surface.

'Don't be afraid,' said Curtis. 'I'm taking you to the others.'

'I . . . see you . . . into. But the others aren't there.'

'I was sent to get you. I'm going to help you get back home.'

'Not *there*!' said Jane. She bowed her head, and as her eyes closed it seemed that the comatose Jane Teal was now somehow fighting to regain possession of her body. But the voice that issued was still the voice of the Traveller. 'Not THERE!'

Curtis moved forward to help. And then the elevator bumped to a halt, the doors sliding open. He looked anxiously over his shoulder, expecting that they would be caught at any moment. He had no idea what the thing was talking about, but they had to get away from the hospital. His luck would not hold out for ever.

'Look . . . can you . . . can you walk?'

Jane's head snapped up. The eyes were bright and glassy once again. The Traveller nodded Jane's head. She looked like a marionette. Eyes still fixed on him, she began to fumble at her arm.

'What is it? Look, we've got to . . . *Jesus!*'

Curtis winced as she tore the IV tube and its tape from her arm, discarding them on the floor. She held her hand out to him. Carefully, Curtis began to edge her from the trolley. They were going to have a much better chance of success if they were on foot. He pulled an arm over his shoulder, and in that moment became aware that he was almost in an embrace with something inside Jane Teal that defied human understanding. Under and inside this warm, damp flesh was something alien.

'The wrong word,' said Curtis grimly, recalling his conversation with Stark. 'Well . . . whatever in hell you are . . . let's go.'

Then they were out of the elevator and heading for the loading bay.

Now Ellis knew what was happening to him.

He had died and gone to hell. That was why the thing inside him was punishing him this way; that was why it was goading him on. He staggered along the embankment, looking down at the motorway traffic. He knew also why he had been brought here, to the place where the crash had occurred. He didn't know the stretch particularly well, but he knew with a deeply felt *instinct* that he was less than half a mile from where it had happened. Moreover, this wasn't the *real* motorway at all. This was a hellish reconstruction, on a different plane. And when he got where the thing inside was taking him, there would be pain and terror and torture waiting for him.

Ellis sobbed and moaned as he scrambled through the bushes.

Perhaps he had never escaped from the car crash at all? He had tried to overtake the coach and it had slammed into him. He remembered the screaming voices and his conviction that his car was on fire and he was burning alive. Yes, that was it. He had burned alive. Everything that had happened afterwards – everything that he *thought* had happened – was just some hellish fantasy. He'd never had the power to kill with a touch. That had all been some kind of . . . some kind of . . . *test*. To see how he would deal with the situation, so that the angels and the devils on the other side of life would know how to deal with him.

'I'm sorry . . . I'm sorry . . .' He began to weep like a child.

He had failed the test, and now he was being taken to a place of everlasting torment. He thought of something then as he moved. Something that stifled the tears and filled him with an even greater dread. Perhaps Dawn, the prostitute he'd murdered, was waiting there for him. Was she to be his tormentor?

'Please . . .' Burwell paused, begging the thing inside to take this nightmare away.

Go on!

He blundered ahead, slipped on the grass and fell cartwheeling down the embankment. Arms and legs flailing, he hit the hard shoulder in a cloud of baked dust and a sliding ripple of shale. Hands bloodied, he staggered to his feet and began to weep again as the thing inside forced him on and . . .

The thing felt Burwell's presence, knew that he was coming to it; knew that he was going to free it from its imprisonment. It still did not understand how it would be done. But it could feel him, staggering along the hard shoulder, getting nearer all the time.

It began to rock from side to side in its cage, like a crooning child.

Both claws were over its no-face.

And then it took its claws away, suddenly wondering.

Perhaps . . . just perhaps . . . its oncoming saviour was also bringing what it had been hunting for in vain.

Perhaps its rescuer was bringing the most precious thing.

Its face.

Curtis had been driving cars for years. But now it seemed that he'd forgotten all the basic instructions. On the way back to his apartment he stalled the engine three times, took a corner so tightly that he mounted the kerb, and almost killed an old man on a pedestrian crossing. When the car juddered to a stop, he hunched forward over the wheel. Suddenly, he couldn't breathe.

Fuck me. I need a cigarette.

He had been through many tight spots in his journalistic life, but nothing like the past few days. The attack in the leisure centre had more than shaken him. He had never been closer to death, and knew that if he dwelt on the possibilities of what *could* have happened he would simply cave in, go back to bed and not get up again until everyone and everything had gone away. But the headlong rush of events that had followed that night had side-lined consideration of his own mortality, and only now was the full impact of it all registering.

'Just give me . . .' He couldn't get his breath. He saw Jane Teal in the rear-view mirror, huddled in one of the corners of the back seat. She had her eyes closed, so he had no way of knowing whether she or the Traveller was 'in charge' at the moment. 'Just give me a minute . . .'

He gripped the steering wheel tight to stop his hands from trembling. Why the hell had he done what he'd done? The doubts about his motivations had crept in once more. He had *kidnapped* someone. What the hell for?

Don't start that again. I did it for the story . . .

And when you've GOT that story, if you see this thing through alive – which you may NOT, Curtis – how are you going to justify your actions, then? You've just committed a criminal offence. There are also two dead men in that leisure centre. You're withholding information from the police. Give it all up. It's gone too far. It's time you handed everything over to the authorities, forgot about this crazy story, and went back to your ordinary life . . .

'Ordinary,' he mumbled under his breath, and that one word held the secret of his behaviour. Yes, Stark was right, he was helping the story along. But it was the very nature of the story which revealed the key. The things he'd seen were more than extraordinary, and nothing he'd ever experienced in his private or professional life came close to the dangerous wonders that had been unveiled since the motorway crash. Layer by layer, with his assistance and involvement, the story was being revealed. He was an integral part of the process, and he knew in his heart that at the very centre of it all was the answer to a Great Mystery. Life, Love, the Universe and Everything. All the big questions. The existence of these travellers might provide answers to all the clichéd yearnings and needs of humankind. And that prospect had transformed everything in Curtis's ordinary life.

'Okay,' he said at last, shoving open the car door. 'It's time to meet your friends.' He paused, waiting for Jane to open her eyes and acknowledge his presence so that he could see who or what he was talking to. But she merely held her hand out like a sleepy child, keeping her eyes closed. Curtis leaned in and helped her from the seat. She felt fragile and helpless, as if she might break if he gripped her too tightly. He had given her his coat as they'd made their escape across the rear loading yard of the hospital to his car. He pulled it tighter around her and walked her carefully to the rear entrance of the apartment block. Once inside, he remembered that the elevator was broken. They'd have to take the stairs.

'Can you make it?'

Jane, or perhaps the Traveller, nodded her or its head, and they continued their slow ascent. As they climbed, Curtis could feel his pulse beginning to race again. Once Jane arrived, they would have enough power to make what Stark had termed 'The Call'. What form would that take? Even now, Curtis was writing up the experiences in his head.

Their movements on the stairs caused shuffling echoes from above and below. The noises sounded eerie, adding to his anxiety.

On the first landing, they paused to allow Jane time to get her breath. She was clearly struggling. When they started up again, Curtis remembered something else Stark had said, something that increased his anxiety tenfold. Somewhere out there was a hybrid thing that had once been the bus driver, George MacGowan. Stark had said that the thing he had become was filled with the energy of the Storm Between, the very power the Travellers would need to get back to their own plane. But Stark had also said that the thing was extremely dangerous. If that Call, whatever it was, summoned the missing two survivors, how the hell were they going to protect themselves from the monstrous thing that George MacGowan had become? Maybe Stark and the others had an answer to that one.

'Unreal,' he hissed, looking at Jane. One hand on the rail, she continued climbing, allowing herself to be led. They reached the landing door leading to the communal corridor on Curtis's level. He ushered her through, suddenly feeling weak with anxiety. She paused, eyes closed, like a sleep-walker. Curtis took her elbow, feeling the small thrill of vibration, and they continued towards his apartment. What the hell would happen if someone opened a door now?

Excuse us. She's possessed by something, and I'm just helping to have her exorcised. And, oh yes, she does look like that woman you've just seen on the television, the one they say was kidnapped from the hospital just a little while ago . . .

Outside his door, Curtis paused.

What exactly would happen when he took her in? He checked to see if there was any reaction, any change on her face. But the marble-white visage was as blank as ever, the eyes resolutely closed as if she didn't want anything to do with this world. Curtis knocked.

There was no answer from within.

Perhaps they were all still sitting and standing in silent communication?

He knocked again.

'Mrs Russell?'

He checked Jane once more. Still no reaction.

'Mr O'Dowd? Chris?'

This was ridiculous. He fumbled for his key, then leant back to lead Jane in gently by the arm. The moment they entered, he could see that the living room was empty. Maybe they'd all gone next door into the bedroom.

'Mrs Russell?'

The door closed behind them, and Curtis looked back, expecting to see that Jane had come out of her trance and had shut it.

But there was a man standing behind the door whom Curtis had never seen before in his life. Tall, with a black leather jacket and looking like a professional boxer. It seemed as if someone had been chopping sticks on the bridge of his nose. He smiled, but said nothing. There was a missing front tooth. And when two other men appeared in the bedroom doorway, also smiling but without any hint of amusement on their faces, Curtis suddenly remembered what the thing inside Jane Teal had said when he'd kidnapped her from the hospital.

But the others aren't there. We have to be together, and they're being taken away.

'Where are the others?' asked Curtis breathlessly as the two men in the bedroom doorway walked calmly into the room. Suddenly, the terror he had felt in the abandoned leisure centre had returned with all its suffocating dread. 'What has O'Farrell done with the others?'

'Someone's been a naughty boy,' said one of the men. 'And someone's going to have to be punished for it.'

'Where have you taken them?'

There was a movement behind him. Curtis half turned, thinking that it was Jane.

But she was standing as still as a statue, and the moment before everything disappeared in darkness Curtis saw the flash of a hand wielding a rubber hose.

'Wake up! *Please . . .*'

Harry was suddenly aware of the hand on his shoulder, shaking him. Groaning, he eased himself to a sitting position, letting his legs fall over the side of the sofa-bed.

Except that this wasn't Curtis's sofa-bed, and when Harry's vision finally focused, he realised that he was no longer in Curtis's apartment.

'Thank God!' It was an unfamiliar woman's voice, but the urgency in her tone was unmistakable. Harry saw a pair of legs, in jeans, standing before him. He looked up, and then remembered the arrival of the young woman called Mercy. There had been a brief moment of understanding then, before everything had faded away. He remembered their need for a fourth, the need to make the call and draw the other survivors. He looked at his watch. Three thirty in the afternoon. When he looked around he could see that they were in a bare room; plasterboard walls, a drawn blind. A single bed and a chair.

'Where are we?' demanded Mercy, glaring down at him.

'What day is it?'

'Don't you know where we are?'

'No, but I don't suppose this is all a bad dream and I'm going to wake up in a minute. Shit, I feel *terrible*.'

'You and me both. You mean you really *don't* know where we are?'

'No. Look, what the hell . . . ? Start again. Let me have a chance to get my head straight. The last thing I remember was meeting you and Martin Russell's wife . . .'

'Sheila.'

'Yeah, Sheila. Then I seem to have blanked out. I think the things inside us were communicating. And then I came out of it for a while and . . .'

'The things *inside* us? What the hell is going on?'

Harry's head began to clear. He recalled now that Mercy would not know about what had happened to them all. Sheila Russell had said she'd told her own side of the story, but there'd been no time to go into details. Harry looked at the door.

'Yes,' said Mercy, 'I thought of that. But it's locked, and I've been hammering on the bastard thing for the past half-hour. I'm surprised the sound of it didn't wake you up.'

'Can you remember anything about getting from Curtis's place to here . . . wherever here is supposed to be?'

'No!' snapped Mercy angrily.

Everything had taken an insane turn in her life, causing her to doubt her own sanity, and she had been hoping that her arrival at Martin's house would put the missing pieces in this crazy puzzle together. But there had been no answers, just more puzzles. Martin had apparently been kidnapped, and Martin's wife had taken her to a newspaper reporter's flat, where it seemed that the same thing had now happened to *her*. She felt even more powerless, and therefore angrier, than ever.

'What happened to me? Some fucker must have put something in a drink to knock me out. I remember arriving at the newspaper reporter's place, remember seeing you and then . . .

nothing after that. So what the hell is going on? What the hell is happening to me?'

'And you can't remember anything about how we got here?'

'Are you fucking deaf or what?' she shouted. 'If somebody doesn't tell me what the hell is happening I swear to Christ I'll kill someone.'

'All right, all right . . .'

'What do you mean, "the things inside us"?'

'Sit down, Mercy. I've got a story to tell you. And then afterwards, we can think about what the hell we're going to do next . . .'

'Something bad's happened,' said Roger groggily, rising from the stained mattress and moving to the sink unit in the corner of their room.

'You could say that,' said Chris. He had been trying to peer through the shuttered window. But there was some kind of blind on the outside too, and he could only see a small patch of grass and a hint of a tree's shadow on the ground below the window. The heat-wave had obviously not come to an end. He was drenched in sweat.

Since Roger had awoken from his death-like sleep in this strange, bare room, Chris had told him everything Curtis had passed on. Throughout, Roger had listened, his pale face with its hollowed eyes betraying no emotion. Even as he recounted the story of the Survivors and of what had to be done, he himself wondered just what the hell they had walked into. He was struggling with an instinctive feeling that this was somehow all part of some other crazy plan. The stuff that Curtis had so seriously talked about could not possibly be true. What was the angle? Some kind of bizarre blackmail plot that had yet to manifest itself fully? But somehow they were both caught up in this living nightmare, a nightmare made worse by the thugs who had suddenly broken into the newspaper reporter's apartment. The sudden eruption had caught both Sheila Russell and himself completely by surprise. Two of the thugs had guns, and when they had laid hands on Roger and the other two whom Curtis had said were

Survivors, they'd offered no resistance. But it seemed as if the spell of communication had been broken by that contact. Like zombies, or sleep-walkers, they had allowed themselves to be led out by the intruders. Chris's one attempt at resistance had been met with a brutal blow to the face which had raised an ugly purple welt under his chin and loosened a tooth. When they had demanded to know who everyone in the room was, Chris had no choice but to tell them. He'd had no chance to offer further resistance before they were all bundled down the back stairs of the apartment block to a van that was waiting in the rear yard. They had been flung inside, and the doors locked. Then the van was roaring off to a destination unknown, throwing its occupants from side to side as it took corners at speed. Chris had tried to communicate with his brother, but it seemed that he, like the others, could not be broken from his trance. It appeared as though something inside Sheila Russell had broken. Her spirit, perhaps. Despite his attempts to speak to her, she kept her head down and her hands cradled in her lap. As if this sudden development were the last straw, and she might never see her husband alive again.

Chris reckoned that they had been driving for over two and a half hours. The heat inside the van had been unbearable, and at one stage he had hammered on the partition wall, on the other side of which he assumed the men would be seated, demanding water or time to take a pee. But there had been no answer.

When the van had shuddered to a halt, he had braced himself. If he moved quickly, perhaps he could dodge past whoever opened the doors and go for help. But the two men standing there, silhouetted by the fierce sunlight, were both holding guns, and Chris had no doubt that these silent figures would have no hesitation in putting a bullet in him if he should try anything. Sheepishly, he had done as he was told and taken his brother by the arm, guiding him out into the bright sunlight.

He had stood there with his brother, blinking and wondering just where in hell they were. They were obviously deep in the countryside. Chris could see a stockade fence on all sides. Beyond, trees were densely crowded around the fence. It looked as if a quarter-square-mile of land had been cleared in the middle of a forest. Ahead of them he could see what seemed, impossibly, to be a church. Just beyond that, a series of wooden chalet huts, like something in a holiday camp.

The others had been dragged out of the van, and they were then force-marched past the church. Chris guessed that their destination was the chalet huts. As they passed the church – a church without windows? – he could see what seemed to be a helicopter landing pad. And now he knew where they must have been taken. Curtis had told him all about Quinn O'Farrell, the abduction of Martin Russell and the attempt on the newspaperman's life. This could only be the Church of the Holy Order.

'Look,' he had ventured, turning as they walked. 'I'm sure we can talk this all out, if you'll just let me know who . . .'

'Shut *up*!' A gun was jammed into his back, and he was roughly forced to face front again. A movement near the church caught his eye, and he was able to half turn and look as another man hurried across to them. This was bizarre. He was wearing what looked like a monk's habit.

'Which one's Sheila Russell?' he called as he drew near.

Chris was aware that the man with the gun was pointing her out.

'He says she's to come to the church. Split the others up, and put them in the chalets.'

Chris was able to turn and look again, in time to see Sheila trying to make eye contact with him. No longer withdrawn, she was attempting to communicate something to him. But before he could glean anything from her, the fake monk had taken her by the arm and was leading her back towards the church. Now they were being split up. Both he and Roger were being led to one of the chalets, Harry Stark and Mercy to another. Chris watched the latter two being led like sleep-walkers. He looked at Roger, in the same condition, and wondered how long they were going to stay like that. He didn't like the fact that they had been split up in this manner. What was going to happen next?

Inside the bare chalet, Roger had said nothing as the door was locked behind them. And Chris had watched in aston-ishment as he walked slowly to the bed, lay down, and then mechanically closed his eyes. Nothing Chris had said over the past half-hour had been of any use in waking him up. Now at last he was awake, and Chris had just told him everything that had happened.

'If we have been taken by this O'Farrell character,' ventured Roger, 'what do you think he wants with us?'

'Your guess is as good as mine. If he kidnapped Russell for the power he's supposed to have, maybe he wants the whole deck. All the survivors, and whatever's in them.'

'But what the hell for?'

'I don't know, Roger,' said Chris impatiently. 'None of it makes sense. None of the stuff that Curtis talked about makes sense at all.'

'You don't believe it? About the Travellers?'

'I don't know what to believe.'

'Chris . . . I know how crazy this is going to sound. But I know . . . I *know* deep down in my guts, in a way I just can't explain, that everything Curtis says is true. Even the stuff I didn't hear personally, about us dying if we don't all get together soon. Even second-hand, I *know* it's true. There's something in me, Chris. Something that survived the crash by hiding in me. And if it isn't released, the way Stark said, then I'll die. We'll *both* die, me and it.'

Chris had returned to the window, trying to peer outside again.

'We've got to get out of here, Chris. We've got to find a way to get the others out.'

'Curtis will have got back to his apartment by now. Whether he's managed to get that Jane Teal or not means that . . . Hello, what's this?'

'What?'

'It's a . . . bloody hell, it's a helicopter.'

Roger joined Chris at the window as . . .

Sheila was pushed through the church doors, and she blinked in puzzlement at what she saw. There were no pews in here, no aisles, no religious frescos on the wall. She seemed to have walked into an indoor gardening centre, with rows of glass frames and what looked like greenhouses, housing extravagant greenery. The ultra-violet lights added to a sense of other-worldiness. Why transform a church into one huge greenhouse? The monk shoved her, and Sheila walked past the glass frames. Up ahead, at the front of the church, was a white double door. She guessed that they were heading there.

She knew where they had been taken. As soon as they had been dragged out of the van and she had seen the church, she knew that this must be the place the Reverend Jameson had called the Church of the Holy Order. And if that was the case, then Martin must be here somewhere. She had tried to communicate that knowledge to Chris, the only other person not in the bizarre trance, but it had been too late. She remembered Curtis's story about Quinn O'Farrell trying to kill both him and Stark. The possibility that Martin had been murdered, for whatever reason, was almost too much to bear. He *must* be alive. She moved ahead anxiously, pausing at the white double doors. The monk pushed past her, holding one of the doors wide. There was a blast of cool air. With fear eating at her stomach, Sheila entered.

There were whitewashed walls on either side. Ahead, a metal staircase.

'Go on,' said the monk, gruffly.

'Where's Martin?'

'Just get the fuck up the stairs and don't ask any questions.'

Sheila ascended. There was movement up above, and bright light.

And then a figure appeared at the top of the stairs.

Sheila paused.

'Ah, Mrs Russell,' said the figure. Despite the weather, he was wearing an expensive three-piece business suit. His hair was iron-grey and curly, his skin tanned. 'We meet at last. What a pleasure.'

'Where's Martin?'

'Come on up.'

The figure beckoned and Sheila continued her ascent, aware of the fake monk just behind her. At the top of the stairs, she could see that she was in an office of some kind. There were banks of machinery against one wall – a computer, perhaps? – and two men in monks' habits were working on keyboards. Neither one acknowledged her presence as the man in the expensive suit stepped to one side. He smiled, seeming to enjoy her nervousness. Now Sheila could see that there were two other men here, both standing with their hands crossed before them, as if waiting for instructions. It seemed that one of them was as nervous as she was.

'Thank you, brother,' said the man in the suit, with more than a hint of sarcasm, and Sheila looked back to see that the fake monk had turned and was vanishing down the staircase once more.

'Would you like a drink, Mrs Russell? It's been a long drive for you in this weather.'

'Where's Martin?'

'Straight to the point. I like that.'

'You're Quinn O'Farrell.'

'That's right.'

'And you kidnapped my husband.'

'Kidnapped? That's a strong word.'

'What would you call it?'

'I'm trying to be nice. It's not working. So let's get this straight, Mrs Russell. You're here for a reason. After the Reverend Jameson's crisis of conscience, I had to make a change of plan . . .'

The uneasy man shuffled. O'Farrell turned to look at him, his face hard. The man stared ahead.

'I knew I'd have to bring you here, along with Mr Curtis. Who has yet to arrive, but is on his way. However, the others are an added bonus. Something I hadn't counted on. But it looks as if what I'd presumed to be a one-man industry might turn into a *real* group enterprise, after all.'

'You killed the Reverend Jameson.'

O'Farrell paused, the smile gone from his face. 'That's right, Mrs Russell. And believe me, I'll have you killed, too. If you don't do what I want.'

'Where is my husband?'

'Very well. Let's start from there. Essen?'

One of the men stepped forward. The nervous man shuffled, looking at his feet.

'Take Mrs Russell to her husband.' He smiled at her. 'He has his own room here, you see. Special treatment, for a man with a special talent.'

Essen held out a hand and Sheila nervously crossed the room to join him. She looked back once at O'Farrell. The smile he gave her was glacial, and frightening. Essen moved past the two monks at the computers, and held open another double door for her.

'We'll speak in due course,' said O'Farrell, maintaining the smile.

Sheila followed Essen through the doors. When they had gone, O'Farrell moved to a drinks tray and poured himself a glass of iced water. Drinking, he looked at Molineux, still shuffling uneasily. When he lowered the glass, he caught his eye.

'So now what's the problem, Molineux? Still got cold feet?'

'I don't understand why you're taking all these unnecessary risks.'

'Risks?'

'Why have you brought all these people here?'

'I had to act when Jameson fell apart. Who would have thought that our intrepid reporter friend could have been so resourceful? One of my best clean-up operatives, electrocuted no less. And poor Reverend Jameson, gone somewhere where he can really be happy at last. No, all that was unforeseen. But things are about to get very interesting now that we have all the party together.'

'I don't understand, Mr O'Farrell. Neither do the others at Central Office . . .'

'Central *Office*?' snapped O'Farrell. 'They're hired hands, like *you*, Molineux! Don't forget it! I'm tired . . . really *tired* of having everything I do questioned.'

'But if we could only understand . . .'

'Nobody expected Curtis's apartment to be full of people. The whole idea was to go and get him, and find out just what he knew. Who could have believed . . . who could have *believed* that he'd rounded up such interesting people?'

'I still don't . . .'

'The ones who act like sleep-walkers. They're survivors of that motorway crash, just like Martin Russell. Did you see them? They're . . . different. That's what Curtis was on to. He knows.'

'Knows?'

'Think big!' snapped O'Farrell, stepping forward to rap Molineux on the forehead. Molineux winced, and stood his ground. 'Look what Martin Russell can do. We've already had four big paying customers here. And why do you think Curtis got on to Jameson, why do you think he rounded up more of the survivors? Because, Molineux . . . *because* something's happened to each and every one of them. Martin Russell isn't unique. The others have got the same powers. That's what this is all about. That's why I've brought them all here. I thought we had a one-man business. But it turns out we've got a whole team of faith healers on our hands now! I'm willing to bet everything I've got that I'm right.'

Molineux opened his mouth to protest again, but could see that O'Farrell had built up a head of steam. To interrupt now was to court disaster. Things were somehow going horribly wrong; O'Farrell was taking risks that were making everyone in the organisation nervous.

'Don't you see, Molineux? We had to bring Russell's wife here. You know how Russell's been since we got him here. We broke him and we used the drugs, but something else is happening to him. One of the medical people told me it's as if his . . . his battery is running down. Every time he uses whatever energy he possesses, it's as if his lifeforce is ebbing. Maybe his wife can coax a little more power out of him. But now that we've got the others, that isn't such a big problem any more, is it? Now we've got three other faith healers. Plenty of time for more experimentation. Even if Russell does die on us the way our medical team think he might, we've got plenty of other raw material. Plenty of time to find out what makes them tick. You just have to have confidence in me, Molineux. That's all it takes, just a little . . .'

O'Farrell moved to a window, and looked out through the blinds.

'I thought I heard something.'

'Sir?'

'A little bird . . . a whirlybird . . . tells me that Mr Curtis and A.N. Other faith healer are just about to arrive.'

Beyond the church, a helicopter was lowering itself on to the pad in a gush of bone-dry dust.

Sheila followed the man called Essen down a short flight of wooden stairs and along a whitewashed corridor. It was claustrophobic here, and she wished she had taken the drink O'Farrell had offered. The heat was overwhelming. Suddenly, Essen stopped beside a door. When he knocked, it was quickly opened. A mumble of exchanged words, and then another of O'Farrell's employees stepped out into the corridor. Both men turned to look at Sheila, silently inviting her to enter.

Heart hammering, she squeezed past both men in the narrow confines of the corridor and stepped into the room beyond. It was dark inside, but a great deal cooler. Blinds were drawn at the single window, and Sheila started when the door was closed and locked behind her.

There was a figure sitting on the single bed in the middle of the room.

'Martin?'

The figure looked up from the bed, and for a moment, Sheila could only stand, fists bunched up to her mouth. Something *terrible* had happened to him. He was wearing the clothes he had worn on the day she'd last seen him, but he seemed to have shrunk inside them. Was it possible that he could have lost so much weight in such a short space of time? His face was sallow, his eye sockets sunken. Martin had been a powerful, well-built man who took pride in his appearance, but now his shoulders were stooped, his hair awry. He seemed twenty years older and so very, very ill. And as he sat there, he was looking at her with no hint of recognition in his rheumy, sunken eyes.

Suddenly, the spell of shock was broken and Sheila ran to embrace him.

'Oh my God, Martin. What have they *done* to you?'

Martin did not return her embrace, and Sheila could feel his ribcage beneath his shirt as she knelt, weeping. Behind them, through the door, she thought she could hear someone laughing. She whirled from the embrace, still holding him protectively, and rounded on the invisible men behind the door.

'You *bastards!* I'll find a way to make you *pay* for this . . .'

'Sheila? Is it you?'

She pushed herself away from him so that she could look up into his eyes. There was a glimmer of recognition there. As she watched, his eyes closed as if a great tiredness threatened to rob him even of the strength to stay awake. Quickly, she laid him back on the bed, ignoring the continued sniggers from the doorway. With great effort, Martin opened his eyes again.

'I'm sorry, Sheila. They . . . they . . .' He gestured weakly at his arms. 'They . . . drugs . . .'

Sheila suppressed a sob, understanding what he was trying to communicate.

And at that moment, she seemed to be teetering on some kind of inner edge, a crumbling brink between her lifelong belief in the powers of good and what had happened to them since the accident. She'd had no doubt that Martin's power had somehow been given by God so that he could do good. The Reverend Jameson had confirmed her belief. But Jameson had been a hypocrite, had deliberately lied to them both for financial gain. And now it seemed that Martin's power had brought them to this point, in the hands of a murderer, Martin sapped to the point of death. The power couldn't be from God. It had all been a lie from the very beginning.

In despair, Sheila clung on tight to her husband and sobbed.

Curtis realised that he was dead.

He had walked into the abandoned leisure centre on a bloody fool's errand, and the man who had been waiting for him there had killed him. Now he knew what it was like to be dead.

There was a great roaring wind, a bright light and flickering shadows. Above him, from where he lay, he could see an angel. Her skin was the colour of a marble statue. Her eyes were closed and her long hair was whipping around her face in the wind. She seemed to be contemplating, and Curtis wondered whether she had been sent to collect his soul. He had no doubt that they were both flying. But as he looked, he could see that the angel's hands were in her lap, so how could she be holding him as they flew up to heaven? And now he was aware that there was a great gnawing pain at the base of his skull where the assassin in the leisure centre had hit him . . . No, the killer had been killed . . . by Stark, in the swimming pool. And surely, if he were dead, he wouldn't feel physical pain.

And then Curtis remembered.

Groaning, he tried to turn. There was a man sitting next to the angel. He grinned as he slammed a foot down where Curtis lay, stamping on his chest and flattening him to the floor of the helicopter.

'Just in time,' said the grinning man. 'We're about to land.'

Curtis twisted his head and realised what was happening. Jane Teal sat next to the man, eyes closed and tuned in to some inner place where the real world couldn't hurt her any more. A blanket of shadow enfolded the interior of the helicopter as it turned away from the sun. Curtis felt the bump as the undercarriage connected with the ground. At last, he was aware of the clattering blades as they began to slow.

The man turned to look at Jane Teal.

'Doesn't say much, does she?'

'Choosy about the company she keeps,' replied Curtis.

'Funny man. Let's see how much you laugh when you get where you're going.'

'And where might that be?'

'Shut the fuck *up!*' snapped the man. Leaning down, he grabbed Curtis by the collar and dragged him to his feet. The sudden change in position, combined with the second blow to his head, engulfed Curtis in vertigo. Moaning, he groped feebly at the coarse, iron-hard hands. Dimly, he was aware of other voices, then a door opening. The sunlight was blinding as he was dragged out of the helicopter. He stumbled, grazing his knees on the rough ground of the landing pad. Cursing, his captor dragged him upright again and frog-marched him ahead. Curtis struggled to regain his balance and senses. He could see that they were being taken to what seemed to be a church. Beyond the church, wooden huts. On all sides, a compound fence surrounded by trees.

The Brothers of the Holy Order.

'Mr O'Farrell always treat his guests like this?' he ventured, hoping that this sudden display of knowledge might unnerve his captor or give him some kind of edge.

'Just cunts like you,' replied the man in a flat voice.

Curtis looked behind, to see that Jane was also being led to the church by another of O'Farrell's men. Blood was running from the wound in her arm where the IV drip had been removed.

'She needs medical attention,' said Curtis. 'Her arm . . .'

'We've got doctors here. They'll see to her.'

Curtis twisted around again to protest.

And then the screaming came from one of the wooden chalets to the side of the church.

'What the hell is *that*?' demanded Curtis.

His captor tried to keep an impassive face, but was clearly disturbed by what they had heard. Was it a woman's voice, in great pain?

'Never mind that,' snapped the man, pushing him ahead. 'Just keep walking.'

Curtis looked back once more, to see that Jane was still in her limbo place as they continued on towards the church. The screaming had not registered with her. Now the sounds had dwindled away, and Curtis was shoved hard towards the church's main entrance as . . .

Mercy sat on the bed with her head in her hands.

Harry had been pacing while he told her the story, and she'd said nothing throughout. Now at last he was finished. He'd outlined the basics, had kept his own grief and experience sidelined; partly because he felt so desperately tired and ill, partly because he could sense that if they were aired again, he might just crumple and fall apart. Although he knew about her power, he had not told her about his own. He moved to the boarded-up window. It wasn't possible to see anything through it, but the light seemed to be changing. The sun was going down and it would soon be dark. When he turned to look back at Mercy, awaiting a response, she was still in the same position, head in hands.

'Mercy?'

'Yeah.'

'Are you okay?'

She laughed. It was a hollow sound.

'I've spent so much time on the move. Running away from things I didn't want. Looking for something. I don't know what. How do I run away from something that's *inside* me?'

'You can't. None of us can. But you *do* believe what I've told you. Don't you?'

'Pretty crazy stuff.'

'Any crazier than everything you've been through so far?'

'No.'

'It's important that you believe it, Mercy. I know you can feel the Traveller now. But listen, we've only got . . .' He checked his watch. '. . . a few hours left. If we're not back on that stretch of motorway between twelve and twelve thirty tonight, we're never going to get out of this alive. The Travellers will die inside us, and we'll die soon after.'

'Then we're going to die, aren't we? We're well and truly fucked.'

'There's still a chance.'

'Oh yeah? All the Survivors need to be together, remember? And in case it's escaped your attention, we're under lock and key here.'

'We've got to get out of here. That's the first thing.'

'Good thinking. How?'

Harry turned away from her then. She watched as he paced back to the window, bracing his hands on the sill.

When he turned back, his face was grim.

'Only one way. Them or us.' He held his gloved hands up to his face. 'Sweet Jesus, I don't want to do this. But it's them or us.'

'What are you talking about?'
'Scream, Mercy.'
'What?'
'I want you to scream.'
'What the hell's the matter with you?'
'Just do it.'

'Jesus Christ!'
Chris swung away from the boarded window, from where he'd been able to get a partial view of the helicopter landing. He had seen Curtis being dragged out by the scruff of his neck. There was a girl with him, who must be Jane Teal. So they'd managed to get him, too. The prospect was both depressing and terrifying. With Curtis still on the outside, there was a chance that he might be able to get help. But their situation looked worse than hopeless.

Suddenly, there had been the sounds of terrified screaming from the chalet next door.

'Sounds like the girl, Mercy,' he said, moving quickly to the locked door.

'What the hell are they doing to her?'

'Leave her alone!' He began to hammer on the door with the flat of his hands as . . .

Brough jumped out of the seat he was occupying outside Chris and Roger's door. He'd been told to keep an eye on this cabin and the one next to it, containing the other two. He had no idea what these people were doing here, but quite clearly they weren't paying guests. Things had been pretty boring of late, even if the money (and the free marijuana as a fringe benefit) was bloody good, and he'd hoped there might be a spot of entertainment planned. But now it looked as though somebody had somehow got into the other cabin and begun the party early. He held up the Uzi and walked gingerly to the edge of the cabin, looking around the side towards the other cabin. It was too bloody hot in his monk's habit and he felt like a fucking idiot. But orders were orders, and it was important that anyone spying on them from the air should see holy men walking around, not armed guards in uniform. He expected to see more monks, perhaps standing in the open doorway and, with any luck, watching and laughing while the bint inside was being given one.

She looked good. My turn next.

But there was no one there, and the door was closed.

He looked across the compound, to where the new arrivals were being taken to the church.

And then the screaming began again.

'What the *hell* is happening?' yelled Roger from behind the locked door.

Cursing, Brough skipped around the side of the cabin and hurried to the doorway of the next. The girl inside continued to yell her head off as he jumped up the wooden steps and hammered on the door. Instantly, she was silent.

'What . . . ?' began Brough.

And at the sound of his voice, she began screaming again.

'Shit!'

He fumbled in his pocket for the key, jammed it into the lock and twisted. As he did so, the screams grew louder, even more shrill. Standing back, he shoved the door in with one hefty kick, expecting some kind of trick. The door was locked, so no one could have let themselves in for any funny business. He had the only key to these two cabins. Now he could see what was happening.

The older man had either cracked or had suddenly had an attack of horniness.

He was pinning the girl back on the bed, one gloved hand at her throat, keeping her down on the mattress. She was hanging on to his restraining arm, thrashing on the bed. Her head twisted towards the door when it crashed open.

'For God's sake, *help* me!'

'Let her go.'

The man ignored him, making a low growling sound in his throat.

Brough levelled the Uzi.

'Get away from her.'

Still growling, the man applied more pressure. The girl began to scream again.

Brough strode into the room, moving quickly to the bed. Keeping the gun levelled at the man, he grabbed him by the shoulder and yanked hard.

And then Harry spun away from Mercy, the ungloved hand suddenly swinging up from where it was hidden at his side.

He clamped the flat of his hand on Brough's face.

Chris began to punch and kick the door when the screams suddenly changed. Before, they had been the screams of a girl. Someone had been hurting her badly. But now, the screams had changed in pitch and intensity. They had turned into one loud, shrill shriek of pain. A shriek that tapered off in dying, sobbing agony.

'What in Christ's name are they *doing* to her?'

Roger grabbed a chair from next to the bed. It was a flimsy effort, but all he could find. He ran back to the boarded-up window and smashed it against the glass, which began to crack and shatter as Chris kept up his attack on the door. There was no time to think through what effect their joint effort might have. They knew only that someone was being tortured, or worse, and that they might be next. Their fear had generated anger.

Chris pulled back from the door and prepared to run at it.

Then he heard the key in the lock.

Roger managed to shatter a complete pane of glass.

'Roger! Wait!'

Chris prepared himself. What if the man on the other side was armed?

Roger turned quickly, holding the remnants of the chair with both hands, ready to use it as a club or a battering ram.

The door swung open and Chris made a rush at it, head down.

At the last moment, he recoiled before he collided with the figure who flinched away from him.

It was Mercy.

'*Christ!*'

'Quick!' she hissed. 'We haven't got much time.'

Amazed, Roger followed her outside, Chris close behind. As they emerged on to the porch of the cabin, they could see Harry Stark, leaning against a door post. He was bent double, retching. Roger looked at Mercy for an explanation.

'No time!' she hissed again. 'Come on, before they find out what we've done. The noise is bound to bring them over.'

Quickly, she jumped down the stairs and grabbed Harry's sleeve. Roger and Chris followed, looking over to where Harry and Mercy had been held captive in the second cabin. Something must be burning in there because a blue haze of smoke was hanging in the doorway. There was no sign of the man who had been guarding them.

'Harry!' snapped Mercy. 'Come on!'

Harry straightened, nodding his head. 'I'm okay.'

'Where?' asked Chris, frantically looking around.

'The fence,' replied Mercy, dragging Harry after her as she headed for the compound fence, fifty feet from them. 'If we get over that and into the forest . . .'

The next moment they were all running hard, Mercy dragging an exhausted and sickened Harry with her as . . .

'Mr Curtis,' said O'Farrell as both he and Jane Teal were brought into the church office at the top of the metal staircase.

'Mr O'Farrell,' replied Curtis, in exactly the same monotone. The man behind him jammed the gun into the small of his back, making him take a step further into the room.

'Good,' said O'Farrell, smiling broadly and showing off a perfect set of capped teeth. 'That's the formalities dispensed with. And this, I take it, is another one of my survivors?'

'*Your* survivors?' asked Curtis as another of their escorts took Jane to one of the chairs. Her eyes remained closed, and she allowed herself to be seated, still with Curtis's jacket over her shoulders. 'You sound very possessive.'

O'Farrell smiled again, looking at Curtis long and hard.

'You're going to be awkward,' he said, as if he'd just worked something out, something that amused him. He wagged a patronising finger at him. 'I can tell. So I think we may have to change tack as regards the way we handle you.'

'You tried to have me killed at the Whitley Leisure Centre. Now you've nearly knocked my brains out, kidnapped me and the others. Why should I be awkward about anything?'

'Yes, a change of plan insofar as you're concerned . . .'

A door on the other side of the room, next to the computer bank, banged open. Molineux staggered in, adjusting his spectacles and breathing heavily. He had obviously been running.

'What the hell is wrong *now?*' snapped O'Farrell, humour evaporating as he whirled to look at him.

'Trouble at the cabins.'

'Trouble? *What* fucking trouble?'

'Perhaps . . . I mean, should we talk about this privately . . . ?'

'WHAT trouble, Molineux?'

'The . . . survivors . . . in the cabins . . .'

O'Farrell strode angrily across the room and took Molineux by the lapels. Suddenly, one of the escorts grabbed Curtis by the shoulder, holding the gun up close to his face, a show of aggression in the hope of pacifying O'Farrell should his anger be redirected towards him.

'What's happened, Molineux?' The anger seemed to have drained from O'Farrell's voice. Now it was calm and cold, and somehow much more threatening that when it had been raised.

'They've . . . escaped, Mr O'Farrell.'

'They've escaped.' Again the calm, cold voice, masking a deadly fury. 'They're under armed guard in the compound. And you're telling me that they've escaped.'

'The guard's dead. Someone killed him. Looks like he's been burned.'

'Well, well,' said Curtis, still in his escort's grip. 'Doesn't look as if things are going your way after all. Does it, *Mister* O'Farrell?'

O'Farrell turned back to look at Curtis, nodding. 'You and I are due a long and detailed talk about our guests, Mr Curtis. And, believe me, you'll co-operate with me . . .'

'Fuck off, O'Farrell.'

'. . . you'll *co-operate* with me, and tell me everything I need to know. In fact, Mr Curtis, you'll *beg* to tell me everything before I've finished with you.' O'Farrell turned back to Molineux. 'They can't get far. Get Essen and Nicolai . . .'

'They've got over the boundary fence. They were seen running into the trees . . .'

'*Get* Essen and Nicolai, have them collect a bunch of the others to cover the forest. They won't get out.'

'But what if . . . ?'

O'Farrell slapped Molineux hard across the face, knocking his spectacles to the floor. Molineux staggered back in shock.

'If you *what if*? me again, Molineux, I swear to Christ and all his angels that I'll cut your fucking head off. Do you understand?'

Molineux nodded furiously, backing off and then stooping to retrieve his spectacles.

'Good. Tell Essen and Nicolai I'm holding them both personally responsible for bringing our guests back. And I want it done quickly.' He turned back to Curtis and Jane Teal. 'Right, take her into one of the rooms in the annexe. There's a place next to Russell's room. Bring Curtis down into the church. Curtis? You and I are going to have a little garden party, and a long, *long* talk about your ladyfriend there. And the others.'

'Go screw yourself.'

'Oh, what *fun* we're going to have, you and I.'

Then Curtis was being bundled down the metal staircase once more, the gun pressed to the back of his neck.

'I can't go any further . . . can't . . .'

Ellis Burwell staggered to a halt on the hard shoulder. Immediately, the thing inside him stabbed him with pain. It flared in his guts, around to the small of his back and then up his spine to his shoulder-blades. He fell to his knees, head thrown back. Now he knew that he was in hell, and all the weeping and cursing and moaning wasn't going to change any of that. As if sensing that he could not be goaded further, the thing inside eased the pain. Burwell gave vent to a loud moaning sigh and pitched forward on to his face.

The sun was beginning to sink on the western skyline.

And fifty yards from where he lay, something stirred in the bushes at the roadside. Something that was aware of his presence, desperate that he reach it and free it from its hideous imprisonment. Something that scrabbled and raked at the bushes, anxious to be free so that it could come and find him. Something that was still afraid of the light, but anxiously peered at the dying rays of the sun, and impatiently waited ... waited ... waited ...

Burwell slept where he lay on the hard shoulder, shadows lengthening all around him.

Molineux followed the guard who was escorting Jane Teal down to the annexe where Sheila Russell had been taken to meet her husband, and paused to look back as Curtis was bundled down the stairs towards the church. As the guard ushered the woman through into the corridor beyond, he adjusted the spectacles on the bridge of his nose, knowing that it was time to put an end to the madness. Cursing silently when he realised that one of the lenses was cracked, he angrily followed the guard and the woman down the corridor. There were two others ahead, guarding Russell's door: Essen and Nicolai.

'Nicolai?'

The man who was known as 'surly bastard' to everyone who worked with him turned to look at Molineux as they came towards him.

'Well, what have we here? A sleep-walker?'

'Never mind that, Nicolai. Put her in the room next to Russell. Essen? There's been a problem with the other guests and Mr O'Farrell wants you and Nicolai to handle it.'

'A problem?'

'They got out ...'

'They *what*?'

'You heard me. One of them was seen jumping over the wire and running into the forest. Brough's dead. Don't *ask* about it, just get some people together and get them *back* again. Mr O'Farrell told me to say that he's holding you both personally responsible for making sure that we get them back. I don't have to tell you how important it is that . . .'

'Don't tell us *anything*, Molineux,' said Essen, taking Jane by the arm and guiding her into the room next to the Russells'. Molineux watched from the doorway as he took her to the spare bed and sat her on the edge. 'We know how to do our job. Keep your smarmy comments for the brain-deads who let them get away.'

Jane Teal remained where she was, sitting on the edge of the bed and facing a blank wall.

'Don't mention it,' Essen said to her. Then, moving quickly back to the doorway, he pushed Molineux roughly out of the way and locked the door.

'Brough's dead, eh?' said Nicolai, ignoring Molineux as they both turned away from him and headed down the stairs that led to the back entrance of the annexe. 'What about that, then? Little bastard owed me ninety thousand quid from a poker game.'

Molineux watched them go, and hated them. Not just because of the relaxed way they'd received the news about the escape, but because they were, quite simply, the worst kind of street thug. They had grown up on the streets with Quinn O'Farrell in the early days and had provided him with his only strong-arm support at a time when his operation was merely a small-time enterprise. As his criminal organisation had grown and spread, O'Farrell had kept both men on, almost like mascots, often referring to them as his lucky talismans. Their dedication to him was total. More than simple bodyguards, they had too much influence for Molineux's liking. They had specialised talents; there was no doubt about that. They had been responsible for breaking Martin Russell's body and his will, and had enjoyed every minute of it. In their own way, they represented the very essence of everything that was now going wrong with O'Farrell and his approach to the job. Things were most definitely out of hand, and something had to be done.

Molineux checked that both annexe doors were locked, and then made his way down the stairs.

Outside, it was early evening, and the shadows from the church, the cabins and the surrounding trees were long and low across the compound area. Molineux watched as Essen and Nicolai organised the cowled figures who were milling around beside the log cabins. This was the first time there had been any real trouble, and it seemed that restoring a sense of control was going to be harder than anyone had anticipated. Molineux heard Nicolai barking orders, watched as Essen knocked one of the cowled figures to the ground when he gave him too much lip. The figure resentfully picked itself up, rubbing its chin, but the intiative seemed to have worked, because now everyone appeared a lot more confident, and a lot more willing to be organised. Two Land Rovers screeched up to the crowd in the centre of the compound. Nicolai directed men into each vehicle. Molineux could see the soft glinting of the fading sunlight on the small-arms weapons each man had been given.

'Bloody, bloody *hell*!' he muttered under his breath.

O'Farrell's guests wouldn't get far in this stretch of forest; of that, Molineux was quite certain. But the fact of the matter was that they shouldn't be here *at all*. Their presence, and the massive complexities that arose from it, was going to undermine everything that had been achieved here, and put the entire organisation in jeopardy. Inside the church, O'Farrell was preparing to amuse himself. But Molineux knew that whatever happened, no one who had been brought here could be allowed out of the place alive. Martin and Sheila Russell. Jane Teal. The other survivors – when they were caught. And Curtis, the reporter. The latter was the most dangerous of all. They would all have to die. All so bloody unnecessary. And what about all those loose ends that had been left out there? Jameson's body had been tidied away, along with the operative who had killed him; but it was just a matter of time before questions were asked about the missing vicar. How could they cover up all the disappearances that O'Farrell's irresponsible behaviour had initiated? And then there was O'Farrell's own employee, healed by Martin Russell, telling everyone who wanted to know, all about it. All those loose ends pointed to O'Farrell. He had brought it all on himself, and put the entire organisation in the firing line because of his obsession with doing things 'his way'. Molineux knew that the Board had been unhappy with the way things had been handled in the past. It was time something was done.

He looked back at the church.

There were still two employees in the office. He couldn't make a telephone call from there. He looked out across the compound to where his own car was parked. The two Land Rovers screeched past it, heading for the main gate as a dozen other cowled figures began to climb the fence beside the cabins, obviously trying to follow the route that O'Farrell's 'guests' had taken. Molineux started out across the compound. There was a personal, unscreened telephone in his car. He would make the call from there.

Behind him, a figure moved through the long shadow of the church to the back door from which he'd come. Head down, Molineux continued on his way. He heard and saw nothing behind him, his thoughts preoccupied with what had to be done.

Inside the church, Curtis walked ahead between the greenhouses, more than aware of the fact that his guard had the gun aimed at the back of his head. He remembered something from his journalist's past, and it filled him with dread. A photograph that had haunted him ever since he'd come across it in the files of the first news agency to employ him. It was a picture from World War II: a refugee, or perhaps a concentration camp survivor, being marched away by a German soldier holding a gun between his shoulder-blades. The look on the old man's face had been what had so affected him. It was an expression of trust; as if the horror of what was happening had been so intense that he had *chosen* to ignore it. The old man had given in to what the soldier wanted, and had made himself believe that he was being taken somewhere safe. But, of course, he was being led away to his death, to the place where he would be shot.

Curtis felt as if he had changed places with that old man. And although he'd come close to death since he'd started on this crazy story about the motorway crash and its aftermath, the headlong rush of events had kept it at bay. But now he knew – without any doubt – that he had reached the point that everyone fears. The point of death. The show of contempt he had put on for O'Farrell upstairs had been a last-ditch attempt to shore up his failing courage. Now every last vestige of courage had left him.

He screwed up his shoulders, waiting for the bullet in the back of his head or between the shoulder-blades.

'What's the matter, Curtis?' laughed O'Farrell from behind him. 'Pissing yourself?'

Curtis heard the man with him laugh, the sycophantic sound of an underling.

'You think you're going to die, don't you?' continued O'Farrell. 'That's what it is. Weren't you listening, Curtis? Didn't I tell you that we were going to have a little talk first?'

Curtis remained where he was, still conscious of the gun pointed at his back.

'See that, Phillip?' O'Farrell could barely contain his laughter.

'Sweating like a pig,' said the man with the gun.

'Turn around,' said O'Farrell then, this time deadly serious.

Slowly, Curtis did as he was told. Somewhere close, a pressure valve hissed. It sounded like a rattlesnake preparing to strike.

And as he turned, opening eyes that had been screwed shut in expectation of the bullet, Curtis saw that O'Farrell had changed places with his underling, who was now standing behind his boss, gun no longer in evidence. The gun had not been at his back since they'd reached the bottom of the staircase. O'Farrell was now right in front of him, standing with his hands on his hips. There was an expression on his face which was supposed to be a smile.

'Relax,' he said, still smiling his no-smile.

And then he punched Curtis full in the face.

The savage blow snapped Curtis's head back, blood flying in a spray from his nose. Arms flying out from his sides, he fell heavily to the soil floor and lay there, stunned, while O'Farrell walked casually around him, looking down at his handiwork. He seemed to be studying him, as if making some kind of artistic judgment about the way he had fallen.

'And *here*, I think,' he said, still casually, before kicking Curtis hard in the ribs.

Curtis cried out in agony, rolling and hugging himself tight.

This time O'Farrell kicked him in the base of the spine. Curtis spasmed, head back and arms groping behind him as his back arched in agony.

'Now we've got the ground-rules established, I think we're probably ready for a talk. Sit him up.'

O'Farrell's underling moved quickly forward and seized Curtis by the hair, dragging him to a sitting position, his back resting against a metal canister containing fertiliser. Steam hissed somewhere behind him as his hands covered his face, fingers probing at his broken nose. Already, it had begun to swell, and he could feel the flesh around his eyes beginning to puff up. He struggled to keep from vomiting; the pain was worse than anything he'd ever experienced in his life.

'You'll probably appreciate, Mr Curtis, that I don't like being fucked around. So I think we'll just get right to the . . . Hey, look at that. You've grazed one of my knuckles . . . Like I say, we'll just get right to the point. Who else knows about your visit to Whitley Leisure Centre?'

'Most of my colleagues, my editor . . .'

'*Wrong!*' yelled O'Farrell, stooping to seize a handful of Curtis's hair and slamming his head back against the canister. 'That was just a test. You've been working on this story alone, so no one knows what you've been up to. And no one knows about the two bodies back there in the Centre, because we had a clean-up operation afterwards. As far as the world outside's concerned, no one . . . but *no one* . . . knows where you are, or what you've been up to.'

Curtis almost said: *Wrong yourself. Brenda knows about* . . . And then he stopped himself. If he mentioned that Brenda knew he had been following the story, had been covering his tracks and keeping everything secret from Ronald back at the *Independent Daily*, he would surely be signing her death warrant. All O'Farrell had to do was remove her from the scenario and then everything would be as he'd said.

'So why the rough stuff?' he asked, feeling a loose tooth with his tongue as O'Farrell stood up again.

'You're right. You're absolutely right.' He turned to look at the man with the gun. 'Why the rough stuff?' he demanded. Unsure, as if everything were somehow his fault, Phillip shuffled uneasily and looked at his feet. 'No need at all for all this violence, is there? You see, Mr Curtis, I let my bad temper get the better of me there. Our friends behaving in such a rude way. Killing one of my people . . . nice boy . . . and then running away like that. It made me angry. I admit it. Now is that any way to behave, I ask myself?' He turned to look at his underling again. 'Well, *is* it?' Still uncertain, Phillip looked at O'Farrell with frightened eyes. 'No, it isn't. I'm sorry, Mr Curtis. Things got off to a bad start. Please accept my apologies.'

'Think nothing of it.'

'Now, let's be more civilised. Who else knows that the survivors of that motorway smash all have the power to heal?'

'They don't.'

O'Farrell paused, looking down at him. Then he looked across at Phillip again. 'Did that make sense to you? I mean, did that sound like a polite answer to my question?'

'It didn't sound polite at all, Mr O'Farrell.'

'No, that's what I thought. And, you see, I can feel myself getting angry again . . .'

'They don't all have the power to heal,' said Curtis. 'Just Martin Russell.'

'I don't like that. It's also not what I asked.'

'Mr O'Farrell,' said Curtis, pulling the loose tooth out and looking at it. 'Pardon me if I seem a little out of order here. But the way I see it, you're going to kill me whatever I say to you. I mean, after everything that's happened, I don't see how you're going to allow me out of here alive.'

'He's got a head on his shoulders,' said O'Farrell, turning to look at Phillip again. 'Hasn't he?'

'Yes, Mr O'Farrell.'

'He certainly has. No doubt about it. And yes, you've put

your finger right on the button, Mr Curtis. You've summed up
the situation in one. But you see, the manner of how you die is
very much predicated . . . Good word, that. Do you understand
it? Of course you do. You're a journalist. Good. As I say, it's
very much predicated on what you tell me now. I want to know
everything that you know. *Everything*. And I should tell you,
I'm very good at knowing when the little bird of untruth is
perched on anyone's shoulder. Now, if you're honest with me,
I'll be good to you. One bullet. Here. Between the eyes. You
really won't feel a thing. Over in the blink of an eye. But if
you're uncooperative, well, I'll just have to make the manner
of your departure very, *very* unpleasant. I think that more or
less sums up the position we find ourselves in.'

'Pardon my manners,' said Curtis, trying to find a spark
of courage inside and praying that he could find a way to
outmanoeuvre the most dangerous man he'd ever come across
in his life, 'but I'm afraid you'll have to go and screw yourself,
Mr O'Farrell.'

'I tried,' said O'Farrell to his underling. 'I really did try.'

Like a parent about to administer a necessary scolding,
O'Farrell stood over Curtis, looking down. When he spoke
again, it was with a note of disapproving sadness.

'All right, Phillip. Hold his legs.'

Burwell awoke, and in the instant of becoming aware once
more, he prayed that everything had returned to the way it
was before. He wanted to be back in the motorway motel,
wanted to be waiting for Klark. He wanted Klark to be alive
again, didn't mind that he was being blackmailed. He had
found the money so far; he would continue to find it. Maybe
even find a way of paying him off altogether. And instead
of driving off on to the motorway in a depressive rage, as
he had done, he'd take it easy. He'd wait for a gap in the
traffic, would join the flow, and then he would find a lay-by.
He would pull in there and watch the coach pass him. He
would switch on the radio and let the classical music soothe
him. And he'd stay there listening to the music, waiting to
hear a bulletin warning that this stretch of the A1 should

be avoided at all costs, because there had been a terrible accident.

An accident that had *not* involved him.

And then Burwell would drive carefully home, and pick up his life from where he had left it before that terrible night.

But his hands were cut and bleeding where he had fallen face first on to the shale. The knees of his trousers were torn, and judging by the smell and the dampness it seemed that he'd lost control of his bladder. There was a sour taste in his mouth and his head felt like hell.

'Oh God, *no* . . .'

And then he was overcome once more by the knowledge that whatever was hiding deep down inside him was still there, still wrapped around the very core of his being. Now naggingly insistent again when he awoke. Burwell pushed himself up to his knees, moaning, as . . .

'Can't wait!' screamed the thing, from inside its hide.

There was still light out there, a hideous streak of it on the skyline. But the waiting was too much to bear, and the instinctive knowledge that its saviour was so close at hand was the final goad.

'Can't WAIT! Want to be ME!'

Clawing at the brambles and the bushes above and around it, the thing destroyed its cage and stood weaving from side to side, looking around for the source of its salvation as . . .

Burwell saw what seemed to be a man bursting from the bushes not twenty feet from where he knelt. The sudden eruption made him flinch, and he froze there, watching as the figure tore brambles and shredded black plastic from its head and shoulders. Its movements were desperate and frenzied, and as Burwell watched, it seemed to him that there was something wrong with the man's hands. At first, he thought that the shreds and tatters that hung from the hands and fingers were just part of the detritus that had been clinging to the tattered clothes. But now, as the figure looked around, he could see that it was the hands *themselves* which were tattered and shredded.

The figure saw him, and raised its head to get a better view.

And in that moment, Burwell knew that he was still in hell.

The face was a demon's face. The hideously mangled and torn face-that-was-not-a-face could not exist in the real world. He looked on the red-brown glistening mask of mutilated cartilage, muscle and sinew ... and he began to weep in terror as ...

The thing swayed, aware of the dying light on its body but unheeding of the pain as it saw the man kneeling on the hard shoulder. It knew that the man had travelled a long way, and it was filled with joy that he had found it at last. Its torment would soon be over, because now the thing could see that the man really had brought the means of its salvation and the means by which it could return home.

'You've brought ME,' said the thing, gazing lovingly at Ellis Burwell's face.

It staggered gratefully through the bushes towards him as ...

Ellis Burwell shrieked, jumping to his feet. Still weak and dizzy, he immediately fell back on to his haunches as the thing came after him, waving its terrible shredded claws and nodding its hideously ravaged head like a berserk, animated scarecrow.

Scrabbling at the shale, he managed to get to his feet at last as the thing stepped awkwardly from the bushes on to the hard shoulder. It paused there, weaving from side to side, watching him as it ...

Wondered why he was making those noises. He had come to save it. Surely he should be as glad to see it as it was to see its saviour. It didn't recognise the face that the man was wearing, and felt disappointed because of it. But soon, when it was wearing it again, it felt sure that everything else would fit into place. Its torment was at an end. It raised one arm in the figure's direction, beckoning for it to come forward as ...

*   *   *

Burwell turned and ran back down the hard shoulder, his steps awkward and lurching. He had no idea how long he had been lying there, but it seemed that his legs were cramped. That, plus the still-present knowledge that he was *dying*, seemed to rob him of any strength. A car zoomed past on the motorway. He flung out a hand, hoping that it would stop, but now it was gone from sight and all Burwell could see was the hideous parody of a living scarecrow as it . . .

Cried out in anger and pain when it saw its saviour running away. The thing flailed along the hard shoulder after Burwell and now he was . . .

Running for his life, with a demon from hell not fifteen feet behind him and closing fast.

'Go away!'

Burwell screamed and pleaded like a child as he ran.

'For Christ's sake, *go AWAY!*'

'Cullen? This is Molineux. You've got to do something . . .'

'The Board is meeting now. Our legal and financial people have been called in to attend. But you've got to understand, there are a lot of nervous people here . . .'

'Believe me, there are a lot of nervous people HERE, too. Listen, you've got to get a message in there, convince them about making the legal and financial transfers in the organisation to cut O'Farrell off completely.'

'The plan's been in place for a long while, but it's going to take a lot of convincing.'

'Then how about this? The people that he kidnapped today have just managed to escape.'

Silence.

'Did you hear that? He had them locked up, four of them, and now they're out there somewhere in Kielder forest. On the run. Do I have to tell you the consequences if one of them manages to flag down a car and get away? The entire facility would be exposed, and there's no way that we can keep the organisation at arm's length from what's going on here.'

'This changes things.'

'Get that message in there, and get back to me on this number as quickly as you can. Something has to be DONE . . .'

Sheila looked up at the door when someone rapped lightly on the other side.

No matter what they said, she wasn't going to leave Martin alone now. They'd have to drag her out of the room, kicking and screaming, before she let them stick another needle full of drugs into his arm.

The rapping came again.

'You *bastards!*' she screamed. Standing at the side of the bed, she cradled Martin's head against her breast. Martin moaned.

'*Sheila!*' hissed the voice from the other side.

It was a young woman's voice. Familiar, but surely it couldn't be her?

'Mercy?'

'Yes, it's me. Are you all right?'

'Yes . . . I mean . . . What . . . what's happening?'

'Just a moment . . .'

And then she heard a screech, saw a streak of faint light down the ridge of the door when something was shoved into the jamb and weight was forced against it. There were mumbled curses from the other side, and now she became aware that there was more than one voice. Another male voice?

The door shuddered, there was another loud crack and this time it flew open. Sheila recoiled in alarm as a man's arm flew around the door, grabbing the edge and preventing it from slamming hard against the wall.

There were three figures in the doorway.

Mercy, Harry Stark . . . and the young man called Roger O'Dowd, who had gone straight into a trance when he'd arrived at Curtis's apartment. All three had looked as if they were going to remain in their trance when they'd arrived at this terrible place, but now they were alert, deadly serious . . . and afraid. Harry was holding the Uzi machine-pistol awkwardly, like an adult unsure of a child's toy, albeit a very deadly toy. He seemed worried that it would go off in his hands if he didn't keep an eye on it.

Mercy rushed into the room as the other two kept an eye on the corridor.

Sheila turned to greet her, still not understanding how they came to be here. Mercy saw Martin sitting on the edge of the bed. She stopped, staring at the big, six-foot-four-inch lorry driver who had such an uncomplicated view of life and who had suddenly become the focus of a formless need ever since the horror had begun.

'They've *hurt* him,' said Sheila, her voice cracking with emotion when she saw Mercy's expression. 'They beat him and filled him with drugs and they . . .'

'Dad . . . ?'

'What?'

'He reminds me of my . . .'

Startled, Sheila stood back in surprise when Mercy suddenly rushed forward and seized Martin in an embrace, crushing his face to her chest in the same pose that Sheila had adopted before the knock on the door. She began to weep then. Silently, as she'd learned to weep over the years, but her entire frame shuddering as she rocked Martin in her arms. Sheila stood and watched and *knew*. She did not step forward to separate them.

'Mercy!' hissed Harry, still nervously scanning the corridor with Roger. 'Sheila! Come on, we have to move.'

Mercy was still then. For a moment, she continued to hold Martin. And then she stood back. Sheila watched the back of her head as she wiped tears from her eyes. When she turned, it was as if she had not been weeping at all. But there was something else in her eyes now. A glint of rage that was somehow the most formidable and dangerous thing Sheila had ever seen in her life.

'Right!' she snapped. 'Where is he? That O'Farrell shit?'

'I don't know.' Sheila moved to Martin. He was sitting in the same pose, on the edge of the bed with his head down on his chest. 'They brought me here to him. O'Farrell stayed back there, in that office place inside the church.'

'We saw Curtis and a girl arrive by helicopter,' said Roger, weighing the rusted piece of iron that he'd found lying outside and which he'd used to force the door. 'I think it was Jane Teal. Did you see them?'

'No, they just brought me straight here,' replied Sheila. 'I think I heard one of the guards outside talking about a sleep-walker, and a girl. That's all.'

'It's *got* to be Jane Teal,' said Roger. 'They must still have her with Curtis, back in the church.'

'How did you get away?' asked Sheila. She had taken Martin's hands, trying to warm them.

'They think we're on the run out there,' said Harry. 'That might buy us a little time. Look, there are four of us here now. We need four to make The Call. But I don't know about Martin. Don't know whether he can help. What do you think?'

'We're not going to make it,' said Roger grimly. 'We've managed to make it this far. But Christ, look at the bloody *time*. We're two hours from the motorway by car. Even if we do make The Call, the other two Survivors could be anywhere in the country.'

'And if we make it now,' said Mercy, eyes still sparking with deadly rage, 'it means that the other two Survivors will head for *here*, where we are. Like you said, we've got to get back to the motorway for it to work. So I reckon we'll have to save that call until we're back there. At the place where the crash happened.'

'There's a car parked by one of the cabins,' said Harry. 'If we can get that . . .'

Roger made an exasperated, hissing sound. He struggled to control the waver of fear in his voice when he spoke. 'Do you know how much time that gives us? Even if we manage to get out of here alive, steal the car and drive to the motorway. Then make The Call. If the other two are at the other end of the country, we've had it.'

'And how long will it take you to make The Call?' asked Sheila. 'Back there in Curtis's flat, when the . . . the things inside you were communicating . . . it took *ages* to find out what you had to do.'

'What else can we do?' snapped Mercy. 'We can't stay here,

because we'll be dead anyway. Harry's right. We steal the car and just get ourselves out of this place first.'

'Curtis,' said Harry. 'And Jane Teal. We've got to get them.'

'There are bound to be others in the church,' said Roger. 'With guns, I mean. Even if we *have* got most of the mad monks out there rampaging through the forest.'

Harry looked at the Uzi in his hands.

'I don't suppose . . .' Nervously, he cleared his throat and looked at Roger. 'I don't suppose *you* know how to handle one of these bloody things.'

Roger shuffled uncomfortably.

Mercy stepped quickly forward and seized it from Harry's gloved hands.

'Let me have it. Harry, you take your gloves off and fry the first fucker you see. Roger . . . Well, Roger, if things turn hairy, you just paint a crazy picture and send everyone mad.'

'Knew I should have brought my brushes.'

Roger moved to the bed and helped Sheila lift Martin from the edge. Putting one arm over each shoulder, they guided him towards the door.

'Let's go,' said Mercy, moving ahead.

'Your brother,' said Sheila looking at Roger as they emerged cautiously into the darkened corridor. 'Where's your brother?'

Roger felt a spasm of fear in his guts.

'*Shhhhhh* . . .' hissed Harry, and the next moment they were heading back along the annexe corridor towards the office church as . . .

Chris crashed through another bush and almost fell in the tangle of greenery. Clawing at the branches, he remained upright and blundered on. There seemed to be a rough path of sorts to his right, but he knew he musn't take the easy route. Presumably O'Farrell's people would know the area well, and he mustn't give them an easy chase. Plunging on ahead into a tangled thicket, he pushed through into the forest. The tree cover here was dense, so much so that the sunlight had difficulty getting through the overhead canopy, and the vegetation on the other side of the thicket was brown and grey, starved of ultra-violet light. Despite the heat-wave, it was cool and dark ahead. Heart hammering, he ran on.

They had decided on their plan of action at the compound fence, knowing that there wouldn't be a lot of time after the screams. Far better to make O'Farrell and his men think they'd got over the fence and away, then double-back to the church and see what they could do. Travelling together in a pack through the forest would mean they would soon be sighted and picked up. Splitting up and heading in different directions was another choice, but with the midnight deadline looming, they knew that their only chance was for the survivors to stick together. Harry, Roger and Mercy were survivors . . . Chris knew that he would draw the short straw, and even before they'd fully agreed he had speeded the decision by quickly scaling the fence. Roger had tried to reach for his leg, as if wanting to pull him down again, but he knew that this was the only way. Chris would head off through the forest. With luck, he might well make it. At best, he would provide a false trail long enough for the rest to be able to do something. As the others shrank back behind the cabin, Chris had remained seated on top of the chain-link fence, waiting.

As soon as figures began to run across the compound towards him, he had dropped quickly to the other side and dashed off into the trees. The sight of him alone had been enough to convince them that the entire group had made their bid for freedom.

Chris paused, gasping for breath and listening. All he could hear was his own hoarse breathing and the beat of his heart. He wondered what Phyllida would make of all this. He had left her a brief message to say that he'd had to travel north with Roger on family business. But what would she make of him now, crouched somewhere in the middle of Kielder forest, on the run from a maniac businessman and his employees, all dressed as monks? And somewhere behind him, a bunch of people – including his own brother – who swore blind that they were all possessed by aliens from space, or some such fucking nonsense.

Somehow, he could not see the humorous side.

Now he was aware of movement somewhere behind him. He could hear the powerful roar of a car engine, possibly a Land Rover. There were shouted voices and the sounds of crashing undergrowth as figures flailed and tore their way through in search of him.

'Shit!'

Head down, fear constricting his rib-cage, making his breathing difficult again, Chris plunged on ahead through the bushes as . . .

Burwell clawed through a tangle of bushes, sobbing for breath. The branches tore at his face and snagged in his hair, but he knew that the thing was right behind him. He could hear it lurching through the undergrowth less than fifteen feet away; could hear the desperately horrible mewling sound it made as it came.

'I didn't . . . didn't . . .' Burwell burst through the bushes, feeling something rip his trouser leg. 'I didn't *mean* to kill her. Sweet Jesus, I didn't mean to . . .' There was a grassed slope in front of him. He clawed his way up, grabbing at tufts of grass. Behind him, he heard the thing thrashing through the bushes. It could be no more than ten feet away now, and Burwell began to weep hysterically as he climbed. He had a vision then. When he reached the top of this ridge, he knew what would lie beyond. It would be a stark, burning landscape of fire and brimstone. There would be jagged peaks and crags, and there would be imps and demons crouched there, waiting for him.

'My . . . my . . .' The thing's voice was a horrifying parody of hunger and rage. 'My face. Give me . . . my FACE!'

'I didn't mean to do it!' shrieked Burwell over his shoulder as he frantically clambered up the slope. 'I didn't mean to kill her!'

The thing erupted from the bushes, blue fire crawling on its arms and legs.

It began to clamber up the slope after him.

'Make a noise,' said Mercy in a voice that sounded almost gentle, 'and I'll fucking *kill* you.'

The two men who had been working at the computer looked up in alarm at the young woman who had suddenly emerged from the annexe corridor into the office. One of them had an arm outstretched across the panel. He kept it there as Mercy stepped into the room and the others followed close behind. She kept her gaze directed at him, seeing his eyes flicker as he looked down at the panel and back at her.

'I don't know just what went through your mind there,' continued Mercy, as casual as ever and now bringing the machine-pistol up to point directly at his face. 'But I wouldn't think about it any more, if I were you.'

The man slowly withdrew his hand from the panel, placing both hands in his lap.

'Where's O'Farrell?' snapped Harry, holding the door open as Sheila and Roger brought Martin into the room and sat him in one of the chairs.

'Are you serious?' said the other man. 'Do you know how many people we have here? Come on. Put the gun down and let's talk . . .'

Mercy stepped forward, eyes flaring as she jabbed the pistol hard at the man's face. The muzzle hit him on the forehead, opening a scarlet weal just above his eyebrow. He doubled over in his seat, both hands flying to his face. The sudden, violent movement caught Harry by surprise. He started back, then watched in startled awe as Mercy hissed: 'We're *serious*! And after everything I've been through . . . and what you've done to Martin . . . I'm . . . I'm . . .' Rage threatened to overwhelm her. The nozzle of the gun was thrust forward again towards the man's head. Harry took a step towards her. It seemed certain that she was going to pull the trigger now and blow his head off.

'All right, *all right*!' In abject fear, the man was holding out both hands towards her. Blood streaked his face. 'They're down in the church.'

'Curtis and the woman?' said Harry. 'They're both down there with him?'

'Just the man,' replied the computer operator, now looking in horror at the blood that streaked his hands. The other man sat open-mouthed, both hands thrust down in his crotch.

'Where's the woman?'

'I don't know,' lied the injured man.

'Shit.'

'What are we going to do with these two?' asked Roger.

'Kill them . . .' said Mercy.

'Jesus!' said the uninjured man. 'Look, we just work here, for Chrissake. There's some electrical flex over there in the corner. Just tie us the fuck up and we'll stay here and keep quiet.'

'Good idea,' said Harry.

Roger looked around, and was finally directed to where the coils of flex were lying. The injured man seemed to have gone into shock. He remained staring at the blood on his hands. Mercy moved to the side window and looked out across the compound. There was no sign of anyone down there. Perhaps they had struck lucky and all the mad monks were still out there chasing Chris O'Dowd through the forest. Roger pulled the first computer operator into the corner, still sitting on his swivel chair, and began to truss him up. When Mercy looked back across the room, she could see that Harry had moved to the top of the metal staircase and was looking down. She knew what he was thinking. If Jane Teal wasn't down there, then where the hell had they taken her? All the survivors would have to be together if they were going to get out of this alive.

She looked at Sheila, cradling Martin where he sat.

Something inside made her want to crumple and dissolve into tears. Then she saw the blood on the muzzle of the machine-pistol and felt the familiar rage flooding her again as . . .

Chris tumbled into a dried-out stream bed.

Two weeks ago, there had been water there, but the heat-wave had finally evaporated the last of its moisture and left a crazy paving of cracked mud. He hit the mud hard, sending up a cloud of dust and a buzzing haze of startled midges. The fall had badly winded him. He prided himself on keeping fit, but even so he felt as if he were on his last legs now. It was one thing to attempt a marathon run through the forest when all you had to worry about was beating your fitness club colleagues, but now he was running for his life and he had underestimated the effects that pure fear would have on his system. He was hyperventilating, and knew it. And there was not one thing he could do to relieve the added burden of terror on his system. He rolled to his knees and tried to control his breathing, but all he could think about was the fact that there were dozens of armed and dangerous men somewhere close behind, intent on catching him and equally intent on never letting him or the others get out of this damned place alive. Something about that *intent*, the pure evil will that Chris sensed, almost made him sit back in the dust and put his hands over his head. He would wait until they found him and just show them that he was so terrified, so helpless and harmless that they couldn't *do* anything to him. They'd just ... well, they'd just chastise him a little, and then they'd tell him to forget everything he'd seen and heard, and go away. Go back south, forget about the Brothers of the Holy Order. Forget about faith healers, and people who could kill with a touch, and people who could kill by sexual intercourse, and by painting insane pictures and ...

Roger and his white face with its dark-hollowed eyes.

The only member of his family left, after the death of their parents.

Back there somewhere, desperately following this ridiculous fairy-tale fantasy to its source. And trying to find a way back to being normal again.

But it was a grim fantasy that was not just his brother's – it was shared by others. And the knowledge that Roger and the others *were* back there, trying to do something to end the nightmare, was enough to break him out of the debilitating terror. Slamming both hands on the baked mud so that his palms stung and a fresh cloud of dust swirled around him, Chris pushed himself up again and scrambled up the other side of the stream bed. The dust made him cough and gag. He retched as he climbed, using the involuntary spasm to force out the fear inside. Pushing through the bushes at the top, he could see that there was a rough dirt track not ten feet from where he stood. He looked back, heard the crashing sounds of his invisible pursuers and rethought his first plan about keeping off well-trodden paths. He scanned the track back and forth. The tree cover here was dense and his view on either side was limited, but surely there must be a dozen such tracks through the forest. They couldn't possibly cover them all, and if he followed this one, surely it would take him to a main road where he might be able to flag some passing vehicle down.

Somewhere behind, someone shouted. Had they found his trail?

The sound of the raised voice decided his course of action. Chris stumbled down the bank to the track and ran ahead.

Did God hate idiots?

A Land Rover roared around the bend just ahead.

Chris watched the passenger suddenly begin to gesticulate wildly as they saw him in the middle of the track. The driver slammed his foot down hard on the accelerator and the vehicle hurtled down on him.

Chris spun in mid-stride, looking from one side of the track to the other for a quick means of escape.

The Land Rover roared towards him.

There was a rotten tree branch at his feet.

He stooped to seize it, running to one side and throwing it awkwardly at the Land Rover as he moved. He saw it whirl end over end towards the oncoming vehicle, and lunged towards the bushes on the opposite side of the track to where he'd emerged.

The roaring of the engine was angry and vengeful and full of malice. It was going to slam him down and crush him. It would take him a long time to die beneath the chassis and the heavy-duty wheels.

But then he heard the crack of the branch slamming across the windscreen and the sudden grinding screech of the brakes as the Land Rover slewed across the track away from him.

And then he was through the bushes and back into dense

undergrowth, running like he'd never run before. The fear was behind him, the consequences and the implications were mere shadows, and his body was leaping and moving through the trees with a purpose and a determination like nothing he had ever experienced in his life. He felt as a bird must feel. Close to the ground, but swooping in between the tree boles, avoiding every one of them by mere inches as he flew deeper and deeper. Low-hanging branches lashed at his face and body, but he didn't feel a thing. He'd found his stride and his stamina was superb and his body was now in better form than anything he'd ever achieved on the squash court. He would circle around, and find the fucking main road, no matter what.

And then something hit him hard from behind.

Something that felt like a hard slap on the shoulder. Enough to propel him a step too hard and fast in his forward flight, enough to make him lose all balance and control. His arms flew out at his side as a tree bole loomed at him. He slammed into it, was enveloped in searing agony, and rebounded to the soft carpet of leaves on the forest floor.

He could see the canopy of leaves above him. The gently swaying branches. The spears of sunlight, trying to find a way down to where he lay.

Then he heard the sound of the gunshot. Less than a split second after the bullet hit him.

It was so out of place here. A sound of thunder, when there could be no storm.

Not here.

Not now, in this peaceful place.

He realised that he could not feel himself breathing.

And then the spears of light dimmed through the branches above.

And faded.

And darkness invaded his soul.

Curtis dreamed that he was back in the church where he had seen Martin Russell performing his laying-on of hands. He was in the same seat, listening to the ecstatic cries of the congregation as Martin moved along by the altar and placed one hand on the heads of the faithful who were kneeling before him.

For some reason, the Reverend Jameson had no face, just a blank, pink mask. It didn't seem to bother him too much, and Curtis found himself wondering how he could possibly breathe.

And then Russell suddenly stopped, looked directly across at him and raised an accusing hand, pointing him out.

'*You don't BELIEVE!*'

His voice sounded like the voice of God here in the church. It made the walls of the building shake. Plaster dust fell from overhead and Curtis heard a sound like a flock of bats up in the rafters, wheeling and shrieking in fear. There was a vibration in the ground now, like an earth tremor. Everyone in the church was turning to look at him, their cries of ecstasy silenced, the glare of accusation in every eye.

'*You don't BELIEVE!*'

Curtis stood up, suddenly afraid and knowing that he had to find the right answer if he wasn't to incur a terrible wrath.

'I just write up what I see, that's all. How can I write something I can't see, can't bring myself to . . .'

And he realised that he had almost used the 'believe' word.

Up front, Quinn O'Farrell was smiling at him from the first row.

'What about HIM, then?' yelled Curtis. 'What's he doing up there if he doesn't believe?'

O'Farrell smiled all the harder.

'You've got it wrong,' he said. 'He's not talking about God. He's talking about you . . .'

And Curtis screamed then as Martin Russell's face swelled gigantically to fill his line of vision, mouth opening wide to devour him. There was pain. A growing, hideous, gnawing pain in his body as Curtis screamed and struggled to be free; but the pain was consuming him, eating him alive as . . .

'That's good,' said O'Farrell. 'Try it again.'

The shock of the second bucket of cold water brought

Curtis out of his unconsciousness. As he gasped for breath and fumbled at his face, he realised that the pain was real and not in his nightmare. He was still sitting with his back against the cylinder, and there was hideous pain in his face and ribs. He also felt as if someone had been stamping on his legs. When he tried to lean forward, the pain in his crotch made him gag and fall back against the metal. Phillip, O'Farrell's underling, stepped into vision, holding an empty bucket.

'Give him a minute,' said O'Farrell, and Curtis could see that he was sitting just opposite him, on a length of pipe that ran all the way down the centre aisle of the bizarre church, feeding nutrients into each of the greenhouses along the way. He had taken off the jacket and waistcoat of his immaculate three-piece suit. His shirt-sleeves were carefully rolled up and he was dabbing at his forehead with a precisely folded, perfumed handkerchief. Phillip carefully placed the bucket on the ground and stood behind his boss, waiting for the next instruction.

Curtis tried to look at his watch, but his vision would not focus. Was he concussed?

'Not going to allow you the pleasure of fading away, Curtis,' said O'Farrell. He was breathless owing to his exertions, damaging Curtis in the most creative ways he could dream up. 'I've seen it done before, over the years. Fade away from the pain, go to sleep. Then die. That's just not on in your case, my friend.'

'Sorry to be a nuisance.'

'That's all right. So far, you've given me a decent work-out. I like to keep in shape, you know? But that's enough exercise for me now, I think. Phillip . . . ?'

'Yes, Mr O'Farrell.'

'Have a look in that maintenance shed over there. Just behind the first greenhouse. See if you can find me some pliers. Better still, pruning shears.'

'Yes, Mr O'Farrell.' Phillip went to do as he was told.

'Isn't this heat a bugger?' said O'Farrell when he'd gone.

'Very uncomfortable,' replied Curtis.

'Don't I know it. Five weeks now, you know? I remember about five years back, I had a lot of hassle from my financial people when I wanted air-conditioning put into my administration offices. Not complaining now, are they? That's the trouble in my line of work. I get a lot of whingeing, you know?'

'Sounds like a pain in the neck.'

'Got it in one. Now . . . your mention of pain brings me back to the problem at hand. That's a good phrase, too. "At hand." A man like you . . . a journalist, I mean . . . depends on the tools of his trade to make a living. Doesn't he? Your hands, that is.'

Phillip was returning from the maintenance shed, tossing something end over end in one hand.

'So, on the basis that you're a tougher man to convince than I'd assumed you were going to be . . .'

'Thank you.'

'Don't mention it. Tough in one respect, a little flabby from a physical point of view. You should look after your body more than you do.'

'I'll bear it in mind.'

'Anyway, let's not digress. I think we should just finish what we've started here. There are problems to sort out, and I don't have a lot of time left. Did you get what I wanted, Phillip? You did? Good. Let me have them. Thank you.'

O'Farrell held up the pruning shears so that Curtis could see, now cleaning imaginary dirt from under one of his immaculately groomed fingernails.

'Now, I'm going to ask you ten questions again. And for each wrong answer . . .'

When O'Farrell nodded, Curtis was seized by Phillip and dragged away from the cylinder. Phillip came behind him and jerked him to his knees. Curtis was too weak to resist as one arm snaked around his neck, holding him tight. Phillip's other meaty fist clamped around his right wrist and held his hand out towards O'Farrell as he stood from where he had been sitting on the pipe. Slowly, he walked forward to stand in front of Curtis.

'Who else knows about the motorway crash survivors?'

'No one but me.'

O'Farrell looked at Phillip, impressed.

'You believe him, Phillip?'

'Yes, Mr O'Farrell. I can feel how scared he is.'

'Phillip believes you. Not really so sure myself. But I reckon the best thing to do is to assume that you *haven't* given me the right answer. So I think I'll just do what's necessary. Then, we can proceed to the next nine questions . . .'

Curtis tried to struggle.

His breath was cut off as Phillip squeezed his arm tight around his neck. His hand was held out towards O'Farrell as he moved forward.

Carefully, almost tenderly, O'Farrell prised his little finger from the bunched-up fist.

'Please,' he said. 'Feel free to express yourself.'

Jane Teal fought with the thing that was inside her.

It wanted her awake, wanted her to emerge from the safe place she had created inside her head. But its sense of anxiety, of the barely focused events that were taking place around its 'shell,' only served to fuel the anxiety that was keeping Jane withdrawn from her world. Her own fear of what her life had become, and what had happened at that Nightmare Dinner Party, was *worse* than the fear that the thing was experiencing. And the more it tried to use its anxiety to wake her, the deeper Jane struggled to remain submerged.

It had tried pain to wake her.

But pain did not matter to Jane any more. There were worse things than pain awaiting her in the world from which she had escaped. And she would never return to it.

The closest the thing had come to emerging was at the hospital, when the distress of the others had communicated itself to it as they'd been kidnapped from their 'commune'. It had been able to surface then, but its host had fought it all the way. And after that brief emergence, Jane had pushed it back into its shell.

Now, as Jane sat on the edge of a spare bed in a cramped and airless room, it tried the only other thing left. There were places inside Jane; places like empty rooms. And in each of these rooms, there were fleeting memories, traces of forgotten perfume, images of faces, once seen, long forgotten. The thing hunted through the rooms while the essence of Jane Teal hid deep away, curled like an unborn fetus, refusing to be born and claim these empty rooms as her own property. Deep in one of the rooms, the thing found a voice . . . and stole it.

Jane, why are you hiding?
   . . . go away . . . leave me alone . . .
Don't you recognise me, darling?
   . . . I'm frightened . . .
I know you are. But it's safe to come out now.
You went away and left me. Why did you leave me?
I didn't leave you, sweetheart. You left me. But that's only natural. You can't stay with your mother all your life. You grew up, that's all.
Daddy hated me.
No he didn't. Not in his heart.
And you're not here any more. It's just your voice.
That's silly. Now come out.
You died.
Only my body.
Tom's dead. I killed him.
Come on out now, honey.
I don't know . . . I'm frightened . . .
Don't be. Tom's gone and no one can hurt you any more.
I don't know . . .

Jane opened her eyes for the first time since her arrival at the compound. Sitting still and silent, she continued to stare at the whitewashed wall before her as the conversation continued inside.

Burwell felt something tear at his trouser leg, something that sliced through the flesh and hooked itself in his calf. He fell headlong to the grassed slope and clutched at the baked earth.

Below him, the thing mewled again and began to drag him down.

There was no pain; his fear overwhelmed it.

Screaming, Burwell kicked out with his other leg, felt it connect with something soft and wet. A cloud of mud dust began to choke him as he thrashed and struggled to be free. There was a ripping sound, whether flesh or fabric he didn't know, but suddenly he was free again. Below, the thing shrieked ... and Burwell scrabbled to the top of the bank.

There were no brimstone crags, no waiting demons.

Just the dying sunlight showing that there were fields and fences and more of the dense shrubbery below and ahead of him. He was still in the real world after all. But he was running deep into the countryside where no one could possibly help him and where he must surely finally collapse of exhaustion and allow the thing behind to get him. Somewhere behind was the motorway, surely the only hope of rescue.

The thing arrested its sudden slide down the slope and began to climb after him again.

Burwell refused to look behind him. If he saw it, he would just collapse on the spot.

The motorway. He had to get back to the motorway.

Sobbing, he plunged over the slope and began to veer to his right. His leg had begun to burn. It would barely take his weight as he tripped and rolled to the bottom of the slope.

Throwing himself into a tangle of undergrowth, he began to claw his way back in the direction he'd come from.

Reaching the top of the slope and seeing him vanish into the thrashing mass of vegetation, the thing shrieked for him to stop and come back.

Weeping, it dragged itself over the rim and slid after him.

O'Farrell nodded, and Phillip let Curtis fall forward.

He slumped into a kneeling crouch, both hands clutched together and thrust down into his lap. His head bowed until his forehead was on the earth floor. Never in his life had he experienced pain like this; the violence of his reaction had been almost enough to tear him free from Phillip's grip, even in his weakened condition. The pain of his broken nose had faded in comparison. Weeping tears of agony, he raised his earth-smeared face again, the scarlet mass of his clenched fists still thrust into his lap.

Casually, O'Farrell tossed the severed finger up and down in his hand.

'Look at that, Phillip. Wonderful piece of engineering, the human body. Even something as small as that. Bet the robotics industry could spend thousands ... no, millions ... of pounds in research, and they'd never get anything as flexible or dexterous as this. Know what "dexterous" is, Phillip?'

'No, Mr O'Farrell.'

'No ... I thought not. Never mind. Mr Curtis knows, I bet. Don't you, Mr Curtis?'

'You ... you fucking *animal!*'

'Ah. Now. We're getting rude again, aren't we? What's to say that what I've just asked you isn't my second question? And you've given me an unsatisfactory answer. What I really wanted to ask was how did you kill my "operative" at the Whitley Leisure Centre? Never seen anything like it. Kentucky Fried Hit Man. Very spectacular. So ... we'll have to make that question three. While you're thinking about it, we'll deal with your wrong answer to question two. Hold him, Phillip.'

Curtis lashed out as O'Farrell's underling came up behind him again. The blow connected with his chest as Phillip held him around the neck once more. Curtis flailed with his other bloody hand, trying to keep it out of Phillip's grasp.

'Don't suppose you need a little finger to type with, do you?' continued O'Farrell. 'Never thought about that. You one of these people who use all their fingers, like a piano player? Or are you like me, just a forefinger on each hand?'

Phillip seized Curtis's wrist. Curtis yelled, a sound of pain and consuming rage.

'The forefinger, Phillip.'

Phillip looked up at O'Farrell, clearly disconcerted.

'The long pointy one,' said O'Farrell, with an exasperated sigh.

Phillip tried to squeeze a finger out of Curtis's clenched fist, but couldn't manage it.

Sighing again, O'Farrell tossed the severed finger aside and moved slowly forward. He stood like an impatient parent as Phillip finally managed to hold out Curtis's hand.

'This little piggy went to market . . .' said O'Farrell, twisting the forefinger free from the bloodied knot of Curtis's fist and bringing up the shears.

Curtis roared at him.

O'Farrell closed his eyes, his brows raised in an expression of indulgence. He paused, while Curtis's voice was choked off by Phillip's forearm across his throat.

And then he put the finger between the blades.

'If you do it,' said a young woman's voice from the double doors leading to the upstairs office, 'I won't shoot you in the face or the head, I'll shoot you in the balls. From here, it'll blow your tackle off. Completely.'

O'Farrell looked up as Mercy strode quickly forward, holding the machine-pistol out in front of her with both hands as the others slapped through the doors and into the church.

'Let him go,' said Harry to Phillip as Mercy hurried to jam the pistol nozzle under O'Farrell's nose. '*Now!*'

O'Farrell lowered the shears, and Mercy snatched them from his hand, throwing them to one side and shattering a glass pane in the greenhouse. Phillip stood back quickly and Curtis fell moaning into his previous kneeling pose. Phillip stared at Harry. He was holding one ungloved hand out towards him as if threatening him with an invisible weapon. The glove was clutched in his other gloved fist.

'He's . . .' Curtis groaned as he straightened again, hugging his hand. 'He's got a gun in his pocket.'

Harry moved forward, looked at his own outstretched hand and then glanced over his shoulder at Roger. Understanding, Roger left Sheila to hold Martin and hurried past him, grabbing Phillip's arm and wheeling him to one side as he searched his pockets. Finding the gun, he shoved him away and then kneeled beside Curtis again.

'You okay?'

'No I'm fucking not,' groaned Curtis, still fighting with his pain and his rage.

'You didn't run away,' said O'Farrell, an incongruous smile creeping over his face. 'I don't believe it. You didn't run away at all.' He began to laugh, despite the fact that Mercy was keeping the gun barrel only inches from his face. 'Clever, clever. You've got most of my people out there, chasing through Kielder forest, and all the time you were still *here* . . .' He burst into louder fits of laughter, moving away from Mercy as if she represented no threat at all, and sitting on the metal pipe. Taking the perfumed handkerchief from his pocket once more, he began to wipe Curtis's blood from his fingers, laughing all the while.

'Shut up!' demanded Mercy. '*Shut UP!*'

She was on the verge of losing control, but O'Farrell remained unimpressed and casual.

'Mercy,' said Harry.

'I said *SHUT UP!*'

'*Mercy!*'

Trembling, Mercy stood back, keeping the machine-pistol pointed at O'Farrell's laughing face. Carefully folding the handkerchief to mask the blood, O'Farrell began to dab at the sweat on his brow, his laughter dwindling to an amused chuckling.

'Where's Jane Teal?' said Roger.

'Precious,' laughed O'Farrell. 'Absolutely precious.'

'Where *is* she?'

'No idea who you're talking about.'

'He told someone to take her to one of the rooms in the annexe,' groaned Curtis. 'Wherever that is.'

'Where's the annexe?' demanded Harry. 'What does that mean?'

'Sorry,' replied O'Farrell, smiling at Mercy. 'Still don't know what you're talking about.'

'It's where we were,' said Sheila. 'Those locked rooms. He called it the annexe.'

'We've just bloody *come* from there!' snapped Mercy, her rage now under control.

'I'll go back and get her . . .' said Roger, heading for the double doors.

'You're just making trouble for yourself,' said O'Farrell indulgently. 'You may have pulled off a neat trick and got my people chasing shadows out there in the trees. But they're not *all* out there. You've been lucky so far. But you can't stay lucky for ever. Now, come on. You've managed to turn things around, I admit. So let's talk about it, see if we can work something out . . .'

'I don't think so,' said Curtis.

'So, I owe you an apology, Mr Curtis.'

'You owe me a fucking finger, Mr O'Farrell.'

'A misunderstanding, perhaps?'

'A misunderstanding you're going to regret.'

'I'm going to get Jane Teal . . .' began Roger.

And then Sheila cried out as Martin pitched forward in her arms. She tried to hold his weight, but fell to her knees as he awkwardly rolled to the ground. In that instant, Phillip lunged at Roger. He caught his collar and tried to put his arm around his neck, at the same time grabbing for his gun. Roger twisted away, his shirt ripping, and O'Farrell was on his feet once more as Phillip fell to his knees, now lunging back at Roger. O'Farrell grabbed for the machine-pistol, seizing the stock as Mercy yanked backwards, still holding on tight.

In that instant, Harry grabbed Phillip's shoulder, intending only to hold him back as Roger sidestepped and raised the gun.

The effect was instantaneous.

There was a piercing crack and the interior of the church was lit by a blinding blue-white flash. The shock of the contact threw Phillip flat on his back, and Harry reeled away. The sudden brilliance had dazzled O'Farrell, but Mercy's back had been turned to the unexpected flash. O'Farrell clung to the machine-pistol as Mercy yanked down hard. But the action meant that his legs were forced apart as he braced himself, and Mercy did not hesitate. She lunged forward and kicked him hard between the legs. O'Farrell yipped. Face contorting in agony, he fell to his knees, clutching at the site of a ruptured testicle.

Curtis had a hideous feeling of déjà vu as a stench of burning filled the air. Still kneeling, he looked from where O'Farrell knelt in a similar prayer-like stance of agony to the smouldering body that lay on the floor. Phillip was lying face down, but there was a ragged smouldering patch on his shoulder where Harry had grabbed him. There was another sound now, like crinkling tissue paper, as his hair shrivelled and smouldered. Beyond him, Harry Stark was staring at his bare hand as if he could not understand what he was looking at. He too was sinking to his knees.

Roger had paused, his face now a blank mask.

Mercy was frozen, still holding the machine-pistol.

And Martin was struggling to raise his head as Sheila tried to turn him over into a more comfortable position.

Déjà vu, thought Curtis. *This has all happened before*.

And then he realised that something like this *had* happened before. He had been kneeling like this on the casualty department floor of Eastleigh Hospital . . . and the survivors of the motorway crash had stood there, somehow frozen beneath the living stormcloud, looking at each other, and silently communicating.

Just as they were all looking at each other now.

Curtis saw the look on Martin Russell's face as he twisted around to get a better view, and then he quickly looked at Harry Stark, seeing something in his eyes which he had experienced both in the hospital and back at his apartment when each of the survivors had gone into silent communication.

The machine-pistol fell from Mercy's limp hands and clattered on the ground.

They all turned to look at each other.

'For God's sake, not *now*!' yelled Curtis, shuffling around on his knees.

'What is it?' demanded Sheila breathlessly, turning to stare at him, still trying to make Martin comfortable.

'Can't you see it?'

The air was filled with something other than the nauseating stench of burned flesh. Now there was a familiar sensation, like static electricity passing invisibly between the silent figures.

'They're making The *Call*! To draw the others. But not now. For Christ's sake, not *yet*!'

O'Farrell scrabbled forward with one hand, reaching for the machine-pistol, but still crippled by agony. Curtis lunged forward on his knees, braced one hand on the ground and snatched up the Uzi with his injured hand. The renewed pain fuelled his anger.

'What's the point, you stupid bastards! Make The Call now, and you'll only draw the other two *here*. You've got to get to the motorway.'

Sheila cradled Martin's head.

'Curtis . . .' she began.

'There's a whole fucking army of gangsters out there. Armed to the teeth. And you're making The Call here? We had a chance to get away. We've *still* got a chance. Stop it! Come on, pull *out* of it . . .'

'Curtis!'

He looked over at Sheila, pushing himself into a sitting position and swinging the Uzi around to point at O'Farrell.

'It's now or never,' continued Sheila. 'Look at them. Can't you see it?'

'But there's still time . . .'

'Look at your watch, Mr Curtis. There's *no* time left. They'll soon be dead. And so will my Martin.'

'Aren't we having fun?' grimaced O'Farrell, still clutching at his crotch as he eased himself back against the green-house pipe.

Curtis shuffled back to the metal canister and braced his back there, keeping the machine-pistol pointed in O'Farrell's direction. Sheila stroked Martin's hair and began to weep softly.

The other figures stood around Phillip's smouldering corpse, and *looked* at each other in silence.

Curtis sighed. A great exhalation of air.

'Give it up,' groaned O'Farrell. 'You're all dead, and you know it.'

'I've still got a trigger finger, Mr O'Farrell,' said Curtis. 'And like Mercy said, from this distance I can just blow the rest of your tackle off. Completely.'

O'Farrell laughed, the action making him grimace in pain once more.

'My men will be back here soon.'

'Let's just wait and see what happens,' said Curtis. 'Shall we?'

Burwell fell heavily.

The pain in his calf where the thing had seized him had spread to the rest of his leg. And the more he struggled and clambered and ran, the worse the pain became. He refused to look at his leg; knew that the sight of the wound and the blood would rob him of his remaining strength. His face was a mask of spider's web scratches where branches and twigs had cut into his flesh like a flagellant's purge. He tried to control his breathing and listened for the sounds of the thing behind him.

But there was no thrashing of undergrowth, no hideous mewling or horrifying cries of hunger and desperation. Had he lost it somewhere in the tangle of bushes and hedgerows? Had the scarecrow found other crows to chase?

He felt something like laughter begin to bubble inside at the thought of a scarecrow uprooting itself like that. He struggled to contain it, because he knew that it was not laughter at all. If he gave in to this impulse now, and laughed even a little bit, he knew that he would never stop. Because it was madness inside. Something that would take him over, and suffocate him.

And the thing might hear him.

And find him.

He pushed himself up and warily looked back the way he had come. No, there was nothing behind him now. He was sure of it.

Something moved ahead.

Flinching, ready to dash back the way he had come, Burwell suddenly realised what the sound had been.

A sound like rushing wind.

The sound of motorway traffic.

He had done it, after all. He had circled around in his mad flight from the scarecrow and come back to the motorway again. No matter what, he would flag something down. A car, a truck, a van. *Anything*. And when he'd got away from this terrible place, he would return home to find that, just as he'd prayed, everything was the same as it had been before the crash. Carefully, he edged forward out of the shrubbery, pushing more of the tangled undergrowth out of his line of vision.

Something flashed past. Something too quick to register. But Burwell had seen it through the ragged screen of undergrowth. He stopped, heart pounding, pain like fire still eating at his leg. It flashed again. Again, the rushing sound of wind.

It was traffic.

Not thirty feet or so from where he crouched.

He pressed on, glancing back over his shoulder, listening intently for any tell tale sounds of movement from the scarecrow back there in the bushes. The baked mud beneath him was spotted with the same red shale that had skinned his knees and palms when he'd first seen the thing. The shale became denser as he crawled, but this time he did not mind the needle-prick of it in the raw flesh of his knees as he moved. Because he knew what the red shale meant. He was close to the hard shoulder. Now he could see it just ahead, through the last tattered veils of shrub. Beyond that, the tarmac. Gathering himself, Burwell gritted his teeth at the pain in his calf, and then launched himself up through the shrubs and on to the hard shoulder.

Straight into the arms of the ragged thing which had been standing there, waiting for him.

Burwell shrieked as the raw meat of the thing's no-face was thrust towards his own. The arms locked around his waist. Spider's web strands of blue fire crackled and stabbed into his flesh where the thing touched him.

'*Give me my FACE!*'

Still shrieking, Burwell clawed at the horrifying open wound that had once been George MacGowan's face. Shreds of cartilage and red-weeping tissue came away in his clawing fingers as the two figures danced in a hideous parody of a loving embrace on the hard shoulder.

The thing's skeletal teeth champed on Burwell's fingers, opening up his knuckles to the bone. There was crawling blue fire in the thing's parody of a mouth.

Burwell clawed and ripped.

And the thing staggered on the shale.

In that instant, Burwell ripped himself free. The thing's claw opened up a gash from his neck to the small of his back as he lunged away from it, straight out on to the motorway in a limping, sprawling, mad gait.

Sobbing in rage and grief, the thing blundered out into the road after him. Burwell was on his hands and knees now, dragging himself away.

But the thing had soon overtaken him.

Something slammed into the small of Burwell's back, widening the gash and pinning him to the sun-baked tarmac. He shrieked and twisted around to see that the thing was standing astride him. It had pinned him down with one foot, blood pooling around its shredded shoe. The sun was in Burwell's eyes. He could see only the silhouette of the thing above him as it stood there, arms weaving at its side, the horribly indeterminate mass that was its face still somehow moving, as if it were trying to speak to him with its vestige of a mouth. The crackling blue energy leapt and crawled in its innards and through the torn fabric of the thing's shredded clothes.

It reached down for his face, as if to stroke his cheek with its hideous claw.

And Burwell felt the laughter coming, after all. The laughter that would drive him insane before the thing tore him to pieces.

But now, the thing was pausing.

As if it had heard someone calling to it.

Burwell looked at the claw, only inches from his face, and giggled.

The thing straightened slowly, drawing its claw back.

It looked around, as if hunting for the sound of the calling voice.

And then something else shrieked at Burwell. The thing remained frozen in the act of 'listening', but Burwell jerked his head around from where he lay to see what it was that had made the sound and was now almost upon them.

It was a diesel truck, bearing down on them with its tyres shrieking on the tarmac as the driver frantically applied the brakes.

Burwell saw the tyres spinning, saw the smoke swirling from the burning rubber, heard the shrieking go on and on . . .

But the thing pinning him to the tarmac remained motionless.

And the radiator grille of the truck roared above Burwell as the thing suddenly decided to half incline its head towards this sudden danger.

The truck smashed into it.

And Burwell knew that he was dead.

You can't stay in here for ever, Jane. You have to come out some time.

Who says I can't stay? There's nothing out there for me, Mother. It's safer here. I don't want to wake up again.

It's not safe to stay. You have to come out.

But Tom . . .

Tom's gone away. He can never hurt you again.

You promise? That he's gone away?

For ever.

I'm not sure . . .

Come out, Jane.

Well, all right, then. If you promise that it's safe.

It's safe.

Her eyes were already open, but for the first time Jane was able to focus on what she was looking at. It was a whitewashed wall. By rights, it should be the wall of her bedroom when she was a child. There should be a picture there. A picture of white horses dancing and leaping in the sea spray of a beautiful, sunny beach. But there was no picture there. Just cracks in the plaster.

Jane looked around.

She saw the single bed and the boarded-up window and then the door. At once, she realised that her mother had not been telling the truth. This was not a safe place. This was a strange and alien place that she'd never seen in her life. She stood bolt upright, as if challenging the reality of where she had awoken to find herself; as if the sudden movement could make the whole room wobble and fade and disappear. But the room remained resolutely solid. It was unbearably hot and stuffy. The fear was returning. Jane hurried across to the door and twisted the handle. The door was locked.

And now the fear had become outright terror once more.

Tom was still alive. He had seen what she'd dreamed about, that terrible nightmare of their burning house, and he had locked her in this horrible, cramped room for ever. Crying out in despair, Jane wrenched at the door handle.

'You lied to me, Mother! You did! You lied . . .'

She backed away from the door, shaking her head.

Inside, the thing tried to regain control.

But Jane's terror was deeper and more profound than the thing could ever have envisaged. Her sanity was teetering on the very brink of madness. Desperately, the thing fought to contain the anxiety, tried to make its benign presence felt. But Jane felt the inner stirrings and could only believe that Tom had found a way to get inside her head as well as her body. Bumping against the bed, she sat again and screwed the bedsheet up with both hands, pulling it up to her face like a security blanket. She began to stroke her cheek with its edge, crooning now as she stared at the door.

The thing had brought her out of coma.

But it had lost the balance of control.

Between waking and dreaming, between this world and the next, Jane Teal stared at the door handle.

The thing thrashed and fought.

The door handle burst into flame. Yellow streaks climbed the panelling.

Jane nodded. It was time to go back to the beginning. Recreate the nightmare of burning, because then she had been in control. And afterwards, she could go back to that sleeping place and not listen to her mother's fibbing voice any more.

She stood again, throwing the blanket behind her and stepping forward to stare hard as the door erupted in flame. Behind her, the bedsheet began to smoulder.

No! cried the thing inside.

'Oh, but *yes,*' said Jane as the room began to fill with smoke.

'Well?' snapped the computer operator with the gashed head.

'It's not easy.' The other man had succeeded in tipping himself and his chair over on to the floor. In the process the wiring that bound him to the seat had been loosened, and he had been working on it ever since.

'Get a fucking move on!'

'This is *wiring*, not rope or plastic or fucking string.' He yanked hard again, cursing when it bit deep into the flesh of his wrists. 'That means it's got bits of fucking *wire* inside, you idiot.'

'If we don't get out of this, O'Farrell will cut our balls off.'

'Can you hear anything? Downstairs?'

'Not since that cracking sound.'

'Maybe they shot him.'

'Chance would be a fine thing.'

One of the wires came loose. 'Good. Not long now.'

'Get a move on!'

'Shut UP!' The second man twisted on the floor again as . . .

'So clue me in,' said O'Farrell, trying to find a more comfortable position. Curtis raised the Uzi from his lap. O'Farrell took the hint and remained still. 'Phillip is dead and he looks to me as if he might be in the same condition as my man in the leisure centre.'

Curtis remained silent. The pain in his hand had muted to a dull ache. It was like feeling the beat of his heart in the palm of his hand. Sheila had wound a handkerchief around the stump and he had kept his hand clenched tight around the barrel of the machine-pistol. She had also retrieved Phillip's pistol from Roger's limp hand and now kept it in her pocket, constantly aware of its unwelcome presence. She had left Martin in a sitting position, still staring at the others, and had gone back to the double doors at Curtis's suggestion to make sure that no one else was coming.

'Something's happening,' said O'Farrell. 'I can tell.'

'Shut up,' said Curtis.

'I've been thinking about what you said a while ago. When I asked you how many of the other survivors have the power to heal. You said they don't.'

Curtis remained silent.

'So I reckon that means they don't all have the same healing power. But they all must have some kind of *other* power. Why else would you have spent so much time rounding them all up? Why else were they all acting like sleep-walkers when we picked them up? Why else are they acting like that now?'

'I said, shut up.'

'The plants in here need regular maintenance. Normally that's done by my people upstairs. But they were due to change shift, and that means it's only a matter of time before someone comes down here from the office. There's a back door in the annexe. Someone will see my men tied up in there. Or maybe someone will just come through the front door.'

'Have you any idea how much pleasure it would give me to shoot you?'

'You're not going to do that.'

Curtis said nothing. He just kept staring at O'Farrell.

'Come on,' continued O'Farrell. 'Give it up. How long are you going to keep us all sitting here? It's been ... what? An hour, two hours?'

Harry took a step forward and wiped his face.

At the same moment, Mercy exhaled and looked around her.

Martin groaned, and Sheila rushed back from the double doors to sit beside him again.

'They did it,' said Roger, his voice dry and cracked as he put his hands to his head. Sheila hastily rose and shoved the gun back into his hand before returning to Martin, glad to be rid of the weapon. Roger looked at the gun for a moment, as if not knowing what it could possibly be. He shook his head again. 'They made The Call.'

'Great,' said Curtis angrily. 'Welcome back. And well done . . . I don't think.'

'Christ,' said Mercy. 'That was unreal. I was here . . . but I wasn't here . . . and I could hear myself, I mean . . . itself . . . and the others. Just . . . just calling. I don't understand it, but I'm not . . .' Suddenly, she was completely aware of what was inside her. She did not understand it, should perhaps have been terrified. But now she realised that fear of the thing inside was not a factor. 'I'm not *afraid* of it. It doesn't mean me any harm. It just wants . . .'

'To survive,' said Martin weakly. He still looked desperately ill, but something in his demeanour seemed to suggest that he was more aware of his companions and his surroundings than before. Sheila hugged him tight.

'Well, they've wasted their chance,' said Curtis, angrily aware of O'Farrell's new grin. 'Like O'Farrell says, it's just a matter of time before the others get back here.'

'There's a car outside,' said Mercy. 'We saw it on the way into the annexe.'

Curtis looked at her with renewed hope.

'Car keys?' asked Roger, trying not to think about Chris out there in the forest somewhere, being hunted like an animal.

'No problem,' said Curtis, now able to return O'Farrell's grin. 'Wouldn't be the first time I'd had to hot-wire a car.'

'Then what are we waiting for?' asked Harry, jamming the glove back on to his bare hand. Striding across the room, he stood over O'Farrell. Suddenly, the grin was gone from the businessman's face. 'Do you want to stand up? Or would you prefer me to "touch" you the way I touched your friend over there?'

O'Farrell struggled to rise, retching at the pain in his groin. Harry waited impatiently as he clutched at the pipe and managed to get into a half-stooped position. Roger helped Sheila with Martin and between them they walked him towards the double doors as Mercy helped Curtis to stand. The sight of O'Farrell's agony served as an incentive to Curtis not to reveal his own. With a broken nose, a broken rib and a mutilated hand, it was hard not to make a noise. But Curtis managed, his only concession being to hand the machine-pistol back to Mercy. She took it, and Curtis leaned on her arm as he hobbled towards the door. Harry made as if to shove O'Farrell forward, but avoided contact, still uncertain about what had happened to Phillip but not wanting the experience to be repeated.

'Not so much to laugh about now,' said Curtis as they moved to the doors. 'Is there, Mr O'Farrell?'

Roger kicked one of the double doors open.

And they all heard the shrieking from the office at the top of the metal staircase.

The door and the bed were ablaze, but Jane remained standing, staring at the door handle. When she blinked, the flames around the door snuffed out. She leaned forward and twisted the handle, the flesh of her hand sizzling in the heat. But she felt no pain as she tugged, and the burned-out, fused metal of the interior lock mechanism cracked and split apart.

She opened the burning door as flames from the blazing bed transferred to the walls and ceiling behind her, fanned by the sudden draught. Slowly, she walked out into the annexe corridor.

'Tom? Are you there?'

She turned in the direction of the office. As she walked, she placed one hand on each wall with each step.

And left a burning handprint in the fabric of the wall as she moved, the flames curling and licking towards the wooden ceiling of the church.

'You shouldn't have hurt me, Tom. You shouldn't have done what you did.'

Inside, the thing fought and twisted at the very core of her being.

But Jane was no longer there. She was here. Back in the nightmare, and ready to relive everything that had gone before, so that she could return to the safe place once again.

At last, she reached the doors leading into the office. Behind her, a dozen blazing handprints in the wall had turned the corridor into a raging mass of flame, just as surely as if the entire length of it had been soaked in paraffin. Somewhere in the spiralling mass of fire there was the sound of shattering glass as the window of the room in which she had been incarcerated exploded outwards.

Jane gripped the door handle, twisted and pushed at the wood with both hands.

It swung inwards, fire crackling like bunsen flame on the varnished wood surface.

There was a man sitting at the computer console, not far from where she had entered. Another was on his knees on the floor, ripping the last of the electrical flex free from his legs, untying himself from the swivel chair. Jane looked at the first man, saw his eyes widen.

'Till death do us part, Tom. That's what the priest said.'

She walked into the room as the second man finally tore himself loose and staggered to his feet. She leaned over the console and touched the first man lightly on the wrist.

And Tom exploded into flame as he jerked back in the swivel seat to which he had been tied. He screamed, high and shrill as his feet stamped and thrashed on the floor. His swivel chair flew in a circle, away from the console, and his hair stood up, as if there had been a sudden blast of air from below. In that same instant, it flared with orange flame, engulfing his head, which twisted maniacally from side to side as if trying to shake the fire loose. And then something seemed to burst in his rib-cage as the swivel chair banged against a wall and overturned. Fire roared from his torn shirt-front to engulf his body completely. Now, only his legs were visible, impotently jerking like those of a burning marionette.

The second man turned to run for the stairs, but his legs

became tangled in the remaining electrical flex and he fell face first to the floor. Uttering hoarse cries of horror, he scrambled on hands and knees, hurling the swivel chair to one side.

Suddenly, there was a hand on his shoulder.

He twisted around, slapping frantically at the hand, and saw the young woman standing over him. She was smiling grimly.

'You shouldn't have done it, Tom,' she said.

And then there was only fire and agony and screaming.

Roger recoiled from the double doors, blundering into Harry. Now they could hear another noise. A fierce crackling, roaring sound.

And then a billowing cloud of smoke and sparks came down the metal staircase, engulfing them.

Harry lunged back, letting the doors slap shut. The smoke curled and gushed against the windows set into the door, momentarily blocked.

'Christ, the place is on *fire!*' said Roger in horror.

Curtis pushed away from Mercy, looking back down the centre aisle of the church. Mercy took O'Farrell by the collar, keeping him at arm's length and the machine-pistol barrel directly in front of his face. She felt worse now than she'd ever done, with hardly any strength at all, and wondered how the others were coping. If O'Farrell should try to pull free now, he would probably succeed with no trouble at all.

'The main doors,' said Curtis. 'We'll have to go that way.'

'But Jane's back in there somewhere . . .' began Harry.

'What *else* can we do?'

Grimly, Harry nodded, reaching into his pocket for his second glove. Jamming it on to his hand, he went to help Sheila and Roger with Martin as they turned and headed quickly down the aisle.

Mercy looked back at the double doors, pushing O'Farrell ahead of her. Smoke was beginning to creep under them now and she could see flames licking against the glass of the windows. In seconds, the fire seemed to have engulfed the entire stairwell leading up to the office.

'O'Farrell's men,' she snapped. 'It must be them.'

O'Farrell grunted. 'Setting fire to a hundred and fifty thousand pounds' worth of drugs crop?' he said miserably. 'I don't think so.'

'You'd better hope that car is in working order,' said Roger ruefully. 'And that nobody tries to stop us.'

Curtis pushed ahead, hurrying to the main doors. He looked back, waving at them to wait while he took a look. They watched him carefully open the door and put his head outside. Behind them, something cracked, and they looked back to see that one of the windows in the doors had shattered. Flames were leaping through the broken glass and into the church, hungry to gain access.

'Shit!' hissed Curtis.

'What is it?' Mercy took O'Farrell by the collar from behind. He did not resist.

'Bad news.'

'They're back, aren't they?' grinned O'Farrell. 'My people have found out that you didn't decide on a game of hide-and-seek in the forest, after all. And they've ... all ... come ... *back*.'

Curtis said nothing, but his expression confirmed what O'Farrell had said. 'Mercy!' he snapped, waving frantically at her. 'Come here! *Quick!*'

Roger moved to O'Farrell, grabbing his arm and keeping Phillip's pistol jammed into his side as Mercy staggered to join Curtis at the entrance. Before she could react, he had seized the machine-pistol from her, hissing in pain when the stump of his finger connected with the stock. He looked down at the pistol as if not understanding how it would work, before twisting himself around the edge of the opened door.

Then he let off a burst of fire, his body shuddering with the recoil.

Mercy drew back in shock. The others tensed. And then Curtis slammed the door shut, looking back at them with a white face.

'They're out there. A bunch of them were making a run for the door.'

'Give it *up*,' said O'Farrell tightly. 'Do you know how many people I have here?'

'We're trapped,' said Sheila, holding Martin tight.

Behind them, something exploded in the stairwell, flinging both doors inward.

Fire roared into the church.

'*Cullen? This is Molineux. The situation here is out of control. Do you hear me? We've got to have an answer from the Board . . . and I mean NOW!*'

'*The meeting's still in progress. I got a message in, but we just have to wait. It's not an easy process. The important thing is that you contain the situation and ensure that our unofficial guests don't get out of the forest.*'

'*The guests are still here. In the church.*'

'*But you said . . .*'

'*We don't have time to fuck around, Cullen. Only one of them got out, and he's been apprehended. The others doubled back and we believe they've taken control of the facility . . .*'

'*They've WHAT? Where the hell is O'Farrell?*'

'*They've got him in there. In the church.*'

'*And what the hell are YOU doing?*'

'*We're in a holding situation. We've got the place surrounded. But you'd better get that decision now, Cullen. Because the annexe to the church is burning.*'

'*Well get some men in there! Get it sorted!*'

'*We tried that. Our guests have managed to get their hands on some weaponry. One of our operatives was cut down when we tried to get access through the main doors. The annexe entrance is burning and we can't effect entry from there. And we don't know how many more of them are armed. Everything here is turning to shit, and we need a decision NOW . . .*'

The surging flame that had enveloped the double doors and the stairwell was suddenly snuffed out. The doors continued to smoulder, the flame that had transferred to the interior walls still leaping and roaring towards the wooden rafters of the church ceiling. But now the area leading into the stairwell was a smoking tunnel. It seemed that the fire was a living, moving thing. Having consumed the stairwell and burned it out, it had entered the church and was hunting for them, devouring and raging as it moved towards them. The central path between the burning greenhouses on either side now looked like the aisle in a Church of Hell.

Curtis was still at the main doors.

'We'll have to give ourselves up!' shouted Sheila. 'We don't have a choice.'

'They'll cut us down as soon as we step outside,' countered Harry.

Overhead, smoke was rising to engulf the rafters. Sparks were gushing in the wooden framework.

'Look,' said O'Farrell desperately, staring back down the aisle at the approaching inferno. 'Use me as a shield. Make me go first. I'll tell them to let you get into the car you saw.' He turned to look at Harry, eyes wild. 'Then you can get away and . . .'

'Oh my *God*,' said Mercy.

They turned to look at what she had seen.

A figure had appeared in the smoking tunnel that had been the stairwell.

It was a young woman, walking slowly through the smoke and apparently unaffected by the swirling, ragged clouds of it as she came into the church. Somehow, she seemed miraculously unaffected by the flames. She appeared to be calling for someone as she moved down the centre aisle, but the roaring of the flames obliterated the sound of her voice. Her hair flew up around her head in the blast of hot air as a greenhouse exploded. A great tongue of flame licked across the aisle, and now it seemed that the woman was no longer impervious to the flames as it caught her hair, making it flare like some hellish orange halo.

'It's Jane Teal!' yelled Curtis. 'Christ, she'll *fry* . . .' Flame belched into the church as if through an opened furnace door. Instantly, the walls on either side flared and began to burn. A cloud of sparks showered down, landing on the greenhouse roofs and setting fire to the nearest frames. Roger had moved towards the doors but stopped, shielding his face, when the heat-wave blasted down the central aisle towards them.

'What have you done?' shouted O'Farrell, his face a mask of rage. 'What have you *done?*'

'There must be another way out.' Roger whirled back and grabbed O'Farrell by the throat. 'There *must* be!'

Somewhere deep within the burning annexe, something else exploded. This time the entire frame of the church was shaken, the vibration making the very ground on which they stood shudder.

'There's no other way. The annexe or the front doors. That's it!'

'Windows?' Harry stepped over a shin-high barrier towards one of the greenhouses, scanning the bare walls. 'You must have windows or something in here.'

'There are *no* fucking windows!' O'Farrell struggled in Roger's grip as the rapacious flame engulfed the greenhouse beside which Curtis had been interrogated. The glass panes began to crack and splinter as the crops inside were consumed in a flaring, surging fireball. 'The annexe or the doors at the front! Make your minds up. I told you to give it up. You can't get out of here alive. Not *now!*'

'There must be a way . . .' Mercy ducked instinctively as the greenhouse on the other side of the aisle was suddenly engulfed in flames.

The fireball was consuming everything it touched with frightening speed. As it transferred to the greenhouses and the walls and the ceiling, it seemed intent on reaching them, pausing only long enough to ensure that everything it touched on its way was burning fiercely first.

Deep within the annexe, there was another shuddering roar.

They watched in horror as the young woman suddenly stopped, the inferno raging around her. Slowly, she knelt in the centre aisle. Her mouth was still working. And then, as casually as a child deciding to have a nap, she lay down on the earth floor of the centre aisle, tucked her hands under her face . . . and went to sleep.

'Jesus . . .'

Roger stared in horror. Somehow, he had been catapulted back to the day of the crash. Raging flame. An overturned coach. Back then, he had managed to save Jane Teal . . . and now it seemed that he must relive the terrible event all over again. Even before he had made a conscious effort, he was running down the centre aisle, unheeding of the others behind him yelling for him to come back. Head down, he ran hard, flinching only when another greenhouse imploded somewhere deep within the raging fire. Above him, he could see that the rafters in the roof were now ablaze directly above where the girl lay. Something cracked and groaned up there.

The young woman lay still and composed, her burned hair smoking.

Pipes containing nutrients had begun to rupture and explode, sending clouds of liquid fire like burning petroleum into the air. A blazing pool suddenly erupted across the aisle . . . but Roger was through it and almost fell over the young woman. Her face was calm, and when he grabbed her he could have sworn that there was a smile on it.

But now he knew that his crazy impulse would be to no avail. This wasn't a rerun of the crash. God was playing a cruel joke. Everything had come full circle. The first time, he had managed to pull Jane out of the blazing wreck, but now he didn't even have the strength to stand. He collapsed to his knees, holding her unconscious in his arms. The fire was closing in on all sides, the heat drying the last moisture from his skin before he cooked. They were both going to die this time . . . both going to burn . . .

'Can't . . .'

He bowed his head.

NOT DIE! the thing inside seemed to shout. *NOT DIE!*

The shout startled Roger. His head came up and he was aware of the searing pain in his right arm where a drop of molten nutrient had burned through his shirt. He brushed it away and looked down again at Jane's little-girl face.

NOT DIE!

'Then do something to *help* me, you bastard!' he yelled into the flames. 'This is all your fucking *fault*, and all you can do is *shout* at me!' Goaded into a terrible rage, he lurched to his feet, dragging Jane up with him. 'I never *asked* for this, you know! Never *asked* for it . . .'

The roaring flames at his side had suddenly become something else. It was the hellish spiral of the painting he had created under the influence of what they had called The Storm Between. It was here now, mocking him. He'd wanted to blow people's minds, and *this* was what he had been allowed to create. Something that brought death, not all the positive, good things he'd wanted his art to bring.

And there was something else in the hellish inferno now, a figure that was running a race of life and death to save them. The silhouette of his running brother.

'*Chris* . . .'

His overwhelming rage at everything that had happened and his fear for his brother suddenly energised him. With his last remaining of scraps strength he whirled back to face the way he had come. The burning pool was flaring, cutting off his way back to the others. He could not see them beyond the curtain of flame. Gritting his teeth, suddenly knowing that he must surely collapse and let the fire take them both, he yelled again and ran ahead through the fire, screwing his eyes shut. His shirt-sleeves flickered as he lunged through. He could feel the pain like fire and ice on the skin of his arms and on his face. His eyebrows were gone, instantly scorched away. His hair was singed.

But he was through and stumbling down the centre aisle again, dimly aware of shapes that had come running to help him. He stumbled on, holding on tight to Jane Teal and weeping at the thought of all the people back there in the coach, burning. And then he fell to his knees, Jane sprawled before him. Steam and smoke rose from his melted shirt and trousers, but he could no longer feel the pain of the burns to his arms and legs. As Sheila and Mercy dragged Jane down the aisle, Harry hurried forward to reach for him. Roger pitched forward, face first, the last of his strength drained. Grabbing him under the armpits, Harry pulled him after them as the exploding nutrient pipes finally set the entire ceiling of the church ablaze.

'There's no other way,' shouted Harry above the sounds of the roaring fire. Grabbing O'Farrell, he shoved him towards the front doors of the church. 'You'd better make them listen to you. Or I swear to God I'll . . .'

'All right, *all right!*' O'Farrell's previous composure seemed to have deserted him. Nodding in hasty agreement, he moved towards the front doors. Curtis turned to look back at the others, and saw Harry's eyes widen in fear as he looked up.

'Curtis, LOOK OUT!'

Curtis heard something crack and splinter directly overhead as Harry lunged for him, grabbing his sleeve and dragging him back into the church. Yelling in terrified rage, O'Farrell broke free and lunged for the machine-pistol. In that same instant, Mercy was on his back, clawing at his hair as the three tangled figures blundered back into the church and away from the door.

Just as the burning rafters above the main door cracked and plummeted down on top of them.

'Cullen, we're not waiting any longer. The fire here is out of control. It's spread from the annexe to the surrounding trees . . .'

'We've got to wait. It's not as easy as you think . . .'

'Christ, man! Don't you understand what I'm saying? We're having to pull back. This fucking forest is dry as tinder from the heat-wave, and the trees are all burning to the west. We've got to get our people out of here.'

'Well, move in! Just move your people in there and take everyone OUT!'

'The church is burning fast . . .'

'Someone's going to have to suffer for this, Molineux. There's a substantial investment in that facility . . .'

'Fuck investments . . .'

'Can I quote you to the Board?'

'And fuck YOU, Cullen! Because this place is burning down, and very soon the whole of Kielder forest is going to be ablaze.

*If we're going to get out of here without being fried, then we
have to go . . . now!'*

*'I can't give you that authorisation until the Board has made
its decision.'*

*'A forest fire means that the emergency services will be here
at any time. Did you get that? The authorities will be here, and
asking questions about how it happened, and who we are, and
what the hell we're DOING here. Now, do I have to spell it all
out for you again?'*

Silence.

'Did you get that, Cullen? Kielder forest is on FIRE!'

'Stay on the line. I'm going into the Board meeting . . .'

O'Farrell had wrenched the machine-pistol from Curtis's grasp
as they fell in a huddle. He twisted it around, trying to get a
proper grip, but now Curtis was on top of him, keeping him
pinned to the ground. O'Farrell cursed and thrashed, trying
to rise, his face only inches from Curtis's own. Before them,
the blazing cross-beams and rafters that had fallen from the
church ceiling had become jammed against the main doors,
creating a burning barrier.

There was no way out of the church now.

The sudden struggle and the falling debris had scattered
the others. Dazed, Mercy had been flung from O'Farrell's
back and was lying not far from them in the centre aisle.
As with Roger, lying unconscious beside her, the last of her
strength was seeping away. She raised a hand feebly towards
the figures who struggled amidst the flames, but she could do
no more than that. She turned, to see that Sheila had stayed
with Martin. He was perilously close to the burning rafters
that had blocked the main doors, and Sheila was trying to
drag him away. His trouser legs were smouldering. Not far
from them, Jane Teal still slept like a little girl on the soil
floor. Mercy tried to move in their direction, but the effort
was too much. At last she could see what had happened to
Harry Stark. A falling spar from overhead had knocked him
aside. It still lay across his back. She could not tell whether
he was dead or merely dazed.

Another nutrient cylinder exploded in the depths of the inferno. The ground shuddered again and Mercy heard the rending crash as the roof of the annexe finally caved in.

There was nothing she could do.

They were going to burn.

She thought of Deinbeck, crumbling and disintegrating and shrivelling away as if he were burning with invisible fire. She wondered if he had somehow got his own back now, and watched helplessly as . . .

O'Farrell twisted from under Curtis, the two men exchanging places as they clung to the machine-pistol. O'Farrell was on top now, trying to squeeze the barrel down across the bridge of Curtis's broken nose, now trying to knee him in the side where he knew he'd broken a rib. But Curtis was refusing to let go, and O'Farrell could feel the searing heat on his back as more of the burning rafters overhead cracked and splintered and groaned . . . and now he pressed all his weight down on the pistol. Curtis turned his head aside to prevent the steel barrel crushing his face; instead, it came down hard across his neck. He couldn't breathe. He felt something stab into his side again and cried out hoarsely. At that moment, O'Farrell lunged backwards, jerking the machine-pistol out of his grasp and staggering to his feet in the centre aisle.

Mercy lifted a hand again.

Sheila turned from Martin to look at O'Farrell in horror, as Jane Teal slept in her safe place.

Roger lay silent, but Harry was struggling to rise now.

And O'Farrell stood in the centre aisle, framed by the blazing greenhouses on all sides. His face was like a mask, a wild, grinning, manic mask. He began to nod his head furiously, as if he had just won some important verbal argument. His grey curly hair was singed and awry, his shirt and trousers smeared with soil and dirt. Expertly, he brought the Uzi to bear on Curtis on the ground before him.

'Looks like you're not going to get the scoop after all, my friend.'

Resigned, broken and ready for death, Curtis looked up at

him. Had it all been worth it? He wondered how Brenda was going to explain what had happened to his editor.

'Just do it, O'Farrell.'

His voice was lost in the roaring of the inferno.

'And to hell with you.'

O'Farrell grinned again, like a wild man.

And pulled the trigger.

Just as the diesel truck exploded through the wall of the church to their right. The wall shattered into fragments as the truck roared into the tangled, burning frames of the greenhouses, sending a cloud of shattered glass and sparks into the interior before it. The nutrient pipes were chewed up under the heavy-duty tyres as the truck bounced, screeching from side to side, the buckling metalwork snarling in the chassis. A section of the church roof caved in on top of the truck, the blazing rafters and woodwork cascading all around it as the swirling smoke suddenly found another gaping aperture to the sky. With a grinding shriek, the truck ploughed across the centre aisle and demolished the burning greenhouses on the other side before coming to rest as . . .

'What the bloody hell was THAT?'

'Molineux? What's happening? For God's sake . . .'

'What do you mean you don't know who . . . ?'

'Molineux? There's something wrong with the line. I can't hear you properly . . .'

'Cullen? Look, for God's sake, get the order to withdraw. Someone's just driven a fucking truck through the side of the church.'

'I can't hear you, Molineux. There's too much interference . . .'

'Where did it come from? We're supposed to have people on the main road to make sure that . . .'

'MOLINEUX!'

'Yes, I'm still here. Look, some mad fucker's smashed through the compound fence and . . .'

'You have permission to withdraw. The Board have agreed to sever O'Farrell from the mainframe of the organisation. The transfers and the covering operation are all active and

enforced. Get your people out of there as quickly as poss-ible.'

'That's all I need to know.'

'There will have to be answers to some very serious questions, Molineux.'

'Check the file, you bastard. You'll find several memos from me to the Board about O'Farrell and his indulgences.'

'I'm talking about how this whole matter has been handled on the ground.'

'Fuck you and goodnight, Cullen. We're getting out . . .'

The shock of the eruption had dazed Curtis, his hands moving feebly to protect his face as something seemed to thunder into the church. At first, he thought that the bullets from the Uzi had smashed into him. Then he realised that he was still hurting, and you weren't supposed to hurt when you were dead. So now he knew that it must be the roof collapsing. He rolled on to his front and waited for the burning beams to slam into him from above. But when fragments fell all around him and he was still alive, he looked back in bewilderment to see what had happened.

O'Farrell was nowhere to be seen.

The diesel truck had ground to a halt. There was a gaping hole in the side of the church through which it had crashed, and although fires still burned around it from the fallen roof rafters, it seemed that the ferocity of the blaze had been subdued by this sudden explosive entrance. The passenger door was flapping open, but there was no sign of anyone in the cab, or behind the wheel. Smoke poured out of the gaping hole in the roof above the truck. Had one of O'Farrell's men done this? Curtis looked around, expecting O'Farrell's employees to be leaping towards them through the ragged aperture. But there was no sign of anyone following. No one could get through the criss-cross of blazing timber. And there was still no way they could clamber through the fire and out through the aperture without being burned alive.

Someone tugged at his arm.

It was Sheila, her face blackened by smoke, coughing as if

she might choke. He rolled to a sitting position, and heard something crash behind the truck. It looked as if the brickwork above the main doors must soon collapse on top of them. Sheila was trying to speak, pointing at Martin, who had found the strength to get to his knees and was crawling towards him.

'Get me . . . get me to the . . .'

'The truck!' shouted Sheila. 'Get us all on the truck before it burns, and Martin can get us out of here.'

'It's burning already,' gasped Curtis. 'Look at it. The bloody thing is wrecked . . .'

Sheila grabbed him under the armpits and dragged him to his knees.

'Will . . . you . . . *get* . . . *UP!*'

Suddenly Harry was at her side, taking over. 'Get Martin . . . and the others. For fuck's sake, come on, Curtis. We need you.'

'I can't . . .' Curtis winced in pain.

'You *can!*'

Curtis staggered to his feet, shaking his head. He looked back at the truck. Was it possible?

Mercy had managed to stand again, and was weaving from side to side. Behind her, another shattered spar fell across the main doors. Some of the brickwork cracked and fell inward in a shower of sparks, but she seemed not to hear it.

'Get the others!' Curtis pushed Harry away from him, and staggered back to the truck. He helped Martin to stand and lean against his wife – and then ran for the cab. There was a burning spar against the opened driver's door. He yanked it aside in a spray of sparks. Steam was rising from the hood. Surely they'd never do it . . . ? But then he was helping Sheila to push Martin up into the empty cab, shoving him hard towards the driving seat. Behind the seats was a curtain, giving access to sleeping quarters for the driver. Could he have been flung back there by the impact? There was no time to look. Martin turned and helped Sheila to climb into the cab. Looking back, he could see that Harry had moved towards Roger. Mercy had rallied and was trying to drag Jane Teal towards the truck.

Something impacted on the roof.

Curtis flinched, dodging to one side as a shower of sparks and soot enveloped him. Another spar had fallen directly across the truck, and now the side nearest to him was beginning to burn. When he looked back, he could see that one of the rear tyres was on fire.

'Martin, can you drive this thing?' he yelled back at the cab as he ran to join the others. 'Christ, speak to me! Can you *do* it?' There was no answer from the cab, but he could see Martin struggling with the wheel. Now he knew that they were all going to clamber aboard the fucking thing and *then* they were going to burn.

Something else roared, and Curtis ducked again as Mercy tried to get Jane Teal to her feet by the passenger door. But this time nothing had fallen from above. And with something like joy, Curtis could see that Martin had managed to get the engine going. The entire frame of the truck was shuddering and roaring in its canopy of fire as Sheila reached down and grabbed Jane, dragging her inside. Mercy followed as Curtis joined Harry with Roger's unconscious body. When Sheila leaned out to grab for his collar, it tore away, the shirt disintegrating in her hands to reveal the extent of the burns to his body. But now Sheila was hauling Roger through the curtains and into the sleeping area to join the others.

A burning length of wood fell on to the hood, obscuring the windscreen.

Harry shoved Curtis up ahead into the cab and lunged down and around, grabbing the spar and dragging it free.

Inside the cab, Martin had dragged the gears into reverse.

'Get in!' yelled Curtis.

The truck shuddered and bucked, its chassis still tangled in the twisted nutrient pipes. Martin jammed his foot down hard on the accelerator, head bowed over the wheel in the effort. Something screeched beneath the front wheels.

'Harry, for God's sake, get in!'

Someone staggered out of the smoke in the centre aisle, not ten feet from where Harry stood. A figure holding a machine-pistol wearily in one hand.

'Jesus, Harry! Look out, it's O'Farrell!'

Curtis saw Harry look back as the figure staggered to a halt and raised the Uzi towards him. And in the swirling smoke, Harry saw the hated face of their kidnapper. He had been badly burned, flung to one side as the truck had exploded into the church. His hair had been burned off completely. His clothes were ragged. It surely could not be possible that this man was still alive. Both Harry and Curtis could see the torn flesh, the blue-white glint of exposed intestine. His hands had been burned and mutilated beyond recognition. And as they looked, they could both see with horror that O'Farrell was *still* burning. There was crackling blue flame around his waist and in his clothes.

And as he stepped forward once more, it seemed that he was trying to smile at Harry. It was a ghastly rictus. And something about the smile had paralysed Harry as the truck growled and lurched and suddenly began to judder backwards, free from its restraints.

'Harry, for Christ's sake, come ON! The roof's coming down!'

But Harry could only stand and look at O'Farrell as the smile became lopsided. Now it seemed that he was smiling the ghostly smile of a circus clown.

'We came,' said O'Farrell, in a voice that was not his own. 'You made The Call and we *came*.' Something was wrong. O'Farrell raised both hands to his face and began to moan, still trying to maintain his lopsided grin.

The truck stalled.

Sparks filled the windscreen and drifted into the cabin.

Curtis leant out through the side window to yell at Harry once more. He saw and heard it all, just before Martin turned the engine over again and the truck lurched backwards through the flames and, tyres burning, began to smash its way through the wreckage and into the smoke-swirling night.

'*I thought I'd found my face,*' said the thing that was not O'Farrell, as the mask of their kidnapper's face slid from the hideous visage beneath and came apart in its claw-like hands. Fifteen feet away, in the ruins of a shattered greenhouse, O'Farrell's faceless corpse lay burning where it had fallen and where the thing that was George MacGowan had leapt from the cab to find the person it felt sure must be its saviour. '*I just . . .*' The thing began to sob, the machine-pistol falling wearily from its grasp. The way O'Farrell's corpse had been holding it, the thing felt sure that it was an important part of its salvation. '*I just want to go home.*'

The thing bowed its head. The blue-fire of The Storm Between crackled and spat from its ragged shirt-front, briefly engulfed the hideous visage and was gone again in an instant.

And Harry Stark stepped up to it, his hand moving to its horrifying no-face.

'It's all right, Caleb. I'm here.'

The thing looked up at Harry, still weeping.

'*Mikal? Oh, take me home, Mikal.*'

And then the truck was roaring out of the church, juddering and bouncing, its four tyres burning like Catherine wheels as rafters and debris rained down on the roof and the hood.

'*Harry!*' yelled Curtis, as the truck slewed out of the ruined church into the smoke-filled night. It careered round in a half-circle before screeching to a halt, jolting everyone in the cab and the sleeping area behind. When it stalled again, Curtis jumped out of the cab and began to run back.

The roof would cave in and collapse.

Harry Stark and whatever the hell had walked out of the flames would be buried beneath it for ever.

But the passage of the truck had ploughed a clear path through the burning debris and back out through the demol-ished wall of the church. Curtis could see both figures, impos-sibly calm amidst the flames. And, oh God, was that *thing* stepping forward to rest its hideously ravaged head on Harry's shoulder?

'Harry! For Christ's sake, will you get the *fuck* out of there!'

Curtis braced himself to make a run back through the rubble.

But Harry was leading the hideous scarecrow out of the flames towards him now. It was an impossibly surreal sight, and Curtis could only stand and watch as they came calmly towards him, walking out of hell. And at last, he realised that it was the thing *inside* Harry which was communicating with the hideous living-dead figure.

They clambered through the ragged gap as another section of the church roof came down in an explosive tangle of fire and debris. The thing staggered on the rubble, and held out a claw to Harry. Curtis almost stepped forward, but couldn't bring himself to approach it. Harry took the claw, and in the next moment they were standing outside the church. At last, Curtis could get a proper look at what he now knew to be one of the missing survivors. George MacGowan, the coach-driver, the Seventh Survivor.

'Harry. Be careful.'

'There's no danger. Not now.'

Curtis tried to look at the thing's 'face', but had to turn away, reaching for Harry's shoulder to help steady him on the rubble and shattered planking as Martin managed to turn the engine over again. He guided them both to the truck. Sheila had pushed the passenger door open.

'Curtis,' said Harry, and when Curtis looked back, he didn't know whether he was talking to the man or the thing inside him. 'Will we make it?'

'Christ knows how we managed to get this far.'

'But will we make it?'

'Get . . . him . . . in the back, and stay there with him.'

They looked back as the roof of the church finally caved in. Beyond, the trees were burning fiercely.

'They're gone,' said Sheila, calling to Curtis down below. 'All those men. They've just *gone*.'

'O'Farrell . . .' asked Mercy wearily, leaning through the passenger door to look down at him.

'Dead.'

'But I saw . . .'

Curtis clambered up on to the footplate. Martin was still revving the engine and fighting with the jammed gears. He had the face of a ghost when he looked up from the steering wheel.

'Think you can find your way to the A1 from here?' asked Curtis.

'No.' Martin struggled with the gear lever. 'But something *inside* me seems to know where it's going.'

'We'll never make it,' said Curtis, looking at his watch.

Sheila tried not to weep. 'But we're free of that terrible man now. And you said that if they all get back to the motorway, where the crash happened . . .'

'There are only six of the Survivors, Sheila. One of them answered The Call. But there's still another one out there somewhere. And that last one could be anywhere. Without him, we'll never do it.'

'Look in the back,' said Mercy. Curtis stared at her in bewilderment. 'Go *on*! Look in the back!'

He quickly followed Harry and the shambling scarecrow around the side of the truck to the back. The flames of the burning tyres had been snuffed out in the frantic retreat through the shattered wall of the church. Now they were smoking furiously. Curtis didn't allow himself to think about how long they might last on a rough track. Harry pulled the loading doors open and guided the shambling thing up into the back of the truck.

From somewhere inside came a terrified moan.

Harry Stark, or the thing inside him, ignored the noise, following after the thing as it climbed inside and found a metal ridge to sit on. But Curtis held the door wide and saw another figure in there, someone who scurried away from the thing and curled up like a fetus in the far corner of the empty truck.

'Don't let it touch me. For Christ's sake, don't let it come near.'

'Nothing will harm you now,' said the thing inside Harry Stark.

'It's . . . it's *electrified* or something. There's blue *fire* in it.'

'You're safe,' said Harry.

'Who the hell are you?' snapped Curtis.

'I'm Ellis Burwell and there's something inside me good Christ there is and that thing tried to kill me it's not alive oh God look at it and it chased me out on the road and something called a sound in my head and the thing heard it too and forgot about me and the truck stopped when it hit the thing and I was right under right *between* those wheels and another few inches and it would have killed me . . .'

'You're the *other* Survivor?' said Curtis incredulously, watching in increasing astonishment as Harry Stark sat next to the hideous living-dead thing and put his arm around its tattered scarecrow shoulders, not flinching at the blood that stained him or the sudden flash of blue light from its tattered shirt-front.

'. . . and the truck driver just jumped and ran when the thing yanked open the door and I wanted to run away but I couldn't because that thing was in my head and it made me climb into the cab with the thing and the thing drove yes oh God it was able to *drive* like hell heading for where we both knew the call was coming from and . . .'

And Ellis Burwell covered his head with his hands and began to weep like a child.

'Will we make it?' asked the thing inside Harry Stark again. When it looked up at Curtis, it was with the same eyes of glass that he remembered Jane Teal displaying in the hospital.

Curtis looked at his watch again, and listened to Martin Russell revving the engine.

'I don't know. But we're going to give it a try.'

'Curtis,' said the thing.

He paused in the act of closing the truck doors.

'Even if we don't get there in time . . . Thank you.'

There was a depth of feeling in the words, and a glittering reflection in the glass eyes, which held Curtis frozen for a moment. It could be the last words the thing might say, and it knew it. Curtis nodded, his face grim. And then he slammed the door, wincing at the stabbing pain in his ribs as he did so. Throwing the latch, he ran past the smoking tyres to the cab. As he climbed inside, Martin was already ramming the gear lever into first. The truck roared away from the burning church.

All around them was the sound of a great, roaring wind.

But there was no wind.

Only the noise of a devouring fire as Kielder forest ignited all around them.

The truck roared out through the gates which it had smashed open on its way in.

The night was brighter than day, with a thousand burning trees on all sides of the track to light their way. All it would take was one falling tree to block the track and consign them all to that burning hell.

But no trees fell, and Martin kept his foot down hard on the gas as the truck roared on through the blazing night.

'And reports are now coming in about a forest fire at Kielder. Emergency services are on the scene but are struggling to contain what is likely to be the worst incident of its kind since 1963. A spokesman for the Kielder Preservation Trust has stated that the conflagration began on the western fringe of the forest but has moved steadily to the centre, destroying tens of thousands of established trees and newly planted saplings. The fire service have as yet been unable to ascertain whether or not a religious sect known as the Brothers of the Holy Order, whose church was established in the west of the forest in the late 1980s, has managed to escape. Aerial shots of the section indicate that the entire area is ablaze and the church itself completely destroyed. It is also understood that a number of burned-out vehicles have been sighted from the air. However, no survivors have as yet been discovered, and rescue services are being severely hampered by the ferocity of the blaze, which has been exacerbated by the recent heat-wave. A fire service spokesman has suggested that the possibility that the fire began in the vicinity of the Order and then spread to the surrounding countryside cannot be ruled out. For a further report on the situation on the ground, it's over to Stuart Costigan who is . . .'

11.59 p.m. . . .
One of the headlights had been shattered as the truck had crashed into the church, the other was badly damaged, and as it roared on into the night Curtis clutched the dash before him, waiting for something to smash through the windscreen at any second. He looked across at Martin, his huge, calloused hands on the wheel, his head bent forward. His eyes were fixed ahead, and Curtis recognised the glassy glint in them. The eyes did not waver, even when the truck hit a rut in the rough track and

Martin had to fight to retain control of the steering wheel. Curtis looked at Sheila, jammed between them in the front seat.

Ask her how she's feeling, said the journalist inside him. Wasn't that what a professional was supposed to do when someone was suffering badly? Hadn't Harry Stark once threatened to kill him for asking that stupid fucking question? Instead, he put his hand on her arm. She glanced at him, and he saw the fear in her eyes. She seemed to be about to ask him something . . .

Will we make it?

. . . but then she bit her lip, clutching the seat as the truck hit another rut and bounced into the air. How long could the damaged chassis hold out? How long before something fell apart beneath them and the truck suddenly ground to a halt? Sheila's eyes were tightly closed. She knew that they were on borrowed time. Part of her still didn't believe that they had got out of the church alive.

Curtis turned to face the front again. As far as he could tell, they were nowhere near the A1 yet. And how far was the accident site from there? He looked at his watch again.

Midnight.

He gritted his teeth and stared ahead into the darkness as . . .

12.01 a.m. . . .
Roger dropped down over the chain-link fence and ran with his brother through the trees. The others had decided to stay and try their luck by heading back to the church, but they needed cover. Chris had decided to do it. Both Harry Stark and the newspaperman were out of condition and carrying too much weight. So it made sense. Chris worked out a lot, was good on the squash court.

And then Roger saw Chris ahead of him, and suddenly he was on the wrong side of the fence. Still with the others, watching his brother run off into the bushes.

'*No!*' He willed himself on the other side of the fence, and the next moment he was running hard after Chris, just as they'd run when they were kids. He was the elder brother, had always been faster than Roger, always won the races. Except for that one time in the back lane when he'd stumbled on a cobble and fallen. Roger had laughed and overtaken him, yelling with pride that he was 'The Winner!' When he'd reached the end of the lane he'd looked back to see that Chris was lying on the ground, hugging his leg. Roger had run back, calling him a cry-baby, but Chris had cracked a shin-bone that day and somehow Roger had never been able to forgive himself for not having stopped to help him.

'The *Winner!*' yelled Chris as he raced ahead.

Roger knew that something was going to happen, that his brother was going to fall again. Shouting his name, shouting for him to stop, he ran after Chris. But here in the deepest part of this dream forest, he could not see where he'd gone. He could only hear the crash and rush of him plunging ahead.

'Stop, Chris! *Stop!*'

And suddenly the trees were gone.

There were only clouds ahead. Dark clouds that swirled like a whirlpool. There was a kaleidoscope of colour at the centre, drawing the eye, sucking at the soul. And now, walking out of the whirlpool, was the silhouette of a man.

'Chris?'

'Yes.'

'You're dead, aren't you?'

His brother's face was blank and expressionless.

'*Aren't* you?'

'Not long now,' said Chris, and turned away from him. The whirlpool was gone. Now there was only brilliant white light, absorbing his silhouette as he walked into its centre.

'Not long for *what*?'

'You're dying. Don't you know that?'

The truck jolted again, and Roger's head banged against the edge of the bunk in the sleeping area, but it did not wake him. Mercy tried to move him to a more comfortable position, but did not have the strength. She turned to stare out of the side window as . . .

12.05 a.m. . . .

She thought about Selina and the kids. They'd probably moved house again, if things on the streets had become as bad as she'd said. She knew that she'd never hear from them again, and that was her last link with anyone from the past. Everyone else was gone; even the sick bastard who had started her off on this long and lonely road.

She looked at Martin, hunched up ahead over the steering wheel. She wanted to lean forward and touch him. But she was too tired. She was slipping away into sleep. Was it sleep, or was it something that only pretended to be sleep? She closed her eyes as . . .

12.10 a.m. . . .
Jane Teal was in her bed at home. It was Christmas morning, and she was looking at the picture on her wall in the darkness; the picture of the horses leaping and dancing in the sea spray. She had heard someone open the door a little while ago, but had kept her eyes firmly closed, pretending to be asleep. And if anyone asked her if she was pretending to be asleep, she would just lie there as still and silent as a mouse and not say a word. She'd heard the rustle of wrapping paper then, as the Christmas presents were placed carefully at the foot of her bed, but she knew that she mustn't open her eyes. Some of the other children at school said that it was the parents who brought the presents and left them there to be found, and there was no such thing as Santa Claus, but she knew that it *was* Santa and that she might just make the magic go away if she ever did open her eyes . . .

And she was never, ever, *ever* going to open her eyes and come back to the real place again. It was much safer for her here. Much, much safer. She tried not to make a secret smile as someone bumped the bed and a big parcel was laid next to it as . . .

12.15 a.m. . . .
'I'm sorry,' said Curtis.

Sheila had been looking at him for what seemed a long time. He had been staring ahead through the cracked windscreen, but could see her out of the corner of his eye. He knew that she wanted to ask that desperate question again, but could not bring herself to say the words. She wanted more reassurance. But they were still travelling through darkness on a rough track, the bright lights of a burning forest somewhere far behind them. And no sign of lights, certainly not motorway lights, ahead of them.

'We still haven't reached the A1, much less the place on the motorway where the crash took place. Harry said between twelve and twelve thirty. I'm sorry, Sheila. It just can't be done.' Still out of the corner of his eye, he saw Sheila lower her head. The truck jolted again, and he winced when the pain stabbed his rib once more.

'We'll make it,' said Martin.

When Curtis looked back, he could see that the glassy glint had momentarily left Martin's eyes. Just like the time . . . a hundred years ago, it seemed . . . when he'd taken Jane from the hospital and the balance of 'possession' between human host and the thing inside had been constantly changing.

'Look at the *time*!' he snapped, and then wished he'd said nothing when Sheila began to sob.

'We'll . . . make . . . it.'

Martin dragged hard on the wheel. The truck screeched from the rough track. Ahead its fractured headlight picked up hedgerows swinging across their line of vision. A tree branch smacked across the windscreen, widening the cracks that were already there. Martin fought with the gears, cursed . . . and then the truck was bouncing and rattling across an open field.

Curtis braced himself against the dash and waited for the front wheels to hit a ditch. Then the chassis would rupture, the axle would crack apart and the whole damned vehicle would turn over. Then the petrol tank would split and they'd be trapped in the truck as the burning petrol engulfed them. He clutched his side, moaning in pain as . . .

12.20 a.m. . . .
Harry was overwhelmed by a feeling of grief.

But this time he knew that it was not his grief. He knew that he was dying, and could not connect with his grief any more.

He was hurt too badly; and the instinctive knowledge that the end of his existence was near had distanced him from the way he had been feeling ever since the crash. For in that dying, there was a natural anaesthetic to this pain that was worse than physical pain. He was aware of the thing within him, had allowed it to surface momentarily as he began to submerge. He could feel its grief, recognised it almost intimately. After all, hadn't they shared the same body and come to understand each other? He knew that his arm was around the monstrous fused thing that had once been the coach-driver; knew that it was a hybrid monstrosity, suffering agonies in its state of spliced personalities. But it wasn't really his arm any more. He had lent it to the Traveller inside himself, so that it could comfort the damaged Traveller inside George MacGowan.

Hadn't he discovered that his inner Traveller and the Traveller inside George MacGowan were somehow lovers?

Now, like an interloper at a scene of intense intimacy, Harry tried to keep himself apart from their reunion. He could hear their grieving, could hear the intimacies, even though no words were spoken. He could *feel* it, no matter how hard he mentally tried to turn away from it. No matter. Soon he would no longer be here. He would have faded away to another place. Soon . . . very soon . . . he would be with Jean and Hilary and Diane and all the suffering would be over as . . .

12.25 a.m. . . .
And yes oh yes I'll be such a good person and I don't care what that thing inside me thinks I'm different now oh yes different and all I needed was a chance I mean a really good *chance* like my fucking mother and father never gave me and I'm sorry I didn't mean to swear like that because I'm a good boy now and everything will be okay there's no hell where things chase you and try to burn you with blue fire and you can kill people by touching them that's just stupid and . . .

'Look out, Martin!' yelled Sheila.

A fence had suddenly loomed up in the angular beam of the fractured headlight, directly in their path. But Martin didn't flinch. He kept his foot on the gas, powering ahead as the fence shattered into pieces. A whirling section flew up to the windscreen. And this time the Plexiglas could take no further impacts. Sheila cried out again as the windscreen imploded into a million tiny particles, flaying their faces and hands with thin spider-laces of blood. The night air flooded into the cabin, but Martin was still staring ahead into the roaring wind as he twisted wildly at the steering wheel and the truck screeched on over the shattered fence, hit a hard surface and swung on screaming tyres on to a bed of red shale.

Curtis stared ahead through the wind.

A car horn screamed at them. There were headlights directly ahead.

'For Christ's sake, *swerve!*' he yelled.

But Martin kept straight on ahead, foot down, and the vehicle that had been heading their way screeched to one side in the darkness and was gone.

Curtis looked ahead at the rushing lights, listened to the howling wind.

Incredulously, he looked over at Martin as he struggled with the wheel, now righting the vehicle and changing gear again as they roared ahead down a clear stretch of road.

'Jesus, I don't believe it!' shouted Curtis. 'We're on the *motor-way.*'

'Cross-country,' said Martin tightly, eyes fixed ahead as he wrestled with the gears. 'Saved a lot of time.'

'How far are we from the site of the crash?' Curtis looked at his watch in wild hope, then his hope was destroyed. Only five minutes. Martin hanging on by the skin of his teeth, the others so weak they could hardly move. Even if they got there, what were they supposed to *do*? He slumped back against the seat as the night wind whipped and howled in the cab.

12.27 a.m. . . .

The thing that had been George MacGowan suddenly tore free from Harry's embrace, tottering from side to side, fighting for balance as the truck raced on down the A1. Harry and his Traveller instinctively made a grab for the lurching figure and Ellis Burwell yipped in the darkness like a kicked dog. The sudden movement snapped Harry back into his own mind again. He could still feel the thing inside. But there was a different feeling now. A feeling of *gathering* inside, as if his Traveller had suddenly withdrawn deep down inside him and was curled there like a foetus. It had gathered some extra strength there now, and was uncurling again, unstretching and *reaching*. It was coming up further than it had ever done before. Harry could feel it reaching and stretching like some Olympic diver, preparing for a spectacular leap, only this diver was coming *up* . . . as the thing braced one claw against the bucking truck wall and gave vent to a long, loud howl. Up in front, Curtis and Sheila jerked around in shock, unable to see what was happening back in the truck because of Mercy, Roger and Jane lying or crouching in the sleeping quarters. Behind and below, the thing continued to howl.

And the crawling blue fire erupted from the thing's waist, where it had been fused together again by The Storm Beyond. The crackling, crawling light swarmed and spread from its waist to its torso as the thing reeled and staggered. Ellis Burwell began to yell in fear as the blue-white energy flowed up to engulf the thing's no-face. Its claws flew to its head as if the energy that spat and sparked there was causing it immense pain, and when the claws were flung away and it stood swaying in a cruciform position, crackling bolts of blue fire stabbed from its hands and filled the interior of the coach. As if filled with St Elmo's fire, the truck hurtled into a line of traffic cones, scattering them in all directions. A cone came hurtling into the cabin through the shattered windscreen, dealing Sheila a glancing blow. She slumped against Martin, who fought to hang on to the wheel as Curtis lurched to look back at what was happening.

And then the strain of everything he had been through finally took its toll on Martin Russell's system. Pain cramped his left arm and smashed into his chest like a steel rod, impaling him where he sat. He was back on the motorway again, in his tanker cab, heading south with Mercy somewhere beside him.

'Something coming . . .' he said, over the noise of the tyres screeching on the tarmac as he lost control of the wheel and it spun from his hands. But this time, the lights on the motorway weren't dead ahead. The light was now flooding into the cabin from the rear of the truck, filling it entirely with a sodium-blue incandescence. Reeling away from the wheel as the heart attack hit him, he was unaware that Mercy had flung herself forward from the sleeping area and had grabbed his shoulders in an embrace, whether to stop the truck from crashing or just to be with him at the last he would never know.

Curtis struggled with the cone that had smashed through the broken windscreen and saw . . .

The same living storm in the rear of the truck as he had seen in the hospital. There was a great writhing blue-white cloud of the electrified mass back there, sending out its lightning bolts in all directions.

The Storm Beyond had returned, the last spark of the energy erupting from the hybrid thing that George MacGowan had become. Now ignited from the sputtering sparks within, which had kept the living-dead thing on its feet since the crash, it had returned in all its spectacular fury.

Ellis Burwell suddenly appeared, trying to scramble away from it by climbing up into the sleeping area. He clawed at the window, and then Curtis saw a bolt of crawling fire stab out from the storm and envelop his face with a spider's web mask of blue threads. Burwell screamed, clawed at his face, and fell back into the cab as . . .

Another blue-white bolt *cracked*! into the cab. Mercy's head flew back, away from where Martin clutched his chest, and at that moment Curtis saw that he had lost control of the truck. There was crawling blue fire in the hands that were clasped there.

The same fire crawled on Mercy and Roger.

It was in Jane's hair. She batted limply at it like a little girl dozing on a summer's day, bothered by a butterfly.

Curtis lunged for the madly spinning wheel, but Sheila was in his way, almost unconscious from the traffic cone that had struck her across the temple. Curtis yelled then, long and loud and wordlessly, as the entire cab vanished in a glowing blue-white phosphorescence, felt the spinning wheel smack hard against his ineffectually glowing and bloodstained hand, and then . . .

The truck hit the motorway embankment with a juddering crash. The front axle shattered, both melted and treadless wheels spinning and leaping into the night as the front of the vehicle buried its nose in an erupting wave of soil and red shale. The fractured chassis, already on the verge of disintegration, cracked from cabin to rear bumper and the entire weight of the truck slammed down hard on the tarmac, raising a cloud of sparks as it slid over the hard shoulder and turned on to its side. The truck spun once, and slid to a halt.

Inside, The Storm Beyond flared and crackled, spears of blue-white light erupting from every fracture and gash in the wrecked vehicle's shattered bodywork, illuminating the night.

Inside, no one moved.

'It's all right, mate. Just lie still. There's an ambulance on its way. Any moment now. No, come on, lie back . . . you're going to be all right. Best not move until a doctor's had a look at you. Christ, you look as if you've been through the mill, but I reckon you're going to be fine . . .'

Curtis's vision finally focused on the shape that loomed before him.

A man with a heavily lined face, and a day's growth of beard. Checked shirt. Craggy, but trying to be friendly. So not one of O'Farrell's men intent on trying to beat the crap out of him in a church without a congregation. Or maybe a doctor or an orderly trying to stop him from kidnapping Jane Teal. Was it Harry Stark? No, it didn't look like Harry Stark . . .

'Thing is,' said Curtis, and the man placed a hand on his shoulder, trying to prevent him from rising. Curtis brushed him aside, and sat up. 'Thing is, it's like this joke buzzer he's got in his hand, see? You know the sort of thing. Shake your hand, and it gives you a shock. Lotsa laughs. Same with him . . . except . . . except mutiply that, like, a *million* times. Can you . . . can you imagine?' The pain returned. His broken nose felt like a bad toothache, all over his face. His rib felt like what his more athletic friends might call a stitch, except ten times worse. And when he felt for the toothache with his hand, he knew there was something missing, but couldn't for the life of him see what it might be.

'I think you're concussed or something,' said the man who had tried to restrain him. 'Come on now. Lie back down and just rest . . .'

And then the confusing images cleared in his mind as he realised where he was, and what had happened.

He was sitting on the embankment at the side of the A1 motorway. The grass was burned, great tracts of it clearly charcoaled, discernible even in the darkness. Down below, on the other side of the roadway, he could see the truck. Lying on its side on the hard shoulder, its rear end sticking out into the road. Someone had placed warning lights around the rear end. Traffic was swerving carefully past it. On the nearside hard shoulder, just below him, were two ambulances and a van. Blue lights flashed and spun in the darkness. A line of red-and-white traffic cones had been scattered all over the hard shoulder and up both sides of the embankment, where the truck had ploughed through them on its way to the site of the accident.

And this was the place.

Curtis knew it well.

Farmers were still complaining about the unnatural blight that had struck the fields on either side and the unexplained effect that the crash had had on their livestock. Down below, he could see carved furrows in the tarmac which the traffic cones had cordoned off until the highway maintenance crews could reinstate the damaged lane. In his mind's eye, he could see the dozens of piled-up vehicles, burning in the night. But now there was only one wreck. The truck that Martin had somehow managed to get back to where the horror had begun. Against all the odds.

Curtis looked at his watch.

The glass was cracked.

It had stopped at 12.28.

He looked back at the flashing blue-white lights of the ambulances below and remembered the last moments in the careening truck, as The Storm Between had erupted in the vehicle and he'd believed that the last vestige of recovered hope was about to be torn away in some cruel cosmic joke. To have gone through so much, with the prospect of failure and death so near that he had almost accepted it, only to find a fierce renewed hope in their last desperate race, and to have that hope cruelly shattered. That last desperation was somehow worse than dying.

The blue-white light was like the energy of The Storm Between. But when he looked at the empty, ruined shell of the truck, the stormcloud energy had gone.

'The others?' he asked anxiously, trying to stand. 'Where are the *others*?'

'Look, the medic's had a look at you and he told me to keep you here. Till the next ambulance shows up. Just two minutes, he said. You start jumping around, getting agitated, you'll get me into big trouble.'

'Where *are* they?'

'All right . . . look, calm down. See, there's the ambulance now . . .' The man pointed down to the motorway, and Curtis first heard the siren and then saw the third vehicle come gliding down on to the hard shoulder. As if on cue, the first two ambulances pulled back on to the roadway, turned and headed back the way the third had arrived, sirens blaring.

'I need to know what's happened,' Curtis pleaded. 'For God's sake, *please* . . .'

The stranger looked down at the ambulance, saw the doors open at the back and the medics jumping out. He waved, caught their attention, and then looked back at Curtis. What he saw must have convinced him that he should keep this accident victim humoured until the medics scrambled up the embankment to take him away.

'You crashed. Down there. Look, I don't know who was driving and I'm not making any judgments. But I was right behind you. And believe me, your truck was all over the bloody road. I mean, all *over*. See, that's my van down there on the hard shoulder. You hit the road cones there, swerved right into that damaged lane. Don't know if you know about this, but there was a big accident down there just a while ago, and the Highways Department haven't had a chance to fix the tarmac and everything yet. Anyway, I reckon you hit that . . . and, well, it turned you over. Thought you were all dead.'

'The others?'

'Well, when I stopped the van and ran over, the whole truck was on fire. I mean, *really* on fire. Looked like the petrol tank had burst or something, 'cause I've seen that kind of fire before. Never thought anyone would survive. The whole truck was *alight*. But then, it wasn't. Just snuffed out, like there wasn't a fire at all. And the bloody strangest thing I've ever seen in my life . . .'

'Please . . . ?'

'The truck wasn't even hot when I got there. Just like it hadn't been on fire at all. But I'd seen blue-white fire all over the thing. Anyway, me and some other people who stopped pulled you all out. Didn't believe we'd find anyone alive. But there you were!'

'Did they make it? I mean, did they all come out of it alive?'

'Look, the medic's nearly here. And you need some help . . .'

'*Tell me!*'

'I don't know, mister. Honest. I heard one of the first medics say he didn't think a couple of them were going to make it. But Christ, *you're* alive, aren't you? And you should thank your lucky . . .'

Curtis moaned, and sank back.

'Here he comes now. The medic, I mean. Now you and your friend here will be safe and sound just as soon as you can say . . .'

'My friend?'

'The other guy. Over there. Now, come on. Take it easy . . .'

Curtis twisted around, gagged at the pain in his ribs, and saw the silhouette standing not ten feet behind him. The figure was facing away from the motorway, looking up at the stars, which Curtis could now see were unbelievably bright and beautiful. He would never have believed there could be so many.

The silhouette was instantly familiar.

'Harry . . .'

But it did not acknowledge him. It stood straight and still, its ragged coat flapping around it in the night breeze, staring up at the stars.

'You're both fine,' said the stranger. 'Dazed, maybe concussion, the medic said. Hey! They're over *here*!'

'Jesus, Harry.' Curtis slumped back to rest on his elbows. 'Never thought I'd be glad to see such an awkward, cantankerous, mad bastard in all my life.'

'Curtis?' said the silhouette.

'Yeah . . .'

Harry turned and took a step forward. It was a curious kind of movement. As if he had been standing there for a long time, listening. And maybe, just maybe, he had caught an echo of a familiar voice, somewhere up there in the stars. Unsure and hesitant, he had taken that step and perhaps even cocked his head as he strained to listen.

'What?' asked Curtis, mesmerised by his strange attitude.

'Give me . . .'

Curtis almost spoke again, but this time the silhouette held up a hand in a plea for silence.

Curtis waited for him to speak again.

'Give me a pen,' he said at last. 'Or a pencil.'

'For Christ's *sake*. I've been beaten, mutilated, burned, hit over the head so many times I can't fucking count it, my nose feels like it's not there any more and you want a . . .'

'*Now!*'

The stranger, still waving at the approaching medics, hurried forward. Fumbling in his top pocket, and obviously keen to placate both of these shocked and concussed survivors, he shoved the stub of a pencil into Harry's hands.

Curtis watched in astonishment as Harry began frantically to search the pockets of his frayed jacket and then his trousers. Finally, and with a great sigh of relief, he found something in the back pocket of his trousers. Pulling it out, he dropped to one knee and spread the crumpled piece of paper across his leg. In his haste, it seemed as if he might overbalance. But he steadied himself and looked up once more at the star-studded sky.

And, looking down again, began to write.

It could not have been more than four scrawled words.

And written with what seemed to be great effort.

When he had finished, Curtis saw him screw the piece of paper up in his hand. Head down and sighing, Curtis waited for him to say something. But then Harry fell backwards, sprawling on the grass.

Just as a medic lunged between them and took Curtis by the shoulders.

'It's all right. We're here to take care of you both.'

'Look,' said the stranger. 'I know this sounds bloody mean. But can I have that pencil back? They're bloody manic back at Admin about stationery and stuff. Got the van logo on the side of the pencil, see? And I don't want to . . .'

And against his will, Curtis faded away from the embankment completely.

EPILOGUE

PART ONE

Attempt at an epilogue, written by Anthony Curtis, late of the Independent Daily, *for the manuscript he has been working on these past months. It's 1.26 a.m. and I've had too much to drink, and looking over everything I've written I'm tempted to finish it all off quickly. Except I can't do that because I still don't have answers to the really important questions that have arisen out of this whole affair, and why the hell am I still typing this up in italics when I could ...*

Be taking a deep breath, and really putting down what I feel and what's been left hanging in the air since the night of the crash. Maybe tonight I *will* (legitimate use of italics there, methinks) be serious and write what I need to write.

First, what happened to everyone in the truck.

When it comes to the finished book, or exposé, or whatever the hell it is I've been working on for so long, I'll probably go into more detail. But just for now, the facts are fairly plain.

Roger O'Dowd made a full recovery. Although he was pretty much out of it during that last, mad race, he hasn't suffered any lasting damage. They were all pretty close to death at the last. Hell, I don't suppose it's possible to get closer. But once The Storm Between erupted in the truck, right on the site of the motorway crash, and freed the Travellers, the human survivors who hadn't already been badly physically damaged in those last days were able to pull through. But, having said that, Roger hasn't reacted so well insofar as his brother, Chris, is concerned.

There's no doubt about it. If it hadn't been for Chris, and his last 'run', none of us would have got away from O'Farrell's place. I think about that last moment, when he jumped down from the chain-link fence and ran into the trees, a lot. I think he knew, even then, that he wasn't going to make it. Afterwards, we held out hope that he would be found. It hasn't been easy since the forest fire to tie in O'Farrell's organisation with what was going on out there at the Church of the Holy Order. Every scrap of physical evidence was destroyed in the fire, and despite intensive searches no bodies were recovered from Kielder.

Until last Thursday.

Then they found a body, in a shallow grave.

Forensic experts confirmed that it was Chris O'Dowd.

I haven't been able to speak to Roger yet, but I know he knows about it.

Jane Teal is still in a coma. She's about to be transferred from Eastleigh to a specialist unit in Surrey. They have some new treatment in development down there, and maybe someday they'll be able to bring her back and we'll be able to help with whatever unknown trauma is keeping her asleep. I've sneaked an unofficial look at some official records about her. Something about growing new skin after her house fire. But not being able to grow new skin after the burns she suffered in the church fire. I don't suppose it's worth telling them all about the strange powers of The Storm Between. Why the hell should anyone believe anything I have to say?

Martin Russell suffered a near-fatal heart attack, and is still recovering. He's no longer in intensive care, and is recovering at home. Sheila is looking after him well, but doesn't go to church as much as she used to.

George MacGowan is no longer suffering the hideous physical and mental torments that he must have been enduring. His body was retrieved from the truck and taken to Eastleigh Hospital, where he was declared dead prior to arrival – by several weeks. They're still arguing about those findings, particularly since a certain truck driver swears blind that he almost ran that unforgettably horrible figure down in the middle of the motorway on the evening of the forest fire. He also swears blind that it climbed aboard his vehicle, dragging the man it had with it, and took off up the motorway 'like a bat out of hell'. The authorities are still trying to come to terms with how a long-dead and horrifying monstrosity like that could steal a man's truck and then crash it further down the A1 later that evening. At the moment, that's their problem. Eastleigh Hospital and the official inquiry are both facing similiar problems of logic about what happened during and after the crash.

Burwell . . . the mysterious Ellis Burwell . . . the one nobody knew anything about. He suffered a fractured skull. He was identified by the truck driver as being George MacGowan's accomplice in the theft of the vehicle. There were further investigations, and although I need to follow this up a little further for the completed manuscript, it seems that someone was able to tie him in with a 'snuff' videotape. A warehouse was raided on Newcastle Quayside after a drugs tip-off, and they found a whole load of porn videos belonging to some chap called 'Klark' who had been recently murdered in a drugs deal gone wrong. The porn should have been destroyed, but a naughty policeman borrowed one of the goodies to enjoy at home with a six-pack and found himself watching a video of the guy they'd rescued from the truck crash, 'offing' a well-known black whore whose murder they'd been trying to tie up for a long time. So, our mysterious friend is serving time for murder. There was some doubt about his mental state. Diminished responsibility and what have you. But he was banged up behind bars. And it seems he's going to stay there.

Mercy . . . nobody has ever found out what her second name was . . . checked out of hospital. Just like the first time. And vanished. But I know that she spent a lot of time with Martin and Sheila Russell beforehand, while her leg was mending. They're reluctant to tell me what they were talking about, and the offer they made. But I think I can guess.

And Harry.

Harry bloody Stark.

The guy who started this nightmare rolling for me.

Can you believe it? He beats me every week at ten-pin bowling. That man has a twist in the bloody wrist that cannot

be beaten. I've tried to copy what he does, that final flick just
before he sends the ball down the alley, but I can't get it even
allowing for a missing finger. I'm going to have to change the
rules. The loser always gets the first two pints of beer in at
the pub on the corner. So far, I'm deeply out of pocket. But
I suppose on the money front, I've not got a lot to complain
about. I got sacked from the *Independent Daily* – naturally
– but then I was asked to take a job as features editor, no
less, at the *Herald*. More money, more prestige. But I was
told to get rid of the anorak. What the hell? I'm prepared
to suffer. Needless to say, Roland was somewhat pissed off.
He'll be even more pissed off when he finds out I'm about to
ask Brenda to take a job here as my assistant.

So, good money. And it's not as if I had to support
a family.

And neither does Harry any more.

Which brings me back to him.

Something happened back then. I was thrown . . . fuck, I
was *catapulted* into a nightmare. Harry Stark was the man
who started it all. When I first met him, I was convinced he
was mad. Maddened by grief. There was a time when I felt
sure he'd kill me. Another time when I knew he was suffering
from paranoid delusions. Then I felt he'd maybe *infected* me
with those delusions. Then things became complicated. I was
running with the story of the motorway crash survivors.
And I'm not going to go back over everything I've talked
about in the manuscript, but I know now – without doubt,
and to my everlasting shame – that I *did* try to spin this
fantastic story out even further than it was destined to go.
The Whitley Leisure Centre still makes me pale, and want
to puke. Not because of what happened to me. But because
I was responsible for engineering it.

And, of course, that was the first time Harry Stark saved
my life.

Against all the odds . . . or is it? . . . Harry and I have become
firm friends.

But even after all this time, there are unanswered questions
about what happened.

Questions to which *he* has the answers.

And do you know something? I've never asked him those questions. Not once since the nightmare. Don't ask me why. I just feel that someday the time will be right. And to ask him now will sully, perhaps even sever, the special bond that has developed between us all since Harry and the others 'collided' with the Travellers.

The bond?

I'd heard of something similar. Investigated and reported on it. The Zeebrugge Ferry Disaster. The Interlaande MonoRail smash. The avalanche at Mount Keir. People who'd lost everything in a terrible incident. The survivors who'd managed to save each other and, in their loss, found something very special and very precious in a new bond with those perfect strangers. Maybe a new outlook on the precious quality of life. Whatever, we're all due to meet up again next week. It's a year after the motorway crash. To the day. A sort of anniversary get-together, I suppose. At Martin and Sheila Russell's place. Their insistence. Harry and I will be there, of course. I've seen him shaking hands since the accident. No one exploded in sparks. Roger is going to try to be there, but he's just landed himself some graphic art job in a Newcastle advertising agency and been given a deadline on a campaign, so we'll have to see if he can make it. So far as I know he hasn't painted any more pictures that have sent people mad. Jane Teal is in hospital. The place hasn't burned down yet. (Maybe it should – they're still pressing charges against me for harassment. Wait until someone finds out about the kidnap.) Burwell's in clink. So that only leaves Mercy. I don't suppose we'll know about her until the day. Sheila told me her story. If there's a God in heaven, he should be looking out for her, or feeling ashamed that he's not. It would be good to see her again, though. Enough, Curtis. You're on the verge of becoming sentimental . . .

But back to the questions.

What *were* the Travellers? And where did they come from? I remember everything Harry said about the parallel realities stuff. But there must be more. I remember that last moment in the Church of the Holy Order. The whole bloody place was collapsing in flames when Martin managed to reverse the truck back out through the wall. And I heard what Harry and that sad, sad thing that was George MacGowan said to each other. The Travellers inside called each other by name.

Kay-leb and Meek-ayl.

I just *know* that Harry knows more about them, and isn't ready to tell me yet.

And what . . . *what* . . . was the last message Harry received as he stood beneath that star-studded sky and heard the last call of the Traveller before it returned safely to the place it had come from? What the hell did he scribble on that piece of paper just at the last moment?

He knows that's the one question I want to ask most.

But I'll wait.

It's got to be the right time.

And when that time comes, I'll have the right ending for my Epilogue.

Which remains

As Always

Unfinished

EPILOGUE

PART TWO

Handwritten note by Harry James Stark. Aged 48. One-time sales representative, but who gives a damn any more. Wife, Jean Marjorie (41). Two daughters, twins: Hilary and Diane (12 years of age).

It seems like a lifetime since the accident.

When I write the word 'lifetime', it's got a special meaning for me now that it never had before. Sometimes, I sit and just say it aloud. And I think about those two syllables, and the hidden depth there.

Strange, the way things turn out.

The man I thought I'd end up detesting more than anyone in my life has become the firmest and most steadfast friend a man could ever have.

And it's strange how sometimes you can discover that the most trivial and apparently meaningless things can contain within them the glimmer of hope and love and optimism for making life not only bearable but ... well, meaningful and joyful. Must show Curtis that phrase. Give him something to laugh at.

I'm writing this note now on the bureau where I found my wife's shopping list.

It's the same shopping list, the same piece of paper, on which I wrote my suicide note. The note that's been in the back pocket of my trousers ever since I died and the Traveller brought me back.

But today, the day before we're all due to meet up for Curtis's reunion party at Martin and Sheila Russell's home, I'm writing this note on a clean, uncrumpled piece of paper. I'm looking at the suicide note now, spread out on the bureau before me. And I'm writing this because I want to get my thoughts straight.

It's taken me a year to really accept what I now know to be a fact.

What I've just written is not quite true.

On that night, when we made that last insane dash in the truck, and managed against every obstacle to set the Travellers inside us free, I think I instantly *knew* the truth. But it was so important ... so vitally important ... that I couldn't allow myself any false hope. I couldn't allow myself to be wrong. Not after everything that had happened. I somehow managed to question my true instinct about it. I needed time to let its reality sink in.

But now, at last, I'm decided.

Tomorrow, I will show Curtis the last message I received. I won't tell him what it says. I'll show him the piece of paper, and what I wrote then.

I hope he'll understand.

If he does, I think it'll change him from the man he was into ... well, I don't know. But I think it'll change him.

And then I need to show Roger.

So he'll know.

About Chris.

You see, Curtis thinks the last note came from my Traveller. But the Traveller had been released by then. Free to go back with the others, to the 'plane' on which they exist. I don't know this for sure, but I have a deep-down gut feeling that the damaged Traveller inside George MacGowan was also released. And that George too was freed. Both of them free from that agony. And maybe both of them ultimately gone to the same place as the others.

And in that moment of release, when my Traveller 'dived' into the stars, something opened up in me. Something that's always been there, but for some reason was withheld from me by a force or forces that I can't ... that I'll never in this life ...

be able to understand. They're the same force or forces that prevented the Traveller from telling me what it really was.

Tomorrow, I'll show Curtis the note, because he's wanted for so long to see it.

And, like I say, he thinks it will be some last message from my Traveller.

But it won't.

It's a note from someone else. Someone the Traveller knew I wanted to hear from, and maybe the Traveller bent some 'rules' at its own cost to let that brief message come through.

I'll show him my suicide note.

And these are the last words scrawled there, on the last night.

Only The Angels Know

I'll show him the handwriting on the shopping list.

And he'll see that it's the same handwriting that came through in the last message. Not the crabbed and tortured scrawling that the Traveller managed, using my hand as a tool. But Jean's exact handwriting.

Now I know.

The Travellers weren't aliens. They weren't Travellers from outer space. They didn't come from another world, they weren't things at all.

They were . . . they are . . . us.

Not some strange alien life-form, but the souls of our own kind.

Dead and departed.

Departed on the next journey of a mysterious and dangerous adventure which only begins with birth and death in this limited and constricting physical existence.

Down here, we're all travelling on roads of our own making. Trying to make some kind of sense of this life. Maybe that journey is more important than we think. All I know is that

Jean and the kids are out there somewhere, beyond Death, all on new and different roads ... roads that we here in this existence can never understand. Their destinations are undreamable here. Their means of travel, their reasons for travel, unknowable. Somehow, for reasons that we'll never understand, we collided with those travelling souls when the fabric of our life and their afterlife was momentarily on the same plane.

But I know they're back out there once more, travelling on those roads again.

Soon, when it's my time – and not before – I'll be a traveller on one of those highways.

Caleb and Mikal found and lost each other in one existence. But they found each other in the next.

By Christ, when my time comes, I'll find Jean and the kids again.

I know I will.

Not now, not in this life. Because the greatest truth I know now is that one should *live* life. That's what it's there for, for God's sake. To live and to give love, even if you never get it back. And to see it through.

And go on.

I hope I can make Curtis see it.

One day, Jean. I'll find you.

One day, Hilary. One day, Diane.

Not now, not next year, maybe not in the next ten years. Perhaps not in the next twenty or thirty. But only when the time is right, and I'm not going to wish for that day before it's due.

Because, before then, I'm going to LIVE.

And when that last day comes.

No matter what it takes, I'm coming to find you.

I'm coming to find you all.

Somewhere.

South of Midnight.